THE BEAUTY AND THE ORCS

A MONSTER FANTASY ROMANCE

FINLEY FENN

This is a work of fiction. Names, characters, places, and incidents are the product of the author's imagination or are used fictitiously. Any resemblance to actual persons living or dead, business establishments, events, or locales is entirely coincidental.

The Beauty and the Orcs

Copyright © 2023 by Finley Fenn

info@finleyfenn.com

ALSO BY FINLEY FENN

ORC SWORN

The Lady and the Orc

The Heiress and the Orc

The Librarian and the Orc

The Duchess and the Orc

The Midwife and the Orc

The Maid and the Orcs

The Governess and the Orc

The Beauty and the Orcs

Offered by the Orc

Yuled by the Orcs

ORC FORGED

The Sins of the Orc

THE MAGES

The Mage's Maid

The Mage's Match

The Mage's Master

The Mage's Groom (Bonus Story)

Sign up at www.finleyfenn.com for bonus stories and epilogues, delicious orc artwork, complete content guidance, news about upcoming books, and more!

ABOUT THE BEAUTY AND THE ORCS

She was ruined by an orc. Now his enraged ex wants to finish the job...

In a world of orcs and powerful men, Kitty Clarendon is a bubbly, beautiful woman about town—until she's dumped by her benefactor, and thrown onto the streets. And as she's drowning her sorrows, she meets... an orc.

He's rash, reckless, and on the rebound—but his laugh is contagious, his touch warm and wicked. And for one perfect, forbidden night, he's all Kitty's darkest dreams come true...

But by morning, there's only shame. Regret. And the orc quickly makes his escape, abandoning Kitty to a devastating discovery...

She's been compromised. With his... *orcling*.

But the orc never returns, and Kitty is left ill, impoverished, and hopeless. Until finally, another orc finds her. Varinn, of Clan Grisk.

The first orc's best friend.

And... his very recent ex.

Varinn can't hide his jealousy, or his bitter, broken rage—but he refuses to leave Kitty behind. And soon she's under his stern supervision, and on her way to Orc Mountain. Back to the orc who so cruelly spurned her. The orc who's been losing his own battles, and still longs for Varinn's firm handling... and his heart.

And can Kitty bring two hostile, heartbroken orcs back together, for her orcling's sake? Or will they break her own heart, too?

To Lauren,
a great Grisk galdr-spinner

1

It was quite possibly the worst night of Kitty Clarendon's adult life.

"What do you mean, you're *severing* our *connection*?" she echoed, staring at the tall, smartly dressed man before her. "Now? *Forever*?!"

Charles didn't even look slightly ashamed, and he coolly patted his gloved hand against Kitty's perfectly curled brown hair. "There's no need to make a scene, Kitty," he replied, with a not-quite-apologetic smile. "We can address this like grown adults, can't we?"

Like grown adults. The heat surged into Kitty's already-rouged cheeks, and suddenly the sounds of the opulent party around them were far too loud, surging dizzy and close. Charles was severing their connection. Here? *Now*?

"You *must* be jesting, darling," Kitty finally said, and she even managed a light, tinkling laugh, a dismissive wave of her gloved hand. "I can't imagine why you would need to sever anything! Our... *connection* has always served us both so well, hasn't it?"

Charles grimaced, and then firmly grasped her arm, and escorted her across the loud, cramped ballroom. And as they passed by their many affluent, well-dressed contacts and acquaintances, Kitty attempted to muster the appropriate smiles and greetings, even as she desperately fought to focus her spinning, seething thoughts on a solution. An answer. Charles could *not* sever their connection. He could *not*. She needed him, needed his funds, his care, his safety...

"I meant what I said, Kitty," Charles told her, as he led her into a small adjoining sitting-room, and shut the sliding door behind them. "I wanted to wait to tell you until after the party tonight, but I've been invited away on a hunting trip in the morning, so..."

He gave a rueful, dismissive shrug, as if his damned hunting trip was some kind of impenetrable defense, rather than the flimsiest possible excuse. And Kitty only vaguely felt her stunned body dropping onto the nearest chaise, her eyes frantically searching his familiar, handsome face. No. He couldn't. *No.*

"But, darling," she said, sounding far too plaintive. "Whatever is the matter? I hadn't realized you weren't quite perfectly content with our—*connection*, and of course if I had known, I would have—"

"Look, it's not you, Kitty," Charles cut in. "It's about the coin, all right? I still haven't recovered from that lost import last month, and I need to reduce my expenses. And I'm sorry, but"—he gave another not-quite-apologetic smile, a meaningful wave toward Kitty's ensemble—"you're *very* expensive."

Kitty's mouth dropped open, and she shot a brief, chagrined glance down at her frothy, frilly fuchsia dress. Yes, it had been very costly—she'd had it shipped all the way from the city—but Charles had been the one to invite her to this party, and to demand that she dress appropriately. *To do me credit,* he'd said. *A prime new prospect will be in attendance, and I'll need you to impress him.*

So Kitty had ordered the dress, and then spent many days

making careful, painstaking alterations—pulling in seams, smoothing out imperfections, and adding subtle padding in several crucial places. Ensuring the frilly pink confection showed off her slim figure, flawless pale skin, and pretty, elfin features to the very best effect.

And then, upon arriving at the party, she'd approached the prospect's wife, complimented her own lovely dress, and eased them all into a light, cheerful conversation. In which she'd casually mentioned Charles' latest successful investment, and several of his most profitable trading ventures, and an entertaining anecdote about a jealous competitor. Leading to the much-desired commitment for a follow-up meeting, during which—if Charles didn't bungle it, yet again—he would gain the final funds required for his upcoming venture out east.

But. Trading was a risky business, one to which Charles wasn't at all naturally suited—and that recent situation with the lost import had proven rather dire indeed. And given Charles' expensive lifestyle, and his casual disregard for his creditors, Kitty could well believe that he was shorter on funds than he'd realized, and now had any number of irate lenders knocking at the door.

All of which meant... Kitty could still salvage this. She could.

"Look, if it's the dressmaker's bill, I'm very sorry, darling," she said quickly, aiming a sheepish smile toward Charles' unreadable face. "I can certainly make adjustments there, and you know how much I enjoy sewing, anyway. And if you need funds that urgently, perhaps I could return some of the gifts you've given me. These earrings, perhaps—"

She winced as she reached a gloved hand to touch one—they were beautifully crafted dropped pearls, and she'd nearly wept when Charles had given them to her last year. But yes, yes, he was nodding, and even smiling down toward her, his eyes brightening with genuine approval.

"You know, Kitty, that would be lovely," he replied. "I'll send James over tomorrow to fetch them all, if you don't mind?"

Oh. Oh. It almost hurt to nod, but Kitty made herself do it anyway, the wavering smile still fixed to her mouth. "Of course," she said. "Whatever will help you, Charles. I deeply value our connection, and I would miss you so desperately if we were parted, so I'm happy to—"

"Wait, Kitty," Charles interrupted, raising his hand. "I don't mean I'm changing my mind. You're a sweet girl, and you've shown me a great time, but"—he made a face, glanced away— "but we've had a good run, all right? No hard feelings?"

What? No. *No.* Kitty's eyes were rapidly blinking now, her throat swallowing again and again, her gloved hand fluttering against her padded breast. No. He couldn't. *No.*

"But—I've shown you more than a good time, Charles," she protested, though her voice trembled. "It's been four *years.* I've given you so much help with your business, and your partners and routes and investors, and—and even your *mother.* I've done you credit at so many events and engagements, we've travelled together, we've enjoyed each other, I've done everything to please you, Charles, *everything.*"

Her voice shamefully cracked at the end, her eyes pleading on his face, while the misery lurched higher, threatened to escape in gulping, gasping sobs. Because gods, she truly had given Charles everything. Her affection, her loyalty, her smiles and jokes and laughter, her attention and knowledge and encouragement. She'd been a perfect partner for him, the ultimate bubbly, entertaining, considerate companion, who'd known him inside out. She'd never once demanded or complained, not even when he'd been dismissive or forgetful or cruel, or made her the target of his unpredictable temper. And for all her efforts, *this* was her reward?

"Look, I'm sorry, Kitty," Charles replied, and for an instant, he did look almost sorry, the grimace twisting his mouth. "I said, you've been a great girl. But"—he gave a helpless-looking shrug—"you must have known it wouldn't last forever between us, didn't you? I mean, you're not exactly the kind of girl a man like me *marries*, you know?"

Kitty couldn't help her recoil, the twitch of her shaky hands up to her hot face, because yes, perhaps, she'd always known how things stood on that front—but Charles had still made so, so many promises. *Come with me to Dusbury, Kitty. You'll do me credit there, and I'll set you up, take good care of you. You'll see.*

"But—you promised you'd look after me," she gasped, and she was on the verge of weeping now, the wetness prickling close behind her eyes. "You *promised*, Charles."

But Charles only looked intently away from her, rubbing uncomfortably at the back of his neck. "Well, and I have, haven't I?" he said defensively. "I mean, your clothes, your apartment, the jewels, your allowance…"

Kitty had to choke back the hitching, hovering sob, because she'd needed all of that—all of it—just to keep up with Charles. To look the part. To fit in with his circle of wealthy, well-established friends and contacts and competitors. To keep herself *fed*, curse him to hell and back.

And even so, she'd still been poor, by every other definition of the word. She'd meticulously planned her budget, scrimping and saving every copper. She'd never hired staff to help manage her apartment or her clothes. She'd often skipped meals, and had surreptitiously eaten as much as she could whenever Charles had taken her out. She'd re-sewn all her dresses a dozen times over, and patched her ill-fitting shoes and threadbare coats. She'd pretended she liked it cold in her apartment, so it wasn't so obvious that she couldn't afford enough wood or coal.

But despite all Kitty's efforts, she'd scarcely been able to save. Charles had extravagant taste, and expected extravagant gifts. He'd often left her to fend for herself on their travels, requiring her to cover any number of unexpected costs. He was frequently thoughtless and forgetful, and when she'd fallen ill with the flu for a fortnight, he hadn't even bothered to visit, let alone bring over food, or pay the month's rent.

"But—what do you expect me to do now?" Kitty croaked at him, through her gasping breaths. "Stuck here alone in Dusbury, without any income or protection? Will you keep paying for my apartment, at least?"

But she knew the answer before Charles even spoke, his lip curling, his eyes again angling away. "Look, I'm sorry, Kitty," he said. "I'll cover the rent for another month, all right? And surely"—he gave her a falsely bright smile—"you can find another fellow to cozy up to, can't you? Or move back home to the city?"

The city. Something cold and clammy was seizing at Kitty's chest, her throat—and suddenly the misery was escaping, streaking hot and betraying down her cheeks. No. No. She couldn't go back there. She'd worked so hard. She'd come so far. *No.*

"I—I can't go back to the city, Charles," she finally gulped, wiping at her face with her trembling hands. "You know what my life was like there. You *rescued* me from all that. Remember?"

Charles still wasn't meeting her eyes, and his mouth thinned, his shoulder jerking a dismissive shrug. "Yes, and I've showered you with gifts and coin for years now," he said, with rising impatience in his voice. "I've spoiled you rotten, Kitty, and aren't you twenty-four—or twenty-five—now? Surely you can manage to stand on your own two feet at this point?"

Kitty's hands kept hovering uselessly at her face, while the wetness streaked faster down her cheeks. "I'm twenty-six, Charles," she choked out. "And I can't afford to get by on my own right now. I don't have any savings, let alone any training, or references, or transferable work experience. I don't have *anyone else.*"

But Charles' expression had gone cold and irritated, now, and perhaps contemptuous, too. "Well, I'm sorry, but that's not my fault, is it?" he said flatly. "And I'm trying to say, you have options. You're a beautiful, helpful, charming girl, you know how to present yourself, and you're a lot of fun, especially in bed. I'm sure you'll be just fine."

But Kitty wasn't fine, she was weeping, and shivering all over, and whipping her head back and forth, and fighting not to vomit all over the plush, opulent carpet. No. No. *No.*

"Look, there's no need to make such a fuss," Charles' voice broke in, grating through Kitty's screaming thoughts. "And look, if it helps for now—here."

He'd shoved something at Kitty—a shiny gold coin—and even as she clutched at it, squeezing the hard metal between her numb fingers, she couldn't stop weeping. No. What could she do. No. *No.*

And before Charles could speak another single horrible word, she leapt to her feet, and fled for the door.

2

Kitty ended up at a dank, dismal pub down the street, pouring glass after glass of sour, sickening wine down her throat.

The pub was a truly decrepit establishment, with terrible service, foul-smelling air, and even worse wine—but it had been nearby, and cheap. And it wasn't a place where Kitty was likely to be recognized, especially with its lamplight turned so dim that she could scarcely make out the shape of the man beside her.

And most importantly, with every glass of the vile wine, the pain and humiliation edged just a little further away. Blunted beneath an ever-expanding dizzy, glassy haze, until Kitty could almost breathe again, think again, despite the incessant hammer of her distant thundering heartbeat.

Charles was done. Gone. Severed their *connection.*

And if Kitty was honest with herself—brutally, painfully honest—she'd always known just how precarious her position with Charles was. She'd known he would never marry her. She'd known how one-sided—how transactional—their relationship had been. And she'd known she had no other training, no real skills, nothing else to fall back on.

But gods, she'd wanted to believe Charles cared. She'd so desperately wanted to believe she was his one and only, his confidante, his compatriot, his colleague. And he'd repeatedly said he wasn't the marrying kind, and he'd seemed so content with their arrangement, with the life they'd made together. While in truth, the entire time, he'd only seen her as... as...

A beautiful, helpful, charming girl. A lot of fun. Especially in bed.

The sobs lurched close again, nearly spilling out, and Kitty gulped down another mouthful of the cheap wine, felt it churn and curdle in her already-nauseated stomach. It had been so long since she'd overindulged like this—since she'd left the city with Charles years ago—and there was no doubt she'd deeply regret it come morning. But right now, all that mattered was pushing it back, cramming it down, making it go away, if only for tonight...

"Are you... well, woman?" cut in a low, tentative voice beside her. "Has aught... harmed you?"

Kitty flailed up, and whirled around on her stool toward the voice—but oh, she'd moved too fast, and the dank room was spinning sharp and sideways. Enough that she could feel her body swaying out, reeling, tilting toward the floor, *no*—

When suddenly, there were hands. Big, warm, capable hands, catching strong and solid on her trembling shoulders. And squeezing, just a little, as they guided her upright, settling her back into place on her stool, before gently drawing away again.

Kitty shivered all over, and for an instant, there was a strange, dizzying urge to clutch back toward those hands, toward that brief, steady safety. To hold on to something, anything, and to finally release all the lurking, sickening misery clamouring in her throat.

But somehow, she gulped down air, and desperately aimed a bright, cheerful smile toward her unknown companion. "Oh, I'm fine!" she announced, though her voice noticeably wavered. "Perfectly all right. Thank you for your assistance."

There was an instant's taut silence beside her, and when Kitty's bleary eyes squinted to look more closely, she realized that her companion was very tall, and he was wearing a large black hood, pulled low over his face. And his hands were wrapped tightly around his tankard of ale, and they were big hands, with long elegant fingers, and...

Black claws?!

Wait. *Wait.* He was... an *orc*?! Kitty was sitting next to an orc? In *public*?!

Kitty gasped and lurched to her feet, turning to sprint for the door—but once again, the room was dangerously spinning, whirling wildly before her eyes. And even as her arms flailed in midair, frantically seeking purchase, something again clasped against her shoulders. Catching her, steadying her, lingering perhaps a little longer this time...

But then the hands firmly set her on the stool, and snapped away again. Returning to clutch against the tankard, before raising it to take a long, gulping drink. And in the faint lamplight, Kitty caught a glimpse of a bright white fang, sharp and menacing against full grey lips. Good gods, he really was an *orc*. Beside her. In *public*.

There was a distant, high-pitched buzzing in Kitty's ears, her heartbeat pummelling against her ribs—and she heard herself laugh, the sound scraping and shrill. No. No. This couldn't be happening. Not now. Not today...

"So you're—you're—an *orc*?" she heard herself say, her voice not at all her own. "Are you going to steal me away, then, and force me to carry your child? Put the final finishing touch on this horrible hellish day?"

An uncontrollable surge of fear raced up her back as she spoke, because damn it, he really was an *orc*. A rabid, rampaging brute, who had probably stolen away a half-dozen women to his terrifying home at Orc Mountain, and then sired his vicious, deadly spawn upon them. Orcs were vile, evil beasts, who wielded powerful ancient magic to gain the gold and sons they craved—and Kitty's stunted thoughts were dragging up vague memories of the decades-long war between humans and orcs, and then the ruckus around that new realm-wide peace-treaty, several years before. And then her mother saying, with a chilly, calculating smile, that orcs paid very well, and some of them particularly preferred women without many scents, and perhaps Kitty would...

"No, woman," interrupted a low, faintly accented voice—the *orc's* voice. And when Kitty flailed to look at him again, his shadowed face was turned toward hers, his head shaking back and forth, as his hands tightened against his tankard.

"No abducting or forcing, ach?" he continued, his low voice deepening. "It's against the peace-treaty. And in truth"—that might have been a grimace on his fanged mouth—"it sounds nightmarish, doesn't it? How any orc has ever sired a son like that, I can't even fathom. *Ugh*."

His tall cloaked figure had actually seemed to shudder, those long clawed fingers again clenching on his tankard. And as she blinked at him, Kitty felt herself very slightly relaxing, though she couldn't stop frowning at his shadowed, unreadable face.

"*Really*?" she asked, her wavering voice sounding very far away. "That's not at *all* what the tales say about orcs."

The orc shrugged, and then took another long, gulping drink, this time showing a hint of a corded grey throat. "Those tales are rubbish," he replied flatly, once he'd set down the tankard again. "*Rubbish*, from rubbish men, who wanna keep you all to themselves. Gods forbid you women actually *enjoy* yourselves with an orc. Find out what you've been missin' all this time."

His voice was slurred, but it sounded surprisingly fervent, enough that Kitty eyed him for another long, uncertain moment—and then she heard herself laugh again, choked and bitter. "I won't argue about the rubbish men," she said, before taking another gulping drink of her foul wine. "I was with

Charles for four whole years, and in all that time, he never once even bothered trying to—"

She bit off the words, shaking her head—gods, she was not talking about this right now, especially not with a random, deadly *orc*?! And what if he used it to take advantage, to drag her out of here by her hair, and destroy what little was left of her already-ruined life—

But there was only a deep, disapproving huff from the orc beside her, sounding almost like a growl. "Ach, I can smell it," he replied. "What a waste. This *Charles* is a fool, and I hope you're now well shot of him, ach?"

Kitty froze, blinking toward the orc—he could *smell* such things? And wait, how did he know it was over between her and Charles? But oh, right, she'd just spoken about Charles in the past tense, hadn't she? And gods, she needed to think, swim through her muddy thoughts, grasp for some kind of answer...

"Yes, it's over between Charles and me," she said, her voice cracking. "As of tonight. He's decided to *sever* our *connection*. After *four years*."

A streak of wetness escaped down her cheek, and she dashed it away, and shot a chagrined glance sideways at the orc. But he was just facing back toward her now, his hooded head tilting, almost as if he was listening. Almost as if... he cared.

"And I thought—I thought it was something it wasn't," Kitty's voice continued, all on its own. "I thought—I thought Charles really cared about me. At least, enough to keep me around, you know? I worked so hard, I was such a good and helpful partner, and now it's just—over, forever. And I'm all on my own again, and—"

She couldn't finish, shaking her head and wiping at her eyes, and she was distantly astonished by the sight of the orc rummaging beneath his cloak, and handing over... a handkerchief? And after a moment's dazed blinking down toward it, Kitty willingly took it from his clawed fingers, and shakily wiped at her hot, sticky face.

"Th-thank you," she said, choked. "I'm so very sorry. I ought not to be dumping this onto you."

The orc shrugged, and then purposefully gestured at the barman for a refill of his ale—and for another glass of wine for Kitty, too. "Don' apologize, woman," he said. "Happy to listen, ach? And I ken this'll sound absurd, but in truth"—he grimaced, shook his head—"same thing happened to me today, too. Gods are mocking us, I ken."

Kitty blinked toward him, and then gratefully accepted the glass of wine the barman brought over. "Really?" she asked the orc, the skepticism far too clear in her voice. "What happened?"

The orc shrugged again, and took a long gulp of his own refilled drink. "My—partner—told me it was over between us," he said, with a slow, shaky exhale. "Forever. Finished."

And now he was the one rubbing at his eyes, and Kitty kept blinking at him, as a rising sympathy began simmering in her chest. And when she passed the wet handkerchief back toward him, he willingly took it, and scrubbed it against his face.

"It's been *years*," he continued, his voice hardening. "So many years. Best friends. Know everything about each other, went through hell together. And I thought—I thought mayhap it was finally working, ach? Thought we were finally sorting it out, after so long."

Oh. Kitty swallowed hard, watched the orc again rubbing at his eyes, his lips wavering against his sharp teeth. "And I ken I'm not perfect," he choked out. "I *ken*. But I tried so fucking hard, ach? Tried to be fun, eager, willing, always there, for *everything*. For the good, an'—the worst. But now it's just— done, between us. *Finished*."

His voice cracked, and he loudly hiccoughed, and blew his nose into the handkerchief. "Sorry, woman," he said, with a broken laugh. "Shouldn't be dumping this on you, either."

But there was only the sympathy now, tangling tight in Kitty's ribcage, and she couldn't help a sad, genuine-feeling smile toward him. "Don't apologize," she replied, echoing his own words from only a moment before. "I'm happy to listen. And I think you must be right about the gods mocking us, too."

The orc barked another strangled laugh, and again shook his head. "Those interfering bastards," he said with a sigh, as he took another long drink. "Fuck 'em all."

Kitty winced, even as she laughed—cursing the gods was a dangerous matter, even when inebriated—and she eyed the orc again, fighting to focus her hazy gaze on his shadowed face. "Did your partner tell you why?" she asked him. "Why she was finished with you? Especially if you really were best friends, for so long?"

And gods, it was surely none of Kitty's business whatsoever, but it was something, anything to keep her swirling thoughts from Charles and her ominous future, and the orc jerked a shrug, huffed another choked laugh. "Said it's because I... I've been drinkin' too much," he replied. "But I haven't, ach? And it hasn't really affected anything between us. If anything, it makes things easier, ach? Keeps me from—"

He grimaced and rubbed at his eyes again, shaking his head. "I was still the best friend, *always*," he said. "An' a good partner, and a damned good time in bed, too. An' I'm not flatterin' myself, because I can damn well smell it, an' I fucking *know*. No matter what—"

He broke off there, his shoulders heaving beneath his cloak, and Kitty's miserable commiseration just kept rising, enough that she nudged her elbow against his on the bar. "I tried so hard, too," she replied thickly. "I was fun and bubbly and eager, too. And helpful, because Charles is in the trading industry, and he's often quite horrendous at it—so I'd always go to his parties and meetings, and help him court his clients, and explain and organize his projects. Gods, just tonight, I helped him get a new investor, and even so"—she gulped a half-laugh, half-sob—"he said he's dumping me because I'm *too expensive!*"

Her voice rang between them, loud enough to make her

flinch—but the orc only snorted into his drink, and shook his head. "Rubbish," he replied sharply. "Dumped you 'cause of the other woman all over his scent, I ken."

Kitty froze on her stool, her eyes snapped wide on the orc's cloaked profile, while her distant pummelling heartbeat thundered closer. No. No. Charles hadn't been seeing anyone else. He couldn't have been. Had he?

But the orc was grimacing, taking another long swig of his ale. "Sorry, woman," he continued, his voice low. "Like I said, he's a fool, and you're well rid of him. An' the other woman's scent isn't nearly as sweet as yours, either. If I had a lovely woman like you, willing and eager in my bed, believe me"—he gave a mirthless laugh—"my nose'd never be wanderin' again."

Oh. And twining together with the misery, the humiliation, the distant rising fury, there was something almost like— longing, clutching deep in Kitty's belly. Gods, what she would give to have assurance like that. Safety like that. To be *wanted* like that, not for how she looked, or how well she could impress a man's friends, or help him with his business, or please him in bed. And maybe being wanted for one's *scent* was just as bad, but in Kitty's strange, hazy state, it sounded almost... appealing. Because it wasn't something she had to work for, was it? Something she could fix or improve with curlers or padding or stylish clothes? No, no, it was surely just... there. Just... her.

And gods, she was going to break down sobbing again, and suddenly the dim room felt far too cramped and crowded, the scent of fetid wine far too strong in her nostrils. Enough that she had to push away from the bar, her hand clamping over her mouth as the room spun around her, reeling out wide and dangerous, until—

The orc. Standing tall and close beside her, grasping her up against warm, solid strength. Holding her, here, in his arms.

And for an instant, Kitty wanted nothing more than to clutch at him, to bury her face in him, to weep until she was empty. To begin begging, perhaps, to demand that he tell her other beautiful devastating things, to ask him what else he liked, how he'd sought to please that ungrateful woman of his, whether he might want to—

But then he purposefully stepped backwards, putting a careful distance between them. His hands falling to his sides, clenching to tight clawed fists, as his hooded face angled away, too.

Oh. Oh. Of course. And Kitty nodded, so forcefully the room flickered—and then she staggered away from him, through the cramped dark pub, toward the door. Just needing to escape him, the wine, the close constricting darkness, Charles, *herself*—

And just in time, she rushed out into the cool fresh air, and vomited into the street.

3

When Kitty's nausea finally subsided, it was with the realization that she wasn't alone in the empty street. That there was a tall, cloaked, twitchy-looking figure standing beside her, uneasily observing every moment of her ongoing mortification.

The orc.

"You all right, woman?" his low voice asked, as he again thrust out his now-soggy handkerchief toward her. "Can I—get you anything?"

Kitty gratefully took the handkerchief, wincing as she mopped at her foul, sweaty face. "No, I'll be quite all right, I'm sure," she rasped back, through her now-painful throat. "I'll just—"

She managed a vague, shaky wave in the general direction of her apartment, but then found herself staggering sideways as the street whirled around her. And suddenly the orc's hands were here again, grasping strong and firm against her shoulders, holding her upright.

"I'm walkin' you home, woman," he said flatly. "That way, ach?"

He'd pointed his claw down the street, in a far more accurate representation of her apartment's direction. And when Kitty gave a wary, uncertain nod, the orc slung his long arm over her shoulders, and began walking. Guiding her along with him, her trembling body tucked in close against his side, his arm warm and heavy around her.

And as they walked down the street together, it distantly, powerfully occurred to Kitty just how damned *tall* he was, her head scarcely reaching his shoulder. And surely she should be arguing this, somehow, pushing him away, something—but she couldn't seem to find the wherewithal to do so. Especially not when he was so warm, so strangely reassuring—and when even putting one foot in front of the other seemed so gods-damned difficult.

"Don' drink like that often, then, I take it?" the orc was saying now, with unmistakable amusement on his own slightly slurred voice. "You're seemin' just a bit outta sorts, here."

Kitty made a sound that might have been a laugh, and she shook her head against the strength of his arm. "Almost never," she replied thickly. "Bear it only for catastrophes. An' for forgetting rubbish men. Because they're rubbish!"

The orc barked an approving laugh, his hand squeezing around her shoulder. "Ach, that's the spirit," he said. "Fuck 'em all, and make 'em weep. 'Cause you know"—he drummed his claws against her shoulder—"that fool Charles is gonna regret it, ach? Lettin' go of a sweet pretty kitten like you?"

Kitty shot the orc a bleary, uncertain glance, but she still couldn't make out his face, not even with the occasional gas lamp lighting the street. "Well, your woman's going to feel the same way," she replied, with a hiccough. "To have someone like you for a best friend, looking out for her, helping her home, trying to please her in bed"—she gave a wavering smile—"that sounds so wonderful. Like something out of a dream."

Her voice had gone blatantly, pathetically wistful, and gods, it was so laughable, so absurd—but the orc didn't laugh. If anything, he pulled her a little closer, his big hand clutching tighter against her shoulder.

"You don' have friends, woman?" he asked, his voice sharp. "Or family?"

Kitty barked a shrill, hiccoughing laugh, but then managed to pull herself straighter, raising her head. "Oh, I've plenty, of course!" she said, as airily as she could. "My social circle is very large. Charles is a very important man here in town."

But too late, there was the sudden, lowering recollection that her social circle was all Charles', rather than her own. And Charles had... *severed their connection*. And when it came to choosing between her and Charles, who would all their friends and acquaintances choose? Was it really even a choice?

"Och, don' weep again, woman," broke in the orc's voice, his hand again squeezing against her shoulder. "Tha' scum doesn't deserve it, ach? No more wastin' your sweet tears on his *rubbish*. Four *years* you already wasted on his sorry useless arse, without even gettin' some proper pleasure outta the deal."

Kitty laughed again, perhaps a little more genuine this time, and attempted a nod against the orc's shoulder. "Too true," she replied, with a sigh. "How I have suffered! He's also cheap, and horribly selfish, and now he wants all his jewels back, too! What kind of lover does that?!"

The orc gave a deeply disapproving frown down toward her, and steered her around a corner, still in the direction of her apartment. "A rubbish one," he said firmly. "I'd never treat a sweet woman like you so poorly, ach? Let alone forgettin' how to use my tongue, and make you scream for me."

Oh, *hell*. And surely it was a sign of Kitty's shockingly inebriated state, but her breath choked in her throat, her feet tripping on the cobblestones beneath her. And her answering laugh sounded too late, too breathless, too... hungry.

"Who knew that Charles would be so severely outclassed

by an orc," she said, attempting to keep her voice light. "The things you learn! I sincerely hope your woman at least appreciated your generosity, and properly returned the favour?"

But at that, the orc's body twitched against her, and his laugh this time was harder, colder. "Not often," he replied. "Would never even give me—och. I wasn't what h—what was... really wanted."

Good gods. Now it was Kitty's disbelief rising, and she shot a brief, affronted frown up at his shadowy face. "More rubbish," she snapped, jabbing a wavering finger toward him. "You're well rid of her too, then. Any man who knows how to use his tongue ought to be amply rewarded. To hell with selfish lovers!"

The orc laughed again, pulling her a little closer against him. "To hell with 'em!" he replied, punching his other fist up into the air. "Make 'em scent it, an' weep!"

Kitty's laugh pealed through the empty street, and she punched up her own fist, too. "An' weep!" she echoed, grinning up toward the orc—to where she could just catch the sight of him grinning back, in the light of a passing streetlamp. And it was a broad, stunning grin, warm and just a little dangerous, sparking something low and dark in her belly...

"Och, is this it?" he abruptly said, his face turning away, toward—oh. The door of Kitty's apartment. And there was a sudden, plunging disappointment, even as Kitty made herself nod, and take a shaky step toward it. Away from the orc, away from his solid warm safety, his stability, her feet already stumbling sideways, and...

"I'll take you up, ach?" came the orc's voice, a little gruff, as his warm strength returned—not over Kitty's shoulders this time, but slipping around her waist, gentle and familiar. "Those're stairs, aren't they?"

Kitty gratefully nodded and smiled up toward him, her face

unexpectedly heating—and as he guided her up the dark, narrow stairwell, she felt her breath catching, her body leaning closer into his touch. His warmth. His easy, wonderful reassurance, his unexpected, astonishing kindness. An orc. An *orc*!

And once the orc had ushered her into her dim, familiar apartment, Kitty found that she couldn't seem to draw away from him. Couldn't seem to even find her voice, or to attempt some semblance of a thank-you, let alone a farewell. And instead, she was frantically noting that he wasn't letting go, either, his long fingers spasming against her waist. And... and his other hand was reaching around, and shutting the door behind them.

Oh. *Oh*. And Kitty's trembling body turned toward him, her hands finally sliding against his warm broad chest, her head tilting up toward his face. Toward where he was exhaling, hard, his sharp fang biting his lip, his big hands spreading wide against her back.

Holding her. Wanting her.

Kitty's heart skipped a beat, the longing soaring bright through her chest—and somehow, somehow, they were both staggering toward the bed together. His hands clutching at her dress, hers fisting tight in his cloak, dragging him closer, down, closer, oh—

She fell back onto the bed with a choked, grateful sob, and he was still here, still here. His warm body settling long over hers, pressing her down, closing her in strong and safe, as the sweet, rich scent of him swarmed her breath. And oh, oh, his face was already ducking into her neck, his tongue seeking hot and slick and hungry, and Kitty moaned for it, arched up into it, as he huffed a soft, shaky laugh into her skin.

"You're sure, woman," he whispered, breathless, as he lifted up to meet her eyes, and his hips circled down, just where she most desperately craved it. "Sure you wanna?"

But Kitty had never, ever been so sure of anything, ever, in all her entire life—and she laughed, or perhaps sobbed, as she nodded, and gripped him as tightly as she could. So tight he would never let go...

"Yes," she breathed, begging, broken. "Yes. *Yes.*"

$$4$$

Kitty awoke to agony. Pure, pummelling agony, punching again and again behind her dry, gritty eyes.

Oh, gods. What... the hell. What had happened. What had she done.

She squinted her eyes open, wincing at even the very dim light from behind the closed drapes. She was in... her apartment. In her bed. And...

She took a shaky breath, and then slowly, deliberately, tilted her head sideways. The movement flaring more unbearable agony through her thundering skull, until—until—

No. *No.* It was—an orc. Sleeping. Sprawled. In her bed. *Naked.*

Kitty yelped aloud, her hand clapping over her mouth, while the room viciously spun, and the memories crashed and churned. She had... met an orc last night. At... that pub. There had been... vile wine. Foul smells. Vomiting in the street. And then...

She squeezed her eyes shut, and her fluttering hand

reached down to brush between her thighs, where... damn. *Damn.* Warm, thick, sticky. Inside her. *Inside* her.

The nauseated disbelief kept churning harder, scrabbling at the vague, distant memories—but there were only flashes, flickers, hazy and dim. His big body moving powerfully above hers. His low, satisfied laugh, shuddering through his tongue, as he'd knelt and feasted between her legs. And then, afterwards, once he'd crawled up over her again, his... teeth. Breaking the skin of her neck, and sinking deep, as his hard, rhythmic swallows had echoed in her ear, in perfect time with his swift, hungry thrusts inside her.

Kitty's tingling, sticky hand flitted up to her neck, feeling the—the *tooth-marks*, oh gods. They'd really done that. And *that*. And maybe even—her throat swallowed, as her tongue brushed against her lips, and registered the unfamiliar sweet taste—that. *Everything.*

The pounding was thudding even louder in her skull, but she squinted her gritty eyes open again, and blinked back toward the orc. Toward where his face was still cast in deep shadow, though she could now make out his thatch of short, messy black hair, sticking out at all angles against the pillow. And his arm sprawled across her waist was long and athletic, his abdomen smooth and muscular, with a taut navel above a line of black hair. And then, his—Kitty's eyes widened, and then squeezed shut again—his soft, dangling grey heft had a *piercing* in it. A thick gold ring, curving out from deep within his slit, and plunging back in below.

Gods. *Gods.* Because here was the memory, just a snatch, of her... *licking* at it. *It's gorgeous*, she'd told him, with unsteady fervency in her voice, as she'd searched his shadowed, watching face. *You're gorgeous.*

What the hell. Honestly, what in the ever-loving horrifying *fuck*. He was an orc. An *orc*.

And it was just then, just as the true depths of Kitty's depravity were beginning to sink in, that there was a rap at the door. A loud, purposeful rap, thudding in distressing tandem with the ache still wailing inside her skull.

"Miss Clarendon!" called a voice, a vaguely familiar voice. "Miss Clarendon, are you in there? It's James. Mr. Tatterham sent me."

Mr. Tatterham. James. Good gods, it was Charles' valet. Because—Kitty's groan came out much like a sob—Charles wanted his cursed jewelry back. Damn it. *Damn* it.

"One moment!" Kitty called, the sound of her own voice studding even more breathtaking pain through her skull—but she somehow shoved her shaky body upwards on the bed, and dragged in a deep, desperate gulp of air. She needed to stand up. Put on her dressing-gown. Get the jewels...

But at that moment, the bed dipped behind her, and a low, hissed curse scraped against her ears. And when Kitty twisted to look, the orc was sitting up too, with his big hand clasped over his mouth, the whites of his eyes just visible in the darkness.

"Oh, no," he whispered, whipping his head back and forth. "Oh, hell, no. Fuck. *Fuck.*"

It was a perfect, horrible echo of Kitty's own thoughts, but the reality of him speaking them aloud—making them into awful, undeniable truth—seemed to hurl even more staggering agony into her sticky, shivering body. He regretted it, too. He hadn't—perhaps he hadn't even wanted it. Because he wanted—he wanted—his *real* woman. The woman who'd dumped him yesterday. The woman who... who surely wouldn't take him back, after this.

Kitty choked down another sudden, inexplicable sob, and somehow she shoved up to her unsteady feet, and swiped for her nearby dressing-gown. But even as she yanked it on, she could already feel the rush of hot, sticky wetness, pouring from inside her, streaking down her thighs. *His* wetness. An *orc.*

He was cursing again behind her, harsh and surprisingly eloquent, and Kitty fought to ignore it as she staggered over to

the jewel-box, and snapped it open. And then she blinked
blankly down toward it, toward all the gifts Charles had given
her these past four years. The beautiful gold locket. The
amethyst earrings. Multiple gold and silver bracelets. Rings
with sparkling, stunning stones. Only lacking—her shaky hand
snapped up to her ear—the pearl earrings.

"Miss Clarendon!" James called again, his voice grating
from beyond the closed door. "Did you hear me?"

Oh, curse every odious man in this godsforsaken realm, and
Kitty sobbed again as she yanked off both pearl earrings, and
hurled them into the box. And then she snatched up the box,
and strode to the door—but just in time, she halted and
whirled around toward the room again. Toward the orc, who
was still sitting up naked in her bed, and staring at her.

But then, oh thank the gods, he jerked a curt nod, and
shoved off the side of the bed, onto the floor. So he at least
couldn't be seen from the door, and Kitty took another bracing
breath, and then pulled the door open a crack. Indeed showing
the highly unwelcome sight of James, Charles' grey-haired
valet, standing impatiently in the hallway.

"Here," Kitty croaked, as she shoved the jewel-box toward
him. "It's all there."

Thankfully, James took it without further comment, though
his beady eyes were glancing past Kitty, peering into her
apartment. "You all right here, Miss Clarendon?" he asked.
"Smells like—"

Kitty's chagrin twisted in her stomach, but she attempted a
smile, and shook her head. "Quite all right!" she replied
brightly. "Just indulged too much last night, that's all. Please
give Charles my regards."

With that, she gave a cheery wave, and firmly shoved the
door closed. And then kept standing there, listening, waiting—
until she finally heard the distinct sound of boots, thumping
down the stairs again.

Oh, gods. Kitty sagged back against the closed door, her

breaths still heaving, her clammy hands dragging over her face. Her jewels, gone. Charles, gone. Her future, gone. The orc... still here.

And curse it, but yes, the orc was still here... and he was leaping up from behind the bed, and yanking on his trousers. And then he pulled on a simple tunic, too, followed by his huge hooded cloak. Once again concealing his spiky black hair, and what little she'd been able to see of his face. As if he was... hiding himself from her. Hiding his regret. His shame.

Kitty's stomach plummeted again, and she shook her head, fought for air, for purchase. This had just been—a mistake. So what if he'd said all those things, done all those things. So what if she'd kissed the ring in his—well. They'd both known it hadn't meant anything, she'd *known*, and—and—

"Och, don't weep, woman," said the orc's voice, so quiet, so... guilty. "You... you don't scent at all of a son, ach? Or even your own seed, either. You ought to—ought to be fine."

Right. Right. *That.* Kitty somehow nodded, blinked toward him through the cursed wetness again collecting behind her eyes. "I—I'm on a strong course of silphium as prevention, too," she said, into the stilted silence. "So—yes. Ought to be fine."

The orc's head rapidly nodded beneath his cloak, and he took a swift step toward her, before halting again. Wanting to leave, perhaps, but not wanting to come closer. Not wanting to speak further, or even to risk a single touch.

And Kitty didn't care, she didn't, but the nausea was churning even stronger, and with it a desperate, pathetic longing. "Will your—your best friend," she began, before she could stop it, "be very angry with you, then?"

The orc's laugh was more like a bark, both his clawed hands rubbing at his face. "Ach," he choked. "Furious, I ken. I have mayhap ruined—"

He broke off there, but his voice had been thick with pain, with regret, with loss. And suddenly there was only more sheer, sickening misery, plunging in Kitty's belly, burying her beneath it. Gods, what had come over her. What had she done.

"Then you'd best go back to her at once," she made herself say, through her constricted throat. "And you'd best just—be honest with her. Tell her it was just—a foolish mistake, that will soon be forgotten. That it—didn't mean anything. For either of us."

The orc was rapidly nodding again, his heavy exhale hitching from his mouth. "Ach," he said. "Ach, woman. Only a—foolish mistake."

Kitty painfully swallowed, but nodded again too, so hard she would have staggered, had she not been still holding onto the door. "Right," she said. "Well. I do wish you all luck, then."

There was an instant's dangling, dismal silence, but then the orc lurched forward, toward her. Or wait, no, toward the door, and Kitty made herself shove aside, leaving it there, for him. So he could leave. Forever.

And he was almost there, his clawed hand was on the latch, his hooded head again turning toward her. And his shoulders rose, and fell, and rose, and fell, and she could hear his cough, loud and awkward in his throat.

"You shall... be well, woman," he said, though his voice was tentative, uncertain. "You shall be well, and safe, here on your own?"

It took just a moment too long, but Kitty found her wide smile, and fervently nodded as she aimed the smile toward him. "Oh, I'm fine!" she replied, through the waver in her voice. "Perfectly all right. Thank you for bringing me home safe last night. I should have been utterly lost, without your kindness."

She'd spoken far too quickly, her voice too high-pitched, but she could see the orc's stiff shoulders slowly sagging beneath his cloak, could hear the weight of his exhale, and his relief. His acceptance, perhaps, that he'd done the right thing after all. And now he could leave, without any lingering guilt or obligation or shame.

And it was just what Kitty had intended, the safest, fastest way to extract both of them from this mortifying situation—so why was her stomach still churning like this, the misery still roiling, threatening to escape…

But yes, yes, the orc was nodding again, quick and determined. Surely about to leave, finally, forever—

And then, without warning, he lurched toward her. His big hand gently gripping her shoulder, as his head bent over hers, and he pressed a soft, brief kiss to her mussed-up hair.

"It was my honour," he whispered. "You're a sweet, eager, beautiful woman, ach? I had—a lot of fun."

Oh. Oh, gods. Oh *gods*. And the misery was so sharp, so strong, so close to escaping—and it was only Kitty's frantic nod keeping it back, shoving it away. "M-me, too," she replied. "Good luck. And safe travels!"

It was so loud, so absurdly banal, enough that even he twitched away—but yes, yes, he had to go, he needed to go, he couldn't *go*. And yes, no, he was going, he was stepping toward the door, yanking it open before him. His hooded head angling toward her for one more brief, halting moment, almost as if—as if—

But then he jerked forward. Away. And the door was slamming shut behind him, as the sounds of booted feet thudded down the stairs, and then faded into silence.

And finally, finally, Kitty sank to the floor, buried her face in her hands, and wept.

5

K itty spent the rest of the day curled up in bed, trying and failing to sleep through the vicious headache still battering her skull.

Gods, what had come over her. What had she done. Foolish. *Foolish.*

And the more she fought to shove away the memories, the stronger they seemed to surface, crowding into her aching head. The orc's laugh. His lean, beautiful body. His tongue. That... ring.

And even worse, his... kindness. His easy generosity. The way he'd made it all seem so... natural, between them. So right. So... *fun.*

Kitty groaned aloud, buried her face in the pillow—but once again, that only made it worse. Because the pillow, she had already unhappily discovered, smelled like him. The entire damned bed—gods, her entire damned *apartment*—smelled like him. Rich. Musky. Sweet.

And not for the first time, there was a sudden, alarmingly powerful compulsion to try to find him again. To return to that pub, perhaps. To seek out places where orcs might gather. To ask, maybe, if they knew a tall, laughing orc with spiky hair, and...

But gods, no. *No.* He hadn't wanted it. Hadn't wanted her. And he hadn't even bothered telling her his name, let alone asking for hers—and she hadn't once gotten a good look at his face, either. And if she were to pass him on the street, would she even be able to pick him out with any certainty whatsoever?

No. No. It had been a stupid, foolish mistake. She had to forget it, and move on. Find a new plan, a new way to survive.

You have options, Charles had said. *Options.*

Kitty almost laughed into the pillow, or maybe it was a sob, because what Charles had surely meant was—she could find another man. Yet another selfish, wealthy man to cling to, and dote on, and impress. And perhaps, if she was very, very lucky, that man might even make her an offer of marriage...

But another choked sob escaped Kitty's throat, because curse him, Charles hadn't been wrong, and men like him *didn't* marry women like her, did they? No. No. They wanted those... *arrangements.* But finding a suitable man for such an arrangement was no easy feat, either—and thanks to Charles, Kitty was now trapped here in Dusbury. Which was primarily a business and university town, not a cosmopolitan hub bursting with wealth and excess and prestige. And Kitty already knew all the potential prospects by name, could list them one by one. Some of them notoriously petty or cruel, some of them deeply in debt, many of them already married to women she knew...

Kitty's nausea was rising again, her head violently shaking against the pillow. No. No. And perhaps—perhaps she could consider the city, after all, just as Charles had suggested. She could run back to her old circles, her old contacts, the various friends and enemies of her ruthless, now-departed mother. She could beg for help, beg for lodging, and in return, she would need to...

The nausea kicked and surged with staggering force, and

Kitty dodged out of bed, and back toward the chamber-pot. Emptying the contents of her roiling stomach again and again, until she sagged forward on the floor, her sweaty face in her trembling hands.

Gods, there had to be another way. There had to be. She could study a trade, something like weaving or dressmaking… but how could she pay the fees? She could seek an apprenticeship… but what reputable master would take on an untested, untrained woman, already well into her twenties? She could set her sights lower, perhaps, try to work as a servant or a housemaid… but how would she gain any of the needed references? Perhaps if she went to Charles, if she begged, he would—

She retched again, but nothing came up this time, and after she shakily washed her face and hands, she curled up in bed again, yanking the blanket over her eyes. If she could just sleep, perhaps she could think again, find a solution, something…

She did somehow sleep after that, but it was jerky and fitful, full of strange, heated dreams. With far, far too many visions of the orc, with his big clawed hands, his warm graceful body, his slick licking tongue. And in the dreams, she could almost—almost—see his face, his eyes. Could see how his eyes glittered, crinkling at the corners when he grinned. When he told her how sweet her scent was, how pleasing she was, how beautiful.

And that image was so clear now, so clear that it might have even happened, perhaps. After she'd kissed that audacious ring of his, perhaps, and told him how gorgeous he was. And then his gentle hands had lifted her face, perhaps wanting to see her eyes.

No, tha's you, his low voice had whispered, almost reverent. *So sweet, woman. So lovely to touch an' taste an' scent. Will never, ever forget this.*

Kitty jerked awake once again, clutching at her churning belly—and after another miserable round at the chamber-pot, she staggered over to the pantry, and attempted to drink a little water, and nibble on a chunk of dry bread. But even that set her stomach heaving again, and soon she was back at the chamber-pot, and then crawling into bed again.

She just had to sleep. To forget. She had options. She would think of something.

But the longer she slept, the worse it all seemed to become. The dreams. The visions of the orc, now mixed up with visions of Charles, with that mental list of men, of *options*. With the memories of all the parties and gatherings and travels, all Kitty's many acquaintances, all her concerted efforts to be bright and witty and cheerful. All of them ending... in this. In being left alone and ill and impoverished, with no income, no prospects, no visitors. Nothing.

Somehow, a full night passed, and then another full day, and an entire night again. And when the third morning dawned, the light peeking in from behind the still-closed drapes, Kitty still hadn't been able to keep down a single bite of food. And the sheer exhaustion seemed even worse than before, despite spending multiple days in bed—and when she stood up, and the room sharply reeled around her, there was suddenly a new awareness, grim and bitter and resigned.

Something was wrong. Something beyond just too much wine. It had been three days. *Three days.*

So with considerable effort, Kitty threw on her dressing-gown, clutched Charles' gold coin, and staggered down the stairs. Down to the apartment of her landlady, Mrs. Schultz. And when Mrs. Schultz opened the door, her steely eyes already narrowed with their familiar contempt, Kitty raised her shaky hand, tried not to notice how pale it had somehow become, how the veins stood out blue beneath her skin.

"Please, Mrs. Schultz," she croaked, her voice not nearly her own. "I've fallen quite—ill. Could you please call a physician?"

Mrs. Schultz sniffed and hummed and hawed, but once Kitty handed over Charles' coin, she finally relented. And then

Kitty crept back to her bed, waiting and waiting and waiting, until finally, there was a knock at the door.

And when Kitty dragged herself over to open it, it wasn't a physician at all, but—a midwife. Kitty's own midwife, Miss Thomas, who had supplied her regular courses of silphium for years. And after a cursory examination, and a discussion of Kitty's symptoms, Miss Thomas sighed, and waved toward Kitty's neck.

Toward... the orc's *teeth-marks*, scarred into her skin.

"Sorry, darling," Miss Thomas said, with clipped, dispassionate finality. "But when you're fool enough to lie with an orc, this is what you get next. His *spawn*."

6

N o. No. It wasn't possible. It wasn't. The orc's spawn. His *spawn*?!

Kitty was... *pregnant*?!

"No," she gulped at Miss Thomas. "No! That can't be possible. I'm on the silphium, right? And it was only a few days ago. Only one night!"

But Miss Thomas gravely shook her head, and began packing up her bag again. "Orc-seed is strong, and affects women in strange ways," she said flatly. "Some worse than others. And it seems as though you're one of the unlucky ones, I'm afraid."

No. No. This couldn't be happening. Kitty was pregnant. *Pregnant*?!

"But—there must be something we can do," she choked, her voice rising. "Something to—address it. Some kind of herbs, perhaps! Or a—potion. *Anything.*"

But Miss Thomas wasn't looking at her now, snapping her bag shut with grim finality. "I'm sorry, darling, but no," she said. "There's no intervention that'll work against an orc-spawn, other than good old sharpened steel. Which, I'm sorry to say"—she did look briefly sorry—"is quite likely to kill you in the bargain, too."

Oh, gods. Kitty's tingling hands were fluttering at her mouth, her head whipping back and forth. "So what—what am I to do?" she demanded shrilly. "What options do I have?!"

Miss Thomas sighed, and gave a jerky shrug. "You tell your orc you're expecting," she said, "and ask him to care for you until you give birth. In my experience, most of them want heirs badly enough that they'll do whatever you ask. And I can't guarantee this, but"—she shrugged again—"I've heard a rumour that there's a decent midwife practicing at Orc Mountain these days, who specializes in orc births—and they may even be able to handle terminations there, too. You'd be wise to seek her out, if you can."

Kitty's mouth had fallen open, her head still furiously whipping back and forth. A midwife... at *Orc Mountain*. The orcs' huge, deadly, dangerous home to the south, teeming with blight and death and disease. And it had to be well over a full day's journey from Dusbury, and how would she ever find her way there alone, especially in this state?!

"I can't," Kitty gasped, or perhaps sobbed. "I can barely walk down the stairs. I haven't eaten anything in *days*."

Miss Thomas grimaced, and snapped her bag back open, pulling out a small folded packet. "Make a tea out of this," she said, "and it should help your nausea. But again, if you can"— her grimace twisted into something much like revulsion—"ask your orc. I'm told their... *emissions*... can sometimes serve a medicinal purpose, in these matters. If... ingested."

Their emissions. If *ingested*. Good gods. Kitty truly could not move, or even speak, and Miss Thomas was obviously taking that as her opportunity to leave, again shutting her bag, and turning toward the door. As if she couldn't bear to even be in the same room as Kitty, now that she'd been so thoroughly compromised by an orc.

"But," Kitty gulped, toward Miss Thomas' back. "What if I—can't find him again. What if I don't even know—his *name*."

Her voice did break into a sob this time, shaky and shameful, and she didn't miss the hard, telltale shudder up Miss Thomas' back, followed by another erratic shrug of her shoulder. "Well, if he's at all like the rest of them," she said, curt, "he'll soon smell it, and come back for you. They've got a disturbing ability to scent these things, even over a large distance."

Her lip curled as she spoke, betraying more visceral distaste, but Kitty was clinging to it, to that one whispering, shining glimmer of hope. The orcs could *smell* it, oh gods. And yes, yes, her orc had spoken of smelling multiple times, hadn't he? He'd praised her scent again and again. He'd been able to scent Charles' lack of effort in the bedroom. And he'd somehow smelled another *woman* on Charles, without Charles even being there.

Yes. *Yes.* The orc would smell it, and come back for her. He had to. He *had* to.

So Kitty didn't argue when Miss Thomas turned to leave again, and she gratefully staggered back to bed, inhaling the orc's sweet, familiar scent on the bed-linens. He would come back. Surely.

She only needed to wait.

7

Kitty waited through the next day, and the next, and the next.

She'd stopped attempting to eat altogether, and had instead focused on drinking Miss Thomas' prescribed tea, and taking careful sips of water. It was enough to curb the vomiting, at least, but the nausea still roiled and festered, and she passed most of each day in bed, slipping in and out of consciousness.

The orc would come. He had to come.

On the sixth day, there was a loud, urgent pounding on the door—and Kitty's heart lurched in her chest, kicking into a furious rhythm as she shoved out of bed and staggered to the door. Flinging it wide open, only to discover—

Her landlady again. Mrs. Schultz.

"I'm here for this month's rent," Mrs. Schultz said flatly, as her narrow eyes swept up and down Kitty's filthy, rumpled form. "It's overdue."

The rent. *Overdue*. The room had already been slowly spinning, and Kitty had to grasp against the doorframe, and pull in long gulps of air. "Ch-Charles," she managed, her voice hoarse. "Mr. Tatterham, I mean. He said—he would pay it. For another month."

And yes, yes, Charles had promised that, hadn't he? At that damned party? So why was Mrs. Schultz shaking her head like that, the contempt flaring higher in her eyes...

"Haven't heard a word from him," she replied. "Sent him multiple letters, even sent my girl over to his place to check. His butler said he's gone off on some hunting jaunt for a month. Didn't leave any word about the apartment."

No. No. No, no, *no*. Charles' trip was supposed to be for a week, he'd said only a week, he had that meeting with his potential funder, he'd said he would pay, he'd *said*...

But the comprehension was slamming into Kitty like a slap to the face, hard enough that she staggered against the wall. Had Charles even intended to pay the next month's rent at all? Or had he only said that so she wouldn't make a fuss, and embarrass him in public? Or, even worse, so she would still hand over all those jewels without complaint? And then he'd ducked out of town, and neatly extracted himself from any unpleasant repercussions...

Oh gods, oh gods, what could she do, and Kitty dragged down deep breaths, and desperately fought to focus on options. She had no coin. No jewels. No savings. No skills. *Nothing*.

"Could—would it be possible to have an extension on the rent?" she finally croaked, toward Mrs. Schultz's increasingly impatient eyes. "Just until Mr. Tatterham returns from his trip?"

But Mrs. Schultz was already shaking her head, and glancing darkly beyond Kitty toward the messy, foul-smelling apartment. "No extensions," she said curtly. "I have expenses, too. And a waiting list."

No. No. *No*. "I could—work," Kitty rasped. "I could—clean. Or some mending, or sewing? I'm good at sewing, I am, you'll see!"

She could hear the desperation, cracking shamefully in her

voice, but Mrs. Schultz's eyes had gone even more contemptuous. First darting down toward Kitty's rumpled nightdress, which she hadn't changed in days, and then back toward the smelly, cluttered, unkempt room behind her.

"No need, Miss Clarendon," said Mrs. Schultz, her voice clipped. "I'll be quite pleased if you can vacate the premises at once."

Vacate the premises? At once?! Kitty's jaw dropped, her heart kicking in her chest, and her head had begun wildly shaking, whipping back and forth. No. No. *No.*

"I can't," she said, pleaded. "I'm ill, Mrs. Schultz. Very ill. And I have no help. Nowhere to go."

But if anything, Mrs. Schultz looked even more disdainful than before, her arms folding over her ample chest. "I'm not running an almshouse, Miss Clarendon," she snapped. "The rent is already late, and my family needs to eat, too. I'll give you until tomorrow noon, and that's final."

Kitty's mouth opened to protest, but Mrs. Schultz was already turning away, and stomping down the stairs. Leaving Kitty to stare after her, unblinking, while a cold, distant terror choked and churned in her chest.

She had to leave. By tomorrow. Noon. Like *this*.

Suddenly the nausea was surging again, bubbling in her throat, and she lurched for the chamber-pot, just in time. Heaving up the minimal remaining contents of her stomach, while her head viciously pounded, and hot wetness streaked down her cheeks.

What could she do. What could she do.

She ended up curled in bed again, fighting for breath, fighting to think through the dread and chaos crashing through her skull. She could try going to Charles' house, or perhaps to one of his friends' houses. One of her acquaintances. She could beg, and plead, and make promises, and...

And then what? She would convalesce there, living on

their pity and contempt, until the orc came for her, and threw the household into an uproar? Or, she would wait until her hosts discovered she was pregnant, and face the consequences then?

And then—even if Kitty claimed that the child was Charles', would it make any difference? Charles had always been adamantly against children—or at least, children with Kitty—and he would insist on having the pregnancy terminated at once. And when the herbs and potions didn't work, what would he do next? And even if she somehow managed to convince him to tolerate the pregnancy, what would he do when he found out the child wasn't his, but an orc's?

No. No. The child needed to be dealt with. The orc needed to be found. And if he wasn't going to come find her, the only option was for Kitty to try to find him.

To go to Orc Mountain. Alone.

Even the thought dredged up more nausea, more bitter barrelling terror—but it was something. It was a plan. A dangling, desperate hope. Maybe she would find the orc. Maybe he would still help her.

She repeated that thought as she dragged herself out of bed, and began the daunting task of sorting through her belongings. Apart from the clothes, accessories, and grooming implements, she didn't have many possessions to speak of, and most of her current wardrobe was utterly impractical for day-to-day living, let alone a gruelling journey to Orc Mountain. Even so, she had to choke down her sobs as she stared down at her tightly packed valise, and then back at all the lovely, costly garments still hanging in her wardrobe. She should try to take them. Try to sell them. Something.

But instead, she ended up back in bed, weeping into the orc's fading scent, until the room began to fade around her, too. She would deal with it in the morning. In the morning...

But when her awareness cut in again, it was with more

pounding on the door. And then Mrs. Schultz's muffled voice, grating painfully into her consciousness.

"Miss Clarendon!" it called. "Unless you've got the rent, you'll be on your way at once."

No. No. No, no, no. But the nightmare was still here, still horribly and brutally real, and Kitty shoved her numb, trembling body out of bed, and back toward the door. To where Mrs. Schultz had brought two large, stern-faced men with her, clearly ready to bodily hurl Kitty from the premises.

So Kitty pulled on her boots, yanked on a shawl over her nightdress, and clasped her valise with shaking hands. And then she stumbled past Mrs. Schultz and the men, lurching down the stairs, and out the door—where she found herself abruptly confronted with the sudden cool air and bright sunlight of the street. And for a long, hanging moment, she could only seem to stand there, staring at nothing, while more sickening, terrified misery plumed in her twisting belly.

Orc Mountain. She needed to go to Orc Mountain. South.

Her first steps were shaky, stilted, tentative—but she was moving, somehow, putting one foot in front of the other. South. Orc Mountain. To find the orc. To find help.

She repeated it over and over as she walked, as the bustling streets around her gradually quieted. Turning into a road with houses and cottages on both sides, and then cottages further apart, and finally just trees. Trees, and the occasional fellow travellers, who often eyed Kitty askance, but thankfully kept their distance. And far too late, she realized that she surely looked downright frightful, wandering down the street in an unkempt nightdress, her face grimy, her hair a tangled mess.

But there was nothing for it, only walking, and walking, and walking. Her steps coming slower, now, her hand clutched over her churning stomach, her mouth parched and dry. Because she hadn't even thought to pack water, oh gods—how *did* one even pack water?—and maybe there would be a stream in the forest somewhere, if she looked?

So she stumbled off the road toward the trees, toward what seemed like a path. Just following into the trees, numb and unthinking, deeper and deeper. Until she tripped over something—a tree root, damn it—and staggered sideways. Nearly crashing into a tree, and she clutched at its solid, scratchy trunk as she gulped for breath, and glanced blearily around her.

Wait. Wait. She was—where? And the road had been— where? Back there, perhaps? Or—wait, no, over there, surely?

She pushed off the tree, staggering back in the direction she'd come—but it seemed to take so much longer this time, with no sign of the road whatsoever. And gods, she was so thirsty, and walking was so tiring, her body both hot and cold, and inexplicably shivering. So shaky she had to grip her hands together, blow on them to stay warm, and why did they look so blue...

But wait, where had her valise gone? At her feet, surely, but no, not there—or maybe back there, by the tree. But the tree was—where, oh gods, where, just as impossible as the road, and Kitty stumbled over another root as she whirled around, as the forest blurred and swooped before her eyes. No. No. She had to think. Why couldn't she think, what was she supposed to do...

The orc. The orc was supposed to come. To help her. But as Kitty stared around at the endless sea of trees, there was no orc, no help, no road, not even a mountain. Just cold, numb emptiness, and with it, a dark, distant wail of panic. She was lost. Sick. Pregnant. Alone.

And the orc... hadn't come. And why, why hadn't he come, what had he said to her, just before he'd left...

You shall... be well, woman. You shall be well and safe, here on your own?

And she'd... dismissed it. Ignored it. Sent him away. *Perfectly all right! Fine.*

The laugh escaped her mouth on its own, or perhaps it was

a sob, ragged and desperate. And the trees were spinning again, catching and juddering, blurring into a mass of grey and brown and green. Alone. The orc hadn't come. Alone. And what came next, was there anything else but this, deeper and darker and colder and crueller, until... until...

Wait. There. A shift of green and grey, in the trees. Something... different. Something... new.

And even before her eyes had properly focused, Kitty choked a high-pitched gasp, and stumbled toward it. Toward the big, bulky grey-green figure standing, staring, unmoving, beside that tree.

The orc. The *orc*.

And she didn't stop, didn't think. Just rushed that last small distance toward him, and threw herself into his arms.

"Oh, thank the gods," she sobbed, into his solid bare chest. "You *came*."

8

For an instant, nothing moved. Not Kitty, and most certainly not the orc. His big body gone utterly rigid against her, as a sound much like a growl shuddered through his chest.

Kitty flinched, inhaling sharp—and wait. Wait. The smell. The rich, sweet scent of that bare skin, warm and smooth beneath her cheek. It wasn't—right?

She flailed backwards, so fast she staggered sideways, her thoughts screeching with panic, her bleary eyes blinking again and again toward the orc. The different orc. Not—*him*.

And no, no, this orc was broader, bulkier, and perhaps shorter, too. His shoulders wide and square, his bare chest and abdomen packed with solid muscle, and scattered with old scars. And his hair wasn't short and messy, but instead it was long and neat, and tightly bound into a shining black braid that fell over his scarred chest, almost to the waist of his trousers.

And... his face. It was a face that might have usually been genial, or even kind, with the broad nose, the upward tilt of his mouth, and those creases at the corners of his eyes. But right now, he looked... shocked. Incredulous. Furious. His black eyes glittering, narrowing, as they swept all the way down Kitty's filthy body, and then back to her face.

But he hadn't yet spoken—his mouth was very hard and set—and Kitty finally gulped for air, for words. "You're—" she began, thick and hoarse. "You're not—*him*."

The orc's lip curled, his jaw flexing in his cheek, and his muscular arms folded tightly over his bare chest. "No," he said, clipped. "You seek Thrain, I ken?"

His voice was low and smooth and velvety, enough to make something clench in Kitty's churning belly, and there was a choked moment's silence as she stared at him, and fought to make sense of his words. *You seek Thrain, I ken.* Thrain?

"I seek what?" her voice blurted out, on its own. "Or who?"

The contempt flashed sharper in the orc's narrow eyes, his big arms flexing against his chest. "Thrain, of Clan Grisk," he said again, far more deliberate this time, as if he were speaking to a child. "My clan brother. You bear the scent of his seed. And his... *son*."

His mouth twisted as he spoke, almost spitting out that final word *son*, and for a dazed, dangling instant, Kitty stared at him, while something powerful clashed and clanged in her chest. A son. She was carrying a *son*. He could... *smell* it.

And in that moment, for perhaps the first time, it occurred to Kitty that this wasn't just a spawn, a sickness, a horrible disaster that had descended upon her and destroyed her life— but a real, living, actual being, growing inside her. A son. *Her* son.

Her hand fluttered to her churning stomach, and she blinked at the orc, at that cold contempt still flashing in his eyes. At how he was... upset by this. Furious. As if it was something... personal.

And wait. *Wait.* Her orc had been upset, too. Because of his real partner, his real woman. And perhaps this new orc was that woman's friend, somehow? A relative? On her side?

"It was just—a—a foolish mistake," she stammered, toward

the orc's angry eyes. "It didn't—mean anything. I know he's still very much in love with his—his real—"

She couldn't seem to finish, and she grimaced, rubbing her shaky hands at her hot, sweaty face. And then she blinked, cringing away, because the orc suddenly looked even more enraged, his hands' black claws visibly lengthening, digging into the meat of his bulky biceps.

"So you did not know Thrain's name," he said thinly, "but you knew *this*? And you yet went forth and *mated* with him, enough to cover yourself with his scent, and spark his *son* upon you?!"

The disbelief was cold and bitter in his voice, in his crackling eyes, and Kitty cringed again, shaking her head back and forth. "It wasn't—like that," she gulped. "I was only upset, and not thinking, and I drank too much wine. Because my— my *boyfriend*—he dumped me, and took away my apartment and all my lovely jewels, and threw me out, so—"

But wait, wait, oh gods, she was losing the thread entirely— but it was already too late, because a harsh, vicious-sounding growl burned from the orc's throat, and his huge taut body flared a little forward, his big hands snapping to tight fists at his sides. Almost as if—as if he'd meant to lunge at her, and then had caught himself, just in time.

"So you then sought a new *boyfriend*, woman?" he hissed, with pure loathing in his voice. "You found a foolish, feckless orc to lie with you, so you might gain his son, and thus his care and keeping—and ach, his *jewels*—for the rest of your days?!"

He was spitting the words by the end, baring a mouthful of sharp white teeth. And Kitty felt herself blanching, her stomach curdling, and she clapped her hands over her mouth, shook her head back and forth.

"No," she gulped at him. "No. Not—like that. I didn't mean—anything. I was only—lonely, and vexed, and very, very foxed. And the orc was so kind, and fun, and handsome, and generous in bed, too, and he just felt so—"

But wait, no, no, that was making it even worse, this orc's bulky body again flaring in place, his growl more like a roar. And his narrow eyes were flashing with more rage, more contempt, and more... pain. Again, as if this was some kind of personal insult, or even... an attack.

Kitty's stomach was truly roiling now, her sticky hands dragging at her face, and she shook her head back and forth, grasped at words, at some way out. "I swear, it didn't mean anything," she choked. "For either of us. I know how deeply he cares for his other woman. He loves her, and he was so upset about how she—"

The orc's menacing snarl drowned out her voice, and his big clawed hand snapped sideways, slicing very near to Kitty's heaving chest. "His *woman*?" he demanded at her. "Thrain told you he has a *woman*?!"

Kitty blinked blearily at his furious face, and lurched a shaky, staggering step backwards. "Y-yes?" she croaked, as the nausea surged higher, closer. "His best friend, and his partner, for years? And she—left him? Because of—his drinking?"

And oh gods, the orc was growling again, his big body vibrating all over, his fists hungrily flexing at his sides. As if he were one moment, one more breath, away from losing the last of his control, and tearing Kitty to pieces where she stood...

"There was no *woman*," he barked at her. "It was me. His best friend, his scent-bond, his *home*. It was *me*, and he was *mine*!"

Oh. Oh. Oh gods, oh gods. And suddenly it was all crashing through Kitty's trembling body at once, the orc's rage, his hurt, his... jealousy. She'd stolen his best friend. His scent-bond. His *home*?!

Kitty couldn't move, could only stare at him for another endless, horrible moment. Her thoughts spinning, her heart thundering, as her stomach kicked and screamed—

And before she'd even followed it, she sank to the ground, and vomited at his feet.

9

Kitty couldn't have said how long her humiliation lasted, her filthy body wracking and trembling at the orc's booted feet.

But when it finally finished, and she'd risked a fearful, ashamed glance upwards, the orc's eyes had gone unreadable, his throat visibly convulsing. And in his clawed hand, thrust out toward her, was…

A waterskin?

Kitty couldn't hide the frantic eagerness in her trembling hands as she grasped for it, and drank, and drank. Desperately craving it, even as her stomach was already roiling again, churning thick and painful in her belly.

"Ach, enough," cut in the orc's voice, far quieter this time, but still with an unmistakable air of command in it. "Too much shall only sicken you again."

Kitty instantly lowered the waterskin, giving a shaky nod, and wiping at her mouth with the back of her hand. Not missing the oddly harsh sound of the orc's exhale, low and irritated, as he fished in his pocket, and thrust something else down toward her.

Oh. It was—a handkerchief. A familiar handkerchief. The

same one the first orc—Thrain—had given her, that ill-fated night. And even as Kitty gratefully took it, mopping at her mouth, she couldn't help another fearful, uncertain glance up at the orc's grim, set face.

"Why do you have—" she began, and then shook her head, cringing backwards, away. Because surely he wouldn't answer, or he would only return it with more rage, and what did it matter anyway?

But the orc's throat was convulsing again, and he glanced purposefully beyond her, his jaw flexing in his cheek. "I used it to track your scent," he said flatly. "I wished to be sure you were not..."

He grimaced, giving a sharp, angry-looking wave of his hand down toward her, and Kitty swallowed hard, crumpling the handkerchief in her fingers. "I didn't want to be," she whispered, desolate. "I was on a strong regimen of silphium. I thought it would be *fine*."

Her voice shamefully cracked, and suddenly the wetness was spilling from her eyes, streaking down her hot cheeks. While the orc just stared at her again, blank and inscrutable— and then his eyes closed, his hand roughly rubbing at his mouth.

"You are alone?" he asked, without inflection. "Are there any others who know of your state, or where you have gone?"

"Just—the midwife," Kitty choked, wiping at her face. "I don't have anyone else. Anything else. Charles—my boyfriend—he severed our connection, and kicked me out of my apartment, and took all the jewels back. And I've been so ill, I haven't eaten for *days*, and I hoped—"

The sobs were lurking in her throat, threatening to consume her voice, and she again wiped at her face, dragged for breath. "The midwife said the orc—Thrain—might come back," she gulped. "But he—didn't. So I wanted to try to—to find him. To see if he—"

Gods, if he what? If he wanted her? If he wanted their son?

If he would support her, or help her, or even care about her predicament in the slightest?

This new orc was looking truly pained now, squeezing his eyes shut, as though he longed for nothing more than to whirl around and walk away, forever. And curse her, but Kitty's fool hand had reached to grasp at his ankle, clutching the smooth, warm leather of his boot.

"Please, sir," she whispered. "Please. I'm desperate. I'll do anything. Anything you want."

At that, the orc's eyes darted sharply down toward her, and Kitty didn't look away. Just held his gaze, let him see the pleading in her wet eyes. Because at this point, she would absolutely do anything, anything he asked...

The orc's eyes slightly widened, his lips parting—and for the briefest of instants, his gaze flicked further down. Down, toward... oh. Kitty's hand. On his boot.

Oh. Ohhhhh. Something swooped in Kitty's belly, hot and deep, and she swallowed hard, felt her tongue brush her lips. And then she slowly, carefully bent forward, and pressed her mouth to his boot.

It was smooth beneath her lips, the scent musky and warm in her nostrils. And as she stayed bent there, breathing it in, it distantly, wildly occurred to her that the orc was watching this. He was... allowing this. Allowing her supplication, her pleading, her... worship.

And when she arose again, meeting his stunned-looking eyes, something seemed to crackle in the air, fierce and heady and aching. And for that single hanging breath, Kitty was almost certain he would agree, he would perhaps push her down onto the earth, and demand she serve him until he relented...

Until, without warning, it was—gone. The orc reeling backwards, away, his hands clawing against his face. And suddenly Kitty could almost taste the rage again, snapping through his bulky body, shuddering powerfully at his shoulders. Shoulders that were rapidly rising and falling, heaving with his deep, erratic breaths.

"Please," Kitty heard herself whisper. "*Please*, sir. I—"

"*Enough*, woman," the orc cut in, his hand slashing out toward her. "Enough. *Ach.* I shall help you."

Oh, thank the gods, and Kitty almost sobbed with relief, and resisted the rising, appalling urge to again begin kissing at his boots. "Thank you, sir," she croaked. "I am forever indebted to you."

But the orc returned it with a heavy exhale, a curt, cursory shake of his head. "There is no debt," he said, his voice wooden. "Only brotherhood."

There was a strange twist on his mouth as he spoke, something between amusement and bitterness. Suggesting, surely, that he was only doing this for the orc he cared for—for Thrain. And once it was done, he would be done, too. Forever.

"Now rise, woman," he said, another clipped command between his teeth. "And come with me."

10

Rise, and come with him.

It seemed a straightforward enough command, and one that Kitty genuinely wanted to follow. So why couldn't she seem to obey it, her hands scrabbling helplessly at the earth, her feet numb and clumsy and useless beneath her...

The orc's sigh felt exasperated, resigned—but then he reached down, his big hands gripping gingerly against Kitty's trembling sides, and lifting her up. Settling her onto her shaky feet with surprising care, before jerking away from her again.

Kitty attempted a grateful smile toward his forbidding face, but she could already feel her body swaying, teetering to the side—until the orc's strong arm caught her, clasping close and firm around her shoulders. Just the way the other orc—Thrain—had done, that night on the street. And Kitty fought the sudden urge to clutch back at him, to collapse into him, to bury her face in his chest and weep.

"Th-thank you, sir," she croaked instead, with a wince. "I'm—very sorry."

The orc sighed again, even heavier than before, and when she risked another look up at his face, he was glancing at the forest around them, his brow creased. And then he inhaled, slow and deep, his eyes fluttering closed.

"You have brought—goods," he said now, his voice still clipped, as he nodded toward the trees. "Over there. Why are these not with you?"

Oh. Right. Kitty winced again, shook her head. "I... don't know," she managed. "I... lost them, I think."

The orc's face looked even more disapproving than before, and perhaps rather incredulous, too. But he jerked another nod, and then began walking in the direction he'd indicated, drawing Kitty along beside him. His movements surprisingly slow and careful, his arm firm and safe around her shoulder.

But even that short distance proved markedly difficult, with Kitty's feet so weak and useless beneath her, with how the trees kept tilting, no matter how she squinted or blinked. And soon the orc had halted again, his breath exhaling harsh, his other hand dragging against his neat braid with obvious exasperation.

"Ach, mayhap you sit and wait, then," he said, as he guided her toward a large fallen log. "And I shall fetch your goods, and return."

Kitty gratefully sank down onto the log, nodding, and then blankly watched as the orc jogged off through the trees. Clearly seeking out her valise by just the scent of it, but she was far too exhausted to marvel at such a feat, or even to keep holding her head up. Far easier to just sag sideways, to close her eyes, for just a moment...

"Ach, woman!" cut in a voice, too close—and when Kitty forced her unwilling eyelids open again, she found herself gazing into a pair of black eyes. The orc's eyes, sharp and disbelieving, and wait, those were his hands, again settling firmly against her sides. Because—oh. She'd somehow fallen off the log, and he was now propping her up against it, taking care that she was fully upright before drawing his hands away again.

"When have you last eaten?" he asked, and she only vaguely realized that he'd opened her valise, and was sniffing at it with obvious distaste. "And why have you brought no food?"

Kitty blinked toward him, and fought to formulate an answer—but once again, nothing would seem to come. "I... don't know," she whispered. "I've been... very ill. For many days."

The orc's square jaw tightened, his clawed hand rubbing at his eyes. But then he nodded and sighed, harsh enough that it fluttered Kitty's loose, sticky hair around her face. "Do you wish to eat now?" he asked, his voice very even. "I have brought some dried fruit and meat, should you wish. Or, I could hunt and cook you some fresh meat, mayhap."

Oh. Kitty's distant astonishment at this generous offer was swiftly overwhelmed by the rebellious roiling in her stomach, and she clamped her hand to her mouth, shaking her head. "No, thank you," she choked, against her fingers. "I—can't."

The orc was still rubbing at his eyes, but he nodded, and then cast another helpless-looking glance around at the forest. "Then we ought to head for Orc Mountain at once," he said firmly. "We have kin there who can help you. Ach?"

Kitty instantly, fervently nodded—gods, in what world would she have ever dreamt of being so desperate to go to Orc Mountain? But the orc was nodding again too, though his eyes were again glancing away, his mouth twisting into another pained-looking grimace.

"It would not be wise for me to journey with you openly thus, on the human road," he said, with a wave of his hand toward Kitty's slumped body. "Lest I wish to risk reproof or attack from humans. Do you ken you could walk upon the road yourself, should I take you there? I could stay near in the wood, and..."

But a highly betraying wetness was already welling behind Kitty's eyes—gods, he couldn't expect her to *walk*, she could scarcely sit up—and thankfully, the orc abruptly stopped speaking, his mouth gone very thin. "Ach," he said. "Then mayhap... I could carry you. Should you wish."

He spoke slowly, and through gritted teeth, as though he wanted nothing more than for Kitty to refuse. But curse it, she was already nodding again, the hopefulness leaping through her chest. "That is—very kind," she gulped, before she could stop it. "Thank you."

The orc's face had gone even grimmer than before, but he slung Kitty's valise on his shoulder, and knelt to slip his arms beneath her. His capable, powerful arms, lifting her up as though her weight was of no consequence, before gathering her body close against his chest.

Oh. Oh, it was lovely, so warm and strong and safe. And for a hushed, hanging moment, curled there into his solid, sturdy strength, into the sweet richness of his scent, Kitty almost felt... relaxed. At peace. He was caring for her. He would keep her safe. He would...

But then the orc began to walk, slowly making his way through the trees. And though she could feel the care in his steps, could feel his palpable efforts to hold her steady and upright, the nausea was already simmering again. Churning higher and higher with every slight jostle of her body, and her deep breaths weren't helping, closing her eyes wasn't helping, oh gods, no, no—

The orc noticed it just in time, roughly thrusting her down onto the ground as she once again emptied her stomach. And afterwards, she could only seem to stay there, trembling, on her hands and knees in the dirt. Gods, what could she do. Why was this happening to her. What if he decided to leave her, no, no, no...

"I'm sorry," she gulped, between choked breaths. "Please don't leave. I'm sorry."

But that was the sound of another sigh above her, a very brief touch of warmth to the back of her neck—and Kitty belatedly realized he was holding up her hair, keeping it out of the mess. "I shall not leave," he said, quiet. "You bear my clan brother's scent, and his son. And thus, I am bound to help you."

Oh. And perhaps it should have felt like an insult—he was only doing this because of the obligation, because of the son—but Kitty couldn't deny the fundamental force of her relief, all the same. He wouldn't leave. He was bound to help her.

"There is a camp near here, beside a spring," he said now. "Mayhap we can rest there, if you can bear to again be carried for a spell."

Kitty wasn't about to argue, and she gratefully nodded, and even attempted a smile toward the orc's face as he again lifted her into his arms. Walking slow and steady, his gaze held straight ahead, his steps even more careful than before.

Even so, they had to stop twice more on the way there, whenever Kitty's nausea became too strong to bear. But finally, she found herself being gently set down on some soft moss, beside a spring of fresh, bubbling water.

"Whilst I ready the camp, you shall drink, and wash, and put on clean garb," the orc told her, the command again clear in his voice. "I shall leave your goods here with you. Call for me when you are done, ach?"

He'd even thrust that handkerchief back into her hand, and Kitty gave a shaky nod, and obliged. Taking slow sips of the spring's cool, fresh water as she thoroughly washed out the handkerchief, and then scrubbed at her hot, sticky face. And next, after a furtive glance around—the orc was nowhere to be seen—she peeled off her filthy shawl and nightdress, and then washed herself all over, too.

Despite the ever-rising exhaustion, it did help, and Kitty gratefully wrapped herself in a clean dressing-gown, and then repacked the valise, before turning to call for the orc. Whose name, she realized, she didn't actually know.

"Um, sir?" she ventured, into the empty forest around her. "Mister... orc?"

But yes, yes, there he was, his big greenish-grey body

striding out from behind a nearby rocky hill. His eyes giving a cursory glance up and down her form as he nodded, and then he once again bent down, and plucked her and her valise up into his arms.

But as he strode back toward the rocky hill, he didn't again speak, not even offering his name. And Kitty's exhausted brain was circling that, again and again, together with the hurtling, incongruous vision of how she'd kissed his boot. How he'd stood there, and watched.

And, too, with how he *had* told her the name of her son's father. Thrain, of Clan Grisk. *My clan brother.*

"So are you... *of Clan Grisk* also?" she heard her thin voice ask, as the orc halted beside a large upright wall of rock, and powerfully heaved his shoulder against it. "Like... Thrain?"

She only vaguely noticed a slab of rock somehow scraping backwards, revealing empty blackness behind it. "Ach," he replied tersely, as he stepped into the blackness, and again shoved at the stone. "I am Grisk."

There was more scraping behind them, and then instant, utter darkness, closing in all around. But rather than the fear Kitty should have felt, there was only more awareness, more understanding. And a quiet, indefensible longing, clutching in her belly, leaning her closer against him...

"Thank you, my Lord Grisk," she whispered. "I don't know what I would have done, without you."

He made a low harrumphing sound, but didn't reply, or argue. Just kept walking through the darkness, which seemed to be steadily tilting downwards, until he finally halted, and shoved his shoulder against something else that scraped loudly in Kitty's ears. And then, after another few steps, he set her down onto something flat, and soft. Something much like... a bed?

And even as he eased away, Kitty found herself foolishly scrabbling for him, clutching his immobile hand with hers. "You'll still stay with me, right?" she choked out. "Please, sir?"

She could hear his exhale, sounding heavy, resigned. But then, to her genuine astonishment, she felt him easing forward again, and settling down onto the bed. Sitting on it, yes, staying with her, even as he nudged her shoulder backwards, away from him, in a silent but very clear command. *Lie down*, it meant. *Sleep.*

So Kitty gratefully nodded, and sank back onto the fur, curling as close to his solid warmth as she dared. She was safe, for now. Protected. Cared for.

And for now, it was enough. More than enough. So she finally closed her eyes, and slept.

11

Kitty couldn't have said how long she slept, or when she awoke again. But when she blinked her eyes open, she found herself in… a room. A small, stone-walled, candlelit *room*.

It was very simply furnished, with a steel trunk, a chair, a small table with the candle, and the bed she was currently lying in. And while the bed was crudely made of hard wood, it was also surprisingly soft, thanks to the large thick fur spread upon it. And it was on this fur that she'd been sleeping, and another fur had been placed atop her, its heavy weight warm and reassuring.

And—wait. The orc. And when Kitty carefully pushed up in the bed, it was to the discovery that he wasn't—here. Was he?

The panic surged through her chest, and with it was the ever-present nausea, already curdling in her stomach. And Kitty groaned aloud as she clasped a hand against her mouth, her eyes searching for the exit, for—

Oh. The orc. Stalking into the room with swift strides, his brow furrowed, his hands clenched at his sides. And gods, even the sight of him somehow seemed to settle the nausea in Kitty's belly, and she fought the highly irrational urge to rush over, and throw her arms around him.

"L-lord Grisk," she said instead, stupidly. "Have I... slept long?"

The orc jerked an irritated-looking shrug, and then grasped for something that had been lying on the bed beside her—oh. A waterskin.

"Drink," he said, his voice flat, as he thrust it out toward her. "Slowly."

Kitty obediently drank, taking slow, careful sips until her stomach's rising protests suggested that continuing was unwise. And once the orc had taken the waterskin back, she drew in a series of long, deep breaths, both hands clutched over her belly, over where—

Wait. *Wait.* Her breath caught, her body snapped to stillness, and she felt her hand tingling as it slowly spread wider over her lower abdomen. Over where it felt... different, somehow. More... solid. Like something new was inside.

Her son.

Kitty could hear her heartbeat, suddenly, rushing in her ears, and she couldn't seem to stop staring toward the orc. Toward where he was looking at her belly, too, his jaw very tight.

"Your son has begun to form," he said, his tone entirely unreadable. "His scent is already strong and hale upon you."

Kitty's breath was still trapped in her throat, her heartbeat still thundering in her ears—yes, yes, she was really having a child, a *son*. And the orc looked almost as unsettled by this fact as she was, and he purposefully glanced away, his hand rubbing at his mouth.

"Do you ken you could eat now?" he said, clipped. "Is there any meat you should favour? Or aught else?"

But gods, even the thought of eating meat was swirling more miserable havoc in Kitty's brain, her belly—she was really having a child, a *son*—and she swallowed hard, and shook her head.

"Thank you, sir, but no," she choked, muffled, over the distant screeching in her thoughts. "Not unless you'd like to try..."

Her voice trailed off, her eyes blinking, as the screeching shuddered louder, closer. Because gods, where the hell had she been going with that? She surely hadn't been about to say—

But the orc's eyes were sharp on hers, his head cocking sideways, his hands again in tight fists at his sides. "What," he said. "Speak this, woman."

And damn it, the command was like a compulsion, already dragging up the words, hovering them close and powerful— and Kitty heard herself laugh, choked and shrill, for perhaps the first time since they'd met.

"The... midwife," she managed. "She told me to ask—my orc—for help, with the nausea. That his—his *emissions*—might serve a—*medicinal purpose.*"

She laughed again, the sound grating painfully in her ears—but before her, the orc wasn't laughing. He only just kept standing there, and if anything, his expression had hardened, gone even more grim and forbidding than before.

"Your midwife was... not speaking false, in this," he finally replied, his voice curt. "Our seed bears many gifts. One of our mountain's clans has been studying this at length, and we have witnessed its truth again and again, over many ages past."

Kitty's mouth dropped open, the disbelief roaring in her chest—wait, this orc really, really believed that?—and before she could stop it, another laugh escaped from her throat. A laugh that again sounded harsh and shrill, scraping horribly through the cozy, candlelit room.

And far too late, she realized that it sounded mocking, too. As if she were *laughing* at this orc, at her exceedingly generous rescuer, for believing something so foolish, so utterly preposterous...

And curse her, but she could see the orc's anger, his contempt, there in his flashing eyes, in his sharp bared teeth. And he'd even lurched a swift step toward her, his hands again clenched to fists, as though he was fighting an all-consuming urge to attack her, to punish her, to make her pay for all the trouble and grief she'd brought him.

"I shall not bear you mocking me or my kin, fool woman," he growled, low and menacing. "*You* were the one who raised this. Do you wish for this from me, or no?"

Oh gods, oh gods, and Kitty cringed back in the bed, and clutched the fur up to her neck. Her heart pounding in her ears, her eyes frozen on the orc's furious face.

And then, gods strike her where she stood, she glanced... downwards. Down toward the front of the orc's trousers. Toward...

Oh. That. A very large, very obvious bulge, jutting against the trousers' too-tight fabric. And as Kitty gaped at it, transfixed, she could actually see it... shifting. *Swelling.*

And—what was that, there, on the fabric. A dark circle, pooling, spreading wider, with every visible shudder of that hardness beneath. And oh, hell, suddenly Kitty could smell it, something strong and rich and sweet. Something that smelled like... like *him.*

Kitty truly could not stop staring, her breath locked in her throat, her body gone utterly still. Except... except for the brief, betraying brush of her tongue, slipping out against her lips.

There was a harsh-sounding exhale from the orc above her, enough to drag her eyes up to his face—but she couldn't read his expression now, couldn't even begin to follow that hard, sharp glint in his eyes, or the purposeful flare of his nostrils.

At least, until his big clawed hand slid over, and... adjusted himself. Grasping that huge bulk with familiar ease, and straightening it in his trousers. And Kitty's breath audibly choked at the sight, her tongue again brushing her lips, and oh, the smell was even stronger now, curling heavy and tantalizing in the air...

"Ach, woman?" came the orc's demand, his command, even sharper and colder than before. "Do you wish for this from me?"

And between his voice, his hand, that sweet succulent scent in the air, the answer was already rising on its own, from Kitty's lips to his fierce watching eyes...

"Yes, Lord Grisk," she whispered, choked and shameful. "I... do."

12

I *do.*

The words seemed to echo out between them, stark and bare and horribly betraying. Expanding Kitty's continued humiliation for the orc's perusal, his judgement, his contempt.

But to Kitty's distant, deeply grateful surprise, he didn't laugh. Didn't even speak. Only stood there for a long, hushed breath, gazing down at her with those sharp, glinting eyes— and then he squeezed his eyes shut, and ran both hands against his hair. The gesture one of frustration, and disbelief, and... reluctance.

"We don't—need to," Kitty choked out, too loudly, as she shook her head, whirling the room around her. "Of course you—wouldn't want to. It's—absurd. This whole situation is just so, so—"

She flailed her hands helplessly between them, and then down at her belly, her stomach, herself. "I think the gods are p-punishing me," she gulped, with a harsh, too-loud laugh. "Your—Thrain—cursed them that night, you know. And I didn't even argue it, which was unthinkably foolish on my part, because the gods already had it out for me, and their judgement has clearly come back upon me, bound to *ruin* me, *forever.*"

She winced at the words even as she heard them escape, and she flailed her hands even more, because what was she thinking, why was she telling him these ridiculous things, how had it all ever come to this—

"Enough, woman," cut in the orc's weary voice, and when Kitty's eyes darted to his face, he just looked grim again. Grim, and resigned, as he heavily exhaled, and then sank down to sit beside her on the bed. Not near enough to touch, but... close.

"Your only punishment, I ken," he continued, steadier than she might have expected, "was having the ill luck to meet Thrain, rather than any other Grisk. We are meant to care for our own. For our brothers, and our women, and our sons."

Oh. Kitty still couldn't detect any anger or mockery in his voice, only that same calm, steady certainty. As if... he really meant this. The Grisk cared for their own. Including her, and her son.

And... wait. Wait. He was dropping his hand, and... pulling at the drawstring on those tight, straining trousers. Loosening them, oh hell, as his other hand reached over to clasp Kitty's shoulder, and began guiding her downward. Toward... his lap.

Kitty didn't resist, didn't even pretend to. Not even when that strong, steady hand guided her head to rest on his big, solid thigh, her face turned toward his torso. Leaving the weight of her body curled up beside him, as if she were a favoured pet, with her head nestled in her lord's lap.

And her lord's other hand was still moving on his trousers, shifting them downwards... and then reaching inside, and drawing something out. Something big and smooth and green, with just a glimpse of glossy pink beneath his fingers...

But between the closeness, and the dim candlelight, and the ongoing presence of his hand, blocking most of Kitty's view, perhaps the strongest impression was the scent of it. That sweet, rich scent, so close now, soothing her, filling her breath.

And her tongue was brushing her lips again, her breath inhaling deep through her nose and mouth, because she could almost, *almost* taste it...

And then—then—she was. She was, because there was smooth warm flesh brushing her lips, and the taste was there, yes, there. Here, oh hell, and Kitty couldn't hide her hoarse, betraying moan as she pressed closer, sought for more...

And oh, oh gods above, it was giving more. The hot, seeping sweetness sputtering slightly as the stream thickened, pooling between her lips. Her lips that were already sucking, opening wider, welcoming that smooth flesh deeper. Deeper, oh gods, deeper, because it tasted so good, felt so good...

There was a low, guttural-sounding hiss above her, but Kitty only dimly registered it, because there was even more of that sweetness, now, oozing steady into her mouth. And she had perhaps never tasted anything so rich, so decadent, so perfect, her throat already gulping in rapid, eager pulses, her tongue seeking out, slipping closer toward the source...

The source was a long, deep slit, cut into that smooth rounded skin. And as Kitty's tongue gingerly delved against it, it almost seemed to reward her, shuddering against her, flooding out more. Perhaps opening even wider, oh hell, thickening the flow even more, and above her the orc hissed again, his strong hand flexing on her hair...

And wait, when had his hand touched her hair—or had it been there the entire time? But surely it meant that he didn't mind, he didn't, and Kitty moaned with relief as her hungry tongue delved even deeper, into that dark clenching heat. Inside him, oh hell, she was drinking from *inside* him, and nothing, nothing had ever tasted so good, so fresh, so pure and sweet and *right*...

She was fully latched to him with her lips, now, locked into him with her tongue. And when his hips canted up, very slightly, she willingly took him deeper. Sliding a little up and down now, and oh, yes, that pulsed out even more. He was alive and huge and hungry in her mouth, he was letting her suck him, he wanted her sucking him, serving him—

"Can you bear—" came the orc's voice, thick, cracked, breathless. "All of it. My—seed."

Oh, hell yes, and Kitty's head was already nodding, jerky and fervent against his thigh. And the orc's moan sounded involuntary, now, desperate, catching in his throat, as his entire body stiffened, his claws scraping at her scalp—

The sweetness surged into her mouth in a rush, flooding her with stunning, staggering force. And just in time, Kitty shifted the angle, opened her throat wide—and oh, oh, yes, that was it, this orc pouring wild streams of his succulent nectar straight down into her belly. Emptying himself for her, giving her all he'd made for her, all he had...

And as he was doing it—Kitty's bleary eyes blinked up, focused on his face—he was watching her swallow it. Watching with that same sharp, glinting intensity, as his nostrils flared, and a low, heated growl purred from his throat. As if... he liked it. As if he'd wanted it. Yes. *Yes.*

And even when the flow finally slowed, his powerful hand on Kitty's head didn't move. Didn't falter. And for perhaps the first time, she felt the strength in it, that same silent command, reflected in those glittering, watching eyes. He wanted her there. Wanted her to stay.

"Swallow it all," he rasped, very quiet. "You shall not waste what I give you."

Oh. Of course. And Kitty was already nodding—as well as she could—and then seeking at him again with her tongue. Running it all over that slowly softening flesh, and then again nudging it inside, into that deep, decadent slit. Indeed finding more sweetness there, and licking again and again, as deep as she dared. Until she'd surely found and swallowed it all, everything, just as he'd asked.

It was only then that the orc's hand's grip on her head loosened, granting her permission, or yet another command.

So Kitty carefully eased backwards, giving a shuddery, regretful exhale at the feel of him falling slack from her mouth. It was over, already, and why was she so disappointed, what had that even been, what was *happening* to her...

But the orc's hand tightened on her hair again, drawing her fluttering eyes back toward his face. Toward where his own eyes were still glinting like that on hers, and he'd even slightly raised his eyebrow. Looking almost... expectant, perhaps, and Kitty swallowed hard, again tasting his decadent sweetness, before clearing her throat.

"Th-thank you, sir," she whispered. "My Lord Grisk. You taste... very good."

It didn't make sense, none of this made sense—not the taste, not the hunger or the relief, not the very slight flare of his nostrils, the approval in his watching eyes. Or maybe... maybe that was even appreciation, the way one might look at a favoured pet who had accomplished a clever new trick.

"Good," the orc replied, low and gruff. "Has this helped?"

And blinking up at his face, it occurred to Kitty that... it *had* helped. That her stomach had finally stopped churning, for what felt like the first time in weeks—and instead, she felt remarkably quiet, sated, full. And even the fog that had previously swarmed her thoughts seemed more distant, more manageable, enough that she almost felt like... herself. Like she'd used to feel, before any of this had ever happened.

"It... did help," she whispered, with a small, genuine smile toward the orc's waiting, watching face. "I'm so grateful to you, sir."

The orc twitched a curt little nod in return, and then he brusquely tucked himself back into his trousers, and nudged Kitty upright again. So she was sitting on the bed facing him, and for a breath, there was an overwhelming urge to lean in toward him, throw her arms around him, cling to him and never let go...

But just as quickly, it was gone. Gone, because he was on

his feet, facing away from her. With both his hands dragging against his bound hair, while his broad bare shoulders rose, and fell, and rose again.

"Now rest," he said abruptly, still not looking at her, his hands dropping to tight fists at his sides. "I shall stay close."

And with that, he strode stiffly toward the door, and left.

13

For the rest of the day—or what felt like the rest of the day—Kitty stayed curled up in bed, slipping in and out of sleep. And every time she awoke, the orc was there—either striding into the room, or sitting rigid and unmoving in the chair against the opposite wall, his arms folded over his bulky chest.

Invariably, he would then frown at Kitty and stalk over, thrusting the always-full waterskin into her hands. And she would carefully drink and drink and drink, and then pass the waterskin back, mumbling her thanks, before falling into sleep again.

So she was surprised—and disconcerted—when she awoke next to find only guttering candlelight, and no sign of the orc whatsoever. Enough that she felt her panic surging, her hands shoving her body up in bed, her eyes darting all around, to the—

Oh. The orc. Lying on his back on the floor beside her bed, with only a thin-looking cloak between his bare upper body and the hard earthen floor. And his eyes, now fluttering open to meet hers, looked bleary and reddened, with visible dark shadows beneath them.

Kitty's stomach dropped at the sight—he was clearly tired, he was trapped here in this tiny underground room, and stuck sleeping on the cold hard earth, all because of her. And she felt her head abruptly shaking, her hand flapping between him and the bed. "No need to sleep down there, sir," she croaked. "Please."

She'd even shoved over on the bed, making space, making her meaning very clear. And for an instant, the orc just gazed up at her, blinking with those sad, tired eyes—but then he sighed, and nodded, and rose to his feet. And once he'd snuffed out the candle, plunging the room into utter darkness, she felt him slip into the bed beside her.

His big body was stiff against hers, and he was lying on his back, occupying a considerable amount of space in the suddenly small-feeling bed. But gods, it was so, so lovely to have him there, so warm and solid and safe, his scent strong and rich in her breath. And despite her best intentions, Kitty felt herself curling a little closer toward him, relaxing, breathing him in...

After that, sleep came even easier than before, enfolding her quiet and close. Holding her in the deep, certain awareness that she was safe, cared for, content. That no matter how this orc felt about her, he would look after her. He would.

And when she awoke again, what felt like a long time later, he was indeed still there, still in bed beside her. Still in the exact same position, as if he hadn't moved a breath—while Kitty, somehow, had fully nestled against his solid shoulder, her hands clutching his muscled arm, her face pressed into his smooth skin.

She winced as she drew backwards, angling a chagrined glance up at his face—perhaps he hadn't noticed?—but damn it, the candle was already lit, and he was already awake. Awake, and watching her, with entirely unreadable eyes.

"Sorry," she made herself say, with an attempt at a rueful smile toward him. "The heat-seeking is ingrained, I think."

The orc's expression didn't change, and Kitty felt her smile fading, her eyes dropping. Right. This was only a job for him. An obligation. Keeping her son alive, and that was all.

But then the orc cleared his throat, and his big body shifted in the bed. "How fare you this morn, woman," he said, without inflection. "Do you ken you could now eat some meat? Or aught else?"

Oh. Kitty's hand dropped to her stomach, which had promptly begun curdling at even the thought of meat—and she shook her head, angling an uneasy glance back up at the orc's forbidding face. "Thank you, but I think—I'd best not," she said, with a grimace. "I'd really rather not subject you to even more of my sicking up. It's honestly a wonder you haven't left me to drown in it yet."

She'd attempted another halfhearted smile toward his face—foolish, *foolish*, because he only glanced purposefully away this time, his clawed hand rubbing at his mouth. "Ach," he replied. "Is there... aught else you might wish to eat or drink, then?"

Kitty blinked at him, fighting back the inexplicable hurt coiling in her chest, because—had he meant he *agreed* with her stupid drowning joke?—and it took far too long to follow the rest of what he'd said. The question he'd asked.

Is there aught else you might wish to eat or drink.

And gods curse her, but Kitty's breath caught, her thoughts suddenly flooding with visions of the day before. Of her head in his warm, comfortable lap, his big hand spread wide on her hair, his hot sweetness filling her mouth, oozing down her throat...

And before she could possibly stop it, her traitorous eyes once again... glanced downwards. Down toward where the orc's lower half was fully concealed under the fur covering them— but oh, he was still very, very there. Here. And wait, was that a bulge, jutting up just slightly beneath the fur, teasing her, taunting her with its riches...

Kitty still hadn't moved, or breathed, her gaze fixed on the sight—but oh, hell, that was her tongue, brushing brief but betraying against her lips. And even as she belatedly squeezed her eyes shut, she could still feel the orc watching her. Could feel his awareness, his swift comprehension of her most unthinkable, inexplicable longings. And would he mock her, reject her, deride her as the abominable fool she was...

When without warning, his warm hand settled on Kitty's shoulder, and... nudged her downwards. Downwards, toward... *that*. The movement firm and purposeful, as if—as if he was truly giving her permission. Or maybe—maybe even another command.

Kitty still couldn't look at him, couldn't draw in a single breath—but yes, gods yes, she was doing it. Shoving herself awkwardly downwards, ducking beneath the heavy fur, while beside her, the orc shifted his weight, turning onto his side. Turning toward her, oh hell, making this easier for her, and she could even feel his hand fumbling at his trousers. Freeing himself, readying himself for her, his scent flooding the thick humid air.

And oh, gods, there he was, gentle and smooth, nudging purposefully against her lips. And Kitty nearly sobbed as she sucked on him, gained her first full taste of him. Almost even better than the day before, rich and sweet and utterly exquisite, and she couldn't stop her moan of pleasure, couldn't resist sucking harder, letting her tongue seek inside...

But the orc wasn't resisting. Wasn't arguing. If anything, that ooze of sweetness had already shuddered, flowing thicker and faster and smoother, as if in response to her lips' hungry kiss. And *gods* it was good, so, so good, and Kitty only distantly felt her shaky hand coming up to grasp at him, to slip around that smooth thick shaft, guide him deeper—

But at the touch, the orc's body suddenly stiffened—and Kitty winced as she drew back, snatching her hand away.

Already opening her mouth to apologize, because clearly that had been too far, and he only wanted—

Or—oh. His hand. Grasping firm but gentle around her wrist, and... guiding her hand back. Placing her fingers there against his swollen heft, just where they'd previously been. And then—after an instant's frozen stillness—he brushed her fingers further below, too. Down to his bollocks, oh hell, soft and round and shockingly heavy beneath her light, tentative touch.

He held her hand there for just an instant too long, before abruptly letting go—but again, it had been permission. A command. And a strange, fierce shiver rippled up Kitty's spine as she gave a nod he couldn't see, and then... obeyed. Curving her eager fingers around those plump bollocks, caressing them with careful gentleness, while her mouth again found his slick head, and sucked him inside.

And perhaps it was because she felt unusually awake, or perhaps it was the certainty of that permission, that command—but she was putting more into it this time, working harder. Sucking him further into her mouth, slipping her tongue into that deep dark slit, shamelessly seeking his decadent sweetness fresh from its source, while her hand kept eagerly stroking him, fondling him, learning him. Marvelling at the sheer size and weight of those bollocks—gods, no wonder he made so much seed—and then at the warm, solid length of him in her mouth, too. Far too large to suck all the way, too thick to even get her fingers around—but it just meant there was so much of him to touch, his skin so soft and velvety, the weight of him pulsing strong and alive beneath her fingers, between her lips.

Gods, nothing had ever felt so good. Tasted so good. And Kitty couldn't hide her gasping breaths now, the way they'd almost begun to sound like groans. The way her mouth was watering around his invading heft, sliding him slicker and easier and deeper, gouging his smooth dripping head against her gulping, convulsing throat.

And instead of gagging at that dangerous, tenuous touch, Kitty almost felt triumphant, more alive than she'd felt in weeks. Because her lord was hard for her, he was throbbing and swelling for her, he was so generously feeding her. And it had to mean something, he had to like it, his bollocks drawing up beneath her fingers, his body stiffening against her—

The blast of seed came in a sudden, shocking surge, flooding Kitty's mouth with molten swarming heat—but somehow, she kept it all in. Gulping it down her throat in hard, desperate swallows, the sounds thick and lurid and obscene. While her greedy, shameless hand kept squeezing his shaft, sliding up and down as she moaned, as if she was trying to pump out more, more, more...

And oh, he kept giving her more. Shuddering it out in long, powerful spasms as she swallowed again and again. Until finally his heft in her mouth gave one last, straining tremor, and then fell slack between her lips, spent.

But it had been so good, so right, so damned perfect—and his order from the day before was already swarming Kitty's thoughts. *You shall not waste what I give you.*

So she again used her tongue, nudged into him, seeking out every last drop. Cradling him, caressing him, until she heard him give a low hiss, his hand gently but purposefully nudging her away.

Kitty instantly obeyed, jerking back from him, and gulping down long breaths of the thick, stuffy air. And for an instant, there was a bizarrely powerful urge to stay there under the fur, hidden and safe, where she could perhaps coax him back to life, do it all over again...

But then she could feel him—moving. Shifting. Easing away from her, out of the bed. And suddenly her face was flooded with cool, fresh air, and she was blinking at the orc's broad back in the candlelight, in the way the muscle moved beneath his skin as he swiftly tied up his trousers.

"Better?" came his voice, husky but clipped. "Do you ken you could now walk?"

Kitty blinked at his back for another long moment, but then swallowed hard, and shoved herself up to sitting. And with slow, careful movements, she shifted herself off the bed entirely, and up to her feet. Feeling the hard earth beneath her, the way the room's stone walls remained solid and still before her eyes.

"I... think so," she managed. "Thank you, sir."

The orc gave a curt nod, glancing briefly over his shoulder—but then he twitched in place, his eyes gone wide and strange. And when Kitty blinked, glanced downwards, she realized that her dressing-gown had fully fallen open, exposing her entire front half to his eyes. Her pale skin, her small breasts with their dusky nipples, and... her belly. Her previously flat belly, which was now slightly... rounded. Rounded, and visibly protruding, in a way it never had before.

Kitty gasped, and belatedly flailed to pull the gown closed—but the orc had already turned away again, snatching up the cloak that had been lying on the floor, and swinging it over his shoulders. Almost as if he were putting up a barrier between them, one that might hide the unmistakable flush creeping up the back of his neck.

"Have you any warmer clothes?" he asked, without looking at her this time. "It shall yet be a full day's journey."

Kitty swallowed, jerking a nod he couldn't see, and then fumbled for her satchel, which was now lying on the floor beside the bed. And as the orc kept standing there, his back firmly toward her, she rapidly yanked out clothes, pulling on a proper shift and dress, and then her boots, as well.

"I'm ready," she told him, hoarse, which earned her another dismissive nod. And still without looking at her, the orc grasped for the still-lit candle, and next for her satchel, and a small canvas pack she hadn't noticed before. And then he spun and strode toward the door, his cloak billowing out behind him.

"Come," his flat voice said, and Kitty scrambled to obey. To follow his big shadowy body through the dark, stone-walled tunnel, while trying not to trip over her uncertain, unsteady feet.

But the orc was walking slowly, at least, casting occasional reluctant glances over his shoulder, and waiting for her to catch up. Until finally he halted before what appeared to be another stone wall, and then snuffed out the candle. And after an instant's loud scraping in the darkness, Kitty found herself bathed in bright blinding light, and inhaling a bracing blast of fresh cool air.

"Gods, that's lovely, isn't it?" she said toward the orc, without at all meaning to, as a shrill, shaky laugh escaped from her throat. "Like coming to life again."

But the orc didn't reply, and Kitty could just make out his jerky-looking shrug in the too-bright light. And then his big body turned back toward the stone wall behind them, shoving the heavy opening closed with another loud, scraping creak.

It left the two of them standing together outside the wall, in the awkward, ever-expanding silence. And now that Kitty could see him better, it occurred to her that he still looked very tired, his eyes even redder than the night before, with deep grey smudges beneath them. And his harsh face was again purposefully looking away from her, his bleary gaze fixed toward the south. Toward, perhaps, Orc Mountain. And wait— Kitty's eyes squinted in the bright light—those scars on his neck—were those faded *teeth-marks*?

"Shall you be able to walk for a spell on foot?" he asked, his voice conspicuously blank, as he glanced toward her, and away again. "Should you need to rest, only speak this."

Kitty attempted a nod and a smile, which the orc returned with a brief harrumph, before turning on his heel and striding off. Leaving her to once again catch up, following him on a narrow path through the greenery.

Her legs still felt shaky and unused, her breaths already coming shorter than they should have, but the orc kept the pace slow and careful, and frequently glanced back toward her. And as they walked, Kitty found herself gradually settling into the steady repetitive rhythm of it, even as her thoughts began stirring, bubbling, far louder and clearer than she'd felt in days.

Gods, this was a mess. *She* was a mess. What had she been thinking, to rush off alone on a long journey like she had, without packing any food or water? And whatever had possessed her to leave the road in the first place? And perhaps most foolish of all, why hadn't she thought to stash away even a few of Charles' jewels, to sell in exchange for safe passage to Orc Mountain?

And truly, how impossibly fortunate was she, that this orc had shown up? That he'd cared for her, and given her a place to rest, and kept her safe? And as unbelievably bizarre as that entire... *feeding* premise had been, the stark truth was, it had clearly worked. Hadn't it? Kitty still hadn't eaten any actual food whatsoever, but here she was, walking again, *thinking* again. And while the nausea was still present, still palpable, it was also distant and quiet, something that could mostly be ignored, rather than the all-consuming calamity it had been before.

And it was all thanks to him. To this tired, taciturn orc, who'd shown her such impossible generosity. While she, on the other hand, had gone and spent the night with his best friend—his partner, his *lover*—and had gotten herself pregnant with his damned *child*. When she'd full well known that her orc—Thrain—had still cared for someone else. She'd known he was still entangled with someone else. With this orc. Enough, perhaps, to leave those teeth-marks on his neck.

It was me. His best friend, his scent-bond, his home. He was mine.

The nausea suddenly surged again, fierce and visceral in Kitty's belly, enough that she had to clamp her hand against her mouth. Gods, what must this orc think of her. How he must loathe her. She'd not only trampled all over his long-term relationship—his *home*, he'd said—but she'd gone and given him a permanent reminder of it with this child. A living, breathing embodiment of so much betrayal and pain.

And now? Now he was still obliged to help her. To care for her, even in the most intimate of ways, to his own active detriment. His own undoing.

And wait, he'd hesitated up ahead, glancing warily over his shoulder toward her. As if he was *concerned* about her, good gods, even as his jaw flexed, and his clawed hand rubbed against his face.

"What is amiss, woman," he said, his voice clipped. "Do you need rest? Food? Drink?"

And now that Kitty could fully see it, follow it, that was surely loathing, or even contempt, glinting dark and bitter in his tired eyes. He hated her. He did. But he was doing all he could to suppress it, to hide it, to show her only kindness and care. Surely not only for her sake, but for her son's, and for Thrain's. For the partner he still loved, to the point where he would do anything. He would do... this.

Suddenly Kitty couldn't bear it, couldn't stand it for an instant longer—and she staggered toward him, reeling shaky and unsteady on her feet. Not missing how the orc's body visibly stiffened, his eyes widening, as she closed the last space between them, and hurled herself bodily to the earth before him.

"I'm so sorry, sir," she choked up at him, both hands clutched over her suddenly hammering heart. "I'm so, so sorry. I've thrown you into such an impossible position, and I can't imagine how you must be feeling. How deeply you must hate me right now."

The orc kept staring down at her, unmoving, unblinking,

and Kitty gulped for breath, for words. "You could have left me to—to die," she continued, even faster. "You could have just walked away, and solved all your problems at once. But"—she hauled in another breath—"you didn't. You saved me. You're still saving me. Even after I helped destroy your—your *home*."

The orc was still staring at her, with unmistakable disbelief on his face—or maybe it was frustration, or once again the loathing. But Kitty couldn't stop, couldn't stand it, and she held his eyes, pleading with him, needing to make him see, needing to make this right.

"You've been so, so good, Lord Grisk," she gasped at him. "So generous. And in return, I'll do anything you want. *Anything*. I swear to you."

He still didn't reply, just gazing down at her, his eyes shifting with something she couldn't at all identify. And maybe Kitty was just making it all even worse, digging herself even deeper, why wasn't he saying anything, what did he—

Wait. Wait. Because... that scent. Rich, sweet, so close. And Kitty's eyes were almost on a level with his groin, on where he was again... swelling. Flexing. Bulging out against those tight trousers, as a visible pool of wetness began spreading before her eyes...

Oh. Oh. And she was fervently nodding, holding his gaze, giving him one more chance to refuse, to mock her, to walk away—but he didn't, he didn't. And suddenly Kitty's hands were desperately fumbling at his trousers, and yanking them down. Exposing a long, plump, pulsing green cock, already leaking a thick string of white from its glossy pink tip.

Oh gods above, and Kitty moaned aloud as she sucked it deep, swallowed it as hard as she possibly could. Already working into that silken slit with her tongue, seeking out his decadent bounty, gulping it down her throat.

He was still watching her, still not moving—but his eyes looked different, now. Not so cold, not so contemptuous, but almost... satisfied. Vindicated. As if he almost wanted to see her on her knees before him, prostrating herself for him, pleading for his favour and his mercy. Like this was fair and appropriate justice, meted out at his whim.

And Kitty understood it, she did, and she let him see it, holding his eyes as she sucked him harder, swallowed him deeper. Already bringing her hands up, too, fondling him how he'd shown her, her rising moans clashing against the slick wet sounds coming from her desperately sucking lips. She had to show him, had to make him see, he wouldn't regret this, he couldn't...

The blast of surging fluid again came without warning, flooding hard and forceful into her throat, but Kitty's moans only rose as she fought to welcome it. To hold it in, to swallow it in deep dragging gulps. To keep showing him, proving this to him, making it up to him.

And even when the flow finally slowed, she stayed in place, carefully seeking and swallowing it all. Showing him that she wouldn't waste what he gave her. Not now, not ever...

He was seeing it, he was, he was—at least, until his eyes squeezed shut, his breath exhaling hard. And in a harsh, jerky movement, he was backing away from her, and tying up his trousers with visibly fumbling fingers. Again purposefully putting distance between them, pushing her away, away, away.

And for an instant, swaying there on her knees in the dirt, Kitty fought back the sudden, unaccountable urge to break into sobs. Gods, what was she thinking. What if she had just made this even worse. What if she was just reading what she wanted into all this, was she truly so desperate to be constantly throwing herself at his feet, and—

"Better?" he asked, thick and gruff, just the same as he had earlier that morning—and Kitty startled as she glanced up at him, at his wary, careful eyes. At where he didn't actually look cold or contemptuous, at least in this moment—and it was enough that she swallowed hard, and maybe even found a smile.

"So much better, sir," she croaked back, and she meant it. "If you're not careful, you're going to have a hopeless addict on your hands. As well as an utterly hopeless traveller."

The orc blinked, and for an instant, that might have been a twinge of amusement, warming his eyes. But it vanished just as quickly, shifting into something that felt almost colder, darker than before—and then he jerked his head sideways. Clearly saying, *Get up.*

So Kitty obeyed, awkwardly clambering to her feet, brushing out her skirts. But this time, instead of striding off ahead of her, the orc waited until she'd steadied herself, and then fell into step beside her.

It was surprising, but certainly not unwelcome, and Kitty felt herself glancing repeatedly toward him as they walked. Toward where his jaw didn't look so tight as before, but instead, his forehead was furrowed, his mouth pursed. As if he was... considering something.

"Did you speak... truth, in this?" he said abruptly, without looking at her. "You wish to... serve my command?"

To serve his command. A strange little ripple flared up Kitty's spine, but she was already nodding, clearing her throat. "Y-yes," she whispered. "You've been—so kind to me, Lord Grisk. You deserve... loyalty. Allegiance."

The words felt laughable, like the most ludicrous thing she'd ever said in her life—but the orc wasn't laughing. No, no, he was again frowning straight ahead, his shoulders rising and falling beneath his cloak.

"Then this is what I wish in return, woman," he said, his voice slow, decisive, deadly. "When we reach my home, your fealty shall not be to Thrain, or to any other. Your fealty shall only be"—his eyes flashed—"to *me.*"

14

Her fealty would be... to him.

Kitty's feet stumbled on the path, her eyes wide and shocked on the orc's face. He wanted... he wanted... *what*?

"How do you... mean?" she heard herself say, too high-pitched. "In—in bed?"

She couldn't stop staring at him, searching the grim, forbidding frown on his face, the still-deep furrow in his brow. A look that certainly didn't speak of desire, or possessiveness, or longing. If anything, it felt almost cold again. Contemptuous. Cruel.

"Not in bed," he replied, clipped. "In all the rest. In how and where you spend your days."

Kitty was still staring, not at all following, and the orc gave a heavy sigh, and ran his hand against his hair. "So long as you bear Thrain's son within you," he continued, slow and deliberate, "you shall stay safe in the mountain, under my care. You shall not leave it, without my guard. You shall follow my terms for the care of you and your son."

Oh. The words seemed to catch and tangle in Kitty's chest,

yanking on too many threads at once. He wanted to care for her. He wanted to control her, confine her. He didn't trust her to care for her son. He...

"And as part of this," he continued, his voice deepening, "you shall not touch a drop of wine, or ale, or berry-juice, or aught else. And you shall not revel with those who do. Should you drink thus to excess even *once*, I shall happily keep you under guard until your son is born."

His voice had gone hard and brittle, his eyes distant, as if with some bitter, painful memory. And now Kitty's own memories were tumbling back, back to that moment in that dank, dingy pub. To what the first orc—Thrain—had told her, about why his partner had ended it between them.

Because I... I've been drinkin' too much.

Oh. So not only did this orc not trust her, but he thought Kitty would—what? Run wild about Orc Mountain, uncontrolled and intoxicated, dragging Thrain along with her? While risking harm to her own *son*?

Kitty's thoughts kept twisting, spinning, cracking—and then catching, tripping on the orc's frozen, forbidding eyes. *Until your son is born*, he'd said. *Until.*

"You... expect me to keep the son, then?" she asked, hoarse, and suddenly that was the most important question, the only question. Could he really want to care for his partner's illegitimate son, for the living embodiment of such betrayal? Wouldn't he want her to... to...

"Do *you* wish to keep the son?" came the orc's reply, clipped, challenging—and his eyes had purposefully flicked to something beyond her. "Should you not wish to keep him, this can be... done."

Oh. Oh. So the midwife hadn't been wrong about that either, then. And Kitty felt her breath stilling, her hand fluttering to that hard little swell in her lower belly, still so new, so strange. Her child. Her son. Who would, by nature of his very existence, earn her this orc's ongoing care, his presence, his attention, until he was born...

No. No. That was a horrible thought, a truly heinous rationale, so selfish it took Kitty's breath away—but even as she inwardly cursed herself, fought to shove it aside... it was still there. Whispering. Tempting.

As long as she kept the son, the orc would look after her. Care for her, and... *feed* her. Keep her safe.

Kitty grimaced, while her thoughts kept throwing up protests, visions, sharper and louder than before. Charles, danger, the son, controlled, confined, her own damned mother, this orc didn't trust her, he didn't even *like* her—

And worst of all, what if he hated it, the entire time. What if he hated her. Forever.

"But if I keep the child, won't you be... angry, to be so obliged?" she whispered, toward his hard, distant eyes. "Especially under these circumstances? Wouldn't you resent it? Resent... me?"

The orc's unreadable gaze briefly flicked down to hers—but then he exhaled, heavy and resigned. "I have no close blood kin left," he said, his voice very even. "My clan is my only kin now, and thus, I should never resent my clan brother's son. Your son is my kin also, ach? My brother. My son. My own."

Oh. And that... that was *longing*, softening his eyes, his voice. He... wanted the son. If nothing else, surely he wanted the son.

And for a hanging, dangling breath, blinking at that hint of warmth in his eyes, it occurred to Kitty, for perhaps the first time, that he looked almost... handsome. Appealing. And he would care for her. Guard her. Keep her safe. Even if he resented her. Even if he hated her. As long as she kept his son. His kin. His own.

"I..." she began, and then swallowed hard, licked her lips. "I... yes, then. Very well. I agree to your terms."

The orc angled another brief glance toward her, his eyes again utterly blank—but then he nodded, jerky and curt. And without another word, he turned and strode off again, his form growing smaller and smaller through the trees.

Kitty blinked after him for an instant, but then hurried to follow again. Earning not even a glance backwards this time, and instead his shoulders stayed square and stiff, his gaze held straight ahead. Almost as if by agreeing, she'd somehow earned even more of his contempt than before.

And wait. Maybe that was—because of his... former partner. Thrain. Because gods, had Kitty even thought about Thrain, in this? About how he might feel, to have his son's care and supervision... *appropriated* like this?

Kitty's stomach was suddenly churning again, her thoughts flooding with visions of Thrain. Of how he'd laughed, how he'd comforted her, how he'd slung his arm over her shoulder, and walked her home. How he'd kissed her, how he'd touched her, how he'd gasped and groaned and praised her.

How he'd... left. How he hadn't come back. Not even now.

If I had a lovely woman like you, willing and eager in my bed, believe me, my nose'd never be wanderin' again.

And gods, this was why Kitty hadn't thought about him, hadn't wanted to think about him—and she surreptitiously wiped at her eyes, took a deep, shaky breath. No. No. She was doing what was best for her, for her son. She'd almost died back there, pregnant and ill and alone. And Lord Grisk was here now, and he was helping her. He deserved her gratitude. He did.

But even so, Kitty's eyes kept prickling, the urgency still rising, crackling, catching in her throat. "You don't think... he'll mind, do you?" she croaked. "Thrain, I mean?"

The orc didn't immediately reply, or even look at her, and Kitty couldn't seem to stop speaking, the words spilling from her mouth. "Just... if he did care, he would have come back, right? He wouldn't have left the way he did, would he? He just made it so, so clear that it was all a mistake, that I meant nothing to him, that he needed to run back home at once, so he could be with..."

With you, she should have said, but she felt her steps abruptly skittering, her eyes frowning at the orc's stiff back. Thrain had run back home, to apologize, to make amends... to Lord Grisk. But Lord Grisk was... here. With her.

So where was Thrain? Wouldn't he have accompanied Lord Grisk here? Wouldn't he at least have wanted to know what was happening? And what his former partner was doing? Unless...

"Thrain isn't... ill, is he?" Kitty gulped, her voice shrill. "Or harmed, somehow? He isn't... you didn't..."

She was cut off by a sharp, grating sound from Lord Grisk, something like—oh. A laugh. And his glance over his shoulder was suddenly hard, glittering, as he shook his head, curt and cold and furious.

"Believe me, woman," he said, "Thrain has no need of *my* help to bring himself grief or harm. Ach?"

The last word sounded strange, somehow, too loud and harsh. And wait, he wasn't even looking at her now, but he'd halted in place, staring straight ahead.

And when Kitty halted too, hovering uncertainly beside him, she could see his lip curling, his hands again clutched to fists at his sides. As if... as if he wasn't speaking to her at all, but instead...

"Ach, Thrain?" he said again, even louder this time, his voice carrying deep and demanding through the trees. "You can wreak your own ruin, all on your own. Though I should never have *dreamt* you should drag in a woman such as this, and a blameless Grisk *son!*"

Wait. Wait. He was spitting the words by the end, his voice a vicious growl, clutching painfully at Kitty's belly. *A woman such as this*. And what did he mean, who was he speaking to, it was—it was—

Oh. *Oh.* It was... *him.*

Her son's father. Thrain. Striding out from the mass of trees up ahead, his body tall and grey, his steps jerky and stiff.

And blinking toward him, Kitty felt her heart skipping, her eyes sweeping up and down his familiar—but still unfamiliar—form. Catching on the lean muscle of his bare chest, on the thick, spiky mess of his black hair—and most of all, on his face. His face that Kitty was finally seeing properly, for the very first time.

And while it was symmetrical, pleasing, surprisingly handsome, it was also... sharp. Sallow. Perhaps... even haggard. His cheekbones standing out stark over the sunken hollows of his cheeks, his brows thick black slashes over his shadowed eyes.

And... his eyes. His eyes were hazy, blank, and gazing at... Kitty. At her face. And then his gaze slowly, purposefully dropped downward, catching on—her belly. Her son. Their son.

There was a moment's horrible, hovering silence as he stared—and then he visibly blanched, and swayed on his feet. And suddenly he laughed, loud and bright and wrong, so, so wrong, as his eyes flashed with shock, and disbelief, and... rage.

"What," he rasped, his voice low, hoarse, scraping up Kitty's spine. "What the *fuck*, Varinn!"

And wait. He was looking at Lord Grisk—wait, at *Varinn?*— and that rage in his eyes was crackling, flashing and blazing higher with every breath, with every rising thud of Kitty's frantic heartbeat...

"What the *hell* is this," Thrain growled, his eyes still fixed on... *Varinn.* "Is this some kind of fucked-up punishment, Varinn? Or revenge? Och, you couldn't stand that I found such joy with another, so you—"

Beside Kitty, Lord Grisk—Varinn—had gone very stiff, a sound much like a growl burning from his throat—and suddenly, he flared forward. Forward toward Thrain, so fast Kitty could scarcely follow, his growl wrenching into a roar—

And with a furious flying lurch, Varinn snapped out his clenched fist, and punched Thrain in the face.

15

Kitty yelped and stumbled backwards, her eyes frozen on the sight before her. On how Thrain's head had jerked back, blood spattering from his nose, as his tall body staggered, tilted—

And then he whirled around, and swung back. His clenched fist catching Varinn on the cheek, in what looked like a painful blow—but Varinn only barked another vicious-sounding growl, and surged forward again. This time throwing his full weight onto Thrain, tackling his taller form down onto the ground beneath them.

"You—damned—selfish—fool!" Varinn shouted, straight down into Thrain's face, as he fought to pin Thrain's furiously kicking body beneath him. "You ken this is a punishment for you? For *you*?!"

Thrain was wrenching and shoving up beneath Varinn, his long arms swinging wildly for his face. "Ach, you overbearing *tyrant*," he shot back, between gasping breaths. "You wish to lord over me, wield all the power over me, just as you always— always—have! And what better way to gain this"—he grunted as he swung harder, faster—"than to put your scent on *my* woman without my leave. And seek to steal away *my* son!"

Kitty's thundering heartbeat skipped in her chest, because—*my woman? My son?* Thrain—he *knew?*

But above him, Varinn loudly scoffed, the sound harsh and mocking in his throat. "You ken I should wish to steal *her*?!" he demanded, with a sharp wave of his hand toward Kitty. "A weak, foolish, thoughtless, *spoilt* woman, with a hundred scents upon her? A woman who eagerly took you to her bed, when she *knew* you were yet bound to another?"

The words seemed to clang through the air, against Kitty's already-pounding skull, and Varinn was hauling in breath, whipping his head back and forth. "A *woman,*" he continued, almost spitting the word, "who haunts these same stinking holes you do! Drowning herself in ale until she *reeks*, whilst seeking to latch onto the first male she can find with a coin or two to his name?! A woman who is for *sale*?!"

Oh. Oh, no. No. No. He—he didn't think those things. He couldn't. *Weak. Foolish. Thoughtless. A hundred scents. Eagerly took you to her bed. Haunts these same stinking holes. For sale...*

Kitty's ears were ringing, her heartbeat wailing against her chest, but he—her lord, her kind and generous rescuer—was still swinging his huge fists toward Thrain beneath him, the rage still spitting from his mouth.

"I should *never* choose a woman like this one," he spat at Thrain's face. "*Never.* But you did, and then you sparked a son upon her, and *left*! What did you ken I should do? Throw away a blameless Grisk son, because his father is a careless, thoughtless, bumbling drunken *fool*?!"

His voice had risen to a holler, his furious fists still pummelling down toward Thrain's face. And though Thrain was still flailing, kicking, arching up, Varinn's big hand had found... Thrain's throat. Clamping tight around it, pinning him there, grinding him into the earth.

"You failed your woman, and your son," he spat. "You left *me* to clean up your mess, again. And ach, I have done this, and saved your woman and your son, at great cost to myself! And you ought to be on your knees thanking me, and begging me for my mercy!"

The words thundered through the air, through Kitty's desperately trembling body, and she felt her head shaking, her hands dragging at her face. No. No. This couldn't be happening. He couldn't be saying these things. He couldn't have thought all those things about her, all that time…

But the truth of it was still here, still screeching pure panic before her eyes, and Thrain's thrashing had begun to slow, his face turning red, almost purple. And Varinn's other fist had drawn up again, ready to smash down into Thrain's face, to crush him, to destroy him—

And somehow, Kitty was already running. Sprinting the short distance between them, staggering on her shaky legs, and hurling herself down onto Thrain's hot, gasping body.

"No," she gulped, pleaded, sobbed. "No. Please, sir. *Please.*"

16

For an instant, everything stopped. Everything but the sound of Kitty's gulping sobs, and the thin, dragging breaths from Thrain's stiff, shuddering body beneath her. The sounds of those breaths whistling in Kitty's ear, loud and shrill and desperate.

But he was here, he was alive, he was *here*—and oh, oh gods, her face was in his neck, and she could... smell him. That rich, sweet, succulent scent, so stunningly familiar from all those days breathing it on her bed, and Kitty sobbed again as she inhaled, as she filled her lungs with it, as deep as it could go.

And beneath her, she could feel Thrain's stiff body— settling. Sagging. And oh, oh gods, that was the feel of two long, warm, trembling arms, folding around her back, drawing her closer, as his chest beneath her slowly filled, too.

"Och, sweet woman," rasped his voice, so close, so broken. "Och, I have missed you. The very *scent* of you."

Oh. Oh. Kitty's head furiously nodded into his neck, her breath again inhaling, long and deep—but it was only then that she caught the other scent in it, too. The pungent, telltale tinge of ale, heavy and harsh, leaching from within his very skin.

He was... drunk?

The awareness was enough to twitch Kitty a little backwards again, enough to see his face. His angular, grey-skinned face, with those gaunt hollows in his cheeks, and those bleary, tired-looking eyes. Eyes that were visibly reddened and bloodshot, blinking at her with strange, hazy disbelief. While his shaky hand awkwardly rubbed at his neck, at where—Kitty swallowed—he had a mess of faded teeth-marks scarred into his skin, too.

"Och," he said again, on a thick, heavy exhale—and for an instant, all Kitty could smell was the ale, strong and sickening on his breath. Enough that she had to jerk backwards, wincing, clamping her hand over her mouth. A movement that Thrain's bloodshot eyes rapidly followed, narrowing just slightly, before flicking down toward... her belly.

"Och, woman," he said, with a twitching little half-smile. "I ken we oughta been more careful after all, ach?"

Right. Kitty attempted a smile back toward him, though it felt faint, wavering. "Y-yes, I suppose so," she made herself say, over the pounding in her skull. "I didn't realize that the silphium wouldn't—work. With orcs."

Thrain's answering laugh was harsh and bright, flooding more of his pungent breath into her face. "Me neither," he said, with a grimace. "Whoops."

Kitty's stomach suddenly, inexplicably plunged, but she attempted another smile. "Indeed," she managed. "It was only the gods' own luck that Lord Grisk found me, and—"

But her voice was abruptly drowned out by another harsh, shrill laugh, even louder than before. "Lord Grisk?" Thrain echoed, his voice incredulous. "*Lord Grisk*?! Och, you mean *him*? *Varinn*?!"

Kitty grimaced, and shot a chagrined glance toward—yes—Varinn. Who had at some point risen to his feet, and was now standing several steps away from them, and watching them with blank, utterly unreadable eyes. And blinking back toward him, Kitty's stomach was plummeting again, the wetness prickling powerfully behind her eyes, as yet more shame and misery pounded through her skull.

Weak. Foolish. Thoughtless. A hundred scents. I should never choose a woman like this one. For sale.

"Lord Grisk my arse," came Thrain's hard, mocking voice, and Kitty realized it was slightly slurred, too. "And Varinn findin' you wasn't luck, woman, or naught else from the accurst meddling gods. Tha' was him sniffing you out like a hound, so he could seek to lord it over me. To steal you away from me. To gain his revenge upon me. After *he* was the one who dumped *me!*"

The pounding in Kitty's skull was thudding louder, the scent of Thrain's rancid breath churning harder in her stomach, and she desperately dragged in air, rubbed at her stinging eyes. Thrain didn't truly—believe all that? That Varinn was trying to steal her? To gain revenge? After all he'd done for her?

"But you," she heard herself reply, recoiling, searching Thrain's narrowed, bloodshot eyes. "You weren't... there."

Thrain blinked back, once—and without warning, he laughed again. Laughed, the sound sharp and shrill, as if Kitty had just made a riotously hilarious joke.

"Och, an' why wasn't I there?" he drawled, his eyes angling up toward Varinn again. "'Cause I was back home pleading and grovelling at his feet, down in that damned stinking crypt, just how he wanted! Just how he's always wanted! An' then he turns around and waltzes out here, and does *this*?!"

His clawed hand was wildly waving between Varinn and Kitty, and Kitty could only seem to blink back at him, the pounding in her head now a staggering, deafening drum. "He... helped me," she whispered, her voice catching. "He saved me."

She couldn't help another brief, fearful glance up toward

Varinn, but he wasn't looking back at her. No, he was looking at Thrain, and his eyes were blazing again, his hands in fists, his big body visibly rigid all over. As if it was taking all the self-control he possessed to hold himself there, to keep himself from again punching Thrain in the face.

But oh, gods, that was Thrain's laugh again, scraping through the too-close air. "Ach, an' what did Varinn want in return?" he demanded. "I ken he wanted you on your knees, woman! Calling him *Lord Grisk*, and sucking his gods-damned *prick*! Wanting you in his thrall, so he can lord it over me, and make me suffer for daring to escape him!"

No, no, no, Thrain couldn't be saying these things, he couldn't actually believe these things... could he? But when Kitty glanced up at Varinn again, he still wasn't moving, he still was just staring at Thrain like that. Like he wanted to attack him, to throttle him, to destroy him...

And suddenly more miserable memories were swarming, surging through Kitty's thundering head. The way Varinn had so dispassionately watched as she'd kissed his boot. The way he'd pushed her head down beneath the fur. The way he'd refused to even tell her his name...

And then, oh gods, that agreement he'd asked for. That... vow.

Your fealty shall not be to Thrain. Your fealty shall only be to me.

And... It wasn't as if he actually... cared. Was it? *Weak. Foolish. I should never choose a woman like this one. For sale.*

No. No. Varinn hated her. He clearly held her in contempt. And now he'd rescued her, or had he trapped her, caught her neatly in a snare, so he could... what? Rule over Thrain? Use her against Thrain, and make him suffer? Just like Thrain had said?

But then—the pounding wailed louder in Kitty's skull—how was Thrain suffering? He hadn't been there. He hadn't come. He hadn't yet spoken a single word of concern, let alone an apology. He was drunk, he kept laughing and making accusations, he...

And had he—had he ever cared, either? Had any of this ever been about her, or their son? Or had it only been about the revenge, the ale, the...

You're a sweet, eager, beautiful girl. I had a lot of fun.

The bile churned in Kitty's throat, and she shoved away from Thrain, up to her unsteady feet. Blinking around for her satchel—there, Varinn had dropped it when he'd rushed to punch Thrain—and grasping for it, clutching it tightly to her chest.

And then, without another word, she spun toward Orc Mountain, and staggered away through the trees.

17

Kitty had only taken a few steps before—oh. Varinn, and Thrain. Both of them dashing around to stand before her, Varinn's eyes wary and watchful, Thrain's wide and alarmed.

"Where are you going, woman?" Thrain demanded, his voice hoarse. "What's amiss?"

And as she blinked between them both, the churning in Kitty's belly began to feel less like nausea, and far more like rage. Rage, and misery, and sheer, surging disbelief. At Thrain, at Varinn, at Charles, at Miss Thomas, Mrs. Schultz, the entire damned world of cursed selfish arseholes.

"What's amiss?" she heard herself echo, her voice far shriller than she meant. "What's amiss is *you*! You made love to me, you made a son with me, and then you left me! And now, here you are, drunk and incoherent and *multiple* days too late, and blaming *him*?!"

She'd waved a shaky, furious hand toward Lord Grisk—Varinn—and felt herself glaring up at Thrain, at his rapidly blinking eyes. "Varinn came for me, when you didn't," she continued, though her voice was already wavering. "He was generous, and considerate, and kind, even when he didn't want to be. He *saved* me, and your son. And he's absolutely right, you should be kneeling and thanking him, and I cannot *fathom* why you haven't! Unless"—she gulped down more air—"you don't actually *want* your son, in which case, then why the hell do you even *care* what he does?!"

Her voice was ringing through the air by the end of it, so loud it hurt her own ears, but the words were still coming, tumbling from her mouth. "And, you let me believe it was *finished* between the two of you," she continued thickly, toward Thrain's still-blinking eyes. "Just the same as me and Charles. But clearly you weren't finished at all! You clearly spent the night with me to get *revenge* on him, and now you have the audacity to say it's *his* fault?"

Her hand was waving wildly at Varinn, who was still standing stock-still before her, his eyes still wide and wary—and Kitty felt her own eyes catching on his, holding, as something crumpled painfully in her stomach. "And *you*," she continued, her voice badly wavering now. "I already knew you hated me, and resented my very existence, and thought I was spoiled and greedy and useless. You didn't need to actually *say*—"

Her voice cracked there, the wetness suddenly spilling down her cheeks. "You didn't need to *say* it," she whispered, dropping her wet eyes toward his booted feet. "I *knew*."

There was a brief, fraught instant of stillness, broken only by the sound of Kitty's shameful, gulping gasps. Gasps that sounded more like sobs with every passing breath, and oh gods, she needed to get away from them, away from this mess, to—

When suddenly, somehow, there were—more orcs. Two more orcs, huge and grey and bare-chested, sprinting out from the trees toward them. The first one looking remarkably like—like *Thrain*, tall and lean with spiky, messy hair, and a bright gold cuff on his arm. While the other orc, racing close behind him, was slightly shorter and slimmer, with a head of loose, shining black hair, and a gold ring in his *nipple.*

"Och, what's this?" demanded the taller orc, as he reeled up beside them, his eyes sweeping back and forth—and then catching, narrowing, on Kitty's waist. "That cannot be—"

He didn't finish, but the second new orc had halted too, and was letting out a long, low whistle as he stared at Kitty's belly. "So there *is* a son, then," he said slowly, angling a narrow, searching glance toward Thrain. "Have you dulled your sense of smell that much, brother?"

Thrain was blinking blankly toward these new orcs, and then back to Kitty again—and he betrayed a visible wince, and rubbed at his eyes. "She wasn't," he replied, his voice hoarse. "Wasn't with child, when I left. It wasn't supposed to happen."

There was an instant's dangling silence, and Kitty felt her stomach painfully twisting again, her eyes dropping. *It wasn't supposed to happen.* And gods, suddenly she just felt so, so tired. Of this, of him, of everything. Enough that they were all slightly tipping, tilting sideways, or wait, maybe that was her—

Until there was—Varinn. Here. Jerking up close and solid beside her, his strong arm circling around her, holding her upright. "Ach, but now it has, and we are most pleased," he said. "And we shall be honoured to welcome a new Grisk son amongst us. Ach?"

There was a sharp note of challenge in his voice, his eyes narrow and flinty as they swept across the other orcs' faces. At where the two new orcs instantly nodded, even as they both kept staring at Kitty, and at her belly. As though she was some sort of bizarre curiosity, an exhibit, something that couldn't quite be real.

But when Kitty shot a helpless sideways glance at Varinn, she could see his irritation fading, in place of... concern. His eyes rapidly searching her face, his strong arm circling a little closer around her back.

"Are you—well, woman," he said, his voice almost too quiet to hear. "Should you wish, mayhap, for a drink?"

Kitty blanched against him, her eyes shocked wide—he couldn't still want that, after everything he'd just said?!—and he grimaced as he shifted something off his other shoulder. Oh. His—pack, and the—the waterskin. Because of course he hadn't meant—that. Of course.

"Th-thank you, Lord Grisk," Kitty whispered back, her voice very small, as she took the waterskin from his hands, and then took a few careful sips. And it was something, gods, anything, to distract from the ongoing hell of this moment— though when she lowered the waterskin again, it was all still here. Still with those two new orcs—and Thrain—all still staring at her, and now staring at Varinn, too.

"Woman, these are—our kin-brothers," cut in Varinn's quiet, pained-sounding voice, as his head nodded toward the two new orcs. "Dammarr, and Thrak, both of Clan Grisk. Thrak"—he waved a shaky-looking hand toward the taller orc—"is also Thrain's elder blood-brother, and thus, blood-uncle to your son. And brothers, this is..."

His voice trailed off there, his mouth wincing as his eyes glanced toward Kitty again. And it took her spinning, shaken thoughts far too long to realize that—oh. He didn't—know her name.

And clearly the other orcs had caught that—or at least, the Dammarr orc had, because he was now elbowing Thrain in the side, and giving him a sharp, meaningful look. But Thrain was still just standing there, staring at Kitty as though—oh. He didn't know, either.

"You cannot mean to tell us that neither of you two fools even know her *name*?" Dammarr finally said, his expression something between amusement and disbelief. "Ach, between you, how many loads have you two poured into her? A half-dozen? Not to speak of the son?!"

Wait. These orcs—they knew that? Just by standing here,

and smelling her? But—wait. Yes. Of course they could, of course they could smell it, and of course Kitty should have already guessed that. And her face was suddenly burning, her hands wringing at the waterskin she was still holding, and she dropped her eyes again, down to the orcs' booted feet.

"My name is—Kitty," she whispered. "Kitty Clarendon."

There was another instant's awkward, endless silence—and then the sound of a laugh. And when Kitty's gaze darted up again, it was the other tall orc, the one Varinn had called Thrak. Thrain's elder blood-brother, he'd said. Her son's uncle.

"Kitty?" he echoed, his black brows raised, his mouth quirking up. "Like a cat? Or..."

Kitty's stomach plummeted, even as she attempted a wretched-feeling smile, and shook her head. "No, like Katharine," she managed, though her voice wobbled. "My mother—she thought Kitty was more... suited, for..."

She couldn't finish, her voice fading, catching on the audible gulp in her throat. And beside her, Varinn cleared his throat, too, and she could feel his arm flexing around her, his hand gripping tight against her waist.

"Katharine has been very ill, these past days," he said, his voice clipped. "I have been seeking to care for her and bring her to the mountain, so she can be better cared for there. Now, mayhap we—"

But he was cut off by a laugh, hard and disbelieving, and when Kitty blinked toward it, it was this... Thrak again. Thrain's brother. And his eyes had gone chilly, surprisingly sharp, glinting on Varinn's face.

"*Caring* for her, ach, Varinn?" he said coolly. "By having her suck your prick? Telling her to name you *Lord Grisk*? Swooping in and building your own mating-bond upon her, so you might steal away my brother's claim, and his son?"

Oh. No. No. Not this again. Not already. And again, no one was arguing it, not even Thrain. Instead, he was just blinking between her and Varinn, his eyes bleary and exhausted. Drunk.

It wasn't supposed to happen, he'd said. *It wasn't my fault*, he might as well have said. *I didn't care.*

And finally, here was the rage again, bubbling up in Kitty's throat. Escaping not in more shouting, or more pleading, or more demands—but instead, in a light, tinkling little laugh, as she leaned a little closer into Varinn's solid form, and even dared to slip an arm around his waist.

"Oh, that wasn't his doing," she said, as smoothly as she could. "The truth is, I begged for him, and his help, and his—care. I do enjoy being looked after, don't I, Lord Grisk? Especially by a big, stern, capable specimen like you."

She'd aimed her most winning smile up at Varinn's face, and didn't at all miss the astonishment—and then the suspicion—flicking across his eyes. But he wasn't denying it, or arguing it, and maybe that was even awareness, now, glinting in those eyes, as they glanced toward a still-staring Thrain, and then back to her face.

"Ach, woman," Varinn said, his voice only slightly unsteady. "I am most honoured to care for you, and your son."

It sounded almost true, enough that Kitty could keep smiling at him, and even stroke her hand a little, up and down the smooth bare skin of his waist. "Thank you, Lord Grisk," she said, and that sounded almost true, too. "Now, as we discussed, could you please escort me the rest of the way to your mountain, so I can meet with your midwife, and be sure our son is still alive and well?"

Her voice had gone thin and strained by the end, now betraying far more truth than she meant. And thank the gods, Varinn jerked a curt nod—and then, with a quick shift of movement, he caught Kitty bodily in his arms, sweeping her up against his safe, solid chest.

"Ach, Katharine," he said firmly, his eyes only on hers. "We shall go."

18

The rest of the day passed in an exhausting, overwhelming haze. In Varinn indeed carrying Kitty for the rest of the journey to Orc Mountain, stopping whenever she felt too ill to continue. And even... *feeding* her, several more times, without prompting or complaint, his eyes unreadable as he watched, his hands warm and gentle on her hair.

Thrain and his brother had gone off to scout ahead, upon Varinn's curt orders, but the other new orc—Dammarr, the one with the nipple-ring—had stayed behind with them. For protection, Kitty now realized, because travelling was still dangerous for orcs, most of all when the orc in question was alone, and carrying an obviously incapacitated woman in his arms.

But thankfully, this Dammarr hadn't made any more rude comments—at least, not ones that Kitty had been able to understand. And instead, he and Varinn had quietly spoken together in a language she didn't recognize, the words rumbling tangled and deep in their throats.

But it had been strangely soothing, too, along with the steady rhythm of Varinn's careful steps, and the blessed lack of ongoing nausea. And Kitty had slipped in and out of consciousness as they'd walked, as the afternoon sunlight faded, and sank into darkness.

When she finally fully awoke again, it was in a strange room, in a strange bed. But Varinn was still here, sitting on the bed beside her, and two more unfamiliar people were leaning over her. One of them was another huge orc, with an alarming scarred face—and the other was a woman, tall and dark-haired and capable-looking.

"Hi there, Kitty," the woman said, with a reassuring smile. "Welcome to Orc Mountain. I'm Gwyn, and I'll be looking after you as your midwife. And this here is Efterar, our physician. If you're comfortable, we'd like to examine you, just to check on you and your son. Is that all right?"

Oh. Yes. Yes, and Kitty was fervently nodding, and gripping tighter at the hand—Varinn's hand?—clasped within her fingers. "Yes, please, thank you," she mumbled. "Anything you need."

Gwyn gave her another reassuring smile, and then began asking a few careful questions, while this Efterar hovered his big hands over Kitty's waist. While something also seemed to prickle *inside* her, following the movements of his hand, almost as if this was some sort of—of *orc magic*?! But Kitty was too exhausted to even marvel at that, and her voice was already slurring on her responses, her thoughts slipping back toward the haze. And to her distant relief, Varinn soon squeezed her hand, and began answering the questions instead. Telling them about the exhaustion, the nausea, the total lack of appetite, but for—*that*. The... *seed*.

But neither Gwyn nor this Efterar seemed even slightly disconcerted by this disclosure, and Efterar even gave Varinn a curt nod, and an approving clap of his hand to his bulky shoulder. "You did the right thing, Varinn," he said firmly. "As far as I can tell, you saved her life—and your son's, too. But with more rest and care, they should both be just fine, don't you worry."

Varinn's throat convulsed, his eyes dropping toward Kitty's, before glancing purposefully away again. And Kitty didn't know what it meant, couldn't even make herself care what it meant, because—she would be just fine. Her son would be just fine. Thank the gods. Thank... Lord Grisk.

And amidst the sheer weight of that relief, Kitty's thoughts finally let go, slipping away into the deep, welcoming darkness. She would be fine. Her son would be fine. Thanks to Lord Grisk.

When her consciousness finally returned again, what felt like a long time later, that relief was still there, steadying her thoughts and her breaths. Even as she sat up a little in the bed, and blinked around at the... room. The unfamiliar, windowless, stone-walled room, lit by the light of a single flickering lamp, set on a nearby shelf.

Now that she could see it more clearly, it was a cozy little room, with soft furs scattered across the floor, and several colourful tapestries hung on the walls. And along with the wide, solid-feeling wooden bed, there was a washbasin standing against the opposite wall, together with two matching sets of shelves. One of the shelves was very neat, with a small wooden chest on top, and multiple rows of folded furs and fabrics beneath. While the second shelf was stuffed to overflowing, spilling out a haphazard array of clothes, boots, and furs.

Kitty's head tilted, her eyes catching on a familiar-looking black cloak—when one of the tapestries swept aside, and Varinn strode in. He was dressed in only a black leather kilt this time, with no trousers or boots, and Kitty felt herself swallowing hard as she looked at him. At his broad bare chest, his muscled legs, his neat braid and carefully distant eyes.

"How fare you this morn, Katharine?" he asked, his voice

clipped, as he thrust out a waterskin toward her. "Better, I hope?"

A strange little spark had thrilled up Kitty's spine—he'd called her *Katharine* again—and she rapidly nodded, and took a long, gulping drink of the waterskin. "Yes, much better," she told him, with a small smile. "Thank you, sir. I remain very much in your debt."

Varinn winced, and reached to take back the waterskin, stoppering it with what appeared to be excessive force. "There is no debt," he replied, almost as if by rote—but then he winced again, and glanced behind him, toward the door. "Ach. Are you well enough to meet guests?"

Oh. Kitty managed another nod, and after an incomprehensible word from Varinn toward the door, several new people strode into the room. Another huge, bare-chested, nipple-pierced orc, together with a pretty, reddish-haired woman, holding... an orc baby?

But yes, yes, that was an orc baby, and he was small and greenish and adorable, and happily squirming in the woman's arms. And when the woman chuckled, and set him down to the floor, he scampered over to Kitty in the bed, pulled himself up on the side of it, and flashed her a bright, beatific grin, showing her a mouthful of tiny white teeth.

Kitty couldn't help an astonished laugh, and she reached down, and lightly patted the tiny orc's messy black head. "Well, hi there, little fellow," she said. "What's your name?"

"This is Rakfi," supplied the woman with a wry laugh, as she strode over, and scooped up the little orc into her arms. "And I'm Ella Riddell, of Clan Grisk. And this"—she nodded toward the new orc—"is Nattfarr, my mate. For the past... oh, eleven years, right, Natt?"

This Nattfarr was giving the woman—Ella—a slow, indulgent smile, his big hand curving with easy familiarity against her bare waist. Because this Ella was very minimally dressed, and her unconventional ensemble consisted of a cape, a short skirt, and a stunning variety of glinting, beautifully crafted *jewels*. Shimmering from beneath her cape, hanging from her ears, spanning across her bare waist—and even flashing in her wild reddish hair.

"Er, hello," Kitty belatedly said, attempting a smile at this Ella, and then toward Nattfarr. Who was dressed much like Varinn, in only a brown leather kilt, but he also sported multiple visible jewels and piercings, glinting all over his bulky greenish form.

"Greetings, new Grisk sister," Nattfarr said, inclining his head toward her. "It is our joy to welcome you here amongst us. I have known Varinn and Thrain since we were all orclings together, ach, Varinn?"

He shot Varinn a broad, toothy smile, and to Kitty's genuine astonishment, Varinn... smiled back. It was quite possibly the first time she'd ever seen him smile, and though it was small and wan, it still seemed to transform his face, turning its stern ruggedness into something warm and handsome and almost... soothing.

"Ach, and I have many scars to prove this," Varinn replied, his voice light, and again Kitty found herself gaping at him, her stomach flipping in her belly. Not only was he smiling, but he was... making a *joke*?

But he was already glancing back toward her, his smile rapidly fading as he cleared his throat. "Nattfarr leads the Grisk clan, in his role as Speaker," he said. "As part of this, he also bears the ancient Grisk gift of Speaking, or truth-seeking. And I ken"—he glanced toward Nattfarr again—"he wishes to seek your truth, Katharine, should you allow this."

Another inexplicable thrill was racing up Kitty's spine at Varinn's use of her name, together with a rising bewilderment—whatever did he mean by *truth-seeking*? But she was already nodding, aiming a hopeful smile toward him, because maybe, maybe he would smile at her, too. "Yes, of course," she said. "Whatever you need, Lord Grisk."

But wait, that was clearly the wrong thing to say, based on Varinn's grimace, and his furtive sideways glance toward Nattfarr. Whose thick black brows had snapped high on his forehead, his head tilting as his gaze flicked toward Kitty's face.

"Ach, then," he said, his voice very steady. "Mayhap you shall tell us, sister, how this has all come about, between you and my brothers."

Oh. Well. Kitty drew in a breath, nodding, meeting Nattfarr's glinting, searching eyes—and then she found, with a strange, jolting alarm, that she couldn't seem to look away. And suddenly she was speaking, her voice rapid and high-pitched as the words poured from her mouth. Telling the entire sordid tale, of how she'd been dumped by Charles, how she'd met Thrain in the pub, how he'd been so funny and sympathetic and kind. How he'd walked her home, how they'd spent such a wonderful night together...

Her face was painfully burning at this point, but she was still speaking, even faster now. Telling of Thrain's generosity in bed, and his magical tongue, and his beautiful ring—oh gods, why was she saying these things—and then, how he'd rushed off the next morning. How she'd begun to grow sicker and sicker, until she'd finally been thrown out of her apartment, and had attempted to find him on her own. How finally, Lord Grisk had found her, and helped her, and cared for her.

"Lord Grisk *saved* me," she continued, breathless and hoarse. "He saved my life, when Thrain was too foxed to notice. And he's been taking care of me ever since, even though"—she hauled in another breath, her voice speaking even faster—"I've made things so painfully awkward between him and Thrain. Which was of course very shabby of me, but I had no conception whatsoever that they were still so entangled, and would never have gotten involved if I'd known! Even if Thrain was the most generous lover I've ever known in my *life*, and I really think we could have been marvellous friends—at least, before he showed himself to be a drunkard who refuses to take any responsibility whatsoever, even after he abandoned me and our son to *die*."

Her panting voice finally stopped speaking there, her torrent of impossibly incriminating words ringing through the room—and far too late, she clapped her hand over her mouth, whipping her head back and forth. Good gods above, what the hell had she just said? And why the hell had she just said it to this strange orc? While this Ella—and Varinn—stood there and listened to every horrible, humiliating word?

And somehow, Kitty's frantic gaze had finally snapped to Varinn, and found him staring straight back toward her, looking just as pained—just as aghast—as she felt. And gods, she'd surely just made all this so much worse, though at least she hadn't spoken of the begging, or the kissing his boot, or that secret agreement they'd made. *Your fealty shall only be to me...*

"You have honoured us with your truth, sister," came a regretful-sounding voice, Nattfarr's voice, and when Kitty shot a fearful glance toward him, he was gazing carefully beyond her, his mouth thin. "We thank you, for speaking this to us."

Oh. Kitty couldn't seem to reply, her throat swallowing hard, her cheeks gone painfully hot. So that had been... more of the orc magic, then. Some impossible gift from the gods. *The ancient Grisk gift of truth-seeking*, Varinn had said. And what was she supposed to do now, to say, and...

And then something moved, across the room. Something... behind the door. And as Kitty blinked toward it, her heartbeat drumming louder and louder in her chest, the tapestry swept aside, and there was... Thrain.

He'd been... behind the door. Listening. To—to everything?!

But yes, yes, surely he'd heard every word of it, his mouth tight and thin, his cheekbones even sharper than before. And his bare chest was visibly heaving, glistening with a sheen of sweat, and his eyes were still bleary and red, with deep dark hollows beneath them. And blinking back toward him, Kitty felt herself wincing, cringing into something small and afraid behind the fur. Because gods, what was he going to say, what if he was drunk again, or he started blaming and yelling again, and—

"Could I—speak to her for a moment, brothers?" he said, his voice cracked and hoarse. "Alone? Please?"

For an instant, there was only stillness, and Kitty realized they were all looking toward her. Nattfarr and Ella with questioning eyes, and Varinn—Varinn with a blank, heavy grimness. All of them waiting for her assent, clearly, and Kitty felt herself jerk a shaky nod. Not missing the very faint flinch on Varinn's form, or the way he instantly spun on his heel and strode toward the door. His back perfectly straight, his head held forward, clearly not even acknowledging Thrain as he stalked past.

He was soon followed by Nattfarr and Ella, Ella giving a regretful smile over her shoulder, while her baby orc eagerly waved his little arm goodbye. And somehow Kitty managed a halfhearted smile back, and a wave, too—but then it all dropped again as she blinked toward Thrain. Toward where he was blinking blearily back toward her, his sweaty chest filling with his breath—

And then he lurched forward. Rushing on shaky steps toward the bed, and then—falling to his knees on the floor beside it.

"Och, sweet woman," he croaked, as he searched her with his red, shimmering eyes. "I'll never, ever forgive myself for how I've wronged you. I'm sorry. I'm so, so sorry."

19

K itty stared at Thrain for a hushed, dangling moment, her body frozen beneath the fur. He was—*apologizing*?

"I'm so, so sorry," he said again, his voice a choked gasp, his eyes blinking as they searched her face. "Gods, I've fucked this up. I've ruined everything. *Everything*."

Kitty still couldn't move, couldn't think, and Thrain dragged in a shaky breath, rubbed a clawed hand at his face. "Never should have left you like I did that morning," he said, hoarse. "Never should have risked it. I—I knew it wasn't right, ach? But I just—I couldn't—Varinn, he's—"

His voice broke off with a gulp, his palms now digging into his eyes. But he didn't continue—just leaving that hanging there, about Varinn—and Kitty drew in a slow, unsteady breath, searched for courage, for truth.

"I—I told you, it wasn't—Varinn's fault," she said, fighting past the sudden surging memories, *weak, foolish, spoilt, your fealty shall only be to me.* "I—wanted his help. I—begged for it. And he—saved me."

It wasn't even slightly untrue, the miserable conviction painfully palpable in her voice, and she could see Thrain's answering shudder, the defeated-looking drop of his stiff shoulders. "Ach," he said thickly. "Ach, I ken. Efterar—our healer—he spoke to us both, after he saw you yesterday. Said you were—very ill. *Dehydrated*, he said, and—and *delirious*, and *starving*. And if Varinn hadn't found you when he did, you probably would have—"

Thrain's voice cracked there, his hand again sharply rubbing his face, and Kitty stared, frozen, as he took another shaky breath. "You almost died," he whispered, on a harsh exhale. "You, and our son. Because I left you. I didn't come back for you. Because I didn't—I wasn't—Varinn—"

Kitty still couldn't move, couldn't reply, could only sit there, waiting, staring at his face, while those unthinkable words—*dehydrated, delirious, starving, you almost died*—rang through her thoughts. And he couldn't be blaming Varinn again, or, or...

"Because—I lost it," Thrain said now, very quiet. "When I came back here, that morning I left you. Varinn smelled you on me long before I got here, and by the time I saw him, he was—*och*. I've never seen him like that before, in all the years I've known him. Wouldn't come out of the crypt—this vile old mess of tunnels and tombs under the mountain—no matter what I said or did. And"—he took another shaky breath—"I couldn't bear the scent, ach? Couldn't bear the taste of his grief, or—or the truth of your scent upon me, shouting of how I—how deeply I'd hurt him. So I opened a barrel of ale I'd been saving, and..."

He trailed off again, grimacing, shaking his head. "Been foxed ever since, I ken," he continued, with a strange, barking little laugh. "Couldn't smell a damned thing, for a single one of those days. The ale blunts it, ach? And I ken it's not an excuse, it's such gods-damned *rubbish*, but"—his shoulders heaved, his mouth bitterly twisting—"if I'd have smelled it, I would've come back for you, and our son. I *would*."

Oh. Oh. Kitty swallowed hard, her thoughts hitching,

catching, cracking. Grasping at pieces, at words, *never seen him like that before...*

"So was it even—over, between you and Varinn, that night?" she heard her hollow voice whisper. "Or was that a falsehood, too? Just like how you said he was—a woman?"

Thrain visibly flinched, his eyes squeezing shut, and he again shook his head, jerky and stiff. "It wasn't—a falsehood," he replied, his voice wooden. "Varinn did—dump me. Threw me out. Said it was finished between us. But..."

But. Kitty kept staring at Thrain, waiting, and he exhaled, dropped his eyes to the fur. "But I knew," he whispered, "it wasn't fully finished, between us. Mayhap it'll never be finished, ach? At least"—his voice cracked—"not for me. Varinn is—my partner. My best friend. My *home*. And I ken he always will be, even if he never touches me again. We've been through too much, and I—I need him. Need him so damned much."

Oh. Oh, gods. And Kitty's eyes were finally prickling now, the painful heat welling close and dangerous. Thrain had lied to her. He'd left her. He'd only ever cared about Varinn, he still only cared about Varinn. And now she was trapped here, trapped having a son with him, when he didn't even...

But then Thrain's head snapped up, his eyes frantically searching hers, almost as if he'd just heard his own words. "I didn't—I don't wish you to think—" he began, wincing, rubbing his palm into his eye. "Och. I will yet—be here, for you, and our son. I will support—whatever you want. Whether you want to keep our son, or not—or whether you want to stay here, or not. Or whether you even want to speak to me—or aught else—or whether you only care for Varinn. Whatever you want, whatever you need, I'll do it. I'll seek to support it, with all my strength."

His voice had hardened, steadied, his eyes glinting powerfully on Kitty's face—and she blinked her prickling eyes, swallowed over the catch in her throat. Gods, he looked so fervent, so miserable, and she so desperately wanted to believe him, but...

"That's—very kind of you to say," she finally replied, her voice a whisper. "But you can't truly mean it, can you? Don't you—don't you remember all the things you said back there, in the forest?"

Thrain grimaced, and he audibly exhaled, heavy and slow. "I can't remember—most of it," he said, quiet. "But Thrak and Dammarr told me. I ken I was raging, and spouting rubbish, and—and being jealous, and a fool. And again"—his eyes met hers again—"I am—so sorry. For my cruel words, and for Thrak's, also. And you shouldn't hold it against him, for he only seeks to defend me, ach? I ken he'll yet be a good uncle—the best uncle—to our son. Should you allow this."

His voice was pleading again, his eyes shimmering as they held hers. "But if you don't allow this," he whispered, "I'll still honour this. I've brought you so much fear and pain and misfortune, and you deserve only peace, and care, and worship. You deserve all I can grant you. And I"—his throat convulsed— "I'm so glad Varinn found you. I'm so glad you welcomed him, and his—his *care* for you, and our son. I know he'll never falter in this, and always treat you as you deserve. He's always longed for a woman and a son, ach?"

Oh. Kitty's throat felt fully constricted, now, too tight to even swallow. Because Varinn didn't truly care about her either, did he? And hadn't Thrain heard Varinn say all those awful things about her, back in the forest? *You ken I should wish to steal her? A weak, foolish, thoughtless, spoilt woman, with a hundred scents upon her. A woman who is for sale...*

But—wait. No. Thrain had been drunk. He only remembered what Thrak and Dammarr had told him. And they... they hadn't been there to hear that part of it. Had they? And surely Varinn wouldn't have spoken of it, either. *Your fealty shall only be to me...*

"But you just said," Kitty began, and it was the wrong point, but she had to say it, she had to, "that you would never stop caring for Varinn. That he's your partner, your best friend, and it will never be finished between you, and you need him in your life. So surely you wouldn't wish to see me, and him, and... and your son..."

Her voice trailed off there, her eyes squeezing shut, because yes, that was exactly what she'd agreed to with Varinn, so why was she questioning it now—and she could again hear Thrain's swallow, and the sound of his hollow, bitter little laugh. "I won't speak false to you," he said thickly. "I don't ken it'll be—easy, ach? But I can only hope, and pray, that mayhap someday I can earn your trust again. Yours, and Varinn's. I'll be the best father I possibly can to our son. And mayhap, with enough time, you'll allow me to yet be—your friend. Or mayhap—mayhap someday you would even—"

He stopped there, blinking hard, shaking his head—and he'd somehow found Kitty's hand, squeezing it tightly in his. And oh gods, his bottom lip was trembling, and that was wetness, escaping from his eyes, streaking down his sharp cheeks.

"I was so close," he choked out. "I was so close, and yet so foolish, ach? If I'd only thought to set down the ale, and to bring you here from the start, before I ever touched you. I ken Varinn would have welcomed you, welcomed this, and—and we could have done this together, sweet kitten. This could have been all our dreams come to life, ach? We could have brought you—such joy."

Oh. Oh gods. Thrain couldn't possibly be saying this, he couldn't truly mean that he and Varinn would have both been—*interested* in her, like that? That they would have— shared? *Welcomed* this? All their dreams come to life?

But no, no, that was impossible. Because even if Thrain *had* done all that, Kitty was still not—*not*—what Varinn wanted. She was clearly not the kind of woman he could respect, let alone care for, or share with his long-term partner. And the wetness was suddenly spilling down Kitty's cheeks too, because oh, gods, what would that have been like, and it was already gone, stolen out of her grasp...

But then she bit painfully at her lip, and wiped hard at her wet cheeks. No, damn it, no. It had never been an option, it had never been in her grasp at all. Thrain had made a drunken mistake, and then he'd abandoned her—and Varinn had come in to clean up his mess. To save him from himself.

And one heartfelt apology—one bad hangover, perhaps—didn't change any of the truth of this. Did it? Thrain had failed her, and rejected her, so she'd made a deal with Varinn instead. And Varinn had been the one to keep his word. He'd been the one who had been there for her. He was the one she could trust. Even if he hated her.

And suddenly here was only a heavy, bone-deep weariness, tangled together with the misery, and the already-whispering nausea. With how Thrain was still looking at her like that, with his own helpless misery shimmering in his wide, pleading eyes.

"I will earn your trust again," he told her, his voice breaking. "I *will*. I'll be the best father you could ask for, and should you allow this, the best friend, also. For this was truth, what you just spoke to Nattfarr, ach? We should have been—*marvellous friends*. We *will*."

The words felt so earnest, so true, and Kitty again wiped at her eyes, gulped down her sob, and somehow felt herself—nodding. Nodding, damn it, saying yes, because gods, she wanted it so much, she couldn't want it so much, she'd made a promise to Varinn, *your fealty shall only be to me...*

But Thrain was nodding too, a feverish-looking light crackling in his eyes. "Thank you, sweet kitten," he whispered, as he brought her hand to his mouth, and *kissed* it. "Och. Thank you. You won't regret this. I swear to you."

Kitty couldn't speak, couldn't think, because he was still... kissing her hand. His mouth warm and gentle and reverent, his tears dripping onto her skin. And he'd even turned over her hand, his fingers easy and familiar on hers, his soft lips now brushing at her palm, her wrist. Sending out light, exquisite flares of heat, of longing—and suddenly, without warning, a memory. A vivid, dazzling memory of him kneeling between her thighs, his eyes dancing on hers, his low laugh shuddering through his tongue...

And oh, hell, maybe he was remembering it too, his breath catching, his eyes angling up toward hers, just like they had that night. And his kisses were slower now, deeper, moving careful but eager up her wrist, her arm. As if he not only remembered, but he would willingly do it all again, this very moment...

But—no. No. Gods, no. Kitty had already done this. She'd seen how it ended. And if she'd learned anything from Charles, it should be this, shouldn't it? She couldn't risk relying on a male's goodwill, on his promises. She couldn't. Especially when—she bit her lip, squeezed her eyes shut—she'd already made promises of her own. She had—a debt. She couldn't, she couldn't, she couldn't—

"Is Varinn—still here?" her thin voice cut in, her hand clutching to her now-churning stomach. "Do you think he would—see me?"

Thrain's head instantly snapped backwards, his lips parted—and no, no, that was pain, flashing across his eyes. Pain, and hurt, and... comprehension. Surely understanding, now, that even if Kitty had accepted his apology—or maybe even his offer of friendship—she was still choosing Varinn. She had to choose Varinn, she had to...

But thank the gods, Thrain was nodding, rapid and curt, even as his too-bright eyes kept blinking, his fang biting sharp at his lip. "Ach," he said thickly. "Ach, Varinn should wish to see you, I'm sure. Ach, Varinn?"

His blinking eyes had flicked over his shoulder, toward the covered door, to where—oh. Varinn was already here, striding through the tapestry into the room, his head held high, his body very stiff. Suggesting that he'd been there the entire time, listening to every damned word.

But amidst the mess swarming in Kitty's brain, it almost... helped. Helped, to know that he was still here, looking after her, as he'd promised. And she somehow found her eyes lingering on his solid familiar form, catching on the bulkiness of his bare chest, the very slight bulge beneath that leather kilt...

And oh, Kitty's breath had stilled at the sight, her stomach flipping in her belly—and that was the feel of her tongue, brushing swift but betraying against her lips. Making something shift in Varinn's flinty eyes, and Kitty could hear the surprising sound of a low growl, hissing from Thrain beside the bed.

But then Thrain lurched upwards, leaping to his feet. And when Kitty blinked up toward him, he was nodding, and rubbing at his mouth, and maybe—maybe even attempting a smile, back and forth between them.

"Ach, I'll leave you both to it, then," he said, his voice falsely bright, even as it wavered. "Only speak, if you have need of me."

With that, he spun away, and rushed toward the door—but just before he reached it, he stopped. And then slowly turned around again, his shoulders squared, his mouth thin and set.

"But again, I'm—sorry," he said, without inflection. "To you both. For all my angry words, and my foolish, thoughtless deeds. I ken I have much to think upon, and atone for. And Varinn"—he inhaled, met Varinn's unblinking eyes—"thank you. Once again, I am in your debt."

He'd bowed his head toward Varinn, his hand clenching in a fist against his chest. And then he turned and fled out the door, leaving the tapestry fluttering behind him.

20

Kitty didn't know how long she sat there, staring at that swaying tapestry, at where Thrain had gone.

I'm sorry, he'd said. *I am in your debt.*

And for a choked instant, those words almost felt like— Kitty's words. They—they *were* Kitty's words. Words she herself had said to Varinn, only a few short moments ago. Words that had been an echo of that first day they'd met.

I'm so sorry. I'm forever indebted to you.

And what had Varinn told her in return? He'd said, *There is no debt. Only brotherhood.* And he'd even looked at her the same way he was now looking at the door, his mouth twisting with sympathy, or bitterness, or both.

"You ken Thrain oft means what he says, when he speaks thus," he finally said, his voice rough, as his gaze angled back toward her. "But this does not... always become truth, ach? Most of all once he has become lost in drink."

His mouth was still twisting, his eyes dark, and Kitty belatedly realized that he was—warning her. Warning her not to believe Thrain, not to trust him, or get too close.

And even as she winced, she already felt herself nodding, and breathing out heavy and slow. She knew. Gods, she knew.

"Has he... always struggled with the drinking?" she asked, her voice small. "You don't seem like the kind of person to readily tolerate such things, in a partner?"

She winced again as she spoke, as those painful words again marched past her thoughts—*weak, thoughtless, foolish*—but when she angled another glance up at Varinn's face, she was vaguely surprised to see the lack of anger there, or contempt. Instead, he was looking resigned, or maybe... maybe even sad.

"For a long time, it was only now and then," he said heavily. "As with any of us, ach? For a party, or a holy day, or mayhap after a trial, or a battle, or—a loss. But these past few years, it has grown worse and worse. And then, a few moons ago, he was granted some long-lost coin from his father, and"—he gave a jerky shrug—"it has been every day since. Every night, and then every morn. Until he never stopped reeking of it."

There was a quiet, aching despair in his voice, in his eyes, and suddenly there was only sympathy, blooming hard and painful in Kitty's chest. "That must have been so difficult for you to watch," she said, her voice low, her eyes searching his grim face. "I assume you must have tried to help him? Tried to urge him to leave it behind? Or given him conditions, ultimatums, that kind of thing?"

She was thinking now of how he'd thrown Thrain out, and if she wasn't mistaken, that was a twitch of surprise, flashing across Varinn's eyes. "Ach," he said, clipped, with a shrug. "All of this. The explaining, the pleading, the threats, even hiding away his coin. But"—his mouth thinned, his chest hollowing—"none of it has helped, ach? It has only served to drive him away, and worsen it all further. Making me into his jailor, and the one to pay his debts, while he has kept on as he wished, and freely spoken his falsehoods to my face. And now, *this*."

He'd given a curt, jerky wave down toward Kitty, toward—their son. And yes, there was the contempt, flaring in his eyes, and Kitty felt her own gaze dropping, as yet more comprehension, more certainty, flickered through her thoughts.

So this—this agreement, between them—this *was* all about Thrain, then. Especially given that promise Varinn had gained from her, back in the forest. *You shall not touch a drop of wine, or berry-juice, or aught else.* This was Varinn desperately trying to grasp control of the situation, of her and Thrain both. And maybe Thrain had even been right, and Varinn was blatantly wielding Kitty and her son against him, in a frantic attempt to bring him back again. To teach him a lesson. To... save him.

"You still want to help him," she said, quiet, toward the fur. "Even after all that? After he... betrayed you?"

There was a moment's silence, and then the sound of a heavy sigh. "Ach, I do," Varinn replied, just as quiet. "I am yet so vexed with him, and so weary of all this—but I cannot just—leave him to this, ach? Cannot just—forget him. Or, now, his son."

His voice sounded helpless, despairing, and when Kitty again found his face, it looked almost pleading, too. Almost as if he needed her to understand, needed someone, anyone to understand, to come alongside him in this goal. Even if it was her, even if he hated her, even if it was all an act. A... transaction. A deal.

But even as Kitty followed it, understood it, her head had distantly begun to ache, the nausea churning higher in her belly. Because gods, what would happen to her, amidst all this? Wasn't this, too, just like Charles, with his expectations, his demands on her behaviour, all his cruel empty promises? And how had she ended up in this again, in such a precarious dangerous mess? *Dehydrated*, Thrain had said, *delirious, starving. You almost died...*

"I—understand, sir," she told him, over the catch in her throat. "I'll do all I can to support you, and repay my debt. But..."

Her voice trailed off, catching on the instant flare of

suspicion in Varinn's eyes, the hard clench of his hands at his sides. "But what," he said, his voice thin. "You wish to alter our terms? To have a drink now and then?"

The hurt bloomed in Kitty's chest, and she blinked back at him, shaking her head. "No, of course not," she managed. "I'm pregnant, remember? Drinking to excess could harm our son. For his entire *life*."

There was a beat of stillness, and then Varinn grimaced, and rubbed at his nose. "Ach," he said, muffled. "Then what do you wish for, woman."

Oh. Kitty drew in a shaky breath, let it out. What did she wish for, in the midst of all this? When Varinn didn't like her, didn't trust her, and surely, she couldn't dare trust him—or Thrain—either. So what would truly help her, once all this was over? Coin would run out, jewels could be taken back, rents could be ignored or forgotten. But...

"Look, you've made it quite clear how you—feel about me," she said thickly. "And that there's no real future for me here. So that means I need"—she drew in a breath, held his eyes— "skills. Training. References. For some kind of real employment. Something I can do—after. To support myself. To prevent something like this from ever happening again."

There was another instant's silence, and blinking at Varinn, it occurred to Kitty that he was suddenly looking rather pale. "Ach," he said, his voice strange. "You are not— unwelcome here, woman. I should not have said—I did not intend—"

But Kitty was choking out a sound like a laugh, and flapping her hand between them. "It's fine," she said, too quickly. "You can't help how you feel, and I wouldn't—expect you to, after all that's happened. And I certainly wouldn't want you to have to—to pretend otherwise, long-term, or else you'll just end up resenting me, and our son, and it seems to me like you've had more than enough of that to deal with already. And"—she attempted another laugh, though she was blinking hard—"I've always wanted to learn a trade. It'll be quite a revelation, to support myself for once."

There was yet more silence from Varinn, his face still strange, blank, entirely unreadable. His hand now rubbing at his mouth, as though he were somehow upset by this, and Kitty belatedly realized that of course he was thinking—about the son again. Right?

"I don't mean I would abandon our son," she continued wretchedly, with a pained-feeling grimace. "I still want to—to be in his life. But—"

But gods, how hadn't she thought about this? How would she ever manage such a thing? Could she even move away from Orc Mountain, and try to support herself, if she wanted to stay in contact with her son? Could they bring him to visit? Or would she now be trapped here between them forever? And what would happen if Varinn found a woman he truly *did* care for? What then?

But Varinn's eyes were shifting again, with something maybe like comprehension, or sympathy, or even relief. "Ach, then, I follow," he said, very quiet. "We shall find a way, ach? And until then, I shall care for you and your son, and you shall help me care for Thrain. And"—he squared his shoulders, gave her a small, tentative smile—"should you truly wish for a trade, I ken we shall find one to suit you."

Oh. Wait. Really? He would? And suddenly Kitty found herself beaming back up at him, truly delighted, for what felt like the first time in weeks. "You really mean it?" she said, breathless. "Oh, thank you, Lord Grisk. Thank you so, so much."

Varinn's throat convulsed, his gaze again locked to hers, and something strange—something new—flicked across his eyes. Something that made Kitty draw in a deep breath, and lean a little closer, toward where he was now standing just beside the bed...

But then she twitched away, and dropped her eyes. No. No.

He didn't like her. He didn't trust her. He didn't care about her. He'd just made that very, very clear, once again. This was just a transaction, just a deal, and that was all...

And then—something moved. Something... beneath his leather kilt, still so close, here before her face. As if... as if...

Oh. And Kitty stared, transfixed, as the kilt again bobbed out, betraying the growing, swelling truth behind it. And when she again glanced up, it was to the sight of a distinctive redness, creeping up Varinn's neck, colouring his cheeks...

But maybe it was—part of the deal. The terms. He would care for her, and her son. And even if she couldn't trust him, even if he couldn't trust her, there was this, just this...

And without thought, without even following it, Kitty's shaky hands fumbled at his kilt, grasping the stiff leather, yanking it open. And when that long green hardness bobbed out, ready and waiting and dripping, she gasped with relief, and sucked him deep into her throat.

It was urgent and frenzied this time, with very little finesse, and only a desperate, bone-deep craving. A craving that seemed to seize her from the inside out, flooding away everything but this. No misery, no uncertainty, no sickness or weakness or foolishness—only this orc's hungry hard flesh filling her mouth, feeding her, funnelling his rich hot sweetness straight into her belly.

Gods, he tasted good, impossibly good, and she moaned as she plunged him deeper, sucked him harder, delved her eager tongue inside him. Teasing out more, more, more, and oh, he didn't even mind, he was just shuddering fatter and fuller, stretching her lips wider around him, his sweetness now pouring in a steady, succulent stream...

Kitty moaned again, low and uncontrolled, and one of her shaky hands somehow found his round heavy bollocks, curving and caressing around them, while her other hungry hand circled the thick solid base of him. Pumping out his sweetness even harder, faster, oh it was good, he was so, *so* good—

And oh, he was even helping, now, his hips gently canting him into her throat, his big hand skittering against her hot face. Holding her in place, oh hell, his thumb pressing into her hollowed cheek, his sharp claw just lightly pricking her skin. So he could use her mouth like this, slide himself in and out, his green skin glossy and glistening with her saliva, the sounds of her lips wet and sloppy against him...

"Good," came his voice, somehow both soft and harsh at once. "Now open wide for your seed, ach?"

Oh yes, yes, Kitty would do that, she would—and she nodded, swallowing him as deep as she could, fighting to relax her throat around him. While still keeping her watering, worshipful eyes fixed to his watching face, to where his black lashes were fluttering low, his gaze dazed and hungry, as a hoarse, heated growl vibrated from his chest...

The seed surged hard and fast, gushing out from that invading head, pouring thick down her frantically swallowing throat. Swarming her mouth with heat and life and sweetness, with promise, with approval.

And as Kitty moaned and gulped it down, blinking up at his flushed face, it distantly occurred to her that he looked almost... satisfied. Triumphant. That this moment—with his flesh filling the throat of the woman he hated, the woman who had entrapped his lost partner—this was part of the deal, too. This was... justice.

And gods, maybe... maybe Kitty didn't even care. Because it was easy, far, far too easy, to keep holding his glittering eyes, to keep seeking all of that sweetness, swallowing every last drop. Until he finally gave a low hiss and nudged her away, his hand still firm on her face, his claw still prodding her cheek. Speaking, perhaps, of his total power in this situation, his command, his control.

And somehow, Kitty still wasn't arguing. Wasn't

disagreeing. And instead, she even found herself twitching a small, shy smile up toward him, her tongue briefly brushing against her swollen, sweet-tasting lips.

"Thank you, Lord Grisk," she murmured, soft. "You're so very kind."

At that, his eyes angled away, and she could see his throat convulsing as his hand abruptly dropped from her face, and straightened out the fall of his kilt. "Is there... aught else you might now wish for?" he asked, rough. "Any other food or drink? Or more rest?"

But Kitty was still feeling so good, perhaps better than she'd felt in days, and she couldn't seem to stop smiling up toward him. "I'm feeling much better, thank you," she replied. "But I'm happy to do whatever you think is best."

His throat convulsed again, but he nodded, and waved a shaky hand toward the shelves. Or rather, toward the neater of the two shelves, which—Kitty peered a little closer—had some familiar-looking fabrics stacked on top of it. Her... clothes?

"Then mayhap you shall ready yourself for the day," Varinn said, quiet but firm. "And then you shall come, and meet your new kin, and see your new home."

21

When Kitty stepped out beyond the room's curtained door, she felt clean, awake, and more certain than she had in weeks. She could do this. She had a plan. A goal. Maybe even a purpose.

And when she found Varinn waiting for her, his eyes briefly flicking up and down her body, it felt almost easy to give a rueful smile in return, and a self-deprecating wave at her current ensemble. "Another highly unfashionable dressing-gown, I'm afraid," she said, as lightly as she could. "Not at all ideal for meeting people you want to impress, is it? I was obviously not thinking properly when I packed for this trip."

Varinn betrayed a faint wince, but then shrugged, his eyes angling away. "You may dress however you please here, and no one shall mark this," he said stiffly. "But"—his nose slightly wrinkled as he evaluated the dressing-gown—"should you wish for other garb, I shall be happy to help you gain this."

"Really?" Kitty asked, with genuine interest, as the vision of Ella's daring outfit rose in her thoughts—and she couldn't help a brief, appreciative glance downwards, toward Varinn's leather kilt. Which was really quite striking, and flattering on him, too, much more so than the trousers. And what would he look like with his hair down, and maybe a few jewels, too, perhaps like Ella's orc mate had worn...

But wait, oh gods, Varinn had caught Kitty looking at him, and he purposefully glanced away, clearing his throat. "Ach," he said, just as stiffly. "I can take you to our clan's storage-room later today, should you wish."

Oh. Kitty's cheeks felt strangely hot, but she drew in a breath, and kept the smile on her face. "That's very kind of you, sir, thank you," she said. "I don't know anything about orc fashion, but"—she angled another lingering glance downwards—"I must admit, this kilt does look very fetching on you. Shows off your assets very well."

The flush of pink up Varinn's neck was instantaneous, and undeniably gratifying, too—and though he glanced away again, he also settled his big warm hand against Kitty's back, and guided her forward. Passing through a circular little alcove, with several more doors embedded in the walls, and then out into a larger, lamplit, stone-walled room. It was furnished with a variety of benches and tables, and it was again surprisingly cozy, with multiple furs and tapestries scattered about. And along this room's walls, there were yet more doors cut into the stone, most of them only showing darkness beyond.

"We are now in our mountain's Grisk wing, in the Speaker's rooms," Varinn said, with a wave of his hand that seemed to encompass the entire area around them. "These rooms are thus all now held by Nattfarr, and he shares them with his Guard— Dammarr, Thrak, Thrain, and me. Together, we serve to keep safe Nattfarr's great gift, and watch over his kin, and all the Grisk clan."

Oh. Kitty couldn't hide her twitch of curiosity at that—had Varinn or Thrain ever spoken of their professions before?— and then glanced around the room again. It really was surprisingly lovely, with the sturdy matching furnishings, the glimmering lamps, the soft furs and textiles, and—

Wait. The orcs. The three familiar, grey-skinned orcs, all sitting together on benches around a nearby table. Dammarr, Thrak, and—oh gods—Thrain himself. And Thrain was blinking toward them with bleary eyes, and then he jerked up to his feet, a basket clutched in his hand.

"Och, it's good to see you up and about, Kit," he said, with false-sounding brightness, as he strode over toward them. "I hope you're feeling better?"

Kitty gratefully smiled back, though she couldn't help noticing that Thrain somehow looked even paler and more haggard than before, a visible sheen of sweat coating his face. "Yes, much better, thank you," she replied. "I'm very grateful to you all for hosting me in your lovely home."

Thrain waved it away with an unsteady-looking hand, and gave her a wan smile in return. "Happy to," he said firmly. "For as long as you please, ach? Oh, and"—he glanced down toward the basket in his hand, and thrust it out toward her—"I fetched you some breakfast from the kitchen, if you might like anything else to eat?"

Oh. Kitty accordingly took the basket, and blinked down at it with genuine astonishment. It was filled to overflowing with an impossible variety of food—fruits, berries, eggs, nuts, greens, several kinds of cooked meat, and even what appeared to be fresh-baked bread. The sight of it didn't seem to instantly turn her stomach, either, and when she carefully took a tentative nibble of bread, she found, much to her relief, that it seemed to settle without difficulty. "Thank you," she said to Thrain, around another careful bite. "That was very thoughtful of you."

Thrain grinned and waved it away again, though the movement was even more erratic than before. "Anything you need," he said. "Though I ken Varinn's seed tastes better than all of it, ach? It's always been my favourite breakfast, too."

Wait. Had he just said—Varinn's *seed*—was his favourite *breakfast*? And Kitty couldn't quite hide her shocked gasp, or the sudden, breathtaking vision of it, rearing to vivid life in her thoughts. Varinn pushing Thrain down in the bed, Thrain looking up at him with those warm, expressive eyes as he lifted Varinn's leather kilt, and swallowed him deep...

But before her, Thrain had begun to look distinctly chagrined, rubbing at his sweaty face, and angling Varinn a wincing, regretful look. "Och, sorry," he said, too quickly. "Sorry. Just—the scent, you know, didn't mean to pry, I wasn't—"

He grimaced again, waving his shaky hand between them—and somehow, Kitty's own hand snapped out, catching his clammy fingers in hers. "It's quite all right," she heard herself say, though her voice was unusually high-pitched. "Varinn does taste very good, doesn't he? It's so generous of you to—er—not mind?"

It sounded far too much like a question, like an admission that perhaps Thrain *should* mind, after all—and she winced as she glanced back at Varinn's stony face, and hurriedly dropped Thrain's hand. But damn it, now Thrain's brother Thrak was shoving up off the bench, and stalking over to join them. His eyes flinty and suspicious on Varinn, as his clawed hand grasped Thrain's shoulder, and give it a firm little shake.

"Ach, my little brother is very generous indeed," Thrak said, with a smile that didn't at all reach his eyes. "For if I were Thrain, I'd be calling you out to a death-match over all this, wouldn't I, Varinn? Mayhap I yet should, ach?"

Varinn's body felt very stiff against Kitty's, his jaw visibly flexing in his cheek—but he didn't reply, or otherwise acknowledge this highly alarming threat. And across the room, Dammarr huffed a loud, irritable groan, and leapt up to stride over toward them, too.

"Ach, and you should likely lose to him, you fool," Dammarr told Thrak, his light voice at palpable odds with the chilly glint in his eyes. "I would never have *dreamt* that Thrain would prove the wiser of you two upon such matters, but I ken I should learn to temper my hopes, ach?"

There was an instant's stillness, and Kitty didn't miss Varinn's brief, grateful glance toward Dammarr—or Thrak's curt, bitter little laugh. "Thanks, Dammarr," he said thinly. "I'll remind you of that, next time you're screaming for mercy on my prick."

Oh. Wait. So did Thrak mean—he and Dammarr were a couple, too? Or no, no, maybe not, based on the look of pure disdain in Dammarr's eyes, and the curling sneer on his mouth. "I ken *you* ought to temper your hopes upon this, also," he said, his voice cold. "For you may be waiting quite some time, ach?"

There was another awkward silence, dangling thick and painful between them—until it was abruptly broken by the rising sound of voices, across the room. And when Kitty jerked to look, there were more people, spilling through the furthest door. Multiple new people, including orcs of varying ages, a woman, and even a smiling teenaged girl, who appeared to be cradling a small black *kitten*.

"Varinn!" crowed one of the younger-looking orcs, as he sprinted across the room toward them. "Your new mate is awake! Can we finally meet her?"

This new orc skidded to a stop close beside Varinn, flashing him a bright, eager smile. And Kitty was distantly surprised to see Varinn smiling too, slow and rueful, before slinging his arm around the young orc's slim shoulders, and pulling him into his side.

"Ach, Timo," he said, with genuine-seeming warmth, as he ruffled his hand in the orc's hair. "This is Katharine—Kitty— from Dusbury. I hope you shall help make her welcome amongst us, as a good Grisk would, ach?"

"Ach, brother," this Timo replied, with a shy, sharp-toothed smile toward Kitty. "Greetings, Miss Kitty. We are so happy to welcome you here, and wish the gods' greatest blessings upon you."

Kitty couldn't help an impulsive smile back, and even a quick little curtsey toward him. "Thank you so much, Mr. Timo," she said. "I'm honoured to meet any brother of Varinn's, and I wish all the gods' blessings upon you, too."

Timo flashed her a delighted grin in return, but then it sobered as he glanced up at Varinn's face. "Ach, well, we are not blood-brothers," he said, with a faint wince. "But close, you ken."

Kitty didn't miss the twinge on Varinn's face too, or the way he pulled Timo a little tighter, and gave him another approving, affectionate smile. "Ach," he said firmly. "Just as close as any blood-brother could be, ach, Eyarl?"

At that, Varinn gave a purposeful nod toward another one of the new orcs—a bulky, kindly-looking older fellow, with silver hair and light eyes. He was standing together with two more orcs, one lean and sharp-eyed and of a similar age, while the other orc—also with light eyes—looked closer in age to Timo, perhaps fourteen or fifteen years old.

"Katharine, this is Eyarl," Varinn said, toward the silver-haired orc. "He has long served as our clan's Chief Scout, and has oft been much like a father to me, and to Timo also. And this"—he nodded toward the lean orc—"is his mate Valter, who also serves as a scout in our clan."

Kitty smiled and curtsied toward them both, earning a toothy grin back from Eyarl, and a brief, polite nod from Valter. While Varinn's warm gaze shifted toward the younger orc, who was watching Kitty with shy wariness. "And this is Eyarl's blood-son Trygve," Varinn continued, "who is just as kind and clever as his father, ach?"

This Trygve visibly flushed and gave Kitty a careful smile, showing off a glinting gold fang. While beside him, Eyarl kept grinning fondly between them all, and then reached to clasp his big hand to Varinn's shoulder. "My best wishes on your great gain, son," he said, in a low, rumbling voice, before shifting his warm gaze to Kitty. "It is a true honour to meet you, woman. Where do you hail from? I ken I scent the city upon you. The Kull district, mayhap?"

Oh. Kitty felt herself slightly stiffening—he could truly *smell* that?—but she drew in a breath, and nodded. "Yes, indeed," she said. "Though I haven't lived there for years, and I'd be quite happy never to return again."

Her voice came out sounding a little too strained, earning a brief sidelong glance from Varinn, but this Eyarl kept smiling, and gave a curt, approving nod. "Then I hope you shall be very happy here with us instead," he said. "You could not have chosen a better mate than our Varinn, ach? I ken he shall take very good care of you."

Wait. A better *mate*? Kitty's body went even stiffer, her eyes reflexively darting sideways at Varinn, and then over toward where Thrain had been—but wait, Thrain wasn't there anymore, and he didn't seem to be among the clusters of new orcs, either. Or even anywhere in the room at all, and Kitty belatedly shoved that awareness away, and dragged her gaze back to Eyarl's waiting, curious eyes.

"Yes, Varinn's been so kind," she said, with what she hoped was a grateful smile. "I've been—very happy indeed."

Thankfully, Eyarl looked thoroughly gratified by this, and gave Varinn's shoulder an approving little shake. And Kitty didn't miss that faint flush, again creeping up Varinn's neck, as he nodded and thanked Eyarl, before guiding Kitty toward the next group of people waiting to meet them. In front was a pretty, beaming blonde woman, clad in yet another unconventional, highly revealing ensemble, and behind her were two more big, bare-chested orcs. One of the orcs was green and genial-looking, grinning at Kitty with unabashed delight, while the second orc was tall, grey, and glowering, though the effect was rather blunted by the tiny, sleeping orc baby, cradled gently in his arms.

"Katharine, this is our Grisk sister Alma," Varinn said, with a genuine-seeming smile toward the blonde woman. "And these are Alma's two mates. Baldr, also of Clan Grisk"—he waved toward the green orc—"and Drafli, of Clan Skai. And their new son, Barden."

For an instant, Kitty could only seem to blink between these two new orcs—*Alma's two mates*, Varinn had said, and *their son*? Wait. As if—as if what Thrain had told her earlier—*we could have done this together*—had been true? And such relationships really were... normal, around here? Accepted?

"We are most pleased to welcome you to our mountain and our clan, woman," said a lilting voice—this Baldr, his grin still warm and wide. "We hope you shall be kept safe and content here, ach?"

Kitty attempted a grateful smile back toward him, though she was somewhat distracted by the sight of this Drafli's grey clawed hand snaking around Baldr's hip, and yanking him close. An action that this Baldr seemed to welcome, turning his head to inhale deeply against Drafli's shoulder, even as his big hand reached to caress the sleeping baby in Drafli's arms. Almost as if the baby was indeed also... *his*.

"Yes, indeed," interjected the blonde woman—Alma—with a bright smile toward Kitty. "We're so happy to have you here, sister. And I hope you're quite comfortable, rooming with Varinn and Thrain? Or would you rather have a space of your own?"

She'd waved across the room, toward where Kitty had been sleeping—and once again, Kitty was caught, blinking, as more disconcerting awareness flashed through her thoughts. That room was *Varinn and Thrain's* room? They'd been serious enough to *live* together, before all this? As these *mates*, perhaps, until she'd barged in between them?

It took a moment for Kitty to find her breath again, and to realize that Alma and her two orcs were all intently looking at her, waiting for an answer. And Kitty's furtive glance toward Varinn found him looking at her, too, his eyes gone narrow, suspicious. Almost as if he fully expected her to instantly jump at Alma's offer, and take the first possible opportunity to escape him, and undermine all the promises she'd made.

But a strange, sudden rebellion was surging in Kitty's chest, rising in her throat, and it was enough to make her square her shoulders, and plaster another smile to her mouth. "Oh, I'm very comfortable, thank you," she told Alma, as cheerfully as she could. "It's such a lovely, cozy room, and Varinn and Thrain have just been so kind to share it with me. And we wouldn't wish to be parted, would we, Varinn?"

She'd aimed her beaming smile toward Varinn's face, and even leaned a little closer into his side. Finding, to her distant surprise, that he'd almost seemed to relax against her, and that the telltale redness was again creeping up his neck. While before them, this Alma was looking distinctly pleased, and flashing them another warm, approving smile.

"Of course you wouldn't," she said firmly. "Varinn is *lovely*. One of the kindest, most generous orcs in this mountain. He'll be such a wonderful mate to you."

That redness kept creeping higher up Varinn's neck, though his eyes had darted warily toward Alma's two mates, who were both frowning back toward him with sudden, surprising hostility. Enough that Kitty quickly cut in with a warm but firm thank-you, and rapidly spun toward the next new person before them.

It turned out to be the human girl with the kitten, and once Kitty had exclaimed over the kitten—as well as the girl's beautiful dress, accented with striking orc jewelry—she soon learned that the girl's name was Cecily, and she was twelve years old, from the clan called Ash-Kai. And her kitten turned out to be a devious little hellion named Floof, who had four equally naughty cat brothers and sisters, all now living with new owners throughout the mountain. And apparently there had been quite a ruckus between the kittens and Ella's dogs, who had gone to stay at her other home for a while, until the kittens had grown enough to defend themselves.

It was a thoroughly enjoyable conversation, but as Kitty cheerfully chatted away, she'd remained very aware of Varinn beside her, of his hand still on her back. Of how that hand had almost seemed to relax a little more, even stroking slightly up and down, as if in silent approval. And when it gently nudged her forward, Kitty accordingly said a smiling farewell to Cecily, and greeted the next orc before them. A big bulky blacksmith named Fjorvi, who Varinn introduced with warm, familiar ease, before guiding Kitty to the next person, and the next. Making it abundantly clear that he intended to individually introduce her to each person who'd come to meet her, and that he fully expected her to make a good first impression on every single one of them.

But Kitty had spent half her life impressing random strangers on command, and she greeted them all with as much witty gaiety as she could muster, while fighting to embed their names and faces into her thoughts. Olarr, who was a warrior in the Bautul clan. Bramdur, a newer arrival to the mountain, who now served as the Chief Cobbler. And Ymir, the bulky, bushy-browed orc who ran the Grisk storage-room Varinn had mentioned—or rather, Ymir informed Kitty with baleful disapproval, the room the rest of the mountain had begun to call the *Grisk Hoard*.

"It's not a *Hoard*," he grumbled in a gravelly voice, his eyes narrowing toward Kitty with surprising fierceness. "You hide a hoard. Brood over it. Keep it secret and safe from your kin. But"—his irate gaze shifted meaningfully to Varinn—"we Grisk *share* our goods. Sell them! To anyone, from any clan! At a fair price! That's not *hoarding*, ach, son? That's good Grisk kindness, that is."

Beside Kitty, Varinn vaguely smiled and nodded, as though he'd heard this particular complaint many times before. But his hand was still on Kitty's back, warm and steady and approving—and without at all meaning to, Kitty felt herself impulsively smiling at this Ymir, and nodding with genuine-feeling agreement. "That does sound very unlike a secret hoard to me," she said firmly. "Perhaps more like a shop, or a boutique. Or a trading-post, or a showroom?"

Ymir, despite having maintained his fierce frown throughout most of this, instantly brightened at the word *showroom*, his green body pulling up to a surprising height. "Ach, a showroom," he announced, pointing a triumphant clawed finger at Varinn's face. "That's it, son. The Great Grisk Showroom-Shop!"

Varinn kept smiling, though it looked rather fixed on his face, and he swiftly guided Kitty away from Ymir, his claws prodding into her back. "The Great Grisk Showroom-Shop?" he hissed, low and exasperated in her ear. "Gods, Katharine, now I shall never hear the end of this!"

But Kitty couldn't help her peal of laughter, her bright grin up at his disgruntled face. "It sounds delightful to me," she said lightly. "Does it have more of these kilts, by any chance?"

She'd given a gentle, teasing tug at Varinn's fetching leather kilt, earning a deep, thrilling growl in return—and for an instant, as she smiled up at his narrow, glittering eyes, it almost felt as though they were the only two people in the room. As if he might drag her over to that wall, or that bench, and yank up that kilt, and remind her what was waiting beneath it...

But then he glanced purposefully away, toward where—oh. *Thrain.* Who had finally reappeared at the back of the room, hovering near one of the doors. Looking slightly less unsteady than before, perhaps, though his eyes were shuttered, downcast, as if he were intentionally avoiding Varinn's narrow, searching gaze.

Kitty could almost feel Varinn's growl, vibrating low and dangerous in his throat, and he abruptly spun away from Thrain, back toward their guests. Toward where young Timo had now sidled up beside them, and was casting a curious glance over toward Thrain, too.

"So is Kitty only mated to you, then, brother?" Timo asked Varinn, chewing at his lip with a sharp white fang. "Or is she mated to Thrain, also? His scent is strong upon her, and I can scent that her son is Thrain's blood also, ach?"

Oh. His words seemed to slice through the air, cutting through the cheerful hubbub of activity around them—and suddenly, there was only dangling, echoing silence. With quite possibly every eye in the room turning toward Varinn and Kitty, waiting for the answer.

Damn it. *Damn* it. And Kitty should have said something, something light and clever and diverting, but her breath had choked in her throat, her eyes darting uncertainly up toward Varinn's face. To where his expression had gone curiously blank, and that redness was again creeping up his neck. Suggesting that this was, perhaps, a question he'd dreaded. A question he didn't want to answer.

But then she felt him squaring his shoulders, and working to bring the smile back to his mouth, the warmth to his eyes. And it looked almost easy, almost natural, as he reached out his big hand, and ruffled it with all apparent approval in Timo's hair.

"Ach, little brother," he said. "This is very good scenting, for Katharine's son was indeed begotten by Thrain, and not by me. But I am yet very eager to meet him, ach?"

His voice sounded only slightly strained, his smile still sincere on his mouth. But even so, the silence seemed to keep ringing out after his words—perhaps because he hadn't actually answered the question, had he? And Timo's head had tilted sideways, and he angled an uncertain glance beyond them, toward...

Oh. Toward where Thrain had pushed off the wall, and was now striding with jerky steps toward them. Coming closer,

closer, his jaw set, his bloodshot eyes hard, intent, on Varinn's stiff, reddening face—

And then, in a sudden movement, Thrain slung his long arm around Varinn's neck, and yanked him close. As if he were... embracing him?

"Och, Varinn, you're too noble, as always," Thrain said lightly, his voice carrying through the hushed, crowded room, as he gave Varinn's shoulder a purposeful little shake. "For of course any son of mine is yours also, ach? I ken you'll be the best father any orcling could ever ask for, and I'd never want to raise a son without you."

Oh. It was... a kindness, Kitty realized. A means of dismissing the question, smoothing it over before all their watching, judging friends. And yes, yes, Kitty could see the relief settling across the assembled observers' eyes, could feel it in Varinn's body against her. Though she didn't miss his sideways glance toward Thrain, either, or the flexing in his jaw, the tightness lingering on his mouth. As if he were fighting back his disapproval, or his dread of what Thrain might do next.

"And," Thrain continued, his voice a little harder now, "Varinn has done me a great honour, in caring for Kitty and our son as he has. I haven't been—there for them, the way I should have been. And"—he drew in a breath—"Varinn has once again covered for my failings, and kept Kitty and our son healthy and safe, in my stead. I haven't deserved his kindness, and he's granted it to me anyway. Just like he always has, for all of us."

His eyes were both flinty and bright, rapidly sweeping over their watching audience, and then glancing back toward Varinn. Toward where Varinn was looking visibly uncertain, unsettled by this public confession, and Kitty could see him swallowing, his gaze holding for an instant on Thrain, before flicking back to the group of watching, waiting onlookers.

"Ach," Varinn replied, his voice steady, carrying through the silence. "And in thanks for my help, until our son is born, Thrain shall fight all our sparring-matches one-handed. And mayhap blindfolded! Ach, Thrain?"

Thrain's glance toward Varinn was astonished, and then delighted—and before them, both Timo and Trygve had crowed aloud, Timo punching his fist triumphantly into the air. And suddenly everyone seemed to be cheerfully chattering at once, anticipating the entertainment to come, but Kitty couldn't seem to pull her eyes away from Varinn and Thrain. From how—in that instant—they looked utterly in accord, Varinn's eyes soft and indulgent, his big hand settling with familiar ease against Thrain's bare back. While Thrain was loudly laughing at something Timo had said, his eyes alight, even as his taller body leaned into Varinn's solid strength, his long arm still hooked tightly around his neck. Looking relaxed, at peace together, for perhaps the first time since Kitty had met them.

But then Timo excitedly rushed off with Trygve, and the rest of the gathered guests slowly seemed to filter away too. And without the audience, Varinn's eyes had rapidly shuttered, and he'd ducked away, out of Thrain's reach. And then he strode toward Kitty with stiff, measured steps, his hand catching on her back, and guiding her across the room, toward one of the adjoining doors.

But Kitty couldn't help glancing back at Thrain, who was blinking after them with bright, strangely wounded eyes. And then he lurched toward them, dodging over to catch up, falling into step beside Varinn. "What is it, Varinn?" Thrain asked under his breath, rubbing at his shiny face. "What's amiss?"

Varinn didn't reply, his eyes held straight ahead, and he kept walking, even faster than before. Guiding Kitty out into a wide, stone-walled corridor, which was softly lit by a series of wrought-iron lamps in the walls. Showing even more doors cut into the smooth stone on either side, but Varinn took no notice of them, keeping his gaze firmly forward, his body stiff.

"Do not play the fool with me, Thrain," Varinn finally hissed, very quiet. "You ken what is amiss."

Thrain flinched, but didn't reply, and kept pace beside them as Varinn guided Kitty down another lamplit corridor, and then another. And then sideways, into a dark, twisty little tunnel, where Varinn finally whirled around to face Thrain, his mouth set, his hands clutched to tight fists.

"You spout all these grand apologies, even before our kin," Varinn bit out, "enough to make me wonder if mayhap you even mean to follow through with this, this time. But in truth"—he gave a sharp wave up and down Thrain's twitchy, haggard-looking form—"here you are, deep in the drink again? Already? After *one day*?!"

Oh. Ohhhh. Because Varinn could... *smell* it. And when Thrain had disappeared like that, back there, he'd clearly gone off and—oh. That. Again.

Thrain was visibly cringing, his mouth opening and closing, his shaky hand wiping at his sweaty forehead. "I'm not," he said weakly. "I mean, I didn't want to, Varinn, I—"

"Do not speak false to me!" Varinn exploded, his eyes blazing, as he jerked a step closer to Thrain's twitching body. "You ken I cannot scent you? You ken because I have covered your failings to our kin—*again*—I have somehow missed the stench of fresh ale on your scent?!"

Thrain was shifting his weight on his feet, his hand still wiping at his drawn, sweaty face. While his bloodshot eyes angled uneasily toward Kitty, and Varinn had clearly followed that too, his own eyes snapping even colder, his lips pulling back to bare his sharp white teeth.

"Mayhap I have not been clear enough upon this," Varinn continued, low and scathing. "You now have two paths before you, Thrain. You can forswear the drink, and regain your son, and mayhap my trust, and Katharine's trust, also. Or"—he jerked another step closer, crowding Thrain back against the wall—"you can keep the drink, and lose all the rest. Me. Her. Your son. *Forever!*"

He'd given a furious wave at Kitty's face, and then—then her *belly*, oh gods. And blinking back toward him, toward Thrain, Kitty realized that this was... the final ultimatum. This was the crux of Varinn's drastic plan, his last-ditch attempt to save Thrain from his failings. By holding himself, and their son—and Kitty—as *leverage*.

And clearly, it was having the desired effect, because Thrain's body was trembling even more violently than before, his bloodshot eyes wide and aghast on Varinn's face. "You wouldn't, Varinn," he breathed. "You wouldn't keep our son— my own blood—from me. You wouldn't."

Kitty winced, shaking her head back and forth, but Varinn's growl again rumbled through the corridor, harsh and fierce. "Ach, I would, and I *shall*," he snarled. "I have told you again and again, and mayhap now it will finally sink into your ale-addled brain!"

Thrain kept blinking, his body still juddering with a strange, erratic agitation, and Varinn growled again, and jabbed his claw into Thrain's bare chest. "I shall *never* allow my son to spend his days with a drunkard," he hissed. "This is not safe. It is not wise. It will teach him that this is how a father behaves, and how he faces his hardships. And it will bring him—and his own sons after him—naught but grief and penury and *death!*"

His voice rang through the corridor, bitter and painful and horribly triumphant. As if this was finally a long-awaited sliver of justice, or maybe—maybe even that revenge Thrain had accused him of. Thrain had hurt Varinn, betrayed him, brought him such anger and pain... and now Varinn could finally fight back against it, with power and reason and utter conviction on his side.

"This is your truth now, Thrain," Varinn growled, his eyes alight with victory and rage. "Now make your choice!"

And even as Kitty was still blinking at it, shaking her head, Varinn clasped her hand, and drew her close. "Come, Katharine," he said, his voice hard. "We are finished here."

And with that, he spun and stalked down the corridor, dragging Kitty away behind him.

22

Kitty stumbled after Varinn down the dim, twisty corridor, her heart hammering, her feet tripping against the smooth stone. While her traitorous eyes desperately searched backwards, back toward where Thrain was just standing there unmoving in the corridor, his eyes bright, his shoulders slumped, his head bowed low. Lost. Miserable. Alone.

"Varinn," Kitty gulped, without at all meaning to. "Lord Grisk. Wait. Please."

Varinn's hand spasmed on hers, but to her genuine surprise, he stopped, halting in the middle of the corridor. And for an instant, his eyes on hers looked almost as bright as Thrain's had, and he rubbed at them with a jerky, unsteady hand.

"What," he said, clipped. "Do you feel ill again?"

Kitty blinked at him, shaking her head, and then glanced back toward where Thrain was—or rather, toward where Thrain had been, just behind that corner. "Just—there has to be—*something*," she said thickly. "Some other way. You just told me you've already tried giving Thrain threats and ultimatums, haven't you? You even dumped him, and kicked him out? And none of that helped, right? Why would this time be any different?"

Varinn was already frowning at her, the disapproval flaring in his narrowed eyes, and Kitty drew herself taller, pulled in a breath. "Look, I agree that this isn't the future I want for my—our—son," she stammered. "But even the *thought* of permanently cutting out one of our son's fathers ought to be a very last resort. After we've tried everything else. Don't you think?"

Varinn's eyes had flared again at that word *fathers*, hinting at something Kitty couldn't quite read—but then he shook his head, his mouth tight and grim. "I have tried all else," he countered, his voice hard. "You have not been here, woman. You have not witnessed all I have done, and all I have borne!"

The furious frustration was too palpable, too strong in his bitter eyes—but he wasn't walking away. Wasn't ignoring her. And instead, he was still standing here, still looking at her, still speaking to her. Still... waiting. Listening.

And without at all meaning to, Kitty lurched a step closer toward him, and settled both her hands against his warm bare chest. Feeling how it was heaving in and out, but how it also... didn't recoil. Didn't twitch away.

"No, I wasn't here," she said, searching his angry eyes. "But I can only imagine, sir. You've been so exceedingly generous toward me, when you didn't at all need to be. So how much more generous would you have been toward him? Toward someone"—her voice lowered to a whisper—"you truly care about?"

Varinn didn't reply, his chest still heaving hard beneath her hands, and Kitty swallowed, kept holding his watching eyes. "So I realize this is me... asking you a favour," she said. "Another one. Please, Lord Grisk. Can we please try other options first. Something. *Anything*. For our son's sake, if nothing else."

Varinn still didn't reply, but he still hadn't moved, hadn't pushed her away. Still watching, still listening—so Kitty dragged in more breath, more courage. More... hope.

"And if there's any way I could help convince you," she continued, quieter, "or repay you... I should be very happy to oblige. Please, Lord Grisk. *Please.*"

The words seemed to dangle there, strange and far too vivid between them. And Varinn just kept looking at her like that, his lips slightly parted, his eyes glinting with something that felt almost... familiar, now. Familiar, and dizzying, and breathtakingly powerful...

And then, oh hell, he glanced downwards. Toward his kilt. Toward... *that.*

And gods, they were still in what appeared to be a public place—and Thrain could very well still be listening, just beyond that bend in the corridor. And Kitty could still taste Varinn's lingering sweetness on her lips from last time, only a short while ago...

But somehow, somehow, she was frantically nodding—yes, yes, *yes.* And then sinking to her knees, kneeling before Varinn, on hard cold stone, in the middle of the damned corridor, in this damned Orc Mountain—

And then moaning, oh gods, as Varinn's smooth, green, dripping-wet head found her mouth, and shoved between her lips. Plunging into her mouth as though he owned it, as though he could do whatever the hell he wanted with it, and maybe— maybe he could. Because Kitty was sucking with all her strength, hollowing her cheeks, sliding up and down that slick length with swift, desperate craving. And even holding his eyes as she did it, watching him watch her as she shamelessly sucked him off in a corridor, because that was what did it for him, wasn't it? That control, the total command over the situation, over her, over her son. And yes, yes, perhaps over Thrain, too.

So Kitty just kept... giving it. Kept sucking him harder, deeper, feeling his powerful flesh swelling and shuddering in her mouth, stretching her lips apart. And she didn't hide her moans, or the sloppy humiliating sounds of it, but instead greedily gulped down that oozing sweetness, and caressed him with both hands, worshipping him with her touch and her mouth and her eyes. Pumping him, plying him, pleading with him, while he just stood there and gazed impassively down toward her, without offering even a single word or touch in return.

But... he was still allowing it. He still wanted it, maybe even needed it. His heavy bollocks tightening as his eyes slightly fluttered, his head tipping back—and oh, oh, there it was. The rush of hot surging sweetness, spewing fast and fierce into Kitty's mouth. Flooding from that jutting, straining cock, straight down her eagerly swallowing throat.

And as she gulped it down, the sounds loud and coarse and obscene, she didn't miss the glint of dark satisfaction, flaring in Varinn's watching eyes. Or maybe even the triumph, as those eyes cut sideways, toward...

Thrain. Oh, gods, toward Thrain, who had somehow, at some point, stepped around that corner. And who was just standing there, and watching all this, his face flushed, his lips parted, his eyes glinting with unreadable intensity. Disbelief, perhaps, or longing, or rage.

Kitty blanched, began to yank away—but wait, *wait*, now that was Varinn's big hand, holding her there, keeping his softening heft in her mouth. And as she glanced questioningly up toward him, her face burning with heat, Kitty again recognized that look in his eyes, that silent, already-familiar command. *You do not waste what I give you.*

So she somehow, somehow, kept going. Kept carefully sucking on him, seeking out every last drop, while his heavy hand stayed there, wanting more. Wanting to flaunt this, maybe, to show it off for Thrain's watching eyes.

And when Varinn finally, finally released the pressure, and Kitty drew back, let him fall from her mouth... the first thing she saw was Thrain. Thrain, now standing far too close, because he was—he was leaning against the damned wall beside Varinn, their shoulders brushing together. And like Varinn, he was watching her, watching this, with blatant, blinking brazenness.

And instead of the jealousy or hurt Kitty had fully expected to see in his eyes, he now looked... stunned. Hungry. His tongue brushing his parted lips, his breath exhaling shaky and slow.

"Gods, Varinn, you're such a damned prick sometimes," he breathed, his voice cracking. "So this is another one of your terms, ach? Showing me what might be on offer, if I can behave as well as she does?"

Oh, hell, and Kitty's breath choked aloud, her eyes wide on Varinn's flushed face. On where he wasn't looking angry, now, or vindictive, or even frustrated. And instead of snapping back at Thrain, or maybe ordering him away, he exhaled, and rubbed at his mouth.

As if... as if maybe Thrain was right. As if this had indeed been... a demonstration, on Varinn's part. A blatant provocation. Another one of his demands, driving that knife deep.

Your fealty shall only be to me.

And for an instant, Kitty wanted to rail at Varinn, shout at him, or maybe even weep at him. To inform him that yes, he was a cold selfish prick, blatantly wielding her desperate desire to please him, so that he could gain what he wanted from her. So he could use her—and her son—as a bargaining tool, and that was all.

But she'd made a promise. And she'd asked for this. So she staggered up to her feet, dragged in a breath, and purposefully turned her face away from Varinn. Looking instead back toward Thrain, searching his tired, twitchy, sweaty face.

"Did you really mean it," she said to him, sharper than she meant, "when you said you want to address this. When you said you wanted to make amends, and be a good father. The best father you can possibly be."

Thrain's throat convulsed, but he held Kitty's gaze, and rapidly, fervently nodded. "Ach," he said, his voice thick. "I meant it. I hate what I've become amidst all this, ach? I hate how I've failed you, and our son, and—and you, Varinn. But I've tried, and tried, and *tried*, and it's—"

He shook his head, and drew in a thin-sounding breath, wiping at his sweaty face with a trembling hand. "It's like the drink has… stolen me," he whispered. "Stolen my peace, and my strength, and all my longings. And it only relents when I pay its price. But"—he took another rattling breath—"I don't *wish* for this, ach? Who would ever wish for this?"

He sounded truly ill, exhausted, lost, alone. And holding his miserable eyes, Kitty lifted her chin, and gave a curt, decisive nod. She had a goal. A purpose. And if Varinn really wanted her fealty, and her help, then he could damn well have it.

"Good," she said firmly. "So we're all in agreement, then. As long as you're committed to changing this, Thrain, we'll do our very best to help you face it, and find a way to address it. In any way we can. Won't we, Lord Grisk?"

Varinn didn't immediately reply, and Kitty's sharp glance toward him found his expression once again gone taut, grim, unreadable. Enough to spark Kitty's rebellion even higher, and she even smiled at him this time, far too brittle and bright.

"Won't we, Lord Grisk?" she said again. "Because I know how, as a Grisk of long standing—and a member of the Speaker's Guard—you're meant to care for your own. For your brothers, and your women, and your sons. And how there's no debt on such kindnesses, but only brotherhood. Right?"

They were Varinn's own words, quoted verbatim from his own damned mouth, and judging from the hard, suspicious disapproval in his eyes, he very well knew it. And Kitty kept smiling toward him, and then leaned closer into him, and even slipped her arm around his stiff back.

"And," she continued, as sweetly as she could, "you wouldn't refuse your new mate such a request, would you? The mother of your son? Who's just—um—*honoured* you in the corridor?"

Beside them, she was almost certain she heard Thrain's cough—but Varinn was only staring toward her, with those same blank, angry eyes. While Kitty kept smiling, and smiling, until...

"Ach, woman," Varinn said, through visibly clenched teeth. "I shall be glad to do as you wish."

Oh, thank the gods. Kitty's shoulders sagged, her smile genuinely brightening as she beamed at Varinn, and then at Thrain. At how Thrain was giving her a wan, grateful smile back, despite how obviously ill he looked. Perhaps just as ill as she'd felt, but she still felt so much better now, in part due to...

"Good," she said, as steadily as she could. "Now, let's go pay a visit to your healer. At once."

23

A short time later, Kitty found herself stepping into a spacious, lamplit sickroom.

It was again a surprisingly lovely room, furnished with a variety of comfortable-looking beds and couches, all separated by tall wooden dividers. Kitty could glimpse a few orcs in the nearest beds, but they all seemed to be asleep, and the healer who'd helped her previously—Efterar—was leaning over one of the sleeping orcs, his hand outstretched. Doing his... *magic.* While a handsome, unfamiliar orc stood close beside him, running a hand up and down his back—at least, until they both glanced toward Kitty, Varinn, and Thrain at the door.

"Ooooh," the unfamiliar orc said, his eyes lighting up, as he promptly spun and strode over toward them. "It's our newest Grisk arrival! I hope you're surviving life here so far, sweetheart? Haven't run for the hills yet?"

He'd flashed Kitty a wry, stunning grin, and she couldn't help an impulsive smile back, or a brief, appreciative glance down at his ensemble. Like many of the orcs she'd met so far, he was bare-chested, and his actual clothing consisted only of tight leather trousers, paired with tall black boots. But in stark contrast to the simplicity of the clothes, he also wore a splendid array of glittering, beautifully crafted jewels. Including a dazzling black pendant, multiple earrings in both pointed ears, rings on his clawed fingers, and even an assortment of shiny silver beads, flashing in his long, loose hair.

"No, she has clearly not *run for the hills*, Kesst," said a flat, repressive voice—Varinn's voice—and when Kitty glanced guiltily toward him, he was aiming a thunderous scowl toward this new orc—*Kesst*, he'd said. And beside Varinn, to Kitty's vague surprise, Thrain was wearing a markedly similar expression, while also casting a bleary, baleful glare up and down Kesst's handsome, glittering form.

"Oooh, a bit touchy today, are we?" this Kesst blithely continued, with another sly, sharp-toothed grin. "Surely we don't have trouble in perfect Grisk paradise already, hmmm?"

At that, Varinn actually growled, low and hard in his throat, and Thrain gave a jolting, shuddering twitch toward the door behind them. "You know what, forget it," he said thickly. "I can just—"

"No, wait," this Kesst cut in, grimacing, as he rapidly flapped his elegant hand between them. "Sorry. Please. What do you need? A comprehensive check-up on your lovely new mate, no doubt?"

He'd given Kitty a rueful, much softer smile, followed by a fluid, graceful bow. "And welcome to our mountain, sweetheart," he said. "Or"—he flicked another brief glance toward Varinn—"I mean, Kitty, right? I'm Kesst, Efterar's mate. And we're honoured to care for you here, as well as your son."

Kitty flashed him a grateful smile in return, even as she followed Kesst's gaze toward where Varinn was still glowering beside her. "Thank you so much," she replied. "But we're actually here about Thrain, if you don't mind?"

Kesst's brows snapped up, his assessing eyes now flicking toward Thrain. Toward where Thrain was taking shallow, shaky breaths, and again betraying the occasional erratic, compulsive-looking twitch, the sweat beading on his pale, haggard face.

"Oh," Kesst said, with genuine-seeming surprise. "I suppose you are. Eft, if you might have a moment?"

He angled a meaningful look behind him, toward where Efterar was already washing his hands in a nearby basin. And then he strode over too, his critical gaze sweeping up and down Thrain's body. "What's this, Thrain?" he said, his voice matter-of-fact. "Trying to ease off the drink, are you?"

Thrain grimaced, but then nodded, his shoulders squaring. "Ach," he said, quiet. "Been wanting to for a while now. But"—he shot a furtive glance toward Varinn—"every time I've tried to quit, I start feeling like—*this*."

"Like what?" Efterar asked, as he reached out his hand, and hovered it over Thrain's head, and then down to his midsection. "Can you explain it?"

Thrain shrugged, gave a slow, shuddering exhale. "Jumpy, shaky, sick," he replied. "Too hot. Can't sleep. Can't stop brooding over finding more drink, until I feel like I'm out of my mind. One time"—he angled another uneasy glance toward Varinn—"I even saw Varinn's dead Pa in the latrine. Sat me down for a good stern talking-to. Sounded just like something he would say, too."

He huffed a choked, brittle-sounding laugh, but on Kitty's other side, Varinn wasn't smiling. If anything, he was looking incredulous, or maybe even appalled. "And you did not think," he cut in, his voice clipped, "to speak to me of this?"

Thrain winced, his eyes now carefully averted, while Efterar just shrugged, and moved his hand back to hover over Thrain's head. "Coming off the drink can be a tricky business," he said. "The sickness it causes is real, and often very severe— enough that I saw it almost kill a man once. It's very wise of you to seek help with it, Thrain."

Thrain winced again, but didn't reply, and beside Kitty, Varinn was still looking appalled, his jaw set, his narrow eyes darting between Thrain and Efterar. "How long does this illness endure, then?" he demanded. "And what comes about when Thrain turns to the drink again? Shall this illness then follow again, also?"

His voice rang through the room, sharp and accusing, and Thrain's wince was more like a flinch this time, his eyes squeezing shut. But Efterar still appeared entirely unconcerned, his brow furrowing as he moved his hovering hand down Thrain's body, and up again. "Most likely it will," he replied. "And anyone seeking to forego the drink is likely to fall back into it at least a few times, especially if they're under strain—its hold over its victims is just that strong. So it's good to be prepared, and don't take it as a personal slight."

He'd glanced toward Kitty and Varinn as he'd spoken, clearly including them in that directive, and Kitty straightened a little, and took a breath. "That's very helpful to know, thank you," she said. "Is there anything else we can do, that you're aware of? Any other ways we can support Thrain, and try to help him through this?"

Efterar seemed to consider this for a moment, his eyes again intently fixed on Thrain's head. "Well, in my experience, if Thrain truly wants to quit the drink, that's half the battle won," he said slowly. "No one else can force or shame him into it, and you don't want to try, either—that'll just lead to grief for all of you, and put strain on your relationship when he's likely to need you most. But"—he shrugged—"giving him a safe place, offering him some distractions from the drink, supporting him in finding other pleasures and goals beyond it—that would probably all help."

Kitty nodded, silently repeating those instructions to herself—safe place, distractions, pleasures and goals—and she found herself impulsively clasping Thrain's sweaty hand, squeezing it tight. And when he shot her a weak little smile, she returned it with an encouraging smile of her own. "We can certainly do all that," she said firmly. "Can't we, Lord Grisk?"

She'd glanced toward Varinn as she'd spoken, and found him—oh. With that telltale redness creeping up his neck, his eyes darting uncertainly toward Kesst and Efterar. Because damn it, Kitty had called him *Lord Grisk* again, in public. And while Efterar still seemed fully preoccupied with whatever he was doing, Kesst's black brows had again shot up on his forehead, his eyes searching Varinn's face with blatant disbelief.

"Ach," Varinn belatedly replied, his voice very stiff. "We shall do all we can for him."

And despite that woodenness in his voice, it occurred to Kitty that he meant it. Surely he meant it, with that grim determination on his mouth, flashing in his eyes. And perhaps Thrain saw it too, because he'd given a choked-sounding little sniff, and a wavering half-smile toward Varinn. "Thanks, Lord Grisk," he murmured. "Again."

The flush crept higher up Varinn's neck, especially when Kesst's head swivelled back toward him, more disbelief flaring in his eyes. But then he rapidly shook his head, as if knocking something out of it, and fixed his narrowing gaze back to Thrain's face.

"And look, Thrain," he said, "if you really want to deal with this, you should also try talking to Rath—my blood-brother, Kitty. Because he's also been there with the drink, and I know he'd try to help you, and maybe direct you to other help, too. Because Eft's right, and"—he pointed a sharp claw between Kitty and Varinn—"it's not fair of you to dump any more of this on them. If I were Varinn, I'd have thrown out your sorry arse long ago—and I wouldn't take you back until you were sober, either. Especially not with a son on the way."

A surprising fierceness had crept into Kesst's voice, his eyes cold and flinty on Thrain's face. And Kitty could see Thrain's throat convulsing, his mouth twisting into a smile that wasn't a smile at all. "Well, you can rest easy, Kesst," he said, his voice low. "Because Varinn's already doing all that, aren't you, Varinn?"

Oh. Wait. Kitty's gaze darted back to Varinn, because hadn't they just agreed to—oh. Perhaps... not. Because yes, Varinn had agreed to help Thrain in this, to support him... but not to take him back. Not like that.

And maybe that demonstration—that ultimatum—he'd given Thrain back in the corridor still stood. Still hung here, dangling in front of Thrain's tired eyes, just like Varinn had wanted. Just like he'd planned.

You can keep the drink, and lose all the rest. Me. Her. Your son. Forever.

Varinn wasn't arguing it, his jaw still tight and set, his eyes gone just as flinty as Kesst's. While a thin, horrible silence stretched out between them, churning in Kitty's stomach, pulsing behind her eyes. She'd barely convinced Varinn at all, then. He was still doing what he wanted, what he'd planned, no matter what she—or any of them—said.

"Well, Thrain, you should stay here for the rest of the day, so I can help manage this," Efterar cut in, his voice firm. "And I'll want you to check in here at least every few days, for the foreseeable future. Maybe bring Kitty with you, because"—he frowned as he turned toward her, hovering his hand over her waist—"this nausea and fatigue of hers is going to keep acting up, too. You'll both need to keep an eye on her, and make sure she gets as much rest and fresh seed as she wants, all right? Whether in her stomach or her womb, it all helps."

Kitty's already-churning thoughts were whirling up even higher—wait, what had he just said?—and beside her, Varinn and Thrain had both noticeably stiffened, Thrain uneasily glancing toward Varinn, while Varinn's jaw flexed powerfully in his cheek. But Efterar hadn't seemed to take any notice, and he was already frowning back toward Thrain, his hand again hovering over his head.

"This really is vicious," he said, almost more to himself than to them. "Mind if I touch you, Thrain?"

But at that, Thrain visibly blanched, and Varinn's already-stiff body seemed to snap even stiffer, a low growl hissing from his throat. "No," he snarled. "No, you may not touch him. As if my nose has not already borne enough assaults, these past days?!"

There was yet more awkward, ringing stillness, echoing out after his words—and Kitty's initial surprise, reflected in Kesst's and Efterar's eyes, rapidly gave way to a sharp, twisting hurt. Because Varinn was—he was talking about...*her*. Wasn't he? *A weak, foolish, thoughtless, spoilt woman, with a hundred scents upon her...*

Kitty's breaths were suddenly coming too shallow, a hard lump growing in her throat, and she only distantly heard Kesst's low, incredulous-sounding scoff. "One would think, *Lord Grisk*," he drawled, "that your mate's health would be far more important than your delicate little nose, hmmm? Or, wait"—he thoughtfully tapped his chin—"I don't actually recall hearing that you and Thrain ever spoke any vows of matehood, did you? And he doesn't seem to bear the full strength of your scent either, does he? Now, I wonder why that could be?"

His coldly glittering eyes on Varinn very clearly suggested what he suspected to be the cause, and Varinn's growl was low and scathing, his body all but vibrating with fury. "Ach, you *wonder*, Kesst," he hissed, through visibly gritted teeth. "When you yourself just said you would not wish to mate a drunkard!"

Beside Kitty, Thrain flinched again, his hand rubbing his eyes, while Kesst's eyes only flashed colder, and he gave a bright, tinkling little laugh. "Good one, Varinn," he said approvingly. "But we all know Thrain's been dangling after you for years, probably decades, long before any of *this*"—he flapped his glittering hand at Thrain's face—"ever came about! Such an extended unrequited passion would almost be enough to drive one to desperate measures, hmmm? Especially when we all know how the drink blunts the scents? Especially for you Grisk, with your over-sensitive noses?"

Varinn's growl had risen to almost a roar, his solid body

jerking in place, his hands clamping to tight fists—and thankfully, Efterar swiftly stepped in front of him, angling a dark, disapproving frown between him and Kesst. "That's enough, both of you," he said sharply, even as his hand slid up and down Kesst's bare back. "It's a sickness, with a mind of its own, and there's no good blaming anyone for it. Our focus now is on getting Thrain the rest and healing he needs, all right?"

Kesst grimaced, his expression already markedly subdued, his head turning into Eft's shoulder. "Right," he said, muffled. "Sorry, Eft. I'll go get us all some lunch."

Efterar's eyes had already softened, and he pressed a kiss to Kesst's shiny hair, which Kesst returned with a surprisingly shy smile. And then he spun and stalked off out the door, while Kitty stared blankly after him, that lump swelling larger in her throat. Varinn had refused to... *swear vows* to Thrain? Thrain had had an... *extended unrequited passion*? Enough to possibly drive him to *desperate measures*?

And yes, Kitty's memories were flashing back, back to that fateful night with Thrain. To how he'd spoken of how long he and his partner had been together, and... how selfish his partner had been. How that partner had refused to return Thrain's affections, because Thrain hadn't been what she—*he*—had truly wanted.

It was enough to raise Kitty's prickling eyes, searching back and forth between them. But there was still only fury, crackling in Varinn's narrow gaze—and if anything, it was Thrain who looked near to weeping. Blinking at Varinn with his bloodshot, too-bright eyes, and chewing at his lip with a sharp white tooth.

"I'd really rather you didn't touch me, Efterar," he said now, his voice a croak. "If you don't mind."

Oh. As if it was another offering to Varinn, a concession, in the face of how Thrain had already so deeply offended Varinn's delicate nose, by tainting it with Kitty's odious scent. And while

Efterar only shrugged at this, Varinn's fury still felt almost strong enough to taste, his hands still clutched to clawed fists.

"Do as you wish," he said to Thrain, his voice clipped and formal. "Kesst was right. We are not mated, and thus, I have no claim upon your scent. If either of you have any further need of us, please only send word."

At that, he, too, shoved off toward the door, striding with jerky, overly controlled steps—and then he halted, and looked sharply back toward Kitty. The furious command flashing far too clear in his eyes, saying, *Come. Now. Or else.*

And with one last, wretched glance toward Thrain, Kitty bowed her head, and went.

24

Kitty stumbled down the corridor after Varinn in choked, miserable silence, her blinking eyes fixed on the hard stone floor beneath her feet.

Varinn hated her scent on Thrain. Hated her. And he was using her, using her and her son, to dangle that damned ultimatum over Thrain's head. *You can keep the drink, and lose all the rest.*

And damn it, why did Varinn even care so much, if he hadn't even wanted to swear vows to Thrain? Why had he gone to such great lengths over any of this? And why had he insisted on dragging Kitty into it, if he couldn't even stand the smell of her?

Kitty's head had begun to ache, the exhaustion clouding behind her prickling eyes, weighing on her feet. Enough that she tripped over a crack in the floor, her body stumbling forward—at least, until Varinn's strong hand grasped her arm, and firmly pulled her upright. His flinty gaze briefly meeting hers, before angling away again.

"Are you well, Katharine," he said, his voice hard. "Is there aught you need."

But Kitty was already blanching, and wildly shaking her head. "No," she replied, high-pitched. "No, thank you."

Varinn loosened his grip on her arm and began walking again, but his steps were slower now, and he kept glancing at her with those hard, angry eyes. "You are sure," he said flatly. "You might not wish for more rest, or food, or—drink?"

Drink. As in—*that.* And his mouth had even twisted as he'd said it, as if he found that prospect just as revolting as he found her scent. So why the hell was he still offering, why the hell was he doing any of this? And why was the breathless, broken rebellion surging again, swirling up in Kitty's chest—

"I would never want to subject you to something that—*assaults* you," her voice blurted out, before she could stop it. "I didn't realize that even my *smell* was truly so disgusting to you. And I can't understand why you keep doing something you hate, to help someone you barely even seem to *like!*"

Varinn's body lurched to stillness beside her, and a hard sound choked from his throat, not unlike a laugh. "You ken I have no *like* for Thrain?" he echoed, the disbelief raw in his voice. "*Thrain*?! You know *naught* about me, woman, or about us!"

But Kitty's miserable rebellion was surging even higher, and she jerked a shaky nod. "I know—enough," she stammered back. "You wouldn't—speak vows to Thrain, or commit to him, when he loved you for years. And"—another distant memory surged—"he did everything he possibly could to please you, and be a good partner! He tried to be fun, eager, willing, always there, for *everything.* For the good, and the bad. And instead"—she dragged in a breath—"now you're threatening him, still giving him all these ultimatums, so you can get your own way? After your constant rejections probably helped drive him to drink in the first place?!"

Varinn whirled around to fully face her, his eyes flashing—but there was something else there too, something almost... hurt. "Did—Thrain speak this to you?" he demanded, his voice cracking. "Or is this only you spitting back Kesst's cruel taunts toward me? Seeking to punish me, for daring to help you, and your son?"

His mouth contorted, his eyes blinking hard, too bright—and when Kitty didn't instantly reply, he stepped closer, his big body towering, twitching, over hers. "I could have left you," he breathed. "I could have walked away, at any moment I wished, and left you to perish alone, just as Thrain did! And"—he hauled in a breath—"you were not here, you know *naught* of how oft Thrain has hidden this, and spoken false to me! Ach, did you not just now hear of how ill he has been, how he has seen visions of my own father? You ken he *once* spoke this to me, or asked for my help?! No, he did not, he traded all his own father's coin for foul men's cheap stinking *swill*, and slunk off and hid this from me, and left me to pay the bills he could not afford! Until the night he creeps off alone to a rank human hellhole, where he finds the first fool woman who reeks of—"

His voice broke there, his body spasming in place, his eyes squeezing shut—and without another word, he whirled around, and stalked off up the corridor. His head low, his shoulders hunched, his steps jerky and swift. And Kitty stared after him, her head pounding, the misery churning wild and panicked in her chest. *The first fool woman, who reeks.* He thought she was a fool, he hated her and her scent, he was leaving her, oh gods he was leaving her, no, no, no—

She rushed up the corridor after him, her feet again stumbling on the stone. But Varinn didn't look back at her, didn't speak, and instead he spun sideways, and into one of the corridor's many doors. The door they'd come out of before, Kitty distantly realized, leading into that cozy fur-strewn sitting-room, and she could have sobbed at the sight of it, her eyes desperately searching for Ella, or Alma, or any of the kind, friendly people she'd met earlier. But there was no one in sight, and Varinn just kept walking, not looking back, heading straight toward another unfamiliar door, on the opposite side of the room.

He strode inside without hesitation, and Kitty drifted over after him, hovering uncertainly at the door. Blinking at the room within, which appeared to be... a temple, or perhaps a shrine. A place of worship, clearly, with a strong scent of incense sweetening the air, and a bounty of soft furs and cushions spread across the floor. And at the front of the room stood a table with a row of stone figures, all of them skilfully carved, and depicting not only multiple orcs, but several humans, as well.

And as Kitty kept standing there, clutching uneasily at the doorframe, Varinn halted and bowed toward one of the figures—a bared, voluptuous human woman, with full breasts, and a swollen, rounded belly. And then he sank to his knees before the figure, his head bent low, his hand over his heart.

Oh. He was—praying. Praying to this figure, this woman, on his knees, in a pose of supplication, or maybe even... desperation. And Kitty could see his mouth moving, forming rapid, silent words that she couldn't at all follow, as a drop of wetness streaked down his cheek, and dropped to the fur beneath him.

Something both cold and hot shuddered up Kitty's spine, and she swallowed hard, the sound far too loud in the silence. But if Varinn heard it, he didn't look up, his mouth still silently speaking, his hand tightening to a fist against his heaving chest.

"Varinn?" interrupted a tentative voice, making Kitty jump, her heart flaring—but oh. It was one of the younger orcs from earlier, the one named Timo. Aiming a cautious smile toward her, followed by a worried glance toward Varinn. Toward where Varinn had lifted his head to look, showing—oh. His wet eyes, his reddened cheeks, his wavering mouth. But Kitty could see him taking a breath, squaring his shoulders, putting on a shaky but sincere-looking smile.

"Ach, Timo," he said, his voice thick. "Is aught amiss?"

Timo grimaced, angling another uncertain glance toward Kitty, before sidling carefully past her, and slipping into the room. And then he settled down to kneel close beside Varinn on the fur, bumping their shoulders together. "Just—scented you," he replied, quiet. "Is aught amiss with *you*?"

Varinn made a sound much like a hiccough, and his big arm circled around Timo's shoulder, and squeezed him into his side. "Ach, well," he began, and then his shoulders sagged, his breath exhaling harsh. "Ach. Thrain is—ill. He is now with Efterar, and I hope he shall be better soon, but—"

His voice cracked, and he roughly rubbed his palm at his eye, shaking his head. "But we cannot know, ach?" he whispered. "He has been ill for so long, now, and I did not once think to see this as—as an *illness*. And now he shall have a son, and how shall he ever be a good father to his son, amidst all this?"

His voice sounded raw, despairing, choking in his throat, and in Kitty's, too. But Timo poked his sharp elbow into Varinn's side, even as he rested his head on his shoulder. "Efterar will heal Thrain," he said firmly. "And you ought not to fret over the son, because *you* shall be his father, too. Ach? And you shall be the best father, Varinn. Everyone knows that."

He spoke with easy, innocent confidence, and perhaps a twinge of wistfulness, too—and Kitty could see Varinn's grimace, beneath his twisting smile. "You unjustly flatter me, little brother," he said, his voice rough. "For I have already offended our son's mother today, and failed to even show her our shrine, and our gods, as well."

Oh. Kitty's breath caught in her throat, because Varinn had angled a brief, regretful look toward her, his chest hollowing. While beside him, Timo's glance toward her was only kind, eager curiosity, and he gave Varinn another nudge with his elbow. "Well, I can scent how sad and distressed you are," he replied. "And this makes it harder to control your words and deeds, ach? Is this not what you always tell me? And that you ought to pray, and seek peace again, and ask your brother for help if you need it?"

Varinn huffed a choked half-laugh, half-groan, but Timo had already leapt to his feet, and fixed Kitty with a wide, encouraging smile. "So I shall help," he said decisively. "Come, new sister, and meet our gods, ach? I am sure this might help ease your distress, also."

And despite everything, Kitty felt herself nodding, and giving Timo a small, wavering smile in return. "That's very thoughtful of you, Timo," she managed. "Thank you."

Timo's grin broadened, and then he waved her forward, toward the row of carved figures. "First," he said, with a little bow toward a hulking orc with a massive pickaxe, "is our father Edom. He came here from across the sea, and together with his mate Akva"—he gestured at the voluptuous human woman before Varinn—"they made our mountain a home, and begat five sons, who became the five clans of orcs. Ash-Kai, Bautul, Skai, Ka-esh, and Grisk."

The names were already blurring together a little in Kitty's thoughts, but she nodded, and listened attentively as Timo explained the five clans' various exploits and preferences, and pointed out their gods. Not all five clans had patron gods, apparently, but the Skai clan was very devoted to Skai-kesh— situated here close beside his mother Akva—and the Grisk particularly revered Akva herself, and also their own heroes and ancestors from ages past. Several of whom were represented among the figures, including a human mother named Jaya, a storyteller named Ruby, and a bulky, bearded orc warrior with his arms outstretched, who was named... *Varinn*?

"Ach, Lord Varinn, or Varinn-kesh," Timo said, with a teasing glance toward where Varinn himself was now watching warily from his fur. "Our Varinn is named after him, ach, Varinn? Varinn-kesh was one of our clan's greatest defenders, and brought us an age of great prosperity and peace. He is oft called our Lord Grisk, as well."

Our... *Lord Grisk*. Kitty's body snapped to strange, sudden stillness, her eyes darting back toward Varinn. Who was intentionally looking away, now, that redness creeping up his neck.

"And Lord Grisk is also one of your forebears, ach, Varinn?" Timo blithely continued. "There is even a clear likeness between you, you ken."

Kitty's eyes had darted back to the carved stone figure, scanning over the bulky body, the bearded face, the kind eyes, with those distinct creases at the corners. And even his pose was one of kindness too, of generosity. Of offering his help.

"Ach, you flatter me again, Timo," Varinn said, his voice still rather choked. "But it is too long past to know, and we have not Lord Grisk's body nor his goods to scent from."

But Timo appeared entirely undaunted, giving Varinn another sunny smile. "Only you would say that, Varinn," he said cheerfully. "The rest of us know it, ach? And your new mate ought to know it, too. And also"—he transferred his gaze back to Kitty—"Varinn's fathers have always served as Speaker's Guards, as far back as memory goes. So should you next bear a son of Varinn's blood, this is sure to come to him, also."

Oh. He spoke not only as if this was expected—as if Kitty would naturally wish to bear Varinn's son next—but also as if it was a great honour, or even a source of pride. And Kitty couldn't hide her wincing glance toward Varinn, who surely held no such sentiments, and was only tolerating her—and her *reek*—as long as he could use her to put Thrain in his place.

And yes, Varinn was wincing too, and reaching out a hand toward Timo. "Thank you, little brother," he said. "Would you be so kind now as to go see how Thrain fares? Mayhap fetch him some water, and a treat from the kitchen, should he wish to eat?"

Timo instantly nodded and clasped his hand with Varinn's, giving it a firm little shake. "Ach, brother," he said. "And you shall keep praying until you are at ease again."

Varinn nodded back, twitching a rueful smile, and then watched with palpable fondness as Timo took off out the door. But then he seemed to remember Kitty, and his smile rapidly faded as he glanced toward her, his mouth again gone tight and thin.

"Should you wish to pray also, Katharine," he said, his voice a little rough, "our gods should be most glad to welcome you, ach?"

Oh. Kitty blinked at him, wide-eyed, uncertain—gods were capricious, dangerous beings, and surely Varinn's gods wouldn't want *her* praying to them, right? But Varinn was studying her with surprising intensity, now, his hand rubbing at his nose, and his exhale was slow, resigned, almost regretful.

"Our gods and forebears are kind," he continued, his voice still rough. "They freely serve and offer aid to all who come before them, and thus, they shall welcome aught you might wish to grant them. Whether this is prayers, or worship, or anger or grief, or silence."

Oh. Kitty swallowed, and angled an uncertain glance toward the figure before her. Toward this... Varinn-kesh. Lord Grisk. With his outstretched arms, and his kind, crinkled eyes. His... help.

It suddenly seemed at stark, incomprehensible odds with the way Thrain had spoken about the gods, with how easily he'd cursed them that night. *Gods are mocking us, I ken. Those interfering bastards. Fuck 'em all.*

But... if the orcs' gods welcomed even anger and grief, like Varinn had just said, maybe—maybe they hadn't minded being cursed, after all. And if they truly wanted to help those who came before them, maybe—maybe it was worth trying. If not for her own sake, at least for her son's.

So Kitty twitched a nod, and dropped to her knees on the fur, holding her eyes on the god's kind face. On his offer of help.

And she needed help. Needed it so much it hurt, between

Thrain's illness, and Varinn's ultimatums and grief. And her own illness, her weakness, the son she'd so foolishly made, amidst all this mess.

And with a shaky little gulp, she lowered her head, and silently began to pray. Begging, and pleading, and even weeping, until the room around her finally faded, and left her only in darkness.

25

Kitty awoke in a vaguely familiar bed, in a vaguely familiar room.

It was the same room from earlier, she realized, as she pulled herself up in the bed, and blinked around her. Varinn and Thrain's bedroom, with the furs, and the lamp, and those two mismatched shelves. But now, standing between the shelves, there was a chair. A large, ornate, heavy-looking wooden chair that certainly hadn't been there before. And seated back within it, his legs sprawled and eyes closed, was Varinn.

Kitty froze beneath her fur, squinting toward him in the flickering lamplight—but he didn't move, or look up. As if he was... asleep.

It was an odd, unfamiliar sight, because Kitty hadn't yet seen him sleeping... had she? And she couldn't seem to look away from him now, from how... different he looked. With his jaw unclenched, and his perpetually creased brow drastically softened. With his big body sprawled lax and easy, his head tilted back, his fingers—with claws drawn in—spread on the chair's wide, ornately carved arms. And his muscled legs were spread wide too, his leather kilt drawn taut over them... and revealing just the faintest glimpse of soft, chubby pink beneath.

Kitty's throat convulsed, and her mouth had begun inexplicably watering, her tongue brushing at her dry-feeling lips—and she belatedly wrenched her gaze away from him, and clutched her fur up to her chin. No. No. Varinn loathed her, and the *assault* of her scent. He thought she was a fool. He'd yelled at her, and tried to abandon her in a corridor, and...

And she'd accused him of being cruel to Thrain. Of helping to drive Thrain to drink, gods curse her. And afterwards Varinn had wept over Thrain, and prayed with such anguished fervour, and he'd still spoken to her kindly about his gods. And then she must have fallen asleep, and he must have brought her here. Here, to his own room, his own bed, while he slept in a damned wooden chair.

Kitty winced, shaking her head—and at that moment, Varinn shifted in his chair, his bulky body jerking up. His mouth grimacing as he rubbed both hands at his face, and then at his neck. Looking stiff, and sore, and surely tired, too.

And as Kitty blinked toward him, suddenly there was only sympathy, and misery, and regret, all clawing together in her churning belly, escaping out her throat. "That can't be very comfortable," her scratchy voice said, before she could stop it. "I'm very happy to share. If you'd like."

She'd shoved herself sideways under the fur, making room—and even the movement called up a sudden, vivid memory of that little room in the cave. And maybe Varinn was thinking of it too, blinking blearily down at the space Kitty had made, and then back up to her face. But not moving, or speaking, maybe because her scent was a *reek*, an *assault*, and because she was only a pawn in his quest to save Thrain, to *threaten* Thrain, and—

Movement. At the door. And when Kitty whipped around to look, it was—Thrain himself. Yes, oh gods, Thrain was here, standing tall and familiar in the curtained doorway, an uncertain little smile quivering on his mouth.

And he looked—good. Better. So much better, in fact, his eyes bright and alert, his skin smooth and clear. His cheeks even looked fuller, the dark hollows almost entirely faded beneath his eyes, and there was no sign of the sweating or spasming whatsoever. Only that uncertain smile, still wavering on his lips, as he glanced from Varinn, to Kitty, to Varinn again.

"Redecorating, Varinn?" he asked, nodding at the new chair, and even his voice was smoother, warm with a tinge of wryness. "I like it. A throne is just what you needed, ach?"

At that, Varinn twitched in his chair, his hands clenching— but then, suddenly, he was on his feet, and striding across the room. Striding straight toward Thrain, his jaw and shoulders set, and then—Kitty startled—he reached for Thrain, and dragged him powerfully into his arms.

Thrain instantly sank into the embrace, his tall body sagging, his long arms slipping around Varinn's bare back. Drawing him even closer, oh gods, so he could duck his face into Varinn's neck, inhaling long and deep.

"Och," Thrain breathed, muffled, his eyes fluttering closed. "Och. Forgot how good you smell, Varinn. *Fuck.*"

Varinn didn't reply to this, though his own face was buried in Thrain's neck too, his breath filling his chest. And Kitty could just glimpse his mouth widening against Thrain's skin, a flash of sharp white teeth—

And then Thrain groaned, his eyes rolling back, his black claws extending against Varinn's bare skin. His face suddenly rapt with ecstasy, with relief, and one of his hands jerked up to Varinn's dark head, his fingers spreading wide. Pressing Varinn closer, harder, as his own head tilted away, giving more room. Giving... permission, because Varinn was—*biting* him? In his *neck*?

But yes, yes, he was, they *liked* that, and the memory of Kitty's night with Thrain was surging again, so strong she betrayed a choked little gasp. And at the sound of it, both Varinn and Thrain jerked apart, twisting around at once toward her. Thrain's expression distinctly hazy, a dazed little smile on his mouth, while beside him, Varinn's face had gone carefully blank. Even as a thick bead of red snaked down his chin, only to be swept up by a swift, darting lick of his long black tongue.

"Um," Kitty said, wincing, as her wide eyes darted between Varinn's mouth, and Thrain's neck—which now displayed a set of fresh red *teeth-marks*, oh gods. "It's... ah... good to see you looking so well, Thrain. How are you feeling?"

Thrain shot back a rueful, grateful grin, as if he knew exactly what Kitty was thinking, and strode over to settle his tall form onto one of the wide arms of Varinn's new chair. "Gods, *so* much better," he replied. "I can't remember the last time I felt this good. And the scents! It's like they're all three times as strong as before, and so much clearer, too. I ken I could probably blow a load just from Varinn's scent alone, ach, Varinn?"

He'd flashed his grin up toward Varinn, who was rolling his eyes, even as he strode over and dropped back into the chair beside Thrain, tugging rather too casually at his kilt. "Spare us," he said repressively, though his mouth quirked, just a little. "Our room has never been so clean for so long, ach?"

Oh. Kitty couldn't seem to stop staring between them, even as something warm and shivery—surprise? Longing? Jealousy?—fluttered in her chest. And then kicking even higher at the sound of Thrain's bright, delighted laugh, his head tilting back, his hand clasping firmly to Varinn's shoulder.

"Well, too bad, Varinn," he said cheerfully. "Because I'm back to make a mess of it all again, ach?"

But at that, Varinn gave an unmistakable wince, and then a rapidly darkening look over toward Kitty, still watching from the bed. And Thrain's smile was fading too, and Kitty could see his head tilting as he studied her, and then glanced back toward Varinn.

"And look, I'm truly sorry about all this, again," Thrain said, his voice far more subdued. "To both of you. You've both been so generous, so much more than I deserve. And it was so good of you, to think of taking me to Efterar today, because"—he exhaled, grimacing—"I never would've thought to do it myself, ach?"

Kitty swallowed, attempting a smile toward him, while beside him, Varinn's grim expression hadn't changed. And Thrain was studying Varinn too, and taking a deep breath. "And Kesst brought Rathgarr by, and we had a good long talk, too," he continued. "And after that, Rathgarr went and dragged in that old Ash-Kai Sken—the one with the Seeing, you know. Nothing like a few harrowing visions of the future to strike some terror into your bones."

He shuddered as he spoke, and Kitty felt herself glancing at Varinn, and finding her own unease—or maybe even her fear—echoed in his eyes. *We cannot know, ach?* he'd said, with such quiet desperation. *How shall Thrain ever be a good father to his son, amidst all this?*

"Rathgarr says I'm to come see him a few times a week," Thrain's low voice added, his shoulders squaring. "Or whenever I'm—craving, too much. And I've vowed not to keep secrets from him, or from Efterar, or"—he drew in another breath—"from either of you. Efterar says the—the hiding is part of the sickness, and just makes it worse. You're ashamed of yourself, so you hide it from the people you're closest to—and then they're understandably angry and hurt, so you hide and lie even more. Until you've pushed away every person you care about, and likely made a mess of their lives, too."

Oh. Kitty exchanged another reflexive glance with Varinn, as Thrain huffed a sound that wasn't quite a laugh. "So I won't lie to you," he said, his voice a little hoarse, now. "I'm not... healed. Efterar's dealt with the worst of what the drink's done to me, but... I still want it. I still... long for it. Mayhap I always will, ach? But"—another deep breath—"I want this more. Want to regain your trust, like you said, Varinn. Want to be a good father to our son."

The silence seemed to spiral out after his words, because was he saying... was he saying Varinn's ultimatum had *worked*? And maybe Thrain was thinking of that too, glancing down toward where Varinn was rubbing at his face, his eyes very carefully fixed across the room.

"But if you still want to throw me out, or keep me away, I—I understand," Thrain continued thickly. "I know I've been absolute rubbish to both of you, and I don't even deserve to be asking you for another chance. Let alone expecting you to keep putting up with me, when you oughta be in here revelling in pleasure with each other."

He twitched a sad, regretful smile toward Kitty, and she fought back her wince, and again glanced toward Varinn. Toward where he certainly was showing no interest in revelling with her whatsoever, and instead was now just... watching Thrain. Watching him with strange, shifting eyes, glimmering between uncertainty, and a stark, unmistakable longing.

And damn him, but Kitty had sworn to help him. She'd made a promise. So she pasted a wide smile to her mouth, and aimed it toward Thrain's regretful face. "Of course we don't want to throw you out," she managed. "We're so happy to hear all this, aren't we, Varinn? As long as you truly want to face this, we want to help you, and support you, as much as we possibly can."

She risked another furtive glance at Varinn, her smile still fixed on her mouth, and she was vaguely surprised to see him swallowing, and giving a curt nod. And Thrain was looking at him too, his eyes blinking hard—and then he abruptly bent down, and pressed a long, fervent-looking kiss to Varinn's hair.

"Thanks, Varinn," he murmured, a little choked. "And you too, Kit. You're both far too good for my rubbish, ach?"

Kitty attempted to wave it away, the smile now feeling more like a grimace on her mouth. And perhaps Thrain had caught that, his head tilting as he studied her, and then he darted another intent, searching glance toward Varinn beside him. Toward where he might have been grimacing, too.

"Well, then," Thrain continued, with a false-sounding brightness. "So tell me, Kit—how are you doing? Still feeling all right? Varinn been following all the expert instructions, and feeding you properly?"

His glance down toward Varinn was warm this time, almost teasing. Almost as if he truly didn't mind about this... *feeding*, perhaps. But Kitty's voice seemed stuck in her throat, her face rapidly heating, and Varinn wasn't replying, either. His expression gone blank and distant again, his body hunching in his chair, his jaw ticking in his cheek.

"Ach, no, then?" Thrain said, his brows furrowing, his eyes flicking between them with genuine-seeming concern. "Thought your scent on her was fading more than it ought, Varinn. What's amiss?"

Varinn still wasn't speaking, and his jaw had gone even tighter, that hard furrow returning to his brow. And suddenly the rebellion was flaring again, surging in Kitty's chest, because Thrain was clearly trying, and they could at least keep trying in return. They could. Damn it, they *would*.

"I've just been a little... worried," Kitty began, tentative, "that perhaps my scent might... bother Varinn. More than he might like to admit."

Thrain's brows rose, and he darted another surprised look down toward Varinn in the chair. Toward where Varinn's eyes were still very carefully blank, his mouth still hard and set—so Kitty took another breath, attempted another wavering smile toward Thrain's watching face. Toward where he still looked attentive, curious, even concerned.

"It's just—if Varinn doesn't even like the smell of Efterar touching you," she said, "then how must he feel about *me*?"

She gave a shaky wave down at her body beneath the fur, what with its *reek*, and its *hundred scents*, which surely Thrain could smell, too. And yes, yes, that was a faint wince on Thrain's mouth, but then he leaned his body forward on the arm of the chair, his elbows on his knees, his hands folded, his eyes earnest on hers.

"Ach, Varinn has a sensitive nose," he told her. "It oft comes with being Grisk, ach? But his nose is one of our mountain's best, and it's a great gift. Helps him look after us all, you ken? He can always scent where his kin are, and oft even how they're feeling—and most of all if there's danger nearby. He's saved our sorry skins a hundred times over, ach, Varinn?"

He'd half-smiled toward Varinn, who was now shifting in the chair, his face slightly reddening. "You bear this gift also, Thrain," he said, a little gruff. "At least, when you have not drowned out your scenting with ale."

Thrain betrayed a faint flinch, but then he jerked a shrug, and shifted his gaze back to Kitty's face. "And ach, it also means you smell *everything*," he continued. "Especially on the people you're closest to. And if the scent feels—wrong, or too strong, or too deep, most of all when you liked it being a certain way before, it's almost... pain. As if"—his brow creased, his eyes gone thoughtful—"as if that person is shouting at you, mayhap. Or waving rotten food in front of your nose—or better yet, skunk-piss. And doing it over and over again, every time they move."

Oh. Kitty's body felt cold beneath the fur, her eyes again trapped on Varinn's face. On where he wasn't at all arguing this, and still wasn't looking at either of them—and his words again rang through Kitty's thoughts, far too loud and clear. *A hundred scents. An assault.*

"And for Grisk, at least, human scents are especially strong," Thrain added, quieter now. "Very bright and distracting, even old ones. They... *linger*, in a way most orc-scents don't. And there's no real way to get rid of them, ach, Varinn? Except..."

His voice faded, his mouth twisting, and Kitty felt herself

sitting up straighter in the bed, her heart kicking in her chest. There was a way to get rid of the scents? Permanently?

"Except, mayhap, for one of our clanmates, Baldr," Thrain continued, wrinkling his nose. "I ken you met him today, Kit? He bears the gift of suppressing scents, and it's been a great boon to many of our kin. But for a Grisk with a sensitive nose"—he shot a wan smile down toward Varinn—"it just leaves the scent of Baldr everywhere instead, ach? And it's the same with Efterar—his healing is a great gift, and one we should never spurn, but it also puts his scent *inside* you. And when that's mixed with the touching, even with something in between, it almost scents as though he's gone and—"

He broke off there, his mouth twisting with palpable distaste, and Varinn was looking distinctly revolted, too. "Ach," he muttered. "Last time Efterar touched you, this took weeks to—"

He winced and shook his head, and his furtive glance between Kitty and Thrain looked almost hunted, as if he hadn't at all meant to say that. And Kitty didn't miss the brief glimpse of surprise, and then satisfaction, flicking across Thrain's eyes.

"Ach, it took weeks for you to cover, with your own scent," Thrain said, with a faint edge of challenge in his voice. "And thus"—he flicked his gaze back to Kitty—"this is the best way to face this, Kit. When you can't bear a scent on someone you're fuc—close to, you cover it with your own, ach? It's as if you're... conquering it. Defeating it. Drowning it where it belongs, beneath the proof of your own claim. Your own strength. Your... domination, mayhap."

His eyes again angled toward Varinn, glinting with a dark, heated meaning. And Varinn was looking back, holding Thrain's gaze for an instant too long, as his hand again slipped down, and surreptitiously adjusted his kilt.

Oh. Kitty's breath caught, a sudden warmth pooling low in her belly—and both Varinn and Thrain glanced toward her, Varinn's jaw clenching again, Thrain's tongue brushing against his lips. "So, Kit," Thrain continued, his voice low. "Varinn's not about to like all those old human scents on you. He can't, ach? Not if you're touching him, too, and sharing his bed. But every time you welcome his touch and his seed instead, you make it a little better. Make his claim a little stronger. Prove to him he's in control. And if there's anything Varinn likes"—Thrain's tongue again brushed his lips, lingered longer this time—"it's being in control, ach?"

Kitty's breaths still felt strangely shallow, her eyes searching Varinn's distinctly flushed face. Because surely he couldn't actually *want* that, she was just a means to an end, and this was still just—just pretending, for Thrain's sake. For the cause. The ultimatum. Right? Right?

But. Thrain was here, wasn't he? He was here, and healthy, and sober—for now, at least. And he still seemed to be supporting this, even—*wanting* this, and maybe... maybe Varinn's plan was working. Again.

And here, too, were Efterar's instructions, rising hazy but powerful in Kitty's thoughts. *Give him a safe place. Offer him some distractions from the drink...*

And yes, yes, Thrain certainly seemed distracted, or maybe even riveted, glancing between Kitty and Varinn with those hungry, eager eyes. As his tall body shifted back to lounge on the arm of the chair, his hand dropping, easy and familiar, to Varinn's bare knee. Gently gripping it, oh hell, and then... guiding it sideways. Spreading Varinn's legs further apart, giving Kitty a better look at what was waiting beneath that kilt. At where that glimpse of pink wasn't chubby and soft at all, now, but swollen, straining, shoving up against that constricting black leather...

Kitty's breath hitched, her throat swallowing, her own tongue brushing her lips—and oh, that was the sound of Thrain's laugh, low and husky and triumphant, as his hand began... sliding upwards. Sliding up Varinn's muscled, hairy bare thigh, slow and proprietary, and blatantly easing the kilt up with it. Up, and up, and up, until…

Until—oh. Ohhhh. That hard, swollen heft bobbed up, jutting straight out of Varinn's groin. Its green length plump and thick, its rounded pink head slick and glossy and smooth. And oozing from that deep slit, there was already a pearly bead of white, growing, growing, until it dropped sideways, trailing down that green skin in a swift, shining streak…

"So what I'm trying to say is," Thrain breathed, his long fingers spreading wide on Varinn's taut thigh, so close, "if his seed's on offer, you oughta take it, ach?"

Kitty swallowed again, licked her dry lips, as her eyes held seized on the sight. On Thrain's hand, so close to that straining, dripping strength, but not touching, because he was offering it to her. *They* were offering it, to *her*…

"But—" she somehow managed. "What about—you. Shouldn't you still—mind. Me doing that. To him."

She'd dragged her gaze back up to Thrain's face, to where his eyes had gone hooded, glinting on hers. "I should mind," he replied, low, "very much, if you were anyone else. Or if you touched anyone else. But"—his tongue again, sweeping his lips—"you bear *my* scent now. *My* son. And for you to bear Varinn's scent also, and him yours—"

His breath caught, and he huffed another heated, husky laugh, shaking his head. "That alone is mayhap enough to keep me off the drink," he murmured. "Sweetest thing I've ever scented in my life."

Oh. Well, then. And Kitty's heart was thundering, now, her eyes darting between Varinn's flushed face, and the brazenly exposed sight at his groin. As if he truly wanted this too, even if it was just for Thrain, just part of the deal, the ultimatum. A way to show Thrain what might be on offer, if he behaved…

"So when you taste him, it's to all our gain, ach?" Thrain continued, breathless. "So come, sweet kitten. Kneel. Drink. Don't waste what your Lord Grisk gives you."

Oh. Oh, gods. Kitty's gasp had escaped her mouth, a sharp thrill running up the full length of her body. And in his chair, Varinn was gasping, too, his lips parted, his swollen, waiting heft visibly shifting, straining. Almost as if it was reaching out toward her, freely offering its bounty...

So Kitty... nodded. Nodded, and yanked her loose dressing-gown tight around her, and shoved out of the bed. And then stumbled over toward him, toward them, falling to her knees on the fur between Varinn's parted legs...

"Good," Thrain murmured, so soft, so approving, and his long fingers finally slipped sideways, circling with casual ease around Varinn's thick green heft. And then, oh hell, guiding it, smooth and eager, toward Kitty's face. "Now drink your fill, ach?"

And with a choked, gasping breath, Kitty leaned forward, and obeyed.

26

Varinn's taste was... divine.

It almost tasted sweeter than ever before, rich and deep and decadent on Kitty's tongue, and she couldn't suppress her helpless-sounding moan, or the desperate seeking of her tongue. Seeking inside Varinn, into that hot velvety slit, just the way he liked—and she only distantly heard his answering gasp, followed by Thrain's low, husky laugh.

"You teach her to do that, Varinn?" Thrain murmured, and she could feel his big hand settling on her head, almost as if he were petting her, approving of her. "Must feel damn good, ach?"

Varinn's reply was a low, incomprehensible grunt, oh gods—and when Kitty's wide, blinking eyes darted upwards, he was watching her, his own eyes dark, unreadable. While beside him, Thrain laughed again, warm and appreciative, while his hand kept stroking Kitty's head, as though she were a particularly pleasing pet.

"Ach, he likes it, Kit," he breathed. "You keep working that sweet little human tongue inside your lord, ach? See how wide he'll open for you."

Oh, *hell*, and Kitty moaned again, instantly obeying, seeking her tongue deeper into that dark, spluttering heat. Earning a growling hiss from Varinn this time, a hard, sustained shudder of his heft in her mouth—and then another laugh from Thrain, even huskier than before. "Ach, that's it," he breathed. "And don't forget to keep sucking too, ach, Kit? He likes it when you work for it. Show him how much you want it."

Oh. Yes, yes, Kitty had forgotten that, somehow, and she couldn't help her grateful glance up toward Thrain as she sucked harder, swallowed a little deeper. And oh, the way Thrain was smiling, sharp and wicked, just like he had that first night they'd spent together, when he'd buried his face between her legs...

"Ach, just like that," he said, his breath hitching, as he again petted his hand against her head. "Gods, she's pretty, ain't she, Varinn? You like having a sweet little human on her knees for you, worshipping you? Sucking your fat, perfect Grisk prick down her throat?"

Kitty moaned again, her eyes desperately darting back to Varinn's flushed, unreadable face. To where he was still just sitting here sprawled in his chair like this, not speaking, not even touching her. Just watching her, assessing her with those strange, glittering eyes.

"Ach?" Thrain murmured again, and Kitty distantly noticed his other hand slipping around Varinn's shoulder, gently squeezing at his neck. "Feel good, Varinn?"

And oh, Kitty was working even harder, sucking deeper, seeking inside, the sounds slick and shameful. While her eyes stayed fixed to Varinn's face, waiting desperately for his answer—but his gaze had cut away, sideways, back to Thrain again...

"Should you not know how it feels?" Varinn asked him, his voice astonishingly smooth. "How many times did she suck you that night? Thrice?"

Oh. The pooling, dizzying warmth had skittered,

shuddered, because how did Varinn know that, surely Thrain hadn't told him that—and Kitty couldn't quite follow the way Thrain's eyes shifted, even as his mouth pulled into a rueful little smile. "In truth, I don't remember," he said. "Sorry, Kit. Kind of a blur, wasn't it?"

Varinn's eyes briefly widened, and then narrowed, frowning back down toward Kitty's face. "Do you recall, then, Katharine?" he asked, his voice cold, and still impossibly steady. "Thrice?"

Kitty blinked at him, fighting to consider that, to wade through the distant foggy memories, even as she kept desperately sucking—at least, until Varinn's strong hand clasped at her face, her jaw. Pulling her off him with a lurid-sounding pop, while his slick length kept flexing and bobbing, close enough that it bumped against her chin.

"Ach, Katharine?" he demanded. "Do you not recall?"

Oh, gods, Kitty couldn't think, couldn't recall a damned thing, and she shook her head, even as her betraying tongue stroked her wet, swollen lips. "No," she breathed. "I mostly remember—his piercing. And that he... he liked it. I think."

She couldn't help an uneasy, apologetic glance toward Thrain, but if he minded, he certainly wasn't showing it. No, instead he was only looking fascinated, or maybe even enthralled, as Varinn grunted again, low and almost satisfied—and with an easy, casual movement, he impaled Kitty's mouth back onto his wet, straining cock. Sliding himself smooth and proprietary between her lips, deeper and deeper, until he butted up against her tight, convulsing throat.

"So neither of you recall this," he said, glancing sideways at Thrain, even as he held Kitty there, skewered deep and firm upon him. "None of this? Truly?"

Thrain was still watching Kitty with wide, arrested eyes, his breaths now audible between his parted lips. "Told you, we were—foxed," he replied, with what seemed to be a palpable effort. "Couldn't scent—a thing. Not—like this."

And perhaps Kitty should have been affronted, offended, especially when Varinn pulled her off him again, and even gave her head a gentle little shake. "What *do* you recall of this, then," he said flatly. "Speak this, Katharine. All of it."

Oh. He sounded surprisingly fervent, and far too coherent, his eyes flashing with command, and Kitty gulped for air, for the distant wispy memories. "Remember him... laughing," she said thickly. "Tasting me. And then—on top. Moving. Biting my neck. Sounded—loud, when he swallowed. And I—I licked his piercing. Told him it was—gorgeous."

She winced as she spoke, again glancing regretfully toward Thrain—but if anything, he was looking relieved, or maybe even satisfied. His claws gently drumming against Varinn's neck, his breath exhaling in a slow, hungry heave.

"See, Varinn?" he murmured. "Guarantee you, she's already had a hell of a lot more pleasure with you than she did with me. This is, what, her ninth time sucking you, now? Got me beat more than twice over."

Wait. And how did he know that, he could really smell that, too? But Varinn didn't look slightly surprised by it, and his grip on Kitty's face had even seemed to soften, his eyes perhaps a little softer, too...

"And I can smell how much she likes you, too," Thrain murmured, his gaze dropping back toward Kitty's face. "You ever tell him, Kit? How much you like him, and want to please him?"

Oh. Oh, gods, wait, he meant he wanted her to tell *Varinn* these things? Now? Like this? And damn it, Varinn's eyes had instantly hardened again, because this was supposed to be for Thrain, not him—but what else did he expect Kitty to do, with Thrain looking at them like that, eager and breathless and hungry, waiting...

"I do—like him," she managed, toward Thrain again, because that was easier, so much easier, than saying it to Varinn's narrow, suspicious eyes. "He's so—kind. Generous.

Handsome, especially in his kilt. And—commanding. Safe. Takes—care of me."

She winced at the last, again darting a furtive, fearful look toward Varinn's eyes. Fully expecting some kind of censure, or shame—but instead finding... surprise. Surprise, and then more of that distinctive red flush, creeping up his neck, beneath the gentle touch of Thrain's black claws.

"Ach, to all of that, Kit," Thrain murmured, and she distantly realized that his other hand was still patting her head, stroking at her hair. "Couldn't agree more. Now show him, ach? Worship your Lord Grisk, as you ought."

Oh, gods, Kitty should not have moaned like that, or lunged for Varinn's hard, slick flesh, so close—but she was, she was sucking him deep between her lips, sinking her tongue into his narrow clutching heat. And bringing up her tingling hands now, too, circling his thick base, caressing those swollen bollocks—and yes, yes, Varinn was gasping, his head tilting back, while Thrain kept watching, kept petting her, his eyes glittering on her face, with Varinn's cock thrust so deep inside it.

"Ach, just so," Thrain breathed, his eyes still alight, his voice a low, dangerous purr. "Look at you, sweet kitten. Bearing my heir in your belly, and sucking our lord's pretty Grisk prick into your tight little throat. You keep sucking like that, swallow him deeper, seek out his seed. And if you're very good, mayhap"—he drew in a ragged breath—"mayhap he'll blow for you, and feed you a nice fat, fresh load from his huge Grisk bollocks—"

His breath choked there, his eyes squeezing shut, his head bending into Varinn's hair, inhaling deep—and oh, oh hell, the seed was suddenly surging into Kitty's mouth, flooding her with fierce, furious abandon. And she was rapidly swallowing, dragging it down in gulp after gulp—gods, there was so *much*— when without warning, her own pleasure flashed out, too. Pulsing hot and wild and uncontrollable between her legs, shuddering her from the inside out, enveloping her whole in the wheeling, reeling relief.

She was trembling all over when it finished, the spasms wracking up her spine—but oh, a warm hand was patting her again, soothing her again, easing the shivers away. But—wait, it wasn't Thrain's hand. It was... Varinn's hand. Because Thrain's own hand was desperately fumbling at his trousers, yanking himself out—

And then he was spraying too, oh hell. His rigid grey cock spewing out a mess of thick white liquid, catching on his gold ring, spattering all over the fur-covered floor. While he himself groaned, low and guttural in his throat, his eyes squeezed shut, as his hand slowly pumped his shuddering shaft, as if to squeeze out every last drop.

And between Kitty's slack lips, Varinn was shuddering too, spurting out another long, sustained burst of hot sweetness. And then another, and another, his blazing eyes fixed to where Thrain was still milking himself out, slower and slower. Until the last of the wetness fell from his gold ring, dangling downwards in an opaque, slowly lengthening string.

"Fuck," Thrain finally said, shaky, breathless, as he shook it off onto the floor. "Fuck you, Varinn. Getting us both off without so much as even touching us, ach?"

He'd angled a not-quite-offended look at Varinn, even as Varinn again shuddered in Kitty's mouth, squeezing out another dollop of hot sweetness. But to Kitty's distant astonishment, his glance back at Thrain was tolerant, amused, maybe even affectionate, his eyes sparkling with wry, shimmering warmth.

"This was not all my doing, ach?" he said, low and smooth. "Had I known you should make such a mess all over our clean furs, I should have brought you a chamber-pot."

Thrain replied with an affronted scoff, even as he grimaced toward the floor. "It's because of the damned piercing, which again, is all your fault," he tartly informed Varinn. "And if you really didn't want a mess, maybe you coulda shared?"

He'd angled a pointed glance down toward Kitty, who was still—curse her—suckling at Varinn's softened heft. And curse *him*, but Varinn's hand gently spread on her hair, holding her there, wanting to watch this, to see her like this...

"No, I could not, for you shall not touch her thus, without my leave," he said, his voice astonishingly cool, proprietary, as if Kitty were truly his now, to offer up as he pleased. "You shall need to earn this right from me, ach? Also"—his brows rose toward Thrain—"I commanded you *naught* about that piercing. Not once."

To Kitty's ongoing surprise, Thrain only scoffed again, reaching to absently paw at the shelf beside him—the neat one—until his hand returned with a folded cloth. "Rubbish, you overbearing tyrant," he said lightly, as he began cleaning himself off, his fingers deft and firm on his softened length. "Know you don't need to tell me a damned thing. Just let it drop, all offhanded, how you like the look of them—especially the ones the Ka-esh make—and then put a few extra credits on my account. Doesn't take a genius, does it, Kit? Best gift I've ever gotten."

He was half-smiling down toward Kitty again, giving a last little tug at his ring with the rag—and then he tossed the rag at Varinn's face. At where Varinn's hand swiftly snapped out to catch it, and then— very briefly—he raised it to his nose, inhaling deep, before hurling it back toward Thrain again.

"Tyrant," Thrain murmured, but he was still smiling, and reaching over for another clean rag. And this time, he brought it down to Kitty's hot face, gently dabbing it at her sweaty cheeks. "You get it all outta him, Kit?" he said, soft. "Or do you have more for her, Varinn?"

Kitty could see Varinn's throat swallowing, his shoulder shrugging, and in return, Thrain dropped his eyes back to Kitty. And then, with an easy nonchalance, he tugged Varinn's softened bulk out of her mouth, and wiped it carefully with the cloth. "You get inside him too, sweet kitten?" he murmured, as he pulled the skin back, inspecting the glossy pink head beneath. "All of it?"

And oh, gods, did he want—but oh, yes, he did, guiding Varinn's soft pink head back toward her mouth. Wanting her to kiss it like this, careful and gentle, seeking inside for every last drop, while Varinn just sat back and watched. Watched them cleaning him, tending to him, worshipping him...

"Good," Thrain breathed, his own cheeks deeply flushed, now, as he guided Kitty's head away again, and gave Varinn's softened bulk one more thorough caress with the cloth. "He'll care for the rest of us until his last breath, without asking for anything in return—but he likes to be cared for too, ach? Even if he'll never admit it."

He angled another warm glance up at Varinn's face, at where Varinn was grimacing back toward him—but not arguing this, and obviously not refusing Thrain's attentions, either. Not even when Thrain slid the cloth downwards, cradling it around Varinn's heavy bollocks, lingering and squeezing with brazen, familiar intent.

"And he'll usually give you another round, too, if you want it," he said to Kitty, with a teasing little grin. "But mayhap we oughta let you rest for the night, ach, Kit? That was a massive load, and we don't want to make you sick on him, either. Been there, done that."

That was said with another cheerful glance toward Varinn, who was now rolling his eyes, and yanking down his kilt over Thrain's hand. "Ach, and it was *foul*," he replied, with a barely repressed shudder. "Even *you* ought to know better than to swallow three full loads in a row."

"*You* fed them to me!" Thrain replied hotly, but he was fully grinning now, and gently drawing Kitty up, onto her shaky feet. "And you oughta scented him, Kit," he continued. "He was all for it, and woulda happily kept going, even after the mess, so long as I kept kneeling and begging for him. Such a Lord Grisk thing to do."

Varinn's smile kept pulling higher, though he gave another longsuffering roll of his eyes. "No orc would spurn a tight hungry mouth on his prick," he said. "This has naught to do with Lord Grisk, and all to do with *you*."

"Whatever you say, Lord Grisk," Thrain blithely replied, his eyes dancing as they dropped back to Kitty's face. "Warning you, Kit. He really is a damned tyrant. Puts on a good, proper, respectable show for the kin, but we know the truth, ach?"

And somehow, Kitty was already smiling back up at him, her body leaning into his solid strength beside her. "Indeed we do," she said lightly, with a teasing glance toward Varinn in his chair. "Though I will say, at least you can't fault his taste, because"—her gaze dropped to where Thrain's ring was still visible, hanging over his sagging trousers—"that ring is excessively flattering on you. Well done, Lord Grisk."

Varinn's brows snapped up, while Thrain barked a loud, merry laugh. "You little traitor!" he exclaimed, slinging his arm around her shoulder, and giving her a gentle shake. "You better watch it, Kit, or else you'll end up stabbed full of his gold, too. It would be just like him, to want us to match."

He grinned back toward where Varinn was, disconcertingly enough, eyeing Kitty with a rather speculative gaze. And though she was still fully concealed by her dressing-gown, for an instant it almost felt like he was looking straight through it, and indeed deciding where he might like to pierce her with his gold...

Kitty's breath caught, the heat again pooling hard and sudden in her belly—but then Varinn's eyes shuttered, and he abruptly rose to his feet, straightening out his kilt. "You ought to rest," he said flatly, frowning between them. "Both of you."

His tone was clipped, decisive, and Kitty meekly nodded, and found that Thrain was doing the same beside her. Though he'd also stiffened a little, and she could hear him swallowing, clearing his throat.

"You're sure about me staying, then, Varinn?" he said, tentative. "And sleeping here again? With you?"

There was a twitch of silence, because right, Varinn had kicked Thrain out—and Varinn was clearly considering the question, his mouth pursing, his breath hissing as he exhaled. "You can stay," he finally replied, "whilst you are sober. But if I scent one *whiff* of drink upon you, you forfeit this right. To our room, to our bed, to *us*. For as long as I see fit. Ach?"

Oh. It was... the ultimatum again. That promise of reward, if Thrain behaved, or punishment, if he didn't. And Thrain clearly knew it, his throat bobbing, his grimace twisting his mouth.

"Ach, I follow," he said, quiet. "Thanks, Varinn."

Varinn jerked a stiff nod, his jaw flexing in his cheek. "Good," he said firmly. "And also"—he glanced downwards, and kicked at the wet fur by his foot—"you shall only stay *after* you have taken these to the scullery, and washed out your mess from them. I shall not bear you leaving all this for our kin to clean on the morrow, ach?"

Thrain groaned aloud, but his body against Kitty's relaxed a little, his uneasy eyes softening. "Ach, ach," he said lightly, with a brief, amused glance down toward Kitty. "Tyrant, I tell you."

But Varinn had folded his arms over his chest, giving an imperious, impatient jerk of his head toward the floor. And even as Thrain huffed another irritated groan, he smoothly dropped to his knees before Varinn, and began gathering up the furs.

But gods, even the sight of it was doing strange things in Kitty's belly, Thrain on his hands and knees at Varinn's feet, his messy head bowed, while Varinn stood there and watched, with those cool, assessing eyes. And oh, wait, Thrain had even put his hand on Varinn's bare *foot*, letting it linger there as his head tilted back, his half-lidded eyes blinking up toward Varinn's kilt, and then his face...

"No," Varinn said, gruff. "It has not even been a day, Thrain."

Oh. Right. Because clearly—clearly this was part of the ultimatum, too. This was another temptation, another reward. Showing Thrain what might be on offer, if he behaved...

Thrain rapidly nodded, dropping his eyes, gathering up the furs with far more speed and purpose than before. And then he rose swiftly to his feet, and flashed both Kitty and Varinn a jaunty grin before heading off for the door. Leaving them both staring in silence after him, Varinn's brow again creased, his hand rubbing at his mouth.

But then Varinn's eyes darted back toward Kitty, and he curtly waved her toward the bed. "Get in, then," he said, clipped. "Unless"—he winced, rubbed again at his mouth—"unless you should rather not?"

His voice was tentative, uneasy, his eyes searching her face. As if the question was about much more than just the bed, perhaps. And as if to confirm that suspicion, he glanced uneasily toward the now-empty chair behind him, his swallow visibly bobbing in his throat.

"No, it's fine," Kitty replied, too quickly, the damnable heat again rising in her cheeks—and she lurched toward the bed, and all but threw herself beneath the fur. Huddling there, facing toward the wall, waiting in the suddenly stilted silence. Until she felt the bed sagging a little beneath her, and then the weight of Varinn's body slipping under the fur, too.

"You are yet... sure of this," came his voice behind her, very low. "There is naught you might wish to alter, or cease, between us. Most of all after"—he exhaled, slow—"all this, today."

Right. All this. The fight they'd had, the accusations, the hurt. And the way it hadn't truly been resolved, not really, but suddenly Kitty couldn't bear to return to it, not now. Not after that. Not with her head still so dazed and crowded, with the heat still churning dangerously close in her belly…

Look at you, sweet kitten. Ach, he likes it. Worship your Lord Grisk, as you ought…

"It's all fine," she said, jerking a shrug beneath the fur, blinking hard toward the wall. "Really fine. No need to stop a thing."

But perhaps it had come out sounding too frantic, because oh gods, what would she do if Varinn stopped now? And wait, why was he even asking, what if he was having second thoughts, what if he—

"Is there anything *you* want to stop?" she asked, high-pitched. "After today?"

There was a moment's silence behind her, enough that her heart kicked in her chest, her breaths coming rapid and shallow. Until—until something squeezed at her shoulder, over the fur. A hand. Varinn's hand.

"No," he said, quiet, decisive. "And I… thank you, Katharine, for your help in this. This was… better than I could have dreamt, ach? To witness Thrain thus again, easy and laughing, seeking help with this, speaking truth to me, scenting of only himself…"

His voice cracked, his hand's grip dropping from Kitty's shoulder. "I shall do all I can to prolong this," he said, hoarse. "All that is within my power, ach? No matter the cost."

Right. And despite the clear desperation in that statement—the admission, again, that Kitty was most certainly a cost, something Varinn was only willing to endure for Thrain's sake—she felt herself relaxing a little into the bed. He was still here. He would still care for her and her son, for now. As long as she kept her vow, did her part, paid her debt…

"So will you tell me, then," she whispered, toward the wall. "Why you *didn't* speak those matehood vows to Thrain? When you obviously care for him so much?"

Her thoughts had flipped back to the way Varinn had

looked at Thrain, the way he'd smiled at him, the way he'd shuddered in Kitty's mouth when Thrain had spoken. The way he'd buried his face in Thrain's neck, and licked that drop of red from his chin…

But there was only more silence behind her, enough that Kitty winced, her body twisting around to look at where—oh. Where Varinn was blinking back toward her, and biting his lip, and looking not angry or offended, but more just… tired. Sad.

"I have always longed… for a son," he said, with an unsteady exhale, an unhappy twitch of his mouth. "An heir. To bear forth my father's scent, and carry his line, and serve our kin after death claims me. And"—another twist on his mouth—"I did not think it right to seek out a woman, and ask her for such a gift, whilst I was bound to another."

Oh. *Oh.* And yes, yes, of course that was it, of course that explained it all, damn him—and Varinn gave another unsteady exhale as he twisted onto his back, blinking up at the stone ceiling. "And I did not think it right to bind Thrain to me," he said, his voice wooden now, "under the threat of someday leaving him for this. Not when he cares for me as he does. Or"—he grimaced at the ceiling—"as he *did.*"

But Kitty was already shaking her head, frowning at his hard profile. "Thrain cares for you, Varinn," she said. "He obviously worships you."

Varinn grimaced again, shrugged against the fur. "Ach, does he?" he said, with a harsh little laugh. "He has hidden so much from me. Spoken false to me countless times. Betrayed me, with *you.* Shattered my scent's claim upon him. And made a *son*, without me. He has done"—he drew in a shaky breath—"all he could have done to wound me. Where he knew it would grieve me most."

His voice was thin, weary, his eyes rapidly blinking at the ceiling, and Kitty felt her own eyes blinking too, her head shaking. "Look, I'm sure it's probably not much consolation," she said, "but Thrain did *not* want a son with me. Not for a single instant. He was absolutely distraught over it all, and terrified of how upset you would be. He ran off the next morning as though the gods themselves were at his heels."

Varinn didn't speak, his breath heaving in and out beneath the fur, so Kitty drew in a deep, bracing breath, too. "And also," she continued, a little steadier, "the hiding and lying is part of the illness, remember? So it's not... *you*, Varinn. He's not trying to hurt you, or punish you, with all this. He's just... sick. Right?"

But Varinn huffed another choked, miserable laugh, rubbing a hand at his eyes. "Mayhap," he said thickly. "But mayhap you and Kesst have the truth of it, and this sickness is—my doing. Mayhap I drove him to this, ach? For I have not always held my ground against him, and too oft I have fallen to my own longings, and welcomed his touch and his comfort and his pleasure. And mayhap"—another broken little laugh— "mayhap in seeking to be kind, by spurning him as my mate, I only showed him cruelty. Mayhap this is now justice upon me. A lesson from the gods, to show me my failings, and teach me my place."

Oh. Oh, gods. And the misery was surging in Kitty's belly, her head shaking, her hand gripping at his stiff shoulder. "No," she said. "No, absolutely not, and I was wrong to say that to you today. Thrain's sickness is not your fault, Varinn. It *isn't*. And"—she drew in another breath, speaking faster—"you just told me that your gods are kind, remember? And apparently one of them is even your ancestor, *and* your namesake—so of course he's going to favour you, and guide you through all this."

She'd shoved up a little in the bed, raising her brows down toward him. And though his eyes blinking up toward hers were still sad, wary, watchful, he wasn't arguing, was he? Wasn't pushing her away?

"So," Kitty continued, braver now, "the only god teaching any lessons around here is going to be *you*, Lord Grisk. And"— she even managed a quirk of a teasing smile—"if these lessons don't involve stabbing Thrain with more of your excellent taste in jewelry, I'm going to be sorely disappointed."

And yes, yes, that was a twinge of warmth, sparking reluctant but unmistakable in Varinn's eyes, and Kitty felt her smile pulling a little higher. "You deserve it," she said firmly. "In truth, we both deserve it, don't we? How many piercings can one orc conceivably have, do you think?"

Varinn's head gave a wry little shake, but his eyes were almost—almost—crinkling at the corners. At least, until they angled meaningfully toward the door, toward where Thrain was striding back through the curtain. And then halting just inside it, blinking uneasily toward Kitty and Varinn in the bed—and too late, Kitty realized what it must look like. Varinn on his back, her leaning up over him, close and familiar, almost near enough to...

"Not interrupting anything, am I?" Thrain asked, a little stilted. "Want me to come back later?"

But both Kitty and Varinn were shaking their heads at once, Varinn lifting up the fur, Kitty waving Thrain forward. "We were just talking about you," she said, as cheerfully as she could. "And discussing all the new piercings Varinn's going to gift you, if you behave."

Both Varinn and Thrain gaped at her, before darting uncertain looks at each other—but then Thrain flashed Varinn a curious little grin, and eased his long body into the bed beside him. "Och, Varinn?" he said, and for an instant, he sounded almost shy. "You're only jesting, I ken."

Varinn angled another brief, almost imperceptible glance toward Kitty, but then gave a too-casual shrug. "Mayhap," he said offhandedly. "We shall see."

But Thrain's grin broadened, his eyes bright and eager on Varinn's face. "Ach?" he murmured, as he shifted a little closer, and ducked his face into Varinn's neck. "Ach, I smell you, you sneaky bastard. *Really*? Why'd you never say?"

And blinking between them, studying that almost-imperceptible shift in Varinn's eyes, Kitty knew precisely why he hadn't said. Because gifts of jewels and piercings, surely, were again something only a mate would offer. A line Varinn hadn't wanted to cross. But now—*I shall do all that is within my power*, he'd said. *No matter the cost.*

And yes, Varinn was looking resigned, but also relieved, or even grateful, as Thrain snuggled a little closer against him, his face still tucked into his neck. And in return, Varinn's arm settled around Thrain, his hand sinking up into his messy hair, his claws carding deep. As if this was a deeply familiar pose, one they'd assumed hundreds of times before...

"You can pierce me wherever the hell you want, Varinn," Thrain murmured now, muffled, into Varinn's neck. "Anywhere, ach?"

But maybe Varinn had already known that too, because his eyes had shifted again, hinting at sadness, and pain. Even as he turned his head to inhale against Thrain's messy hair, the breath slow and deep and reverent, so tender that Kitty almost wanted to weep.

At least, until Thrain opened one eye, squinting toward her—and then he reached out, and tugged her downwards. Down onto Varinn's other shoulder, oh, and Varinn had even obligingly settled his arm around her, just like he had with Thrain. Tucking her into his warm, solid side, almost as if he wanted her there, almost as if he could bear her, for now, for this.

"He's the best pillow, ach?" Thrain mumbled, yawning, as he stretched against Varinn, and snuggled himself even closer. "Gods, I've missed this. Smell so good, Varinn, so good it's *deeply* unfair, you have no damn right to—"

"Quiet, *krútt*," Varinn cut in, soft but sharp, his claws gently yanking on Thrain's hair. "You need sleep, ach? All of you."

All of them. And wait, he was surely counting Kitty's son in that statement—or rather, *their* son. And oh, even Varinn's hand had somehow curved down over her side, spreading against her waist—and suddenly Thrain's hand was there, too. His fingers widening over Varinn's, or even tangling together with them, holding tight.

It was unlike anything Kitty had ever felt before, tucked close and warm and safe beneath the fur, with those big hands spread over her son, these sweet scents mingling in her breath. And with Varinn's firm, solid body beneath her, all around her, caring for her and her son, just like he'd promised...

And with one last deep, contented breath, Kitty closed her eyes, and slept.

27

It was quite possibly the loveliest night Kitty had spent in her life.

Sleep felt so easy, so safe, with Varinn and Thrain both so close, their big hands still clasped against her waist. And when she'd awoken in the middle of the night with a pressingly uncomfortable bladder, Varinn had silently escorted her to a nearby latrine, his arm firmly around her as they'd padded through the pitch-black sitting-room. And then, after he'd guided her back the same way, he nudged a still-sleeping Thrain sideways in the bed, and drew Kitty back in beside him. Once again gathering her close, nestling her head against his warm solid shoulder, while Thrain shifted and stretched on his other side, and then sprawled his long arm and leg across them both.

And if Kitty sleepily turned her head, and pressed a furtive, grateful kiss to Varinn's warm skin, he didn't seem to notice, or complain. And when she awoke again, what felt like some time later, she was still there, still tucked into his arm, still cocooned in warm, drowsy safety. And across from her, Thrain was still lying on Varinn's other shoulder, and looking just as relaxed as she felt. Giving her a slow, sleepy smile as he leisurely stretched out against Varinn, his long arm again sprawling across them both.

"Sleep all right, Kit?" he murmured. "How're you feeling this morn? And our son?"

Right. Kitty's hand reflexively dropped to her belly, which—somehow—already felt slightly more swollen than the day before. And now that she was thinking about it, her breasts even felt a little fuller, and decidedly tender, too—and even a whisper of the nausea had returned again, gnawing quiet but consistent in her stomach.

"Need a bit of breakfast, I ken?" Thrain murmured, angling a quirking smile upwards. Toward where Varinn was already awake too, glancing with unreadable eyes between them. While Thrain smoothly slipped his hand down from Kitty, toward... Varinn's groin.

"Just need to warm him up a bit first, ach?" Thrain continued, with another grin toward Kitty, as his hand moved with blatant, suggestive ease beneath the fur. "I'm still in disgrace with him, so it'd best be—*och*, Varinn. Why the hell'd you wear this thing all night?"

He shot a disgruntled glance up at Varinn's unreadable face, and irritably shoved down the fur covering them, revealing—oh. His own hand, fumbling at the leather belt holding Varinn's kilt closed, because yes, apparently Varinn had worn it all night, just as Kitty had worn her dressing-gown. While Thrain's trousers had clearly vanished at some point, because his tall grey body was now fully bared against Varinn's side, his long leg hooked over Varinn's knee. And—Kitty's throat swallowed—his half-hard length was propped on Varinn's thigh over his kilt, a thick bead of white already pooling against his gold ring.

"No need for prudery between us now, is there?" Thrain blithely continued, followed by a grunt of satisfaction as he yanked Varinn's belt open. "We've all seen it all by now, haven't we?"

Oh. Well. Because—no. They hadn't. Or at least, Kitty hadn't, had she? Because despite all the times she'd—*drunk* from Varinn, he hadn't once—oh. Oh. Because Thrain had already drawn Varinn's kilt all the way open, yanking it out from beneath him, and tossing it aside. And beneath it...

Kitty's breath rushed from her lungs, and she'd somehow shifted up to look, her eyes wide and greedy on the sight. On Varinn's hard, muscled, bulky bare form, just lying here like this between them, exposed, *gorgeous*. With the broad chest, the rippled abdomen, the hairy, powerful thighs. And there, resting heavy and full on his belly, was that smooth, rapidly swelling green length, its dripping pink tip just peeking out from beneath its soft green hood...

"Much better," Thrain murmured, as his long fingers trailed up Varinn's thigh, over that hard abdomen, until it paused to gently tweak at a deep green nipple. "Pretty, ain't he, Kit? Could look at you all day, Varinn."

He shot a wicked little grin up toward Varinn's face, which was looking distinctly flushed, despite the narrowness of his watching eyes. "*Thrain*," he said, a sharp note of warning in his voice—but Thrain just kept smiling toward him, giving that green nipple another slow, deliberate tweak with his black claw.

"What?" he said lightly. "Just showing off the goods for your sweet new mate. Just as any old friend might do, ach?"

Varinn groaned, or maybe it was more of a growl, but he hadn't pushed Thrain's hand away, either. And clearly Thrain was taking that as permission, his hand widening with proprietary ease against Varinn's chest before sliding back down. Moving slow and smooth and heated, as his wicked gaze flicked toward Kitty, gleaming with bright satisfaction.

And oh, Kitty was utterly arrested, her eyes unblinking, her mouth gone entirely dry. Because gods, the *sight* of this. Their two bodies pressed together, Thrain's hand blatantly caressing down Varinn's hard front, pausing to tickle at his taut navel. A touch that prompted Varinn's swollen length to strain upwards, sputtering out a slick bubble of white onto his belly—while Thrain's own hardness, still propped sideways on Varinn's thigh, was now leaking from its ring in a long shining strand, dangling down between Varinn's slightly parted thighs.

"You can touch him too, Kit," Thrain murmured, waggling his brows toward her, as he nudged a finger against Varinn's slit, and then trailed the finger sideways, downwards. Drawing a thick, viscous line down the full length of Varinn's green cock, as it bobbed and flexed beneath his touch, sputtering out more of that thick white onto his belly. "He likes it, ach?"

Kitty couldn't help another darting glance up at Varinn's flushed face, at where he was still balefully frowning toward Thrain. But still not arguing, not even as Thrain's gently tracing hand slid down to his bollocks, rolling them in his fingers. "Ach, Varinn?" he breathed. "Like to be petted and played with, don't you? Like to have your pretty prick plumped up, and your fat bollocks urged full to the brim, made ready for your spilling?"

And oh, Varinn was still just watching, his breaths now heaving hard through his chest, as Thrain kept caressing those swollen weights, blatantly encircling them, squeezing them, even gently bouncing them on his deft, teasing fingers. "Ach, just so," he continued, with a devious smile toward Varinn's face, almost as if he'd spoken aloud. "Don't want to do a damned thing to get yourself off right now, do you, Lord Grisk? No, because that's what we're here for, ain't it?"

Kitty's breaths were heaving nearly as hard as Varinn's, now, her gaze desperately darting between Thrain's deft playing fingers, and his glinting, hungry eyes. "We're here to fill you up and empty you, ach, Lord Grisk?" he breathed, as he slowly traced a finger back up Varinn's swollen, straining length. "To keep that good, potent Grisk seed flowing. So we can cover ourselves with it, drink it inside us, and make ourselves reek of you. Just the way good little worshippers should."

Oh, hell, because that was finally a low moan, hissing from Varinn's parted lips, even as his narrow eyes cut toward... Kitty. And Thrain easily followed it, his grin curving higher, as his hand snaked toward hers, catching her wrist in his long fingers.

"Touch him," he purred, so soft. "He wants you to, ach?"

And surely Varinn could say no, surely he would—but Thrain had already settled Kitty's fingers against Varinn's warm, heaving chest, and Varinn was still just... watching. Just watching, with those narrow, intense eyes, even as that swollen heft on his belly spurted out another thick splash of white.

"See?" Thrain murmured, eyes dancing, as his own hand began sliding back downward. "Told you, Kit."

Kitty swallowed hard, darting another look up at Varinn's flushed face, his heated eyes. And suddenly, his words from the night before were surging, skittering through her thoughts. *I shall do all within my power. No matter the cost.*

And yes, yes, Thrain was here, still sober, bright and warm and alive, his body in Varinn's bed, his hand on Varinn's cock. With Varinn very much in control of the situation, even as he lay here silent and unmoving. And what had Thrain said, about this? *If there's anything Varinn likes, it's being in control...*

So Kitty drew in a breath, and slipped her hand downwards. Sliding it over Varinn's warm, greenish-grey skin, feeling the silken smoothness of it, the way it was shuddering beneath her touch. The way the hard bulk of his chest gave way to his slightly softer abdomen, the ridges of solid muscle within it. The way the muscle spasmed whenever his cock spurted out, and oh, Thrain had taken him fully in hand now, holding him upright so Kitty could touch his belly beneath. Her fingers slipping into those spots of wetness, now, streaking them wide across his skin...

"Ach, that's it," Thrain murmured, his glittering eyes fixed on the sight, as his hand gently began pumping up and down that green length, milking out more thick white, spattering it across the back of Kitty's hand. "You like it too, ach, Kit?"

There was no refuting it, not amidst her shaky breaths, or her heated cheeks, or her hungry stroking fingers—or, damn it, the furiously pooling heat between her thighs. And it didn't make sense, Varinn didn't even like her, and her hazy thoughts were dredging up memories—not all unpleasant—of her many other experiences with men, with Charles. Most of them far more involved than this, than lying here fully clothed, carefully touching a male's belly...

But they all seemed so faint, suddenly, muted and distant and dim. And then shattering altogether, vanishing into the distance, at the sound of Varinn's low grunt, the utterly enthralling sight of his spurting wetness thickening into a smooth, steady stream. Pouring down over Thrain's knuckles, off his still-stroking hand, dangling toward Kitty's fingers beneath...

"There we go," Thrain said, with dark satisfaction, and an approving grin up at Varinn's flushed face. "When he starts leaking steady like this, Kit, that means he's ready, ach? Ready to plug whatever hole you're offering, and pump it full of his good Grisk seed."

Oh, hell. Kitty's moan had escaped on its own, far too loud and betraying, but Thrain's grin only broadened, his tongue brushing his lips. "Though if he's set on one hole over the other," he murmured, "he'll let you know, ach, Varinn? But right now"—his wicked eyes glanced between them—"it's gotta be Kit's tight little mouth again, ach? Healer's orders, and all."

Gods curse her, because Kitty had moaned again, and maybe Varinn had, too. And that lengthening strand of white, still dangling from Thrain's knuckles, had finally caught the backs of her own fingers. Stringing between her, and Thrain, and that deep, glossy pink slit. Oozing out from all the way *inside* Varinn, from where he was making it for her, ready for her, oh hell...

And oh, Thrain had released his hand's grip around Varinn's cock, letting it fall back to his belly—and then, without warning, he brought his wet knuckles up to Kitty's mouth. Brushing her parted lips with that slick liquid, sparking sweet and succulent in her breath, on her tongue—because oh, she was kissing his skin, licking fervent and frantic, her heated moan shuddering out her throat. Gods, it tasted so good, he felt so good, he was feeding her Varinn's seed and it was—

"*Thrain*," hissed Varinn's voice, deep and disapproving, freezing both Kitty and Thrain at once—and in a jerky movement, Thrain's hand snapped away from Kitty's mouth, his eyes instantly apologetic on Varinn's face.

"Sorry," he murmured, a little breathless. "You just—smell so good, ach? Both of you. Need to scent your seed on her. Inside her."

His darting gaze between them was pleading, now, and Kitty could almost see Varinn relenting, could see the shift in his glinting eyes. And oh, that was the feel of his hand, gripping her shoulder—and then guiding her downwards. Downwards, toward that. Wanting this. From her.

Kitty wanted it too, craved it, needed it so much it ached, and she was already nodding, obeying. Shoving herself downwards over him, letting that firm hand guide her between his legs. Until she was kneeling between his bulky thighs, oh gods, and Thrain's hand had slipped down again, encircling Varinn's thick green base with proprietary ease, and guiding it up toward her gasping mouth.

"He's telling you to suck it, Kit," he hissed, his previous contrition utterly vanished, in favour of sharp, urgent command. "Now."

Oh, gods, yes, and once again, Kitty was already obeying. Lowering her mouth to that shining sputtering head, dragging in a shaky inhale of its heady sweet scent—and then sucking it deep and desperate between her lips. Taking him as far inside as she could go, gouging him into her convulsing throat, and Varinn's answering hiss sounded almost approving, almost satisfied, as his hips canted up, sinking him even deeper...

"*Ach*," came Thrain's voice, shaky and strangled, and when Kitty's eyes snapped upwards, he'd buried his flushed face in Varinn's neck, his chest visibly filling with his breath. "Ach, Varinn. You show her who's in charge here. You show her whose seed she's gonna swallow down that tight little throat."

Both Kitty and Varinn groaned at once, Varinn's invading heft swelling even fuller in her mouth, and Thrain made a sound like a half-laugh, half-moan, muffled into Varinn's neck. "Ach, that's it," he breathed. "You feed her that good Grisk prick, Varinn. You be a good Grisk lord, just like your forebear, and share your rich seed with your clanmate's sweet little woman. Feed her with you, fatten her up on you, make her *yours*—"

His voice cracked into a groan, while beneath Kitty, Varinn made a sound much like a cry—and suddenly his hot sweetness was swarming her mouth, surging out so fast she couldn't keep it all in. And it was blubbering out her lips, streaking slick and messy down her chin, while both orcs blatantly watched. Varinn's eyes dark and hazy, Thrain's blazing with bright, arrested craving. His entire body gone stiff against Varinn, his hips grinding up hard against Varinn's thigh, his moan low and guttural and—

"Ach," Varinn muttered, his hand snapping away from Kitty's shoulder—had it been on her shoulder, this whole time?—in favour of groping down beside the bed. And when it re-emerged, it was holding—a steel basin?

But yes, yes, he was, and he was thrusting it purposefully into Thrain's chest—and Thrain barked a choked-sounding laugh as he fumbled for it, shoving it beneath him, twisting his body up and sideways. Rising to his hands and knees over it, oh hell, so Kitty had a vivid, unbroken view of his long, lean back arching, his rigid cock giving one last shuddering, sustained jolt—and then spewing out. Pouring down into the basin in a sharp, messy spray of white, so forceful it splashed over the sides, spattering Kitty and Varinn both.

And then it just kept going, and going, and going. Spraying out strong and steady from that straining green length, while Thrain's breaths kept heaving, his head thrown back, his muscles taut, his skin covered with a sheen of sweat. Until the flow from his slit finally slowed, and then sputtered to a thick, streaming drizzle, dangling down into the basin from that slick gold ring.

"Fuck," Thrain breathed, shaking off the string with an unsteady-looking hand, and sinking back onto his heels on the fur. "Fuck you, Varinn, again, because—what?"

He was glancing between Kitty and Varinn, his brows rising, because—oh. Because they'd both been blatantly gaping toward him, and watching this. Varinn with his lips parted, his tongue sweeping against them, while Kitty's own lips had gone slack around Varinn's still-hard heft, still buried deep in her mouth. And Thrain's glances between them had become increasingly amused, his mouth quirking up into a curious little grin.

"What?" he said again, lighter this time. "A fellow can't get off into a basin without getting gawked at? Was just following your orders, Varinn! And not making a mess on the clean furs!"

Kitty could see Varinn's throat convulsing, his lips pressing tightly together, his exhale shuddering through his chest. "You *have* made a mess," he said reprovingly, though his voice was hoarse. "You shall need to take these furs for cleaning, too."

He'd waved a shaky-looking hand toward where Thrain's spraying wetness had splashed over the basin's sides, and though Thrain rolled his eyes, he was still smiling. "Ach, ach," he said. "Such a tyrant, Varinn. And speaking of which"—his eyes angled toward Kitty—"you're not wasting that, are you, Kit?"

Oh. He was referring to where Varinn's thick sweetness was liberally dripping from Kitty's still-occupied mouth, down her chin, and onto Varinn's belly. And now Varinn was looking too, his brows rising, his eyes glinting with unmistakable command. As if, despite however he currently felt toward Thrain, he was still in full agreement with him on this particular point. *You shall not waste what I give you.*

Kitty's face was heating again, but she was already nodding, obeying. Searching her tongue against Varinn's softened heft, delving inside him, sucking out every last drop, until there was nothing left. And when she pulled away, letting that soft flesh fall from her lips, she found that Thrain's hand had settled against her head, guiding her downwards. Down toward the mess on Varinn's belly, oh, and Kitty's face burned even hotter as she licked at it, as Thrain's hand caressed slow and approving against her hair.

"Ach, that's it," he murmured. "You lap up all your lord's good Grisk seed, and don't waste a drop. He's made it just for you, pumped it out those big bollocks for you, to grow you hearty and hale for our son, ach?"

An inexplicable gasp choked from Kitty's throat, even as Varinn's previously soft cock flexed up, brushing her chin. And beside them, Thrain was chuckling, low and satisfied, his gleaming eyes darting toward Varinn's face. "And maybe he'll make you even more, ach?" he said. "If you keep worshipping him properly, as you ought?"

But at that, Varinn's hand snapped up, rubbing at his eyes, and his other hand grasped Kitty's shoulder, guiding her sideways. "No," he said firmly. "We have much to address today."

Oh. Kitty's stomach inexplicably plummeted, something much like hurt clutching in her chest—and Thrain's glance toward her was far too knowing, his hand again stroking her hair. "And that's Varinn-speak for later, Kit," he said softly, with a twitch of a smile. "Likely by noon. Ach, Varinn?"

Varinn was already shoving out of bed, wrapping his previously abandoned kilt around his waist before striding to the washbasin. And though he hadn't looked back toward them, he wasn't arguing, either, and Thrain waggled his brows toward Kitty, his eyes alight. "Wait for it," he said cheerfully, as he leapt out of the bed, and then guided her up to her feet after him. "And then tell him I told you so."

Kitty couldn't help a relieved laugh, and then a furtive glance at Thrain's lean, fully bared body, just standing here before her. All lithe muscle and smooth grey skin, with that dangling length at his groin, surrounded by soft black curls. And oh, he was lazily stretching up, extending his long arms high over his head, and then running an easy hand through his hair, standing it all on end. Looking impossibly rakish, impossibly compelling, the too-aware wickedness flashing in his eyes...

"Thrain," cut in Varinn's sharp voice from the washbasin, where he now appeared to be shaving, drawing a small steel blade down his cheek. "*Dress.*"

Thrain's glance at Varinn was swift and sheepish, and he instantly dropped the pose, and strode toward the messier of the two shelves. "So what do you think, Kit," he said, as he began yanking out clothes. "Said you liked Varinn's kilt, didn't you?"

Kitty darted another uncertain look toward Varinn, but he still seemed entirely intent on his shaving. While before her, Thrain kept yanking items from the shelf, not even seeming to notice when several kilts fell haphazardly to the furs at his feet.

"Well," Kitty said, as she surreptitiously rescued the fallen kilts, and took a swift, critical look at each one. "This one needs repairing—the leather's all but torn off here, see?—and I can't imagine this one fits you at all. It seems to be built for someone broader... perhaps it's Varinn's?"

She'd risked another glance toward Varinn, but he still wasn't looking back, and Thrain snatched for the kilt, drawing it to his nose, inhaling deep. "Ach, that *is* Varinn's," he said, as he tossed it over toward Varinn's shelf, and tugged out another one. "And this one is, too. Although..."

He was half-smiling toward a small, short leather kilt, with a beautifully intricate gold chain woven into the top. "Although I ken it's from when you were what, twelve summers old?" he asked over his shoulder toward Varinn. "Always liked this gold in it. Beautiful Grisk forging, ach? Suited you."

His voice had gone wistful, his fingers tracing against the gold with palpable reverence, and Kitty found herself studying him, and then glancing curiously toward Varinn, too. "So you two have really known each other for that long, then?" she asked. "How did you first end up getting together? As more than just friends, I mean?"

She'd thought it a relatively innocuous question, but Varinn was purposefully looking away again, while Thrain's gaze had gone very intent on the kilt. "Och, one thing and then another, I ken," he said, a little too casually, as he carefully folded the kilt, and placed it back on the shelf. "You ken how it is."

Kitty didn't, but she could take a hint well enough, and fought to shove away the whispering uncertainty as Thrain cast her an apologetic look, and then tossed a few more items onto the floor. "Not those, either," he said, too quickly, with an obvious attempt at changing the subject. "All still scent of ale, and it takes an age to fully wash out. Do you ken Ymir would take 'em at that giant hoard of his, Varinn?"

Kitty briefly met Varinn's eyes, and felt her smile reluctantly pulling up together with his. "It's not a hoard," she informed Thrain, as lightly as she could. "It's the Great Grisk Showroom-Shop, right, Varinn?"

Varinn rolled his eyes, but he was still smiling, and looking distinctly relieved, too. "The Grisk *Shop*," he said, though his tone didn't at all match the warmth in his eyes. "And ach, I ken Ymir would be glad to take them. This is good thinking, Thrain, on your part."

His voice had lowered, his gaze soft and approving on Thrain's face. Enough that Thrain visibly blushed, before turning back to the shelf, and thrusting out a few more garments toward Kitty. And once she'd sifted through them all, she pulled out the best-looking kilt, and held it up before him. "How about this one?" she asked. "It looks about your size, and it's very well-made, too. Beautiful stitching on the leather."

Thrain promptly took the kilt, and wrapped it around his hips without hesitation. And once he'd fastened the buckle closed, and smoothed down the leather front, Kitty could see that it had been an excellent choice indeed. Its fit close but not constricting, and hanging low enough to show off the lovely sharp cut of his hipbones.

"Very nice," Kitty said lightly, with a genuinely appreciative glance up and down his lean form. "Suits you very well. Now, you only need a few of Varinn's piercings, and you'll be all set."

She'd angled a teasing look toward Varinn, who seemed to be eyeing Thrain rather intently, too—but he wasn't smiling, or responding. While Thrain jerked a twitchy-looking shrug, and flashed Kitty a grin that didn't quite reach his eyes.

"I yet ken Varinn was just jesting about the piercings, ach?" he said, a little stiff. "He wouldn't give jewels to someone who isn't actually his..."

But his voice trailed off there, because Varinn had abruptly turned toward his own shelf, and snapped open the small wooden box on top. And after blinking into it for an instant, he drew out something long and gold and glittering. An intricate, beautifully wrought chain—not unlike the one Thrain had admired on the kilt—and it was studded with shining gold beads, and what appeared to be *teeth*?

"Here," Varinn said, his expression unreadable, as he strode over toward them. "Shall this suffice, for now?"

Thrain's mouth had fallen open, and he stood stock-still as Varinn lowered the chain around his neck, settling the beads and teeth against his bare chest. Where they looked bright and bold and vivid, and perhaps just a little dangerous, too. Perhaps—perhaps just like Thrain himself.

"It's perfect," Kitty murmured, without quite meaning to,

but perhaps Varinn thought so too, giving a decisive, satisfied nod as he stepped backwards again. While Thrain's eyes were still wide and stunned, and his shaky-looking hand twitched up to touch the chain, his fingers fumbling against the beads and teeth, as though he needed to feel every one, to make sure they were real.

"But this was... your Pa's *thyrja*, Varinn," Thrain finally said, his voice thick. "You can't mean to—*give* it to me. Ach?"

Varinn's mouth pursed, his gaze intent on the chain—the *thyrja*, Thrain had said—against Thrain's skin. "Mayhap," he said. "If you can show me you are worthy of this."

Oh. It was... more of the ultimatum. Again. And Thrain clearly knew it, judging by the dangling, stilted silence, and the sound of his audible swallow. But then he rapidly nodded, his hand tightening against one of the teeth. "Ach," he said. "Ach, I follow."

There was another instant's silence, but then Varinn nodded too, short and curt, before turning and striding back to the washbasin. Leaving Kitty and Thrain standing there looking at each other, Thrain still clutching at his *thyrja*, so tightly his knuckles had gone pale.

"And naught for Kit, Varinn?" Thrain finally said, clearing his throat. "Doesn't seem fair for you to grant me such a gift, and not your own sweet new mate?"

Kitty couldn't hide her wince, and Varinn had similarly stiffened at the washbasin, his hand spasming on what appeared to be a toothbrush. While Thrain gave a jerky shrug, and then a wan little smile between them both. "Ought to have a mating-gift, Kit," he said. "Long Grisk tradition, ach? Brings blessings from the gods upon your union, or some other such rub—"

He broke off there, clearly catching Varinn's sharp, narrow glare—but then Varinn snapped his toothbrush down beside the washbasin, and again stalked toward his shelf. Where he flicked the box back open, and yanked out another long, dangling gold chain. One that was far more delicate and intricate than the first, but it was obviously by the same maker, with the same style of smithing, the same gleaming gold beads. And Thrain's eyes had widened at the sight of it, and then flashed with unmistakable satisfaction.

"Ach, there we go," he murmured, followed by a low, appreciative whistle. "You'll need to lose the dressing-gown to put it on, though, Kit."

Oh. Wait. He didn't mean—or did he? Because Varinn had halted before Kitty, the gold in his hands, his brows lifted, waiting. And when she jerked a shaky nod, Thrain slipped around behind her, and gently drew the dressing-gown down over her shoulders. Undressing her, oh gods, for Varinn's eyes, and yes, Varinn was watching, waiting, as Thrain tossed the gown away, and showed him... everything.

And Varinn was still looking. Looking at Kitty's slim body, her small breasts, that slight swell in her belly. And perhaps that was even the familiar redness, creeping up his neck, as he stepped forward, lifted the gold chain, and lowered it over her head.

And it wasn't just a single loop, Kitty realized, as she felt the cool metal settling against her shivery skin. No, it was an entire complex connected web of glittering gold, with larger openings at the sides and front. And at Thrain's gentle nudge beneath her elbows, she slipped her arms through the side openings, and found that the rest of the gold chains settled down the full length of her upper body, curving around her breasts, and the swell of her belly. Almost as if surrounding them, exposing them, flaunting them, for—for Varinn.

And oh, he didn't like it, or did he, the way his throat visibly bobbed, his eyes still sweeping up and down. And Kitty felt herself swallow too, far too loud between them, because, because—

"But this is—too much," she said, her voice catching, her

hand fluttering up to touch at the gold resting against her collarbone. "You can't mean—you're not—"

She clamped her mouth shut, too late, before she betrayed something she'd regret—and suddenly there was only longing, twisting in her chest, so fierce and desperate it stole all her breath. Gods, he couldn't. Not after that night. Not after all that pleasure. Not after all those impossible words that she would never, ever forget.

Ach, Varinn. You be a good Grisk lord. Feed her with you, fatten her up on you, make her yours...

But no. No. No. Varinn had made himself very clear, again and again. He was doing everything within his power. This was still about saving Thrain, and that was all.

But Varinn wasn't replying. Wasn't taking his beautiful gift back. Was still just looking at Kitty like that, while Thrain gave a low, husky laugh behind her, his warm hands slipping around to her front. Skating over the gold, over her skin, brushing very lightly against her peaked nipples, curving slow over her belly.

"No need to protest, Kit," he murmured. "A *thyrja* is a good Grisk gift, ach? Expected of him, by all his kin. And it's for his benefit too, 'cause not only does it mark you as his mate, but it shows you off for him, see? Flaunts to him what's his."

Oh gods, oh please, because Thrain's hands had again slipped up to her nipples, gently circling them with his thumbs, bringing them to hard, straining peaks. And Kitty couldn't think, couldn't breathe, because Varinn was watching it, his eyes dark, half-lidded on the sight. On Thrain touching her like this, leaving her nipples flushed and rigid, and slipping his big hands back to her belly again. Caressing it, showing it off, for Varinn's hungry eyes, and Kitty's own eyes were fluttering, her head tilting back into Thrain's shoulder, as his hand slid further downward, toward—

"*Thrain,*" Varinn hissed, a low, dangerous growl in his throat, and Thrain's hands instantly dropped, his body easing back, away. But not before he gave Kitty a brief, meaningful little nudge toward Varinn, as if, as if...

"Thank you, Lord Grisk," Kitty said to Varinn, before she could possibly stop it, the words spilling fervent and choked from her mouth. "It's such a stunning gift, and I'm honoured to wear it, to bear your mark and your scent. I'll do my best to please you, and do you credit as your mate. I swear to you."

And yes, yes, his eyes were softening again, and as Kitty blinked up toward him, it occurred to her that she meant it. Gods, she meant it, and she wasn't supposed to mean it, Varinn didn't even like her, he was only doing this for Thrain, doing all that was within his power, driving those damned ultimatums. And she was supposed to be doing the rational thing for once, learning a trade, planning for her future. So why couldn't she look away, and why wasn't he looking away, either...

"Not going to kiss her, Varinn?" came Thrain's voice, very far away. "Seal the mating-gift between you?"

And oh, was that something they were supposed to do, maybe it was, maybe. Because Varinn's lashes fluttered, his breath exhaling—and then he slowly bent forward, and brushed his mouth to Kitty's.

It was light, soft, sweet, barely a kiss at all. But it still seemed to swarm up Kitty's spine, fizzing in her chest, sparkling behind her eyes, tingling on her lips. He'd kissed her, he'd really kissed her, and no kiss had ever felt like that, *ever*, and—and—

Then he jerked backwards, around, away, back toward the washbasin. Where he promptly plucked up his toothbrush, and began brushing his teeth. As though his gift—his kiss— was a forgettable, everyday occurrence, one that meant nothing to him at all.

And maybe Kitty would have been hurt, or insulted, if not for the feel of Thrain's fingers, tickling lightly at her back. And when she turned to look, he was smiling at her, warm and teasing, with just a twinge of that satisfaction still shimmering in his eyes.

"He likes it," he murmured, so soft. "By noon, I tell you. Och, Varinn?"

And at the basin, Varinn rolled his eyes, snatched up a hairbrush, and hurled it at Thrain's head. But Thrain was still grinning as he caught it, his eyes bright and eager on Kitty's face. Almost, for an instant, as if he really meant this, as if it wasn't just a debt, just a deal...

"You'll see, Kit," he said, his voice rich with promise, with hope. "You'll see."

28

When Kitty finally stepped out of the bedroom, with Varinn and Thrain by her side, she still felt far too flustered, and fluttery all over. Her face too hot, her breaths too short, her clammy hands clutching at her clean dressing-gown, at the still-unthinkable truth of that beautiful gold *thyrja* hidden beneath it.

It had again been too lovely, painfully lovely, getting ready for the day together. She and Thrain had also taken turns at the washbasin, and then Thrain had unravelled Varinn's long braid—which had gotten a bit mussed during the night—and brushed out his hair into long, shining black waves. The sight doing more strange, shivery things in Kitty's stomach, Varinn's head tilting back with obvious indulgence as Thrain's deft fingers parted his hair into three, and re-plaited it with rapid, familiar ease.

"Wanna pick a kilt for him too, Kit?" Thrain had asked as he'd worked, giving her a devious little wink, and Kitty had accordingly sorted through Varinn's shelf, folding Thrain's messy recent additions as she went. And when she'd shyly held out a beautifully crafted kilt, made of wide strips of hanging leather, Thrain had flashed her a wicked grin, and told her, his voice far too light, that proper Lord Grisks shouldn't have to dress themselves, either.

Again, Varinn had shown no sign of refuting this, or perhaps even of hearing it, so Kitty had again obeyed. Her cheeks burning hot as she'd unfastened Varinn's current kilt—still the one from the day before—and again revealed those hairy muscled thighs, his firm rounded arse, the chubby, half-hard heft at his groin. All of which she'd desperately fought to ignore as she fastened the new kilt on, securing the belt around his hips, and fussing with the leather strips until they fell properly over his thighs and arse, showing only tantalizing glimpses of his skin beneath.

"Very nice choice, Kit," Thrain had cheerfully said, as he'd snaked a hand around Varinn's front, slipping in between the leather strips with audacious ease, and stroking at what was beneath. "Make him extra easy for us to access."

Varinn had replied with an exasperated-sounding growl, knocking Thrain's hand away, but Thrain hadn't looked even slightly daunted, flashing Kitty another bright, devious smile. "Now for you," he'd said. "You'll like to dress as Lord Grisk's mate should, ach?"

But in that, he'd soon been disappointed, because Kitty's dismal selection of remaining clean dressing-gowns had left much to be desired. And after perusing them with increasing impatience, Thrain had cast a dark, almost accusing look toward Varinn. "Can't expect her to get by on just this," he'd said flatly. "Ymir's all but your personal lackey, why haven't you taken her to plunder his hoard—I mean, his shop—yet?"

At that, Varinn had glanced toward Kitty, a glimmer of surprising regret in his eyes. "We had meant to do this yesterday, ach, Katharine?" he'd said. "Mayhap we shall go there next, after breakfast and prayers."

Oh. Kitty's face had heated again, and though she'd stammered an incoherent thank-you, they'd both firmly waved it away, even Varinn. And once she'd put on her best remaining dressing-gown, hiding most of her lovely new *thyrja* away, they'd guided her out the door together, into the adjoining sitting-room.

At first glance, the room was mostly empty, apart from a cluster of now-familiar people at the nearest table—Thrak, Dammarr, Nattfarr, Ella, and little Rakfi. And while Ella and Rakfi were cheerfully waving toward them, Dammarr and Nattfarr both looked surprised, and Thrak's expression had gone downright disapproving, his narrow eyes flicking between Varinn and Thrain.

But then Nattfarr leapt to his feet, striding over toward them, and hooking his bulky arm around Thrain's shoulder. "Ach, it is good to see you all up and well," he said, with a genuine-seeming grin. "And it is good to see Vrangr's *thyrja* again also! A great honour, brother."

Thrain's head ducked in response to this, his pointed ear-tips gone rather pink. "Ach," he said, muffled, with a sidelong glance toward Varinn. "A great gift."

Nattfarr's brows rose again, his eyes angling toward Varinn, too. Toward where Varinn was looking decidedly stubborn, his jaw tight and set. Almost as if he expected to be challenged on this, on giving Thrain a gift like this—and yes, wait, Thrak was barking a harsh little laugh, and lurching up to stride over, too.

"So what's the game with the priceless family heirloom, then, Varinn?" Thrak asked, his voice cold. "A bribe? A payment? Rewarding my brother for finally giving you the son you've always wanted, mayhap? Or mayhap you're now floundering to keep his eyes on you, instead of his new woman? Trying to make up for not even granting him your full *scent*?"

Varinn stiffened even more, a low growl hissing in his throat—but Thrain had already snapped out a hand to Thrak's arm, his claws digging into his grey skin. "Leave it, Thrak," he said, harder than Kitty might have expected. "It was a gift. And he gave Kit one also, the one to match. His mother's."

Oh. Wait. That beautiful *thyrja*, still nestled against Kitty's skin, was an heirloom from Varinn's *mother*? And he'd given it... to *her*?

That strange fluttering had returned in her chest, especially when Thrak frowned toward her, his narrow eyes catching, holding, on the glimpse of intricate gold at her throat. "So what, are they mating-gifts, then?" he demanded. "Did you finally stoop to speak vows to my brother, Varinn?"

There was a moment's horrible, awkward silence, in which Thrain flinched, Nattfarr grimaced, and Varinn looked even more furiously forbidding than before. But no one spoke, and finally Kitty cleared her throat, and attempted her most winning smile between them.

"We just felt that Thrain's very fetching kilt just needed something a little extra, didn't we, Varinn?" she said, as lightly as she could. "The *thyrja* is such a stunning piece, and suits him so well, don't you think?"

There was another instant's silence, but then Nattfarr nodded and grinned again, giving Thrain a cheerful shake, while Thrain himself angled Kitty a warm, grateful look. And perhaps Varinn's shoulders had even sagged a little, though he was still frowning toward Thrak, his lip curling with distaste.

"And at least I have done what is called for amongst our kin, after claiming a mate," he said, his voice clipped. "I could have given them no gifts at all, ach? Even in the face of their many gifts toward me."

His gaze had dropped purposefully down toward the gleaming gold cuff on Thrak's arm—and in return, Thrak's eyes flashed with cold anger, and Thrain and Nattfarr winced in unison. Suggesting that Varinn's remark had been pointed, personal, and Nattfarr had indeed angled a brief, telling glance over toward Dammarr. Who was still sitting at the table with Ella, and looking rather pale around the mouth.

"You smug, overbearing *prick*," Thrak's hissing voice cut in, as he clutched at his gold cuff, and lurched a step closer toward Varinn. "How dare you—"

But before he could finish, he was interrupted by two young orcs, bursting into the room. They were perhaps seven or eight years old, and the first one was slim and wide-eyed, and dragging the second, plumper little orc behind him.

"Varinn!" the first orc demanded, as they rushed across the room. "Varinn, Vragi needs your help! You shall help him, ach, brother?"

Varinn's expression instantly shifted, the anger softening into genuine concern, and he promptly knelt before the young orcs. "Ach, I shall do my best, Bram," he said to the first one, before shifting his gaze toward the second. "What is amiss, Vragi?"

The plump orc—Vragi—blinked rapidly toward Varinn with wide, shimmering eyes, as a streak of wetness dropped down his round, greenish little cheek. "It's Arni," he stammered. "M-my new kitten. She's gone! What if she is lost forever?!"

But Varinn's mouth had already pulled into a warm, reassuring smile, and Kitty could see him drawing in a slow, deep breath before angling his eyes upwards, and to the left. "You might try the kitchen, little brother," he said. "I ken she might be hunting a tasty breakfast there, ach?"

Both little orcs instantly brightened, and they excitedly chattered together as they rushed back toward the door. Leaving Varinn still kneeling, the smile lingering on his mouth as he watched them go, and Kitty found herself inexplicably glancing toward Thrain. Toward where Thrain was glancing toward her, too, his eyes soft and rueful as they flicked brief but meaningful toward her belly, and then back to Varinn. Saying, oh gods, that he really wanted this, he wanted...

But no. No. It was just a debt. Just a deal. And Kitty desperately glanced away from Thrain, toward—toward where Thrak had thrown up his hands, casting a baleful glare toward Varinn. "Och, fine," he snapped, as he stalked back toward the table. "Have you three eaten yet? We have fresh pork, and eggs, and bread."

Oh. Kitty blinked uncertainly between Thrak and Varinn, but Varinn was already rising to his feet, and nudging her toward the table. Toward where Thrak had dropped his lean body down to sit close beside a still-pale Dammarr, elbowing him purposefully in the ribs, while Ella flashed Kitty a bright smile, and waved her over toward the nearest empty bench.

"Yes, come, eat," Ella said cheerfully, "and ignore all their bickering, for it's just how they tell each other they care. Right, brothers?"

This was greeted by a round of groans and sighs, but no one actually argued her point, and Nattfarr chuckled as he settled back down beside Ella, and circled his arm around her. "Ach, my lass," he murmured into her hair. "You only grow wiser and sweeter with each passing day, ach?"

Across from him, both Thrak and Dammarr made loud gagging noises, and even Thrain made a face as he drew Kitty down to the bench between him and Varinn. "Breakfast, then," he said. "So what's the clan's news today, Speaker?"

Varinn had already pulled the tray of breakfast closer, plunking a loaf of bread into Kitty's hands, while Nattfarr began speaking, answering Thrain's question in surprisingly comprehensive detail. First discussing an outbreak of flu in a nearby camp, and then a delay installing lamps in the southwest Grisk wing, and an incoming shipment of goods from the north. And then a rumour of a woman pregnant with a Grisk son to the west, an injured orc to the east, and an elderly Grisk orc to the south who had been asking after Varinn all week.

"Dammarr and Thrak went to see him yesterday," Nattfarr was saying, with a regretful glance toward Varinn, "but he would not even allow them inside. I ken you shall wish to spend a few more days here with your new mate, brother, but mayhap later this week, if you should not mind—"

But he abruptly stopped there, angling a tolerant look up toward the door, because another orc was stalking into the room. It was one of the orcs Kitty had met the day before—Valter, Eyarl's mate, who worked as a Grisk scout—and his keen eyes settled with visible relief on Varinn as he swiftly strode toward him.

"I need a scent placed, son," he said, thrusting out what appeared to be a broken, rotten stick of wood. "Should be quick."

Varinn was already nodding, standing up to take the stick, and drawing it to his nose. Again inhaling, slow and deep, as his brow furrowed, his head tilting. "It is Grisk," he said, "but not an orc I have met. Young, between ten and fifteen summers. From the west, by the sea. South of Osada, I ken."

Valter nodded, and clasped Varinn firmly on the shoulder before snatching back his stick, and striding from the room. Leaving Kitty blinking with undeniable awe toward Varinn, because—had he really been able to tell all that from smelling an old stick?

But if any of the others seemed surprised, they weren't showing it, and Thrain was half-smiling toward Kitty, a knowing warmth glimmering in his eyes. "Told you Varinn's got a brilliant nose," he said. "You'll need to get used to him being interrupted a dozen times a day, whilst he also runs himself ragged all over the province, sniffing out all our clan's messes to clean up, and visiting ancient orcs who refuse to see anyone else. He's far too good-hearted to tell them all to leave him the hell alone for once."

But on Kitty's other side, Varinn was visibly bristling, frowning toward Thrain with palpable disapproval. "This is what we are meant to do, as our Speaker's Guard," he said firmly. "We are called to serve the Grisk, and uphold our clan as best we can. We are happy to help our kin, and support them, whenever or wherever we are needed. Whether in matters great, or small."

No one argued this—Nattfarr was gravely nodding, arching his brows toward Thrain—and Thrain was already raising his hands in mock apology, still smiling at Varinn, looking entirely undaunted. "Ach, ach, I ken," he said, with a roll of his eyes. "I bow to your superior wisdom, Lord Grisk."

But at that, all the orcs' heads—plus Ella's—swivelled toward Varinn, and then back toward Thrain. Because of that *Lord Grisk* mention again, oh gods. And Kitty could feel Varinn stiffening beside her, that redness again creeping up his neck—while Thrain just kept smiling, and then shrugging as he swiped a hunk of meat off the tray, and tossed it into his mouth.

"What?" he said lightly. "Suits him, doesn't it? Most of all with how he tends to us all, just as his forebear did."

Nattfarr's brows were still high on his forehead, and across the table Thrak snorted, wrinkling his nose with obvious distaste. "Ach, and didn't Lord Grisk collect all his fallen brothers' women, after that war?" he demanded at Thrain. "Took them all to his bed, fattened them on his seed, and then claimed their sons as his own?"

He shot a dark, pointed glance toward Varinn, who was already glowering back—but wait, Varinn wasn't denying this rather scandalous version of events around Lord Grisk, either. And suddenly there was the vision of it, blooming far too strong in Kitty's thoughts. Varinn sending her away after their deal was done, so he could *feed* other women, take them to his bed, raise *their* sons instead? And no, no, no, surely he wouldn't, he could *not*—

Varinn was darting her a strange, startled look, while on his other side Thrain laughed again, and reached over to clasp at Kitty's knee, giving it a reassuring little shake. "No need to worry, Kit," he said. "I ken our Varinn's got his hands full with the two of us already, ach?"

Wait. Wait, Thrain meant that they'd all just somehow *smelled* her reaction to that, oh gods—and Kitty's cheeks were flooding with heat, her eyes chagrined on Varinn's face. But he didn't actually look angry, did he? Or even... displeased?

"Ach, this is truth," he told her, with a wry, almost-sincere smile. "Even Lord Grisk himself could scarce handle Thrain alone, I ken."

At that, Thrain loudly scoffed, and punched Varinn in the shoulder—and to Kitty's genuine surprise, Varinn chuckled, and punched Thrain back. And in a flurry of sudden movement, Thrain bodily lunged at Varinn, and tackled him to the fur-covered floor beside the bench. Where they rolled around together, kicking and elbowing at each other, their laughs and yelps ringing through the room.

Kitty couldn't help a relieved laugh too, and more of that fluttery warmth rippled through her chest as she watched. The two of them so obviously in accord, their shared glee lighting up their faces, crinkling the corners of their eyes. And oh, the sound of Varinn's laugh, rich and velvety and deep, as he finally pinned Thrain beneath him, one big hand slamming Thrain's wrists to the floor above his head, the other hand clamped firm and familiar against his neck.

"Got you, you vexing *krútt*," he hissed, his tone not at all matching the glimmering warmth in his eyes. "Too easy. Again."

Thrain's grin back at Varinn's face was just as warm, alight with bright, eager affection. "Ach, you have me, Lord Grisk," he purred. "Now what'll you do with me next?"

Varinn's nostrils flared, his lashes fluttering, his chest slowly filling with his breath. And for an instant, Kitty's own breath was caught, her heartbeat skipping with a strange, heated anticipation. Needing to see this, to know what Varinn would do next, if he would...

"I did *not* miss this," announced Thrak across the table, as he hurled a piece of bread at Thrain's head. "There's an orcling present, you arseholes."

Varinn froze, glancing up over his shoulder toward where

little Rakfi was indeed watching them with keen, bright-eyed interest. Prompting Varinn to lurch hurriedly to his feet, intently smoothing out his kilt, while Thrain cast Thrak a decidedly incredulous look, and threw the bread back toward him.

"As if you're any better!" he exclaimed. "Maybe if you'd thought to get Dammarr a mating-gift, he'd be jumping you over breakfast, too."

Thrak's eyes flashed again, but Varinn had hurriedly cleared his throat, and reached to pull Kitty to her feet. "Ach, we are due for prayers, I ken," he said loudly. "Come along, both of you."

Neither Kitty nor Thrain argued this, following Varinn over toward the shrine. But once they'd reached the door, Thrain hesitated just outside it, angling an uneasy look toward the row of carved figures inside.

"Look, why don't you two go ahead," he said, "whilst I go cool down a bit. Meet you in the hoard—I mean, shop?"

Kitty couldn't quite read the look on Varinn's face, or the sudden stillness on his form—at least, until Thrain sighed, and gave a purposeful wave down toward his kilt, which was sporting a distinctive bulge in front. "Not going off to—*misbehave*, Varinn, I swear," he murmured. "Just—really need to deal with this, if I'm going to function this morning. Unless you wanna take pity on me, after all?"

Kitty could see Varinn's shoulders abruptly relaxing, the warmth returning to his eyes. "No," he said coolly, even as he reached a hand, and absently straightened out Thrain's new *thyrja* against his chest. "Not yet."

It was no doubt another one of those ultimatums, but it sounded almost like a tease, or even a promise. And Thrain's answering grin was broad and bright and stunning, and he even gave a firm, proprietary little pat against Varinn's own distinctive bulge before turning around, and striding jauntily away.

Varinn watched him go, his expression both exasperated and fond, his gaze lingering on Thrain's arse. Until he seemed to remember Kitty beside him, and he angled her a furtive, almost guilty look as he waved her toward the shrine.

"You do not... mind, ach?" he said, once they were alone inside the cozy, sweet-scented room. "If I might... keep taking pleasure, thus, with Thrain? I only..."

He cast Kitty another helpless, guilty grimace, almost as if he thought he needed to keep denying Thrain such things, denying himself such things, until Thrain proved his worth. Until Thrain proved he could keep all those damned ultimatums, perhaps. And Kitty was already shaking her head, and even slipping her hand into Varinn's arm, guiding him over toward the carving of Lord Grisk. Who, despite all those shocking new revelations, looked even kinder, more welcoming, than before. His mouth gently smiling, his eyes crinkling, his bulky arms outstretched with such warm, generous ease.

"Of course I don't mind," she told Varinn, as firmly as she could. "It's something that connects you, something you both obviously enjoy, and Efterar said pleasure might help too, didn't he? And"—she drew in breath, settled to her knees before Lord Grisk—"you've already made it very clear that you won't be intimate with him when he's drinking, right? So whyever would you deny it when he's sober, too? When he's obviously trying so hard to make an effort on this?"

She could hear Varinn's heavy exhale, the swallow in his throat—and then he nodded, and even gave her a brief little smile, as he dropped to kneel beside her on the fur. His head bowing toward Lord Grisk, his braid falling over his shoulder, his hand in a fist over his heart. His elbow just nudging hers as his chest rose and fell, the words already forming silent but fervent on his lips.

Oh. Well. So Kitty prayed too, kneeling there beside Varinn, before his own ancestor, while feeling that light brush of his arm, the truth of his lovely *thyrja* against her skin. Feeling almost right, somehow, almost safe, and she felt her breaths coming slower, her heartbeat settling in her chest. While the silent prayers rose, quiet and heartfelt, shimmering with too much gratitude, too much longing. *Ach, Varinn. You be a good Grisk lord. Make her yours...*

She didn't know how long they stayed there, but when Varinn nudged her upwards, it felt easy, too easy, to oblige, to smile at his own softened eyes. And then to accompany him out into the corridor, where he not only greeted every orc they passed, but regularly paused to make more introductions, as well. And when a tiny ball of black fluff suddenly sped down the corridor toward them, Varinn lunged to catch it in his big hand, ignoring its affronted little mewls as he promptly returned it to a grateful, wide-eyed Vragi, who had frantically rushed out of a nearby door.

"Kittens," Varinn said lightly, as he watched Vragi happily scamper down the corridor again, his kitten clutched to his chest. "Naught but trouble, ach?"

He'd angled Kitty a sheepish, meaningful look—because wait, he was *teasing* her?—and she couldn't help her bright, merry laugh as she elbowed him in the side. "Kittens are a *delight*," she informed him. "They're sweet, and soft, and they purr when you pet them..."

"Ach, mayhap," Varinn said, with another wry half-grin toward her. "But they also need endless watching. And tending. And feeding."

Kitty scoffed with mock disbelief, and tossed her hair over her shoulder. "Many kittens are *very* well-behaved," she replied archly. "And it's not their fault if the milk their lords are offering is so damned delicious, is it?"

She waggled her brows toward Varinn's face, the playful grin still curving on her mouth, and she didn't miss the slight flare of his nostrils, or the clench of his hand on her back. The way he didn't look angry, or annoyed, but maybe—maybe even hungry? Approving?

But then his gaze purposefully angled away, and his hand nudged her toward—oh. A new door. One that led into a large, unfamiliar, lamplit room, fronted by a long counter, with rows and rows of shelves beyond. And standing behind the counter, eyeing them with expectant, irritated impatience, was Ymir.

"There you are, son," he said, without preamble. "It's about time you finally brought your new mate to the Great Grisk Showroom-Shop! The grandest room in all the realm!"

Varinn was looking both pained and amused, and Kitty's merry laugh had already escaped her mouth, her hand giving an audacious little squeeze to Varinn's arm. "I've been so eager to see it," she told Ymir, as she cast a brief glance toward the rest of the large, sprawling room behind him. "It already looks so intriguing! What kinds of goods do you sell here?"

Ymir's chest puffed out even more, and he rapidly waved his hand, beckoning Kitty and Varinn behind the counter. "Come, come, and be amazed," he said firmly. "I shall show you it all!"

Kitty only barely heard Varinn's sigh of resignation beside her, but she flashed him her most winning smile, and gave another squeeze to his arm. And then, without waiting for him to follow, she willingly trotted after Ymir behind the counter, and soon embarked upon a grand tour of the Great Grisk Showroom-Shop.

And to her ever-increasing delight, it was utterly *marvellous*. With multiple rows of long, fully stocked shelves, all bursting with an impossible variety of goods. Tools and weapons, barrels and basins, cooking-pots and pans, lamps and tents and tarps and supplies. And then furs, and textiles, and—Kitty's breath caught—clothes. A truly staggering quantity of clothes, stacked neatly on shelves, hanging in racks, packed into open chests and trunks. More clothes than she'd ever seen in any shop, even back in the city—and she felt herself slowly spinning in place, her mouth fallen open, her hands clasped tightly to her chest.

"It's wonderful, Ymir," she said, breathless. "I've never seen anything like it in my *life*. Truly the grandest room in all the realm."

Ymir replied with a deep, satisfied-sounding grunt, while beside Kitty, Varinn's expression was again reluctantly amused, or maybe even tolerant. "I ken Katharine is as fond of finery as you are, Ymir," he said lightly. "Such a greedy little kitten, ach?"

And wait, he was teasing her again, and Kitty gave another incredulous peal of laughter, and a poke of her elbow into his side. "You're the one who brought me here!" she exclaimed. "You should know better than to bring your hungry kitten into such a stimulating environment!"

And oh, the way he chuckled, the sound low and warm, his eyes crinkling at the corners. "Ach, naught but trouble," he said, with an exaggerated sigh. "Could you grant us a moment alone, Ymir?"

Kitty's heart skipped in her chest, her eyes widening, because yes, yes, Ymir was giving a knowing little smirk, and striding away up the aisle. While Varinn's brows rose toward Kitty, his nostrils again flaring, as his eyes shifted, and angled downwards. Toward... his kilt.

And when Kitty followed his eyes—oh, gods—she could glimpse something new, peeking out between those thick leather strips. Something long, green, hungry, now parting the strips around it, brazenly swelling up and out toward her. The sight so suddenly, sharply compelling that she whimpered aloud, biting her lip—and then darted a brief, wide-eyed glance at the shop around them. Which seemed otherwise empty, thank the gods, because Varinn was still watching her, still with that cool, amused command flickering in his eyes.

"Soothe yourself, then, kitten," he said, his voice very low. "Sate your hunger, and suckle your sweet milk. Ach?"

Oh, *hell.* Kitty's breath choked in her throat, the heat

pooling hard and furious in her belly, as her shocked eyes searched Varinn's face, the creeping red up the back of his neck. But he wasn't taking it back, oh gods he could not, *not*, take it back—and before Kitty could speak, breathe, think, she'd jerked a fervent nod, and dropped to her knees on the hard floor before him.

She only distantly heard his gasp, or saw the long, sustained shudder of that jutting green heft, because oh, oh, it was already here, prodding thick and firm against her lips, pushing into her mouth. And Kitty moaned aloud as she sucked it in, as she gained her first taste of that decadent sweetness, oh gods, oh, *gods*.

She moaned again as it sputtered thicker, as he swelled larger, stretching her lips around him—but when her blinking, pleading eyes glanced upwards, she found him... looking away. Away, toward the shelf before him, as he casually picked up a folded piece of clothing, and brought it to his nose. His eyes closing as he inhaled, his chest slowly filling—and then a slight shake of his head as he set it back on the shelf, and picked up another.

Wait. He was... *shopping*?!

Kitty's moan sounded even louder this time, with a distinct edge of indignation in it, but if Varinn noticed, he didn't acknowledge it. Only inhaling the next item he'd picked up, and then frowning, and setting it back again. Even as his hips canted a little forward, nudged his swollen, leaking length deeper into Kitty's throat.

Kitty moaned again, hoarse and shameful, and felt that hardness in her mouth shudder even fuller—but Varinn still wasn't looking, wasn't betraying the slightest hint that he'd even noticed her efforts. Not even when she wriggled her tongue against that smooth slit, seeking deep inside—or when her hungry hands slipped up to touch him, stroking and caressing just the way he liked. And gods, it only seemed to whip her desperate craving up higher, harder, because despite everything else he'd wanted this, he still wanted this, he had to, he *had* to...

And before she could stop it—before she'd even followed it—she let her teeth scrape against him. Not hard, no, but enough that he surely felt it—and yes, yes, he was glancing down, the displeasure flaring in his eyes. And in a flash of movement, his hand snapped down into her hair, gently gripping it, and yanking her backwards, off him entirely. Leaving his slick green length to bob and dangle before her, dripping a thick strand of white toward the floor.

"No, *kisa*," he said, the strange word sounding both harsh and soft on his mouth. "Behave, whilst I tend to you. If you please me, then, mayhap, I shall pay heed to you."

Oh, hell. Kitty whimpered again, even as she rapidly nodded, her eyes wide and chagrined on his. But he didn't let go, his brows rising, his rigid length still poised and leaking before her face. Wanting more, wanting this, oh...

So she swallowed hard, drew in a breath, licked her slick, swollen lips. "Forgive me, sir," she croaked. "May I try again? Please, Lord Grisk?"

And yes, yes, that was satisfaction, triumph, *craving*, glittering in his heated eyes, as he shrugged, and released his grip on her hair. And as Kitty first gratefully kissed him, and then swallowed him deep, he again returned to his perusing, so careless and indifferent, as if she weren't there at all...

But he liked it, he had to like it, and maybe—surely—this was just... something else he needed. Part of him taking that control back, by lording his easy power over her, and perhaps over Thrain, too. By granting her his seed and his favour, his generosity and his justice, while she sucked and begged on her knees, fighting for his attention and his sustenance and his praise...

"Och," said a thick, familiar, choked-sounding voice, and when Kitty's wide eyes darted to look, it was—oh. Thrain. Standing there looking dazed and stunned in the aisle, his body still, his mouth fallen half-open. "Didn't even make it to noon, ach?"

There was a very slight edge on his voice, a glinting look in his eyes that might have been jealousy. But above Kitty, Varinn only gave another dismissive shrug, and picked up another garment, sniffed it, and set it back again.

"She needed more feeding," he said, as he picked up another one. "I only seek to serve, ach?"

Thrain's eyes shifted again, his throat visibly bobbing—but then he strode the rest of the way toward them, his steps jerky and quick. "Such a martyr, Varinn," he snapped, a little hoarse, as he snatched the clothing out of Varinn's hand. "Give me that. And pay some heed to the sweet little kitten on her knees for you, ach?"

And oh, the way Varinn's mouth twitched, his eyes almost warm, amused, as they caught on Kitty's face. And perhaps she was even smiling too, rolling her eyes at him—and earning in return another firm grip of his hand to her hair, a gentle, warning little shake.

But then his eyes fluttered, his head tilting a little back, because wait, Thrain had eased up close behind him, his head bending into the crook of Varinn's neck, his big hands slipping around his front with swift, possessive familiarity. And Varinn wasn't even resisting, not even when Thrain tweaked at his nipple, and nibbled at his shoulder. Because maybe—maybe this was part of it for Varinn, too. Both of them serving him, wanting him, tending to him at once.

And yes, yes, that was a contented little growl in Varinn's throat, his eyes slipping closed, his head tilting further back toward Thrain. As a distinct satisfaction glinted in Thrain's eyes, glancing down toward Kitty over Varinn's shoulder, his tongue brushing his lips...

"Tastes so good, Kit, doesn't he?" he murmured. "You keep sucking him, ach? Keep showing your lord how sweet you are, how well you behave. How much he's gonna enjoy having two worshippers on hand to serve him, whenever he damn well feels like it."

Kitty betrayed another hoarse moan, her mouth sucking Varinn even deeper, and she was distantly surprised to see his eyes blinking open, and angling a tolerant glance toward Thrain over his shoulder. "Two wayward fosterlings to care for, you ken," he murmured, but there was no malice in his voice. "And to keep safe, and well fed."

Thrain huffed a loud, disgruntled scoff, even as he kept plucking at Varinn's nipple, the other hand stroking wide over his hard abdomen. "Don't see you feeding me here, do we?" he said lightly, with another nibble at Varinn's throat. "What am I supposed to do, starve? What kind of good Lord Grisk would allow that?"

Varinn's eyes were still warm, indulgent, his hand still resting easy on Kitty's hair as she sucked him in and out. "I cannot spare seed for you," he said mildly. "Not when I have an extra mouth to feed. You shall need to find aught else."

That might have been more jealousy, flaring in Thrain's eyes, but it was gone just as quickly, replaced by an impish, devious warmth. "Ach, I follow," he replied, as his hands slid back around Varinn's hips, toward his arse. "You won't begrudge me this, then, will you?"

And *this*, oh hell, was Thrain dropping to his knees, too. Dropping down behind Varinn, just like how Kitty was kneeling in front of him, good gods. And though she couldn't at all see what Thrain was doing, she could hear Varinn's sudden, sharp intake of breath, could feel his entire body jolting to shocked, perfect stillness. His head thrown back, his eyes squeezed shut, his hand clenching tight on Kitty's hair. And even his heft in her mouth had stilled, rigid and straining, even harder than before...

Behind Varinn, Thrain's laugh was muffled, triumphant—and then Kitty could hear the sounds of his ministrations, slick and sloppy and obscene. Because he was kissing Varinn, licking him, using that long black tongue, perhaps even—even slipping it *inside* him. While Varinn gasped and startled again, his hips plunging forward, gouging himself deeper into Kitty's throat.

"You like that, Lord Grisk?" came Thrain's heated, drawling voice, still tantalizingly muffled between Varinn's arse-cheeks. "Like having your two worshippers on their knees for you at once, with both their hungry tongues seeking inside you?"

Varinn's gasp sounded choked this time, helpless, because yes, yes, Kitty was seeking her tongue into his slick pulsing heat again, while Thrain surely did the same behind him. And oh, Varinn's hips were moving steadily now, rocking back and forth, as if desperately needing to impale himself on each of their tongues in turn. While Thrain's hands gripped his hips, guiding him faster, and Kitty could hear him laughing again, the sound even slicker and filthier than before.

"Ach, that's it," Thrain's breathless voice said. "You show us who's in charge. Show us your great Grisk kindness, by using both our mouths at once. Letting us both eat you, feast on you, *worship* you—"

His words choked into a moan, into the sounds of more slick sloppiness, and oh, the look on Varinn's face, the sheer stunned ecstasy, his head upturned, eyes closed, lips parted. His heft now slamming in and out of Kitty's mouth, gouging deep into her throat, and she needed it, craved it, ached for it, please, please, please—

The sweetness sprayed out in sharp, sustained pulses, surging out again and again, pouring down Kitty's throat. And she moaned as she sucked it back, urgent and frantic, seeking out every last drop, while behind Varinn, Thrain was moaning too. The slick slurps now sounding choked, helpless, and Kitty could see his hands trembling as they kept clutching Varinn's hips, his knuckles pale, his claws digging in deep.

"Ach," Varinn finally breathed, or groaned, almost like a prayer, and his hand gently patted Kitty's hot face as he drew his softened length out, all the way—and then he turned around, toward a kneeling, sweaty, red-faced Thrain. And when Varinn slid his hand into Thrain's messy hair, tilting his head back, Thrain didn't resist. Only blinked up at Varinn with hazy, worshipful eyes as Varinn leaned forward, and fed his soft, glistening heft between Thrain's slack, parted lips.

Thrain's moan was instant, harsh, desperate, as he urgently sucked Varinn deep, his eyes rolling back—and oh, hell, that was his own white mess, streaming down from beneath his kilt, spattering across Varinn's feet. Painting them with his pleasure, with his gratitude, his worship, while Varinn just stood there, tall and silent, and accepted it. Accepted it as his rightful due, his offering.

And perhaps... perhaps this, again, was justice. Or even kindness, with the way Varinn's hand was gently carding through Thrain's messy hair, standing it all on end, while Thrain's eyes fluttered closed, his head leaning heavily into Varinn's touch. As the stream from beneath his kilt gradually slowed to a drizzle, pooling on the stone floor between his knees, until it finally stopped.

It was only then that Varinn drew away, tugging his half-hard length out from between Thrain's swollen lips, and reaching behind him for a tunic. One of the ones he'd clearly put in his reject pile, and he handed it toward Thrain without a word. Watching impassively as Thrain nodded, wiping shakily at his own face, before meekly beginning to mop up the mess at Varinn's feet.

Kitty couldn't seem to look away from it, from the strange hitching longing in it—and maybe Thrain had felt that, glancing over toward her. Toward where she was still kneeling, too, both of them still on the floor before their lord. And Thrain twitched her a crooked, knowing little smile, and then licked his black tongue at his lips.

"Tyrant, right?" he said, even as he angled a warm glance

upwards, his head tilting against Varinn's still-petting hand. "Can't help himself."

Varinn gave a creditable huff of irritation, though his own cheeks were distinctly flushed, his swallow convulsing in his throat. "I had *naught* to do with this," he replied, his voice husky, so smooth. "You are the one who cannot fetter your hunger, or keep from soiling yourself at your lord's feet."

Thrain's crack of laughter was bright, incredulous, amused—and his grin toward Kitty was just as warm, his hand reaching to clasp hers as he rose to his feet, drawing her up after him. "What he means to say, Kit," he murmured, "is that he liked it. Ach, Varinn?"

Varinn clearly wasn't deigning to answer that, even when Thrain lowered his head to his shoulder, and gave a light little nip against his skin. "Thanks, Lord Grisk," he said. "We liked it, too. Mayhap you'll let us do it again sometime?"

Varinn's shoulders rose and fell beneath Thrain's mouth, his throat convulsing—but then he nodded, curt and short. And Kitty could see the relief in Thrain's eyes, and maybe even a sudden brightness, before he rapidly blinked it away.

"And thank you, Kit," he continued, glancing toward her. "We make a good team, ach? Work him over 'till he relents."

Oh. His voice was light, but his eyes were still a little too bright, too intent. And for a brief, dangling instant, as Kitty held his gaze, it almost felt as though Thrain could see inside her, down into her deepest, darkest thoughts. Into all her memories, all her secrets, all this tangled mess between them. As though he could see it all, and he still wanted it all, wanted her and Varinn both. Just... just the way she wanted them both, too...

But no. No. It was just a debt. Just a deal. Just until Thrain was well again. And that was what Kitty wanted too... right? She needed to learn from Charles, from almost dying, needed to keep her distance and not get attached. Needed to ignore how Varinn was still just standing there looking at her, flushed and dazed, while Thrain gave a low, husky laugh, his arms slipping tighter around Varinn's waist.

"And now, Kit," Thrain murmured, his eyes warm and impossibly tempting on hers. "Come, and let us dress you, and show you as Lord Grisk's true mate."

29

Kitty spent the rest of the morning in a haze of clothes, furs, and sheer, sweeping happiness.

"You can't mean—I can have anything I want?" she'd asked Varinn and Thrain at first, her voice breathless with disbelief. "But what about the cost? I don't have any coin. Or anything else to offer in return."

But Varinn and Thrain both waved it away, and Thrain grinned fondly at Varinn, and slung his long arm around his neck. "You're Varinn's mate now, Kit," he said cheerfully. "And even if he wasn't so damn responsible, and didn't have likely the largest credit-account in the whole clan, Ymir would probably still hand over whatever the hell he wants, ach?"

Varinn rolled his eyes at this, but then grimaced, glancing darkly toward the mountain of clothes around them. "But I should not yet wish to gain *all* of this," he said flatly. "And there are many scents I could not bear to smell all day long. If"—he grimaced at Kitty this time—"you should be willing to take this into account."

But he was offering to buy her an entire damned wardrobe, and Kitty was already nodding, and grinning delightedly back toward him. "Of course, Lord Grisk," she said firmly. "I would never want to impact you unnecessarily. Perhaps you could choose your preferred items by scent first, and we can go from there?"

An unmistakable surprise flashed in Varinn's eyes, followed by a twinge of genuine-seeming appreciation. And beside him, Thrain laughed, reaching for a neat stack of clothes on the nearest shelf. "He's already begun, you ken," he said. "Sorting scents while you're getting your prick sucked, Varinn, *really*."

That telltale red was creeping up Varinn's neck, but he didn't argue, and Thrain laughed again, thrusting the stack of clothes toward Kitty. "Any in there you like, Kit?" he said. "If so, mayhap you'll try them on for us?"

He waggled his brows toward her, and Kitty felt her own face heating as she began to sort through the stack. It held a few human-made garments—a dress, a shift, a large tunic—but the bulk of Varinn's choices were obviously orcish in style and provenance. Furs, kilts, capes, leather bands and belts, and several items that Kitty couldn't even begin to identify.

"Och, that's meant to wrap around you, I ken," Thrain said cheerfully, as Kitty frowned at a narrow rectangle of thin red silk. "Here, lose this, and I'll show you."

This was Kitty's dressing-gown, already sliding downwards under the purposeful tug of Thrain's hand. And Kitty's uncertain glance toward Varinn found him dispassionately watching this, as if waiting, or even approving—so she nodded, and carefully shrugged off the dressing-gown. Leaving her standing there fully undressed, but for Varinn's beautiful gold *thyrja*, which suddenly felt far too heavy, too present, against her prickling skin.

But Varinn's eyes were still looking, lingering, sweeping up, down, up again. As if he truly did approve of this, of seeing her like this—and maybe of seeing Thrain touch her like this, too. Gently lifting up the *thyrja*'s chains so he could slip the strip of red silk beneath, settling it snugly against Kitty's bare breasts. And then he pulled the ends around her back, tying them closed, so that her breasts were concealed, while the rest of her—including the small swell of her belly—remained very, very exposed.

"We Grisk know you humans don't always like to show everything off," Thrain was blithely saying, as he plucked a leather kilt from Varinn's approved stack, and slung it around Kitty's hips. "So we aim to please, ach?"

Kitty couldn't help a choked, flustered laugh, because even with the kilt—which barely reached her mid-thigh—she was still exposing shocking amounts of skin, even more than Ella or Alma's daring ensembles had shown. But oh, the way Varinn was still looking at her, his eyes half-lidded, his head jerking a curt, decisive little nod.

"Ach, we shall take this," he told Thrain, his voice firm—but then he winced, and cast an apologetic glance at Kitty's face. "Should you wish, Katharine."

But there was suddenly no thought of refusing, not with that look in Varinn's eyes, not with that longing clutching in Kitty's chest. "Of course, Lord Grisk," she replied, smiling shyly toward him. "We willingly bow to you, and your excellent taste."

The surprise flared again in Varinn's eyes, followed by more unmistakable warmth, and Thrain laughed again as he unfastened Kitty's kilt, and reached for the next item in the pile. "You're a quick learner, Kit," he said lightly. "Mayhap next you'll ask him to pick out a piercing for his sweet new kitten. Or a pretty Ka-esh *kraga*, to go around your sweet little neck?"

His voice was teasing, but his eyes glancing toward Varinn were a little too hungry, or maybe even envious. And Varinn had clearly caught that too, his jaw tightening in his cheek— and Kitty found her head rapidly shaking, her hand briefly reaching to squeeze Thrain's arm. "Oh, no, I won't," she said cheerfully, "because those piercings are *all* yours, Thrain.

Dozens of them, right, Lord Grisk? Wherever you might enjoy stabbing them most."

She didn't miss Thrain's breath hitching, or the eagerness glinting in his eyes. And oh, maybe it was there in Varinn's eyes too, flaring in his nostrils, in his tongue brushing against his lips. "Mayhap," he said coolly. "If he behaves."

Thrain half-laughed, half-groaned, and muttered a curse under his breath—but it had seemed to dispel the lingering tension, replacing it with bright, cheerful anticipation. Making it easy to laugh and joke and tease each other as they excitedly dug through piles together, as Thrain helped Kitty try on outfit after outfit, each one more unconventional than the last. Leather kilts and belts and loincloths, fur wraps and capes and cloaks, fluttery silks and fine fabrics.

And if Varinn seemed to tend toward more orcish—and even more revealing—choices as they went on, Kitty found that she couldn't quite care. He did have good taste, with an excellent eye for quality craftsmanship, and there was something strangely gratifying in the way he kept looking at her, alternately assessing and approving, while Thrain fixed and fussed and adjusted the unfamiliar clothes around her, and then gleefully threw more items on the pile.

"Why don't you try on a few things, too?" Kitty asked Thrain, once her stack of approved items had grown to truly shocking proportions. "I'd love to see the orc equivalents of some of these, and get a better sense of the styles?"

Luckily, neither Thrain nor Varinn seemed opposed to this suggestion, and soon Kitty was the one adjusting the clothes on Thrain, and merrily laughing as he modelled them for her and Varinn. Not only strutting brazenly up and down the aisles, but also striking utterly shameless, ridiculous poses that showed off his lean, beautiful body to both stunning and comical effect.

"What do you think of this one, Varinn?" he crooned, as he spun in a backless loincloth, wiggling his fully bared arse toward Varinn. "Giving you any ideas?"

Varinn's eyes were warm, his mouth quirking up—and without warning, his hand snapped out, striking against Thrain's bare arse with a firm, ringing slap. To which Thrain yelped and jumped, lurching away—but then something shifted in his expression, turning it sly and hungry. And then he sauntered back toward Varinn again, reaching a hand between the strips of Varinn's kilt, and giving an audacious little squeeze.

"Ach, I smell you," he murmured. "Will you buy it for me, Lord Grisk? Have me wear it for you? Show off to you what's yours?"

Varinn's nostrils were flaring again, a low growl rumbling through his chest, and Thrain's lashes fluttered as he leaned in closer, pressed the full length of his lean body up against Varinn's shorter, bulkier form. "Ach, Varinn?" he breathed. "You wanna dress me? Make me?"

For an instant, there was only taut, breathless silence, and then the sight of Varinn's hand moving. Slipping over to spread wide against Thrain's bare arse, yanking him closer—

Until there was a loud cough, from the end of the aisle. And when Kitty whipped around to look, it was Ymir, his arms folded over his chest, his head jerking toward the corridor.

"Sorry to hinder you, but young'uns on the way," he said flatly. "For you, son, I ken."

He was talking to Varinn, surely, because Varinn had already jerked away from Thrain, one hand rubbing hard at his nose, the other yanking down his kilt. "Ach," he said, with a grimace. "I swore to Timo that I would take him hunting this afternoon, for I have spurned him all this past week. But mayhap I ought—"

He grimaced again, angling a regretful look toward Kitty and Thrain both, but Kitty was already waving it away, and found Thrain doing the same beside her. "Ach, go, Varinn," Thrain said. "I ken it'll do you good, ach? Kit and I'll finish up here, and then I'll take her to the sickroom for a spell. Healer's orders, for us both, remember? And then mayhap I can show her around the mountain a bit more, too."

Varinn's eyes were still uneasy, but after another glance over his shoulder toward Ymir, he nodded, and turned to go. And then paused as he looked back, and reached to give a purposeful little tug at Thrain's loincloth. "Buy this," he said. "And *behave*."

That was clearly meant for Kitty, too, his eyes briefly catching on hers, before he spun and strode away. Leaving both Kitty and Thrain standing there behind him, Thrain still with an unmistakable tent at the front of his loincloth.

"Och," he said, with a sheepish glance toward Kitty, as he pulled awkwardly at the loincloth. "Sorry, Kit. Don't mean to keep elbowing in on your fun. And your mate."

His eyes had sobered, shifting into something like real regret, and Kitty waved it away, and gave him a sincere smile. "It's fine, truly," she said. "This was so much fun. For him too, I think."

Thrain's grin back was wry and warm, and he reached for his own previously discarded kilt. "Ach, I wish you coulda scented him," he said lightly, as he snapped on the kilt, and then tossed his new loincloth on the pile. "Had no conception playing dress-up would fire him up so much. Woulda offered to dress for him *years* ago, if he'd ever given me a single damned hint."

Kitty was still smiling, even as she considered that point, and Thrain huffed a curt, too-loud laugh. "Never had even a whiff of his Lord Grisk fix, either," he said, with an unmistakable twinge of bitterness in his voice. "I mean, always knew he felt a kinship with that randy old galoot, but for him to up and—"

He stopped there, wincing, rubbing at his eyes. "What I mean is, clever of you to hit on it, Kit," he said, too quickly, his voice too bright. "It's plain it really does it for him, ach? Feeds right into that control fix he has, too. Shoulda thought of it myself."

But Kitty could feel her smile fading, and she shook her head, as rapidly as she could. "Look, Varinn certainly didn't tell me that on purpose," she said. "That whole Lord Grisk situation only came about because he refused to give me his own name. Because he was so—"

But wait, wait, she was not supposed to be betraying any of that—though maybe Thrain had already caught it, his eyes shifting with something she couldn't quite read. But then he glanced away, and his throat bobbed, a sad little smile twisting on his mouth.

"Ach, but mayhap that's part of the control fix also, you ken?" he said, quiet. "Keeping from you what you most wish for. I've oft wondered if that's why he refused to speak vows to me, or grant me his seed. The vows I could bear, I ken, but being denied his full scent, too, again and again, after so damned long—"

Oh. Kitty blinked at him, and her thoughts flicked backwards, to how Thrak—and Kesst—had both brought up the scent, too. "What... do you mean?" she asked uncertainly. "You and Varinn have been... intimate. For years. Right?"

But that was another bitter laugh from Thrain, a jerky shrug of his shoulder. "Ach, we have, but it's yet the seed that binds the scent deepest, remember?" he said. "Most of all if it's put... *inside* you. Not just down your throat, but an actual good old fucking, all the way. No pulling out, no spilling the seed elsewhere. And I know I talk a good game about it, because I know Varinn likes it, and he likes fucking me, too, but"—his voice cracked—"he hasn't actually spilled his seed like that, inside me. Not ever. Not one piddly little load."

Kitty was still blinking at that, and Thrain laughed again, not a laugh at all. "We Grisk oft don't," he continued woodenly, "most of all if we're fooling around with one another. No one wants to end up full-on scent-bound to someone you can't stand, ach? But when it's been going on for years, and you're sharing a room, a bed, a job, a gods-damned *life*?"

The sympathy was catching in Kitty's chest, tangling with more confusion, more uncertainty. "Scent-bound?" she echoed. "What does that mean?"

Thrain's brittle smile abruptly faded, his chest hollowing as he exhaled. "It's when someone bears your scent, and only yours, all through them," he said. "It... binds you both. Flaunts your claim over them, and theirs over you, and makes it so much easier to find and track and sense each other. It's... an offering, when you grant only one other person your scent. A great gift."

Oh. Kitty's thoughts were tumbling backwards, now, back to the forest, and her hand fluttered to her mouth, her chagrined eyes searching Thrain's face. "But," she began, "when Varinn and I first met, he told me—he said *you* were scent-bound. Both of you. Right?"

It was me, Varinn had told her, with that fury in his eyes. *His best friend, his scent-bond, his home. It was me, and he was mine.*

Thrain's eyes widened, and he stared at her for a long, silent moment. "No, he didn't," he finally said, though it sounded blank, uncertain. "He couldn't. He wouldn't. He's never once—I don't—he hasn't even been my only..."

But his voice trailed off there, his face gone pale, something panicked and almost pleading in his eyes. As if he expected Kitty to agree, to deny it, but she could only seem to shrug, and give him a wretched little half-smile, half-grimace.

"I'm sorry, but he definitely did say it," she replied. "He said you were his best friend, his scent-bond, his home. He said"— she grimaced again—"you were *his*."

Thrain's face looked even paler than before, his eyes blinking again and again. "No," he said again, shaking his head. "He couldn't, Kit. Never. Not without the—"

His voice broke, a hard swallow convulsing in his throat, and suddenly he looked appalled, or maybe even distraught.

And his head was shaking faster, his hand clapping over his mouth, his eyes wide and frenzied and—

"Fuck," he choked. "Fuck. I just—could you please—wait here, just for a moment, I—"

And without waiting for an answer, he spun around, and sprinted for the door.

30

Kitty stood in the aisle for a long, dangling moment, uncertain and bemused, staring at where Thrain had gone. Had he... fallen ill? Had she been wrong to tell him that, about Varinn? And surely he wouldn't be gone long, right? He would keep his word, and return soon, and explain?

But curse it, already here was the memory, flaring too bright in her thoughts, of how Thrain had disappeared the day before, and sneaked off to... drink. And now that Varinn was gone, out of the mountain, perhaps far away enough not to scent it, Thrain could...

Kitty shook her head, hard, and abruptly turned toward the nearest shelf. Which they'd left in a state of abject disarray, with clothes and furs scattered everywhere—and after dragging in a deep, fortifying breath, she began folding and stacking, fighting to keep her attention focused on what she was doing. Not on the way her heart was still pounding, or the way she suddenly felt a strange, unsettling affinity with Varinn. Nervous about where Thrain had gone, what he was doing, what state he might be in when he returned. If he might rage and shout again, make more bitter, painful accusations, tell Varinn that she'd shared his secrets, betrayed his trust...

Kitty shook her head again, and straightened out her neat new stack on the shelf before reaching for the next item. Another kilt, one that Varinn hadn't liked the scent of—and as she held it up, she couldn't seem to stop blinking at it, while an unexpected lump caught in her throat. Gods, what the hell was she doing. This was just a deal. Just a debt. Varinn didn't care about her, he didn't even like her—and even after all the times they'd been intimate together now, he still hadn't once made the slightest attempt to touch her. Let alone to grant her pleasure, or to allow Thrain to do so, either. It was just like Charles all over again, and Kitty needed to learn from her mistakes. Remember that she still needed to leave, after all this, and then...

"Ach, sister," said a voice, a new voice—and when Kitty spun around toward it, her heart skipping in her chest, she found a new orc. A bulky, green-skinned orc with a long black braid, and a careful, toothy smile on his mouth. "Did my brothers leave you here alone, to clean up after them? There's no need, you ken."

Oh. Kitty blinked uncertainly back toward him, and it belatedly occurred to her that she was still wearing one of her revealing new outfits—a short fur kilt and matching cape, showing off the entirety of her bare torso, and Varinn's beautiful *thyrja*. And it was a sight that the new orc clearly hadn't missed, his brows rising as he glanced up and down, his eyes lingering on the slight swell in her belly.

Kitty drew in a breath, and it took a concerted effort to pull the smile to her mouth, and attempt a dismissive wave of her hand. "Oh, no, I'm very happy to help tidy up," she said brightly. "We made quite a mess of this aisle, didn't we? And Thrain only needed to run out for a moment, and I'm sure he'll be back very soon."

But this new orc was giving a too-knowing smile, a wry little shrug. "Ach, let us hope," he said lightly, as he turned and picked up a fallen pair of trousers, folding them into a surprisingly neat square before setting them on the shelf. "And you're Kitty, ach? Varinn's new mate?"

Kitty twitched an uncertain little nod, which the new orc returned with another warm, knowing smile. "Welcome to our clan, woman," he said. "I'm Harthr, of Clan Grisk. I've known Varinn and Thrain since we were all orclings, ach? I oft work with Ymir here in the shop, shipping goods in and out."

Oh. Kitty felt herself slightly relaxing, and she nodded as she turned her attention back to her own folding. "Managing this place must be quite the job," she said, as steadily as she could. "It's a very impressive establishment. I'm ashamed to say, but I would never have *dreamt* of finding such a large or well-stocked shop in Orc Mountain."

Harthr laughed and shook his head, folding another pair of trousers with a quick flick of his hands. "This is because you're new to the Grisk," he informed her. "Our clan has long nursed a deep fondness for goods, and a need to gather them safe and close. If left be, I ken we could hoard ourselves straight out of a home, ach?"

Kitty smiled and relaxed a little more, straightening out her newest pile before starting another. "So how do you keep it all in check, then?" she asked. "Can anyone buy or sell here? Do you use human coin? Or trade anything beyond the mountain?"

Harthr's eyes brightened, and soon he was regaling Kitty with a detailed explanation of Orc Mountain's system of trading-credits, which essentially seemed to function as an internal currency. Credits could be earned, sold, or traded for human coin, and it was the Grisk clan—and particularly Ymir—who managed the rates, payouts, and exchanges. And Harthr currently led a small team that ran the mountain's broader trading efforts, and worked closely with Grisk scouts like Eyarl and Valter to move goods and payments between the mountain and various orc camps across the realm.

"The other clans and camps oft wish for goods, but it isn't so easy for them to seek them out, or keep them close and safe, as we do," Harthr said, with obvious pride in his voice. "So when we Grisk gather the goods and sell them to our kin, it brings great gain to us all, ach?"

That made sense, and Kitty glanced around the shop with even more appreciation than before. "I used to have—er—*friends* who were involved in trading," she said. "It certainly can be a very rewarding venture, especially if you can develop new markets, and secure investors to support more ambitious imports and routes."

"Ach, is that so?" Harthr said, as more enthusiasm flashed in his eyes. "We've oft spoken of working more with human traders to expand our routes and goods, and we ought to—"

But he stopped there, his eyes darting up beyond Kitty, to where—oh. Thrain had returned, striding down the aisle with long, swift steps, his gaze decidedly wary on Harthr. "Ach, Harthr," he said, his voice clipped. "You have met our mate, I ken."

Harthr's smile didn't quite reach his eyes, but he shrugged, and resumed his folding. "Ach, for she was left here all alone," he said blandly. "And I ken I heard she was *Varinn's* mate? Or have I been misled?"

Thrain's eyes narrowed, and he reached to swipe up their stack of approved clothing—still perched on the opposite shelf—before clasping Kitty's hand. "C'mon, Kit," he said thinly. "Oughta sort these out with Ymir, ach?"

Kitty didn't argue, and gave a halfhearted wave toward Harthr as Thrain led her away. And though Harthr readily waved back, his eyes remained focused on Thrain, his claws drumming absently on the nearest shelf. "Whilst you're here, brother," he said, toward Thrain's back. "Shall we order you the same as last time? Two kegs? Mayhap some berry-juice, also? Or should you rather human wine this time?"

Thrain's steps froze beside Kitty, and he grimaced as he slowly turned around again. "Thanks, but no, Harthr," he said. "I'm off the drink. For good."

Harthr's brows rose, his smile curious, or maybe even amused. "Again?" he asked lightly. "Mayhap we yet ought to order it in, just in case?"

"No," Thrain replied, his voice harsh. "I don't have the coin. And Varinn won't pay it this time, either."

That smile was still lurking on Harthr's mouth, and his eyes purposefully dropped toward the teetering stack of clothes in Thrain's hand. "No?" he asked. "Who's paying for all this, then?"

Thrain growled, low and angry in his throat, and Harthr abruptly raised his hands, his smile apologetic. "Forgive me, brother," he said. "Only wishing to help, ach? It's only good Grisk kindness, to make sure our hardworking Speaker's Guards have all they might need."

Thrain sighed, rubbing at his eyes, and muttered a curt thank-you under his breath. And then he again drew Kitty down the aisle, his hand clammy on hers, until they'd reached the front of the shop again. Where Ymir was already standing behind the long counter, and writing in some kind of ledger.

"We're taking these, Ymir," Thrain said thinly. "On Varinn's account."

Ymir looked up and curtly nodded, as if he'd expected nothing less, and began sorting through the stack. While beside Kitty, Thrain's body seemed to keep stiffening, his hand wiping again and again at his mouth. And when Ymir finally finished, Thrain snatched up the clothes without a word, and strode from the room.

"Are you... all right, Thrain?" Kitty asked him, tentative, once they were well down the corridor again. "Should I not have spoken to Harthr, as I did? I didn't realize he was..."

Your supplier, she'd been about to say, and she bit it off just in time—but Thrain had surely caught it anyway, grimacing toward the floor as they walked. "Ach, the blame for this isn't his," he said stiffly. "He did only as I asked. As I would mayhap do again, had I not—"

He grimaced again, shaking his head, and then barked a short, bitter little laugh. "As I almost did, just now, when I left you," he continued, his voice hollow. "Longed for naught more than a drink, ach? Might've even gone and done so, had I not scented Harthr with you. And imagined what a towering rage Varinn would be in, if he'd come back to find me in my cups, and you and our son alone with *Harthr*. He'd never dare trust me again, and I'd damn well deserve it."

Oh. So Kitty's suspicions—hadn't been wrong, then. And her stomach was already dropping, a chill racing up her spine, as Thrain laughed again, a choked, gulping sound in his throat. "Ended up sicking up in the latrine instead," he said thickly. "Naught like learning you're even more selfish and useless than you thought. On top of learning that your lifelong love truly thought you *scent-bound* to him—until you went off and fucked that up, too."

Kitty swallowed hard, the sympathy and misery and unease all curdling in a tight knot in her belly, but she somehow drew in a breath, let it out. "But you said—Varinn didn't actually tell you he felt that way about you, remember?" she managed. "And—you *didn't* fall into the drink, Thrain. You *didn't*. You fought off the temptation, and came back, and kept your word, and told me about it. You took a true step forward, achieved a true victory, and you should be proud of yourself, not angry. Right?"

Thrain's eyes glancing toward her were far too bright, shimmering with something between grief and gratefulness. "You're—too sweet, Kit," he said. "But you shouldn't even be dragged into all my rubbish in the first place, ach? You're the one who's growing our son, the one who's still recovering from what I did to you. You're the one who needs taking care of."

Kitty shrugged, and gave him a tentative, hopeful little smile. "Well, you've been ill, too," she replied. "And you're also recovering, right? So we can both help take care of each other, can't we? For Varinn's sake, if nothing else?"

At that, there was a very slight shift in Thrain's bleak eyes, so Kitty kept at it, elbowing him in the side, and attempting a jaunty grin. "Because you cannot argue that Varinn needs a break," she said firmly. "It cannot be healthy for him to be thrown into towering rages all the time, while also dealing with your contrary brother, scenting out orc trouble across the realm, spending time with Timo, and chasing wayward kittens all over the place! And constantly needing to feed them, too!"

Her voice had gone light and teasing, her grin warm on Thrain's face, and in return, he slowly smiled back, his eyes still glimmering with gratefulness. "Ach," he said, choked. "Ach, this is truth. I—thank you, Kit."

Kitty attempted to wave it away, but found that Thrain had caught her hand in his, and brought it to his mouth. "I thank you," he murmured again, his lips soft and warm against her skin. "Now come, and let me take you to the sickroom. Gain you some of the care you deserve, ach?"

Kitty couldn't argue, not with those warm lips on her skin, those earnest eyes still shimmering on hers. And after a quick stop in the Grisk wing to drop off their new clothes, they indeed headed to the sickroom, where they met not only with Efterar, but also with Gwyn, the mountain's midwife. And together, Gwyn and Efterar conducted a thorough examination of Kitty, during which Gwyn asked a variety of questions, and Efterar again soothed her nausea—and her gradually increasing tiredness—with truly miraculous ease.

"And how are you feeling today, Thrain?" Efterar asked, once he'd finished with Kitty. "Craving the drink quite strongly again, no doubt?"

Thrain blinked, angling Kitty a decidedly regretful look, but then he sighed, and nodded. "Ach, very much," he said. "It's been easier to ignore when I'm feeling good, or having fun, or being otherwise occupied. But earlier, when I was worked up and alone, I almost—"

He made a face, shaking his head, and Efterar absently nodded, hovering his hand over Thrain's forehead. "That's very normal, and to be expected," he said. "All you can do is keep picking yourself up, and moving forward. Keep seeking out those distractions, putting your mind elsewhere, finding new habits and pleasures. And this should help a little, I hope."

He clearly meant whatever he was currently doing with his impossible orc magic, and Kitty could see Thrain's shoulders gradually relaxing, his head jerking another nod. "Ach, that's much better," he said, on a slow exhale. "Thanks, Efterar. Very grateful to you."

Efterar shrugged and waved it away, while Gwyn—who had been washing up in a nearby basin—came back over, smiling between Kitty and Thrain. "Have you shown Kitty around the mountain yet, Thrain?" she asked. "Perhaps you might like to bring her to see the garden, and give her some sun and fresh air? And something to eat, too?"

Thrain's eyes sparked with unmistakable interest, and Kitty eagerly agreed, too, grinning excitedly between them. And after a short trek through the mountain's dim, cozy Bautul wing, Kitty followed Gwyn out through a heavy stone slab of a door, and into a large, sun-dappled garden.

It was truly an astonishing sight, tucked up close against the south side of the mountain, and bursting with colour and life—flowers and berries, herb and vegetable patches, and even full-sized trees. And it turned out that Gwyn's mate Joarr worked in the garden too, and that the small, bright-eyed orcling strapped to his back was their son, Joakim. And together, they took Kitty and Thrain on a cheerful, impromptu tour, while Kitty's surprise slowly turned to genuine, heart-stopping awe.

"This is incredible," she told Gwyn, her voice thin with disbelief, and with a bare, betraying longing. "Nearly as incredible as the Grisk Shop. You're so *lucky* to live here."

Gwyn's glance back toward Kitty was warm, but a little confused, too. "Well, now you live here too, right?" she said. "And you're welcome to stop by the garden anytime you like. It's excellent for your health, and your son's, too."

Right. Kitty fought back her wince, and pasted on a bright, grateful smile—because gods, as far as any of them knew, she was happily mated, and staying here, forever. Not repaying a debt, not pretending to be Varinn's mate, and most certainly not... leaving.

But damn it, Thrain was eyeing her very carefully, now, his head cocked sideways, a questioning smile on his mouth. "Ach, Kit," he said, a little too lightly. "I ken you'll love living here with us. We'll have so much fun together, ach?"

And though Kitty fervently agreed, flashing him her best, brightest grin, it soon became clear that Thrain was determined to demonstrate his point. Plying her with cheerful jokes and commentary—and multiple tasty snacks—as they finished touring the garden, and then, once he'd ushered her back inside, continuing his tour with merry, unbridled enthusiasm. Guiding her through each of the five clans' separate areas in the mountain, explaining their differences, and showing her an astonishing array of intriguing rooms along the way. Forges, fighting-pits, shrines, common-rooms, meeting-rooms, and even several more trading-posts, though none of them came close to rivalling the Great Grisk Showroom-Shop.

And as they went, Thrain also made an obvious effort to introduce Kitty to a variety of women, and to their orclings, too. A plump, pretty Bautul named Stella was wrapped in a cozy shawl, and nursing a stout little orcling named Skoll, while a tall, handsome Skai woman—Maria, wearing a dagger and a large men's tunic—proudly introduced her two adorable orc sons. And finally, in what appeared to be an otherwise empty *schoolroom*, they met three more women—Jule and Geva, both from the Ash-Kai clan, and Rosa, from the Ka-esh.

"We're so glad to finally meet you, Kitty," said Jule, who was tall and capable-looking, and clad in loose-fitting men's clothing. "We've all tried to visit you already, of course, but your mates have been *very* particular about your well-being."

She'd angled a half-annoyed, half-amused glance toward Thrain, who—to Kitty's vague surprise—had assumed an entirely unconvincing expression of innocence. While beside Jule, this Rosa—who was short, blonde, and heavily pregnant—pointed an accusing finger at Thrain, her pretty face contorted into a thunderous frown. "You and Varinn wouldn't even let me deliver my comprehensive *Orc Mountain Manual for Modern Mates!*" she said crossly. "I would never have imagined *Grisk* to be so anti-intellectual!"

Thrain betrayed an unmistakable wince, and awkwardly rubbed his hand against the back of his neck. "Och, I ken you've got the wrong end of it, Rosa-Ka," he replied. "Mayhap we've both read this most excellent Manual in full, but we don't wish to frighten off our sweet new woman with it, ach?"

Rosa's fierce expression wavered, hovering somewhere between gratified and insulted, but before she could continue, this Geva—whose stylish human dress also showed off a distinctively swollen waist—put her brown hand to Rosa's arm, and gave Kitty a reassuring smile. "Maybe we could offer to directly answer any questions Kitty might have instead?" she said. "Oh, and Thrain, I know Rathgarr would be happy to see you, if you'd like to check in with him for a few moments."

She'd jerked her head—full of beautifully beaded braids— toward the next room, and Kitty belatedly recalled that Rathgarr was Kesst's brother, and the orc Thrain had agreed to meet with regularly. And when Thrain glanced uncertainly toward Kitty—perhaps not wanting to leave her—she quickly smiled and nodded, and cheerfully waved him away.

It left her entirely alone with the three new women, but they seemed friendly enough, and after a few careful questions from Kitty, they were all easily chattering together. First about Orc Mountain's clans and leadership structure—it turned out that Jule was mated to the captain of the entire mountain—and then about the orcs' language, which was apparently called Aelakesh. This soon led into a detailed discussion of the room they were currently sitting in, which was part of Orc Mountain's new school. The school was co-directed by Geva and Rathgarr—who was also Geva's mate—and it provided a comprehensive education for young orcs of all ages. And, to Kitty's surprise, apparently Varinn was not only a member of the school's leadership committee, but he was also a regular guest instructor, and taught scenting classes almost every week.

"Varinn's a wonderful teacher," Geva said warmly. "Kind, patient, encouraging, and extremely skilled at scenting. I suppose I can see why he might not want to be represented by the Manual, Rosa."

She'd flashed a teasing smile toward Rosa, who was looking affronted again, and puffing out her chest. "But that's exactly when we need the Manual most!" she exclaimed. "I'm sorry, Kitty, but orc culture is often very different from our own, and that never-ending war affected them in truly horrifying ways. And as a result, even the kindest orc in the mountain is statistically *very* likely to stab you in the heart for their kin—metaphorically, of course—and feel entirely justified in doing so! Even the Grisk, and"—she jabbed her finger toward the next room—"I've begun to suspect that beneath their sweet exteriors, they might actually be the worst offenders of them all, because their mates never see it coming! We all know what Nattfarr did to Ella, right? Or what about Baldr and Alma?"

Wait. Really? Kitty's body stilled in her chair, her hands clutching against her knees, her eyes uneasily searching between Jule and Geva. But neither of them even attempted to argue Rosa's point, and instead, they were exchanging a brief, speaking look. "Right," Jule said, with an unmistakable wince. "Rosa, I don't suppose you might have an extra copy of the Manual on—"

But before she could finish, Thrain had suddenly reappeared, striding out of the next room with long, purposeful steps. "Och, I ken it's time to go, Kit," he said, with a teasing smile that didn't quite reach his eyes. "Not willing to hear any slights upon my clan, and most of all upon Varinn. He'd *never* betray or harm a woman. Most of all one who bears his own son."

His voice had gone cool and clipped, his hand tightly clasping Kitty's, pulling her to her feet. And once she'd said a quick, regretful thank-you and farewell to the women, Thrain swiftly drew her from the room, and back down the corridor.

"You ken Varinn would never, ach?" he said thinly, though he wasn't looking at her, his face held straight ahead. "If he's sworn a vow to you, he'll keep it. To his last breath."

Kitty smiled and rapidly nodded, even as something plunged in her belly, harsh and bitter and cold. Because Varinn hadn't actually spoken that kind of vow to her. She was only here to repay her debt, to help him rescue Thrain. And then...

Thrain angled a narrow, sidelong glance toward her, and his hand tightened on hers, pulling her to a halt—and without warning, he tugged her into the nearest door. Into what appeared to be a meeting-room of some sort, with a table and low benches, but it was currently unoccupied, and illuminated only by the dim lamplight from the corridor. Enough that Kitty could just make out Thrain's eyes, searching her face with a sharp, uncertain intensity.

"Listen, Kit," he said, his voice quiet. "You, and—Varinn. You're—happy with him, ach? He's been good to you so far? A good mate?"

Kitty couldn't stop the convulsive swallow, but thankfully

her smile came easy, along with a fervent nod. "Yes, Varinn's been so kind," she said, too quickly. "So excessively generous. Very, very good to me."

But Thrain's uneasy expression hadn't changed, and his head tilted as he leaned in closer, his eyes still searching hers. "Ach?" he asked, still very low. "How so?"

Kitty's throat convulsed again, but she kept smiling, even as her hands groped backwards, finding the cool hard stone of the wall behind her. "He—rescued me," she said, a little steadier this time. "Even when I know it—wasn't easy for him, at first. And he helped me, he stayed with me, he kept me safe and fed, he only spoke to me with kindness. He saved my life."

And thank the gods, Thrain was nodding now, and giving a faint little smile, even as he came a slow step nearer. "Ach, I ken," he murmured. "And then what?"

He was so close now, his vividly familiar scent suddenly flooding Kitty's breath, swarming her thoughts—and she couldn't seem to move, somehow, couldn't think, couldn't look away from his intent, searching eyes. "And then—we—came here," she stammered. "Right?"

And yes, yes, that was right, and Thrain was still smiling, still nodding, even as he leaned a little closer, his hand now flat to the wall behind her. "Ach, we did," he agreed, still so soft, so easy. "And when Varinn... spoke this vow to you? What did he say?"

Oh gods, oh gods, what was he doing, what was he implying, and Kitty had to fight for words, for air. "He swore— to take care of me," she gulped, toward Thrain's strange, glinting eyes. "Me, and our son."

And oh, the way Thrain's body suddenly sagged against her, his eyes fluttering closed, the exhale heaving harsh and shaky from his mouth. His elbows thudding against the wall on either side of her head, while his own head bumped softly against it, his hard swallow audible in Kitty's ear.

"Good," he said, his voice hoarse. "Good, Kit. Varinn will keep this vow. Keep you both safe. *Ach.*"

He sounded relieved, grateful, almost painfully so, and his body gave a full-length shudder against hers, his hand slipping down to graze against that bare swell of her waist. His long fingers spreading wide and protective over it, his claws very lightly skittering against her skin.

Oh. He'd been worried—for their son. For their son's safety. And for an instant, trapped there beneath his trembling touch, Kitty could almost taste his longing, and his desperation. His overpowering need for Varinn's vow to be true, because maybe—he still didn't trust himself. He didn't trust himself to care for her, or their son.

Something seemed to crumple in Kitty's chest, and she felt her own hand slipping out, finding Thrain's solid warmth. Finding his heartbeat, feeling how it was thundering, clamouring fast and frantic beneath his skin.

"But you'll be there for us, too," she whispered. "I know you will, Thrain. You'll keep your word, and be a good father. You *will.*"

Thrain made a strange choking sound, his breath juddering from his lungs. But then he nodded, as his head lowered over hers, his mouth pressing soft and reverent against her hair.

"Too sweet, Kit," he said, his voice rough. "Too good for all my rubbish."

Kitty laughed and shook her head, though she still felt quivery all over, and her body sagged a little forward, into the warm strength of his touch. Into where he'd suddenly stiffened, his head whipping sideways, his body lurching backwards. Because—wait—

It was Varinn.

31

Varinn was here. *Here.* Standing in the door, staring toward them. Toward where...

Damn it. *Damn* it. Kitty was still backed against the wall, her face flushed and hot, her breaths heaving, her hand pressed flat to Thrain's chest. While Thrain looked just the same, except for—oh. That unmistakable bulge in his kilt. Bobbing out against the leather, betraying him, betraying them.

And without a word, Varinn spun around, and left. Strode out the door, his shoulders hunched, his hands in furious fists at his sides. Leaving Kitty and Thrain staring at each other, the panic surging up between them—and then they both rushed for the door at once, Thrain's hand clasping tightly on hers, dragging her along after him.

"Varinn!" Thrain hollered, his voice harsh and hoarse. "Wait. *Wait!*"

Varinn's steps didn't slow in the slightest, his fists flexing at his sides, and Thrain groaned aloud, pulled Kitty along faster. "Varinn!" he called again. "It was naught. *Naught!*"

Varinn returned that with a sharp, contemptuous glance over his shoulder, his eyes far too bright, and he spun sideways, into a familiar-looking door. Into their quarters, Kitty realized, and Varinn stalked through the sitting-room with his head down. Not even glancing toward where Ella, Nattfarr, and Thrak were all watching from their usual table, Ella and Nattfarr with obvious confusion, Thrak looking darkly grim.

"It was naught," Thrain insisted, as he doggedly followed Varinn into their bedroom, his clammy hand still clasped tight on Kitty's. "Scent me, Varinn. It was naught. I swear to you!"

His voice sounded desperate, almost panicked, and finally Varinn spun around, his eyes blazing with fury. "Ach, I scent you, Thrain," he hissed. "I could scent you from halfway across the mountain! You ken *I* could forget how your hunger smells?"

He gave a furious wave toward Thrain's kilt, and Thrain groaned aloud, dragging both clawed hands against his face. "Ach, and you ken I haven't scented thus for the whole of this day?" he shot back. "You grant me this *thyrja*, you let me touch you, taste you, please you—and next you leave me alone with your sweet, lovely mate, after you've dressed her thus, and granted her your fresh scent! How am I not to smell and see this, and long for this?"

Varinn's jaw spasmed, his mouth rigid and thin. "Ach, I may have believed all this," he spat, "had I not then walked in and *seen* you!"

He gave another furious wave toward them, toward—Kitty, this time. And Kitty felt herself blanching, her head shaking, and she gulped for air, fought to find her voice. "It truly wasn't that, Varinn," she said thickly. "It wasn't, I swear. We never would, without you."

But Varinn's scoff was harsh and instantaneous, almost like a laugh—because wait, damn it, she and Thrain had already proven her claim abjectly false, when they'd spent that damned night together at her apartment. And no wonder Varinn was upset, no wonder he was suspicious and hurt, and Kitty's hands were wringing together, the words lost in her throat. She and Thrain should have realized how that would look, they should have been more careful, and whatever had possessed them to even risk such a thing, when they knew how strongly Varinn felt about it? When they knew—or at least, she knew—how much Varinn was trying to trust Thrain, and help him, and make this work?

But wait, now that was a low growl, hissing from Thrain's mouth, and Kitty felt his twitchy hand settling to her back, his fingers spreading wide. "You don't blame Kit for this, Varinn," he said, his voice hard. "You wish to blame someone, blame me. And ach, I ken I've done much to deserve it, but"—he drew in a shaky breath—"if your trust in me is so broken, to think I would have *dared* to seduce your mate after all this, let alone even touch her with a *drop* of my seed, without your leave— then why do you yet bother with me at all? Why do you taunt me as you do, with all your threats and promises? Why not just send me away, and forget me?"

His voice had gone low and plaintive by the end, his eyes pleading on Varinn's face, and Varinn shook his head, rubbed hard at his nose. But he didn't reply, didn't argue, and after another moment of dangling silence, Thrain barked a harsh, bitter little laugh. "Och, I ken it's the control fix again, is it?" he said, his voice very steady. "You wish to keep me close under your heel, where you can watch me flail and suffer beneath you? You can flaunt your lovely woman before me, flaunt your scent and our son upon her, and punish me if I even *dare* to touch our son without your leave?"

It was an unmistakable echo of what he'd told Kitty earlier, and suddenly it sounded far too much like those drunken accusations from the forest, too—and Kitty didn't miss that flash of hurt in Varinn's eyes, as an incredulous growl burned from his throat. "You ken I wish to do this?" he demanded at Thrain. "You ken I take *pleasure* from this?!"

But Thrain laughed again, the sound bright and cold. "Ach, mayhap," he said, clipped. "You love naught more than to command me, and lord over me, and deny me what I most long for! Ach, even after denying me your scent for so long"—his laugh twisted, hardened—"you yet thought us *scent-bound!* But you never *once* spoke a word of this, for you would never grant me the power of knowing this, and holding a claim upon you!"

His words rang through the room, angry and accusing, and the hurt flared again through Varinn's eyes, followed by a sharp, narrow glance toward Kitty. Knowing, surely, that she'd been the one to tell Thrain this, to betray his confidence. But even as she opened her mouth to speak, he'd already turned purposefully away from her, and back toward Thrain. His shoulders squaring, his breaths heaving through his chest, as if he were trying to steady himself, to find an answer, to explain—

But now Thrain was spinning away from him, pacing across the room, dragging his hands through his hair. "Och, don't deny it, Varinn," he choked. "It's always been thus, ach? It's always been about the control for you. About you holding your power over me, whilst I worship and beg for whatever scraps you'll deign to give me. It's you reminding me I'm second best, I'm your backup plan, and I always fucking will be!"

Oh. The pain in his voice felt too powerful, too real, wringing through Kitty's belly, and Varinn had begun to look truly ill, his breaths still shuddering through his chest. "No, Thrain," he said, his voice a rasp. "This was never my intent. You ken I have only ever done this for your own—"

"Och, for my own good!" Thrain finished, with a half-laugh, half-snarl, as he spun back around to glare at Varinn, his mouth quivering. "Because it's always been a woman you really want! And even without that, I'm too weak, too stupid, too much of a drunken fucking *waste* to actually earn your respect, or your vows, or your trust! Let alone your gods-damned seed!"

Varinn flinched, his eyes squeezing shut, his body visibly swaying on his feet. Almost as if Thrain had reached out and struck him, drawn fresh blood with his misery and his rage, and it distantly occurred to Kitty that perhaps—perhaps they'd never had this conversation before. Beyond that vicious fight in the forest, perhaps, when Thrain's wild accusations had been drunken, reckless, easily ignored. And suddenly she could almost see it, could see Thrain smiling and laughing and waving all this darkness away, desperately trying and failing to gain Varinn's trust and his favour, while the bitterness and loneliness kept tearing him apart.

I wasn't... wanted. I tried so fucking hard. Tried to be fun, eager, willing, always there, for everything. For the good, and the worst.

And oh, something was already shifting on Thrain's face now, as awareness—and then chagrin—flashed through his eyes. And then the sudden, certain regret, stark and miserable, as he staggered backwards, and sank down on the bed, his head in his hands.

"Och," he mumbled, his voice cracking. "Och, Varinn, I'm sorry. I ken how it is, I ken I'm the one who's kept pushing myself on you, all these years. And I *am* a drunkard, and a failure, and I *know* you'd never grant your seed or your vows to a—"

But thank the gods, Varinn had finally lurched toward him, clutching his big hand against Thrain's messy bowed head. "Quiet, *krútt*," he rasped. "Ach, do not speak thus. Please. I— you—you were never second best. *Never.*"

Thrain made a sound that might have been a scoff, or a sob, and Kitty could see Varinn struggling for breath, his hands fumbling at Thrain's face. Tilting it up, so he could see his wet cheeks, his red, miserable eyes. "Never, *krútt*," he said again, to Thrain's eyes. "You have always been precious to me. *Always.* And this—this is why I have always fought so hard for this power, ach? It was not to rule over you, but to—to rule over *me.*"

Thrain's bright eyes were incredulous on Varinn's, but he wasn't looking away, and Varinn caressed his face, wiped the wetness from his cheeks. "I cannot trust myself with you," he continued, choked. "I have never trusted myself with you, *krútt*, not since—ach. But I have yet longed so deeply for a son, and I *know* no woman would wish for this. No woman would wish for a mate who—who is so entangled with another. So... *enthralled*."

Right. That again. And Kitty swallowed hard as Varinn grimaced at Thrain, still holding his eyes. "No true mate would wish for this," Varinn repeated, almost despairing. "For me to be always watching you, *krútt*, and longing after you, and growing hard in my kilt each time I caught my scent upon you! This would not be right for her, or for you, and thus I"—he drew in a shaky breath, let it out—"I have fought to control this. To control *us*. Not because I do not respect you, or care for you, but because—because I *do*."

His voice had gone so quiet, so pained, aching with raw truth in Kitty's chest. So strong that it was only when Thrain's uncertain eyes glanced sideways, toward her, that she realized what Varinn had said. What he had just... betrayed.

No woman would wish for this. No true mate would wish for this.

No true mate.

And damn it, damn it, now Varinn was glancing at Kitty too, his eyes wide and alarmed. As if he, too, had just heard the danger, the gods-damned confession, in what he'd just said. Because she wasn't really his mate, and they both knew it. And he was already wincing, surely seeking some answer, some tidy falsehood—

And suddenly Kitty couldn't bear it, couldn't bear any more lies or pretending from either of them. She'd promised to help them, she had a deal, a debt—and gods curse them, she was seeing it through.

"But lucky for us all," she began, as sweetly as she could, "then you found *me*. And nothing would make me happier"— she smiled brightly toward Thrain—"than to see my mate plough you until you scream, and make you *reek* of his good Grisk seed."

In another day, another moment, Kitty might have laughed at the look on Varinn and Thrain's faces. Both of them staring at her with eyes that were equally dumbfounded, and then wary, and then deeply, undeniably suspicious.

But Kitty had already expected that, of course, and she sauntered over to the bed, and sat down primly beside Thrain, crossing one bared leg over the other. "I trust Lord Grisk implicitly, and I know he'll take good care of me, and be a good mate to me," she said archly, though she couldn't quite hold Thrain's gaze. "Why should I care if he gets hard in his kilt for you? He's a lusty, virile orc, who's descended from an actual *god*, and his fat bollocks are bursting with good Grisk seed. Surely enough for us both to share, don't you think?"

Thrain's eyes were still suspicious on hers, but the awareness was there in Varinn's now, sharp and regretful. Knowing exactly what Kitty was doing, damn him, and she felt her smile go a little brittle as she deliberately leaned over, and unfastened the belt of his kilt. Her hands only slightly trembling as she drew it downwards, displaying—yes, yes—

where his hardness beneath was already bobbing up, swelling fuller with every breath.

"And if I'd realized, Lord Grisk," she continued, still smiling at his shifting eyes as she neatly dropped his kilt on the floor, "that you've been denying yourself this particular pleasure with your most loyal subject because of some misguided responsibility toward a future mate like *me*, I should have corrected you at once. Because I understand, just as he does"—her eyes angled brief but meaningful toward Thrain—"that you ought to have your full choice of pleasures. You ought to have your good Grisk prick milked dry any way you might please."

And yes, yes, the suspicion in Thrain's eyes had finally begun to fade, in favour of hunger, and something almost like appreciation. While the sound in Varinn's throat had been without question a gasp, even as his fluttering eyes narrowed on Kitty's face, their warning far too clear.

And maybe—maybe that was because Varinn had still been doing this for the next woman. The one he would find after her, the one he could truly care for. But gods, even the thought of that was swirling up irrational jealousy in Kitty's thoughts, and with it, a dark, dizzying vindictiveness. If Varinn had been trying to keep himself pure for that woman, or some other such rubbish, well, too bad for her, and for him. He'd be secretly lusting over Thrain and growing hard in his kilt no matter what he said or did, and gods curse him, Kitty was doing him a damned favour.

But wait, maybe he and Thrain could smell her jealousy again, both of them now frowning toward her—so Kitty sat a little straighter, and tossed her hair over her shoulder. "Of course, you're well aware this only applies to *him*," she told Varinn, her voice crisp. "If you should ever try to grant your lordly blessings to anyone beyond the two of us, I will personally claw their eyes out, and feed them to the kittens."

She didn't miss the brief, strangled laugh from Thrain, or

that shift of reluctant, amused comprehension in Varinn's eyes, too. Because he had to know she wasn't jealous of Thrain, she'd never once even thought of it. Not when she wanted this so much, she wanted...

"But, Kit," Thrain said, choked. "Varinn hasn't—he hasn't even done it with *you* yet."

Right. That. And damn it, of course Thrain could smell that, of course he would know she and Varinn hadn't gone near there yet. And perhaps that was something they should already be doing, something else that risked the entire plan—and surely something Varinn didn't want from her, either. And Kitty belatedly waved it away, and twitched what she hoped was a casual shrug.

"We've been taking our time and enjoying one another, haven't we, Varinn?" she said smoothly, without looking at him. "And now I'm exceedingly glad of it, because it seems far more appropriate to me that he should take such an important step with you first. Since you've been together for"—she briefly faltered at that uncertainty—"for so long. And this way, I'm able to witness it, and enjoy it. And take great satisfaction in my powerful mate's excessive virility."

She gave Varinn her sweetest, most innocent smile, before dropping her eyes back to the heft at his groin. To where it was already fully swollen now, heavy and twitching, and liberally leaking that slick white from his slit. Because of course he wanted this, he'd always wanted this, it was crackling in his eyes, in the air between them—and oh, Kitty could hear Thrain's swallow, could see his head nodding, his eyes locked on Varinn's flushed face.

"Please, Varinn," Thrain breathed, as his hands suddenly scrabbled for his own kilt, yanking uselessly against it. "Please, Lord Grisk. If you really want to. I *beg* you."

Something hot and hungry burned from Varinn's throat, but he wasn't moving, his eyes now fixed on Thrain's fumbling hands. And without at all meaning to, Kitty batted Thrain's hands away, and unfastened the kilt's belt properly, revealing Thrain's lean, shuddering body for Varinn's eyes. His gold *thyrja* glinting against the sheen of his skin, his pierced length already rock-hard, and liberally leaking against his belly.

"Yes, Lord Grisk," Kitty echoed, hoarse, as her audacious hand gently pressed against Thrain's bare chest, nudging him backwards onto the bed. "Look how pleasing he is, how handsome. How hungry he is for your good Grisk ploughing."

Varinn's heaving breaths had undeniably hitched, his hooded eyes fixed on Kitty's hand—so in another burst of courage, she carefully stroked up and down the hot silken skin of Thrain's chest, felt him jerk and shudder beneath her touch. "He wants to scent of you," she continued. "He wants to open for you, and reek of you, and scream for you. He wants to be yours, Lord Grisk, *yours*."

And oh, yes, yes, Varinn was slowly shifting down onto the bed too, his knees shoving up close against Thrain's arse, and Thrain instantly jerked his thighs higher, his eyes wide and wild on Varinn's face. On where Varinn was inhaling slow and deep, his nostrils flaring, as a heated groan rumbled from his chest. "Keep begging," he breathed, so low Kitty almost didn't hear it. "Keep showing me what is mine. Both of you."

Oh, hell, and both Thrain and Kitty were rapidly nodding in unison, Thrain already lifting his thighs higher, blatantly opening himself wide, while Kitty kept stroking up and down his torso, even daring to pinch at a taut grey nipple. "Please," Kitty choked, or maybe that was Thrain, or both of them. "Please, Lord Grisk. More."

Varinn's nostrils kept flaring, his tongue sweeping against his lips, and he leaned closer over Thrain on the bed, shoving his legs wider apart. So he could brush his jutting, dripping pink tip just against—

"Fuck," Thrain gasped, his body arching up, because yes, yes, Varinn was already pressing in, pushing that slick head a little forward, as a low, husky growl rasped from his throat.

Betraying, perhaps, just how much he wanted this, and Kitty couldn't look away from him, from them. From the way Varinn's chest filled as he inhaled, his hooded eyes lingering on her hands, on how she was still eagerly stroking against Thrain, showing off his hunger, his reckless, shameless beauty.

"Please, Varinn," Thrain gasped again, and Varinn rewarded him by pushing a little deeper, making him arch up higher. "Please. Give me more. All of you."

But Varinn was taking his damned time, breathing in so slow and deep, his blazing eyes flicking to Kitty's face. Because she'd stopped begging, damn it, and in apology her hand dared to slip a little lower, circling around Thrain's straining length. "Please, Lord Grisk," she breathed. "Look how gorgeous he is. How much he wants you. How much he needs you."

Thrain was frantically nodding, his hands now clutching at Varinn's hips, fighting to drag him closer. "Need you," he gasped, pleaded. "More of you, Varinn, oh gods. Inside me. Please."

And yes, yes, Varinn was finally shifting further forward, his swollen green flesh sinking deeper between Thrain's parted legs, as Kitty's hand began stroking up and down Thrain's shaft. Driving Thrain's moans even louder, his movements jerky and fervid, his eyes alight.

"Ach," Thrain sobbed, as Kitty kept stroking, harder, faster. "Ach. Please. Please, Lord Grisk, oh gods, please. Need you. All of you. More than anything. *Please.*"

There was a deep, satisfied growl, low in Varinn's chest—and then he slammed in without warning, without hesitation. Driving that swollen cock deep between Thrain's legs, splitting him apart, while Thrain thrashed and shouted, his whole body arching up, convulsing around Varinn's invading flesh. Sucking it in, welcoming its brutal breach of him—and maybe even welcoming the way Varinn was circling his hips, grinding himself even deeper. His big powerful arms now holding up his rigid, straining upper body, so he could watch Thrain flounder and flail beneath him, trapped, impaled, clamouring for more.

And when Varinn drew back, slowly easing that slick, shiny pole out again, Thrain growled with displeasure, his shaky arms fighting to grip tighter against Varinn, to keep him there, pull him back. And gods, the way they both moaned as Varinn obliged, far slower this time, feeding himself in breath by breath, until he was again fully seated inside, his full bollocks grinding taut against Thrain's arse.

Kitty had almost forgotten how to breathe by this point, her hand again gone slack on Thrain's straining cock—but a meaningful glance from Varinn set her moving again, stroking and caressing Thrain for him, while he drew his fat, gleaming length out again. Watching it emerge bit by bit, until it bobbed free with a slick-sounding pop, hovering brazen and obscene before the dark, spasming opening he'd made.

"What do you say now, *krútt*?" Varinn's voice purred, softly mocking, utterly certain. "What do you wish for next?"

And oh, the way Thrain trembled and groaned in return, his lean sweaty body arching up, his clawed hands still uselessly fighting to drag Varinn downwards. "Again," he gasped. "Please, Varinn. Give it to me. Please."

Varinn's laugh was both a caress and a conquest, his blazing eyes hitching into something almost like affection—and then he slammed in again. Making Thrain spasm and choke, his entire body surging up beneath it, but Varinn just kept grinding even deeper. As if to open Thrain up for him, to lay irrefutable claim to him, once and for all.

"I should tell you to beg for even more, *krútt*," Varinn's voice breathed, another heated liquid caress, as he kept circling his hips, watching Thrain shout and writhe upon him. "But I ken you are already full, ach?"

Thrain's body spasmed again, and he made a strangled sound that might have been a laugh—but his blinking eyes on Varinn were pure, reverent worship. While his hands kept gripping Varinn, holding him there, as his own hips hitched up into the shaky stroke of Kitty's clutching fingers.

"Still need more," Thrain gasped, his worshipful eyes bright and blinking, his voice a croak in his throat. "Please, Varinn. Lord Grisk. Need it so much. You have no idea how much. *Please.*"

Varinn's eyes briefly closed, his head bowing, and Thrain drew in another ragged, whistling breath. "Please," he gasped. "Please, forgive me, forgive me, for all of it. Tell me I'm still good. Still feel good. Still bring you ease, make you laugh. And you'll never send me away, never let me go, never leave me, never forget me, *please.*"

Oh. The words felt desolate, suddenly, painful, laced with fear and lost, hopeless longing. So wretched they choked in Kitty's chest, clamped around her heart—and she nearly sobbed at the sight of Varinn giving a harsh, heavy exhale, and then nodding. Nodding, and even bending down, gently pressing his mouth to Thrain's, before easing into a slow, steady rhythm. Rocking himself out and in, seeking his glossy pink crown into Thrain's opened body again and again.

"Ach, *krútt*," he murmured, as he kept pumping, filling Thrain, reassuring him. "You ken I care for you. You ken I shall never leave you, or send you away from me. Ach?"

Thrain rapidly, desperately nodded, his eyes pleading on Varinn's face, as Varinn made that low shushing sound, rumbling in his chest. "Good," he purred. "Always so good, *krútt*. Better than aught else I have ever known."

Thrain's groan was guttural again, helpless, his hands now frantically clawing at Varinn's back, his arse. Scoring deep red marks into Varinn's smooth skin, but Varinn didn't even blink, his hooded eyes only on Thrain, on how he choked and trembled with every thrust of his thick wet cock, still driving steadily in and out.

"Good," Varinn purred again, caressing a hand against Thrain's hot, sweaty cheek, while Thrain kept looking back at him with such bright, reverent worship in his eyes. As if this was deliverance, a revelation, and Varinn was truly a god's favoured heir, innately worthy of his worshippers' suffering, their service, their adoration. As if in return, the god might deign to offer his kindness, or his care, or his…

His seed. Because oh, fuck, Varinn was going rigid over Thrain, arching up, his groan raw and guttural—and then he plunged deep. Plunged deep and poured out, all the way inside. And Kitty could see Thrain's choke of wild surprise, could feel it flaring between them—and then came his juddering cry, shaken and shocked, as he sobbed, and shuddered all over. His expression one of almost panicked abandon, his eyes rolling back, as if he'd never tasted anything so glorious, never known anything so wondrous, such fiercely, utterly perfect bliss.

And oh, the way Varinn was watching it, his eyes blazing, intent, and almost painfully fond, as he finally filled Thrain with his seed, with his scent. Freely giving him this—*great gift*, Thrain had called it, after so long. Doing all within his power, perhaps, to keep this, to save this…

And then, to Kitty's ongoing astonishment, Varinn's glinting eyes swept toward her, and then purposefully downwards, behind them. Toward—oh. That basin, sitting empty and innocuous by the bed.

"Get that, *kisa*," he said, with breathtaking coolness, even as he kept pouring himself into Thrain. "Empty him into it for me. And"—his eyes went soft, almost amused—"mayhap I can help you gain your own relief, also."

What? Kitty stared back for an instant, his words jumbling strange and slow through her thoughts—but then she twitched, and nodded, and obeyed. Grasping the basin, lurching back toward where Thrain's swollen length was uncontrollably bobbing, straining up, clearly about to burst…

And in a swift, desperate movement, she'd snatched Thrain in hand again, eagerly stroking him toward the basin, while Varinn's own firm, warm, capable hand slipped between her thighs. Grinding hard and purposeful against her, pressing just there—and then, oh hell, came the ecstasy. The furious flares of sharp, shivering pleasure, surging not just from deep in Kitty's own belly, but also from Thrain's rigid, pulsing strength in her fingers. Pouring out of him in a fierce, forceful stream, spattering white and messy through his gold ring, streaming into the basin. While his cries sharpened into something frantic, almost feral, fraying thick and muffled through the hot, sweet-scented air.

Kitty's own pleasure was still pulsing, shuddering through her shaky body into Varinn's warm pressing hand—but as it slowly settled, she could see Thrain's body sagging, too. His pouring white finally slowing, sputtering to a steady drizzle, dangling from his ring. And his cries had slowly faded, too, shifting into muffled, weak-sounding whimpers, and after a brief little pat against Kitty, Varinn drew himself backwards, out, away from them both. So he could set the basin safely on the floor, and then sink down onto the fur beside Thrain. To where Thrain was already surging into his side, the movement reflexive, vulnerable, almost helpless.

But yes, yes, Varinn was already gathering Thrain close, stroking his big hand firmly up and down his sweaty, trembling back. As his own flushed face bent into the wild mess of Thrain's hair, his breath inhaling slow and deep.

"Ach, *krútt*," Varinn murmured, in that rough, silken purr. "So good. So good."

Thrain fervently nodded, and Kitty could see him inhaling too, his upper body expanding, as his black tongue fluttered out of his mouth, almost as if to scent the air. "Can you smell me, Varinn?" he croaked, with a choked-sounding bark. "Fucking smell me, Varinn!"

Varinn was actually chuckling at this, and inhaling again, gathering Thrain closer. "Ach, I smell you, *krútt*," he murmured. "Scents good, upon you. So good."

Thrain made that sound again, and Kitty truly couldn't tell

if it was a laugh or a sob, wrenching through his sweaty body. "You'll never be rid of me again, Varinn," he said, and suddenly it sounded bright, joyous, almost gleeful. "Never. Ever. *Again.* You'll be able to scent me across the realm! Beneath the earth! In a city of *millions!*"

And surely Thrain couldn't see Varinn's face, not with how he was still desperately nuzzling into his chest, but Kitty could see. Could see the soft, sad, pained-looking affection glimmering in Varinn's eyes as he smiled down at Thrain, and pressed another kiss to his hair. "Ach, *krútt*," he said, with a very faint crack in his voice. "Shall now never stop scenting you."

But perhaps his tone had caught something, jerking Thrain's head back up, snapping a sudden tension back through his previously languid form. "You... meant to, Varinn," he said, though it sounded uncertain, now. "You wanted to do it. Ach? It wasn't just because—Kit goaded you into it? Or because I was being an arse to you? Or saying I don't like you being in charge? Because you know I do, Varinn, especially when it comes to fucking, but in the rest of it, I just—"

His voice was again plaintive, almost pleading, and Varinn's hands were already stroking, easing the tension away. "Ach, I ken, *krútt*," he murmured. "And ach, I—wished for this. Wished to—regain your trust in me."

Thrain's softening body had flared up again, his narrow eyes searching Varinn's face, and Kitty could see Varinn taking a breath, letting it out. "It was not—right of me," he began, with visible effort, "to treat you as mine, for all that time, and see you as my scent-bond, when I gave you no claim in return. When I—denied you what you most longed for. Made you feel—second best."

They were all direct quotes of Thrain's accusations from before, and Kitty didn't miss the shock, flashing through Thrain's body, choking in his throat. "Really?" he asked, incredulous. "In truth, Varinn?"

Varinn drew in another deep breath, giving a slow, decisive nod. While Thrain kept frantically searching his face, as if he didn't believe it, couldn't dare believe it. "And you don't think you'll end up... regretting it?" he said uncertainly. "Or resenting me, or Kit, or—"

He'd cast a brief, panicked look over at Kitty, as though he'd just remembered she was there—and oh, that was his hand, reaching to clasp tight and clammy against hers, drawing her closer toward them. "And Kit, it was so sweet of you, again, but"—his eyes seemed to clear slightly, blinking toward her—"but wait, I'm doing it again, barging in on your mate, coming between you, when I barely deserve to be in the same room with you. And fuck, what happens when you finally realize you're sick of my rubbish, what then?"

His voice was rising, gone high-pitched and afraid, and Kitty couldn't help her own impulsive, weepy-feeling smile, the rapid shake of her head. "I told you, I don't mind," she said thickly. "I wanted it, too. I want you two to work through this. I want us all to be happy together."

She had to bite back her wince, because damn it, those were dangerous words, risking far too much—but beyond Varinn's brief, narrow look toward her, he didn't acknowledge it, and Thrain's grin again looked too bright, too tenuous, too grateful. "You're too sweet, Kit," he said fervently. "Too good for us. She's such a good mate for you, ach, Varinn? You'll be so happy with her?"

With that highly alarming question, he'd flopped toward Varinn again, burying his face back in his chest. But oh, gods, Varinn was again glancing at Kitty, his glinting eyes now holding on hers, looking almost suspicious, or angry, or even—betrayed.

"Ach, *krútt*," he murmured, his soft voice at total odds with his eyes, as he again caressed Thrain's back. "Now quiet yourself, and sleep for me. Let my scent settle and deepen upon you."

Thrain rapidly nodded, nuzzling his face even deeper against Varinn's skin, and huffing a happy, squeaky little sigh. Reminding Kitty, with a sudden, bizarre vividness, of little Vragi with his kitten, and she couldn't seem to stop blinking toward him as his breaths slowly deepened, his body curling closer into Varinn's. Neither of them appearing to have even slightly noticed that they were still sprawled sideways on the bed, or that—Kitty winced as she glanced down toward it—there was a slowly growing wet spot beneath Thrain on the fur.

"Leave it," Varinn said, his voice quiet—and when Kitty darted a wide-eyed glance toward him, he was suddenly just looking tired, his hand still stroking at Thrain's back. "I shall see to it later."

Oh. Kitty swallowed and nodded, though her eyes had again found Thrain. Holding on where he already seemed to be fast asleep, his chest steadily rising and falling, his face smooth and peaceful. "Is he... well?" she asked, uncertain. "Are... you?"

Varinn's throat convulsed, but he jerked a shrug, his eyes dropping back to Thrain. "He is only fuck-drunk," he said thinly. "It... happens, now and then. He shall be more himself again come morning."

Oh. Kitty silently nodded, distantly noting that he hadn't answered the second part of her question—but suddenly she couldn't bear to push it, or even to meet his eyes. Because gods, this had been so much, so intense, and she'd been— responsible for it. Entirely at fault. But she couldn't seem to find any guilt for it, either, and even the memories of it were making her belly clench, catching on a sharp, twisting longing. She did want them to be happy together. She wanted it for both of them, wanted it so much it ached—but once they were reconciled again, where did that leave her? Alone, away, working for herself, until...

"I—I'm sorry I told him how you felt about the scent-bond,"

she heard herself croak, abrupt, into the silence. "I didn't realize—he didn't know."

Varinn jerked another shrug, took another long inhale of Thrain's hair. "No, he was right," he said, with a sigh. "He ought to have known. I cannot rebuke him for speaking false to me about the drink, when I did the same to him in this, ach? This was... small of me. Selfish."

Oh. Kitty's eyes dropped to her hands, a sudden miserable rebellion surging in her thoughts. Because despite that grand statement, Varinn still *was* speaking false to Thrain in this, wasn't he? With this deal they'd made, this secret vow, this debt? With how he didn't really care about Kitty in the slightest?

But then again, amidst all this tonight, he'd also... touched her. He'd involved her in it, and willingly brought her pleasure. And why had he done that? For Thrain... right?

"You ought to sleep also, Katharine," cut in Varinn's voice, again sounding tired, resigned. "You need rest, ach?"

Right. Kitty still couldn't seem to look at him, at how he and Thrain were still wrapped tightly together. And if Varinn wanted her to have any further part of it, he surely would touch her now, draw her closer—but he wasn't, he hadn't. So Kitty stiffly set herself down on the bed, her back toward them, her blinking eyes facing the wall. Her fingers clutching at her beautiful new *thyrja*, because she would need to leave that behind too, and then...

"Sleep well," came Varinn's voice, even wearier than before. And though Kitty rapidly nodded, and even attempted to obey, she could only seem to stare at the wall, and fight back the ever-rising misery, swelling behind her eyes.

33

Kitty's sleep that night was light and fitful, full of strange dreams, and far-too-vivid memories. Of Varinn hovering over the bed, looking at her with such softness in his eyes, his hand touching her with warm, firm gentleness...

It wasn't helped by the way she again needed to empty her bladder in the middle of the night, or the way Varinn had again seemed to sense it. Silently extracting himself from Thrain's still-sprawled body, and escorting Kitty to the latrine, his hand warm and careful against her back. But afterwards, instead of lying down again, he'd mumbled something she hadn't been able to hear, and then he'd spun around, and left the room entirely.

It took far too long for Kitty to fall back to sleep, even despite Thrain's soft, contented snores beside her. And when she finally blinked awake again, she found Thrain yawning and sitting up next to her on the bed, with the fur still over his lap, and Varinn still nowhere to be seen.

"Where's Varinn?" Kitty asked, wincing at the too-thin sharpness in her voice. But if Thrain noticed it, he didn't let on, and instead he flashed her a warm, easy grin as he drew in a deep breath, leisurely stretching his long arms over his head.

"Och, I can scent him over in the baths, with Baldr," he said cheerfully. "Oft likes to swim at unseemly times in the mornings—for his health, he says. Such a Varinn thing to do."

His grin pulled up higher, bright with affection and amusement, and Kitty could see him inhaling again, even slower and deeper this time. And then—she blinked—he turned his head to sniff at the thatch of black hair beneath his upraised arm. Drawing in another long, leisurely breath of it, and then giving a sustained, full-body shudder as a harsh groan escaped his throat, and something visibly twitched beneath the fur.

Kitty couldn't help wincing at the sight, her thoughts darting back to Varinn's fury from the day before—and Thrain swiftly dropped his arms again, shoving irritably at the fur. "Sorry," he said, his grin gone sheepish. "Need to better watch that, I know, I..."

His voice trailed off there, because he was inhaling again, his head drifting toward his shoulder this time—and then he barked a sudden laugh, the sound ringing with sheer, contagious joy. "Och," he said, as he gave another taut, full-body shudder. "Och, I smell so good. So fucking *good*, Kit."

His gleeful eyes were dancing and shimmering on hers, as if he needed nothing more than to share his utter delight with her. And despite Kitty's still-present unease, she couldn't help smiling back, watching with rising amusement as he eagerly shifted closer, and thrust his arm toward her. "Smell," he said eagerly. "I bet even you can scent the difference, ach?"

Kitty duly obliged, carefully sniffing at his arm, and finding—to her surprise—that he did seem to smell different, somehow. A little darker and richer, a little more like—like Varinn.

"It is good," she told him, with another warm smile toward him. "I'm so happy for you, Thrain."

But at that, Thrain's eyes shifted. Sobered. And he abruptly dropped his arm again, folding his clawed hands tightly together in his lap. "Are you... sure, though, Kit?" he asked, far quieter than before. "You really didn't mind?"

Kitty blinked, and then shook her head, waved it away—but Thrain was still watching her, his eyes searching, intent. "Because Varinn's still your mate now," he continued slowly. "Not mine. And after what I did to you"—he grimaced, his breath heaving out—"you'd be well within your rights to never want to see me again. To never want Varinn to speak to me again. Let alone to sit there and watch him granting his pleasure and his seed to me, when he oughta be granting it all to you. Most of all"—he grimaced again—"after he told us both he only *wanted* to grant it to you."

Oh. Something tightened in Kitty's throat, but she again attempted to wave it away, and paste another smile to her face—at least, until Thrain's warm fingers grasped her wrist, and gently drew it back down to the bed. "Look, you don't need to put on the act for me, Kit," he said, even quieter. "I know I do it too, and I'll confess that I'm realizing how rubbish it is, because"—his smile went apologetic, maybe even sad—"I can scent you, ach?"

Right. Right. Kitty's throat convulsed again, her heart kicking in her chest, because damn it, where was Varinn, what was she supposed to say, she had to keep this secret, keep her vow, repay her debt...

"Look, I truly—don't mind," she finally managed, toward Thrain's searching, patient eyes. "I want to see you both reconciled again, and I'm happy for you to take whatever pleasures you like together, especially if it helps distract you from—other things. But it's all just very—new, still, and I just don't always know where I fit, between you, and how it will..."

And oh gods, she was veering far too close to the truth again, and she belatedly shook her head, clamped her mouth shut. But there was no judgement in Thrain's watching eyes, only that same easy patience, his head slowly tilting as he studied her.

"Is it because he's been putting off fucking you properly, too?" he asked softly. "You'd like to have your turn now, I ken?"

Kitty blanched, her face instantly flushing hot, her head shaking—but Thrain was smiling again, warm and impish, with something almost like relief glimmering in his eyes. "Ach, now, that's an easy fix, Kit," he said, his voice husky and low. "I know you said you were taking your time with it, but you ken that's not because Varinn doesn't want it, ach? That's just him being a damned noble martyr again, and not wanting to push his sweet new mate into pleasing him. So don't worry"—his eyes gleamed on hers—"we'll goad him into it. Just like last night, ach?"

Oh. Kitty couldn't stop her choked-sounding laugh, or the strange, inexplicable *hopefulness*, unfurling in her chest. "I was *not* trying to goad Varinn into anything," she replied, with as much primness as she could muster. "I was only seeking out my own satisfaction. My own selfish entertainment."

But Thrain was fully grinning at her now, waggling his eyebrows with devious, highly suspicious eagerness. "Ach, of course," he said lightly. "So you won't mind if I do the same, ach?"

Wait. Wait, because Thrain was already leaping up to his feet, and before Kitty even realized it, he'd tugged off the little cape she'd still been wearing, and then her kilt, too. Leaving her utterly bared on the bed, adorned in only Varinn's beautiful *thyrja*—but wait, Thrain was only wearing his *thyrja* too, and he was now lunging toward the washbasin, and returning with a... hairbrush?

"You leave it to me, Kit," he said firmly, as he promptly drew her hair back over her shoulders, and began brushing. "We'll get you fucked good and proper, ach?"

Kitty's face still felt far too hot, her hands helplessly fluttering in midair, and a shrill, too-loud laugh escaped from her mouth. "*Thrain*," she said, her voice thick with exasperation, and perhaps with longing. "You can't actually want—"

"Oh, I do," Thrain cut in, with a clipped, easy certainty. "Believe me, Kit, I do, especially after last night. Varinn's yearned for it all his life, and I want to witness him gaining it, ach? Want to"—his voice lowered—"be part of it. With him, and with you. Like you were with me."

Oh. Kitty swallowed hard, darting a glance up over her shoulder, and found Thrain's eyes intent on his brushing. On how he was gently stroking at a shining lock of her hair, touching it with something almost like reverence.

"And I ken it's me being greedy and selfish again," he continued, a little rough, now, "but I've sworn to be truthful with you, so—och. I *want* Varinn's scent on you, thus, just like I wanted his vow to you. I want what it grants you. His fealty, his care, his safeguarding over you, and our son. If I fuck this up again"—he huffed a shaky exhale—"I want him there. I *need* him there, Kit."

Right. Kitty couldn't seem to find a response to that, her throat spasming against a sudden tightness. Because Thrain was saying, again, that he still didn't trust himself. Still wasn't sure he could do this.

When suddenly—Kitty startled—Varinn himself strode into the room. He was wearing only what appeared to be a small damp *towel*, slung low around his hips, and water was dripping from his face, streaking down his chest. And most compelling of all, his usually neat braid was dishevelled, and long tendrils of black hair were fanned out over his broad shoulders, clinging to his wet, shining skin.

"What," he said, stopping up short, eyeing both Kitty and Thrain with decided wariness. "Is aught amiss?"

Kitty blinked uncertainly back toward him, because wait, he'd left them alone together again, for all that time—and perhaps that had been on purpose. Perhaps it had been an attempt to follow up on yesterday, to offer up his trust, to show them he meant it. And behind Kitty, Thrain had already set down the hairbrush, and was striding toward Varinn with rapid, eager steps.

"Naught amiss at all," he murmured, almost shy, as he slipped his tall, bared body up against Varinn's side, ducked his head into his damp neck. "Just scenting you, and missing you. Have a good swim?"

Varinn cautiously nodded, his eyes darting toward Kitty, even as he bent his own head into Thrain's messy hair, and took a slow, deep inhale. His lashes visibly fluttering, and oh, that was again that low, purring growl, rumbling deep in his chest.

"Smell good, don't I?" Thrain mumbled, nuzzling a little deeper into Varinn's neck. "You like it, ach? Glad you finally did it?"

Varinn didn't reply, but perhaps his inhale spoke for itself, his rumbling growl steadying, deepening. And Kitty could see Thrain's happy, contented smile, curling sweetly at his mouth, even as his hand snaked toward the front of Varinn's towel, and gave it an audacious little squeeze. "Feeling a bit full there, Lord Grisk," he murmured. "In need of some milking, I ken? Need to empty out all that good Grisk seed?"

Varinn's growl unmistakably hitched, his eyes again darting toward Kitty in the bed, toward where—oh. She was still sitting up, still wearing only his *thyrja*. Fully flaunting her breasts, her peaked dusky nipples, the small swell in her belly. And thanks to Thrain's brushing, her hair was arranged in smooth, shining waves over her shoulders, and she was biting her lip, looking at Varinn looking at her, as Thrain chuckled into Varinn's neck, his hand still stroking against the towel with shameless eagerness.

"Och, we've been waiting for you, Lord Grisk," Thrain continued, with a gentle little nibble at Varinn's neck. "Your sweet little kitten most of all, ach? Look how hungry she is, longing for some fresh milk from her lord."

Kitty's breath spasmed in her throat, and she couldn't help a sharp, reproachful glance toward Thrain's satisfied face—to which Thrain merrily laughed, and gave another proprietary nibble at Varinn's neck. "Och, and I ken she's getting a little feisty, too," he said, with immense satisfaction. "Wants to sink her little claws into me, for always draping myself all over her mate. Distracting you, and stealing away your scent for myself, when you promised it all to her, ach?"

Varinn was frowning toward Thrain, his eyes gone narrow and suspicious—but when he glanced toward Kitty, she could see his chest hollowing, his mouth twisting. Looking almost guilty, or even regretful, and Kitty fought down the surge of genuine surprise by frantically shaking her head, and flapping her hands toward him.

"I *wanted* that last night, remember?" she said, too loudly. "Very much indeed! So I'm perfectly fine, and very happy for you both. I want you to be happy."

The words sounded true, they *were* true, but Varinn was still looking at her like that, and Thrain's smile had faded, his head drawing back, so he could search Varinn's face. "Too sweet, as always," he said, under his breath. "You'll tend to her next, ach, Varinn? Remind her that she was right to trust you, and you'll always care for her, too?"

Varinn betrayed a very faint wince, his gaze darting between Kitty and Thrain, and now Thrain was looking at Kitty too, with something much like sympathy in his eyes. "Don't like to scent her, thus," he continued, even softer. "How long's it been since she's had your seed, almost a whole day now? Worry for her health, too, and our son."

Varinn's throat visibly spasmed, and to Kitty's ever-increasing disbelief, he—nodded. Nodded, and drew away from Thrain, so he could stride toward her in the bed. His shoulders square, his jaw set, his eyes flinty and determined. And Kitty couldn't stop staring, her mouth fallen open, as he halted to stand beside the bed before her, and—pulled off his towel. Revealing the rigid, swelling green length behind it, already steadily leaking, and bobbing toward her mouth.

"Forgive me, Katharine," he said, his voice sounding careful, almost formal. "I held no wish to forsake your care for so long, or deny you what ought to be rightfully yours."

Oh, hell. Kitty's eyes were still gaping, her breath juddering out harsh, and she couldn't help a furtive, grateful little smile up toward his face as she drifted forward, her mouth already watering, her tongue brushing her lips. Gods, it really had been almost an entire day since they'd done this, and she really had missed it, to an astonishing degree, and...

"Ach, wait, Varinn," came a distant, disapproving voice, Thrain's voice, and that was his hand, slipping around Varinn's bare waist from behind, drawing him back. "Ordering her to suck you isn't much of an apology, is it? Surely Lord Grisk's favoured heir can do better than that?"

Varinn huffed an irritated-sounding exhale, his eyes again angling narrow toward Thrain. But Thrain only frowned back, and shoved Varinn toward the bed—and to Kitty's ongoing astonishment, Varinn actually obliged. Sinking down heavily onto the fur, so he was seated beside her. His big body suddenly seeming far too close, too present, too powerful... especially that heft at his groin, now propped thick and full against his belly, sputtering its white fluid onto his skin.

"I ken your sweet kitten would mayhap like to be petted, Varinn," Thrain was blithely saying now, setting a knee to the bed on Varinn's other side, and shifting around to nibble at his shoulder. "Mayhap in your lap."

Varinn's glare toward Thrain was instant, and distinctly incredulous, maybe even offended—and Kitty blanched at the sight of it, twitching backwards, as a sudden bitter misery plunged in her belly. Gods, what had she been thinking, going along with any of this? Of course Varinn didn't actually want to do it, he still didn't care for her in the slightest, he was just doing this for Thrain, and that was all...

"Och, watch it, Varinn," Thrain hissed, his eyes darting toward Kitty, his voice gone surprisingly sharp. "If you're going to keep sparking that much hurt in her scent, mayhap you'll let me comfort her instead?"

At that, Varinn's big body spasmed, a low growl scraping from his throat, and he'd even bared his teeth toward Thrain, his lips curled back. And wait, wait, it wasn't making sense, why was he *angry*—and for an instant, Thrain looked almost as confused as Kitty felt, his head tilting, his eyes studying Varinn's face.

"I ken," Varinn finally said, his breaths oddly laboured, "that Katharine—ought to speak—what *she* wishes for. Not you."

He'd angled Kitty a brief, apologetic look, suggesting that— oh. He thought—he thought *she* didn't want it. He thought she wouldn't want to be held, petted in his lap, fussed over, cared for...

Kitty's mouth had gone inexplicably dry, her cheeks again burning hot, her eyes frozen on Varinn's face. While beside him, Thrain chuckled, the sound husky, almost relieved. "Ach, now I follow," he said softly. "But I ken your kitten is still a bit skittish of you, Lord Grisk, and mayhap too shy to speak what she truly wishes from you. At least"—he winked toward her over Varinn's shoulder—"when it comes to her own pleasure, ach?"

Oh, gods damn Thrain, and maybe Kitty was even proving his point, sitting here stunned and staring like this, her tongue too tangled in her mouth. "Look, I'm not—" she began, and drew in a shuddery breath, tried again. "I'm quite all right. Very well indeed! And there's no need whatsoever for any petting, or comforting, from either of you. And I'm sure Varinn has many other important matters to attend to, and other places he needs to be, so..."

But her voice trailed off, because neither of them appeared to be listening. And instead, Varinn was grimacing toward

Thrain, whose expression was bright again, gleeful, maybe even smug. "See?" Thrain said, with satisfaction, before flicking his gaze back toward Kitty. "You'd like Lord Grisk to comfort you, wouldn't you, Kit? You'd like"—his voice lowered, softened again—"to curl up safe in his lap, to feel him pet you, and kiss you, and care for you?"

Oh, hell, because Kitty's breath was rushing from her lungs, escaping in a sound much like a moan, or a whimper. And damn Thrain, again, because he was smiling at her with such warm, indulgent approval, his eyes dancing with delight. "And while he's at it," he murmured, "maybe he'll grant you that good Grisk load he's been nursing in those fat bollocks of his, too."

Kitty couldn't hold back another whimper, or the way the stark, stunning longing was swirling, surging up in her chest. Enough to draw Varinn's strangely hazy gaze back toward her, as his chest filled with his breath, his broad shoulders squaring. As his big hand slowly, carefully slid over, and...

Caught on Kitty's bare hip. Curving warm and gentle around it, so he could... draw her up. Closer. Toward him. Toward his... *lap.*

Kitty startled all over, because he didn't mean it, he didn't want it, he couldn't—or could he? Or could he, because his other hand was here too, settling against that slight swell in her belly, spreading wide over it. And she couldn't at all read that look in his eyes, dark and glittering, as he tugged her closer.

There was no fighting it, no will to fight it, nothing. And somehow, after a moment's awkward scrambling, Kitty found herself indeed seated in Varinn's lap, her legs straddling his waist, her eyes blinking wide and shocked toward his face.

But he didn't look away. Didn't falter. Just settled her a little closer, her bare arse pressing against his bulky bare thighs, the heat between her legs blatantly opened toward him, oh. And he was inhaling again, slow and deliberate, as he held her eyes, and slipped his big warm hands up her sides. Touching her. Petting her.

Kitty couldn't stop the reflexive shiver, the scattering gooseflesh beneath his touch, and she only distantly heard Thrain's laugh, low and satisfied behind Varinn. "Much better," he murmured. "She likes it, ach?"

If Varinn heard, he didn't acknowledge it, not even when Thrain again ducked his head into his neck, nipped at it with his teeth. While his own hands settled on Varinn's bare sides, fingers spreading wide.

And when Varinn moved his warm hands down again, back to Kitty's hips, Thrain did the same to him. Stroking slow and easy and languid, and Kitty could already see how Thrain's touch was relaxing Varinn's shoulders, easing the tension in his jaw. How it was even softening the touch of Varinn's hands against her, sliding them smoother, spreading his fingers wider. Scattering more light, sparkling sensation across Kitty's skin, drawing it deep into her chest, her belly, her exposed quivering heat.

Her breaths were already gasping, her body arching against Varinn's caress. Against where one of those big warm hands had slipped around her back, skating lightly over the links of his *thyrja*, until it rose all the way to her neck. Flaring out more shimmering heat, more sharp wheeling hunger, especially when that hand circled, so very gently, around her neck. Enclosing it almost entirely in his light, careful grip, almost, almost a threat, but not quite. And Kitty shouldn't have moaned like that, shuddered like that, the longing surging and aching, catching in his watching, glittering, too-knowing eyes.

"Ach, she *really* likes that," murmured Thrain, from where his own teeth were scraping at Varinn's throat. "Really oughta give her that *kraga*, Varinn."

Varinn didn't seem slightly inclined to argue with this, his black tongue brushing his lips, as his sharp claw very gently nudged at the hollow of Kitty's throat. Holding her entire life in his hand, in this one claw, in this moment—and surely that was truth, it was only due to his mercy that she was even here, even alive, let alone shuddering all over with such desperate, agonizing pleasure.

And Varinn knew it, he saw it, tasted it, his eyes again flaring with dark, dangerous power as he slipped his warm hand down Kitty's front, his claw very gently scraping her hard, peaked nipple. Driving another choked, frantic gasp from her mouth, and oh, that might have even been a twitch of a smile on his mouth as he did it again. Just brushing his claw against that straining peak, watching her shiver and gasp, utterly caught beneath his touch, his whim, his control.

"So much better, ach?" Thrain's heated voice was murmuring, still into Varinn's neck. "Scents so sweet, Varinn. Don't stop. *Ach.*"

And thank the gods, Varinn wasn't stopping, his other hand come up to her other nipple, stroking it, too. While Kitty gasped and moaned against him, now helplessly pressing into his touch, pressing closer, until—oh. Something nudged against her lower belly. Something hard, hot, insistent, streaking its slick wetness against her bare skin.

Kitty's gasp was almost a cry this time, her wild eyes desperately darting down toward the sight. Toward that thick, rigid jut of hungry flesh, now pressed up close between them, and steadily pouring from its deep-cut slit. And oh, now she couldn't seem to stop looking at it, especially when Thrain's audacious hand slipped around to touch it, and then began... stroking it. Slipping smoothly into that thick, oozing white, sliding it up and down, smearing it all over...

"You want Lord Grisk inside you now, ach, Kit?" came Thrain's voice, so smooth, so damnably tempting. "You want to sit your pretty little form all the way down upon him, and milk his good fresh seed into your sweet little womb?"

Kitty gulped, shuddered all over, and felt herself helplessly nodding, as the longing stabbed sharp, deep, devastating. As

Thrain's hand kept stroking, kept milking, polishing Varinn's oozing cock to a slick, glossy shine. The sounds now lurid and obscene, Varinn's thick seed liberally pouring over Thrain's knuckles, coating his hand, the sweet scent humid and musky in the air...

"Ach, look at him, Kit," Thrain's low voice continued, soft with satisfaction. "All ready for you, ach? Ready to fill you up with him, and his scent."

Kitty's gaze snapped back to Varinn's face, to his flushed cheeks, his glinting eyes. To where he wasn't denying this, not in the slightest, and behind him, Thrain was chuckling again, and then shifting even closer, too. His knees now straddling Varinn's hips from behind, his face buried into Varinn's neck, his hand still stroking, still milking out that thick pouring sweetness...

"Wants to make us match, I ken," Thrain breathed, even hotter. "Wants us both walking around here reeking of him. Leaking his fresh seed every time we damn well move."

Varinn's eyes flashed, fluttered, and that was a hard, husky growl, burning low from his throat. The wetness from Thrain's pumping hand spattering straight up, now, streaking across Kitty's belly, and oh, oh, Varinn's big hands were finally clamping on her hips, drawing her up. Positioning her over him, oh hell, over where Thrain was guiding that slick, dripping head up toward her...

And yes, yes, that was it, that was him, there, nudging so large and smooth up against her open, frantically convulsing heat. Touching her, seeking against her, spluttering his slick fluid inside her. *Inside* her, easing his way, because oh, he was already pressing, flashing out an unmistakable twinge of pain around him. Or maybe that was her, bearing downwards, needing to feel him opening her, breaching her, making her his...

Until Varinn's hands clenched on her hips, stopping her, just perched there on the head of him. And she could see his heated eyes flicking down, holding on the sight, on where—oh, hell—Thrain's hand was still stroking between them, still milking him, easing out more, into her, *into* her.

"Easy, *kisa*," breathed Varinn's low voice, rough and silken all at once. "Slow. Cannot risk harming you, or our son."

Oh gods, oh gods, Kitty couldn't think, couldn't move, her eyes wild and almost panicked on his face. Because she needed him so much, needed this so desperately, needed to please him and to honour him and bear his scent, gain his protection and his care, please—

"But I need it," she choked at him, begged him, unthinking, her hands clutching against his chest. "Need you, my lord. Need you inside me, need your scent, you have no idea how much, I—"

An unmistakable surprise had flashed across Varinn's hazy gaze, but then he nodded, *nodded*. And that might have even been warmth, approval, flickering in his eyes, as he guided her down just a little more, opened her just a little wider. "Ach, I ken," he murmured, so soft. "But slow, *kisa*."

Right, right, the gratefulness and the relief swerving up, shuddering in Kitty's ribs, in her fingers clutching at his chest. In how Varinn was still steadily sinking in, guiding her down, stretching her out around him. And oh, gods, she could feel the full overpowering girth of him now, so much, too much, not enough, not enough—

"Oh gods," she gasped, trembling all over, as she felt herself clamp around him, around that full width of him, impaling her, holding her wide open upon him. And oh, wait, she could feel Thrain's hand now, too, still stroking between them, but there was less room, less to milk and squeeze, because Varinn was halfway into her now, sinking deeper with every slow, excruciating breath. And finally Thrain's slick, dripping fingers fluttered up, slid against Kitty's chin, into her mouth. Tasting of Varinn, of them, enough to shock her to utter stillness upon him—and then she belatedly began sucking, while both Varinn and Thrain watched. Varinn with a surprisingly cool indulgence, Thrain with a wild, feverish light in his eyes.

"Keep going, Kit," Thrain hissed, hot and harsh, through his bared teeth. "You don't stop until he says."

Kitty groaned, fervently nodded, cast an alarmed apologetic look at Varinn's watching, patient eyes. "Please, Lord Grisk, please," she babbled, as he sank a little deeper, a little deeper. "Please, oh gods, please, don't stop, I need it, need you, need your scent, please—"

The words kept coming, kept escaping her mouth in a steady shameful stream, but she scarcely heard them now, shivering all over like this, grasping helplessly at Varinn's chest, his broad shoulders. Lost in that impossible stretching strength, still opening her, conquering her, occupying her, making its claim. Until there was nowhere left for it to go, stabbed so tight and full inside, with Kitty writhing upon it, upon him, trapped, wide open, utterly exposed and bared and—

"More, Kit," came Thrain's hot voice, silken and unrepentant. "You wanted Lord Grisk's ploughing, you fucking take it. All the way."

Oh gods, but it was already so much, so, so much, and maybe Varinn saw the panic in Kitty's eyes, felt it in her fluttering hands—because he reached up, firmly grasped Thrain's head, and thrust it down into his neck. And then he gathered Kitty closer, tucking her against his broad heaving chest, as his hands swept up and down her shaking, trembling back.

"Quiet, *kisa*," he breathed, and she could hear that low, shushing purr, could feel it rumbling through his chest. "This is good. So good."

Oh, oh he didn't mean it, he couldn't, but Kitty already felt herself melting into him, into that safe solid warmth. Into how it was all around her, and buried deep inside her, holding her here tight and close upon her lord. And if she clutched even tighter at him, wriggled herself deeper upon him, he didn't seem to mind. Just kept caressing, stroking, soothing, as that low steady rumble filled her chest, her heart.

"Good," he breathed again. "Good, *kisa*. You honour me. You honour our clan, our forebears, our son. You shall carry forward our scents, our line, and our home. Our *life*. Ach?"

He said *life* like it was a precious thing, a thing worth guarding, worth treasuring, worth revering. And Kitty nodded, frantic and fervent and forever lost, forever caught, clamped and clinging and craving, until—

Varinn gasped as he sprayed out inside her, his body pitching forward, catching her in his arms. As the all-consuming strength locked within her powerfully pulsed, again and again and again, pouring her full from the inside out, painting her with his scent, with his fresh Grisk seed. Giving it to her, offering it to her, and Kitty wanted to weep with the truth of it, the stark sheer promise of it, carrying forward their scents, their home, their... life.

And amidst that truth, that impossible awareness, Kitty's own relief flashed dark and dizzying, seizing so strong it escaped in a scream, in her entire body spasming, thrashing wild against him. Against where his big arms just kept cradling her, keeping her held tight, safe against the waves crashing over her. Until finally, finally, it somehow faded, leaving Kitty gasping, clinging to Varinn with all her might, while shameful wetness streaked down her hot cheeks.

But if Varinn was embarrassed, or offended, he again showed no sign of it. Only just kept caressing Kitty with those big warm hands, smooth and steady, as her breaths gradually slowed, her thoughts settling into a strange, stilted disbelief.

She'd... done that. With Varinn. With *Varinn*, who was still locked deep inside her, but that didn't seem to bother him, either. And instead, he kept on stroking her, again and again, even bringing up a hand to gently wipe the wetness from her cheeks. As if this was entirely to be expected, and he'd dealt with tearful overwrought lovers many, many times before. And wait, maybe—Kitty twitched a little backwards, searching for Thrain—maybe he had.

And yes, yes, Thrain had lifted his head from Varinn's neck, blinking back toward her—and in another moment, another life, Kitty might have been shocked by the red streaked all over his mouth, or the ragged teeth-marks he'd left in Varinn's skin. But right now, there was only the wry, knowing sympathy in his red-rimmed smile, shimmering in his warm, contented eyes.

"You all right, Kit?" he asked thickly. "Still in one piece?"

Kitty couldn't help a choked, shrill little laugh, a jerky shrug of her shoulder. "I... I think so," she managed, with a mortified glance toward Varinn's watching, hooded eyes, still surprisingly easy on hers, despite a distinct dark haziness. "That was..."

There truly were no words, no way to explain it, and Thrain gave a low chuckle, a wry shake of his head. "That's what happens when you fuck a god's favoured son," he murmured. "You'll get used to it, ach? And lucky for us"—his glance toward Varinn was teasing this time—"he's usually good about it. Once you give him his due, at least."

Oh. A quivery little shudder ran up Kitty's spine, even as she winced toward Varinn, and shook her head. "But I didn't even—" she began, and felt her face heating, her eyes dropping to his chest. She surely hadn't been a good bedmate just now, not at all the kind of fun, eager, desirable partner she'd always strived to be. The kind of bedmate men liked to keep around, the ones they would pay for, and care for...

"Och, Kit," Thrain said, his hand brushing at her shoulder, drawing her head up. "If this is because of anything I said"—he grimaced—"it was rubbish, ach? Got carried away, you know, like I usually do. Doesn't mean Varinn agrees with me, ach, Varinn?"

His eyes darted uneasily toward Varinn again, toward where Varinn's expression was still mild, hazy, surprisingly soft.

"I rarely agree with you, Thrain," he said, still with that silken huskiness on his voice. "So ach, Katharine, you ought to ignore all he says, and listen only to me."

Kitty gulped another hoarse little laugh, even as a distant whispering voice pointed out that Varinn had, perhaps, liked quite a bit of what Thrain had said, amidst all that. And yes, Thrain was scoffing at Varinn, rolling his eyes, and giving a painful-looking nip at the mess of teeth-marks he'd left on Varinn's neck. "Tyrant," he muttered, with another sharp nip. "I really do want to see her take you all the way, though, Varinn."

Varinn gave a halfhearted sideways hiss toward Thrain, before settling his mild gaze back on Kitty. "I ken she shall, soon enough," he said, with a cool, thrilling certainty. "Ach, Katharine?"

Oh, gods, he meant they were going to do it *again*, and Kitty couldn't stop her helpless-sounding groan, the reflexive clutch of her hands to his chest. Or the clutch of her tender-feeling heat against the slightly softened bulk inside her, which—she blanched—seemed to release a sudden surge of hot fluid between them, pooling thick and viscous out onto Varinn's lap.

"Ach," Varinn muttered, clearly displeased by this threat to the furs—but Thrain was already leaping off the bed, and returning with a rag, and the clean basin. And soon they were all laughing together as they attempted to maneuver the rag and basin, and catch the worst of the mess.

It should have felt shameful, or even humiliating, but Varinn was still just so easy, so relaxed and warm and indulgent, while Thrain almost radiated a bright, delighted glee. Especially once Kitty had finally been fully cleaned up, and Varinn had moved the rag to his own messy, seed-streaked groin—and then hesitated as he glanced, brief and affectionate, toward Thrain. Toward where Thrain had been intently watching, his tongue greedily brushing his lips—and with a soft chuckle, Varinn firmly grasped Thrain's head, and guided it down toward his groin instead.

Thrain's moan of pleasure was hoarse, reverently grateful, and he instantly sank to his knees on the floor, and began lavishing Varinn with feverish abandon. While Varinn leaned back on the bed and coolly watched, his arm circling easily around Kitty's waist, drawing her into his side. Until his eyes briefly fluttered, his head tilting back—and then he again poured out into Thrain's throat, while Thrain choked and gasped, and stroked himself out into the basin.

But afterwards, Thrain was even more gleeful than before, laughing and prancing around their room, and tackling Varinn to the floor more than once. And they once again helped each other dress, except that this time, Kitty had her lovely stack of new clothes for them to choose from. And after a good amount of bickering back and forth—in which Kitty discovered that her old dressing-gowns had inexplicably disappeared—she ended up dressed in yet another short kilt, with only a piece of fluttery fabric covering her breasts, together with, of course, Varinn's *thyrja*.

"Are you sure this is appropriate?" she doubtfully asked them, tugging uncertainly at the fabric—but Thrain only grinned, waggling his eyebrows, while Varinn gave a sharp, curt nod.

"This is customary Grisk garb," he said firmly. "And any mate of mine ought to dress thus, ach? This shows me great honour, before our kin."

Oh. It was enough to send another warm, trembly thrill up Kitty's spine, especially when Varinn turned toward that box on his shelf, and snapped it open. And then—Kitty's breath caught—he brought out something new. Something that flashed and glittered against his fingers as he strode back toward her, his eyes not quite meeting hers.

"Ought to have earrings, also," he said, a little husky, as he held one up against her ear. "To match the *thyrja*, ach?"

Oh, gods, he didn't mean it, he couldn't, and Kitty nearly whimpered as she stared down at the other earring, still glittering in his hand. It was a cluster of intricate, beautifully crafted dangling chains, ones that would shimmer and sparkle whenever she moved, and they were surely by the same maker as the *thyrja*, meant to be a matched set. And Varinn was already slipping the first earring into her earlobe, his fingers very careful against her skin, while Thrain snatched the other one from his hand, and did the other side. And then they both stepped back to look, Varinn giving a decisive little nod, while Thrain flashed her a stunning, approving grin.

"But—you can't," Kitty gulped at Varinn, at both of them, shaking her head, and oh, she could feel the beautiful earrings moving, softly brushing their gold against her skin. "It's—too much. So much. Again."

But they both waved it away in unison, and Thrain lifted his hand to touch the earring again, running the chains through his fingers with something almost like reverence. "Suits you, though, Kit," he said. "Gorgeous smithing, too. Much better to see them on you, rather than leaving them to moulder in a box, ach?"

Varinn was nodding, too, a small, approving smile on his mouth—and then he spun back toward the box, combing through it with his claw. "Now you, Thrain," he said, his voice far too smooth. "Mayhap this?"

This. It was another earring, surely, but it was thick and round, a single perfect loop of bright, gleaming gold. And Thrain's breath stilled as he stared at it, as Varinn snapped the earring open, revealing a glinting, sharpened point. And then he pulled over their nearby lamp, holding the point into the steady flame, turning it back and forth. And once he seemed satisfied, he turned back toward Thrain, his shoulders squared, his jaw set.

"Here, ach?" he said, huskier, as he held the ring up against the flushed, pointed tip of Thrain's right ear. "Should you wish?"

Thrain rapidly nodded, and Varinn visibly swallowed as he

nudged Thrain downwards, onto his knees. So Thrain was kneeling on the fur before him, his face upturned, his eyes almost worshipful on Varinn's face. While Varinn carefully stroked at the delicate flushed tip of his ear, pulling it taut— and then he stabbed the piercing deep.

Thrain gasped, harsh and hoarse, his face twitching with pain, or pleasure, or both. But already, Varinn had bent over him, gently drawing that pierced ear-tip deep into his mouth. And Kitty could see Thrain's expression softening, his body leaning into Varinn's touch, his shaky hand gripping at Varinn's muscled calf.

And when Varinn drew away again, Kitty couldn't stop staring at that lovely, gleaming gold ring, now embedded in Thrain's ear. At how it perfectly suited him there, looking both rakish and refined, glinting against his messy black hair.

Varinn clearly liked it too, his hand slipping into Thrain's hair, tilting his head up, as something again bobbed in his throat. And Kitty felt herself swallowing too, and sidling closer to get a better look. "It looks lovely on him," she said, soft. "You truly have such excellent taste, Lord Grisk."

Varinn's mouth curved into something very like a smile, while Thrain grinned broadly up toward her. "Ach?" he said, eager and perhaps a little shy. "You like it, Kit?"

Kitty fervently nodded, making her own earrings sway against her skin, and beside her, that was a nod from Varinn too, or even a telltale twitch at the front of his kilt. But then he cleared his throat and stepped purposefully away, straightening out his kilt, and smoothing out his braid.

"Now, come, you two," he said. "We have much to address today, ach?"

Thrain shot Kitty a wry, resigned grin, but leapt to his feet, and brushed out his own kilt, too. "Ach, whatever you say, Lord Grisk," he replied lightly. "We are yours to command."

Varinn nodded, glancing briefly between them both, as if he fully expected that now, as if it was his right. And maybe it was, and gods, maybe Kitty even wanted it that way. Wanted his supervision, his care, his beautiful impossible gifts, his...

"Good," he said firmly. "For today, Thrain, we shall return to our duties in earnest. Whilst Katharine, should she agree"—his eyes settled on hers, his shoulders squaring—"shall begin to learn a trade, as an apprentice in the Grisk Shop."

34

itty blinked at Varinn for a hushed, dangling moment, while his words seemed to rattle and echo through her skull. He was sending her to learn a trade? In the Grisk Shop?

And yes, yes, a distant rational voice pointed out, that was exactly what she'd wanted, what she'd asked him for. And the shop *had* been truly delightful, and an apprenticeship as a shopkeeper sounded surprisingly appealing, and well in line with her skills and interests. So why was her heart hammering like this, and why did it feel like such a... an *insult*, after everything they'd just done? Why had she thought that sharing such intimacies with Varinn would change things, why had she thought it would make any difference at all?

I shall do all within my power, Varinn had told her, *no matter the cost*. And surely all that—him soothing her, caring for her, making love to her, even giving her these beautiful earrings—it had been, once again, about Thrain. Not her.

But when Kitty's blinking eyes darted toward Thrain, he looked even more unsettled than she felt. His mouth half-open, his body rigid, his eyes narrow and suspicious on Varinn's face.

"What the hell do you mean, Kit's going to work?" he demanded, his voice sharp. "She's pregnant, Varinn!"

Varinn's gaze angled toward Kitty, but he squared his shoulders, and gave a curt nod. "Ach, I ken," he said, very steadily. "But her health is now much improved, and Ymir has sworn to grant her leave to rest, whenever she needs this."

"Ymir?" Thrain echoed, even sharper. "You're really sending her off to apprentice with that ornery old codger? To spend every damned *day* with him?!"

Varinn's eyes flared with something Kitty couldn't read, but he nodded again. "Ach," he replied. "You ken Ymir should never harm a woman, Thrain. And he is quite taken with Katharine, and says she should well suit the work. He shall teach her well, and keep a close watch over her."

Thrain's mouth was opening and closing, the disbelief in his eyes now clashing with something much like rage—and far too late, Kitty stumbled forward, and grasped his arm. "I—I asked Varinn for it," she said, in a rush. "I asked him to find some work for me. I—I've always wanted to learn a trade, and have a way to support myself. It's something I've never had a chance to do before, and—"

But Thrain's eyes on her were incredulous now, or maybe even hurt. "But you don't *need* to support yourself, Kit," he said, almost pleading. "Not now, not anymore. Not as long as you have"—he grimaced, twitched his head—"Varinn to take care of you, ach? You can trust he'll never fail, in this. Especially not now. Ach, Varinn?"

He'd angled that hurt, pleading look toward Varinn, who was now rubbing at his nose, and looking intently away—but then he nodded, short and curt. A response that only seemed to agitate Thrain further, his eyes wildly darting between them, his body bobbing on his feet.

And gods, why couldn't Kitty move, and she finally cleared her throat, and squeezed his arm a little tighter. "It's got nothing to do with not trusting you, Thrain, truly," she said, high-pitched. "It's just—I've always depended so much on—others—in the past, and it's led to some... difficulties, for me. And this is just something I've wanted to do, for—for myself, and for our..."

She bit off the dangerous word *son*, just in time—but Thrain might as well have heard it, his eyes again incredulous, disbelieving, hurt. "You ken you need to toil away as a damned *shopkeeper* to support our son?" he demanded, his voice angrier than Kitty had ever heard it. "You really think that little of us? Of me, ach, I ken I deserve that, but *Varinn*?!"

Oh. Something cold and painful was scraping up Kitty's spine, shivering her all over—but oh, thank the gods, Varinn was here, stepping toward her, rubbing his big hand up and down her back. "You will leave this *now*, Thrain," he hissed. "We shall listen to Katharine's own wishes, and honour them. If learning a trade shall fulfill her, and grant her peace, then we shall uphold this, with all our strength. This shall only serve to all our gain, and our son's gain, also."

His voice was hard, authoritative, utterly certain, and despite her still-whispering hurt, Kitty felt herself sagging into his touch, into his strength. Into his... permission, even, her right to choose this, to be supported in this. To have a man—an orc!—want what... what *she* wanted.

And surely Thrain had followed that, understood that, his unhappy eyes first searching hers, and then Varinn's. And then he nodded, and even smiled, though it didn't at all reach his eyes.

"Ach," he said thickly. "Ach, I follow. I ken I"—he bowed his head, squeezed at his eyes—"I ken it is mostly the thought of leaving her with Ymir all day, ach? And all those greedy, coin-grubbing hoarders like Harthr, too. *Harthr*, Varinn! *Ugh*."

He gave a palpable shudder, and beside Kitty, Varinn's mouth slightly grimaced, too—but then he pulled up taller, his hand spreading wider on Kitty's back. "Enough, Thrain," he said flatly. "You are a Speaker's Guard, and you ought not to speak thus of our kin, who work tirelessly for all our gain. And Ymir shall take good care of her, ach? And you ken no Grisk would *dare* to touch or harm *our* woman."

Thrain's head snapped up at the *our woman* part, his eyes strangely alight on Varinn's—but then he nodded again, rapid and swift. "Ach," he said. "Ach, I ken Ymir will do his best to care for you, Kit—for Varinn's sake, if naught else. If you can truly bear him and his rubbish all day."

He shot Kitty a wan little smile, and she couldn't help a quick, genuine smile back. "I really don't mind Ymir," she said. "He's just... very enthusiastic about his shop. Rightfully so, though, because it *is* quite spectacular, don't you think?"

The eagerness was clear in her voice, and she could see Thrain's shoulders sagging a little more, his eyes again meeting Varinn's. "Ach, just so, Kit," he said, with another attempt at a smile. "I ken they'll be lucky to have you."

Well, then. Kitty felt herself beaming toward Thrain, and then toward Varinn, too. And Varinn's slow, approving smile back was enough to settle her shoulders, and soothe the fluttering unease in her chest. He'd made love to her. He'd given her beautiful gifts. He'd found her an apprenticeship. And he'd given Thrain so much happiness too, by granting him his scent, and that piercing. And maybe, maybe...

The hopefulness kept rising as they ate a cheerful breakfast with their kin—ignoring Thrak's repeated dark looks at their new earrings—and then headed for the shrine. And though Thrain again made his excuses at the door, mumbling something about needing to pack their goods for the day, Kitty found that the prayers again seemed to help, too. And there was something strangely powerful, meaningful, about kneeling before Lord Grisk together with Varinn, their elbows touching, their hands over their hearts.

Afterwards, it felt even easier to smile at Varinn, and to cheerfully chat and joke with him as he took her to the Great Grisk Showroom-Shop. To where Ymir was already waiting for them behind the counter, his eyes bright and eager on Kitty's face.

"There you are," he said, without preamble, as he enthusiastically waved her around the counter. "Now come in, come in, and we shall begin!"

Kitty nodded and smiled, and made to oblige—at least, until she found that Varinn's hand had tightened around her waist, holding her close against him. And when she shot an uncertain glance up at his face, she found him looking surprisingly intent, or perhaps even—nervous?

"You shall rest whenever you feel weary, Katharine," he told her. "And you shall not leave Ymir's scent, ach? Nor leave the shop, without a trustworthy guard. And if you hunger, or thirst, or need the latrine—or feel ill at ease for any cause—you shall only call for Ymir, and he shall help you at once. Ach, Ymir?"

Ymir's expression was something between indulgent and impatient, and he jerked a curt nod toward them. "No need to fret, son," he said firmly. "You ken I'll keep her well guarded for you. Most of all now that you have fully claimed her as your own."

With that, he gave them an approving wink, sending that distinctive red flush up the back of Varinn's neck. Because wait, Ymir meant he could smell Varinn on Kitty, could smell what they'd done that morning, and—and wait, did he really think Varinn had fully *claimed* her now? As his own?

"I thank you, brother," Varinn said, his voice stiff, his eyes not quite meeting Kitty's. "And Katharine, I shall come to fetch you once we are done our day's work, ach?"

Right. He was leaving her alone here, for perhaps the entire day. And once again, that whispering unease skittered up in Kitty's chest, and despite her nod and her smile, she was still hovering up against him, searching his distant eyes.

"And will you be... nearby?" she asked, before she could stop it. "Or will Thrain, perhaps?"

Varinn winced and jerked a shrug, his gaze still fixed

beyond Kitty's head. "This hinges upon what kin need us most," he said. "We shall go wherever we are needed, whether within or beyond the mountain. This is the work we are called to do, ach?"

Oh. Kitty's nod and smile felt a little forced this time, but she made her best attempt, and wrenched herself away from the warm safety of his side. "I wish you much success, then," she said, too brightly. "And safe travels!"

Varinn's chest hollowed, his hand rubbing at his nose, but he nodded too—and then he spun and strode out, without so much as a farewell. Leaving Kitty blinking uncertainly after him, while Ymir loudly snorted, and again waved Kitty behind the counter.

"That boy's always worked too hard," he informed her. "No sense seeking to bully it out of him, either, for he'll just dig in his claws out of spite. Stubborn little wretch, just like his father."

He spoke with genuine-seeming fondness, and Kitty felt her hurt slightly fading, beneath the twitch of rising interest. "You knew Varinn's father?" she asked. "Before he... passed?"

Her thoughts were darting backwards, catching again on how very little she knew of Varinn and Thrain's histories, or their families. And in truth, she held no desire to dredge up her own past either, but it suddenly still seemed like another slight, another unhappy reminder of her place. Varinn didn't really care about her. She wasn't a real mate. It was just a debt. Just for Thrain...

"Ach, I knew Varinn's father well," Ymir absently replied, as he waved Kitty after him, down into one of the shop's aisles. "Vrangr was a good Grisk, a good father and mate, who gave all to care for his kin. Varinn is much like him, ach?"

Kitty opened her mouth to ask what had happened to Vrangr, but Ymir was already trotting faster, his eager eyes fixed straight ahead. "Now come, woman," he said, over his shoulder. "We have a new shipment today! This will please you, I ken."

Kitty nodded and hurried to catch up, following Ymir into a large, open space at the far end of the aisle. And there, piled haphazardly on the stone floor, was a huge, teetering stack of... chaos. Furs, clothes, blankets, lamps and cutlery and jars and hammers, and even what appeared to be several long, fresh-cut pieces of *timber*.

"Plenty of work for your first day," Ymir said, with satisfaction, as he plucked up an item from the top of the pile—a wool blanket—and inspected it before shaking it out, neatly folding it, and setting it on a nearby cart. "Need to look through it all, sort out what's got value, and what doesn't. Then it needs to be scented through by an orc with a good nose— Varinn oft helps when he can—and I'll tally it up, and pay out the credits to the sellers."

Kitty hadn't fully followed all that, but she accordingly picked up an item—a tunic—and shook it out, too. "Er, so why does it all need to be—*scented through*?" she asked, as she took a careful sniff of the tunic. "Does that affect the value, somehow?"

"Ach, now and then," Ymir said, as he yanked a pair of trousers out of the pile. "But most of all, we need to be sure of the source. A scent will speak of who's made or owned the good, and oft whether it's been taken under duress. If a piece reeks of pain or death, or if it rightfully belongs to one already living here, we can't be selling that, ach? Taints the stock, and the good name of the Great Grisk Showroom-Shop!"

His chest proudly puffed out, and Kitty couldn't help a brief, amused grin toward him. "That sounds like an excellent policy to me," she said. "And what if"—she held out her tunic, showing him a small rip in the hem—"an item needs repairs? Do you refuse to take it?"

"Ach, no," Ymir said, glancing over at the rip. "But we'll lower the payout, and send it off for repair. Usually to the Skai tailor, Gamall, but he's a busy fellow, who doesn't like to be bothered with smaller jobs. But, woman"—his eyes glinted as they narrowed toward her—"I ken you've got some sewing skill too, ach? One of the reasons Varinn recommended you so highly."

Wait. Varinn had recommended her because of—her sewing skill? But they hadn't ever discussed her sewing, had they? Or really, any kind of skills or experience Kitty might possess whatsoever, or—in truth—even her suitability for an apprenticeship like this. Right?

But clearly Ymir had caught Kitty's confusion, because he gave her an apologetic smile as he sifted through the huge stack, and yanked out a familiar-looking item. One of... Kitty's old dressing-gowns?

"Varinn brought them all in last eve," he said. "Told me how he couldn't bear the man's scent on them, and how henceforth you'd be dressing for him as a good Grisk mate. But"—he brandished the gown's hem toward Kitty—"that's your stitching, ach? And this is your work on the lace and pleats, too? It's got your scent all over it."

Oh. It was still taking Kitty far too long to follow this—Varinn wanted her to keep dressing for him, as a *good Grisk mate*? And he'd gone and sold off her dressing-gowns, because he hadn't liked Charles' scent on them? *And*, he'd been observant enough to notice her own scent on the stitching, and then to use that as a recommendation to Ymir?

"Er, yes, that's all mine," she belatedly replied, blinking down at the dressing-gown, and then back at Ymir's face. "I've always done a lot of sewing, it was very necessary in my old..."

Her voice faded uncomfortably away, but Ymir didn't seem to notice, and gave a short, satisfied nod, rubbing his hands together. "Good, good," he said brightly. "Just what we needed, you ken. So we'll set you up with a spot for mending, mayhap over there"—he'd nodded toward the shop's very back corner, which currently held a few chairs and a large looking-glass—"where you can work away at any smaller repairs that come in, so Gamall can focus on the bigger jobs. And if you'll chart your work, we'll charge that to the sellers, and add a portion to your salary, also."

He'd been speaking very quickly, the excitement almost contagious in his voice, but once again Kitty was blinking uncertainly toward him, and feeling genuinely baffled. "My... salary?" she asked. "What do you mean?"

Ymir gave her an odd look, and yanked a fur out of the pile. "You work, you earn payment," he said. "These most oft would be trading-credits, but you can trade these for human coin, also."

Kitty was still blinking at him, shaking her head. "But— usually apprenticeships involve paying fees," she said. "For your time in training me, and any supplies I might need, and..."

Ymir loudly snorted, and shook out his fur. "You humans," he said. "No wonder you have naught that rivals the Great Grisk Showroom-Shop!"

Kitty shot a warm, grateful grin toward him, and for the rest of the morning, she threw herself into the work with as much enthusiasm as she could muster. First helping Ymir sort through the entirety of the pile, and then familiarizing herself with the shop's layout, learning what was in each aisle, and how Ymir preferred to arrange each section.

And then, while Ymir carefully placed gems into a large glass display case in the clothing aisle, she even stood at the front counter for a while, greeting shoppers as they came in, and guiding them to whatever goods they were seeking. Luckily, thanks to Varinn's steady stream of introductions, she already knew most of them by name—Valter, Bramdur, Baldr—and to her relief, most of them seemed pleased to see her again, and several of them even congratulated her on her new role, as well.

"Ooooh, it's our lovely new Grisk!" exclaimed a vaguely familiar voice, late that morning. "Wait, have they put you to *work* in here?"

Kitty's head snapped up, from where she'd been studying

Ymir's complicated general ledger—and found herself blinking at Kesst, the lean, handsome orc from the sickroom. And hovering close behind him was a much larger but equally handsome orc, who was beautifully dressed, and sporting a tasteful variety of glinting jewels all over his bulky form.

"Er, hello," Kitty said, with a tentative smile between them, as she fought down the unpleasant memories of her previous encounter with Kesst. "Welcome to the Great Grisk Showroom-Shop! I'm Kitty, and is there anything I can help you find today?"

Kesst's brows shot up, but thankfully, the bigger orc flashed her a broad, toothy smile, and gracefully waved her question away. "We are only here to peruse the day's new goods," he said. "We come here near every day, so you shall be seeing much of us, I ken. You are Varinn and Thrain's new mate, ach?"

Kitty nodded, still a little uncertain, and the orc gave a satisfied nod back. "I am Rathgarr of Clan Ash-Kai, Kesst's elder brother, and also his heart-father," he said, with distinctive pride in his voice, as he slung his big arm over Kesst's shoulders. "Thrain has oft spoken of you, woman. You have already done him much good, I ken."

He accompanied this with a genial wink, and Kitty felt her shoulders relaxing, the smile pulling at her mouth. So this was the orc Thrain had agreed to meet with regularly, and—her thoughts twitched backwards—he was the lovely Geva's mate, too.

"It's a pleasure to finally meet you, Rathgarr," she told him, with a quick little curtsey. "We're so grateful to you for taking the time to help Thrain, the way you have been."

"Ach, I am honoured to help," this Rathgarr replied, inclining his head toward her. "I ken it is not an easy trial to face. For Thrain, and for you and Varinn, also."

His eyes had gone sympathetic on hers, and beside him, Kesst visibly winced, and gave a quick shake of his head. "And look, Kitty, I've been wanting to apologize for stirring things up between the three of you the other day," he said. "It was petty and unnecessary, I know. I just sometimes get a bit"—he winced again—"*defensive*, when it comes to Eft."

"A *bit?*" Rathgarr scoffed, but he was good-naturedly grinning at Kesst. "You become a vicious little demon-spawn, son. I am sorry you had to bear this, woman."

Kitty laughed and waved it away, and—after eyeing their jewels again—asked if they'd like to see the new gems Ymir was putting away. This earned her two stunning, near-identical grins, and soon they were all poring over the glass case together, while Ymir eyed them approvingly from down the aisle.

"Ach, Kesst, this one should well suit you," Rathgarr eagerly said, jabbing his claw at an exquisite garnet, so richly coloured it was almost black. "Mayhap in another *hálsmen*. But shorter, so you could wear it with Efterar's, as you wished."

He'd poked absently at the current chain around Kesst's neck—one with a glittering, dangling black jewel—and Kesst seemed to be considering this, biting at his lip. "But we already have four jewelry orders in with the Ka-esh smiths," he said doubtfully. "And you know how they groused when I asked for a short *hálsmen* last time! Complaining that it wasn't standard, because it wasn't either a proper snug *kraga*, or something Eft could properly chain me up with!"

At that, he and Rathgarr gave identical-looking shudders, followed by darkly baleful glowers toward the case. And when Kitty darted a helpless glance down the aisle at Ymir, he was jerking his head meaningfully toward—oh. Where he'd just placed a few pairs of crisp new trousers on what Kitty had already begun to think of as the trousers-and-kilts shelf.

"Well, perhaps you'd like to peruse some of our other new stock, then?" she asked Kesst and Rathgarr, as brightly as she could. "I know Ymir's just put out some new trousers, and one pair was actual silk, wasn't it, Ymir?"

Kesst instantly brightened, spinning excitedly toward the

trousers-and-kilts shelf, and soon he and Rathgarr were happily comparing trousers together. And once they'd made their choice—the silk pair, naturally—Ymir helped Kitty write up the sale, and gave her a decidedly smug grin as Kesst and Rathgarr left again.

"Those Ash-Kai love naught more than throwing their coin at shiny new goods," he said, with satisfaction. "But I ken"—his grin slightly faded—"we'd wring even more from them if we could fulfill the jewelry orders ourselves, ach? But the Ka-esh are our best goldsmiths now, and they're overrun with work—and damned finicky about what they'll take on, too. I don't suppose"—he frowned at Kitty again, a speculative gleam in his eyes—"you've got any experience in jewels, either, woman?"

Kitty shook her head with genuine regret, but thankfully Ymir didn't seem daunted, and was already waving her toward where another orc was striding into the shop. He was one Kitty hadn't met before, tall and lean with glinting, impatient eyes, and once she'd offered her cheery welcome and introduction, he inclined his head toward her, and coolly introduced himself as Killik, of Clan Skai.

"I need ropes," he announced flatly. "The strongest you have."

Kitty accordingly took him over to the tools-and-supplies aisle, where he frowned at all the available items, before finally choosing a generous length of heavy braided rope. And though he didn't even thank Kitty as he left again, he looked rather wickedly pleased, enough that she found herself smiling after him, and counting that as a success, too.

Ymir watched Kitty write up the sale this time, and then went back to his stocking, while she turned toward the morning's next customer. Which turned out to be none other than Dammarr, sweeping his long, lovely black hair over his shoulder, and eyeing her with a wry, sympathetic amusement.

"How are you faring, sister?" he said lightly. "Ymir has not run you off yet, I see? Or buried you under a mountain of goods?"

Kitty laughed and waved it away, shaking her head. "Not at all," she replied. "I'm actually—really enjoying it so far."

She was vaguely surprised to realize that she meant it, and maybe Dammarr looked a little surprised, too. "I am glad to hear this," he said. "I still cannot believe Varinn sent his pregnant mate off to work thus, in her first week here. It is just like him, ach?"

He'd smiled again, still with a twitch of sympathy in his eyes, and Kitty gave another dismissive wave. "I asked him for something to do," she replied. "And besides, I know he and Thrain have their own work to address all day, too. Perhaps not even here in the mountain."

Her voice had dropped at the end, sounding damnably dejected, or even hurt—and there was an instant's silence from Dammarr, an unmistakable grimace on his mouth. "No, I ken they are out," he finally said. "They are out almost every day, now, for Varinn is mayhap our best scenter, and he is always in high demand amongst our kin, ach? But"—he gave her a reassuring smile—"I am here for the day, if there is aught you might need. And they asked me to look in upon you, also."

Oh. Well. Kitty attempted another smile toward Dammarr, but perhaps didn't quite manage it, because his own smile had faded, his arched brows furrowing. "*Are* you well, sister?" he said. "Not only in this"—he gave a vague wave at the shop— "but with Varinn and Thrain, also? I shall admit, I do not envy you in the slightest, for coping with an Aetha Grisk is chaos enough on its own, ach?"

His mouth twitched back into a thin smile, and Kitty blinked toward him, her head tilting. "An *Aetha* Grisk?" she echoed. "What does that mean?"

"Aetha is the name of Thrak and Thrain's line," Dammarr replied, with a shrug. "And Nattfarr's, also. Their fathers were brothers, ach? Brothers with the power to make their kin laugh and romp and play"—his smile went rather grim—"even as they strewed naught but havoc in their wake. Just as Thrak and Thrain do with us now."

Oh. Kitty swallowed, her thoughts darting backwards to that earlier conversation with Ymir. To how little she knew about Varinn and Thrain's families, or their pasts, or how they'd even gotten together in the first place...

"Oh, but surely they aren't that bad," Kitty finally managed, with another attempt at a smile. "I mean, Thrain is *lovely*, truly. You can't help but adore him."

But Dammarr's laugh was instantaneous, and a little too sharp, too. "Ach, but that is just the problem," he said. "Why do you ken Varinn was all but mated to Thrain, when he truly wished for a woman and son, and bears the self-control of a saint? And why do you ken I"—his voice hitched—"stay bound to a chronically thoughtless orc who cannot be bothered to grant me the *least* that is due to a Grisk mate?"

Oh. Kitty couldn't at all seem to find an answer to that, and Dammarr shrugged again, his mouth twisting. "I will admit, Thrak at least seems highly vexed by all Varinn's sudden gifts to you and Thrain," he continued. "He would not have expected to be so cast in the shade by Varinn, ach? But you ken"—he huffed another hard laugh—"he would never then seek to learn from this. Let alone offer up mating-gifts of his own, even after I granted one to him."

His voice had gone low and bitter by the end, and despite her own lingering disquiet at all this, Kitty felt a sharp, sudden sympathy, surging up high in her chest. Dammarr was unhappy, and he was—jealous. And gods, she knew all too well how awful that felt, most of all when it came to lovely clothes and jewels that were fully out of one's reach.

"Well," Kitty said, pulling herself up straighter behind the counter. "It seems to me that Thrak *ought* to be vexed by his thoroughly shabby behaviour toward you. And if he's not willing to offer you the gifts expected of a mate, you ought to ignore his rubbish, and treat *yourself* to whatever gifts you please."

Dammarr's brows shot up, his eyes blinking—but then he winced, and shook his head. "Ach, sister," he said thickly. "I ought not to have spoken so harshly. I should never wish to turn you against Thrak and Thrain, and I am not always an easy mate either, and I ken Thrak did not know the... full truth of this, before. I am only..."

His voice faded, and he rubbed at his eyes—but Kitty wasn't being deterred at this, not now. "Look, you're only standing in the grandest shop in all the realm," she told him, as firmly as she could. "And you're long overdue for a lovely gift from yourself! And it's my first day, and I'd love to help you find something that suits you. Please?"

She shot him her brightest, most winning smile, and she could see his shoulders slightly sagging, his smile tugging back up. "Ach, very well, sister," he said, on a slow exhale. "I am in your hands."

Kitty beamed back toward him, and eagerly waved him around the counter. "Then come in, come in!" she said, belatedly twitching at just how much like Ymir she sounded. "What would you like to look at first? Some jewels? Or new clothes, perhaps?"

Dammarr gave a distracted-looking shrug, but he was indeed following her into the shop, glancing uncertainly around them. "Ach, a new tunic, mayhap," he replied. "All mine have been near clawed to shreds by wild little kittens, I ken."

Kitty half-laughed, half-winced, and led him over into the clothing aisle. "What kind of styles do you prefer?" she asked, glancing down at his bare chest—with that gleaming gold nipple-ring—and the loose, rather dishevelled-looking trousers he was wearing, their messy hems pooling over a pair of soft leather boots. "Something comfortable that you can move in, perhaps? And perhaps shows off your lovely piercing, as well?"

Dammarr blinked, glancing downwards, and then jerked another shrug. "Ach, mayhap," he said, a little stiffly. "I have never liked tight clothing much."

Kitty nodded, and turned toward the nearest stack of tunics, which she now knew were conveniently arranged by size. And once she'd discerned which pile was closest to Dammarr's size, they began sifting through the stack together, pulling out a few that seemed best suited.

But once Dammarr had tried the tunics on, it turned out that none of them showed his ring properly, and the fabrics—which were often stiff and starched—seemed to either pull on his neck or shoulders, or set him uncomfortably scratching. And Kitty didn't miss his frown of distaste toward the rest of the stack, or his brief, lingering glance across the aisle. Toward—oh. The row of hanging dresses, many with low-cut fronts, and light, fluttery fabrics.

Kitty blinked for a moment, considering that—and then she spun toward the dresses, carding through them in rapid succession. "Have you thought, perhaps, of something like this instead?" she asked, as she drew out a dark green robe that was made much like a dressing-gown, with an open front and a loose silken sash. "The fabric would likely be more comfortable, and this kind of neckline would show off much more of your chest, don't you think?"

Dammarr stared at her, and then down at the dress, his mouth fallen open—but then he snapped it shut, and shook his head. "Ach, no," he said flatly. "This is a dress for a human. A *woman*."

But Kitty shrugged and held the dress up against him, gauging the width of the shoulders against his. "So?" she asked. "Varinn told me quite clearly that anyone may dress however you please here, and no one would mind—and I'm sure he would know, wouldn't he? And if *I'm* dressed in orc clothing"—she gave a self-deprecating wave downwards—"much of it likely meant for males—why can't *you* dress in human clothes, if you prefer?"

Dammarr didn't reply to that, his mouth pursing, but he was again glancing at the dresses, his eyes lingering with unmistakable intensity, or perhaps even longing. So Kitty thrust the green robe into his arms, and began working her way through the rest of the rack. "What colours do you like best?" she asked, over her shoulder. "Perhaps something like this? Or this?"

She'd drawn out a clingy black silk robe, along with a more elaborate pale blue number—and Dammarr choked a laugh as he shoved the blue one back toward her. "*Not* this," he said flatly. "It should look ridiculous, against Grisk skin. But..."

His eyes had strayed back to the black one, so Kitty thrust that toward him, too, followed by a similar one in navy. And by the time she'd finished sorting through the entire rack, Dammarr was holding eight or nine dresses, and blinking down at them with decidedly stunned bemusement in his eyes.

"Now, perhaps you can go try them on?" Kitty asked brightly. "There's a looking-glass at the back of the shop, and I'm happy to help you, or leave you alone with them. Whatever you like."

Dammarr's glance down at the dresses was again almost baffled, and he twitched an uneasy shake of his head. "I should not know the first thing to do with them," he said. "So if you should not mind..."

"Of course not," Kitty said, with a delighted grin. And once she'd eagerly waved him toward the looking-glass, she plucked out the silken black robe, and helped him pull it on over his broad shoulders. And then she fussed with the sash at the waist, tying it over his trousers for now, before stepping back to admire her handiwork.

And at first glance, it certainly looked—unconventional. The black silk pulled taut over Dammarr's shoulders, the front—which would have fully closed on a woman—opened wide to show his muscled chest, and the glinting ring of his piercing. While the bottom half—which did close around his waist—hung fluidly from his narrow hips, reaching just to his knees, and showing off the snug fit of his tall black boots beneath.

But the more Kitty looked, the more it seemed to suit him—especially with the shining black fall of his loose hair, and the gold earrings laddered up both his pointed ears. And perhaps Dammarr thought so too, staring like that at his reflection in the looking-glass, his grey cheeks flushing with a becoming shade of pink.

"I think it looks lovely on you," Kitty said firmly. "Very elegant, and surely more comfortable than all those starchy tunics, too. Don't you think?"

Dammarr's throat visibly convulsed, and he distractedly moved his arm up, and then out to the side. "It loosens at the front when I move thus, though," he replied, waving down toward his groin. "I should rather not flaunt *that* to all I meet, ach?"

But after a brief inspection of the hems there, Kitty waved it away, and beamed up at his still-flushed face. "No trouble at all," she said. "Ymir's setting me up with a mending station, and I can put a few fasteners in here for you. If you've decided on this one, that is? Or perhaps you'd like to try on a few more first?"

Dammarr's eyes darted toward the rest of their pile, and he jerked a furtive little nod. And soon Kitty was exclaiming over the next dress, and the next, while Dammarr's face progressively went redder and redder, and he stared at himself in the looking-glass with stark, unmistakable longing.

"This one is gorgeous on you," Kitty fervently told him, once he'd tried on a deep crimson silk number, trimmed with intricate black lace. "Absolutely stunning, Dammarr. You'll be turning every head in this mountain."

Dammarr certainly didn't seem to disagree, twisting from

side to side in the looking-glass, and even tossing his long hair over his shoulder. Showing off the beautiful contrast of the soft crimson silk with his smooth pearly skin, and the glinting gold of his piercing. And he was even biting his lip, running his trembling hands down his front, and Kitty couldn't help nodding, and grinning broadly at his face.

"If you don't take it, I'm setting it aside for you, and buying it for you with my first salary," she archly informed him. "And begging you to wear it. For all our sakes."

Dammarr choked a laugh, and shook his head. "You are too kind, sister," he said hoarsely. "But—it is to no one's gain for me to dress thus. To draw... notice, thus."

Right. Because it would undoubtedly draw attention, that was true—but Kitty felt her head tilting as she considered it. "But it *is* to our gain, to know that you're comfortable and content," she replied. "And it does us all credit if our brother is dressed so beautifully, doesn't it? Just like"—she gave another sheepish wave down at her own daring ensemble—"Varinn says it's to *his* credit when I dress like this."

Dammar rolled his eyes, but his shoulders had slightly relaxed, so Kitty kept going, thinking it through. "And it's to *your* credit most of all," she continued. "When you feel at home in your own skin, and your own clothing. That's going to help grant you peace, isn't it? It's going to make you a better brother, and a stronger supporter of your kin. And that's just what you're called to do as a member of the Speaker's Guard, right?"

She could hear the conviction ringing in her voice, could see it easing into Dammarr's eyes. And he chuckled as he finally gave a resigned little nod, and shrugged off the dress. "Ach, sister," he said, his voice slightly wavering. "I ken you shall make a formidable shopkeeper."

Kitty couldn't help another delighted grin toward him, especially when he plucked out four of the dresses—including the black silk, the deep green, and the crimson-and-lace—and thrust them toward her. "I shall take these," he said. "Tell Ymir to charge them to my account, ach?"

Kitty eagerly nodded, and nearly skipped to the front of the shop. To where Ymir was already waiting, quill in hand, his eyes gleaming on the bounty of dresses in Kitty's arms. "Good work, woman," he said, under his breath. "Very, very good."

Kitty almost preened at the praise, and then carefully noted each dress in Ymir's ledger, and—at his prompting—added a note about the needed fixes to the black silk, too. And once she'd pulled that dress aside, she neatly wrapped up the others in paper, and thrust them out toward a still-bemused-looking Dammarr.

"I should have the black silk ready for you in another day or two," she told him. "I can't *wait* to see you in it."

Dammarr wryly smiled, and tucked the package under his arm with palpable care. "I thank you, sister," he said, with a brief little bow toward her. "And I salute you, Ymir, on gaining such a helpful apprentice. I ken I have not spent so much on clothing in all my life."

Ymir returned this with a decidedly gleeful grin, and waved Kitty away again, back toward the shop—at least, until Dammarr loudly cleared his throat. "But also," he continued, "I ken Kitty ought to come eat a meal, and rest for a spell. You have been working since early this morn, ach? Since Varinn and Thrain left?"

Kitty uncertainly nodded, and Dammarr's eyes glinted with something she couldn't quite read. "Then I ken you are finished here for the day, sister," he said, clipped. "She shall return tomorrow, Ymir, if she feels well enough for this."

Kitty didn't attempt to argue—she *was* feeling rather weary, after all the day's activity—and she said a grateful farewell to Ymir before following Dammarr out into the corridor. Eyeing his frowning profile as he led her back in the direction of their quarters, that paper package still carefully tucked under his arm.

"I ken you wish to do Varinn credit, sister," he said abruptly, without quite looking at her. "But you shall need to learn to speak for yourself also, ach? He holds himself to such a high measure, that he does not easily follow when others cannot do the same. Mayhap those close to him most of all."

Oh. Kitty swallowed, considering that, as her thoughts unhappily twitched back to the debt, the deal. "That... makes sense," she said, with an attempt at a shrug. "I just—want him to be pleased with me, you know? So maybe he'll—"

She belatedly winced, snapping her mouth shut—gods, maybe she was more tired than she'd thought—but Dammarr was already frowning, his eyes angling narrow toward hers. "Varinn *is* pleased with you," he replied. "You are all his deepest dreams come to life, ach? A sweet, lovely woman who seeks to support him, and honour him before all his kin? Even enough to toil away all day in a shop, and make friends of *Ymir*?"

Kitty's stomach flipped, and she felt her face heating, her hand attempting to wave it away. Earning another narrow look from Dammarr, a hard shake of his head. "Varinn is not the kind of orc to waver in his loyalty," he said. "If he has deemed you worthy of his care, he will never falter in this—whether you reach his measure, or do him credit, or no. Just look at Thrain, ach?"

Oh. Kitty couldn't seem to look away from Dammarr now, from how he was fully frowning back toward her, his expression utterly certain. "And I know what I said before about Thrain, and the Aetha," he said, quieter. "But Varinn truly cares for Thrain also, ach? And you caring for Thrain as you do—this is a great gift to Varinn, and a great relief for him, also. For I ken he needs Thrain as much as Thrain needs him, ach? He needs"—he made a face—"the... power Thrain so freely grants him, mayhap. The... freedom, to just be as he is. For we have not had much of this in the rest of our lives, ach?"

He'd angled a rueful glance down to the package under his

arm, and Kitty felt herself blinking, and then twitching a quivery smile back toward him. "I absolutely understand," she said, a little choked. "And—thank you, Dammarr, for telling me all this. And for being such a patient test subject today, too. Learning a trade is maybe"—she drew in a rushed breath—"my own way to... seek power. And it really meant a lot to me, to be able to help you today."

Dammarr waved it away, but his smile was warm, or maybe even indulgent. "The joy was all mine, sister," he said lightly. "And I *did* look stunning in those dresses, did I not?"

Kitty gave a bright, relieved-sounding laugh, and grinned back toward him. "You were *dazzling*," she said, with as much conviction as she could muster. "Truly, Dammarr. I can't wait to see you in them. And I can't wait to see Thrak's face when he sees you, too."

Her voice had gone light and teasing, her eyes dancing, and she didn't miss the flush creeping up Dammarr's pierced ears. "Ach, well, if he even notices," he said dismissively. "Now stop caring for me, and go care for yourself, ach? I ken Varinn left some food in your room, so you ought to go eat, and rest. And he will come to you the instant he returns home, I am sure."

Kitty blinked at that—Dammarr really thought Varinn would come to her, as soon as he returned?—and gave him an uncertain little smile. "Thank you," she said, "but—how will he even know where I am?"

Dammarr's answering laugh was easy and bright, his head shaking. "You *reek* of Varinn's fresh scent, sister," he said. "He could sniff you out across the realm, ach?"

Oh. Well. Kitty couldn't seem to reply to that, but once Dammarr had escorted her to their familiar bedroom, she again earnestly thanked him, and waved farewell. And then found that he'd been correct about the food, too, because there was a basket of fruit and dried meat sitting on Varinn's chair, along with a bulging waterskin.

The warmth seemed to shimmer through her chest as she

ate and drank, and then curled up in the bed's warm, sweet-scented furs. Varinn had made love to her. He'd given her beautiful gifts. He'd found her a trade, one she'd genuinely enjoyed. He'd left food for her. And Dammarr even thought he liked her, and maybe... maybe...

Kitty must have dozed, drawn deep into those twining, too-tempting thoughts. And when her awareness lurched back again, the lamp had almost gone out, and—someone else was in the room. Someone pacing back and forth, someone who was—oh. Varinn.

Kitty shoved up in bed, blinking toward him, because he looked—wrong. His shoulders hunched, his hands in tight fists, his brow heavily furrowed. And his eyes, darting briefly toward her, were wild, and hurt, and... miserable.

"What's wrong?" Kitty asked, her voice hoarse. "What happened?"

Varinn barked a laugh, rough and bitter in his throat, but didn't reply. And Kitty glanced uneasily around the room, toward the door, toward...

"Are you alone?" she asked, quieter, as her heartbeat skipped in her chest. "Where... where's Thrain?"

And even before Varinn opened his mouth, she knew the answer, plunging like that in her belly. Thrain was...

"Where do you ken he is?" Varinn said, with another choked laugh, not a laugh at all. "He is at a stinking human pub, pouring ale down his throat."

35

Thrain was... at a pub. Getting drunk.

The truth of it almost felt like a blow, suddenly, swaying Kitty in the bed, spinning behind her eyes. Drunk. *Drunk*. After last night, after all his words, all his happiness, all his damned promises. His promises to her, to Varinn, to their son.

The rage surged in Kitty's chest, just as harsh and dizzying as the shock had been, and she could see it reflected in Varinn's flashing eyes, could almost smell it curdling in the air. "After all these past days," he growled. "After all the grace I have sought to show him. Granting him my scent. My gold. My father's *thyrja*. This is akin to *vows* amongst much of our kin, and now he wears it as he breaks all his own promises to me, yet *again*?"

His voice cracked at the end, and Kitty's own eyes were prickling, blinking rapidly at his desolate face. Because— because damn it, Varinn had clearly been trying. Despite his initial reluctance, and all those ultimatums, he'd still been trying the new way, like she'd wanted, like she'd asked, like Efterar had said. Giving Thrain a safe place. Offering him distractions. Guiding him to other goals, other... pleasures. Everything Efterar had told them, down to the letter.

And suddenly there was just sadness, just sympathy, catching in Kitty's throat, closing off her breath. "I'm so sorry, Varinn," she choked, and somehow she'd lurched out of bed, and stumbled over toward him. "Gods. I'm so sorry."

Varinn's eyes widened, his big body stiffening—but when Kitty foolishly flung her arms around him, he didn't resist. Didn't move. Just stood there, breathing hard against her.

But then his body sagged, his breath sharply exhaling, and his arms slipped around her back. Holding her there against him, warm and close and firm. Almost... almost as if he wanted her there.

So Kitty squeezed him tighter, as tight as she possibly could, as she buried her face in his chest, and inhaled the familiar richness of his scent. Gods, it wasn't fair, he didn't deserve it, not when he'd tried so hard, and done all he could. Not when he'd given Thrain so much—giving up so much of that power he craved—only for Thrain to turn around and betray him, again.

And Kitty was supposed to be helping. She needed to help, needed to do whatever she could. And what did Varinn want, what did he need, what could she offer him...

And without thinking, without even following, Kitty flailed downwards, falling to her knees on the fur. Fumbling at the belt of Varinn's kilt, shoving it off onto the floor, so she could find the half-hard heft at his groin... and then swallow it deep into her mouth.

Varinn's groan was low and guttural, his head instantly tilting back, his hand clutching on her hair. Welcoming it, wanting it, needing it—so Kitty kept going, throwing herself into it, into every single thing she knew he liked. Her lips sucking hard, her tongue seeking inside, her hands stroking and caressing, cradling those bulging bollocks in her fingers. While he swelled harder and fuller in her mouth, sputtering out that hot sweetness for her, thicker and steadier with every desperate breath...

And when he twitched backwards, toward his chair, Kitty awkwardly followed, still sucking, still clinging. Even as he sank heavily down onto it, his big hand guiding her head into his lap, as he let his own head fall back against the stone wall, his eyes squeezing shut. Looking, for an instant, like a wounded fallen lord, taking solace in whatever comfort he could find—and somehow, somehow, it was enough. Enough for Kitty to keep going, keep working him over with every bit of effort she could muster, until—

Until... his hand nudged her upwards. The movement small, almost imperceptible—but most certainly intentional. And when Kitty's wide eyes darted up, she found him looking at her, his eyes heavy and hooded, as he nudged her upwards again. Toward... his lap.

Something roared in Kitty's ears, and she instantly nodded and clambered up onto him, straddling his hips in the chair. Keeping her eyes on his face, on the way he was still watching her beneath those hooded, hazy eyes. On the way he... wanted this. Wanted the support she could offer him, the relief. And surely... surely he wanted the power, too. Wanted a willing, obedient lover in his lap, eager to comfort him, to worship him.

And when Kitty's tingly hands fluttered down to the fabric beneath her *thyrja*, Varinn's gaze willingly followed, and held there. Watching with unmistakable intensity as she pulled the fabric off, away, and then fumbled to yank off her kilt, too. Leaving her clad only in the *thyrja*, showing him everything, everything that was his.

And yes, yes, he was still looking, his half-lidded eyes sweeping up and down, as his cock twitched and shuddered, splattering more white across his own bare belly. Wanting this, clearly, but maybe still wanting more of that power, too...

"Will you—allow me, Lord Grisk?" Kitty heard herself whisper, her voice not at all her own. "To—to drink your good Grisk seed inside me?"

And oh, the way Varinn seemed to consider it, his head

tilting as he studied her, as if evaluating her worth—but then
he twitched a brief, dismissive nod. And then—Kitty's breath
choked—he again closed his eyes, and tilted his head back
against the wall. For all the world as if he didn't care, as if he
were well accustomed to receiving such offers, and to casually
doling out his seed to worshipful maidens upon request.

Kitty's twisting thoughts had leapt back to the real Lord
Grisk, to all those women he'd made his own—and somehow it
only seemed to spike the frantic longing higher, harder. She
needed to show him, please him, prove her worth. And maybe,
maybe...

"Thank you, sir," she whispered, as she shifted a little closer
on his hips. "I am—so grateful to you, for granting me your
scent, and your seed, and your kindness. Your protection."

The breath heaved from Varinn's chest, but he still didn't
open his eyes, and Kitty hitched forward a little more, her gaze
dropping to that fat, swollen heft between them. Now pouring
steady with white, ready to fill whatever hole was on offer, and
pour it full of sweet seed...

But wait, Thrain had taught her that, and Kitty swallowed
hard, shoved that thought away. And fought to focus on her
own tingling, audacious hand, slipping downwards, catching
around that smooth green weight. Feeling it shudder and swell
beneath her touch, wanting this, yes—and then, in another
burst of inexplicable daring, she settled that silken, seeping
head against her own wet, wide-open heat.

Her gasp was harsh, hoarse, and that might have also been
a hiss, from between Varinn's parted lips. But he still didn't
move, didn't even look, and Kitty gulped down a shaky breath
as she spread her knees wider, settled a little deeper. Feeling
that slick head opening her, stretching her around it, sinking its
way inside. Inside her, Varinn was truly inside her now,
pouring out his gifts for her, and Kitty gasped again as she
pressed downwards, as he gave her more. And more, and more,
filling her breath by breath, splitting her apart.

And even if he wasn't looking at her, there was no denying the truth of what he was doing. Filling the womb of his bared, trembling worshipper, and blatantly flaunting the depth of his power over her. And—Kitty moaned aloud this time—even tilting up his hips a little in the chair, wanting to go deeper, wanting more...

"You feel so good, Lord Grisk," she gasped, as she ground back down against him, as the furious sensation whipped and whirled deep within. "So, so good. *Gods.*"

And wait, that had earned her a brief, slitted glance beneath those black lashes, so she drew in another shaky breath. "I need you, my lord," she whispered, sinking deeper, deeper, meeting another gentle roll of his hips. "Need you inside me, need your scent and your seed. Need to honour you, and please you—"

Her voice choked, because oh, hell, she'd managed to take him all the way this time, she was sitting flush on his bare hips, with him fully buried inside her. And it was so good, impossibly good, the pressure and the power pulsing out higher, harder, until—

The rush of pleasure flashed with sharp, shattering fierceness, seizing Kitty all over, squeezing his strength within her again and again. Clamping on him, pumping him, pleading with him—until oh, yes, yes, he was groaning aloud, his body jerking forward. And the pole inside her was surging, spraying, spurting out fast and harsh, pouring her full to the brim with his good Grisk seed. With his indulgence, his approval, his pleasure.

And maybe—Kitty's eyes fought to refocus on his face, as the shudders kept trembling through her body—maybe even his gratitude. His relief. Because his eyes on hers were different now, softer, and his hands had finally, finally, slipped toward her, spanning wide against her bare hips.

"This was... very kind," he murmured, very low. "I... thank you, *kisa.*"

His gaze had dropped down between them, to where Kitty was still sitting flush upon him, with his strength buried all the way inside. And curse her, but Kitty almost felt giddy at the sight of it, at the ridiculous accomplishment of it. She'd taken her lord fully inside her, and earned his seed, and his touch, and his praise.

"It's my honour, Lord Grisk," she murmured back, with a shy smile toward him. "Thank you, for indulging me."

Varinn's throat bobbed, his chest hollowing, but then he nodded, his eyes again catching on her face. Still looking softer, easier, without any of the rage or pain from before.

But the more Kitty looked, the more she could still see the sadness there, the grief. The genuine hurt and loss over such a betrayal, from someone he loved so much.

"I'm sure Thrain didn't mean to hurt you, Varinn," she said, tentative, searching his eyes. "It's a sickness, remember? And Efterar did say that it was normal to sink back into it, at least a few times, right? And that"—she grimaced—"we shouldn't take it personally?"

Varinn grimaced too, his breath exhaling again, but he didn't reply. And Kitty kept considering it, casting through her memories, grasping for truth, for hope. "And didn't Efterar also say," she began, "that a relapse is especially likely to happen under duress? And Thrain even said that too, that the temptation is strongest when he's upset and alone, right?"

Varinn's forehead furrowed, his head tilting. "I have not heard him say this," he said, a little clipped. "He said this to you?"

Right. Thrain had told her that when Varinn had been out with Timo, damn it, and Kitty considered that too, her hands settling against Varinn's warm chest. "He did," she replied, quiet. "But it seems to me that you shouldn't take that personally, either. He's obviously desperate for your approval, and your good opinion of him—so he's not likely to open up and tell you all his weaknesses, is he?"

Varinn made a low sound in his throat, maybe a groan, or a growl. "He ought to," he said, with genuine heat in his voice. "And then I could face this, address this, and direct him as he ought!"

The words seemed to ring out between them, flat and harsh and laced with fury, or even contempt. And when Kitty twitched slightly backwards, blinking uncertainly toward him, she was vaguely surprised to see Varinn wincing, rubbing his hand at his eyes.

"Ach," he said thickly. "I ken, *kisa*. I ken."

Oh. Kitty couldn't help a strange, relieved little laugh, her hands spreading wider against his chest. "Was Thrain... alone today?" she ventured, carefully now. "Or upset? Did anything happen that might have affected him?"

Varinn's chest filled and emptied against her hands, his mouth grim. "Ach, he was alone for much of the afternoon," he replied. "We had many kin to see, after spending so many days at home, so it seemed faster to do this apart. And when I caught up to him in the pub"—he took another long, shaky breath—"he was already deep in the ale, and I did not... ask."

He didn't need to elaborate further, because clearly he'd launched into one of his rages, and left Thrain behind. Left him alone in a pub, with the added despair of Varinn's fury, his broken expectations, heaped upon his head. And Kitty's thoughts were flicking backwards, catching on Dammarr's words from earlier. *Varinn holds himself to such a high measure, he does not easily follow when others cannot do the same...*

"Is Thrain... still there, then?" Kitty asked, still tentative. "At the pub? Can you... tell?"

Varinn drew in an unsteady breath, his throat bobbing. "Ach, I can scent him," he said. "He is... coming home, now. Halfway here, mayhap."

Oh, thank the gods. Kitty's own breath exhaled in a thick, relieved rush, and she attempted another smile at Varinn, rubbing her hands up and down his chest, squeezing at his stiff shoulders.

"Then that's good, isn't it?" she said. "And maybe we could go to the shrine for a while, and seek some peace while we wait?"

She kept smiling at him, as brightly as she could, and she could feel his shoulders sagging, his head twitching a curt little nod. And then he reached sideways, grasping for a rag from the shelf, and passing it into Kitty's hand.

It was clearly an order, and he watched with strangely glinting eyes as she gingerly drew off him, and attempted to mop herself up as best as she could. And not missing, once she'd finished, how he'd made no attempt whatsoever to clean himself up, just sitting back like that with his legs sprawled, his softened length lying chubby and slick against his lower belly.

Thrain's words were rising again, far too strong—*he'll usually give you another round, if you want it*—so in another inexplicable lurch of bravado, Kitty dropped to her knees before him, and again drew him into her mouth. Sucking him clean with careful gentleness, while also distantly revelling in her own taste upon him, her tangy flavour a compelling contrast to his own rich sweetness. Because he'd been inside her, he'd willingly done that with her, again. And oh, gods, it was working, he was swelling between her lips again, was he giving her more, he was giving her more—

She moaned as she frantically worked him over, sucking and salivating, slipping her tongue inside, burying him deep down her throat. Caressing him and worshipping him with all the desperate eagerness she could muster, until he choked a hoarse little gasp, and again emptied himself out inside her.

Afterwards, it felt too easy to smile at him as she dressed herself again, and then—in another burst of daring—she grasped his hand, and pulled him out of the chair. So she could dress him again, too, fastening the kilt properly around his waist, and brushing it out until it fell just as it should.

"Ach, Katharine," Varinn said once she'd finished, his eyes shifting on hers. "I did not even think to ask how this went today, in the shop. Was Ymir kind to you? I hope the work was not too strenuous? And that no one set you ill at ease?"

Kitty flashed him a brief, surprised smile, but waved the questions away. "It was lovely," she said firmly. "Ymir was very kind, and so was everyone else. And I truly enjoyed the work, too. Thank you for recommending me."

She couldn't at all read that look in his eyes—surely it wasn't regret?—but he nodded, and gave her a small smile. "I am glad to hear this," he said, a little rough. "I wish to help you gain all you might long for."

Oh. Something flipped in Kitty's chest, surging too hot and close in her throat, and she managed a nod, and another wavering smile toward him. "That's so generous of you, Lord Grisk," she replied. "Although, speaking of the shop"—she took a breath, and poked a teasing finger into his chest—"when were you planning to tell me that you went and sold off all my dressing-gowns?"

Varinn's smile twitched a little higher, and he gave a too-dismissive shrug. "Your Grisk garb is far better suited, ach?" he said, his voice light. "Scents much better upon you, also."

So he was admitting that he hadn't liked Charles' smell on them, then, and the warmth again surged in Kitty's chest, escaping in a choked little laugh this time. "You *are* a tyrant, Lord Grisk," she cheerfully replied. "Thrain was right about you, you know. On all fronts."

But wait, that was again the sadness, darkening Varinn's eyes, dragging down his shoulders. And Kitty couldn't even seem to find a single word of comfort, beyond clasping his arm, and tugging him out toward the shrine.

The sitting-room was empty as they passed through, and the shrine was nearly pitch-black inside. But Varinn guided her across the room, and then drew her down to kneel beside him. And Kitty willingly joined him in prayer, her head bowed, her hand still clasped around his arm. Pleading for guidance, for

Lord Grisk's strength, for protection, for peace. Not only for her and Varinn, but for Thrain most of all.

At one point, she felt Varinn twitch, heard his sharp inhale of breath—suggesting, maybe, that Thrain had returned—but he didn't otherwise move, or speak. So Kitty just kept praying, now leaning a little into Varinn's solid bulk beside her, until finally she felt him exhale and straighten, his forearm flexing beneath her touch.

"Thrain is here now," he said, on another heavy exhale. "Should you wish to come see him with me?"

Kitty nodded, and willingly accompanied Varinn out of the dark shrine. Passing through the quiet sitting-room, and then into the dim, empty corridor. Leading toward...

"The shop?" Kitty asked uncertainly, glancing at Varinn with genuine surprise. "Why would he..."

Varinn's mouth thinned, his shoulders sagging. "Your scent, I ken, and our son's," he said, very quiet. "For I... forbade him, earlier, from coming to me."

Oh. He'd ordered Thrain not to come to him, and she'd been with him, so Thrain couldn't come to her, either. And Thrain would really want... to smell her? And their son? To the point where he would be holing up in the shop, alone?

But when Kitty and Varinn stepped into the shop, there was no visible sign of Thrain anywhere. Only the rows and rows of dark shelves, leading into utter blackness, and Varinn paused to pull a lamp from beneath the counter, lighting it with a flick of his claws. And then he clasped her hand in a surprisingly tight grip, and led her down the dry goods aisle, toward the very back of the shop.

And there, sitting hunched and small on the stone floor, was Thrain. His knees pulled up to his chest, his messy head bowed over them. His shoulders rising and falling, visibly shuddering with every breath.

Varinn drew Kitty to a stop before him, his own breath exhaling sharp—and finally Thrain looked up. Showing them his pale, haggard face, his bright, brimming-wet eyes, the tracks of wetness streaking down his cheeks.

"Please don't say it, Varinn," he said, his voice a croak, as he shoved upwards, onto his staggering feet. "Please. I know. I'll go."

36

He would go?

Kitty stared at Thrain for a blank, frozen moment. Blinking at how he'd ducked his head, bent his shoulders, turned his usually tall body into something small and afraid, as he made to edge past them, and back down the aisle.

"Wait," Varinn said, his voice gruff, as his hand snapped out, caught against Thrain's arm. And in return, Thrain betrayed a full-body flinch backwards, and Varinn instantly let go, his brow furrowing, his swallow bobbing in his throat.

"Right, right," Thrain said, too rapid, high-pitched, as his trembling hands fumbled at—oh. Varinn's *thyrja*. Yanking it off over his head, and thrusting it back toward Varinn, its beads and teeth slightly rattling. "Here. I—I thank you, for the chance to wear it. It really—meant a lot to me."

He twitched a shaky little bow toward Varinn, toward where the *thyrja* was now hanging slack from Varinn's fingers. And then he spun away and strode off down the aisle again, walking with rapid, jerky steps.

Kitty blinked after him, her eyes wide—and then, without

thinking, she rushed to follow him, clasping his wrist in her own trembling fingers. "Thrain, wait," she gasped at him, at his stiff, slumped back. "Could we—talk for a moment? Please?"

Her heart was hammering, the urgency clamping at her throat, and thank the gods, Thrain slowly turned around again, a miserable, twitching little grimace on his mouth. "Sorry, Kit," he said, his voice cracking. "There just—isn't much to say, ach? Varinn gave me his terms, and I've broken them. Broken my promises to him, and to you, and our son. I"—he hauled in a breath, rubbed at his wet eyes—"I can't do it, ach? Can't keep my word. Can't be a good father, let alone a good mate, to either of you. You can't trust me. *I* can't trust me."

The tightness clamped even tighter in Kitty's throat, her head shaking, but Thrain only huffed a miserable laugh, dragging both hands at his face. "Varinn even gave me his scent," he choked. "His fucking *scent*, Kit, after so long, because he was being that fucking good to me. Trying to trust me, to help me, to give me another chance. To make this work, between all of us, in the face of what I've already done to him. And what do I do? On the next damned *day*?!"

He'd flailed a furious hand at his chest, himself, hard enough to leave red scratches on his skin. "I'm fucked, Kit," he gulped, his eyes pleading on hers. "I'm so, so fucking useless. I'm—broken, ach? I can't do it. I can't. I'm sorry."

Oh, gods, he couldn't be saying these things, and the wetness was escaping Kitty's eyes now too, streaking down her cheeks. "That's not true, Thrain," she began. "It isn't. You—"

But his laugh was too loud, too painful, drowning out Kitty's voice. "No, Kit," he hissed back. "You don't defend me. You've already borne enough, and you're just too sweet for this rubbish, ach? You need to understand"—he clasped her hand, squeezing too tight, his eyes bright and wild on hers—"I'll make you miserable. I'll fail you, and hurt you, and—destroy you. You deserve better. So much better."

Kitty's head was still shaking, the misery lurching higher, and Thrain abruptly released her hand, stumbling backwards, away. "You deserve Varinn," he said thickly, with a firm, decisive nod toward him. "You deserve to be cherished, and guarded, and cared for. You deserve someone who can keep his vows to you."

The misery kept rising, escaping in a strange little sob from Kitty's mouth, because Varinn was never going to make a real vow to her. His loyalty was to Thrain, no matter what. And Thrain couldn't truly believe all these things, he couldn't do this, he couldn't—

"You won't regret it, ach?" Thrain continued, with another jerky nod toward Varinn. "He'll be such a good mate to you, he'll take good care of you, and make you his own. You'll be so good together, you'll be everything good Grisk should be—and good parents to your son, most of all. I couldn't ask for better, truly."

He was even smiling between them, the sight unnervingly wide on his wavering mouth. Because he'd said... *your son, yours,* for the first time, ever. As if he was truly just—giving up, leaving, just like that? Forever?

But damn him, and damn Varinn, because Thrain was just conceding to Varinn's ultimatum, wasn't he? Honouring the terms of the promise he'd made. *You can keep the drink, and lose all the rest. Me. Her. Your son. Forever.*

Kitty's hands were wringing in midair, her head still shaking—no, no, no—and she nearly staggered with relief at the sight of Varinn. Varinn, finally striding up between them, his eyes flashing, his jaw set, his hands in fists. About to fight this, again, to make more demands and ultimatums, no, and—

"What went amiss today, Thrain?" Varinn said, rasping and quiet. "What came about, after we parted?"

Thrain twitched, blinked, the uncertainty flaring in his too-bright eyes, and he shook his head, barked a strange little laugh. "Naught at all," he said, his voice shrill. "All the same as always, ach? Troubled orcs, angry humans who might attack at any moment, and bored lonely orclings. Och, I spent half the afternoon"—he choked another brittle laugh—"tracking a half-grown orcling who'd run away from his mother on a lark, down into the vilest little tunnel. Damn thing *reeked* of gas, would've fucking killed the little menace if I hadn't dragged him out in time. Just the sort of rubbish I'd have pulled at his age, ach?"

He laughed again, far too loud and harsh, and then flapped his clawed hands, frantically shook his head. "So—naught went amiss," he said, in a rush. "Naught, if that's what you're trying to say, Varinn, if you're trying to scrounge up some tidy excuse to defend me. We've dealt with far worse, every second day, and you damn well know it. It's our damned *job*, my own damned *birthright*, what we're called to do as Speakers' Guards. I don't fucking deserve your kindness, I don't, just let it go, I—"

But without warning, Varinn's hand snapped up, and—shoved something into Thrain's *mouth*. A ball of silken fabric, perhaps a handkerchief, one he must have snatched from a nearby shelf. And Thrain choked and gaped at him, wide-eyed, as Varinn swiftly grasped both his wrists, and yanked him closer. So he was looking directly into Thrain's eyes, holding them on his.

"Quiet, *krútt*," he said, low but firm. "I ken how it is with tight tunnels, and the scent of gas, and frightened orclings most of all. You ought not to have needed to face this. Most of all with your scenting now so much stronger than before."

Thrain made a strangled noise around the gag, but he didn't try to spit it out, and Varinn kept him there, kept holding his eyes. "I ken you did what you had to do," he continued, his voice softening. "I ken, *krútt*. But you are yet sick, ach? I ought not to have left you alone thus, without help. Ought not to have risked this, so soon."

Thrain was shaking his head again, his eyes wide and almost panicked on Varinn's face. While Varinn just kept looking back, and now he was sliding his big hands up Thrain's arms, and down again. "So hush, *krútt*," he murmured. "I am not angry with you, ach? I am glad you came home. Glad you sought out Efterar and Rathgarr, and sought to make yourself sober again. And"—he swallowed—"I am glad you honoured my wishes, and gave me time to think and pray upon this."

Wait. Wait, Thrain had sought out Efterar, and Rathgarr, and given Varinn time to think and pray? But yes, yes, that made sense, Thrain had clearly returned some time ago, and he didn't *seem* drunk, did he? Not like before, not with the shouting and the anger—and wait, he didn't even smell of the drink, either. Did he?

Thrain still wasn't arguing with Varinn on this, was only staring at him, now, with a desperate longing in his eyes. While Varinn's big hands slipped to his lean bare torso, his flanks, sliding up and down with smooth, easy familiarity. As if petting Thrain, soothing him, as that low steady rumble began purring from his throat.

"This was all good, *krútt*," he continued. "Very good, ach? You knew I should not wish to find the fresh scent of ale tainting my own new scent upon you. And you came home to us, and our son. You fought against the sickness' claim upon you, in favour of ours."

Thrain's eyes were so wide, so bright, so painfully, pitifully hopeful. And Varinn just kept stroking, kept purring, and he even leaned forward, and gave a gentle little nibble at Thrain's throat.

"I have thought much upon what you said to me, last eve," he continued, his voice rough. "Of how my commands and threats have harmed you, and your trust in me. How I have carelessly wielded my power over you, and thus"—he exhaled, slow—"I took something that ought to have only been for both our pleasure, and twisted it for my own gain. For what I wished from you."

Oh. Thrain was staring at Varinn, shaking his head, as if he hadn't said all that in the least—but maybe, maybe he had.

And beside Varinn, Kitty was nodding, catching Thrain's wide eyes—and now Varinn was glancing at her too, letting out a slow breath.

"So henceforth," Varinn said, squaring his shoulders, his flinty gaze back on Thrain, "when you come to me thus, and seek my help, seek to honour my claim upon you"—he brushed a clawed thumb against Thrain's nipple—"I shall seek to reward you, ach?"

Thrain's gasp was audible through the gag, his shock almost palpable in the air. And that was a full-body shiver, trembling him all over beneath Varinn's steady stroking touch, beneath the sudden simmering heat in Varinn's eyes.

"So bend over, *krútt*," he murmured, his voice low, rich with hunger and promise. "And show me what is mine."

Thrain's eyes snapped even wider on Varinn, his moan muffled, frantic—and in a flurry of furious motion, he whirled around, turning his back to Varinn, and yanking off his kilt. Showing off the entirety of his lean bare body, already bending forward—and thrusting out his exposed arse toward Varinn with sudden, shocking shamelessness.

But Varinn didn't look shocked. If anything, he looked satisfied, or even triumphant. His glinting eyes sweeping up and down Thrain's bared, bent-double body, as his big hand slid to caress that rounded arse, squeezing it tight—and then drew back, and gave it a firm, ringing slap.

"I said, show me," he said, his voice all deep, smooth velvet. "Honour me, *krútt*."

And gods, the way the shudder wracked up Thrain's body, as he blatantly arched his back, and scrabbled his legs out wider. Now displaying absolutely everything, his wide-open crease, his heavy bollocks hanging beneath. While Varinn just kept looking, with that cool satisfaction glittering in his hooded, hungry eyes.

And then—Kitty's breath choked—those eyes glanced

toward her. Lingering, strange and speculative, before dropping purposefully to... his own kilt.

"Come, *kisa*," he said, still such smooth, silken heat. "And ready me to take him, ach?"

Oh, hell. A strangled moan escaped from Kitty's mouth, but she eagerly nodded, and lurched toward him. Scrabbling at the belt of his kilt, yanking it apart, pulling the kilt off. Leaving him entirely bare, too, his swollen length already bobbing and sputtering, spattering slick white across the grey skin of Thrain's arse.

But he wasn't pouring steady yet, wasn't quite ready, and Kitty gulped as she caught some of that sputtering fluid in her fingers, and then grasped him, and began gently stroking. Slipping her hand up and down, coating him, plumping him, priming him—and yes, yes, he was already shuddering fuller in her fingers, pouring out thicker, smoother, painting Thrain's skin with more sticky white. So Kitty kept stroking, a little harder now, smearing the seed all over him, coating him to a slick, glossy, sweet-scented shine.

She only stopped when Varinn jerked a nod, and then he purposefully glanced sideways, toward a small wooden chest on the nearby shelf. A chest Kitty vaguely recalled seeing earlier, but Ymir hadn't made any particular note of it, had he? No, not like the way Varinn was nodding at it, something new and meaningful flickering through his eyes.

"Fetch that, *kisa*," he said, husky. "Show me what is inside."

Kitty instantly nodded, and rushed to obey. Bringing the chest over, snapping open the lid, and holding it out for Varinn's perusal. And while she couldn't quite make out the chest's contents in the dim light, he clearly could, his gaze sweeping over what was inside.

"That gold ring," he said, with a decisive nod toward a glinting item. "Place this upon me, *kisa*."

Kitty's hand was already groping for it, and setting the box aside—and only then did she realize what she was holding. A solid, smoothly rounded gold ring, a little larger than a lady's bangle, but not quite large enough to serve as a choker. And what did Varinn mean by this, did he want it on his arm, or...

But then he again... glanced downwards. Down toward his slick, swollen, sputtering length, still spurting wetness across Thrain's bared backside. And the comprehension was dizzying, fizzing through Kitty's thoughts, because it was *that* kind of ring, and he was going to wear it for Thrain, reward him with it, oh—

So she fervently nodded again, twitching closer toward Varinn, taking him back in hand. Carefully guiding the ring over his slick dripping head, down the full length of him. And it was surely too large for just this, and after another searching glance at his face—yes, yes—she cautiously cupped his bollocks, and guided them through, too. Until she could settle the gleaming gold ring all the way beneath, flush and firm against his skin.

She nearly whimpered at the feel of it, the sight of it— because gods, what it did to him. Circling his considerable assets close, and bulging them out even larger and fuller than before. Looking shockingly huge, impossibly obscene, flaunting his potency and his power. Framing the way his plump, straining length was now pouring steady from the slit, drizzling straight down into Thrain's still-open crease.

"Good, *kisa*," Varinn murmured, though he was looking at Thrain's arse too, watching his thick white pooling into it, readying it. "And now?"

Now. Kitty's breath choked again, because he was ready, he needed this, they needed this—so she again grasped that gorgeous, swollen strength, and gently guided it downwards. Guided it toward Thrain, toward his bared, split-apart crease. Toward where she could just make out that small, fluttering pucker of skin, exposed, waiting...

Thrain shuddered and moaned as she brushed it there, as Varinn's slick, dripping head spasmed, and sputtered out more.

Settling there, seeking, finding its place, and Kitty couldn't breathe as she watched, as her shaky hand slipped up Varinn's length again, and began stroking. Milking him out into Thrain, easing the way, just like Thrain had done for her. And yes, Varinn liked that, he had to like that, the steady growl again purring from his throat as he eased forward, pressing, breaching.

And it shouldn't have looked so easy, or so compelling. Not with Thrain's body fully heaving, now, vicious-looking shudders wracking up his spine, as Varinn kept pressing forward, sinking so smoothly inside. As if Thrain was offering no resistance whatsoever, as if he'd already been readied and opened wide, rather than swallowing this impossible invasion whole at its very first touch.

But he was, it was, and gods, Varinn liked it, both his hands now grasping Thrain's trembling arse, opening him wider, so he could watch. Could see his fat, glossy, gold-encircled pole disappearing into Thrain's upraised arse, into what he owned, where he belonged.

"Good, *krútt*," Varinn breathed, his chest heaving as he sank deeper, deeper. "So good. Ach?"

Thrain's messy head frantically nodded, his moan thick and muffled through the cloth, and Varinn angled another brief, meaningful glance toward Kitty. "Take that out, *kisa*," he told her. "Wish to hear him beg for me."

Oh, hell. Kitty's own moan was nearly as loud as Thrain's, and she instantly nodded, and obliged. Twitching around to kneel before Thrain, so she could gently tug at the silk cloth, drawing it out from between his dry lips. Earning a choked, grateful gasp from his mouth, a flash of his hazy, still-bright eyes on hers. Still looking—helpless, suddenly, disbelieving, or even desperate.

Kitty's hand fluttered to his sweaty cheek, her gaze darting uncertainly up toward Varinn—and to her distant surprise, he nodded. Nodded, giving her permission to keep doing this, oh gods—so she settled a little closer before Thrain, and brought up the cloth she was still holding, stroking it at his flushed face, wiping at his wet eyes.

"All right, Thrain?" she whispered. "Do you—need anything?"

But his head was already shaking, his eyes flashing with more bright, desperate gratefulness. "Just—more," he choked. "More, Varinn. Please. Please. I *beg* you."

The huff of breath from Varinn might have been relief, or even laughter, and he nodded, his gaze again dropping to the sight of their joined bodies before him. "Ach, you shall have more, *krútt*," he murmured. "If you keep begging."

Thrain's cry was anguished, elated, and he gulped for air, arched his back even more. "Please, Varinn," he gasped. "Please. Give me more. All of you."

Varinn's chest hollowed, his hands slipping to grasp Thrain's hips, holding tight—and then his own hips snapped forward. Driving a harsh, strangled shout from Thrain's mouth, his eyes rolling back, his body writhing all over. Because Varinn was surely buried deep, caught all the way inside him, and it almost looked like more than Thrain could bear, his teeth biting sharp into his lip, the water again streaming from his eyes.

"Still good?" Kitty whispered, before she could catch it— but another furtive glance at Varinn showed him waiting too, watching, listening. Until Thrain rapidly nodded again, his wild eyes refocusing on hers.

"Och," he gasped, though his head slightly tilted, pressing into the touch of her hand, still hovering against his cheek. "Och. So good."

Kitty exhaled her own shaky relief, and began stroking at his face again, wiping the wetness away. "Good," she murmured back. "You're doing so well, Thrain. Offering yourself up to our Lord Grisk so sweetly, showing him the honour he deserves."

Thrain moaned and nodded against her hand—and oh, perhaps even Varinn had gasped, his eyes crackling on hers. So Kitty gulped down more air, brought up her other hand, cradled Thrain's sweaty, staring face in her fingers.

"So good," she told him, her voice hitching. "Welcoming our lord inside you like this, sucking him deep. And maybe"— she hauled in another breath, darted another look at Varinn's crackling eyes—"maybe, if you're good, he'll even give you more. Maybe he'll feed you all that good Grisk seed. Make you *reek* of him, even more than you already do."

That was definitely a gasp from Varinn now, his hips grinding against Thrain's backside, while Thrain choked another helpless cry, his head furiously nodding. "Och," he rasped. "Och. Please, Varinn. Oh gods. Fuck. Please, plough me. Give it to me. *Please.*"

And yes, yes, Varinn's hips were already canting faster, harder, and Thrain scrabbled and whimpered beneath it, arching up into it, his face straining into Kitty's hands. "Ach," he gasped. "Please, Varinn. Need you—so much. So fucking much. Oh gods, oh gods, oh gods—"

Varinn's hips were snapping deep and forceful, now, plunging himself in again and again, but there was no pain on Thrain's face, still cradled in Kitty's hands. Only more frantic, furious pleasure, and Kitty kept caressing him, stroking him, as a soft-sounding purr hummed through her own chest, too. "So good, *krútt,*" she whispered. "Look at you, taking your lord's pounding so well, swallowing his fat Grisk prick inside you. You keep sucking him in, keep pleasing him, begging for him, just as he deserves."

And gods, what was she even saying, but the way he and Varinn were moaning in unison, now, Thrain's eyes rolling so far she could only see the whites of them, the sweat streaking down his red cheeks. And he was begging, again, but now in words she couldn't understand, babbling rapid and high-pitched, while Varinn's hands clamped against his sides, his head tipping back, his eyes hooded, almost closed—

But then he glanced downwards again, his narrow eyes briefly sweeping across the nearby shelves, and then catching—on Kitty. "Suck him, *kisa*," he ordered, short, breathless. "All of it."

Wait. Wait, he was—wanting—ordering—what? And Kitty and Thrain had both frozen, Kitty's eyes shocked wide on Varinn's face—but at another sharp jerk of Varinn's head, she scrambled to obey. Lurching further beneath Thrain's bent-double body, toward where his pierced, swollen length was wildly bobbing and leaking, clearly about to burst—and Kitty lunged for it, sucked it deep, just in time. Just as Thrain shouted, ragged and raw, and poured out hot and furious into her mouth.

He tasted so different, and yet so familiar, the rich spraying sweetness, the hard gold of his ring beneath her tongue. Surging Kitty through with a shocking, sparkling craving, strong enough to spin the room around her, to flash flying white behind her eyes—and then her own pleasure crashed through her, striking again and again. Shaking her all over, so powerful she nearly lost the suction—but somehow she caught it again, swallowing it deep, as Thrain again cried out, long and loud and shrill.

And wait, wait, now Varinn was groaning too, hoarse and rasping, and she could feel his hands gripping powerfully at Thrain's hips, yanking him tighter, impaling him whole— because he was pouring out, too. Filling Thrain with his scent, and his seed, again, while Thrain did the same to Kitty, shuddering out ever-smaller pulses of sweetness into her mouth.

And for a strange, surreal moment, it was as though they were all floating together, lost in the relief, the pleasure, the peace. The bare, powerful certainty of this moment, of Lord Grisk granting his worshipful subjects yet more of his great gifts. One of his worshippers bent over for him, welcoming his conquest deep up his backside, while the other knelt before his altar, drinking up the bounty he offered. While also... keeping the floors clean?

Kitty blinked at that thought, that uncertainty—and then distantly noted that Varinn was nudging at her with his foot. Wanting her up, away, and she drew back with genuine regret, pressing a furtive little kiss against Thrain's lovely gold ring, before letting his softened heft fall from her mouth. And then she awkwardly clambered out from beneath Thrain again, and shoved up to her feet before Varinn. Eyeing him with a tense, rising unease, because had he really wanted all that, had he wanted her to do that, or had it just been about the mess, about Thrain, and...

And without warning, Varinn's big hand slipped around her back, and swept her close. So he could—tilt her head up, and... *kiss* her.

Kitty froze for an instant, blinking—but then moaned as she sank into it, into the warm softness of his lips, his tongue. Into the realization that he was tasting Thrain, on her. And a bright, shivery relief was streaking up her back, as her own hands slid reflexively around his waist, her fingers spreading, as she opened wider, welcomed him deeper, oh—

But then Varinn drew away again, giving a brief little pat to her arse, before turning back toward Thrain. Toward where his trembling body was still bent double, still fully impaled upon him. And Varinn's big hands again stroked up and down Thrain's flanks, strong and soothing, until his shivers finally stilled, his breath heaving harsh through his sweaty body.

"Bring me that again, *kisa*," Varinn said now, his voice husky, as he again nodded toward the small wooden chest. And once Kitty had obliged and fetched it, he drew his claw through it for a long moment, until finally he pulled out another large, polished gold item. It had a very distinct, bulbous shape, as if it were made of a row of connected, gradually larger beads, until its final bead was as thick around as Kitty's forearm. And at the very end, connected to that bead, there was what almost appeared to be a circular gold handle, as though it was meant for...

And yes, oh hell, Varinn was glancing down, to where he was still buried deep inside Thrain—and then he bent Thrain even lower before him. Holding him there, his hand firm and proprietary on Thrain's back, as he carefully drew himself out, his chubby, shiny-slick bulk emerging breath by breath. Until it fell free of Thrain with a soft squelch, revealing—oh. A large, gaping opening, where he'd split Thrain wide upon him. Where Thrain was already leaking out a thick string of white, dangling toward the floor.

For an instant, Varinn just looked, his breaths stilled, his sharp fang biting his lip—but then he caught the string of white with the very tip of the gold length, and guided it back up. Brushing it against Thrain's waiting, wide-open cleft, and gently nudging it inside, while Thrain shuddered and keened.

Kitty was breathless, suddenly, watching with wide, disbelieving eyes as Varinn slowly, purposefully, slipped the first full gold bead inside. Into where it easily disappeared, while Thrain visibly spasmed, and attempted to close around it—but clearly he couldn't quite accomplish it, and Varinn huffed a soft little laugh as he slid the next bead in, and then the next. Until the largest one had slipped in, too, and there was only the circular handle left, jutting up bright and obscene out of Thrain's open arse. And Varinn was still holding it, even giving it a gentle little circle, along with a light slap of his other hand to Thrain's trembling flank.

"Close up around your new *rassja, krútt*," he murmured. "You will not waste what I give you, ach?"

Oh. He meant he was blocking off the scent with this—*rassja*, trapping it inside, and Thrain clearly knew it too, as he fervently moaned and nodded. And Kitty could see him fighting to obey, his stretched-out body working to tighten around the gold filling it—until finally, somehow, he seemed to manage it. Gripping the *rassja* tight, showing only the gleaming handle, nestled close between his firm arse-cheeks.

"Good," Varinn said, breathless, as he bent forward, and pressed a gentle kiss to Thrain's sweaty back. "So good, *krútt. Ach.*"

And for an instant, suddenly it was him who looked reverent. Worshipful. His eyes fluttering closed, his breath inhaling slow and deep against Thrain's skin. As if he was savouring the scent, the taste, and surely he was, surely. Because he—he'd given Thrain his seed, again. His scent. His kindness. His... forgiveness. Just as—Kitty's throat convulsed— just as a true god's son should.

And when Varinn finally drew Thrain up again, and turned him to face him, Thrain looked just as dazed as she felt. His eyes hazy, far too bright, his face deeply flushed, still covered with a sheen of sweat, and betraying distinct tracks of water down his cheeks. And his shoulders were heaving, his mouth opening, closing, opening again, as if he'd forgotten how to speak.

"You—" he began, shook his messy head, briefly squeezed his eyes shut. "You—shouldn't have, Varinn. You—I—you—"

He was blinking at Varinn again, his lip quivering, but Varinn just gave a small smile back, a quick jerk of his head. "Here," he said, as he reached to grasp something on the nearest shelf. "This is yours. Should... you yet wish for it."

It was Thrain's abandoned *thyrja*, and Thrain was rapidly nodding, snatching it close, clutching it to his chest. "Ach, I wish for it," he choked. "Ach. I—I thank you, Varinn."

Varinn twitched a brief nod, another soft little smile—and then he dropped his hand downwards, toward his groin, where he was still wearing that thick gold ring. As if—wait, he was going to take it *off*, oh gods, and Kitty only distantly felt herself yelping, and lurching close toward him.

"You are *not* getting rid of that, are you?" she hissed at him. "You cannot, Lord Grisk. It is *stunning* on you!"

Varinn blinked at her, once—and then he was smiling again, even more indulgent than before. "You and your taste for finery, *kisa*," he murmured. "Ach, mayhap I shall keep it for you. But you must not expect to be spoilt with it all the time, either."

Kitty's sudden, eager grin had swiftly turned to a displeased pout, and she heard Thrain huffing a shaky-sounding laugh behind her. "Tyrant, I tell you, Kit," he said, his voice wavering. "And gods, it's so fucking *good*, ach?"

His eyes were still so bright, blinking like that toward her, as if he desperately needed her to agree—but Kitty was already nodding, and smiling shyly back toward him. Because oh, she'd gotten to taste him again, gotten to feel that lovely ring against her tongue, and Varinn had kissed her afterwards, Varinn had liked it, hadn't he?

"Now come to bed, you two," Varinn cut in, his voice firm. "I ken we all need it, ach?"

Kitty and Thrain both nodded, and after a few moments' fumbling for clothes, they were flanking Varinn as he strode down the corridor. Kitty's hand again clutched to Varinn's arm, while Thrain was fully leaning against him, his head bent into his shoulder.

But once they'd all cleaned up, and piled into bed together— with Kitty tucked warm and safe in the middle between them— she couldn't quite seem to fall asleep. And maybe Varinn and Thrain couldn't either, Varinn's body still a little too stiff against her back, Thrain's still betraying the occasional telltale twitch.

"Och, I really am sorry," Thrain's low voice finally said, into the quiet darkness. "I—I really thought it might fix it, Varinn, to finally have your scent. Your... security, after so long. Made me careless today, ach? Stupid."

Varinn's body went a little stiffer, but he didn't reply, and Thrain drew in a slow, rattling breath. "It was always easier, I ken," he continued, "to tell myself that I was drinking so much... because of you. Because of what I didn't have. And I had to keep doing it, to keep things easy between us. To keep my thoughts away from it all, ach? From always"—Thrain huffed a heavy sigh—"being your second best."

There was more stiff silence from Varinn, and then a swallow, an inhale, as if he were about to speak—but then Kitty could feel Thrain kicking at him, catching their legs together. "I ken, I ken," he said, his voice cracking. "But I *did* think it, and it was an easy thing to blame, ach? Especially with us always arguing over it, and you giving me all those ultimatums over it—I ken it tangled it all together, like you said. Made me feel justified in being defensive, and resentful toward you. But in truth..."

His voice cracked, and Kitty could feel Varinn's breaths coming harder, rustling against her hair. Listening, waiting for Thrain to continue, and Thrain was breathing heavy now too, his body spasming against her.

"But it wasn't you, Varinn," he said thickly. "Or you, Kit, or anyone else, either. It was just—me. It's always just been—*me*."

His voice sounded drawn, now, despairing, and Kitty could feel his chest shuddering as he exhaled. "Like I told you," he continued, "I just—I can't do it. I'm—fucked. Broken. I can't handle things like—like you do, Varinn, or the rest of our kin does. Something unexpected happens, whether it's a lost orcling, or getting dumped, or fighting with you, and I just—I lose it. I can't control it, I can't be trusted, I make a fucking rubbish heap out of everything I care about. That's all."

His voice was cracked and quiet by the end, his despair almost a palpable ache in the air, and Kitty felt herself blinking hard, her hand finding his chest, spreading wide against it. "But it's not *you*, Thrain," she said into the silence, the conviction catching in her voice. "It's not. It's the sickness, remember? And as much as we'd all like it to just disappear forever, it's not going to work like that. We need to expect setbacks. We need to just keep learning, and moving forward."

Thrain's body lurched a little closer in the bed, but he wasn't arguing, so Kitty drew down another breath, kept going. "And Efterar said that strain was the most likely thing to cause those setbacks, right? And it sounds to me like you were under excessive strain today. Needing to rescue a lost child trapped in a poisonous tunnel? That's *horrifying*, Thrain."

Thrain barked a too-loud laugh, his body convulsing against her, and Kitty could feel Varinn's arm abruptly drawing him closer, stroking up and down his back, while that low steady purr rumbled from his throat. "Katharine speaks truth, *krútt*," he said softly. "You have been ill, and I ought not to have pushed you into working again, as I did. I ken I thought it would—keep your focus elsewhere, but our work is not easy, and I did not think of how it might affect you. Most of all with your scenting at full strength again."

But Thrain just laughed again, harsh and short and miserable. "But it's fine for you," he choked. "It's fine for Thrak and Dammarr and Nattfarr. It's still just—*me* who's fucked, Varinn. Me who's rubbish at just—existing. When by all accounts, my life is—good, ach? I have you and Kit, I have a son on the way, I have food in my belly, clothes, friends, kin, a home. I have everything I need, and I'm still just—*failing*."

The despair was again so heavy, so wretched in his voice. But thank the gods, Varinn was still here, still stroking, still with that steady, soothing purr rumbling through his chest. "Ach, our lives are good now, *krútt*," he murmured, very low. "But they have not—always been thus. And you have borne much, ach? More than mayhap any of us."

Thrain betrayed a faint but undeniable flinch against Kitty's hand, and she blinked into the darkness, cleared her constricted throat. "How so?" she asked, before she could stop it. "What—what happened?"

Thrain flinched again, his laugh cracking almost painfully

through the air. "Och, just the usual, you ken," he croaked. "My father was rubbish, never knew my mother, war and death and trapped and—och. Just the same as the rest of us!"

His voice was high-pitched, frantic, and now it was Kitty flinching as Varinn's purr dropped into something like a growl, his hand catching, stilling, on Thrain's back. "Quiet, *krútt*," he said, deep and authoritative. "It was not the same, and there is no shame in seeing this. And henceforth"—his voice hardened—"you shall stop working as a Speaker's Guard, both here in the mountain, and out in the realm. Until I grant you leave otherwise."

Oh. Kitty's uncertain curiosity was still clanging through her thoughts, but against her, Thrain's body heavily sagged, his breath hitching with stark, staggering relief. Suggesting that he very much welcomed Varinn's command on this, and would happily capitulate—at least, until he stiffened again, and gave a low, resigned sigh.

"But—I don't want to disappoint Thrak and Nattfarr and Dammarr, and all our kin," he said. "And—you most of all, Varinn. I know how you feel about our work, our calling. And even if you say this now"—he dragged in a shaky breath— "how will you feel when you have to watch me larking around here, shirking my duties, and failing our kin? Leaving you and our brothers with even more work and strain than you already need to bear?"

But Varinn's hand was still stroking Thrain's back, that low purr again rumbling from his chest. "I shall speak with Nattfarr," he said firmly. "We shall find other ways. Our kin's wellbeing does not all hinge upon you, ach? And"—his voice softened again—"I shall not think less of you for taking time to heal, *krútt*. I wish you to be well."

Thrain was leaning even closer, tilting into Varinn's touch, even as he huffed another thin, choked little laugh. "But—I wouldn't get to spend my days with you anymore," he whispered. "What if you realize how much better it is, without me? What if—what if you forget me?"

Kitty could hear Varinn's hard swallow, the brief catch in his purr, in his steadily stroking hand. "You ken I shall never forget you, *krútt*," he said, a little rough. "I could not, even if I wished to, ach?"

Thrain choked another sound, much like a sob, but he didn't reply, and Varinn didn't, either. And finally Kitty drew in a breath, and attempted a smile up toward Thrain's face in the darkness. "Of course he couldn't," she said, as lightly as she could. "He absolutely adores you, Thrain. I mean, he's given you his scent, and stabbed you with his piercings, and now he's gone and shoved a golden pole up your—"

She broke off there, genuinely flustered, but thank the gods, Thrain's laugh was sudden and bright, shaking his chest against her. "Ach, Kit, just so," he said, between chuckles. "And I thought I scented gold, but then thought—och. Is the *rassja* really gold, Varinn?"

His voice sounded shy, suddenly, and Kitty could feel him slightly squirming, perhaps touching at it, feeling how it was still there, still surely far too present inside him. While Varinn made a low huffing noise, not at all displeased.

"Ach, gold-plated," he said, a little too offhandedly. "My credit-account shall soon be lain to utter waste, between the two of you."

Oh. Well. Because he meant he wanted to keep dressing them, keep giving them his jewels, making them his own. Caring for them, like a real god would, and for an instant Kitty couldn't speak, over the sudden clutch of gratefulness in her throat.

"Well, as usual, your taste is exquisite, Lord Grisk, because it was a lovely piece," she finally said, as easily as she could. "And it looked very compelling in—er, *on* you, Thrain. I do hope you'll be wearing it for us often."

And now it was Thrain's throat catching, and Varinn huffing

a low, tantalizing laugh. "Ach, I ken he shall," he said smoothly. "If he beha—"

But he broke off there, and Kitty could almost feel his wince, his chagrin. His realization, surely, that he'd fallen into his habit of commanding Thrain again. Not only in this, but perhaps about their work, too.

But now it was Thrain's arm moving, rubbing up and down Varinn's back, easy and reassuring. "Och, you ken I want to behave for you, Lord Grisk," he murmured. "Want you to keep telling me to, ach? Want whatever rewards you might be willing to offer me. I just"—he swallowed—"just want you to listen, too. Want your... support. Your respect. For me, and for what... what *I* want. Like you did... with Kit. With the shop."

Oh. His voice sounded tentative again, uncertain, as if again, this was something they'd never discussed before. Something Thrain had never dared to ask for, perhaps. And Kitty could feel Varinn's breath, again rustling in her hair, as he rapidly nodded, and drew them both closer against him.

"Ach, I follow, *krútt*," he replied, his voice so raw, so soft. "But then you must also tell me if I am—not honouring this. If I am trampling over you about your work, or your garb, or—my gold in your rump."

Thrain's laugh rang through the air, the sound warm and wonderful, and Kitty could feel him happily wriggling closer. "Och, you ken I like that kind of trampling, Varinn," he said lightly. "Most of all with the gold, ach? And"—his voice lowered—"and supporting me with the work thing, too. I... thank you."

Varinn might have shrugged, but his hand had shifted up to catch Thrain's hand against him, grasping it tight. And then Kitty felt Varinn guiding both their hands to—her. Settling together against her waist, their fingers interlaced, their touch warm and solid and safe.

"Now if you truly wish to behave, you shall sleep," Varinn said, in a tone that brooked no argument. "All of you. Now."

A delicious little shiver snaked up Kitty's spine, and she nodded, and curled up closer against him. Her back tucked into the strong, sturdy heat of his chest, while her front was facing Thrain, her hand spreading against the steady beat of his heart. He was here, he was sober, they were working it out. And maybe... maybe...

And after a wide, contented yawn, Kitty closed her eyes, and drifted into the darkness.

37

When Kitty awoke the next morning, she still felt calm, relaxed, utterly at ease. Especially upon discovering that both Varinn and Thrain were still in bed with her, their bodies all tangled together, Thrain's face buried deep in Varinn's neck.

"Morning, Kit," Thrain murmured as he drew away to grin blearily at her, revealing his red-rimmed teeth, chaotic hair, and messy, red-streaked face. "Sleep all right? Feel all right?"

Kitty nodded, smiling back toward him, and he leaned in closer, inhaled deeply against her hair. "Good," he said. "Smell so good, too, with my scent and Varinn's both blending fresh in your belly. Ach, Varinn?"

Kitty couldn't help a brief, disbelieving little laugh, a furtive glance toward where Varinn didn't seem to be arguing this— but then she felt her smile fading, her eyes guiltily darting back toward Thrain's. "You don't—mind, though?" she asked, before she could stop it. "That we did it last night without—"

Without you, she'd meant to say, angling her guilty glance up toward Varinn this time. Toward where Varinn was carefully watching Thrain, his brow creased—but Thrain didn't look even slightly concerned, and he shifted downwards in the bed, inhaling deep against Kitty's belly this time. "Och, no," he said, husky, as he pressed a warm, gentle kiss to her skin. "Varinn's your mate, isn't he? Want him to keep building his scent upon you. Want him bound to you, and our son."

Oh. It was again perhaps a confession, admitting that he still didn't trust himself in this, and he kissed Kitty's belly again before lifting his head, twitching a small smile up toward her and Varinn. "And also," he continued, "he came to you last night, Kit, instead of going down to brood alone in that godsforsaken crypt. It's what he usually does when I dump my rubbish onto him, and it makes him *reek* of rot and death."

He betrayed a revolted little shudder, together with a regretful wince toward Varinn's face. But to Kitty's vague surprise, Varinn only wrinkled his nose, and gave a tolerant ruffle of his hand in Thrain's messy hair. "This is bold of you to say, Thrain, granted how you yet carry the stench of that foul human pub," he said crisply. "Now, you shall both come and bathe with me, ach? At once."

A bath did sound delightful, and soon Kitty was wrapped in a cozy towel, and accompanying Varinn and Thrain into a room she hadn't yet encountered. It scented distinctly of sulphur, but it was large and steamy and wonderfully warm, and boasted several huge pools cut into the smooth stone floor. And in one of the pools, there were already three people swimming and splashing together—Alma, and her two orc mates Baldr and Drafli.

"C'mon, Kit," Thrain said, winking cheerfully toward her, as he tossed off his own towel onto a large nearby rock. "No clothes in the pool, ach?"

Kitty hesitated, glancing first toward Thrain's lean, fully bared body, and then toward Alma and her mates—who indeed seemed to be undressed, too. And Alma had even paused to wave at Kitty, before hurling herself onto Drafli's shoulders, and splashing back into the water—and wait,

Varinn was already yanking off his towel, too, and diving headfirst into the empty pool.

So Kitty tentatively pulled off her own towel, fighting to ignore the feel of the open air on her bare skin, the awareness that Alma and her mates could see this, and anyone else could walk in, at any moment. But Thrain was grinning at her, nudging her toward the pool, and Varinn had already resurfaced, shaking the water out of his hair as he swam back to meet them.

"Do you know how to swim, *kisa*?" he asked, holding out both hands toward her, and Kitty nodded as she gratefully leaned into his touch, and allowed him to guide her into the warm water. While behind her, Thrain whooped and leapt in beside them, creating a gigantic splash that sprayed Kitty and Varinn both.

"Thrain!" Varinn said reproachfully, wiping the water out of Kitty's eyes, but Kitty was already laughing, and waving it away. Watching with rapidly rising amusement as Thrain paddled up beside Varinn, mischief dancing in his eyes—and then he tackled Varinn bodily into the pool, splashing even more water straight in Kitty's face.

When they surged up again, Varinn was reluctantly grinning too, and then he pounced back toward Thrain. And soon the two of them were wildly wrestling and playing together, chasing each other in circles around Kitty, while she alternately cheered them on, and laughed until her stomach ached.

It somehow ended with Varinn hopping up to sit on the edge of the pool, his muscled legs sprawled wide, his bare cock already bobbing out ruddy and swollen from his groin. And though he hadn't said a word, he was looking at Kitty and Thrain with that hungry, hazy glint in his eyes—and then he jerked his head toward them. Saying, very clearly, *come*.

But Kitty hesitated again, glancing toward Alma and her mates in the next pool—and though the three of them were still frolicking together, taking no notice whatsoever of this, it distantly occurred to Kitty that Varinn's beautiful, muscled body was now fully on display, for anyone who might wish to see. And even if Alma was already happily mated, perhaps there were other women who weren't, other women like the ones Varinn would truly prefer. Like the woman he would find after he and Thrain worked this out, after he sent Kitty away...

And suddenly, for the first time in days, here was the memory, bitter and miserable, of what Varinn had said about her, back when they'd first met. *You ken I should wish to steal her? A weak, foolish, thoughtless, spoilt woman, with a hundred scents upon her?*

"Och, Kit," cut in Thrain's voice, and Kitty twitched at the feel of his hand on her back, and then the sight of his warm, searching eyes. "Your mate's trying to get your attention over here, ach? You're not about to disappoint him, are you?"

Oh. Kitty's gaze darted back toward Varinn, who was watching her with his head tilted, something almost like confusion in his eyes. But he certainly wasn't arguing Thrain's point, and Kitty swallowed as her eyes drifted downwards, towards—*that*. Already swelling even fuller, bobbing toward her, inviting her to come closer...

But she couldn't help hesitating again, angling another uncertain glance over her shoulder, toward where—oh. Alma and Baldr were both clinging to Drafli, Baldr's mouth bent into Drafli's neck, suggesting that perhaps they were about to be similarly occupied. And Thrain's hand was stroking Kitty's back now, moving with familiar, easy reassurance.

"Don't worry about them," he told her, his voice soft. "Or about anyone else. They'll all be able to smell it, so if they don't want to see it, they won't. And Varinn's always scenting too, ach, Varinn?"

Varinn twitched a curt nod, and Kitty felt her body relaxing in return, her hunger simmering higher in her belly, her eyes again dropping to the sight at Varinn's groin. And with a breathless, jolting burst of courage, she swam a little closer, and took him into her mouth.

Her moan escaped on its own, her lashes fluttering, because oh, he tasted so good—and beside her, Thrain's laugh was amused and approving, his hand again stroking up and down her back. "Good, Kit," he murmured. "Ach, you're so sweet, aren't you? So pretty, with a good, fat Grisk prick filling your mouth?"

Kitty nearly choked, but kept going, delving inside Varinn with her tongue, deepening the suction as much as she could. Teasing out that hot sweetness in heady little spurts, oh gods, while Thrain kept stroking her, and Varinn just sat there, watching with those glinting, hooded eyes.

"Good, Kit," Thrain said again, huskier. "You love pleasing our lord, don't you? Love seeking your sweet little tongue inside him, plumping up his big bollocks for you? Coaxing out his good Grisk seed for you?"

Kitty moaned again, fervently nodding as she held Varinn's eyes, as Thrain gave a low, heated groan beside her. "Ach, he's so good, isn't he," he breathed. "Tastes so sweet, just like the gods' very own. Wish I could—"

His voice broke, and when Kitty darted a glance sideways, he was wincing, angling an apologetic look between her and Varinn. But Kitty had easily followed his meaning, and she drew back from Varinn, meeting his glinting, watching gaze.

"Would you mind—if we shared you?" she shyly asked, through her swollen-feeling lips. "Please, Lord Grisk?"

And oh, the hunger, and then the soft amused indulgence, flitting across Varinn's eyes. "Ach, should you wish, *kisa*," he said, his voice impossibly smooth. "But you ken my full load is for her, *krútt*."

He'd arched an imperious brow toward Thrain, who was already rapidly nodding, blinking between Varinn and Kitty with worshipful eyes. And then he swam closer, toward that wet, tantalizing length, jutting out between Varinn's hairy thighs—and without an instant's hesitation, he put his lips to that glossy head, and sucked it deep and greedy into his throat.

Kitty's breath caught, because oh, the way Thrain *looked*, with the water still streaming down his face, plastering his spiky hair to his skin, while he eagerly sucked on the hard, slick length filling his mouth. And his eyes on Varinn were bright, blatantly reverent, especially when Varinn slipped down a hand, and sank it into his wet, messy hair. Guiding Thrain's head back and forth, plunging himself in and out with such casual, entitled ease.

But then Thrain pulled off, releasing Varinn's bobbing length with a loud, blatant slurp, before winking at Kitty, and nudging her back again. Watching with warm, approving satisfaction as she again took Varinn's shining, dripping head between her lips, and swallowed him deep.

"Good, Kit," Thrain murmured, hoarse. "You keep sucking your lord, like a good little kitten. We're gonna work together and milk him dry for you, aren't we? Plump him up nice and full, and then suck out every last drop he can make for you?"

Kitty betrayed another choked gasp, and oh, Varinn liked it too, his head tilting back, his strength swelling even fuller between her lips. While beside her, Thrain chuckled and leaned in closer, and then began nibbling up the inside of Varinn's thigh. Kissing him, lavishing him, twining his long black tongue into that thatch of dark hair, as Kitty kept sucking him deep into her throat. And then, when she drew back a little, slipping her tongue deeper into that leaking slit, Thrain promptly began licking at Varinn's exposed shaft, curling around it with his long tongue, easing up toward Kitty's mouth...

And somehow, oh hell, they were almost kissing, but not quite, passing Varinn's slick rounded head between their lips— and now Thrain was sucking on it, while Kitty kissed down the full length of it, into the coarse hair at Varinn's groin. Breathing in his musky rich scent, revelling in the feel of his damp thigh twitching against her cheek, his hand slipping into her hair. Wanting this from her. Approving of this, from her.

So she kissed her way back up his pulsing length, more eagerly this time, until she'd again reached Thrain's mouth. And oh, it was willingly meeting hers, and passing Varinn's swollen, seeping head back to her again. The sounds slick and messy between them now, the wetness smearing across Kitty's face—only to be thoroughly licked away by Thrain's firm sweeping tongue, before he again took Varinn from her lips, and sucked him deep.

And this time, Kitty kept kissing at Thrain's mouth, at the impossible feeling of Varinn's hot, pulsing cock jutting inside it. At the twinges of sweetness she could taste between Thrain's lips, as they again met hers, and nudged that leaking head back toward her. But this time, Thrain's tongue came with it, slipping greedily between her already-stretched lips, because oh, Varinn was close, he was tightening, gasping, and—

Kitty moaned as the hot sweetness surged into her mouth, flooding it full. Dousing not only her tongue, but Thrain's, too, and Thrain choked a harsh, desperate cry as Kitty belatedly, fervently swallowed, gulping Varinn's rich bounty down her throat. While Thrain kept blatantly kissing her, kissing them, slick and hungry and obscene, making this moment—this gift—not just hers, but theirs.

And when the flow faded to a steady drizzle, Kitty slipped Varinn's softening head back into Thrain's mouth again, watched him suck it whole, his eyes rolling back—and then he passed it to her again, even softer now. Cleaning up together, making sure to find every drop, while Varinn just sat there, and watched them with such easy, indulgent eyes.

"So greedy, *krútt*," Varinn finally murmured, once Thrain had drawn off again, licking at his wet, swollen lips. "Should you ever wish me to put him in his place, *kisa*, know that you only ever need to ask."

Kitty choked a laugh as she drew away too, smiling shyly

between the two of them. "You're too kind, Lord Grisk," she said lightly. "And you know, if you really are offering"—she waggled her brows—"I certainly wouldn't mind seeing you stab him with more of your lovely taste in jewels."

Now Varinn was coolly raising his brows toward Thrain, who was gaping at Kitty with delighted disbelief. "You devious little hellcat!" he exclaimed. "He already... you don't actually want to..."

But his voice trailed off there, his eyes darting uncertainly up toward Varinn. Toward where Varinn was jerking a nod, and then smoothly leaping to his feet. "Come, then," he said. "I ken I have one in mind."

The disbelief again flashed through Thrain's eyes, but he clambered out of the pool too, drawing Kitty up behind him. And somehow, it felt far less awkward as they dried off together, and Kitty even called a cheerful goodbye to Alma— who was still similarly involved with her mates in the pool— before they left.

And once they'd reached their room and dressed again, Varinn indeed pulled over his box, and produced a small, glinting gold jewel. One that appeared to be another earring, but it was shaped like a crescent moon, with a slightly thicker middle, and sharp points at either end.

"For here," Varinn said, a little too casually, as he held it up against... Thrain's *nose*. "If you are sure it should not be too strong for your scenting?"

But Thrain's breath had caught in his throat, his tooth biting his lip, as abject longing flared through his eyes. "'Course not," he croaked. "Getting to scent your gold with every breath, Varinn, it would be—"

He swallowed hard, flashed Varinn a suddenly weepy smile. And Varinn smiled too, warm and affectionate, as he went to heat the ring in the lamp's flame, and then strode back toward Thrain, nudging him down to sit on the bed. Tilting his head back, drawing him close—and then Thrain gasped, flinched, as Varinn stabbed the piercing through.

But when Varinn drew back again, there was no blood, no pain on Thrain's face. Only that glinting new gold, jutting out curved and sharp from each of his nostrils. Looking decidedly wild, daring, even a little dangerous—but gods, it suited the rest of him so well, contrasting beautifully with his messy hair, his earring, his bright flashing eyes. And without quite meaning to, Kitty lurched across the room, grasping Thrain's *thyrja* from where he'd left it on the shelf—and Varinn murmured a husky thank-you as he took it from her hands, and slipped it on over Thrain's head.

"Perfect," Kitty breathed, drinking up the stunning sight of him, bared in all his striking, beautiful jewels. "Excellent choice, Lord Grisk. Again."

Varinn was clearly in full agreement, his tongue brushing his lips, his hand tilting Thrain's face up. "We shall go see Efterar after breakfast, ach?" he said, his voice not quite steady. "And you will follow all he asks of you, to make sure it fully heals, and does not affect your scenting."

"Ach, ach," Thrain replied, with obvious exasperation, but there was a small, quavering smile on his mouth. "I... thank you, Varinn. Again."

Varinn curtly nodded, drawing backwards again—at least, until Thrain clasped his hand, squeezing it in both of his. "I—I mean it, Varinn," he said, very quiet. "You didn't have to do any of this, last night, or today, or—or ever. I don't deserve it, and I'll do whatever I can to make it up to you."

Varinn's chest hollowed, and his hand squeezed back on Thrain's, his claws nudging into his skin. "Ach, I am glad to help," he replied, just as quiet. "And if you truly wish to honour me, you shall keep seeking to rest, and heal. And when I come home tonight"—his mouth quirked—"I wish to find you sober and waiting for me, and wearing your jewels. *All* of them, even if Katharine needs to help you. Ach?"

He clearly meant that golden *rassja*, too, and Thrain visibly flushed, his head ducking as he nodded. "Ach," he said thickly. "And you're *sure* you don't mind me staying here today, Varinn, and leaving you to do all the—"

"I am sure," Varinn cut in, his voice firm. "I have already spoken with Nattfarr upon this, whilst you slept. And in truth"—his eyes flicked toward Kitty—"I shall be glad to have you here to keep a scent upon Katharine, also. You were right to raise this with me yesterday, for Dammarr told me she reeked of weariness when he saw her, and had not eaten, either. I"—he swallowed, met Thrain's eyes—"I ought to have better listened to you upon this, *krútt*. I am—sorry."

Oh. Something strange and shivery was pooling in Kitty's belly, especially when Thrain smiled back at Varinn like that, slow and shy and grateful. Enough that the redness was creeping up Varinn's neck, and he roughly cleared his throat, and nudged them toward the door. Out into the sitting-room, where Thrak, Nattfarr, and Ella were already eating breakfast at their usual table, while little Rakfi scampered around their feet.

"Morning!" Ella said cheerfully, waving them over. "How are you, Kitty? I've been hearing raves about your work in the shop yesterday. And"—her warm eyes angled toward Thrain—"is that a new piercing, Thrain? It's lovely."

Thrain's face flushed, but he nodded as he gingerly sat down next to Thrak on the bench, and swiped a strip of meat off the platter before them. "Ach," he said, a little too offhandedly. "Another gift from Varinn."

Ella's brows shot up, but she gave a pleased-looking smile toward Varinn, who had guided Kitty to sit beside him on the empty bench, and placed some bread into her hand. While across the table, Thrak was frowning darkly toward Varinn, his mouth pursed.

"But you haven't yet spoken matehood vows to my brother, have you, Varinn?" Thrak said stiffly. "So what's the meaning of all these gifts, then? Bribes, mayhap, to keep him trapped here in the mountain, and serving you at your whim? Instead of doing his damned *job* with us, and helping us support our kin, as a Speaker's Guard ought?"

There was an instant's silence, in which Varinn's jaw went very tight, and Thrain visibly grimaced. But then, to Kitty's vague surprise, Nattfarr gave a disapproving harrumph, and kicked at Thrak beneath the table. "If Thrain needs some time away from our work, we are happy to grant this," he said firmly. "We have no wish to push him against his will, and thus build anger or resentment between him and our kin. Also, he now has a woman and son to care for, ach?"

But at that, Thrak's chilly gaze flicked toward Kitty, holding with disconcerting intensity. "Ach, but has your *woman* spoken vows to you either, brother?" he said coolly. "Or bothered to grant you a mating-gift?"

Kitty instantly blanched, blinking wide-eyed toward him— had she been supposed to give Thrain a mating-gift, too?!—and thankfully, Thrain frowned, and sharply elbowed Thrak in the side. "You don't bring her into this, brother," he said, his voice hard. "She doesn't owe me a damned thing. And look, I *want* the time off. I told you"—his throat bobbed—"I'm trying to get off the drink, ach?"

But Thrak didn't look convinced, again darting a narrow, disapproving glare toward Varinn. "Och, and Varinn thinks leaving you to sit here bored and alone on your arse all day is going to help with that?" he demanded. "How can you yet know *naught* about my brother, Varinn, after all these years?"

Varinn's mouth thinned, but he didn't reply, despite the visible flex of his jaw in his cheek. And again, it was Thrain who growled, and began to speak—at least, until his eyes snapped sideways, across the room. Toward where Dammarr had just stepped out of one of the adjoining doors, and was now striding over toward them.

And—Kitty felt her eyes lighting up—he was wearing one

of his new dresses. The lovely dark green one, its rich colour contrasting beautifully against the pearly grey of his skin, and showing off his muscled torso—and his nipple-ring—to stunning effect. And though his face and ears were flushed a deep pink, he was holding his head high, and tossing his sheet of glossy black hair over his shoulder as he strode across the room toward them.

"What news this morn?" he asked, perhaps a little too casually, as he sank down onto the bench beside Ella. Not seeming to notice the multiple eyes goggling at him—and in particular, the way Thrak's mouth had fallen open, his hand hovering uselessly over the platter of breakfast.

"What," Thrak croaked, "in Akva's name are you *wearing*, Dammarr?!"

Dammarr's cheeks had gone even redder, but he didn't instantly reply. And this time, Kitty felt her own shoulders squaring, her eyes narrowing across the table toward Thrak's face. "Dammarr came by the shop yesterday, and was kind enough to be my first proper client," she said, speaking a little too quickly. "That colour is gorgeous on him, don't you think? It's a beautiful garment."

There was another moment's dangling silence—all the orcs were still staring, and Ella, too—and finally Thrain was the first to stir again, casting an apologetic glance toward Kitty. "Ach, Kit," he replied. "Very nice. Looks good on you, Dammarr. Ach, brother?"

He'd firmly elbowed Thrak in the side, to which Thrak twitched, and then snapped his mouth closed. "Ach," he said hoarsely. "But you don't mean—to wear it—*out*, Dammarr. Ach?"

But Dammarr's head was still held very high, his eyes not quite meeting Thrak's. "Why should I not?" he said. "It hides more skin than your own garb, if this is what you mean to say."

He'd given a dismissive wave toward Thrak's own kilted, bare-chested form, and Thrak accordingly glanced downwards, his sharp tooth biting his lip. "It is not—*that*," he said thinly. "It is…"

But his voice had trailed off, his eyes darting helplessly between Nattfarr and Varinn. But Nattfarr had begun to look decidedly amused, while Varinn just shrugged, and reached again for the platter. "It is that you do not wish others to notice how well Dammarr wears this, mayhap," he said coolly. "Or how he does *not* wear any of the jewels that would mark him as mated to a Grisk, ach?"

Thrak's eyes narrowed toward Varinn with sudden, visceral dislike, but Kitty didn't miss the brief flare of gratefulness in Dammarr's eyes, or the way his shoulders sagged beneath the lovely green silk. While Thrain again elbowed Thrak in the side, and shot him a teasing, reassuring smile.

"Or, my brother's just jealous that Dammarr got to you first, Kit," Thrain said, with a wink toward her. "Mayhap you'll dress him next, ach? Put him in one of those tall hats your human men favour. Or some pointy shoes. Or a ballgown?"

Kitty choked a laugh, and then made a show of looking Thrak up and down, tapping her finger against her chin. "He *would* look lovely in a caped greatcoat," she said thoughtfully. "Perhaps with a patterned necktie, and a pair of fawn breeches beneath? And a curled white wig, of course."

Thrain barked a bright, merry chuckle, reaching up to yank cheerfully at Thrak's spiky hair, and to Kitty's heartfelt relief, Thrak twitched a reluctant little smile back. "Och, and give every bloodthirsty human a target to aim at?" he said wryly. "Mayhap Dammarr has the right idea after all. Wearing green, to blend in."

He'd cast an apologetic look toward Dammarr, who seemed suddenly preoccupied with inspecting one of his claws. "But you have not seen the blue dress yet," he replied, a little too casually. "Or the red."

Thrak's mouth fell open again, but before he could speak any further, Varinn rose to his feet, and signalled for Thrain and Kitty to rise, too. "Come, you two," he said firmly. "Katherine, Ymir is expecting you. But Efterar first, ach?"

Kitty and Thrain both meekly obliged, saying a quick farewell to the others before following Varinn down the corridor to the sickroom. And after a brief examination from Efterar—including a thorough inspection of Thrain's new piercing—Kitty and Thrain were both cleared to go, Kitty with more firm instructions to rest if she needed it.

"And Thrain shall be scenting you for any sign of weariness, Katharine," Varinn told her, once they were all out in the corridor again. "Or illness, or hunger, or aught else. *Without* bothering her work. Ach, Thrain?"

Thrain rolled his eyes, but smiled and nodded, and Kitty nodded, too. She still felt remarkably well, with very little of the nausea she'd suffered previously, but it was still strangely comforting to know Thrain would be nearby. And Varinn gave a firm nod in return, before leaning in to press a brief, solid kiss to Thrain's mouth. And then—Kitty froze—he stepped closer, and brushed his mouth against hers, too. His lips gentle, his breath warm and sweet against her skin.

"Behave today, both of you," he said, a little husky, as he drew back again. "And I shall tend to you both when I return this eve."

Oh. Well. Kitty's lips were still tingling, her face flushing hot, but she nodded again, and found Thrain doing the same beside her. And when Varinn spun and strode off down the corridor, she couldn't seem to stop staring after him, blinking at his neat braid and kilt and broad shoulders, as a strange little ache shivered up her back. He was still only doing this for Thrain... right? For the debt? The deal? For that... other woman, after her?

She couldn't quite meet Thrain's eyes as they walked the rest of the way down the corridor, and he seemed unusually quiet, too. At least, until they stepped into the shop, and found

Ymir already waiting behind the counter, eyeing Thrain with palpable impatience in his glinting eyes.

"You've brought her late, boy," he snapped. "We've another shipment to unload. Come along, woman."

But Thrain's growl was sharp and instantaneous, his hand circling tightly against Kitty's waist. "She's not late, Ymir," he said, with surprising, chilly malice in his voice. "And you're not working her nearly as hard today, either. For I'll be nearby and scenting everything, ach?"

Ymir muttered something back that Kitty couldn't follow, and then turned and stalked off into the shop. Leaving Kitty to flash a quick, grateful smile toward Thrain, followed by a furtive kiss to his cheek. And thankfully, he was smiling back now too, and leaning in to inhale deeply at her hair.

"Too sweet, Kit," he murmured. "I'm off to meet with Rathgarr next, but just holler if you need me, ach?"

It was again surprisingly comforting, and Kitty shyly nodded as she waved goodbye, and then rushed to catch up with Ymir. Who was swiftly striding down the aisle, toward where there was something new, standing in the middle of the floor. Something that looked like... a cart?

But, yes, it was a huge, overflowing cart with large steel wheels, just sitting here at the back of the shop. And behind it, cut into the previously smooth stone well, there was a yawning black chasm that certainly hadn't been there before—had it?— and Kitty blinked at the sight of a second cart, rolling out through the opening. It was being pulled by three orcs, their bulky green bodies sweaty and straining against the steel chains strapped around their powerful arms, and Kitty belatedly recognized the nearest orc as Harthr, the trader she'd met the other day.

"This comes all the way from Osada, brother," Harthr was saying to Ymir, between heavy breaths, as he and the other two orcs drew the cart to a halt behind the first. "There are even some orc-forged jewels. Ought to fetch a good price, ach?"

Ymir was eagerly nodding, rubbing his green hands together with palpable glee, while Harthr angled a warm, curious glance toward Kitty. "Back again, sister?" he asked. "Ymir hasn't brought you to help unload, has he?"

But the glinting look in Ymir's eyes suggested that he'd expected exactly this, and to Kitty's distant relief, Harthr laughed and dragged over a large nearby table. "*We* shall unload," he said firmly, "whilst you start sorting. There's a great deal to work through, ach?"

He wasn't exaggerating, Kitty soon discovered, because both carts proved to be tightly packed full with an astonishing variety of goods. Not only shocking amounts of clothes and shoes and blankets and furs, but also dozens of sacks and crates and barrels. Grain, flour, salted pork and fish, dried fruit, syrup and honey, and even fresh vegetables.

But despite the daunting quantity of it all, sorting through it proved to be a highly engrossing project. Some of the clothing was lovely—Kitty had already set aside a dress that would likely suit Dammarr—and it was fascinating to see the sheer bizarre variety of goods that a mountain of orcs might require. And once again, Harthr was a friendly, cheerful conversationalist, and though his two colleagues—Grein and Knorr—both seemed reticent at first, they answered Kitty's curious questions willingly enough. And soon they were all chattering and joking together, and then discussing Harthr's plans for expanding their trade routes.

"Did you say you had some contacts in the north, Kitty?" Harthr asked, as he heaved another armful of clothes onto her pile. "Any other traders or sellers, mayhap, who might not ask too many questions of who they're trading with?"

Kitty could easily call several names to mind—Charles had never been scrupulous about his trading partners—and soon she and Harthr were bent over the table together, writing out a list with a paper and quill. Which led to more in-depth discussion of possible routes and opportunities, not only in the north, but closer to the mountain, as well.

"Ach, there are a few nearby human traders we've been weighing," Harthr said eagerly, as he scanned down the list. "In Dusbury, the foremost one is this *Charles Tatterham*, if you've ever heard of him?"

Charles Tatterham. Charles. *That* Charles. And for a brief, dizzying instant, Kitty could only seem to stare at Harthr, while something kicked and plummeted, deep in her belly. Of course it was only natural that Charles' name would come up, of course it meant nothing, but why did she suddenly feel so ill, so... tainted. Like even the thought of Charles, having any connection whatsoever with this mountain, this shop, this *life*—was a violation. An insult. A threat.

"Er, yes," Kitty belatedly managed, through her laboured breaths. "I do know Charles Tatterham. But I wouldn't— recommend working with him, if at all possible. He's—cheap, and careless, and unreliable. You'd surely come to regret it."

It was all true, every word of it, and thank the gods, Harthr only vaguely smiled and nodded, and made a note on his list. But Kitty still felt strangely dizzy, disoriented, and she mumbled what she hoped was an appropriate excuse, before turning and stumbling back up the aisle. Back to the safety of the counter, to where—she froze again—someone was already waiting.

And it was someone—new. Someone—wrong. He was far too tall to be a human, but his skin was pale, so light it was almost translucent. And his claws impatiently tapping the counter were long and curved and wickedly sharp, longer than any orc-claws Kitty had ever seen—and instead of hair on his head, he seemed to have... tattoos. Tattoos in a strange, repeating pattern, almost like lines of cramped text written across his bare scalp.

But most alarming of all was the way he was glowering toward her. His mouth contorting with vicious disapproval as his narrow gaze raked up and down her body, lingering on her revealing ensemble with blatant, sneering contempt.

"Er, hello," Kitty made herself say, though she couldn't help a shaky, tentative step backwards. "Can I help you find anything?"

The orc curled his lip toward her, and spoke a few words she didn't recognize, the sounds thick and strange in his harsh, deep voice. And when Kitty winced and shook her head in reply, he drew something out of the sack at his belt, and tossed it onto the counter with a *thunk*.

It was a rock, large and grey and jagged, likely as big as Kitty's head. And the orc was gesturing angrily at the rock, and then at her, clearly expecting some kind of response—so she jerked a shaky nod, and reached out a hand toward it. Perhaps he wanted her to take it, or give it to Ymir, or—

The orc's growl was sudden and terrifying, his sharp-taloned hand slicing between her and the rock with furious intent, and Kitty stumbled backwards, wiping her trembling hands on her kilt. "I—I'm very sorry," she stammered, "but I can't understand you. I'll just go fetch Ymir, and—"

But the orc growled again, loud enough to make the hairs on her neck stand on end. And Kitty's heart was thundering, her body fixed in place, as the dizziness spun harder, and the darkness seemed to crawl higher, closer, curling around her throat. Trapping her here, trapping her breath, and oh gods, she couldn't breathe, couldn't speak, and where were Ymir and Harthr and please, gods, please—

When suddenly, something new rushed into the room, and leapt over the counter. Something, someone, warm and safe and familiar, drawing her close, dragging her into his strong, steady arms.

It was Thrain.

38

Thrain was here?

"Och, Kit," Thrain said, his voice a rushed little croak, as his hands ran rapidly up and down her back. "Och, I've got you. No need to scent thus, ach? Naught's going to harm you. *Naught.*"

Oh. The relief was staggering, flashing dark and dizzy behind Kitty's eyes, and she sagged heavily into Thrain's warm, safe arms. And found, to her distant humiliation, that she was dangerously close to weeping, her eyes blinking rapidly against his solid chest.

"I—I'm sorry," she managed, hoarse, high-pitched. "It's so silly, so stupid, I didn't—I don't—I—"

"Hush," came Thrain's voice, low and soothing, and for an instant, he almost sounded like—like Varinn. "Just breathe, ach? Slow and deep. Draw in my scent."

Oh. Kitty fervently nodded, dragging in a deep, desperate breath of his rich warmth, so close—and she could feel him humming his approval, his hands again rubbing up and down her back. "Ach, just thus," he murmured. "Naught to fear. Most of all from Filak, ach? He's only short-tempered, and doesn't speak your common-tongue, for he's a northern Ka-esh, ach? Strange, surly loners, all of them, who barely come up from underground. It's honestly a wonder they've ever managed to reproduce at all."

Kitty sagged a little more, her breath exhaling in a choked little laugh, and she even managed a brief, uncertain glance back toward the orc at the counter. Who was scowling at Thrain with equally angry disapproval in his eyes, and again growling more harsh, incomprehensible words, while waving furiously at his rock with his pale clawed hand.

Thrain snapped something back toward him, and though the words sounded slightly less tangled in his throat, his tone was still surprisingly harsh, even angry. And to Kitty's surprise, something shifted in the new orc's eyes, and he muttered something that sounded almost apologetic. To which Thrain curtly nodded, and after a gentle squeeze to Kitty's arse, he turned back toward the counter—and then he visibly startled, his brows snapping high on his forehead.

"Och, Filak!" he said, with genuine-seeming delight. *"Er það smaragður?"*

To Kitty's rising astonishment, the tattooed orc—Filak— seemed to instantly relax at this, jerking a curt, satisfied little nod, and muttering an incomprehensible reply back. And in return, Thrain gave a low whistle, and then carefully reached to pick up the rock, turning it over, and showing Kitty what was beneath. A bright line of shining, glittering green.

"Look at that, Kit," he said, with palpable awe in his voice. "Pure untouched emerald. Grisk love emerald—the green, you ken—and we'll get some real stunners out of this one. And this probably means he's found more of it, too, not that he's about to tell us where, ach?"

He still seemed truly pleased by this, grinning broadly toward this Filak, and then back toward the stone, tilting it so the green glinted in the lamplight. While Kitty watched with increasing bemusement, glancing between him and this Filak, who continued to look distinctly gratified at having his rock properly appreciated.

"Er, so maybe I should go fetch Ymir, then?" Kitty ventured, to which Thrain eagerly nodded—but then he winced and glanced up again, searching her eyes with unmistakable concern.

"Or I can come with you," he said. "Or we can go back to our room together, and rest. Whatever you want."

But Kitty waved it away with as much certainty as she could muster, though her hand was still very slightly trembling. "I'm fine," she said firmly. "I just... thank you."

The last part came out quiet, her throat swallowing, as she gave Thrain a small, apologetic smile. Earning a slow, affectionate smile in return, and a gentle squeeze of her hand. "Happy to help," he said softly. "I ken Ka-esh are oft the most terrifying of us all, ach?"

Kitty couldn't help a high-pitched little laugh, and it felt far easier to move again, and head for the back of the shop. To where Ymir and Harthr seemed caught in a heated discussion over a large metal trunk, although at Kitty's mention of emeralds, they both startled and straightened at once. And then they rushed off toward the front counter, too, where they joined Thrain in excitedly exclaiming over the rock, while Filak watched with cool, haughty satisfaction.

However, it wasn't long before their discussion devolved into loud, increasingly aggressive haggling over the rock's price, and Thrain soon guided Kitty away from the turmoil, and back toward the rear of the shop. "You still all right, Kit?" he asked. "Sure you don't want to go rest for a spell?"

But Kitty again waved it away, and gave him another grateful smile. "Truly, I'm fine," she replied, as she glanced toward the towering piles of clothes and goods all around them. "Although"—she drew in a slightly unsteady breath—"there's still a lot to do today, so if you'd have any interest in staying for a while, I'm sure Ymir wouldn't mind having the extra help. If you'd be so inclined?"

Her voice had gone tentative, and damnably hopeful, too—and she was deeply relieved at the sight of Thrain's instant, decisive nod. "Ach, I'll stay," he said. "Though I ken you might be wrong about Ymir welcoming my help, ach?"

But Kitty waved that away too, beaming back toward him, and pulling him closer toward the table. And then, while Thrain listened with surprising attentiveness, she explained Ymir's sorting process, including the crucial part about first separating the items by scent.

"Och, I remember Varinn speaking of this," Thrain said, as he gingerly picked up a nearby tunic, giving it a careful sniff—but then he wrinkled his newly pierced nose, and thrust the tunic away with obvious distaste. "Blood. Ugh. Ripped, too."

"Yes, exactly," Kitty said, again beaming toward him. "So perhaps you can do the initial sorting based on scent, and I'll work on organizing what you approve? And anything you disapprove, Ymir can review later?"

This plan seemed to work well enough, and soon they'd found a swift, steady rhythm together. Leading to multiple stacks of neatly folded clothing before Kitty, while several haphazard, ever-growing stacks of rejects congregated about Thrain's feet.

"What's this?" Ymir demanded, once he'd finally reappeared, cradling Filak's rock reverently against his chest. "Thrain is not to be bothering your work, woman!"

"Oh, but I knew you needed this done today, so he's very generously offered to help," Kitty replied, flashing Ymir her brightest, most winning smile. "That's the blood-and-death pile, right, Thrain? And that's the previously-owned-by-someone-living-here one, and those all need repairs. And these"—she waved at her own neat piles—"are the good ones. For your review."

Ymir still looked deeply suspicious, eyeing Thrain with

marked dislike, but he sidled forward, and sniffed at the various stacks around Thrain. And then he sniffed at Kitty's neat stacks, too, before giving a loud, resigned-sounding harrumph. "This is... acceptable," he said stiffly. "But I shall be watching you, boy."

He accompanied this with another dark look toward Thrain, and then scurried off up the aisle again. Leaving Kitty grinning delightedly toward Thrain, who gave a longsuffering roll of his eyes, and a wry shake of his head.

"Ymir's never liked me," he said, as he sniffed at another tunic, and passed it toward her. "Doesn't think I'm good enough for his precious perfect Varinn. Old grudges between the Grisk houses, you ken?"

But that was news to Kitty, and she eyed Thrain thoughtfully as she folded the tunic, and set it on the appropriate pile. "The Grisk houses?" she echoed. "Different families, you mean? Like how yours is the Aetha?"

Thrain glanced up with surprise in his eyes, but nodded. "Ach," he said. "We don't oft speak of them, for we don't wish to divide the clan—but we all know them, ach? It's deep in every Grisk orc's scent, and it's part of how we weigh each other, most of all upon first meeting. There are six Grisk houses now, I ken, but I've heard tales of another one or two out in the realm, also. Never scented one myself, though."

Kitty considered that as she folded a kilt he'd passed over, and then a blanket. "And are Ymir and Varinn from the same house, then?" she asked. "Not the Aetha?"

"Ach," Thrain said again, as he frowned at a ripped tunic, and tossed it into the repair pile. "Their house is called Thjoth, and they're all brilliant scenters, who care for their kin above all. Baldr's also a Thjoth, and Eyarl and Timo, too. Doesn't mean they're close blood kin or anything, but if you go back far enough, they're all related at some point."

That made sense, and Kitty nodded as she folded the next

tunic. "And how about the Aetha?" she asked. "Are there many of you, as well?"

Thrain shook his head, gave a smile that didn't quite reach his eyes. "Just a few of us left," he replied. "Me, Thrak, and Nattfarr, and now Rakfi, and"—his gaze dropped toward Kitty's waist—"our son. We're good at getting ourselves killed, ach?"

Kitty's thoughts instantly flicked back to the night before, to all those hints of war, of darkness. But before she could prod further, Thrain cleared his throat, and snatched the tunic out of her hands. "Look, you oughta take a break and eat, Kit," he said firmly. "What do you say to lunch in the garden?"

It was a delightful suggestion, and soon they were walking out in the dazzling sunshine, eating fresh fruit and meat as they chatted and laughed together. And once they'd returned to the shop again, Kitty did feel decidedly refreshed, and she returned to their sorting project with renewed enthusiasm. Until she and Thrain had gone through nearly the entire pile, and Ymir abruptly reappeared, now cradling a small wooden box against his chest.

"I don't suppose, boy," he snapped at Thrain, still with obvious distaste, "you can scent jewels, also?"

Thrain frowned back toward Ymir with equal dislike, but then his gaze dropped to the box, and glinted with surprising interest as he watched Ymir snap it open. "Mayhap," he said offhandedly. "What've you got?"

It turned out that Ymir's box was stuffed full to overflowing with glittering gold items—surely the jewels Harthr had just shipped in—and Kitty didn't miss how Thrain's eyes lit up at the sight, his breath exhaling in a low, appreciative whistle. "Och, look at that," he murmured. "Orc-forged? From Osada?"

Ymir's answering grunt sounded both pleased and annoyed, and he jerked an irritable nod. "All needs to be scented and sorted, just the same as the garb," he said flatly. "And I'll scent if you seek to pocket even a *mite* of it."

Thrain's eyes instantly darkened, and he barked a low,

menacing growl back toward Ymir. "I am *not* a thief," he hissed. "No good Grisk *steals* his gold. Gold is to be earned, and *given*."

There was a twitch of surprise across Ymir's face, his gaze darting down toward Thrain's *thyrja*, and then up to his earring, and the new piercing in his nose—but then he nodded again, and trotted away. Leaving Thrain to glare after him, before shaking his head, and dropping his decidedly eager eyes back toward the chest.

"Look at this *hálsmen*, Kit," he said, his voice hushed, as he drew out a long, beautiful gold chain. "Every link is hand-forged, and exactly the same. Stunning, ach?"

Kitty fervently agreed, and watched with rising curiosity as Thrain brought the chain to his nose, and inhaled slow and deep against it. His eyes fluttering, his chest filling, as a low, contented-sounding growl rumbled from his throat—and then he drew the chain out long, and sniffed down the next section, and the next. Apparently scenting every single separate link, before passing it over to Kitty with a rueful little smile.

"It's harder to follow scents on jewels and metals than on clothing," he explained. "But the jewels also smell so much better, ach?"

Kitty could certainly see that, and her curious amusement kept rising as she watched him work his way through the box, evaluating each item with surprising care. Smelling and sorting rings, earrings, chains, *thyrjas*, and even a few more *rassjas* of various shapes and sizes, while his eyes went increasingly hungry and glazed, his tongue sweeping again and again against his parted lips.

"Och, this *hálsmen* is broken," he told Kitty, with a genuinely sad-seeming sigh, as he held out another beautifully forged chain, with a twisted, jutting clasp. "Though I ken mayhap I could fix it in the Grisk forge, if Ymir would allow this."

Wait. Kitty's interest had sparked even higher, her eyes

studying Thrain's dazed, wistful face. "Really?" she asked. "You know how to… forge things?"

Thrain gave a dismissive shrug, a too-casual wave of his hand. "Not very well," he replied. "Never ended up finishing a proper apprenticeship, after—och. But my great-uncle, before he died, he was a great Grisk goldsmith, one of the best. Oft had me in his shop working for him, doing jobs here and there. Said it kept me busy, and out of trouble. He was a clever orc, ach?"

He flashed Kitty another one of his wry grins, but Kitty was blinking back at him, her thoughts whirling up all at once. "But that's—*brilliant*, Thrain!" she exclaimed. "Ymir said he needs a Grisk to do jewelry repairs, because"—her head tilted, rapidly casting backwards for the memory—"because the Ka-esh are the best now, but they're too busy to keep up with demand, or something to that effect. Although"—she bit at her lip—"you just said there's a Grisk forge, right? And I'm sure I've met several Grisk smiths already, so perhaps it isn't…"

Her voice trailed off, but Thrain was holding her gaze, and his expression had gone thoughtful, too. "Ach, we have good smiths," he replied slowly, "and they'll do their best with jewels, when they're asked. But it's tricky work, and none of them were trained up to it, so they'd usually rather keep at their tools and weapons. We don't have any proper Aetha goldsmiths anymore, ach?"

He twitched another sad little smile, and gods, that might have been *longing* in his eyes—so Kitty pulled herself up straighter, and thrust the broken chain back toward him. "You *will* fix it, Thrain," she said firmly. "And if Ymir won't allow it, I'll have Varinn come and talk some sense into him. He'll get through to him, you'll see."

Thrain's eyes blinked, once—and then they flickered with warmth, and with something almost like appreciation. "Och, I ken he will," he said, husky, as he carefully took the chain back. "I'll try, then, if Ymir allows it."

Well. Kitty beamed toward him, and then peered back into the wooden chest. To where there only seemed to be one item left—a strange, intricate gold contraption that looked almost like a coiled spring. It was attached to a large, sturdy-looking ring at one end, not unlike the one Varinn had worn during their pleasures the night before—but at the coil's other end was a small gold ball. And attached to the ball was a slim rod that extended all the way back down inside the coil, perhaps the width of Kitty's smallest finger.

"What's this one?" she asked, glancing toward Thrain—and finding his eyes even more glazed than before, his cheeks visibly flushed. And his throat audibly swallowed, once, again, as he picked up the item, and held it out before her.

"It's... a *typpavír*," he said, his voice a low rasp. "To adorn and flaunt your prick. Or to keep it safe, or stoppered, or untouched. Whatever you—or your mate—might wish."

Wait, really? Kitty stared at it, her mouth fallen open—but when she darted a shocked glance up at Thrain's face, he swallowed again, and then lowered the item to hover over the front of his kilt. Demonstrating, good gods, where the thick gold ring would sit—encircling the full base of him, just as Varinn's ring had the night before—and how the flexible gold coil would then curl its way up around the length of his shaft. All the way up to that large gold bead at the end, with the slim rod pointing back down the middle...

"That doesn't go," Kitty managed, rather shrill, "*inside* you?"

But Thrain's shrug was far too nonchalant, his cheeks now a bright red. "Ach," he said thickly. "But it's naught, really. Most of us Grisk have pricks that open up easy, ach? It's why we all long for your sweet little tongues."

Well. Kitty's own cursed tongue was currently brushing her lips, her wide eyes still staring at the—the *typpavír*. At how Thrain's hands were still holding it there, and very slightly shaking, as his glazed eyes stared down toward it, too. As if he... he...

"You... want it?" Kitty whispered, through her strangely constricted throat. "You want to wear it?"

Thrain's swallow was again unusually loud, and he rapidly shoved the *typpavír* away, back into the otherwise empty chest. "It's a rare piece, and the cost is far too steep, I'm sure," he said, with a too-dismissive wave of his hand. "And as I said before, Grisk gold is meant to be earned. Given."

Oh. Kitty still couldn't seem to speak, her mouth uselessly opening and closing, and she finally reached her own shaky hands for the chest, and snapped the lid closed. "I'll just—go let Ymir know we're—finished," she stammered. "If you'll just—wait here, for a moment, while I speak to him."

Thankfully, Thrain still seemed far too dazed to argue, gazing at the chest in Kitty's hands with abject yearning in his eyes. And it took a considerable effort for Kitty to turn away, and then to seek out Ymir, who was again working in his ledger at the front of the shop.

"We're finished," she told him, her voice hoarse. "Except for one broken *hálsmen*, which Thrain is going to fix in the forge, with your permission. Also"—she drew down a shaky breath, and thrust the chest toward him—"Varinn wants to buy this *typpavír*. As soon as he returns today."

She had to bite back her wince as she spoke, but she didn't correct herself, either. Just stood there, her face burning hot, as Ymir frowned toward her, and then down at the box. "He does, does he?" he asked, with entirely unveiled suspicion. "This'll fetch a high price, woman. Mayhap more than even he can afford."

"Then put my salary toward it, until it's paid off," Kitty said, steadier now. "Please, Ymir. This is—important to me. And to Varinn."

One of Ymir's bushy grey brows arched up, but then he shrugged, took the chest, and tucked it beneath the counter. "I'll speak to him when he returns," he said blandly. "Also, if that boy damages *one link* of my *hálsmen*"—he jerked his head back toward Thrain—"you shall be buying that also, ach?"

His eyes had sharply narrowed, but Kitty was already grinning delightedly back toward him, and even giving him a quick little curtsey. "Thank you, Ymir," she said fervently. "Thank you so, so much. And is there anything else you need done today?"

Ymir was looking distinctly mollified again, and he waved it away, glancing down toward Kitty's waist. "No, you have done good work today," he said. "And I scent Varinn returning now. He shall wish you finished to meet him, I ken."

Oh. Of course. Something warm was fizzling in Kitty's chest, and she grinned gratefully toward Ymir again, and stammered her thanks. And then nearly skipped back toward Thrain, who was still staring dazedly off into the distance, his chest heaving with his breaths.

"We're all finished for the day," Kitty told him, clasping his slack hand in hers. "And Varinn is on his way back, so perhaps we ought to go—er—prepare?"

Her cheeks were again heating, the anticipation thrumming up her spine, and Thrain's hand twitched as his eyes dropped to hers. "Ach, I can scent him," he murmured, sweeping his tongue against his lips. "We'd best go ready ourselves for him, as he asked."

Kitty eagerly agreed, tugging Thrain toward the door—but instead of turning down the corridor toward their room, Thrain nudged Kitty the opposite way, in the direction of the kitchen. "He'll want to find us fed, you most of all," he said. "And we'll fetch him supper, also."

Right. Kitty didn't argue, though she was admittedly distracted as they waited in line for the kitchen's meal offerings—some kind of savoury meatballs, with crispy sweetened carrots and greens—and then companionably chatted with Ella and Nattfarr as they ate together in their usual sitting-room. And finally, Thrain led her back to their familiar bedroom, where he'd already set an overfilled plate of food—and a bulging waterskin—on Varinn's empty chair.

"Och, so what do we wish to wear?" he asked now, his voice almost shy. "Mayhap we could choose for each other?"

Kitty instantly grinned and nodded, making at once for Thrain's overstuffed shelf, where she rapidly began sorting through options. While Thrain, too, carefully sifted through her own clothing, comparing multiple items, until he finally strode back toward her, with several pieces in hand.

"Varinn will like this," he told her, holding out the shortest, flounciest kilt she owned. "And this, for the top."

This was a sheer little slip of white fabric, one Kitty had nearly forgotten about—but once Thrain had helped her tie it on, and set her *thyrja* over it, she couldn't seem to stop blinking down toward it. It almost seemed more scandalous than wearing nothing at all, her nipples peeking out against the sheer fabric, while the gold *thyrja* sparkled and shimmered against it.

The kilt was just as revealing—it turned out to have a slit up the front that Kitty hadn't noticed before, allowing for extra-easy access—and she felt her face burning even hotter as Thrain slowly circled around her, trailing his claws lightly against her waist. "Very pretty, Kit," he murmured, once he'd halted before her again. "Only wish we had more jewels, for—och. What'd you pick for me?"

His curious eyes darted toward his shelf, and Kitty willingly went to collect her choice. It was, of course, the backless loincloth Varinn had so obviously admired that day they'd gone shopping, and Thrain chuckled at the sight of it, and promptly dropped his current kilt to the floor. Revealing his hard, bobbing length, already dripping from the tip, but Kitty did her best to ignore it as she drew the loincloth around his lean hips, and fastened it in place. And now it was her turn to walk a circle around him, eyeing his piercings, his *thyrja*, his firm, blatantly exposed bare arse.

"And what about your *rassja*?" she asked, through her too-dry mouth. "He wanted you wearing it, right?"

Thrain jerked a nod, his own cheeks flushing bright red as he strode toward Varinn's jewel-box. Drawing out a long, cloth-wrapped item, and then bringing it back to Kitty, unwrapping it with slightly trembling hands. Revealing the polished gold beneath, so clean and shiny that Kitty could see her reflection in each of the rounded beads.

"What now?" she asked, breathless, and Thrain huffed a choked-sounding exhale as he dropped his hand downwards, pulling aside the front of his loincloth. Again revealing his swollen, bobbing length, already dripping white from the slit.

"Need to slick it up," he said, hoarse, taking himself firmly in hand. "Too hard to take otherwise, ach?"

Right. Kitty truly could not move, not even to nod, as she watched Thrain drop the *rassja* down to his already-leaking tip. Hovering it there, oh gods, guiding it back and forth, pumping out his oozing, shining fluid onto it. Coating it all over, while Kitty's breaths quickened, her hands tingling, her eyes fluttering as Thrain ran his hand up and down and around the gold length, easy and familiar, slathering it with his seed, his hunger.

"Don't s'pose," he murmured, very briefly meeting her eyes, "you could help me put it in?"

Kitty startled, her breath spasming in her throat, and Thrain winced, his face even redder. "Just—not sure I can do it, without help," he said. "But Varinn—said he didn't mind, ach?"

Right. Because Varinn *had* told her to help Thrain prepare if he needed it. Right? And Kitty was already nodding, desperate and urgent, snatching the *rassja* from Thrain's hands, while the relief—and the hunger—flashed across his dazed eyes. And then, with stilted movements, he turned away, toward Varinn's chair, and gripped both hands to its solid wooden arms. Bracing himself there, oh gods, so he could bend over, and bare his firm backside toward her.

Kitty gasped, far too loud and shameful, but she was in this now, committed to this now. Though it still felt like someone else, looked like someone else's hands, guiding that slippery gold pole downwards, and nudging its first, smallest bead between those firm, twitching arse-cheeks.

Thrain's gasp was choked, his body jolting at the touch, but then he shifted, lining it up. So Kitty could feel more give beneath the *rassja* now, could feel the way his body was pulsing against it. Resisting, and then relaxing, resisting, relaxing. As his breath shuddered out slow, his back arching, his hands flexing against the chair.

"Push harder," he breathed, harsh. "Won't hurt me, ach?"

Oh. Kitty twitched a nod he couldn't see, and attempted to comply. Pressing, circling, harder and harder, until she felt something give—and oh, hell, now the first bead was inside, and she could see Thrain's taut skin, stretched out thin and strained around it, as he gasped and shuddered and keened.

"Ach, thus," he breathed, burying his face in his shoulder. "Again."

Kitty's body was shivering and tingling all over, now, her eyes wide and unblinking on the sight. On her own hands doing it again, circling, pressing, opening him, stretching him—until the next bead slipped inside, too.

But that left three more, and Kitty had to gulp down deep, dragging breaths as she kept pressing, her hands tingling and trembling against the smooth gold handle. And wait, Thrain's head snapped sideways, a desperate groan hissing from his throat as another bead slipped inside.

"Och, he's coming, Kit," he hissed. "We ought—"

But then, oh gods curse them, here was Varinn. Striding into the room with quick, purposeful steps—and then halting, his head tilting, at the sight of them. At Thrain bent double over his chair, his arse brazenly bared, with a pole of gleaming gold still jutting halfway up out of it.

The shame and the alarm felt almost like a slap, striking

Kitty where she could, and there was no possible way to speak, or even attempt to explain. Only staring at Varinn, and then slightly cringing, because what would he say, oh gods, oh gods—

But then—Varinn's mouth... twitched. And he strode over toward them, his big hand first patting against Kitty's back, before giving a light slap to Thrain's exposed, quivering arse.

"Having trouble, you two?" he said, his voice damnably light. "My gold too much for you, *krútt*?"

And at that, Thrain—laughed. The sound shaky, relieved, trembling through his bent-double body. "Ach, you tyrant," he replied, breathless. "Help a poor fellow out, will you?"

But that was another twitch, wry and amused on Varinn's mouth, and he grasped at the *rassja*'s upraised handle, giving it a gentle little shake. To which Thrain arched and moaned, and very nearly lost his footing, while Varinn's smile pulled higher, into something almost wicked.

"Mayhap later," he said coolly. "You make quite the sight, *krútt*. Now, is that my supper?"

He'd nodded toward the plate, still lying on the chair before Thrain, and Thrain choked another laugh as he jerked up to standing, and waved Varinn toward it. But for an instant, Varinn just looked at him, at his bared, sweaty body, clad in the scandalous loincloth, with that gleaming gold length still jutting out from behind.

"All yours, Lord Grisk," Thrain murmured, husky, and oh, he knew exactly how Varinn was taking that, how to draw that low, heated purr from his throat. And Varinn had even stepped closer, bending his face into Thrain's neck, inhaling slow and deep.

"Ach, *krútt*," he murmured, so quiet Kitty almost couldn't hear it. "It pleases me, to find you ready for me thus."

Kitty could see the distinct sag in Thrain's shoulders, the soft, happy smile toward Varinn's face—but then he glanced toward Kitty, his smile pulling even higher. "And Kit too, ach?"

he murmured, into Varinn's shoulder. "Poor thing worked even harder than I did, I ken."

But at that, Varinn's eyes flicked back toward her, and there was something... different in them. Something amused, and thoughtful, and almost speculative. Or again, maybe even... wicked.

"Ach, I ken," he replied, his voice deceptively light. "But along with this, Katharine spent near all my gold today. *Without* so much as asking me."

Kitty blanched, staring at Varinn with genuine alarm—while Thrain whipped to look at her, his brows instantly furrowing. "Och, no, she didn't," he snapped. "Did you, Kit?"

But Kitty was biting painfully at her lip, still staring at Varinn with wide, chagrined eyes. Surely displaying every bit of her damned wretched guilt, for both of them to see. And Thrain was frowning between them now, while Varinn's eyes shifted again, into something dark and dangerous...

"And thus, *kisa*," he purred, "I shall have naught more to do with you, until you are punished."

39

Until she was... punished.

Kitty's entire body shocked to stillness, her eyes again wide and searching on Varinn's face. He would have naught more to do with her, until... until...

And then he turned away, and plucked up the plate of food before sinking down into his chair. Tossing one of the meatballs into his mouth, while still watching Kitty with those cool, strangely speculative eyes.

"Well?" he asked once he'd swallowed, sliding his gaze toward Thrain, his brows lifted. "You allowed this today, *krútt*, so this is upon you to address."

Thrain was still looking just as stunned as Kitty felt, his eyes blinking—but then it occurred to her that his cheeks were still bright red, and his lips were parted, his tongue brushing against them. And when he finally glanced toward her, his gaze was heavy, hungry, half-lidded, shifting with something she couldn't at all read.

"You really sneak away from me today, and do that, Kit?" he said, his voice very low. "Spend all Varinn's coin, without asking?"

Kitty blanched again, but her own face was heating too, her throat swallowing hard. "Um," she managed. "Yes?"

Thrain's eyes shifted again, and he came a smooth, prowling step closer. "That's not how Lord Grisk's sweet kitten is supposed to behave," he murmured, and though the words were an admonishment, his tone was something else entirely. "Do you need to be taught a lesson, Kit?"

Oh, hell. The comprehension flashed so hard it was almost dizzying, swirling around Kitty in a wild wheeling stream, and she swallowed again, licked her dry lips. "I'm—sure I don't know what you—mean," she stammered. "I mean—the coin wasn't doing him any good—just sitting there, right?"

But Thrain was slowly shaking his head, making a low sound of disapproval in his throat, while the eagerness—yes, eagerness—flared hungry and bright in his eyes. "Och, wrong, pretty kitten," he replied, so soft. "Lord Grisk's coin is his alone. If we want it, we please him, or we beg. Naught else."

Kitty choked, the heat shuddering her all over, pooling hard and powerful in her groin. And Thrain was inhaling, his eyes fluttering, as he came another prowling step closer, close enough to grasp her chin in his light, gentle fingers. "And what did I tell you just today, sweet kitten?" he purred, even softer. "Grisk gold is earned, or given. Have you already forgotten this?"

Kitty shuddered again, her wide eyes darting toward Varinn in his chair, who was just... eating. Eating his supper, and watching this, his eyes patient and calm. As if he was approving of this, wanting this from her, from Thrain. And another rippling shudder wrenched up her spine, clamping, clawing...

"I didn't—forget," she said, her eyes back on Thrain's face. "I just—wanted it."

And oh, the hunger, the delight, crackling in Thrain's eyes. "Wicked little kitten," he murmured softly. "This is not how you honour your lord, who has shown you such kindness.

Now"—his voice dropped even lower—"it's your turn to bend over for me, ach?"

Oh good gods, Kitty's mouth had again fallen open, her eyes darting once more to Varinn. Who was still just watching this, waiting, and tossing another meatball into his mouth. And then making a little circular motion with his claw toward her, saying, *Get on with it.*

So somehow, somehow, Kitty... nodded. Nodded, at him, at Thrain—but when her helpless eyes held on Thrain's, perhaps silently begging him for what to do next, he again smiled so sweetly toward her, and grasped both her hands in his. And then bent her forward, so she was facing the bed, with her arse in its too-short kilt aimed toward Varinn in his chair.

"Need to show Lord Grisk," Thrain murmured, as his warm hand slipped to her thigh, and began sliding her short skirt up. "Need to prove you can learn your lesson for him, ach?"

The shivers were wracking Kitty all over, now, racing fierce and furious up her spine, and Thrain's hand briefly hesitated, tightening a little against her upper thigh. "All right, though?" he breathed, even quieter. "All good?"

But Kitty was rapidly, desperately nodding—gods, he couldn't stop, they couldn't, not now—and she could hear Thrain's slow exhale, shaky and relieved. "Good, Kit," he murmured, as he gave a gentle squeeze to her arse. "Now, deep breaths, ach?"

Kitty nodded again, dragged in deep—and without warning, Thrain's big hand drew back, and landed with a light, firm little slap. Not nearly enough to hurt, but still enough to shake Kitty all over, and drive a hoarse, high-pitched moan from her throat. While Thrain's big hand caressed her, smoothing against the too-hot skin—and then drew back, and landed in another firm slap, a little harder this time.

The sound from Kitty's mouth was more like a cry, her body again writhing all over—and then again, and again. The sensation whirling up so strong, so impossibly overpowering, consuming all other thought, all fear and worry and unease. Leaving only this, only being corrected, attended to, cared for, by the two orcs she craved so much, the orcs she needed so much. Both of them looking at her, here with her, the steady strikes of Thrain's hand so warm and solid and safe, while Varinn's watching eyes—his perusal, his *approval*—felt almost as palpable, almost as real, as a touch.

But then, Varinn purposefully cleared his throat. And when Kitty glanced backwards, he was reaching into the side of his kilt, and drawing out something small, and slim, and... gleaming. "I ken she yet needs a little more, *krútt*," he said, his voice a husky purr. "Mayhap this shall help?"

Thrain's groan was low and hoarse, and he fervently nodded as he lurched toward Varinn, snatching up the item with shaky fingers. And when he strode back toward her, his steps still a little shaky, Kitty realized it was... another *rassja*. One of the ones from the new shipment that day, in fact. And though it was far smaller than Thrain's, it had the same shape, the same row of progressively larger beads, even the same little gold handle at the end. And Varinn had—bought it? For—for *her*?!

Kitty's breath choked, her mouth fallen open, her eyes darting back to Varinn's face, searching him with stunned disbelief—but he was settling back in his chair again, that amused smile again curving at his mouth. "But be gentle with my mate, *krútt*," he said smoothly. "Be sure to slick it well for her, ach?"

Oh, hell. Kitty and Thrain both groaned at once, and yes, yes, Thrain was flipping aside the front of his loincloth, so he could begin... coating the *rassja* for her. Just the same way he had with his own, pumping out his slick, shining fluid onto it, all over it, until it was glossy and dripping, the white seed dangling toward the floor.

"Now, open up, Kit," he murmured, his breath hitching, as he jerked back toward her, his hand settling against her tender, inflamed arse. "Show Lord Grisk how well his disobedient little kitten can behave, ach? How you can welcome his great gift inside you?"

Kitty wildly nodded, arching herself out toward him, even as her face burned with more fierce flaming heat. Because oh, gods, what must this look like, all her most secret places opened wide, shamelessly bared, and Thrain was even giving a choked, husky chuckle as his gentle fingers spread her a little wider, and nudged the slick *rassja* against—there.

Kitty yelped and gasped, felt herself clench and arch against it—but Thrain just held it there, waiting for her to soften again. Wanting her to open up for Varinn's gift, for his eyes, and Kitty gulped down a deep, dragging breath as she arched back a little further, and... obliged. Willed herself to relax, to open, to even press back a little against the gold's smooth, solid touch.

"Och, that's it," Thrain's strangled voice said, as she pressed a little further, felt the first bead slip inside. "Good little kitten. You want Lord Grisk's gold inside you, deep up your pretty little rump? Want to show him what a well-behaved little worshipper you can be?"

Kitty fervently nodded, opened up more, felt the next bead slip inside—and Thrain laughed again, thick and approving. "Good," he breathed, and oh, that was again a slap of his other hand, light but purposeful against her inflamed arse-cheek, as the gold kept pressing, sinking deeper. "And while you're at it, don't you think you oughta thank him? For his kindness toward you, in the face of your disobedience?"

Oh, gods. Kitty choked and nodded, twisting around to again meet Varinn's eyes. To where he was still watching all this, sprawled so casually in his chair, his eyes glittering as they flicked between Kitty's face, and the gold still slipping so brazenly into her arse beneath Thrain's pressing fingers.

"Th-thank you, Lord Grisk," Kitty somehow croaked, and she even arched back more, opened a little wider for the still-plunging gold, so he could see it, so he could know she meant it. "Thank you for—granting me—such a gift. In the face of my great—disobedience."

And oh, that look on Varinn's face, the hunger, the satisfaction, as she felt the *rassja* finally slip all the way inside, its handle nudged close and tight into her crease. As Thrain murmured his approval, and his hand began caressing her bare arse, slow and smooth. As if showing it off for Varinn, flaunting her for Varinn—and then another light, gentle slap. The sensation even stronger now, vibrating through that gold deep inside her, and Kitty cried out, shivered all over, fought to keep breathing, keep showing him, please...

"That better, Lord Grisk?" Thrain rasped, as his hand struck her hot skin again, again, again, shattering impossible sensation all through her with every touch. "Your kitten on her knees behaving for you, bravely learning her lesson? Sucking your gold up her tight little rump? Showing you what's yours?"

Kitty was shuddering all over now, her eyes fluttering too hard to see Varinn's face, but she kept fighting to accept it, breathe, to show him. To earn his approval, his forgiveness, his favour. As her steady cries kept sharpening, lurching higher with every strike of Thrain's hand, until her last cry came out sounding more like—like a sob.

And suddenly that was a low growl from behind her, an abrupt stillness in Thrain's touch against her skin. "Ach, enough," said Varinn's voice, heated and low. "Bring her here."

Kitty's body seemed too shaky to move, but Thrain's firm warm hands somehow managed it for her, lifting her up, rubbing up and down her sides. And then guiding her stumbling, unseeing body over toward the chair. Toward Varinn's warm, waiting arms, drawing her close into his broad, heaving chest. As if he wanted to hold her, comfort her, caress her on his lap, but suddenly Kitty needed so much more than that, needed everything, everything, and she was shifting and clawing at him, finding that heft beneath his kilt, sliding it up beneath her own—

She nearly sobbed again as she felt him sink smoothly inside, filling her without hesitation or complaint, while that low, husky purr rumbled from his throat. And oh, he felt even stronger, more overpowering than before, with his huge heft plunged in front, his gold still buried deep behind. But he was here, he was touching her, inside her, and his warm hands were stroking firm up and down her back, smoothing over her slightly stinging arse, as if to ease the pain away.

"Good, *kisa*," he murmured. "So good. So brave and hungry and sweet."

Kitty shuddered hard against him, around him, still clinging to him as tightly as she could. Only distantly hearing Varinn say something to Thrain, his hand lifting from her back—but then, oh, there was Thrain's warm, strong body behind her, settling close in the chair. Perching on Varinn's lap, too, the three of them tucked together, and Kitty moaned and tilted her head at the feel of a warm, gentle mouth, kissing at her neck.

"You all right, Kit?" Thrain murmured, a little choked. "Hope I didn't take that too far, ach? Never—*never*—wish to vex you, or harm you. *Never*."

But Kitty was shaking her head, and somehow finding his trembling hand, and clutching it tightly in hers. "I—liked it," she managed. "Loved it. Too—too much. And the gold, too, it's so—so—"

She couldn't finish, but Thrain's laugh behind her was shaky, relieved, his hot mouth kissing down the line of her shoulder. "Och, I ken," he murmured, between kisses. "It's all Varinn's fault, ach?"

Kitty somehow laughed too, strangled and high-pitched, and despite Varinn's low answering growl, he again ran his hands up and down Kitty's back, even firmer than before. "Turn around, *kisa*," he said, soft. "So you can touch him."

Wait. Wait, he wanted her to—touch Thrain? But she was already nodding, and attempting to oblige. Awkwardly lifting up in the chair, shifting around, twitching at the press of the *rassja*'s gold handle against Varinn's belly. But oh, it still felt so good, especially with how Thrain was already grasping Varinn's slick leaking length, and guiding it back up inside her. Locking them together again, except that now her back was to Varinn's chest, and she was blinking at Thrain's flushed, wryly smiling face.

"So sweet, Kit," he murmured, as he shifted a little closer, his long legs now straddling both hers and Varinn's on the chair, his hand hungrily caressing at where Varinn was still buried deep inside her. "Scents so good, when he's inside you."

Kitty moaned and helplessly nodded, her tingling hands settling against his sweaty chest, feeling the stunning strength of him, of them. Of how they were circling her, surrounding her, Thrain so close and alive before her, while Varinn's strength was all behind her, inside her. And one of his big warm hands was skating protectively over her nipple, her *thyrja*, her belly, while the other hand—Kitty's breath caught— had reached around behind Thrain, clearly grasping at his own *rassja*. Finally plunging it the rest of the way in, perhaps, based on how Thrain's eyes instantly rolled back, his hips bucking firm and reflexive against Kitty's belly. While his gold-tipped length hungrily prodded out from behind its loincloth, streaking white across her skin.

But it was even better, oh gods, better than anything Kitty had ever seen or felt in her life. And when her shaky hand found Thrain's pulsing, leaking heft, that sparked up even more pleasure, set Thrain writhing and arching upon them, while Kitty clamped hard at Varinn, felt him shudder fuller inside. Both of them bound together and watching Thrain, pleasuring him at once, while he thrashed and gasped upon them, shameless, utterly on display for them, just the way she'd been, oh hell. And the distant awareness of that seemed to wrench the craving even higher, hotter, Varinn wanted this from her, from them, and he was pulsing even fuller inside her, while Thrain did the same against her fingers, and—

"Up, *krútt*," Varinn rasped, sudden and hoarse. "In her mouth."

Thrain's eyes snapped wide, his moan cut short—but then he jerked up, back, one foot still on the chair, the other hopping to the floor. So his leaking, gold-tipped length was in perfect line with Kitty's mouth, and they both moaned aloud as he plunged it deep inside. Flooding her senses with more rich, heady sweetness, with his wild bucking hips, the growl that was almost a roar, as Varinn jerked to stillness behind her—

And suddenly Thrain was pouring out, they were both pouring out, both of them streaming into her at once. Filling both her mouth and her womb with their hot, rich sweetness, Thrain's hands skittering on her face, Varinn's shaky fingers stroking at her groin, his head ducking into her neck. And at the barest touch of his teeth against her skin, Kitty's own pleasure flashed and flared, surging through the whole of her body with blast after blast of pure, unthinkable bliss.

She had no memory of actually swallowing, but she must have done so, because Thrain finally drew back with a shaky-sounding hiss, and then sank heavily to his knees before them. His eyes bright and shining, darting between Kitty and Varinn with rapid, worshipful awe—and without warning, he lurched his face forward, toward... there. Into where Kitty and Varinn were still locked together, though Varinn's thick fluid was already seeping out between them—and Kitty shivered again at the slick, shocking touch of Thrain's tongue. Licking eagerly against them both, oh gods, not wasting a drop, and Kitty's darting glance back at Varinn found his eyes gone mild, indulgent, his hand slipping down to sink into Thrain's messy hair.

It meant he liked it, he wanted it, again—and it was enough to allow Kitty to relax again, sagging back into his solid bulk behind her, despite the stunning, sparkling sensation of Thrain's tongue between their legs. Not only licking what was there, but—Kitty gasped—even slipping up inside her. Squeezing its way in beside Varinn's softening strength, so he could seek out more, more, as his throat audibly, rapidly swallowed, oh hell.

But Varinn still didn't seem to mind, just watching Thrain with that same mild, tolerant approval in his eyes. Looking, just for a moment, like a god's favoured heir, sprawled on his throne with the day's favoured woman still impaled and debauched upon him, and his favourite supplicant kneeling at his feet. Worshipping his lord with all his strength, kissing his most intimate places, freely seeking the dregs of his lord's bounty, even after that bounty had been granted to another.

But then the vision shifted, snapped back to reality again, because Varinn was—purring. Purring, his chest vibrating against Kitty's back, as one of his hands stroked her rounded belly, and the other kept caressing through Thrain's hair. Speaking so clearly of his deep, generous affection toward Thrain, and toward their son. And maybe—maybe he even felt something toward Kitty, after all, what with how he'd held her, and touched her, and given her that *rassja*, and even—punished her. With how he was allowing his favourite orc to kiss her, taste her, drink out from inside her, shivering her ever deeper into his own solid embrace.

And then—Kitty shuddered again—with how he was tugging Thrain back upwards again. Back onto his lap, too, and while that meant the loss of his glorious licking tongue, it also meant that Kitty was once again cradled close between them, her breasts pressed tightly against Thrain's warm, sticky torso. Feeling his breaths shudder all through her, as he sagged forward, burying his face into Varinn's shoulder.

But Varinn's chest was still rumbling with that soft, steady growl, his big hands now stroking up and down Thrain's back, and Kitty could feel Thrain relaxing beneath it, too. His body sagging closer, his limbs heavier, his breaths coming slower, easier, steadier again.

"So was this better, today?" Varinn's low voice finally asked. "For both of you?"

Kitty blinked at that, but then twitched an uncertain little nod. And against her, Thrain was doing the same, his breath exhaling slow through his chest. "Ach, it was better," he replied, his voice still muffled against Varinn's skin. "A lot—easier, without adding everyone else's mess into my own. Thanks, Varinn."

Varinn didn't reply, but his hands kept stroking, and Kitty could feel Thrain relaxing even more, and even choking a short little laugh. "Also, it was good I was here," he continued, "for that damned northern Ka-esh Filak showed up in the shop, and started railing on at Kit in Aelakesh when she didn't understand him! Sparked up her fear something fierce. Those louts oughta be dragged to their own clan's common-tongue classes, ach? So much for being the clever ones around here."

Varinn had noticeably stiffened at this revelation, his hands stilling on Thrain's back. "I hope you addressed this, and made sure it will *not* happen again?" he demanded, his voice sharp. "And where was Ymir, amidst all this?"

Thrain shrugged, but now he was the one rubbing at Varinn, sliding his hand up and down his arm. "Ach, I sorted it out, Varinn," he said. "And Ymir was off haggling over goods, or some such. But he's also not gonna see a Ka-esh as any kind of threat to Kit whatsoever, you ken?"

Varinn's body still hadn't relaxed, and he huffed a displeased-sounding grunt. "Henceforth, you shall keep a close watch upon this," he said flatly. "And stay near to Katharine at all times, ach?"

"Ach, ach," Thrain said, with palpable amusement in his voice, but he was still stroking at Varinn, too. "Naught to fear, Varinn. Kit even went and sweet-talked me into helping her in the shop, and"—he huffed another wry laugh—"even doing some jewel repairs in the forge. If our smiths will bear me fumbling about amongst them."

Varinn's body shifted again, perhaps into something more like surprise. "Ach, *krútt*?" he said, his voice far softer than before. "Ach, I am glad of this. Mayhap I shall speak to Fjorvi upon this, also."

Kitty vaguely recalled that Fjorvi was one of the Grisk smiths she'd previously met, and though Thrain gave another disbelieving little laugh, he didn't actually argue this plan, either. And instead, he'd seemed to relax even more against them, nibbling at Varinn's neck.

"And how did *you* fare today, then, Varinn?" he asked, his voice light again. "You miss me?"

The tension had again oddly flared through Varinn's body, but he shrugged. "Ach, it was quiet," he said, a little too offhandedly. "But there was naught I needed you for."

Thrain's laugh was bright with disbelief, and when Kitty twisted to look at him, he was again nipping at Varinn's neck, hard enough to leave marks on his skin. "Tyrant!" he exclaimed. "I hope you're swarmed with a horde of bored, shouting Bautul orclings tomorrow. You'll miss me then, you ken?"

Varinn groaned, but he chuckled, too, and then reached for the nearby shelf, groping for a rag. And then began wiping down between them, doing it himself, and Kitty couldn't help glancing uncertainly toward his face, searching his eyes. How they were still a little distant, his body still slightly tensed against her. Almost... almost as if he *had* missed Thrain, but didn't want to admit it.

But perhaps Thrain hadn't noticed, again nibbling happily at Varinn's neck, and Varinn briefly met Kitty's gaze, before clearing his throat. "And how did you fare today, Katharine?" he said, a little too stiffly. "Mayhap you now wish for a rest? Most of all after..."

He'd glanced guiltily down toward her arse, but a shiver of

warmth ran up Kitty's spine, and she flashed him a grateful little smile. "I'm fine, I swear," she said. "And in truth, I don't feel tired at all. That was very... invigorating."

She didn't miss the palpable relief in Varinn's eyes, or the way his body finally relaxed beneath her. While Thrain eagerly pulled back from his neck, and grinned down between them. "Och, we scented you, Kit," he said cheerfully. "There's naught like a little stern correction from your lord now and then, ach? Most of all when it comes with gifts attached."

Kitty couldn't help another hungry little shiver, to which both Varinn and Thrain laughed, Thrain's light and merry, Varinn's still husky with relief. And now Thrain was pulling back further, glancing between Kitty and Varinn, his eyes dancing with bright, eager curiosity. "So did you really spend all Varinn's coin, by the way, Kit?" he asked. "Or was that just him winding us up?"

Kitty's eyes briefly met Varinn's again, and he gave a too-casual shrug. "Ach, mostly," he said dismissively, with a gentle clap of his hand to Kitty's flank. "Now, what should you two wish to do this eve? Mayhap some quiet time by the fire?"

But Thrain's eyes were still dancing, and he hopped back up to his feet, stretching his arms over his head. "Nice try, Lord Grisk," he drawled. "But we pleased you tonight, so now it's your turn to please us. Ach, Kit?"

Kitty blinked toward him, but felt herself slowly smiling at his contagious grin, at the devious sparkle in his warm eyes. "C'mon, you two," he said, "and let's go have some fun."

40

Thrain's idea of fun, apparently, began with a sparring-match.

It turned out that Thrak and Nattfarr were already wrestling in an adjoining sparring-room, while Ella and Rakfi watched from the sidelines. And when Ella caught sight of Kitty, she eagerly waved her over, while Thrain excitedly dragged Varinn toward the match. And soon all four orcs were shouting and flailing on the floor together, while Kitty and Ella laughed and cheered.

Ella also showed herself to be an easy, cheerful companion, first asking kindly about Kitty's pregnancy, and how she was faring with Ymir in the shop. And then she regaled Kitty with several highly amusing tales of various disagreements between Ymir and Nattfarr, and how these days all shop discussions went through Varinn, for the sake of everyone's well-being.

"Varinn is such a gift from the gods, truly," she told Kitty, with a quick, rueful smile. "I don't know what we would do without him. He never makes a fuss, and he's always where he needs to be, just getting the work done. Natt relies on him for so much, and I'm not sure he even realizes the half of it."

She'd shot a fond smile toward where Nattfarr currently

had Thrak in a chokehold, while a cackling Thrain wildly flailed against Nattfarr's back, and a laughing Varinn fought to drag him off. All of them looking so relaxed, so utterly at ease, and Kitty's thoughts seemed to catch on that, comparing it to the careful distance Varinn had borne earlier, when he'd spoken of not missing Thrain.

"I know Varinn does take his work very seriously," Kitty belatedly replied, with an uncertain glance toward Ella. "But with Thrain staying here for a while, have you thought about perhaps giving him more support? I mean"—she grimaced—"not that he probably needs it, or would ask for it... but just in case?"

Thankfully, Ella didn't appear offended, and she nodded, giving a slow sigh. "Natt actually tried to convince him to take some help today," she said, "but he refused everyone he suggested. Which is understandable, of course, because it's often sensitive work, and requires not only good tracking and defense skills, but also a lot of people skills and patience. And saddling Varinn with someone who can't keep up, or worse, makes it more difficult for him"—she sighed again—"that's more disruptive than sending no one at all, right?"

Kitty nodded, though she felt the unease still twisting, even when Ella gave her a companionable bump with her shoulder. "And I'm sure Thrain will be back to his usual self very soon, anyway," she said firmly. "He already seems so much better lately, don't you think? It's clear he loves having you here, and having things settled between the three of you."

Kitty gave a wan-feeling smile back, but couldn't seem to find a reply. And thankfully, at that moment, Nattfarr and Varinn had seemed to gain their victory, pinning both Thrak and Thrain beneath their heavier-looking bodies. Prompting Ella to begin loudly cheering at their success, while Rakfi escaped from her arms, and dashed over to scramble up onto his father's shoulders.

"Och, that was a good one," Thrain said brightly, once he'd

dragged a sweaty, smiling Varinn back toward Kitty again. "Although fighting against you two great boulders at once is the worst, Varinn, you know we're much better as a team, ach? And where the hell was Dammarr, anyway, he always adds a—"

But his voice broke there, because Dammarr himself had indeed appeared at the door. But he certainly didn't seem ready to fight, because—Kitty's mouth pulled into a delighted smile—he was wearing the stunning red dress, looking truly resplendent in its flowing silk and intricate black lace.

Thrain gave a low, appreciative whistle, to which Varinn elbowed him sharply in the side—but Dammarr's brief glance toward Thrain was distinctly grateful. Followed by a far more uncertain glance over toward Thrak, who'd still been lying sprawled and sweaty on the floor—and who had now shoved up onto his elbow, staring toward Dammarr with his mouth hanging open.

Dammarr raised his chin, looking suddenly, stubbornly defiant—at least, until Thrak leapt smoothly up to his feet, striding across the room toward him with long, purposeful steps. Not slowing, not stopping, until he'd grasped Dammarr's wrists with both hands, and pinned them to the stone wall above his head.

Dammarr gasped, his eyes wide and shocked—but then his head tilted back, his eyes fluttering closed, as Thrak's lean, sweaty body firmly pressed him into the wall. His hips grinding against Dammarr's with unmistakable purpose, as his hand gently drew the red silk aside, so he could bend his head into Dammarr's bare shoulder, his breath inhaling deep.

"Akva curse you, Dammarr," he mumbled, nearly inaudible. "Can't keep *doing* this to me."

Dammarr didn't reply, his eyes still squeezed shut, but his hips were grinding back toward Thrak's, meeting his movements with easy familiarity. While beside Kitty, Thrain gave an amused-sounding huff, and nudged her and Varinn toward the door. "Och, time to go," he said lightly. "The Ash-

Kai oughta have some music going tonight, Kit, if you'd like to hear it?"

Kitty eagerly agreed to that, and after a short trek up through the mountain, she soon discovered that not only did the Ash-Kai have music—thanks to a group of large, capable-looking drummers—but that it was also part of a lively little gathering with games, food, and dancing. And while there were many people present who Kitty didn't know, more faces were familiar than not, and she soon found herself cheerfully caught up in greeting and chatting with all her new acquaintances, including all the women she'd met so far.

"Oh, you met *Filak*," Rosa said, with a wrinkle of her pert little nose, once Thrain had casually dropped that particular tidbit into their conversation. "Yes, those northern Ka-esh are quite something, aren't they? We've dealt with them very rarely until now, since they live so far away, and usually stay deep underground. But thanks to some recent diplomacy efforts"— she irritably flapped her hand toward an amused-looking Geva beside her—"they've been coming around more often. Especially now that they know *some* people"—she swivelled her disgruntled face toward Varinn and Thrain—"will pay truly shocking amounts of coin for their ore!"

Thrain hastily assumed an unconvincing expression of bewilderment, to which Rosa pursed her lips, and jabbed a pointy finger toward him. "John-Ka told me that thanks to demand from Grisk like *you*, Ymir offered Filak *three thousand trading-credits* for some absurd emeralds he scrounged up!" she snapped. "And now Filak's decided to cool his heels in the Ka-esh wing and start shopping his rock around the mountain, in hopes that he'll get an even better offer from somewhere else!"

She'd glanced darkly across the room, toward where Rathgarr and Kesst seemed engrossed in conversation together. Both of them arrayed in a beautiful selection of jewelry, but distinctly lacking—Kitty couldn't help noticing—any emeralds. While beside Thrain, Varinn's eyes had sparked with unmistakable interest, his hand nudging at Thrain's elbow. "You did not say Filak brought *emeralds*," he said, his voice low. "How large? What colour? How did they scent?"

Rosa gave a surprisingly deep growl, and threw up her hands in palpable frustration. "There really ought to be a process," she said loudly, over Varinn and Thrain's reverent-sounding emerald discussion. "With consistent prices across the mountain, and only *one* point of contact, to prevent this kind of unscrupulous wheeling and dealing! I can't deny to you, Kitty, that it's been most exasperating to have these—these *illiterate mercenarie*s wandering about willy-nilly, undermining all our clan's scientific progress and educational efforts with—with *base commerce!*"

Kitty couldn't help a laugh, but her head was tilting, too, her thoughts turning it over. "It's true, though, that there ought to be an agreed-upon standard of pricing, to protect both buyers and sellers," she said. "I know many trading markets have similar restrictions in place. Along with mechanisms to ensure that some of the funds traded are used for the community's greater good, as well."

Rosa's eyes lit up, and soon she and Kitty were embroiled in an intensive trading and taxation discussion. One that eventually drew over the capable-looking Jule, who had a huge, alarming orc in tow—apparently her mate, Grimarr, the captain of the entire mountain. Who listened to their discussion with surprising attentiveness, and then asked Kitty and Rosa if they would work with their clan kin to develop a proposal for proper review.

At this, Rosa beamed beatifically toward him, and Kitty couldn't help grinning, too—especially at the realization that Varinn had been hovering behind her, listening, and his big hand was now stroking up and down her back with obvious approval. While this Grimarr gave a satisfied nod toward him, and a brief, appreciative smile. "I salute you on your clever new mate, brother," he said firmly. "It is right, I ken, for the Grisk and the Speaker's kin to help lead this for us. To build a safer, stronger home for our sons."

He'd nodded purposefully toward Kitty's belly, and then toward Jule, too. And beside Kitty, Varinn was looking both pleased and proud, his face flushing as he drew Kitty closer beside him, and gave a brief bow toward the captain. "I thank you, Captain," he said, a little hoarse. "We are honoured to serve our home, and our kin."

He was still looking pleased as they parted, his warm eyes glimmering on Kitty's face. "I did not know you held such knowledge of these things, Katharine," he said, his head tilting. "How did you—"

But he broke off there, because Thrain—who had previously been chatting nearby with several Grisk orcs, including Harthr's trading colleague Grein—had abruptly lurched toward them. His claws out, his eyes strangely glittering, as his tongue flicked against his lips.

"Och," he said thickly, "I ken they're bringing out—the ale. And the scent, it—"

He grimaced, his eyes gone almost pleading as they darted between Kitty and Varinn. But Varinn was already grasping Thrain's arm, steering him bodily toward the door, while Kitty rushed to follow. And once they were out in the corridor, Kitty clasped Thrain's other arm too, stroking it with rapid, fervent approval.

"That was a fun party, Thrain, thank you," she said, as lightly as she could. "But I bet you'll have even more fun once Varinn has you bent over and screaming for him, right, Varinn?"

Her eyes were still perhaps a little panicked as they caught Varinn's, but he firmly nodded, and gave a low, tantalizing little growl. And once they'd reached their familiar sitting-room— which was far dimmer than before, with a small fire guttering in the fireplace—Varinn marched them straight toward the fire, his hand clamped on Thrain's arse beneath his kilt.

"Ach, *krútt*," he murmured, as he spun Thrain toward the fire, and kicked his legs apart. "It shall grant me great joy to care for you. To reward you for coming to us, and seeking our joy, instead."

Thrain was already groaning, nodding, because oh, Varinn's hungry hands were bending him over, and flicking up his kilt. Exposing that now-familiar bare arse, still with—Kitty's breath caught—Varinn's gold *rassja* jutting deep inside. And Varinn's hand was already grasping the handle, gently drawing it out, and gods, how that looked, how it sounded, squelching smoothly out of Thrain, and leaving him slack, wide open, in its wake.

"Hold this, *kisa*," Varinn told her, with damnable coolness, as he carefully passed the *rassja*'s handle into Kitty's fingers. "And hold my kilt, also."

Oh, hell, but Kitty was already nodding, obeying, one-handedly unfastening Varinn's kilt as quickly as she could, and draping it over her arm. Revealing the mouthwatering sight of his fat, dripping length, already seeking toward Thrain's lax, waiting opening... and then, in one swift, easy thrust of his hips, Varinn plunged himself deep inside, all the way to the hilt.

Thrain staggered and moaned, his claws scrabbling at the stone wall above the fireplace, because oh, Varinn was already pumping in and out, his hands gripping Thrain's hips, his eyes intent on the sight. While the sounds rose slick and obscene between them, together with the firm, steady slap of skin against skin.

"Ach, *krútt*," Varinn breathed, as he picked up speed. "Look at you, so soft and open and ready for me. Swallowing me whole without even the slightest struggle. So good."

Thrain moaned again, hoarse and desperate, his head twitching back and forth. "But probably not—as good for you," he gasped, between dragging breaths. "Not as tight. Most of all after you've had—"

He'd shot a chagrined sideways look up toward—toward Kitty, and she was suddenly, fervently grateful when Varinn reached up to grasp at Thrain's chin, aiming it firmly back toward the fire, before slipping a possessive hand around his neck. "No, *krútt*," he hissed, slamming his hips in harder, faster. "It is perfect. You feel perfect. Perfect, for you are *mine*. Both of you. Ach?"

And wait, wait, he was—he was talking about Kitty, and he even glanced toward her, holding her eyes for the briefest of instants, before looking back at Thrain again. And Kitty's heart was roaring, suddenly, writhing in her chest as she watched her powerful, wonderful lord holding his favourite vassal by the neck, bending him double before him, taking his pleasure from him with fierce, furious purpose. Making it true, bringing it to impossible, inconceivable life between them. *Perfect*, he'd said, *mine. Both of you.*

"Empty him, *kisa*," came Varinn's cool command, his voice not even hitching. "Into the fire."

Wait, he couldn't—he wasn't—but Thrain was groaning, his own bobbing length flexing and swaying beneath his kilt, leaking toward the stone floor. And in a flail of movement, Kitty clasped that hot pulsing length in hand, milking it up and down, as Varinn ground deep, a harsh growl rumbling from his throat—

And with a loud cry, Thrain jerked and sprayed out. His heft furiously pulsing against Kitty's fingers as the molten white streamed from him, spattering thick and messy across the flickering flames. Enough that the fire soon fizzled away altogether, hissing and billowing into sweet-scented smoke instead. Smoke that Varinn was visibly inhaling, his chest filling, his eyes fluttering, as he kept grinding into Thrain, surely pouring out his own seed, too.

"Ugh," said a familiar voice from across the room, and when Kitty jerked to look sideways in the much-dimmed light, it was Dammarr, sidling out of one of the adjoining rooms, with a distasteful grimace on his mouth. He was holding a waterskin, and his red dress was hanging loose and disheveled from his shoulders, blatantly displaying the fresh red teeth-marks on his neck. "Did you *really* need to make the whole room reek of him, Varinn?"

Varinn appeared entirely unperturbed by this, that familiar mild warmth back in his eyes, and he slowly drew out of Thrain again, leaving him even more stretched open than before. "The fire needed to be doused anyway," he said blandly, as he coolly reached to pluck the *rassja* from Kitty's slack hand. "And Katharine had already swallowed his full bollocks' load before this, and I do not wish to make my *kisa* sick, ach?"

Oh. There was something in how he'd said that, how he'd clearly considered all that, and Kitty hungrily stared as he casually brought the *rassja* back to Thrain's still-opened cleft, and began smoothly sliding it in again. As if this were a perfectly acceptable, even ordinary, thing to do, while another orc stood there, and watched. Even as it set Thrain gasping and trembling again, and his slackened heft—still in Kitty's fingers—squeezed out a few last, straining spurts onto the still-smoking fireplace.

"How thoughtful of you," Dammarr finally replied, his voice thin, and it belatedly occurred to Kitty that he had indeed been watching, a rather dazed expression in his eyes. "Open the damned vent when you're done, at least?"

Varinn absently nodded, his attention still fully fixed on what he was doing, while Dammarr sighed, and then stalked in the direction of the latrine. Leaving Kitty blinking blankly after him, her own breaths still coming far too quickly, her heart still thundering in her chest. *Perfect*, Varinn had said, *mine. Both of you.*

And that look was again there in Varinn's eyes as he finished settling the *rassja* in place, watching as Thrain again fought to close against it, to hold it in place. And once he'd finally managed to do so, Varinn gave a low purr of approval, and drew him up to standing again. Turning him around, revealing his sweaty, reddened face—and then leaning in, and pressing a soft, lingering kiss to his mouth.

"So good, *krútt*," he murmured. "This pleased me."

Thrain's eyes fluttered as he kissed back, his arm slipping around Varinn's waist—and then his other hand purposefully reached toward Kitty, drawing her close, too. And oh, Varinn was doing the same, pulling her in tightly against them, and that felt so good too, so perfect. Both their sated, sweaty bodies warm and strong against her, the sweet-scented smoke still filling the air.

"You ken Kit might get sick of this, though, Varinn," Thrain finally mumbled. "She oughta have all your tending to herself, ach? Also"—he glanced at the still-smoky room around them—"pretty sure pregnant women aren't supposed to be breathing in smoke, either."

Varinn twitched a nod, and jerked away to flick at something in the wall—the vent, surely, from the way the smoke instantly began trailing toward it. "Ach, but it pleases her to watch me use you however I wish, ach, *kisa*?" he said as he strode back toward them, his voice far too smooth. "Just as it pleased you to punish her for me tonight, *krútt*. You ken I cannot scent all your deepest longings?"

Oh. Right. Of course. And Kitty's cheeks were again burning hot, her eyes briefly meeting Thrain's, her smile pulling up at the sight of his swift, wry grin. "Tyrant," he murmured, glancing back up at Varinn's face. "And don't pretend I can't scent you, too, Varinn. You fucking *love* it. It's all your most dissolute Lord Grisk dreams come to life, ach?"

Varinn didn't even pretend to argue this, and instead herded them back toward their room, and into bed. While Kitty couldn't seem to stop smiling, at either of them, because Varinn had called her *his*, he was scenting for her deepest longings, this was all his dreams come true. And she'd pleased him today, she'd done him credit before his captain, and Thrain had done better today too, and had come to them when he needed help. And it was all so good, so easy to keep smiling as she curled up between them, as their big hands again settled wide and safe against her belly.

Sleep came easy, too, sweeping Kitty into soft snug darkness, into whispering hopeful dreams. And the usual nighttime latrine break was dazed and dreamy too, her body tucked safe beneath Varinn's arm as she drifted through the still-sweet-scented air. And once he'd tucked her back into bed without him—about to head off for his swimming, or whatever he often did at nights—Kitty clasped his hand, and even pressed a furtive little kiss against it.

"Come back in the morning?" she whispered, and though he didn't reply, she could have sworn she felt something warm brushing against her forehead. And when morning came, he was indeed somehow here again, slipping back into bed beside her and Thrain, his hair and body still dripping wet, and scenting of the baths.

But that was so good too, so perfect, and Kitty joined Thrain in working him over together. Their touches and kisses sleepy and sloppy at first, but gaining wakefulness as they went, and soon Kitty was kneeling over Varinn, sucking his leaking head desperately into her throat, while Thrain lay sideways beneath his sprawled hairy thighs, his tongue twisting up deep in between.

Varinn's choked cry as he came was deeply, darkly satisfying, and so was the way he wildly bucked between their mouths, pumping into Kitty's throat—at least, until he sat up, coolly patted both their heads, and slipped out of bed. Smirking down at their flushed staring faces, damn him, before spinning on his heel, and striding for the washbasin.

"If you both keep behaving today," he said over his shoulder, "I shall again tend to you this eve, ach?"

It was a starkly powerful motivation, and Kitty still couldn't stop smiling as they washed and dressed together, and then ate a cheerful breakfast with their kin. Even Thrak seemed in a far better mood than usual, casting frequent furtive glances across the table toward Dammarr. Who was eating very primly in his beautiful navy dress, which contrasted quite compellingly with the still-red teeth-marks in his neck.

"Take care today, both of you," Varinn told Kitty and Thrain, once he'd walked them both over to the shop. "And you shall again keep a close watch over her, ach, *krútt*?"

Thrain was already nodding, leaning in to nibble at Varinn's neck, while Kitty impulsively flung her arms around his waist. "And you take care, too, Lord Grisk," she said shyly. "We'll miss you."

Varinn replied with a strange-sounding harrumph, but then kissed her hair, and gave her arse a gentle squeeze. Almost as if he'd liked that, or even appreciated it—but when she glanced back up, he'd already turned away, striding off down the corridor. Leaving Kitty behind with Thrain, who was looking just as fondly affectionate as she felt.

"Och, we'll get him tonight," Thrain murmured. "Good for him to be thinking about it all day too, ach? Want him looking forward to coming home to us again, and making his sweet *kisa* scream for him."

The warmth was again fizzling in Kitty's chest, the smile painfully hopeful on her face. "You know, I still have no conception of what *kisa* even means," she said, before she could stop it. "He could be secretly thinking of me as a dung-beetle, all this time. Or some sort of cockroach infestation, perhaps."

And wait, curse her, she was perhaps betraying the truth about all this again, when she'd been doing so well—and she was deeply relieved when Thrain barked an amused, merry laugh, and slung his arm over her shoulder. "It means *kitten*, of course, Kit!" he exclaimed, giving her a little shake. "A sweet, soft little marvel that he gets to tend and cuddle and play with. Just as he's always wanted, ach?"

Oh. Kitty's disbelief was surging, together with more of that hot fizzing warmth—and she was smiling up at Thrain again, leaning into his touch. "And what about *krútt*, then?" she asked. "Does it have a meaning, too?"

And now it was Thrain's face visibly heating, his throat bobbing. "Means—*little darling*," he said, with a bashful half-smile toward her. "'Course, I was a lot smaller when he first started up with it, ach?"

Kitty's head tilted, but Thrain didn't elaborate further, and instead nudged her purposefully toward the shop up ahead. Clearly avoiding the topic of his past, yet again—but even so, the warmth was still bubbling in Kitty's chest, eager and damnably hopeful. Varinn had been calling her *kitten*, all this time. *A sweet, soft little marvel. Just as he's always wanted.*

And somehow, it felt even easier to throw herself into another busy day's work at the shop, especially with Thrain's close, reassuring presence nearby. He again proved to be a considerable help, first lending a hand in packing up Harthr's latest outbound shipment—meant for a few Grisk and Skai camps to the west—and then sniff-sorting the next round of items that had been traded in. And when a frowning, glowering Filak showed up again, apparently in search of mining tools, Thrain easily dealt with him, to the point where even Ymir was looking grudgingly satisfied.

They ate another lovely lunch out in the garden together, and afterwards, at Kitty's prompting—and with Ymir's permission—Thrain joined her in taking the broken *hálsmen* just a few doors down the corridor, to the warm, brightly lit Grisk forge. To where one of the vaguely familiar Grisk smiths—the Fjorvi Varinn had mentioned—immediately set down his hammer, and lumbered over to greet them.

"Varinn said you would be coming to work today, brother," he told Thrain, with a genial, toothy grin. "It shall be good to have an Aetha goldsmith back at the hearth again, ach?"

Thrain's head ducked, his pointed ears unmistakably flushing, and it belatedly occurred to Kitty that he was...

nervous. Nervous about not being properly trained for this kind of work, perhaps, or about finding it difficult, or even failing at it altogether. So she pulled herself a little taller beside him, and gave Fjorvi her brightest, most grateful smile.

"Thank you so much, Fjorvi," she said. "The thing is, though, it's been quite a few years since Thrain trained with his great-uncle. It would be exceedingly lovely of you if you might be willing to show him around, and let him know how you run things here? And"—she cast an uncertain glance toward the large nearby worktable, and the array of bizarre-looking tools scattered across it—"will he need to bring his own equipment, or other materials, or…"

Thankfully, Fjorvi was already nodding, and launching into a complicated-sounding discussion of the forge's current goldsmithing tools, materials, and processes. This apparently included regular deliveries of ore from the Ka-esh, along with plates and draw benches for making wire, a variety of lamps and blowpipes for soldering, and hammers, saws, files, and chisels for shaping and engraving.

It all made very little sense to Kitty, but Thrain seemed to follow it easily enough, and even asked several equally incomprehensible questions in return. And once he and Fjorvi were poring over the large worktable together, intensively discussing something called wax casting, Kitty finally took that as her cue to leave, giving Thrain's hand a companionable, reassuring squeeze before cheerfully waving goodbye.

There were already a few new customers waiting at the shop—Ymir was off to the side, seemingly embroiled in deep discussion with Kesst and Rathgarr—so Kitty promptly took her place behind the counter, and greeted the next orc in line. It was the lean Skai Killik again, seeking out heavy chains this time, and once he'd been sorted, Kitty helped Valter and Trygve purchase some fresh inks and parchment. Next was little Vragi with his kitten Arni, searching for a cat toy—and when it turned out that they didn't have any ready-made cat toys on hand, Kitty quickly comforted a dejected-looking Vragi, and helped him tie a bit of fur to a string instead. Which turned out to be so successful that he was soon shrieking with laughter, while his tiny kitten careened and caterwauled after her new quarry.

Kitty was still grinning when she turned to meet the next customers at the counter—which turned out to be Timo and the human girl Cecily. And with them was a lean, frowning young orc—also about Timo's age—who was apparently named Sune, from the Skai clan.

"We have come to gain Sune some new boots, sister," Timo told Kitty, with a shy smile. "Cecy's kitten went and clawed his last pair to shreds, ach, Sune?"

Sune didn't reply, but pursed his lips as he glanced darkly toward Cecily. Who was in turn looking highly offended, and crossing her arms over her chest. "Those boots were already in atrocious condition!" she exclaimed at him. "Such a typical Skai, to walk around looking like something *ate* you. Floof was doing you a *favour*."

Sune only raised his pointy chin at this, staring down his nose toward her, while Timo laughed and grasped Sune's hand, lacing their fingers together. "So please, sister, take us to the boots," he said, "so I no more need to bear their squabbling, ach?"

Kitty chuckled, and willingly escorted them to the boots, where it soon became apparent that Cecily had very strong opinions about which boot styles suited Sune best. And Kitty's amusement only rose at the gradual realization that Sune was perfectly willing to concede to Cecily's wishes, despite his continued frowns and sniffs of disdain toward her. And their one true disagreement—whether the brown or black pair suited Sune better—was soon settled by Timo, who firmly insisted that Sune choose whichever pair was most comfortable, and that if Cecily wanted him to dress in a particular colour, she could give him a proper gift instead.

This led to more enthusiastic wandering around the shop, Sune and Cecily now arm in arm, while Timo followed along behind with Kitty. "So how are you faring now, sister?" he asked shyly. "I hope you and your son are well? And that Thrain is feeling better, also?"

Kitty nodded, and gave him a genuine, grateful smile. "I've been doing very well, thank you," she said. "And I think Thrain is, too. Varinn has been taking very good care of us both."

Timo's smile back was quick and approving, and he gave a firm little nod. "Ach, I am sure he is," he said. "He has always taken such good care of me, also, and all the rest of us. Although"—his voice trailed off, his eyes angling away—"did I scent him leaving alone again this morn?"

Kitty wasn't quite sure how to read that, but she nodded. "Yes, Thrain's staying here at the mountain for a while," she said carefully. "But Varinn's been quite adamant that he doesn't mind working alone."

Timo's brow furrowed, his tooth chewing at his lip—but when Cecily called for him from the next aisle, he promptly perked up and jogged over. Just in time to work through another squabble, apparently, this one about whether a used dagger was an appropriate gift for Sune. But Timo again settled the dispute with surprising decisiveness, pointing out that daggers were important Skai gifts, and that Cecily ought to wait until she could consult with at least one grown-up Skai upon it. Which soon led to Cecily perusing the jewelry section instead, where—after much consideration—she finally chose a beautiful braided gold cuff.

"I like this one," she said decisively, holding it up against where Sune was already wearing a gold armband, of a contrasting but complementary style. "It'll match the one you gave him, Timo, but it's different enough to be interesting, don't you think?"

Timo cheerfully nodded, and Sune was looking surprisingly pleased, too, his cheeks flushing pink. But once he'd slipped it on his arm next to the first cuff, his face abruptly fell, because the new cuff was clearly a few sizes too big, already sliding down to dangle uselessly against his elbow.

Cecily wailed with disappointment, and Timo's glance toward Kitty was alarmed, and perhaps even pleading—and without quite meaning to, she waved her hand between them, and gave them her brightest smile. "Not to worry at all," she said, with as much certainty as she could muster. "I'm sure we can manage an alteration. Perhaps we can take some measurements, and you can leave it with us for the evening?"

Timo's grin toward Kitty was wide and grateful, and Cecily and Sune both looked pleased too, grinning shyly toward one another. However, once the sale had been finalized—for a considerable amount of trading-credits—Ymir whirled around, and fixed Kitty with a deeply suspicious frown. "You aren't expecting Thrain to alter that, woman?" he demanded. "That's tricky work, on a costly piece. I ken you'd best put it in the Ka-esh queue for next month, and go tell those young'uns you were mistaken."

Kitty winced, her stomach plunging in her belly—but before she could speak, Thrain himself strode into the room. He was wearing what appeared to be a thick leather apron, and his arms and hands were streaked with copious amounts of black soot and ash. But he was broadly grinning, and glinting in his hand was the broken gold *hálsmen*. Which—Kitty gasped, and lurched closer to look—had been fixed. Hadn't it?

"Finally managed it, after spending half the morning burning through gold, bungling my tests," he said wryly, although his eyes on Kitty were already narrowing, and then darting toward Ymir. "And what's wrong, Kit? Not feeling ill, are you?"

Kitty waved it away, beaming at him, and then at the *hálsmen*. "I knew you could fix it," she said proudly. "And I just—I may have promised Cecily and Sune that you could alter this cuff for them, too. But then Ymir made the point that it's very difficult work, and likely ought to go to the Ka-esh instead."

She thrust the gold cuff out toward him, and Thrain carefully took it from her hand, frowning at its intricate gold coils. "Sorry, Kit, but I ken he's right," he said, with a grimace. "I ken the Ka-esh are the only ones who would know how to..."

His voice trailed off, his claw carefully pulling at the edge of the cuff, drawing it out into a single shimmering length—and at that moment, a beaming Rosa strode in, with a book clasped to her chest, and an unfamiliar, genial-looking orc trailing along behind her.

"Greetings, all!" she said brightly. "I'm here to discuss our pricing and taxation proposal, Kitty, if Ymir can spare you for a few moments? And"—her keen eyes glanced toward Thrain—"we Ka-esh know what, now?"

Thrain gave Rosa a tolerant smile, and briefly showed her the braided cuff, and explained how they often needed alterations to fit properly. Though Kitty couldn't help noticing that his gaze repeatedly glanced toward the genial orc hovering behind her, and soon Rosa waved the orc forward, and introduced him as Gary, one of the Ka-esh smiths.

"Gary has very kindly offered to advise us on our proposal, Kitty," Rosa said, beaming toward him, "as he's our own clan's principal gem purchaser, and not about to fall for the machinations of a devious creature like Filak! But"—she reverently touched at the delicate gold choker she was wearing—"he's also an absolutely brilliant goldsmith, aren't you, Gary?"

Gary's face visibly flushed at the praise, but he also nodded toward Thrain's cuff. "Ach, I have worked on these before," he said, in a soft, smooth voice. "To alter its size, you shall need to remove equal links from each part, so it keeps the same balance, and moves how it was meant to. You can see how the links are smaller here, but larger here?"

Thrain was already nodding, and eagerly pulling the cuff

even further apart, until it was a single long, shimmering gold chain. "Ach, that I follow," he replied, "but what do I do with the terminals? They won't align and lock thus once the links are removed, ach? Would you remove them also, and re-cast them on again?"

Gary's answer was nearly incomprehensible, and Thrain's next question even more so—and Kitty was distantly grateful when Rosa waved her away, toward the end of the counter, where she'd begun spreading out sheets of paper. "Now," she said firmly, "here are a few preliminary thoughts and numbers I've pulled together, in discussion with a few other Ka-esh. Perhaps you and Ymir could review together?"

Ymir had been watching all this with a slightly disgruntled expression, but he accordingly came over, too. And soon the three of them were caught in a surprisingly fascinating discussion about Ymir's current pricing processes, and how a system of price regulation—and possibly taxation—might best be implemented.

At one point during the conversation, Thrain and Gary had excused themselves to head to the Grisk forge, Thrain pressing a brief kiss to the top of Kitty's head. And when he returned, Kitty was surprised to realize that a considerable amount of time must have passed, because he was even more coated with ash and soot than before, and proudly holding the gleaming cuff in his hand.

"Done," he told Ymir, with a wide, satisfied grin. "And it's not bad, either, ach?"

Ymir snatched the cuff from Thrain's hand, frowning at it with obvious suspicion—but once he'd pulled it apart, and shaken out the full length of it, the look on his face shifted to something more calculating. "Not bad at all, boy," he said, with a sharp look toward Thrain's face. "Gary do most of the work, though?"

"A bit, especially with the casting," Thrain said, reaching to finger at the cuff's tricky-looking end-clasp. "But I did all the link removal and soldering. Picked the right links to cut, too."

His chest had swelled with palpable pride, while Ymir cast him another narrow, shrewd look. "Hmph," he said, pursing his mouth. "Ach, then, boy. As of tomorrow, I'm sending you down to apprentice with the Ka-esh smiths, and you'll begin to cover all our jewel repairs, ach?"

Thrain blinked, and Kitty didn't miss the brief flare of eagerness in his eyes—but then they narrowed again, as he gave a choked, disbelieving laugh. "What?" he demanded. "I don't work for you, Ymir. And also"—his gaze angled toward Kitty—"I need to stay close to Kit, ach? The Ka-esh wing is way too far if she needs me."

But beside Kitty, Rosa had brightened, beaming back and forth between them. "But you can both come!" she exclaimed. "The library isn't far from the Ka-esh forge, Kitty, and we can keep working on our proposal together there. I'm sure Thrain would have no trouble scenting you from the forge."

Thrain wasn't arguing this point, chewing his lip as he frowned toward Rosa, and then toward Kitty. Looking hesitant, uncertain, and Kitty shot an encouraging smile back toward him, and reached to clasp at his sooty arm. "It sounds like an excellent plan to me," she said, "as long as Ymir doesn't mind me going, of course. How much time would you need to spend there each day?"

"Only as much as I want," Thrain replied, angling another dark look toward Ymir, "because I *don't work for you*, Ymir."

But Ymir hadn't even spared Thrain a single look, and was still studying Kitty, his mouth pursed. "I can spare you for a spell late each morning, woman," he said curtly. "And while you're down there, boy, you'll focus on chains first, for I could place a half-dozen new orders from those Ash-Kai alone."

Thrain huffed an irritated groan, but no one—except Kitty—seemed to pay any attention. And Rosa had already begun gathering up her papers, clasping them to her chest before heading for the door. "I'll arrange it with Gary," she said over her shoulder, "and we'll see you in the library tomorrow morning. Until then!"

Kitty couldn't help a wry chuckle as she glanced back at Thrain, who was still looking decidedly nettled. But he seemed to have given up trying to argue, even when Ymir reached beneath the counter, and plucked out what appeared to be a bracelet, a pair of earrings, and a belt.

"These all need fixing today too, boy," he said flatly, as he shoved them across the counter toward Thrain. "As for you, woman"—he turned back toward Kitty—"I've put all the mending together at the back, so you'll go set up your station, and spend the afternoon working on repairs, too."

Kitty exchanged another amused glance with Thrain, but didn't miss how he'd already pulled the little pile of jewels closer, his fingers running reverently against the belt's tarnished gold buckle. "I can't wait to see what you do with them," she told him, giving a squeeze to his arm. "See you again soon?"

Thrain nodded, and pressed a kiss to her forehead before leaving again. After which Kitty followed Ymir to the back of the shop, where he'd indeed set up a table with a mound of mending, several lamps, and a variety of sewing supplies.

"I've gathered a few things for you," he said gruffly, "but you may choose whatever you need from the shop, also."

Kitty perked up at that, and soon she was eagerly roaming the aisles, collecting items for her station. Another little table, a stool, several pillows, a small mirror to help direct light, and even an old dress-form that had been shoved beneath a shelf.

And once she'd set it all up to her satisfaction, she sat down and just stared at it for a moment, her heart hitching in her chest. Gods, she wanted this. Wanted all of it, Varinn, Thrain, this shop, this *life*—so much it ached. And if she just kept working, just kept trying, maybe, maybe...

So she sat up straight, pulled over the first item—a tunic

with a ripped hem—and set to work. Mending it as quickly and carefully as she could, her stitches small and neat, and almost imperceptible from the rest of the hem. And then moving on to the next, and the next, until she had a respectable pile beside her, and—something caught her eye, and her head jerked up—someone was standing before her. Varinn.

Kitty's mouth broke into a delighted smile, and she leapt to her feet, her heart skipping in her chest. "You're back already!" she exclaimed. "Or wait"—she glanced uncertainly around at the otherwise quiet shop—"it's not suppertime, is it?"

Varinn's already-warm eyes glinted with amusement, and his mouth pulled into a surprisingly fond-looking smile. "Ach, it is, *kisa*," he said, a little husky. "How was this, today? I hope you are feeling well?"

"Oh, all very good, thank you," Kitty said dismissively, as she kept beaming toward him. "How about you? Did everything go well?"

Something shifted in Varinn's eyes, but he waved it away too, the smile pulling even higher on his mouth. "Ach, all was well," he said lightly, as he reached over to clasp her hand, drawing her out from behind the table. "And do I scent Thrain still in the forge? How has this gone?"

Kitty eagerly slipped up against his warm, solid side, and as they left the shop together, she rapidly explained about all that had happened that day. What with Timo and Cecily and Sune, and the cuff, and Gary, and Ymir's apprenticeship demand, and their subsequent agreement to work together in the Ka-esh wing. While Varinn's brows rose higher and higher, his eyes glinting with undeniable disbelief.

"You have been busy, little *kisa*," he said gruffly, as he guided her toward the door of the forge. "I am most glad of all this. And—"

He'd pulled up short just inside the forge's door, his eyes fixed on—oh. Where Thrain was still working behind the large, cluttered worktable, his sweaty skin still covered in soot and ash, his hair standing all on end. And he had a long, strange-looking *pipe* caught in his mouth, and his steady hand was holding its opposite end over a brightly burning lamp-flame, which was flickering sideways with his breath. And beneath the blown flame, Thrain was holding Ymir's broken bracelet with a pair of large metal tongs, its gold glinting in the light of the forge's larger nearby fire.

It was an admittedly bizarre sight—but an oddly compelling one, too, especially with the flame blowing so smoothly from the pipe in Thrain's mouth, the focused intent flashing in his eyes. And Kitty didn't miss the spasm of Varinn's hand on her back, or the visible bob in his throat as he strode over toward the workbench, drawing her close behind him.

"Sorry, you two," Thrain said with an apologetic grin, once he'd lowered the pipe. "Just wanted to try to finish this up, as I'm almost done! Had to make these three new links here, and then solder them on, ach?"

He'd nudged his claw at the bracelet, at where—apart from their darker colour—the three new links seemed nearly indistinguishable from the rest. And when Kitty eagerly pointed out that fact, Thrain's already-red face flushed even redder, a pleased little smile tugging at his mouth. "Och, well, they aren't polished yet," he said offhandedly. "Hopefully won't be able to tell the difference once it's done, ach? Well"—his eyes glanced toward Varinn—"except for the scent, mayhap."

His smile had gone a little uncertain, his eyes searching Varinn's face. Where Varinn was still looking rather stunned, his gaze fixed on the bracelet—but when Kitty surreptitiously nudged at his back, he twitched all over, and flashed Thrain a smile that looked almost... shy.

"This is stunning work, *krútt*," he said, quiet. "I ken I forgot how much time you spent with Thyrikr, when we were young. He sought to train you up as his successor, did he not?"

Thrain's eyes relaxed again, his smile a little bashful, too. "Ach, mayhap," he said. "Though he could do this kind of job"—he waved at the bracelet—"in a few moments. Not half an afternoon."

"Ach, but you are yet learning," Varinn said, with a decisive little nod. "The more you train upon this, the easier it will become. And Gary is mayhap the mountain's most skilled goldsmith, and it speaks much of your skill that he has agreed to teach you."

Thrain's face flushed even redder, but his eyes were still uncertain, searching Varinn's face. "But you're still sure you don't mind, Varinn?" he asked. "You didn't... need me today, for anything?"

"Not at all," Varinn said firmly, his eyes flinty on Thrain's. "Except..."

Thrain visibly hesitated, waiting, uncertain again—but then a slow smile spread across Varinn's mouth. A smile that spoke of warmth, of hunger, of bright, gleaming wickedness.

"Except to reward you, mayhap," he purred. "Both of you. Now finish your work, *krútt*, and come."

41

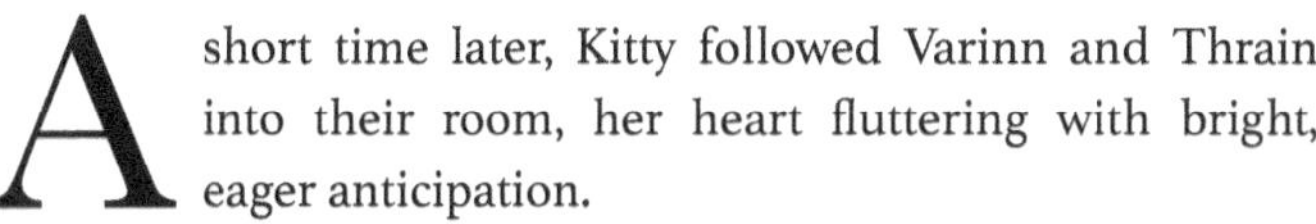 short time later, Kitty followed Varinn and Thrain into their room, her heart fluttering with bright, eager anticipation.

Varinn had kept that look in his eyes as he'd taken them first to wash up, and then to eat supper in the kitchen. And even as he'd spoken politely to their kin—and cheerfully exclaimed over Vragi's new cat-toy—his eyes had kept wandering back toward Thrain and Kitty, glinting with unmistakable hunger, and perhaps even eagerness.

"Ready each other for me," he ordered now, his voice damnably cool, as he sank down to sprawl in his chair. "I wish you both in only your jewels."

Oh, hell. Kitty's breath escaped in a moan, her eyes meeting Thrain's—and together they nodded, and hurried to obey. First fully undressing each other, until they were only in their *thyrjas* and piercings, and then Thrain brushed out Kitty's hair, too. And next—Kitty gulped—Thrain went to fetch both their *rassjas* from the shelf, their polished beads gleaming in his fingers.

"D'you ken, Varinn," he began, angling his gaze toward

him, "we could use your seed to slick them, this time? Might make it easier, ach?"

Varinn inclined his head at this, waving a magnanimous hand down toward his kilt. But otherwise making no effort to oblige, and Kitty bit back another moan as she and Thrain lurched over to Varinn together. Her hands quickly unfastening his kilt, pulling it aside, so Thrain could grasp him, and begin... milking. Pumping out Varinn's sweetness onto both *rassjas'* smooth gleaming gold, while Varinn himself just sat there, and watched. Waiting patiently as Thrain moved the gold back and forth against him, turning them over again and again, until they were both coated with thick glossy wetness.

"You first, Kit," Thrain murmured now, his eyes hooded on hers, as he nudged her bare body downwards. Until she was lying face-down over Varinn's lap, oh gods—and Kitty could feel them both watching, their eyes prickling on her skin, as Thrain's careful fingers spread her apart, settling that gold tip just there against her. And then—she flailed up a little—he pressed it in, slow and gentle, while she gasped and shuddered and keened.

But it went easier this time, smoother, and Thrain gave her an approving little slap as the *rassja* settled fully inside. "You like Varinn's seed in there?" he murmured. "Me, too, Kit. Mayhap he'll even fill you there properly someday, if you're a good little kitten."

Kitty's hunger surged even higher, her breath hitching in her throat, and Thrain chuckled as he drew her up again, and slipped his own slick *rassja* into her hands. Because it was his turn, oh gods, and she hungrily watched as he turned sideways, and put a shaky-looking foot up onto the arm of Varinn's chair. Giving them both a truly shocking view of everything in between his legs, his crease spread wide open, his bollocks hanging heavy below.

But if Varinn was shocked, he certainly didn't show it. Only licking his lips with his black tongue, and then glancing inquiringly toward Kitty, and the slick *rassja* in her hand. So she nodded, and carefully set the first gold bead in place against him, while Thrain twitched and gasped beneath it.

But when she began pressing, circling, it also seemed easier this time. Perhaps because of Varinn's seed, like Thrain had said—or perhaps because he'd had more practice with it now, too. But whatever the case, the gold beads sank in smoother, faster, disappearing one by one, even as Thrain's body shuddered all over, his gasps already turned to low, hoarse moans.

"Good, *krútt*," Varinn murmured, once the *rassja* was fully in place, with only its gold handle visible. "And *kisa*, also. It pleases me, when you both take my jewels without complaint, as you ought."

Kitty and Thrain both groaned in unison, and Kitty watched with riveted, fluttering eyes as Thrain stood tall before them again. Now exposing his own swollen, dripping length, jutting out straight toward Varinn's eyes—and Varinn was indeed eyeing it, his gaze cool, almost contemplative, as he reached toward his nearby shelf, and drew something out from beneath his stack of kilts.

And it was... the *typpavír*. The intricate, coiled gold jewel from the shop, the one that was meant to go around—and *inside*—an orc. And at the sight of it, Thrain's jaw dropped, his body twitching all over, his exposed length bobbing with highly betraying hunger.

"You—you *didn't*, Varinn," he gasped, his shocked eyes snapping back to Varinn's face. "The—the cost! And how did you even know—"

But Varinn's brief glance toward Kitty was explanation enough, and Thrain twitched as he followed his eyes, searched Kitty's face. "Och," he said, his voice hitching. "Och, so that's why he punished you yesterday, Kit, and it was so, so sweet of you to think of it—but gods, Varinn! To spend that kind of coin, on me, when I've been such a damned—"

But Varinn cut him off with a sharp sideways slice of his hand, a firm shake of his head. "I wished to," he said firmly. "We both wished to, ach, Katharine? And"—his eyes slightly darkened as they flicked between her and Thrain—"next time your stubborn brother *dares* to claim that Katharine did not grant you a proper mating-gift, *this* shall be your answer."

Thrain's mouth was still hanging open, and maybe Kitty's was, too—especially when Varinn coolly nudged the *typpavír* into her slack fingers. "So here, *kisa*," he said, a little husky. "Grant him your gift for me."

Oh, hell. Kitty stared at Varinn for a taut, dangling instant—he'd truly bought this on her behalf, so she could have a proper *mating-gift* to offer Thrain? When Thrain wasn't actually her mate, and Varinn still wasn't, either...

But Varinn's eyes on hers hadn't changed, and he gave a meaningful nod toward the *typpavír* clutched in her shaky fingers. And Kitty bit her lip as she blinked down at it, and then over at Thrain's hard, jutting length. It needed to go around him, *inside* him, and Varinn wanted her to do that for him... but how? How did one even *begin* to do such a thing?

But thankfully, Varinn gave a low chuckle, and reached to grasp the thick gold ring at the *typpavír*'s base, snapping it off with a jerk of his fingers. "You begin with this, *kisa*," he said softly. "And then the rest clasps onto it, ach?"

He snapped it back together again, showing Kitty the clever little attachment on the ring, and she somehow managed to nod, and then to repeat what he'd done, pulling the *typpavír* apart. And then, after thrusting the coiled section back into Varinn's hand, she clutched the gold ring, and turned back toward Thrain. Keeping her gaze firmly on her hands as she slowly, carefully, brought the ring to his bobbing, leaking shaft, and began guiding it down over it.

At least this part was familiar, thanks to how she'd done it to Varinn the other night—and Thrain certainly didn't seem to mind, his breaths audibly gasping as she first slid it to his base, and then gingerly guided his heavy bollocks through, too. Until the gold ring was tightly encircling all of him, lying flush against his groin, and flaunting his own bulging jewels with sheer, mouthwatering shamelessness.

Kitty could only seem to stare for a moment, her breaths dragging through her chest—and then Varinn nudged the rest of the *typpavír* back into her hand. The long coiled part, with that slim gold rod inside it, and Kitty truly could not move as she glanced between it, and Thrain's dripping, gold-encircled length. And most of all at his glossy head, with that deep cleft, and that neat little opening that suddenly seemed far too small...

But thank the gods, Thrain's warm hands had settled on hers, and when she glanced up, his eyes were dazed, hot, hungry. And oh, he was helping her now, guiding the *typpavír* closer, easing its gold coils over his shaft—until the smooth rounded tip of that slim gold rod settled against his slit, driving a strangled little gasp from his throat.

"Wouldn't recommend ever—doing this, thus, with a human, ach?" he breathed, his hazy eyes now fixed on the sight of that rod, nudging up just against where Kitty could see his opening slightly convulsing around it, spurting out its thick liquid against it. "At least, not without lots of practice first, and cleaning. But for orcs, especially with all our seed to ease the way, it's a—"

His voice broke, his eyes rolling back, because oh, the rod was slipping inside him, its gold length vanishing slowly but surely, deeper and deeper. And he was scarcely even touching the *typpavír* now, but it just kept sinking, almost as though his prick was... sucking it inside. Drawing it in, wanting it there, enclosing itself in its gleaming gold coils. Further, further, until the rod had vanished fully inside, and the round gold bead at its head was nudged up tight against Thrain's slit, and his own gold piercing. Almost blocking him off entirely, good gods, and Kitty nearly choked as she watched him pull the flexible coil even further downwards, toward the ring at his base. Adding even more pressure against the gold rod inside him, surely, and he sharply groaned as it snapped into place, enclosing him whole within it, around it.

And gods, how it looked. His pulsing length swollen fuller than Kitty had ever seen it, surely thickened by not only the ring constricting his base, but by the gold rod threaded inside him. By how he was now fully, flagrantly trussed up on the *typpavír*, stretched out, opened up, on display—but also closed off, blocked off, entirely trapped. And even his usual dripping fluid seemed to have slowed significantly, escaping in only a few oozing droplets from around the gold blocking his slit.

Kitty only distantly noticed Varinn's hand, making a turn-around motion—but oh, yes, now Thrain was turning, his movements jerky but eager. Showing them his bare back, his firm arse, and how it was filled with gold, too. How he was bejewelled on both sides, now, for Varinn's satisfaction, and his pleasure.

And yes, yes, Varinn was looking darkly, wickedly satisfied, his half-lidded eyes drinking up the sight—and when Thrain had turned to face him again, Varinn beckoned him forward, and then gently nudged his claw against the gold bead at the *typpavír*'s end. The tiny touch enough to make Thrain gasp and shudder all over, his eyes rolling back, his hands clutching to fists at his sides.

"Very pretty, *krútt*," Varinn murmured, still with that wicked smugness flashing in his eyes, as he nudged it again. "It pleases you to wear my mate's gift, I ken?"

Thrain gasped again, his head frantically nodding, and Varinn slowly smiled as he leaned lazily back into his chair, his eyes shifting into something speculative, or almost amused. "So mayhap," he continued, "you shall now thank her, as you ought. Grant her as much pleasure as she has granted you."

And wait, wait, Varinn was waving them—toward the bed.

He was—giving them permission, giving Thrain permission, to touch Kitty, to grant her pleasure? Without him?

But yes, yes, surely he was, especially with how—oh. His own prick was still swollen and dripping, lying propped against his bare belly, and his eyes were again holding on Thrain's *typpavír*, and glinting with more of that cool, wicked satisfaction. Because—because now that Thrain was locked away like this, stoppered up, he couldn't possibly take Kitty, like that. He likely wouldn't even be able to lie down against her, and instead would only be able to use his hands, or—or his tongue. And gods, it shouldn't have felt so powerful, so compelling, so damned impossibly arousing...

The hunger was flashing across Thrain's eyes, too, and he jerked sideways, as if about to instantly obey, and leap toward the bed—but then he stilled again, his eyes searching Varinn's face. "You're—sure, Varinn," he gulped. "Anything I— we—want."

His eyes darted toward Kitty, flared with unmistakable longing, with disbelief—but Varinn was still smiling, and settling back further into his chair. "You shall not spill your seed, without my leave," he said coolly. "And"—his gaze flicked back toward Kitty—"you shall be sure to make her soft and open for me, so she can next bear my good strong ploughing."

Oh, gods. Now Kitty was the one gasping, her eyes wildly darting between them, and Thrain's eyes were doing the same, his chest hollowing, his gaze dropping to the swollen heft at Varinn's groin. "Ach, Lord Grisk," he replied, hoarse. "I shall be honoured to serve you, and ready your mate for your strong ploughing, and your good Grisk seed."

Kitty couldn't find a way to speak, to even respond to this— except to allow Thrain to clasp her hand, and draw her over toward the bed. And when he nudged her down onto it, she willingly went, sinking her tingling, bared body back on the soft furs, feeling the twinge of the *rassja* shifting inside her. While Thrain eased up onto his knees over her, his long legs straddling her thighs, his caged heft slightly bobbing, jutting out over her belly. And his throat was bobbing, too, as his eyes swept up and down her front, and then angled back toward Varinn in his chair.

But Varinn was still just watching this, his body sprawling a little wider, his elbow propped on the armrest, his chin resting on his fist. As if he had truly settled back to observe this, to enjoy this—and his fingers even made a brief, indulgent little gesture toward them. Saying, surely, *Keep going.*

So Thrain rapidly nodded, angling his hazy gaze back to Kitty again. His shoulders rising, falling, as he slipped his hands toward her, and spread them wide against her bare waist.

Kitty shuddered all over at the warmth of his hands, the carefulness of his touch—and in return he huffed a low groan, his tongue licking his lips. His long fingers spreading a little wider, before slipping upwards, skating over her *thyrja*. Brushing her sides, her ribs, and then—*oh*—her breasts.

Kitty gasped and arched up, her hard nipples already straining against his warm palms, and Thrain huffed a chuckle as he circled his hands there, caressing, gently squeezing. And then drawing back to brush his thumbs against those too-sensitive peaks, watching her twitch and gasp—and then, oh hell, he bent over, and slipped one into his mouth.

It felt glorious, like tickling sparkling wonder teasing out from his clever lips, his gently flicking tongue—and Kitty was already moaning, her head tilting back, her body pressing higher into his touch. Into where he was moaning too, the sound vibrating into her very skin, oh, *oh*—

His warm hands were touching her again, too, caressing up and down her sides, her hips. And somehow, Kitty was already clutching back against him, her own hands greedily stroking and seeking, re-learning the feel of him, the powerful shifting heat of him, the silken smoothness of his skin. While his eager wandering tongue kept kissing, tasting, now slowly seeking up her collarbone, toward her neck, his teeth gently scraping her skin—

"No teeth, *krútt*," came Varinn's order, mild but certain, and Thrain instantly nodded, yanking backwards from her neck, while Kitty's fluttering gaze found Varinn's face. His eyes still so indulgent, even approving, as one of Thrain's searching hands slipped up the inside of her thigh, toward, toward—

Kitty arched and moaned again, but kept her fluttering eyes fixed on Varinn as Thrain's warm hand settled against her hungry heat, slipping up against where it already felt heavy and swollen. Against where she was already pulsing back against his touch, needing more, more—and oh, yes, that was his long, blunt-tipped finger, stroking all the way down her crease. Pausing to tease at the *rassja*'s gold handle, making her writhe and whimper, oh, before slipping back up to nudge against her slick, clutching openness. And when Kitty whimpered, glanced wildly toward his face, Thrain was hovering up over her, his eyes glittering, his face deeply flushed.

"You keep watching your Lord Grisk, Kit," he murmured. "Let him see just what he's doing to you, ach?"

Kitty moaned and nodded, glancing back toward Varinn's hungry, approving eyes, as Thrain slipped further down between Kitty's thighs, spreading them wider apart. And then—she yelped, wrenched all over—Thrain kissed her. There.

And oh, the memories were whirling back again, sharp and staggering. Images of that forbidden night together, of how he knelt so eagerly before her, and buried his face between her legs. How his clever lips had stroked her, caressed her, while that long, sinuous black tongue had slithered up inside her, just—just—like *that*. Enough to make Kitty cry out, clutch at him, and perhaps even open up wider, welcoming him deeper, oh—

But somehow it was even better this time, more

pleasurable, more perfect. Maybe because Kitty's senses were fully awake, alert, alight with this gift, this impossible ecstasy— or maybe it was because of Varinn. Because of Varinn sitting there, so coolly watching Thrain lick and suck and kiss between her brazenly spread legs. Watching them, and approving of them, because this time they were acting on his behalf, upon his order.

And even the truth of that, the impossible certainty of that, was arching Kitty up higher, the pleasure tangling with a shuddering satisfaction, and perhaps even relief. Because this was how it should have been that first time, with no whispering unease, no danger, no regrets. With only sheer rising hunger as Varinn watched them, approved of them, coolly waited his turn...

The craving whirled up at that reminder, clamping Kitty powerfully against Thrain's blatantly slurping tongue—and oh, it was at that very moment that Varinn finally rose to his feet. Inhaling slow and deep as he prowled toward the bed, toward her, while Thrain instantly drew back, shifted sideways. But his hand was still between Kitty's legs, his fingers playing with easy familiarity against her, even as Varinn reached to draw him close, and kissed him on the mouth. Surely tasting Kitty on him, oh hell, and Varinn even licked his own lips as he drew back, his hand patting Thrain's flushed, sweaty cheek.

"Thank you, *krútt*," he murmured, giving him a small, affectionate smile, before dropping his gaze downwards. To where Thrain's fingers had still been inside Kitty, but were now guiding her slick, pulsing heat even wider open. As if exposing her for Varinn, showing off his handiwork for Varinn's judgement...

"Your mate should be all ready for you now, Lord Grisk," Thrain murmured, his voice thick. "Nice and wet, and wide open for your fat prick's good Grisk ploughing, ach?"

Varinn gave a brief, approving little nod, his eyes still lingering on the sight beneath Thrain's fingers. But not moving yet, no, because perhaps that, too, was Thrain's job. And yes, Thrain's other hand was already finding Varinn's swollen length, circling around it—and then smoothly pumping it, milking it, his movements deft and swift. Making sure Varinn was fully ready for this, too, his seed now pouring out of him in that steady oozing stream.

And then—Kitty gasped—Thrain drew Varinn's heft downwards, guiding it toward her waiting, wide-open heat. Until that slick, oozing head nudged up against her, pulsing its wetness against her, parting her even wider around it...

"Good?" Thrain breathed, as Varinn slowly, slowly began to press forward. Sinking in so smoothly, so gently, spreading her wide, splitting her open. The sensation shuddering out from him, lurching together with his gold already deep inside her, whirling and sparkling up through Kitty's groin, her belly, her chest. And she was clutching at him, too, needing him deeper, more, more—

"Ach," Varinn gasped back, his eyes fluttering as he bore in deeper, deeper. "Good work, *krútt*. This is the wettest she has been for me yet."

Kitty moaned again, clamping hard against him, and in return he seemed to swell a little fuller, his breath hissing out as he pressed in deeper. And Kitty only distantly noticed Thrain still kneeling beside them, eagerly running his hand up and down Varinn's back, his arse, and—Kitty groaned again— even slipping down further, feeling Varinn steadily sink inside her...

"Ach, I can feel it," Thrain rasped. "Just how it oughta be. Your sweet mate's tight little womb stretched wide open for you, dripping wet for you, sucking you inside. Offering up what's yours, for you to make use of however you wish."

Varinn's groan was harsh and approving, his strength pressing in even faster, deeper, oh—and Thrain's greedy gaze had dropped to Kitty's face, his tongue brushing his lips. "You keep sucking up your lord, Kit," he said, a dangerous heat in his voice. "All the way. It's what he deserves, after he was kind enough to have you opened up for him, ach?"

Kitty gulped and fervently nodded, dragging in breaths, spreading her thighs even wider—and oh, how Thrain was smiling, approving, as Varinn finally sank all the way in. His groin grinding flush against hers, their sharp groans rising together, as Kitty wildly spasmed around him, as he pulsed and seeped out deep inside...

"That's it, Kit," Thrain murmured, his eyes still alight. "That's so good, isn't it? To know you've honoured your lord, and given him what's his? A soft, wet, wide-open little womb to plough, and pump full of his good Grisk seed?"

Kitty was still desperately nodding, moaning, clutching Varinn closer—but he wasn't moving, just holding himself up over her on his hands, watching her with strange, glinting eyes. While Thrain's eyes flashed with something she couldn't read, and his wet hand slipped up, gave her rigid nipple a light little pinch.

"He likes it when you ask, Kit," he said, harder than before. "Remember? So if you want your lord's good ploughing, you need to beg him for it. Show him you deserve it."

Oh. Oh. Yes. And Kitty was nodding again, dragging her eyes back up to Varinn's face, gulping down more shaky breaths. "Please, Lord Grisk," she gasped. "Please, give this to me. Please, grant me your favour. Your—good ploughing. Please."

And yes, yes, Varinn was already rocking his hips a little, his eyes still glinting powerfully on her face, and Kitty found more air, more words. "You feel so good," she gasped. "So, so good. And I just need more of you, so much more, anything you'll give me. Please."

Varinn's grunt was low, but unmistakable, as his hips slowly moved harder, faster. Drawing out a little, now, before sinking that dizzying, all-consuming strength even deeper into her. Rocking her entire body with it, but oh, it was everywhere, everything, all her lord's power here, inside her, making her his own...

"Yes," she choked. "Yes, Lord Grisk, please. Use me. Take me. Grant me your ploughing, your power, your—purpose. Your scent, and your seed, and your—son."

Varinn groaned aloud at that one, his hips plunging even faster, deeper. Fully doing this now, driving into her, taking her, like he'd never done before. His upper body sinking lower over her, his powerful warmth lying long atop her, pressing her into the furs. As his hot impaling strength kept pumping into her, hard and deep, jolting her beneath him with every furious thrust.

"Good," Thrain's voice was murmuring, from where he was hovering over Varinn now, his face buried in his neck, his breath inhaling deep. "Keep begging, Kit. Beg for your lord's good prick, his good ploughing, his good seed. His *son*."

Varinn growled above her, his eyes briefly closing, but Thrain's eyes were on fire, flashing on hers. And Kitty kept clinging, kept nodding, sucking in breath, air, anything, anything—

"Please, Lord Grisk," she begged, her voice hitching with every deep, dizzying thrust inside her. "Please, give me your seed. Your sons. As much as you want, as many as you want, all reeking of you—"

And oh, that, that drove him in harder, slamming in so deep it was almost painful. Grinding in as far as he could go, as his chest heaved against her, his eyes blazing on hers...

"Say that again," he breathed, almost too quiet to hear. "Again, *kisa*."

Kitty gulped, nodded, held his beautiful burning eyes. "Need you," she gasped. "Need your scent, and your sons. As many as you want, as many as I can give you. All reeking of you, of you, because I—"

I need you, she'd been about to say, *I love you, I love you*—

But thank the gods, she'd bitten it off just in time—right?

Or had she, because Varinn and Thrain were both groaning together now, Thrain's eyes rolling back, his hands frantically fumbling at his groin, at his *typpavír*. And somehow it was Varinn batting his hand away, grabbing the *typpavír*, dragging Thrain by the cock up toward—Kitty's face. So she had a shocking, unbroken view as Varinn's shaking hand snapped the *typpavír*'s coil off the ring, releasing it, so—

So the rod could shoot out of Thrain, its gold shiny and slick, its attached coil snapping into Varinn's hand—because behind it, there was the seed. Spraying out of that stretched-out hole in a wild, surging stream, splattering across the bed, across Varinn's hand, across Kitty's cheek. Until Varinn swiftly grasped Thrain's pouring length, and shoved it into—Kitty's mouth.

And now she was moaning, Thrain was shouting, his fluid flooding furiously into her as she rapidly, desperately swallowed—and as Varinn thrust hard and firm and deep, one more time. And suddenly she could feel him pouring out, too, pulsing powerfully inside her, as Thrain did the same to her mouth. Both of them again emptying into her at once, oh hell, and nothing had ever felt so right, so good, so perfect.

They finally seemed to slow in tandem, their bodies inside her gradually shuddering, softening. And it was Thrain who eventually began drawing away first, slipping his slackened heft backwards—but then just hovering it there, at Kitty's lips. As if wanting her to keep sliding her tongue against him, nudging into his stretched-out cleft, slipping deeper than she perhaps ever had before...

But then Varinn nudged at him, guiding him backwards, and Thrain hissed as he obliged, giving both Kitty and Varinn a clear glimpse of his wide-open slit. And Kitty didn't miss how Varinn's eyes fluttered at the sight, a low groan rumbling through his chest—and then the sound softened, deepened, as Thrain flopped down to sprawl beside them on the bed, his arm thrown over Varinn's back, his face bent into Kitty's shoulder.

"Did you mean it, Kit?" Thrain murmured, his voice slightly catching. "About granting Varinn a son of his own blood, too? After this?"

Oh. It was only thanks to Varinn's heavy body over her—inside her—that Kitty didn't twitch, or flinch, or otherwise betray her alarm. But her eyes had darted uncertainly up toward Varinn, toward where his own eyes had gone suddenly wary, the low purr catching, stilling, in his chest.

"Ach, there is—no need to speak upon this now, Thrain," Varinn cut in, his voice flat. "Katharine is surely weary, and ought to rest. And"—his eyes shifted, sharpened—"you are not in pain, ach, *kisa*? Or feeling unwell?"

Kitty shook her head, attempting a smile up toward him, but it didn't quite seem to work—and curse it, Thrain had lifted his head, frowning between her and Varinn. "Look, I mean it, Varinn," he said, low. "Because—*have* you two talked about it? Kit knows how you feel about a son, ach?"

Kitty was already nodding, attempting another wretched-feeling smile toward Varinn's blank eyes, because yes, of course she knew, of course—but of course he would still never want that... with her. Never. It would be that other woman, the one who would come after her, the one without the scents that he could truly care about...

But he wasn't speaking, and Kitty heard herself swallow, far too loud in the silence. And finally that was Thrain's sigh, hitching slow and heavy from his throat. "Och, you two," he said. "You ken I can't smell you? What's amiss with it, then?"

The question seemed to hang horribly between them, clutching at Kitty's belly, choking at her breaths—and finally, Varinn cleared his throat, and frowned back toward Thrain. "It is not fair of you—of either of us—to push Katharine upon this," he said, his voice hard. "She has scarce begun to grow our first son, and knows not how she will fare with his birth, or what is next to come. She cannot speak to *aught* beyond this."

But Thrain's frown was still just as stubborn, his eyes

surprisingly flinty on Varinn's face. "But you've still been honest with her, though, ach?" he said. "You've told her how much a son of your own blood means to you? How you've always wanted it more than anything—*anything*—else? Even more than..."

He winced and stopped there, searching Varinn's eyes, and gods curse it, Kitty just needed to fix this, to find some way to escape this. Because no, Varinn had never wanted this, not from her, not ever. And she'd sworn to help him, to help Thrain, to leave them alone after this, but what was she supposed to say, oh gods—

"So, er, yes, of course I know Varinn wants a son," Kitty cut in, far too loud, too bright. "But, um, he's right, and I'm just— not sure how this all will go, and it's all still so new, right? And"—she hauled in a breath—"if a son is so important to him, I'm sure he might want to wait a while, too. To make sure I'm the right kind of woman, you know, someone he would really want to carry on his father's scent with."

It made sense, it was all a very logical and reasonable explanation—right? So why was Thrain looking at her like that, like she'd just said something laughably unthinkable— and now he was staring at Varinn like that, too. As if he was waiting for Varinn to cut in and correct her, perhaps, but Varinn had gone silent again, his eyes uncertain, uneasy, on her face.

"The right kind of woman?" Thrain finally echoed, his voice unnaturally shrill. "You're not going to just lie there and let her spout this rubbish, ach, Varinn? What more do you ken he could wish for, Kit? What the hell have you done that isn't *exactly* what he's always wanted?"

Kitty blinked at Thrain, her thoughts swaying, swerving, tangling together—and he flapped his hand toward her, his eyes flaring with stark disbelief. "You do—*this*, with us," he said. "With both of us. You welcome Varinn's command, and my touch, and you haven't once fussed or fainted over any of it, ach? You've watched him plough me again and again, you've sucked him with me, played with his *rassjas* with me, milked me into his damned *basin*. Gods, Kit"—he barked a strange laugh—"you conspired with him to buy me a *typpavír*! You ken I should have ever even *dreamt* that a human would even think of giving such a gift? Let alone wanting to see an orc *wear* one?"

Kitty's throat felt oddly dry, her eyes held to Thrain's face— and he laughed again, shook his head. "And even without all that," he continued, "you're doing all this work in the shop. You've made friends of *Ymir*. You already remember more Grisk names than I do. You dress like the most shameless Grisk mate imaginable. And you keep putting up with my rubbish, and helping me, and pushing Varinn to help me, and supporting him as he helps me, and—"

He broke off there, grimacing, but his eyes were still holding hers, glimmering with an unnerving brightness. "You're all we've ever wanted in a woman, Kit," he said, a little choked. "Both of us."

Oh. Oh. He couldn't mean it, he couldn't possibly mean it, and Varinn surely, surely didn't mean it—but Kitty's frantic glance toward Varinn's face found it looking alarmingly inscrutable. As if perhaps he didn't at all approve of Thrain saying these things, meaning these things. Because Thrain was his, only his, and he was only doing this for Thrain, and that was all. *I will do aught within my power…*

And Kitty had to fight it, to break it, and what could she say, what could she do. "But," she managed, and suddenly her heart was plummeting, the cold tightness clawing at her chest. "But you—you don't know me, not really," she whispered. "Either of you. You don't know how I've—how I've—"

She had to stop there, fight to breathe, fight to make herself keep going, going. Had to make Thrain believe it. Varinn was only doing this for Thrain, she was supposed to be helping him, making it easy for him to cut her out forever, and find— and find—

"And look, I still don't really—know you," she made herself say, through her constricted throat. "Either of you. I don't know—what happened, to either of your families. I don't know why Varinn's parents aren't here to wear their *thyrjas*, or why Vrangr had to give everything to care for his kin. And I don't know what happened to Thrain's great-uncle, or why Thrain stopped apprenticing as a smith. Or why he and Thrak see things so differently, or why he's been doing a job he doesn't even seem to *like*, all this time! And most of all"—she hauled in more air—"I don't even know how you two first got together, or why, or why you didn't just go and seek out a mate together *years* ago. Because you're both just so lovely, and so very kind, and of course any woman would love to have both of you in her life, and—"

And she was losing her way, losing the truth of it, and she desperately grasped backwards, gulped down more thin, unsteady breaths. While both Varinn and Thrain just kept staring at her, Thrain with that same shimmering disbelief in his eyes, Varinn's expression still entirely blank.

"Och, Kit," Thrain finally said, his voice hoarse. "You could have just—asked. We weren't trying to—"

But Kitty's stomach was plummeting again, and she made a sound like a laugh, not really a laugh at all. "But I did try to ask," she countered, her voice too thin, too shrill. "And you dismissed it, multiple times, and"—oh gods, she was losing it again—"and that's fine. Perfectly fine! Because I know my place, I know I haven't told you everything either, I haven't told you how I—"

The words choked in her throat, she couldn't say them, she couldn't—at least, until she felt Varinn shifting over her, inside her. And oh, gods, he'd been inside her, all this time, and now he wasn't, he wasn't. And she was making a mess of his furs, and making a mess of this, but he wanted her to make a mess of this, he was only doing this for Thrain—

"What have you not told us, Katharine," Varinn said, his voice low, menacing. "Speak this. Now. To Thrain's eyes."

And what was that look on his face, was it anger, judgement, contempt—but Kitty was nodding, pained and desperate, and obeying. Holding Thrain's strange, shimmering gaze as she fought to breathe, to say it aloud, where it could never be taken back...

"I'm not the kind of woman you want to keep," she whispered. "Because I'm a woman who's always been—for sale."

42

For a moment, there was only silence. Silence, as Thrain's eyes kept holding, glimmering, on hers, as she could feel the too-close intensity of Varinn's eyes, too. Surely judging her, surely helping her ruin this, just as he wanted...

"My mother—she ran a house, in the city," Kitty's voice continued, faster now. "It was—high-class. For—respectable gentlemen. Who wanted—social companions, as well as bedmates. So I learned"—she jerked a painful shrug—"to be a good companion. To dress however the clients liked, to impress their friends and families, to help them with their careers, to do whatever they pleased in bed. To not be—shocked by what they wanted from me, and even"—she felt her face burning—"to enjoy it, as much as I could."

Thrain was still staring at her like that, holding her caught, trapped, in his gaze, and Kitty gasped for more air, more truth. "But it wasn't—easy work," she managed. "At least, not for me, not the way my mother expected from me. The work never stopped, and I got attached to my clients too easily, and some of them were married, or many years older, and some could be— quite cruel. Dangerous. And when I couldn't bear it any longer,

I—I latched onto the most promising client I could find, and moved with him across the realm to Dusbury, so I could become his full-time mistress, instead. That was—Charles, and he wasn't my partner, or my boyfriend, or my husband. He was"—she cringed, made herself say it—"my employer."

And was that it, please let that be it, but the shame was still clawing at her, the fear, the misery. "So no, I hadn't seen a—*typpavír*, before," she whispered. "But I've done—so many other things. I'm—good at pleasing men. Being fun and eager in bed, and not asking too many questions. Giving them whatever they want from me."

Her voice had gone very small, and gods, she wanted to look away, why couldn't she look away. But Thrain wasn't looking away either, and he was biting his lip, shaking his head. Choking out a sound that could have been a laugh, harsh and disbelieving.

"Och, Kit," he said, his voice thick. "There's no need to scent of shame over any of this, and I ken we—we already knew most of it, ach?"

Wait. Wait, what did he mean, they already—*knew it*? And Thrain was grimacing again, shaking his head, and finally glancing away, with something almost like guilt in his eyes. "You're sharing Varinn's bed, Kit, and bearing his seed," he said. "You ken he wouldn't find all this on your scent, more and more with every day that passes, and every day his own scent becomes clearer upon you? And whatever he couldn't learn from scent alone"—he jerked a shrug—"I ken Eyarl and his scouts have learnt for him instead, ach?"

Oh. He was truly saying—Varinn had been—investigating her? Learning about her, and looking into her past? And why hadn't he ever said anything, why hadn't he told her? Why hadn't he just—asked?

But Varinn's eyes were still so damned inscrutable, his body so stiff and unmoving beside her, and she twitched at the feel of Thrain's hand on her arm, snapping her gaze back toward him. "We just thought—you didn't wish to speak of it, ach?" he continued, quieter now. "For we can both scent your anger and pain embedded in your mother's scent upon you, and how—how the scents of many of these men are so entangled with your fear, and are far older upon you than they ought to be. You ought never have been treated so cruelly, ach?"

Kitty's throat spasmed, her eyes blinking hard, because he couldn't be saying this, he couldn't actually think this—but yes, good gods, that was sympathy in his eyes, and maybe even a glint of anger, too. "You're so sweet, Kit," he murmured. "So good, and generous, and true. You deserve kindness, and care, and all else we can grant you. And I ken you've been stuck dealing with far too much of my rubbish, but that doesn't mean—"

He paused there, something shifting in his eyes, as his breath drew in, slow. "But that doesn't mean," he said, very carefully now, "we *expect* that sweetness from you, ach? You ken you don't need to try to please us? To... give us what you think we want from you?"

Kitty froze in place, her eyes again trapped on his, as a sharp, desperate ache streaked through her chest. *But I need to,* she wanted to say, the words clamouring up, so close. *I promised Varinn. I made a vow. I have a debt to repay. I need to please him, to give you your son, and then get out of your life forever.*

But somehow she kept the words inside, kept the vow, clinging to it with all her strength. "I know you don't expect it," she gulped, and she was talking to Thrain now, only Thrain, but maybe he wouldn't read it that way, maybe. "And I've truly wanted to do—all of this, with you. Both of you. But I just—"

She had to stop there again, dragging in deep breaths, because all the words were a betrayal of Varinn, of their vow. *I need to please him. I want to make him happy. I want him to like me, and hunger for me, and care for me. I want to have his son. I want to stay.*

Thrain was still waiting, still studying her, with something far too much like suspicion sparking in his eyes, and Kitty gulped down more air, searched for something, something. "But I do want to please you both, very much," she said, in a rush. "And I think—maybe because of that—I think Varinn won't ever be able to—trust me. And it would be better, for him, for me, for you, if we—if we consider—parting ways, after all this. So he can find"—the ache plummeted again— "someone else. Someone who doesn't have—my past, who— hasn't betrayed him, or tainted any—any scents. Who could be a good—a good Grisk, to carry on his father's—"

But Thrain's eyes had flashed with something like incredulity, or maybe even fury, as they finally snapped away from her, toward—Varinn. Toward where Varinn was looking deathly pale, suddenly, his face gone almost haggard, his eyes so blank and empty on hers. And without warning, he'd lurched away, out of bed entirely, and Kitty almost whimpered at the loss of him, no, no, no—

"I need—a moment," he rasped, his shoulders heaving. "Need to be—alone, for a spell. Forgive me. I—"

But he didn't finish. Didn't look back. Only snatched up his kilt from the floor, and rushed from the room, without a single look back.

43

Kitty didn't know how long she stared after Varinn, or when the wetness began to escape her eyes, streaking down her cheeks. She'd done what he'd wanted. She'd kept her vow. Right? So why had he left, what else could she have done...

And finally, from somewhere behind her, there was a low, aggravated groan—and suddenly Thrain was leaping over her, out of bed, too. Striding toward the washbasin, and snatching up a wet cloth, before hurling the *rassja* and the *typpavír* into the basin with a furious-sounding splash.

"That overbearing, self-immolating fool prick *tyrant*," he hissed, as he strode back toward her, his eyes still glinting with a sharp, cold anger. "He told you to say that, didn't he? Told you he didn't want you having his son, for some absolute rubbish reason?"

Kitty didn't speak, still couldn't, and Thrain barked a harsh laugh as he sank down beside her on the bed, and began wiping her up with a gentleness that didn't at all match the look in his eyes. "Because it's rubbish, Kit," he snapped. "It's his usual suffering, save-the-world martyr *rubbish*. He wants you. He sure as hell wants a son with you. He'd be as happy as an orcling rolling in fresh meat if you gave him a half-dozen sons, all of them reeking of you both. Ach?"

Kitty couldn't stop staring, shaking her head, and Thrain laughed again as his careful fingers found her *rassja*, and slowly slipped it out, too. "I can scent him," he countered, as he tossed the *rassja* over into the washbasin, and gently resumed wiping. "I *know* him, Kit. He's never scented like this before. He dotes on you, and he damn well loves doing it, and you better believe he sees you as his, and *only* his. He's drenched you in his scent, he's spent all his savings to please you, he's given you all these jewels. And ach, he pretends to be so high and mighty and enlightened, but if you ever tried to leave him, or shunt him off onto someone else, he'd absolutely chase you across the realm, and drag you back here again!"

His voice was clipped, carrying, utterly certain, and Kitty was still shaking her head, betraying it, betraying Varinn, oh gods. "But I'm still not," she choked, "what he really wants, long-term. He wants..."

"Rubbish," Thrain cut in, sharper than before. "Sorry, Kit, but it's rubbish. It's him not wanting to put pressure on you, or to make you feel like he expects something from you—maybe because of all those rubbish men you were stuck with before, ach? But he still wants you. He *does*."

The certainty in his voice was almost dizzying, swirling wildly through Kitty's tilting thoughts. "But—all the scents," she whispered. "The other men. He—doesn't like them. He— he *said*."

And gods, she wasn't supposed to be betraying that, either—but Thrain only scoffed again, and shook his head. "Already told you, it doesn't matter," he said flatly. "You know how he gets off on the control, ach? And there's only one thing better than having a sweet mate scent-bound to you, and that's knowing, with every breath, that you've beaten out a hundred men to gain her, and drowned out all their weak scents beneath your own. That's power, Kit, and he gets hard just fucking smelling it. I *know*."

Oh. Kitty's throat spasmed, her eyes blinking unseeing toward where Thrain was tossing the cloth back into the washbasin, too, and reaching to snap some clothes off the shelf. "So don't you worry," he said, his voice softening, as he strode toward her again, and gently swung a kilt around her waist, before fastening one of her little capes over her shoulders. "We'll get this sorted out, ach?"

Kitty kept gazing blankly toward him, still not quite digesting all this—at least, until he snatched up the lamp, and then grasped her hand, and drew her out of bed. Leading her toward the door, toward—

"Where—are we going?" she asked, too shrill. "We're not—*following* Varinn? He said he wanted to be—"

"More rubbish," Thrain replied, as he led her through the quiet sitting-room, and out into the dim corridor. "He's gone down to brood in that godsforsaken crypt again, and he can't be left alone in that stinking hellhole. It's a gods-damned death-trap waiting to *gobble* him, is what it is."

Oh. Kitty couldn't help a choked, high-pitched little laugh, leaning closer into Thrain's solid, certain warmth. Not missing his brief, approving smile back toward her, though it didn't quite reach his eyes. "That's the spirit, Kit," he said. "We'll knock some sense into him, and drag him out before the skeletons can get to him."

Kitty chuckled again, and somehow the dread and the misery had seemed to loosen, the ache not quite as sharp in her chest. "Thank you, Thrain," she said, with a shaky exhale. "You're always just—so lovely."

He huffed a little laugh too, but it was almost sad, and he shook his head. "Afraid not, Kit," he said, lower, as he settled his long arm around her shoulder, and drew her closer into his side. "Didn't realize all this had been festering, ach? Should've told you about—before. And I still forget, sometimes"—he huffed a heavy sigh—"how you can't scent Varinn. Can't scent how much he adores you. What it does to him when you smile at him, and oblige him so sweetly, and beg for him, like you do. How damned good it feels for him, when he's buried inside you, pouring out his seed into you."

Kitty's breath hitched at even the thought of it, enough to earn her another wry smile from Thrain—but maybe that was part of it all, too, tangling up in her thoughts. "But I still don't want—to come between you two, either," she replied, searching his eyes. "I don't want to monopolize Varinn's attention, or—his pleasure, when you've been in his life for so much longer. When *you're* the one who should be his mate."

Her voice had dropped again, the grimace twisting on her mouth, but Thrain only shrugged, and let out a slow exhale. "But see, Kit," he said, "it's also been better between the two of us since you came along, ach? Him giving me his jewels, his full scent, his rewards—he *never* did that before you. And look, if it helps"—he shrugged again, his voice dropping—"I know he's still mine, too. I know how he scents when I tease him, or make him laugh, or kneel for him, or suck him. I know every time he's looking at my arse, and thinking about fucking it wide open. I *know* how he scented today, when he watched me put on that damned *typpavír*."

Oh. Kitty's smile back was curious, and not just a little relieved, and Thrain's arm gave her shoulder a gentle, companionable shake. "This just—gives him more, ach?" he added, husky. "More holes to fuck, more pleasure to find, more worshippers to own and command and lord over. He loves that, Kit, gets off on it like naught else, and in truth"—his voice lowered again—"I love giving it to him. Love how he scents, when he's all swelled up on power, and having his wicked way with us, however he damned well pleases. Can't say a real god would scent any better."

Kitty felt herself nodding, the tightness in her chest loosening a little more as she flashed him another relieved, grateful smile. And then glanced around them, toward where the corridor had become darker and narrower, the only light now flickering from the lamp in Thrain's hand. And there were no other orcs here, either, at least until—Kitty nearly tripped, clutching at Thrain's arm—a ghostly white wraith loomed out of the darkness up ahead, its eyes sunken black hollows in its skeletal face.

"Och, it's only Filak," Thrain said, patting Kitty's shoulder, and Kitty sagged back against him, warily eyeing Filak as he approached. He looked truly eerie in the lamplight, his pale skin almost luminous, the black script across his skull standing out stark and vivid against it. And he didn't spare them a single look as he strode past, though he did wrinkle his nose in palpable distaste.

"Just ignore him," Thrain said, guiding her around a corner, and then up toward what appeared to be a flat stone wall. "Until he brings you more of those emeralds, at least."

Kitty half-smiled back at that, and watched as Thrain purposefully pressed at seemingly random places on the stone wall—and then it creaked open, the sound loud and scraping in the too-close corridor. And behind it, Kitty could see that the corridor kept going, even darker and narrower than before.

"This way," Thrain said, as he clasped her hand again, and led her through the huge stone door. Which was already closing again behind them, shutting with a hard, decisive-sounding crunch. "Pretty grim, ach?"

He was smiling again in the flickering lamplight, but Kitty could see the unease in his eyes, now, too, the stiffness in his shoulders. The way he winced as he inhaled, and led her further down the ever-darkening corridor.

And as they walked, deeper and deeper, Kitty felt her own unease creeping higher again, circling against her chest. Varinn was down here. Varinn had come here, to get away from them, from *her*—and he surely still felt angry, hurt, betrayed. And no matter what Thrain said, no matter how many reassuring claims he made, Varinn himself hadn't said any of it, had he? No. Varinn had told her his priority was Thrain. He'd told her he only wanted her obedience. He wanted her to repay her debt. To keep the vow she'd made.

But she kept walking, kept taking shaky breaths of the musty air, as Thrain led her through another massive stone door, and then another. And finally—Kitty hesitated, and blinked around at it—into a large, round, silent stone antechamber, with a high arched ceiling, and two life-sized stone figures standing at the centre of the room.

"Over here," Thrain said, his voice thin now, as he led her across the room, past what appeared to be multiple stone urns and coffins. Heading straight toward one of several stone doors carved into the wall, which turned out to lead to another dark, narrow passageway. One that was lined on both sides with wide flat bunks, carved into the stone.

And carefully placed inside the bunks, there were... bodies. Bodies wrapped up tightly with thick strips of fabric and furs, but the forms were still far too distinct, far too real. And Kitty's unease kept growing as she blinked around at them, as Thrain drew her deeper and deeper. Around a sharp corner, into a side passageway, down a twisty winding tunnel...

And then—Kitty's breath choked—up ahead. A figure. A living, breathing, upright figure, standing in the middle of the narrow passageway, his hands gripping the stone bunk, his head bowed low. Varinn.

And gods, even the sight of his familiar bulky form was a stunning, staggering relief, despite the uncertainty still pounding in Kitty's chest. Varinn was here. Alive. Safe. And she could hear his exhale as he dropped his hands from the bunk, and turned around to face them.

But he wasn't speaking, just looking at them with a strange bleakness in his shadowy eyes. And to Kitty's vague surprise, Thrain drew her straight down the tunnel toward Varinn, and then—*into* him. Into his warm, safe arms, settling around them both with something that almost felt like... eagerness. Gratefulness.

"Och, Varinn, you gotta quit coming down here like this," Thrain said, muffled, into Varinn's shoulder. "It's unhealthy. Unhygienic. Gonna set death-rot growing in your lungs, gods damn it."

There was an odd sound from Varinn's throat—maybe a laugh—and then the feeling of him drawing them both a little closer. His hand spreading wide on Kitty's back, and even rubbing up and down, almost as if—as if he didn't mind her being here. As if—he even *wanted* her here.

"Ach, I ken," he replied, hoarse, with a heavy sigh. "Just wished to scent—"

He didn't finish, but when Kitty angled a look up, his eyes had glanced toward the bunk before them. The bunk that only held one large, still, silent figure, wrapped tightly in cloth and fur.

"His father's father," Thrain's voice supplied, very low. "Vitharr. His closest blood kin he can yet scent."

Oh. There was something important in that, surely, and Varinn nodded, his breath inhaling again, his hand spasming against Kitty's back. While Thrain cleared his throat, and then nudged at Varinn's belly, enough to make him twitch.

"And you ken, Varinn, that Vitharr would *not* approve of your rubbish," Thrain said, in far more his usual tone of voice. "He wouldn't walk away from his mate like that, let alone leaving her scenting of so much pain and sadness. I ken you're upset too, but"—his voice hardened—"you need to fix this. *Now.*"

Kitty flinched, stiffening, because that hadn't been at all what she'd meant, or why she'd come down here. And should she try to make more excuses, to tell them everything was fine, perfectly fine, and she was already drawing away, taking a breath—

When Varinn—nodded. Nodded, meeting her eyes in the

flickering lamplight, and then—he reached to clasp her hands. Holding them gently in both of his, holding her here in place before him, trapped, exposed.

Kitty's unease was flailing up again, skittering into something almost like panic—and Varinn winced, his hands both clenching a little tighter against hers, as his oddly intent eyes held to her face.

"Ach, Katharine," he said, a little formally. "I—I have not always been truthful with you, about—our future. In my anger, when this first began between us, I led you to believe"—his eyes glanced, very briefly, toward Thrain—"that I was not—fully sure of this. Of you."

But—wait. Wait. Was he talking about—the vow? About their agreement? Or about the debt? Or was it just about Thrain, surely it was about Thrain, he had to be doing this for Thrain... right? *I shall do all within my power...*

"But," Varinn continued, his shoulders squaring, and oh, gods, he looked so earnest, so regretful. "But now that we have better learnt one another, I see I was—wrong, to have done this. For Thrain was right, Katharine, once again, and"—his breath exhaled, shaky—"you are just what I have wished for in a mate. In a mother for my sons. You have welcomed my clan, my home, my touch, and my care. And most of all, you have welcomed Thrain, also, and helped him, and helped me. You have helped—*us*."

Oh. He was glancing toward Thrain again, holding his eyes, as though he meant this, but he couldn't—mean this? But Thrain's own eyes were softening, his shoulders relaxing, his hand slipping up to stroke against Varinn's back. Making Varinn's shoulders soften, too, as he glanced back to Kitty again.

"I could never have hoped for more than this, *kisa*," he continued, husky. "In you, the gods have blessed me, and answered all my prayers. So I wish you to know"—his throat convulsed—"how deeply I care for you. How deeply I long to be your mate, and your lord, and—your friend."

Kitty's face was swarming with heat, her heart hammering, her eyes still caught on his impossibly earnest face. Because he couldn't be saying this, he couldn't truly believe this, he couldn't mean it... could he? It was still the vow, still the debt, still Thrain... right?

"But," Varinn continued, his head tilting, and yes, this was the catch, it had to be. "I ken you have borne much, from us. From me. And I ken"—his mouth tightened—"you have long sought to please others, rather than yourself. And I have not—helped this, in asking you, *expecting* you, to please me, as I have. Just as I have also done"—his eyes were pained as he glanced sideways—"with Thrain."

Kitty's heart was thudding even faster, her hands surely sweaty in his, but Varinn was again looking at her like that, with that strange, startling sincerity in his eyes. "So it should please me even more," he said, very quiet, "if you take your time upon this, *kisa*. If you keep learning more of us, and think deeply upon this—and then speak your truth to me. Not the truth you ken I might wish to hear, but"—his mouth twisted into a sad little smile—"your own thoughts. Your own truth."

Her own truth. No, no, no, he didn't mean that, he couldn't—but he was nodding, and even raising one of her hands to his mouth, so he could... kiss it. His lips warm and soft against her skin, his tongue's touch brief and gentle, and this couldn't be happening, it wasn't, was it?

"And whatever this truth is," he continued, lowering her hand again, his eyes now flinty on hers, "I will honour this. We will honour this. Whether you wish to stay, or you wish to mate only one of us, or both. Whether you wish to bear one son, or more. Whether you wish to finish learning your trade, and"—his mouth slightly spasmed—"and then leave us, and mayhap run your own shop, whilst—"

But oh, gods, he couldn't, Kitty couldn't bear to even hear him say it, and she was whipping her head back and forth, and squeezing his hands as tightly as she could. "I don't want to leave," she said, in a rush. "Please. I want to stay with our son, and I want him to know you both, and love you both. I should never have even *suggested*—"

She broke off there, still shaking her head, her eyes darting chagrined toward Thrain. But to her distant astonishment, he didn't look surprised, or upset, or even unnerved that she might have once suggested such a thing. If anything, he was looking... satisfied. Relieved. His eyes glinting with genuine warmth on hers, as he gave a curt, approving little nod.

And before her, Varinn was looking distinctly relieved, too, the slow smile pulling at his mouth. "I am most glad to hear this, *kisa*," he murmured. "But I yet wish you to think upon it, ach? This, and all the rest. And whatever you choose, we shall do all within our power to honour this."

All within our power. The words slicing through the chaos swarming Kitty's thoughts, flashing shock through her breath, her eyes—but Varinn's eyes were still so steady, so serious, on hers. "Though mayhap you ought to know," he said, quieter, "that I shall not leave my home, or my kin. And most of all"— his eyes darted again toward Thrain—"I shall not leave Thrain. For amidst all this, I have learnt more than ever"—he twitched a wry little smile—"how I cannot bear to live without him."

And oh, the look in Thrain's eyes, blinking with genuine disbelief—and then lighting up with pure, childlike glee. His mouth flashing into a broad, truly stunning grin, as he leaned forward, and gently nipped at Varinn's neck. "Took you long enough," he murmured. "You won't regret it, ach?"

Varinn's eyes had softened on Thrain, his head turning so he could inhale, slow and deep, against his messy head. "Ach, I ken," he murmured back. "I love you, *krútt*."

Oh. Kitty could hear Thrain's hard swallow, the sharp, betraying sniff of his nose. The way he buried his face deeper into Varinn's neck, his shoulders slightly shuddering, as if he couldn't quite bear to look up, not yet.

"Love you too, Varinn," he whispered. "And—will you please—tell Kit? All the rubbish from—before?"

And now it was Varinn's shoulders shuddering, as he took a long, resigned-sounding breath—but then he nodded. Swallowed. Met Kitty's eyes.

"Ach," he said. "I shall."

44

Varinn would tell her.

Kitty hadn't missed the grimness in his voice, or even the reluctance—and even as she opened her mouth to try to dismiss it, wave it away until later, he cleared his throat, and drew in a breath.

"You ken how orcs and humans were at war, for so long," he began, his voice very smooth, very steady. "On our side, this war was led by the Ash-Kai clan, and their cruel captain Kaugir. But we were not all in agreement upon this war, and the Grisk stood against it mayhap most of all. For we did not wish to fight our mates' kin, ach? We did not wish to risk losing our mates, and our sons, and the lines of our blood, our houses. Our *life*."

Kitty swallowed, nodded, and Varinn drew in another slow breath. "Our clan was defended by strong leaders, back then," his voice continued, still unnaturally steady. "Foremost amongst these were two Aetha Grisk—Nattfarr's father Rakfarr, and his blood-brother Thakfarr, Thrain and Thrak's father. Both brothers bore the great gift of truth-seeking, which only runs within the Aetha. You remember Nattfarr's great magic in this, ach?"

Kitty nodded again, recalling far too clearly how disconcerting it had felt, spilling out all her secrets at Nattfarr's most innocuous questions—and Varinn nodded too, his hand absently stroking against Thrain's messy head, still buried into his shoulder. "Rakfarr's skill was just as strong as Nattfarr's," he said, "and by wielding it against the Ash-Kai, he was able to earn the fear of even the cruel Kaugir—and thus he gained the Grisk some measure of distance and safety from the war. Whilst Thakfarr"—his eyes glanced briefly toward Thrain— "most oft wielded his gift... in other ways. Oft in battle, or in games of chance, or toward... humans. Women most of all."

Oh. The thought of that spasmed in Kitty's throat—was Varinn implying that Thrain's father had used his magic... to sway women into his *bed*? But yes, the look of distaste on Varinn's mouth suggested just as much, especially together with Thrain's harsh, muffled laugh into Varinn's shoulder.

"Varinn doesn't like speaking ill of the dead," he cut in, without looking up, "so what he's trying to say is, my father was rubbish. A handsome, smooth-talking rabble-rouser who fucked his way across the realm, leaving pregnant women in his wake. Used his truth-seeking, you ken, to pry out exactly what his conquests wanted from him—until he got bored of them, and left. My poor mother fell for his song and dance twice, so thus, you get Thrak, and then me, and then she never spoke to any of us again. And"—he huffed another bitter laugh—"your father *hated* mine, ach, Varinn?"

Varinn grimaced, but didn't deny it, and glanced back toward Kitty again. "My father—Vrangr—was oft the one to clean up Thakfarr's messes," he said. "To sniff out his forgotten women, and his sons, and grant them the clan's care and safety. My own mother, Karinn, was"—his breath hitched as he exhaled—"one of these women. She near met death birthing Thakfarr's son, and the son died, also—but my father cared for her, and nursed her back to health again. And then—"

He twitched a rueful little wave down toward himself, while

Thrain gave another choked-sounding laugh into his neck. "Best thing my father ever did, I ken," he said thickly. "And don't get the wrong idea, Kit, because Varinn's parents adored each other. Adored him, too."

There was an unmistakable longing in his voice, and Varinn kept stroking his hair, his claws carding deep. "I was— very blessed," he said, quiet. "But even so, it was not... easy for my father, to always be at such odds with one of the orcs keeping our clan safe. Most of all as the war kept deepening, and Rakfarr and Thakfarr began to speak of moving the Grisk away from the mountain. Away from the captain, who had only become crueller with time, and longed to wield our clan's numbers in his war."

Kitty was searching Varinn's eyes, following the bleakness in them, the frustration. "My father fought with all his strength against this move," he continued, "for he had oft seen—and scented—the risks faced by orcs and their women away from the mountain. He knew how men could not tell one clan from another. He also could scent Kaugir's growing hatred toward the Grisk, and"—he drew in a breath—"he did not think Kaugir would leave such a slight unpunished. Instead, my father wished to stage a rebellion, and defeat Kaugir from within. Failing that, if a move was truly what the clan thought best, my father wished to ally with the Ka-esh to build a new home far from here, deep beneath the northern mountains. Or mayhap even to leave the realm altogether, and sail across the sea. But none of these were good choices, and the clan was bitterly torn upon this."

His voice had gone quiet, his shoulders rising and falling, and Kitty felt herself easing a little closer into his other side, slipping her hand tentatively against his back. "And were you and Thrain... friendly, in the midst of all this?" she asked carefully. "Or did you hate each other, too?"

Varinn angled a brief glance toward Thrain, who barked another laugh into his shoulder. "You know Varinn's too good to hate anyone, Kit," he replied, hoarse. "Most of all a wild little motherless Aetha, whose father usually forgot he existed. Thrak was always my father's favourite, ach? Even though I had the... the..."

His voice trailed off, his face grimacing into Varinn's shoulder, and Varinn grimaced too, his hand tugging a little at Thrain's hair. "You have not told her of it, *krútt*?" he asked, as he cast a sharp, searching glance toward Kitty. "Ach, I am sorry, Katharine. I ought to have thought to—"

"No, no, you shouldn't," Thrain broke in, and then he sighed, heavy, and drew up from Varinn's shoulder. His eyes unmistakably red, his face shiny and bright. "I should have told her, and I didn't do that, either."

Kitty's breath was caught in her throat—he hadn't told her what?—and Thrain squeezed his eyes shut, ran both hands through his messy hair. "I have some of—the gift, also," he said, his voice rapid and thick. "Not as strong as Nattfarr, and I've never trained it, not since I was small. Never wanted to use it, ach? Never wanted to deal with being Speaker, or risk becoming like—my father. And it draws out truth from both sides, you ken, not just the other person—and I don't want to spout all my rubbish for anyone to hear, ach? But I ken I do still use it, now and then. Not on purpose, but just..."

He grimaced again, and suddenly Kitty's thoughts were tripping backwards, back to all those brief, strange moments when Thrain had held her eyes, and... asked. *You're sure, woman. What's amiss. You all right, Kit? When Varinn spoke this vow to you... what did he say?*

And gods, even just before this, back in their bed. When Varinn had told her, *Speak this. Now. To Thrain's eyes.*

Because he'd known. They'd known. They'd both known, and they both hadn't told her. Again.

"I'm sorry, Kit," Thrain's voice continued, too quickly. "I just—I hate speaking of it, hate thinking of him, ach? If I could get rid of it, I would, in a gods-damned instant. It's useless, and *rubbish*, when you can't even believe the pretty lies people tell you to keep the peace, and—"

Kitty's heart skipped in her chest, something distantly shouting at the back of her thoughts—but Varinn's hand was stroking up and down her back now, swift and reassuring, and perhaps doing the same to Thrain, too. "Hush, *krútt*," he said. "You bear a great and rare gift, one that has long been revered in our clan. But"—his voice lowered, his eyes darting toward Kitty—"it is well within Katharine's right to be angry with us over this, also. Most of all if she did not know our son may carry this gift, also."

Thrain's mouth was twisting, and he gave a jerky nod, his eyes still bright and apologetic on Kitty's face. While Kitty's tingly-feeling hand dropped to her belly, because Thrain really meant—their son might have magic? *Magic?*

They were both still looking at her, awaiting some kind of response from her, and Kitty fought through the mess in her thoughts for something, anything. "So what happened next?" she made herself say. "Did your clan end up moving away from the mountain, after all?"

Thrain's throat convulsed, his eyes closing, and it was Varinn who nodded, his jaw tight. "Ach, we left," he said. "Against all my father's efforts and arguments and pleading. We moved to a camp called Meinolf, mayhap a day's journey from here. Almost all above ground. Far too large to be fully hidden."

Oh. There was a dark, quiet foreboding in his voice, his shoulders again rising as he drew in breath. "But my father also went, despite this," Varinn continued. "He was one of the clan's best scenters, so he sought to sniff out danger as best he could, and keep our kin safe. He also brought in Ka-esh to begin digging out beneath the camp, to offer us even more safety. But it was not easy, and the strife within the clan only grew, until..."

His voice had faded, his eyes now fixed blankly on the shroud of his grandfather, and now it was Thrain heaving in a breath, letting it out. "Until the attack," he said, without inflection. "By a whole army of men. In a huge rainstorm, which hid the scents until it was too late. Found out much later"—he barked a hoarse laugh—"it was Kaugir behind it. Gave the humans goods with Rakfarr and Nattfarr's scents, so they could use dogs to track them. And Kaugir even told the bastards how to hide their own scents, too. To use the rain."

Oh. Oh, gods. A cold, vicious shudder was ripping up Kitty's spine, her body frozen against Varinn's, her eyes aghast on Thrain. Watching him laugh again, the sight almost alarming on his pale, bitter face.

"It was a bloodbath," he continued. "Everyone they could get to. Even elderly, women, orclings. My great-uncle. I had"—his voice cracked—"two little half-brothers. The only reason any of us survived was—"

His breaths were rattling, now, and he again buried his face in Varinn's neck, dragged down a shaky inhale. And Varinn was breathing in his scent, too, his eyes shut, his hand stroking Thrain's back. "My father," he said, quiet. "As soon as he scented the men, he—came for us. The sons. Any of us he could find. Threw us all underground, into the half-finished tunnels, and—collapsed the entrances, as best as he could."

The ice was crackling in Kitty's chest, cold and stark and horrifying, and Thrain laughed again, the sound almost sickening in the air. "Singlehandedly saved dozens of us," he choked. "The whole next generation of Grisk. He was truly a god's son too, Varinn."

Varinn's throat audibly spasmed, but he nodded, his too-bright eyes again on his grandfather's shroud. "My father gave us life," he said, very quiet. "Life, out of so much death. Even his enemy's sons."

Thrain nodded, fervent, into Varinn's neck, and then laughed again, a little less sharp this time. "And then—*you*, Varinn," he said, with a hiccough. "I broke my leg when it happened—ended up tumbling down into the deepest tunnel.

Couldn't walk, couldn't climb out, could barely even move. Until *you* found me. Sniffed me out down there."

Varinn was still stroking Thrain's back, still blinking at his grandfather's shroud, and Thrain drew away a little to look at Kitty. "Everyone else ran back to the mountain, as soon as the battle was over," he continued thickly. "Even Thrak. Not that I blame them, our parents were all dead, and it was absolute hell. But Varinn still—stayed with me. Tended me. Fed me. Helped me sleep and drink and piss, even scented gas and aired it out, when otherwise it would've killed me. Until"—he shuddered out another breath—"I could finally walk again. Took an entire fortnight, ach, Varinn? And then another week to make it back to the mountain. It's a fucking *miracle* we weren't killed."

The horrified disbelief was again roiling up in Kitty's chest—they'd been trapped underground together, for weeks? Alone? Amidst deadly gas, amidst a terrifying battle, amidst the sudden, harrowing deaths of all their parents, all their kin?

There was truly no possible response to this, no conceivable answer, except to keep staring at them, while the shock kept sinking deeper, colder. No wonder they hadn't wanted to speak of it. No wonder Thrain struggled with his work, and had struggled with rescuing that young orc, with the tunnel and the gas. And maybe... maybe it was no wonder Thrain had turned to the drink, too. No wonder he was so devoted to Varinn. Who had found him, stayed with him, saved him—and then, all these years later, he'd turned around and... saved her. Their son. Just as... just as his own father had.

"And I ken it wasn't easy on you, Varinn," Thrain continued, with a strange little gulp. "You adored your parents, and you—you smelled them dying. Smelled their scents fading. Smelled all that death, enough to make you sick, ach? But you didn't leave me. Not even to go bury them, or burn them, or collect their clothes to scent from, or—"

His eyes were glimmering on Varinn's face, true grief

pulling at his mouth. But Varinn gave a small shake of his head, and drew Thrain a little closer. "They were gone," he said, very quiet. "Keeping you alive was more important, and they both would have been in full accord upon this. And"—his eyes dropped, his hand gently skimming against Thrain's *thyrja*—"they had already hidden away our jewels, ach? They... they knew."

Oh. Oh, gods, and now Varinn had saved Thrain and Kitty both, saved their son—and even in the face of their betrayal, he'd given them his mother and father's jewels. These stunning, impossible gifts that had clearly meant so much to him, that spoke so strongly of the parents he'd loved so much. And why had he done this, why had he done any of this, how could one orc be so kind, so generous, so beautifully, painfully—*good*.

And that—the comprehension was staggering through Kitty's thoughts, her chest—that had to be part of why Varinn longed for a son of his own. Why it was so important to him. *To carry the scents*, Thrain had said, because Varinn had forever lost the scents of his own parents, by keeping Thrain alive. And Thrain wanted to give it to him, needed to give it to him. Needed to repay his debt, just as she needed to repay hers...

And without at all meaning to, Kitty was clutching at Varinn, staring up toward him, holding his unhappy eyes in hers. "If you still—want it, after all this," she gulped, "I would be honoured to have your son, Varinn. Truly."

He blinked at her, the sadness shifting away into surprise, and his mouth opened, surely to protest—but Kitty clutched him tighter, furiously shook her head. Because she needed this, needed him to see this, needed to give him this, so much it ached. "Please," she said, steadier this time, to his astonished eyes. "I—I want to. I want a son who scents of your father, of your mother, of *you*. Your line needs to be carried on. It *needs* to be."

The disbelief was still there in Varinn's eyes, his head

shaking—maybe because he'd just told her he wanted her to take her time, to think it over. And Kitty swallowed hard, searched his face, felt the heat and the life of his big shifting body beneath her hands. "I'll still—think about it," she managed. "About all the rest. But the son is—still yours, if you want it. No matter what. You *deserve* it, Varinn."

He kept shaking his head, his eyes almost bemused, now, so Kitty's hands began stroking, caressing down his solid chest, over his abdomen, all the way to his groin. To where that familiar bulge was already shuddering, swelling beneath his kilt, as his nostrils flared, his breath hitching into his chest.

So Kitty swallowed, nodded at his eyes, kept going. Slipping up beneath his kilt, now, brazen and hungry. Feeling the hot silken skin, feeling how he pulsed and filled beneath her touch. He was here, alive, alive, and they were here, because of him. And Kitty needed to keep touching him, needed to see that hunger kindling in his eyes, burning away the sadness, the loss, the grief.

"Good, Kit," came Thrain's hushed, husky voice, and now those were his hands, big and warm, slipping up beneath her own kilt, grasping at her bare arse. And then—Kitty blinked, but obliged—he was guiding her around, away from Varinn, facing her toward... toward one of the stone bunks, on the opposite side. But this one was empty, thank the gods, and Thrain was gently lifting her upper body onto it, into it. So her arse was facing out, her feet scrabbling to catch on a little ledge, cut into the stone...

And oh, Thrain's hands were still here, lifting up her kilt, exposing her to the air, to—to Varinn. And she could almost feel Varinn's watching gaze, heavy and intent, as Thrain's hand slid up and down her crease, settled against her slick opening. And then slowly, shamelessly spread it wide apart, so Varinn could see...

"She's already wet for you, Lord Grisk," Thrain breathed, so soft. "Fill her with your life, ach? With your good Grisk seed."

There wasn't a reply, not even a sound behind her—but then, yes, yes, there it was. Varinn's round, slick, familiar hardness, settling in place between Thrain's fingers—and then driving deep inside in one hard, jolting thrust.

Kitty shouted, arched up, scrabbled against the stone—gods, he was big, he was everywhere, everything—and oh, oh, he was doing it again. Drawing out, slow and smooth and certain, and then sinking back inside. And then again, and again, setting up a swift, steady rhythm, plunging in again and again. Taking her in a way he never had before, raw and fierce and frantic, his hands gripping her hips as he slammed in faster, deeper. Wringing up Kitty's cries even higher, harsher, but oh it felt so right, so perfect, so good. To have her lord finally taking her, using her, needing her—

And yes, yes, Kitty's desperate glance over her shoulder found Varinn's eyes bright, hard, flashing with something possessive, hungry, proud. While Thrain stood close behind him, his long arms circled tight around his torso, his face still buried deep in his neck. Wanting this too, needing it as much as she did, needing to spark and stroke and seek out Varinn's pleasure, and his life. To savour it, maybe even to save it. Just the way he'd saved theirs.

And gods, how it looked, how it felt, when Varinn's head arched back, his hips grinding hard and deep—and that powerful flesh filling her jerked, and erupted. Spraying out all its hot Grisk seed deep inside her, pumping it out in rushing, furious torrents. While Kitty gasped, groaned, perhaps even begged for more, pinioned whole upon her lord, bent over into an empty grave.

But then, without warning, Varinn drew out of her, away—and where he'd been, there was only hot, slick, sticky seed. Surging out in thick gurgling pulses, streaking down Kitty's legs, spattering the crypt's stone floor beneath her. But Varinn wasn't cleaning her up this time, wasn't even touching her now, because somehow he—he'd lunged for Thrain. Grasping his arms, twisting him around—and then shoving his upper body down beside her, and yanking up his kilt. So Thrain was bent double, too, open and exposed, and Kitty gasped at the sight of Varinn's huge, dripping-wet heft, still sputtering fresh white as it bobbed toward Thrain's parted, wide-open crease.

Thrain startled and choked as he felt it, his body straining up—and then he shuddered all over as Varinn drove inside. Slamming into Thrain even harder than he had with Kitty, the sound of skin striking skin echoing through the tunnel—but even louder was Thrain's shout of pleasure, of pure, untrammelled ecstasy. Ringing even sharper, louder, as Varinn drove in again and again, filling him, taking what was his. While his glinting, greedy eyes flicked between them both, catching on Kitty's still-bared arse, on the mess still streaking down her thighs.

And then, oh gods, he grasped Thrain's hips too, his claws digging in, his eyes rolling back—and Thrain shouted again as Varinn ground deep and poured out, flooding him full of more hot, thick seed. Giving him this, just as he'd given it to Kitty— and then, oh, even drawing out, the same way, and hissing a breathless little command toward Thrain. So now Thrain was the one pouring out fresh seed, sputtering out from within him, streaking down his legs, spattering across the old musty stone.

And Varinn just kept standing there, just... looking. Looking at them both, dressed for him, bent over for him, bared for him. And fully, utterly drenched for him, leaking his good Grisk seed, while something like satisfaction—like relief—flashed across his eyes.

It was Thrain who stood up first, stretching his arms over his head, and Kitty only distantly noticed that he'd sprayed out too, painting the stone beneath him with a growing pool of fresh white. And his half-hard length was even still dripping onto the floor, good gods—but uncharacteristically, Varinn didn't seem to mind that either. Instead, his eyes had even dropped to linger on the sight, holding there with soft, easy approval, as his hand reached to catch at Thrain's waist, drawing him close into his side.

Kitty stilled a little, her face heating as she watched—but oh, now they were both reaching for her too, pulling her up, and into their safe, steady warmth. Neither of them seeming to notice the ongoing mess, not even Varinn, and instead he was bending his head to Kitty's hair, and inhaling slow and deep.

"Thank you, sweet *kisa*," he whispered, his voice both rough and soft. "I am so glad the gods brought you to us."

Oh. Oh, gods, he still couldn't actually mean that, and Kitty's disbelieving eyes glanced upwards, catching on Thrain's flushed face. On where, for an instant, he looked almost regretful, almost—guilty? But then it swept away again, his mouth quivering up a little, his eyes warm on hers.

"There's naught that blocks out the reek of death like some good fresh seed, ach?" Thrain murmured, with a wink. "Although ploughing us into your own damned vault is a bit much, Varinn. Even for you."

Kitty's wide eyes darted to the empty bunk—that was supposed to be *Varinn's* vault?—and when she glanced up at him, he gave a too-casual shrug, his gaze angling away. Suggesting, again, that doing this, like this, had maybe been important to him, somehow. Life, out of death. In the face of death. In spite of it, even.

"Well, I think it's quite meaningful," Kitty said, as firmly as she could. "And just the kind of thing a god's son would do. Reminding us that even if he isn't immortal"—her shy eyes glanced again toward his face—"his goodness will carry on after him, right? In his deeds, and his scent, and his sons. Just like his own father, and even like Lord Grisk himself."

Varinn's eyes blinked, flaring with surprise, and then—with gratefulness. Yes, gratefulness, raw and almost painful to look at, as he twitched a fond little smile toward her. While Thrain stared between them both, and then threw back his head and laughed, the sound blithe and merry in the too-cramped darkness.

"Not you too, Kit!" he exclaimed. "It's the skeletons and their death-rot infecting you, I swear. Next thing I know, I'll come down here and find you two happily fucking away inside that damned vault itself! No, Varinn, gods damn it. *No.*"

Kitty couldn't help a bright, choked laugh of her own, especially at the undeniable glint of *interest* in Varinn's eyes. But he was smiling too, his eyes flicking soft and indulgent between them both, as his strong arms drew them both a little closer.

"I... thank you both, for coming to find me," he said, hoarse. "Are we all... well again, then? Is there aught more we should speak of?"

At that, Kitty's eyes caught Thrain's again—and for an instant, blooming up in her thoughts, were more questions, even stronger than before. Had Varinn truly meant all that, about wanting to be her mate? About wanting her to take her time, and think about it? And had he accepted her offer of a son? Had he known how deeply she'd meant it?

But—was it still part of her debt, somehow? Was Thrain? And did Thrain have a debt too, one he was trying to repay? With doing all that work he'd so disliked, with companionship, with laughter, with pleasure? With... with...

He's always wanted a son. More than anything anything—else...

And they'd both still—kept secrets from her. About Thrain's magic. About their past. About already knowing Kitty's own past. And maybe even about why Thrain had been so drawn to the drink in the first place, and why Varinn had been so desperate to save him, again. Because it was his legacy, his father's sacrifice, and it was all so tangled, so heavy, so much to be borne...

But looking at Thrain's eyes, at the tight little grimace on his mouth, Kitty found that she couldn't seem to say any of it. And instead, she gave a small smile back toward him, and then up at Varinn's watching, waiting face.

"All good," she said, as lightly as she could. "Perfectly all right. I'm so grateful to you both for telling me all this, and making this such a... *memorable* evening. Although"—she couldn't help a wincing glance downwards—"what do you think about a bath? This might be all well and good for the skeletons, but surely not our clean furs?"

And yes, thank the gods, that was Thrain's merry laugh again, and Varinn's quieter laugh, too. And as they traipsed out of the crypt together, cheerfully chattering as they went, Kitty could almost—*almost*—forget all the death surrounding them, and that whisper of guilt in Thrain's eyes.

45

For the next few days, neither Varinn nor Thrain mentioned the crypt. Or their past, or all those horrifying revelations, or the question of sons. The question of Kitty... thinking about it.

And instead, if anything, they seemed to smile and laugh more easily. Teasing each other, touching each other, enjoying each other. With Varinn making those heated promises every morning before he left, and then carrying them out with brutal, beautiful certainty when he returned. Coolly ordering Kitty and Thrain to dress for him, to pleasure him, to worship him.

Gods, it was good, and it was without question the happiest Kitty had ever been in her life. Especially with her ongoing work at the shop, which had also begun to settle into a steady but highly intriguing rhythm. Combining the more mundane work—sorting new stock, mending garments, helping customers—with several highly fascinating projects. Including ongoing discussions with Harthr around trade routes and potential partners, plus regular meetings with the Skai tailor Gamall, and—most intriguing of all—Rosa's pricing and taxation report. Which had continued to find Kitty and Thrain spending some time deep in the Ka-esh wing each morning, Kitty cheerfully chatting with Rosa in the library, while Thrain worked down the corridor with Gary in the Ka-esh forge.

And if some uneasy part of Kitty had wondered whether Thrain might eventually lose interest in the smithing—especially once it clearly proved to be hot, gruelling, tedious work—she was deeply relieved to be proven wrong. Because not only had Thrain eagerly continued it each day without complaint, but he'd shown a level of dedication bordering on sheer fanaticism. To the point where he usually ended up eagerly chattering about it in bed to Kitty and Varinn, telling them all he'd done that day—drawing wire, repairing a tricky amulet, working on wax casting techniques, re-learning filigree. Most of which Kitty—and surely Varinn—scarcely understood, but they both listened attentively anyway, and asked questions wherever they could. And afterwards, Varinn would invariably kiss or caress Thrain, and murmur praise and encouragement, and roundly dismiss any questions about whether he needed help in his own work.

"Naught at all," Varinn firmly told Thrain, perhaps a week after the night in the crypt. "I am most happy to have you here, where you can keep watch over Katharine, and build your skill at smithing. Ach, just today"—his voice softened even more—"Gary told me you are the most promising apprentice he has seen in years! This is a great gift, *krútt*. A return to the old ways of the Aetha, after all that has been lost."

It was the first time he'd so much as hinted at all that darkness, and Kitty didn't miss how Thrain shuddered, and buried his face in Varinn's neck. To which Varinn kissed and caressed him, rumbling that low purr through his chest, until Thrain had sprawled limp across him and Kitty both, snoring softly into Varinn's shoulder.

But Kitty could still feel Varinn's quiet, watchful wakefulness, and for an instant, she thought he might bring up the crypt again, all those lingering questions—but instead, he cleared his throat, and drew her a little closer into his other side. "So, *kisa*," he said, low. "I have been seeking out new rings for Thrain, to pierce his nipples with. But I have found naught worth buying, and the Ka-esh waiting list is many moons long. I wonder if, mayhap"—he pressed a kiss to her hair—"you could devise some clever way to have him make them for me, without knowing they shall be his? Say they are a gift for another, mayhap?"

Kitty beamed up at him in the darkness, and fervently agreed. And after some mulling it over the next day, she found a willing accomplice in Ella, who had come by the shop with an excitable, tattered-looking Rakfi to buy him some new clothes.

"I swear, he's never met an article of clothing he couldn't destroy," Ella said, with a wry grin toward where Rakfi was already scampering up and down the aisle. "And of course I'd love to help with Varinn's rings. Just tell Thrain they're a surprise gift from me to Natt, why don't you? I imagine they'd probably have somewhat similar preferences, being so close— and related, too?"

Kitty eagerly nodded and thanked her, but found her thoughts catching on that last statement, on all those dark, horrifying secrets from the crypt. "So were Thrain and Nattfarr close when they were younger, too?" she ventured. "Varinn and Thrain recently told me about... about the past, with the clan. All the in-fighting, and the camp, and the... the attack."

And I just need to talk about it with someone, she very nearly said—but despite Ella's wince, there was unmistakable understanding, or even sympathy, in her too-aware eyes. "Gods, it's an awful story, isn't it?" she said, her voice lowering. "And they're all so good at dismissing it, pretending it never happened, and that they're completely over it. It's taken me a long time to understand how deeply it affected Natt, and how the aftermath almost—*broke* him. I"—she swallowed, gave Kitty a wavering little smile—"I've had a lot to learn."

Oh. Kitty's own smile faded, her eyes searching Ella's, and Ella grimaced as she turned toward the nearest stack of baby clothes, and halfheartedly began sifting through it. "But yes, I think Natt and Thrain were always close," she said. "And Thrak, too. But as they got older, it sounded like all that mess with the clan really pulled them apart. Thrak and Thrain's father was—volatile, and he treated them very differently. And I know Natt's father was trying to do his best for the clan—but he didn't cast his wayward brother out, either. Didn't listen to the people he should have trusted."

Kitty's thoughts flicked back to Varinn's father, to how he'd known the risks all along—and perhaps Ella had followed that too, giving another grimace toward the clothes. "Natt actually spent a lot of time with me, on my family's grounds, during those years," she said. "I know he loved me, but I also didn't realize at the time that he was—escaping it all. It actually saved his life, in the end, because when the attack happened, he was—with me. But then afterwards..."

Her voice had cracked, and she was gazing blankly at the clothes now, her hands not moving at all. "Afterwards, it was hell for all of them," she continued, quieter. "Natt—didn't come back here, for a long time, but the ones who did—well. It sounded like they were extremely lucky to still have Varinn's scenting. To have him looking out for them, just like his father did."

Oh. Kitty's stomach clenched, because gods, they hadn't even spoken of that part—had they? And Ella grimaced as she began sifting through the clothes again, far faster than before. "So after that," she said, "Natt's always made sure to keep Varinn close, and listen to his counsel. And Dammarr's, too, because Dammarr's fathers were both brilliant warriors, and they viciously fought against the move. They weren't afraid to tell Natt's father exactly what they thought—just like you, Dammarr."

She'd angled a wavering, grateful smile down the aisle,

toward where—oh. Dammarr himself was striding toward them, with a squirming Rakfi in his arms, and a bemused little quirk on his mouth. "You lost something, sister," he said lightly, as he hitched a grinning Rakfi a little higher on his hip, and rustled a hand at his messy hair. "Too busy over here dredging up the best-forgotten past, are you?"

Ella gave a relieved-sounding laugh, and reached to pluck Rakfi out of his arms. "I'm afraid so," she said. "Kitty asked, and I want to make sure she's not—surprised, by any of it. Because if it was up to all of you"—she raised her brows toward Dammarr—"you'd never tell us anything, ever. You'd just float along pretending like none of it ever happened, and that you're all perfectly delighted with your lot in life."

"Well, we are, are we not?" Dammar replied, a little too smoothly. "The war is over, Kaugir is dead, the clan is at peace. Nattfarr has all he has ever wanted—you, Rakfi, the role of Speaker. Varinn is doing the work he has always felt called to do, and he has two lovely, obedient pets to wear his jewels, and worship at his feet. Whilst Thrain has apparently up and decided to become the next great Grisk goldsmith, and Thrak is just happily blundering along being Thrak. Whilst I... I..."

He shot a brief but betraying glance downwards, toward where—oh. He wasn't wearing one of his lovely dresses, but was again clad in a rather sloppy-looking pair of trousers. His hair was dishevelled, too, and as she studied him, Kitty realized that there were dark circles under his eyes, a distinct tightness around his mouth.

"Are you here to do a little more shopping?" Kitty finally asked, into the too-taut silence. "Harthr brought in a shipment of beautiful new clothes from the city yesterday, and I'm sure I saw a few things that would suit you."

The interest unmistakably sparked in Dammarr's eyes, but then it faded again as he glanced away. "Ach, mayhap later," he said, his voice hollow. "Look, have either of you seen a kitten? Vragi's has become lost again."

Kitty and Ella both exchanged bemused glances, shaking their heads. "Those kittens," Ella said, with an obvious attempt at a smile. "I can't believe I offered to keep my sweet pups at the house to help those ungrateful little furballs settle in! You'd best go find Timo, he'll sniff the little menace out. And"—a militant glint entered her eye—"my dogs are coming back here sooner rather than later, kittens be damned."

Kitty laughed at that, and thankfully Dammarr was reluctantly smiling, too, before ruffling Rakfi's hair, and stalking down the aisle again. And after eyeing his sagging trousers for a moment, Kitty made a mental note to set aside those dresses for him, and maybe a few accessories, too.

Her forethought was rewarded that very afternoon, when none other than Thrak himself showed up at the shop counter. Flashing Kitty a broad, rakish smile, though it didn't quite reach his eyes.

"Hello, sweet sister," he said cheerfully. "Don't suppose you might have a suitable gift for a gorgeous but pissed-off orc mate? Preferably one he won't murder or mock me over? Not sure which is a worse fate, really."

His mouth twisted into a wry wince, and after blinking for a moment, Kitty beamed brightly back toward him. "You know, I actually do," she said, excitedly waving him behind the counter. "There were a few items that came in yesterday that I thought would suit him very well."

Thrak followed her willingly enough, all the way to the back of the shop, where she'd tucked the dresses beneath her mending station. "So Dammarr really likes silk, and rich colours," she said, shaking out a deep purple robe. "This one is gorgeous, don't you think? It would show off his piercing so well, and a sash like this"—she held up a leather strip studded with gold beads—"would be lovely with it. And add a bit of orcish flair, too."

Her enthusiasm was clear in her voice, earning her an amused grin from Thrak—but then his smile faded as he studied the purple robe. "Sorry, sister," he said thickly. "I—I can't buy him something like this. Not after I've already fucked up so much with it, ach? He'll think I want him to wear it—that I expect him to wear it, or I like him better in it. I can't even tell what *he* likes to wear most of the time."

He smiled again, but his gaze on the robe looked almost sad—and then he squared his shoulders, and glanced purposefully away. "So mayhap—some kind of sweet treat, if you have any?" he said brightly. "He's such a fiend for any kind of maple or taffy—that'll always kick him out of a funk. Or mayhap a new fur for our room, if you've got something nice and soft? Or a feather pillow, he loves those."

Kitty didn't recall seeing any taffy or maple come in, but there had been some furs with Harthr's latest shipment, so she led Thrak over toward them, and proclaimed their various merits as eagerly as she could. But even so, Thrak's reaction to the furs seemed decidedly listless, his head shaking as he stroked one, and then another, and another.

"Needs to be softer," he said, with another smile that didn't reach his eyes. "He's such a prickly little possum, he needs the softness just to settle himself sometimes, ach?"

Oh. It seemed like unusual thoughtfulness, from someone who hadn't previously seemed to exhibit such a characteristic—and Kitty felt herself chewing her lip as she studied him. "Thrak," she said slowly, "I hate to pry, but—is this why you haven't bought Dammarr a mating-gift? Because you—you didn't think he would like it?"

Thrak's mouth spasmed, and he twitched a jerky, highly betraying shrug. "He'd be bound to wear it all the damned time," he said, his voice thin. "Pretty shit of me if it makes him feel like rubbish, ach? Makes him feel—*out of his skin*, like he says things do, sometimes. And it's one thing if it's a family heirloom or some such"—he nodded toward Kitty's *thyrja*—"since that's not so much *my* fault if it's all wrong. But our fool father didn't think to stash the jewels before he got himself killed, ach? So now it's just—on *me*."

The comprehension was flashing through Kitty's thoughts, surging up against a tight, twisting sympathy. "And you can't just—talk to Dammarr about it?" she asked carefully. "Ask him what he might like most?"

Thrak barked a sharp, bitter laugh that sounded eerily similar to how Thrain's sometimes did, and shook his head. "Och, no," he said. "We don't talk about clothes. We can't. *He* can't. I was"—he laughed again—"jolted, in truth, to see him in the dress that first day, and I ken that's why I was such an arse over it. For he never said a *word* upon it to me before that, ach? Made a lot of sense after, though."

Oh. This was all sounding strangely, painfully familiar—*if it was up to all of you, you'd never tell us anything*, Ella had said—and Kitty drew in a deep breath, and considered it for a long moment. "I don't suppose," she ventured, "you might remember what your family's heirlooms looked like? Or would Thrain remember, maybe?"

Thrak shrugged, glanced away. "Some, probably," he said. "Thrain more than me, I ken. He was always the one into the jewels."

But Kitty was beaming again, and drawing herself up a little straighter. "So you could have Thrain remake one of them for you," she said firmly. "Something you liked. And that way it's special, it's something meaningful to you—but it's still not so much pressure if it doesn't work for Dammarr. And if it doesn't, I'm sure Ymir would buy it from you, too."

Thrak was blinking blankly toward Kitty, his brow furrowing. "But—*Thrain* can't do that," he said uncertainly. "Can he?"

"Well, why don't we go ask?" Kitty replied, as decisively as she could—and after another moment of suspiciously eyeing her, Thrak nodded, and followed her down the corridor to the forge. To where Thrain was once again behind his workbench, holding a tiny gold chain with one hand, while using the other hand to twist it with a pair of red-hot tongs.

"Och," Thrain said toward them, once he'd set down the chain and tongs, and wiped at his flushed, sweaty face with his arm. "Is aught amiss, brother?"

His eyes were wary on Thrak, his mouth pulling into an uneasy smile, while Thrak gave a similarly wary smile in return, and then glanced down at the gold chain on the bench. "No, just—" he began, and then bent lower, peering at the chain with genuine surprise in his eyes. "You didn't—*make* that, brother?"

Thrain's face flushed even redder, and he shrugged, waved it away. "Not all of it," he said. "Just this half, here, expanding it. Ymir's got me doing alterations all over the place, like I'm his own personal repair shop."

His expression was something between disgruntled and pleased—maybe both—and Thrak studied him for a too-long moment, his head tilting, his claws tapping on the workbench. "You actually—*like* this, though?" he asked, a little tentative. "More than being out and busy all day? With *Varinn*?"

There was an unmistakable emphasis on Varinn's name, sounding almost accusing—but Thrain shrugged, dropped his gaze back to the chain. "Ach, I miss Varinn," he said. "But in truth, I don't miss the work. At all. I was tired of dealing with other people's rubbish all the time. Was never good at leaving it behind at the end of the day, like you can. Ended up drinking a lot of it away, I ken."

Thrak's claws were still tapping on the counter, his head tilting further. "Och, I follow," he said, his voice a little thick. "Really oughta be sending someone else out with Varinn, though. Bit risky to be going alone all the time, even for *him*."

That note of emphasis—maybe even dislike—was still there, but Thrain's eyes glancing up again were warm, and surprisingly grateful. "Ach, I ken," he said. "Keep trying to tell the stubborn bastard, but he doesn't listen to a damned word I say. Even worse than Dammarr, brother, really."

"He is not," Thrak countered, as a quick, relieved grin flashed across his mouth. "Dammarr is the most obstinate orc in this mountain, and I won't hear a word otherwise! Yesterday he refused to eat in the same room as me, because he remembered the time I ate those moose-antlers!"

"Ach, and you sicked up everywhere," Thrain said, with a gleeful grin back toward him. "It was vile, brother. I ken I don't want to eat with you anymore now, either."

Thrak barked a loud, scoffing laugh, and threw something from his pocket—a ball of old *lint*—across the workbench toward Thrain. To which Thrain cackled and threw one back, and soon they were caught in an involved lint-throwing battle, while Kitty took several steps backwards, and watched with increasingly revolted amusement.

But once they seemed to settle again—Thrak had claimed victory, and Thrain hadn't argued it—Kitty finally cut in, and explained the original reason they'd come. About needing a mating-gift for Dammarr, and how—Kitty briefly caught Thrak's increasingly narrow eyes—he hadn't found quite the right one yet, and how perhaps an heirloom replica might be more meaningful.

"Ach, I could see that," Thrain said thoughtfully, stroking at where Kitty knew he was still wearing his own *thyrja* beneath his apron. "Were you thinking the *thyrja*? Or the emerald cuff, or his signet ring? Although"—he made a face—"you oughta have had the ring, brother."

Thrak blinked at Thrain, and then down at his own hand, as if that thought hadn't before occurred to him. "I—don't know," he said, a little helplessly. "If I give him a *thyrja*, he'll think I'm just copying Varinn, with you two. And I don't think he'll like having something tight and heavy like a cuff on his arm all the time, so—"

He grimaced, his hand absently rubbing at his own gold

cuff, while Thrain kept looking thoughtful, drumming his claws against the worktable. "What about the *kíróna*, then?" he said. "You might not remember it that well, because Father never had a mate to give it to—but it was a really good piece. Would look nice with how Dammarr wears his hair."

Kitty was swiftly losing the thread on this, but Thrain was already glancing toward her, and making a circling gesture around his head with his claw. "A headpiece," he explained. "Kind of like... a coronet, maybe, in human terms. Ours was really striking, with lots of tiny coloured stones, to catch the light. Shouldn't be beyond me to copy it, either, especially if Gary helps. And I could try to keep it pretty light for Dammarr, too, if you think weight's an issue."

Thrak's eyes were looking astonished again, but then softened into a bright, surprisingly genuine gratefulness. "That sounds good, brother," he said. "I do remember it now, and ach, I ken—I ken mayhap it would suit him. I—thank you."

Thrain shrugged and waved it away, but they were both grinning at each other again. And once Thrak had said farewell, Kitty also took the liberty of adding Varinn's gift—or rather, Ella's gift—to Thrain's list. A project he accepted with all apparent magnanimity, despite Kitty not quite meeting his eyes on the Ella point—and she couldn't resist ducking behind the worktable, and pressing a brief, furtive kiss to his sweaty cheek.

"You're wonderful," she told him, beaming up toward his smiling, still-flushed face. "I can't wait for tonight."

Thankfully, the rest of the afternoon passed quickly, and included—to everyone's relief—Timo's recovery of Vragi's kitten, who had been hiding in a cupboard. And Varinn returned just in time to congratulate Timo on his accomplishment, slinging his big arm over his shoulder, and giving him a companionable shake.

"Good work, little brother," he said firmly. "You have again proven yourself one of the best noses in our mountain, ach?"

Timo blushed and grinned, and then shyly asked whether

Varinn might have a few moments for some sparring after supper, since he'd been so busy of late. And after Varinn's uncertain glance toward Kitty—which she returned with an encouraging nod—he smiled at Timo, and told him he would be honoured.

This soon led to a highly entertaining round of matches in the sparring-room, with more Grisk seeming to get drawn in with every round. Alma's mate Baldr turned out to be a vicious fighter, who was only defeated by a joint effort from Thrak and Thrain, and Eyarl put up a good showing against his mate Valter, while Trygve and Timo shouted and cheered. And Varinn and Timo actually turned out to be an excellent fighting team, which—Timo breathlessly explained as he sank down beside Kitty—was because they could scent one another's movements so well.

"It is why he and Thrain are such a good team also, ach?" he said shyly. "I am sure Varinn sorely misses him, whilst he is out working."

His voice had sobered, his brow furrowing as he watched Varinn and Thrain in the ring, gasping and laughing as they rolled around on the floor together. "I ken Varinn would likely never allow," Timo continued, very tentative now, "for an untrained orc to come along with him instead, ach? Even if the orc—stayed very quiet, and out of the way?"

Kitty blinked at Timo, genuinely taken aback—he was how old, fifteen?—and he rapidly flapped his hands at her, his eyes wide with alarm. "Ach, of course not," he said, too quickly. "Please do not mention it to him, I am sure he should not wish to—ach! There is Sune."

He leapt up and dashed across the room, toward where a frowning Sune was indeed standing in the door, surveying the ongoing brawl with reluctant-looking curiosity. But upon seeing Timo, his frown faded, and soon he was almost— almost—smiling as Timo tugged him over toward the ring, too.

The fun only ended when someone brought out a keg of

ale, much to many participants' obvious excitement. But Thrain—who at this point had been cheerfully chatting with Kitty and Alma and Ella, and helping to wrangle Rakfi—had suddenly stiffened on the bench, his throat bobbing as he glanced across the room. And while Kitty knew how hard he'd continued to work at this—including his ongoing visits with Rathgarr and Efterar—she also knew how much he still struggled with being exposed to any kind of drink, or even scenting it in the air. So she quickly made their excuses to Alma and Ella, and grasped Thrain's arm, guiding him out the door as swiftly as she could. And finding, thank the gods, that Varinn had already caught up with them, his braid dishevelled, sweat streaming down his face.

"Good, *krútt*," he purred, as he nudged both Thrain and Kitty to the side of the lamplit corridor, into a hidden alcove she hadn't noticed before. "Very, very good."

He was already crowding into Thrain, his head nuzzling deep into his neck, and Thrain gasped as his head tilted back, his hips already bucking into the easy stroke of Varinn's hand. To where Varinn was yanking off his kilt, tossing it to the floor, and—Kitty gasped—nudging her downwards onto it.

"Kneel and suck him, *kisa*," he ordered, husky and hot. "Make it good for him, ach?"

Oh, gods, Kitty was already nodding, obeying, falling to her knees on the kilt. Swallowing Thrain as hungry and deep as she could, while Varinn kissed and nipped at his neck, then slipped purposefully around behind him, spreading his legs apart. And then surely breaching him there, oh, because Thrain hissed a guttural moan, and swelled even fuller in Kitty's mouth.

"So good, *krútt*," Varinn murmured, as that purr rumbled through his chest, and his hips began rhythmically slapping against Thrain's arse. "So hot and soft and eager. Just what I have always longed for."

Thrain arched and moaned even more, bucking helplessly

into Kitty's throat, and Varinn kept purring, thrusting, kissing, caressing. "So good," he breathed. "So pretty, so hungry. So brave. Such a rare, precious gift, my sweet *krútt*. Mine."

Thrain cried out, his head arching back, and Kitty plunged him deeper, seeking inside him, sucking as hard as she could, while Varinn's voice went darker, hotter. "Mine," he hissed. "Mine, and my *kisa*'s. You have always been mine, my pretty Aetha prize. And thus, you will"—his voice went ragged—"you will bend over for me, whenever I wish. You will open all your holes wide for me. You will empty yourself at my command. You will wear my jewels upon you, and also deep within you, where naught has touched but *me*—"

He broke off there, and oh, Kitty could hear Thrain's choked gasp as Varinn bit down, could feel it in her own throat—and suddenly Thrain was spraying out, pouring into her mouth in torrents of thick sweet heat, as he helplessly shouted his pleasure.

But she kept sucking, swallowing with hungry gulps, while Varinn did the same at his neck. Until Thrain finally sagged back against Varinn, his breath exhaling in a low, laughing groan. And Kitty could see that Varinn had pulled a little away from Thrain's neck, now gently licking and kissing at it, and he reached down to guide Kitty back upwards too, drawing her close into them.

"Good, *kisa*," he murmured, as he tipped her head up, and pressed a soft, salty-tasting kiss to her mouth. "I wish you could scent him, when your sweet little mouth is upon him. Divine, *krútt*."

Thrain laughed again, still husky and breathless. "Tyrant," he said lightly. "And such a tease, too. Giving me such gifts. Saying all these sweet things you don't mean."

But at that, Varinn drew back to look at him, his eyes strangely intent. "Ach, I mean them," he said, low. "You... ken I do not?"

Thrain huffed another laugh, shorter this time, even as his

eyes searched Varinn's. "Dunno," he said thickly. "If you did, mayhap you would…"

He swallowed, glanced away, but Varinn grasped his chin, tilted it back toward him. "What, *krútt*," he said. "Speak truth to me, and I shall speak it to you."

And wait, oh, Kitty knew what that meant now, as Thrain licked his lips, his shoulders rising and falling. "Mayhap you would," he said, his voice a rush, "speak vows to me. As you have—with Kit."

Oh. Right. That. *That*, waiting, hovering between them, and Varinn angled a brief, unreadable glance toward Kitty. Because—because he still hadn't spoken a real vow to her, not like that. And Kitty still couldn't decide whether that discussion in the crypt had really meant what she'd hoped it meant, and she had to fight down the unease fluttering in her chest, fight to keep her eyes steady. Waiting, waiting, as Varinn drew in a slow breath, let it out.

"Mayhap I only wish to give this… more time," he finally replied, a little gruff. "As I have asked for with Katharine, also. I ken I have oft been a… tyrant, as you so oft say. For in truth, I should"—he drew in a shaky breath—"be very glad to bind you to me for life, and compel you to obey me, and command you to never touch the drink again. But we have gone through much, these past weeks, and I wish to learn from my past failings, ach? I wish to respect you, and your right to… to keep choosing me, also. To keep choosing our *kisa*, and our son. To keep… finding your own path, mayhap."

It sounded true, it felt true, it had to be true, his eyes held steady, unblinking to Thrain's. And the fluttering in Kitty's chest had seemed to settle again, turning into a strange crushing longing. Because Varinn was saying he'd meant it, he wanted to, he had to, he had to…

"I have come to see, these past weeks, just how much power I have held over you," he continued, quieter. "Since those days when I held your life in my hands. And after that, I have always kept you close to me, in our work, and our play, and—all else. It is only now that you have begun to push against this, and I only—I wish to be sure. I wish *you* to be sure, for I love you so, *krútt*."

His voice was rough and hoarse, his eyes blinking hard, and Thrain was blinking too, rubbing at his eyes with his palm. And then giving a deep, choked-sounding growl as he dragged Varinn close, clamped his long arms tightly around his broad back. "You know I'm sure," he breathed, into Varinn's neck. "And you know I *wanted* to stay close to you, all that time. But—ach. Whenever you're ready. When *you're* sure."

Varinn was nodding into Thrain's neck, his own eyes squeezed shut, and Kitty realized it was still—a promise. A promise between the two of them, or—or maybe even the three of them, as Thrain groped out toward her, and dragged her in. Squeezing her tightly between them, breathing her in, making it truth. Maybe even making it stronger than the debts, the deaths, that distant whispering unease...

And it made it even easier to smile and talk and joke together as they went down to the baths, and then piled into bed together. Easier to sink into the feel of their hands on her belly, to Thrain telling their son goodnight in soft, affectionate Aelakesh. And easier to take their pleasure the next morning, Varinn again wet from the baths as he took long, luxurious turns with them, kissing them both slow and deep as he emptied himself inside.

Afterwards, Kitty felt so hazy and wonderful that she drifted through breakfast and prayers, leaning into Varinn's warm side as she silently thanked Lord Grisk for all her blessings. It wasn't until Varinn was saying goodbye to Thrain—who'd skipped out of prayers as usual—that she remembered that conversation with Timo from the night before.

"Have you ever thought about taking Timo out with you, for the day?" she asked Varinn. "I know he's missed spending time with you lately, and you two seem to get along so well. He seems very responsible for his age, too."

She was thinking of how Timo had found Vragi's kitten, and even how he'd sorted out those various disagreements between his friends. And perhaps Varinn was thinking of it too, his eyes blinking, his brow furrowing—but then he rapidly shook his head. "Ach, he is far too young," he said firmly. "And he yet has schooling, and this is far too risky. And I should never wish to—"

But to Kitty's surprise, Thrain cut him off with a sharp little growl, a tight grip of his hand to his arm. "Och, Varinn, it's not always risky, and you know it," he said. "Where are you going today, south? You likely won't even scent a human all day. And you know Eyarl and Rathgarr would welcome an apprenticeship for Timo, ach? And Kit's right, he's not gonna cause trouble for you, and he'd love every moment of it. You probably would, too."

Varinn was still frowning at Thrain, looking very much as though he wanted to keep arguing, but Thrain growled again, and even stepped a little closer. Almost staring Varinn down, good gods, his taller height suddenly seeming far more noticeable than usual.

"It's a good idea, Varinn," he said, his voice hard. "You say you want to respect me and listen to me, well, do it. You need help, Timo's a hard worker, a good fighter, and he can probably scent you better than anyone else but me. And"— his chin lifted higher, his brows rising—"he's like a son to you, and you've been constantly ignoring him for us lately. And that's a pretty rubbish thing to do to him, isn't it? Especially to a young, fatherless orc who looks up to you as he does?"

His eyes were flashing with satisfaction, with victory— because yes, those last points would perfectly prick at all Varinn's sympathies, all his lofty self-set standards. And Kitty had to bite back her chuckle at the sight of Varinn visibly deflating, and looking helplessly toward her—to which she clasped his other arm, and smiled sweetly up at his face.

"It sounds like a wonderful idea to me," she said. "And we'll both be far less worried knowing you're not alone out there, won't we, Thrain? I'm sure feeling less anxious will be beneficial for my health, and our son's health, too."

Varinn was looking deeply pained, now, or perhaps even panicked, to which Thrain laughed aloud, and gave him a reassuring little shake. "Och, Kit, now that's cutting him too deep," he said cheerfully, with a light little nip at Varinn's neck. "We'll be fine either way, Varinn, but—please?"

Varinn groaned a sigh, but finally threw his hands up, and rolled his eyes. "I shall speak to Timo and Rathgarr," he said flatly, "and think upon this. But this is *all*."

Thrain didn't seem at all perturbed by this, again nipping at Varinn's neck, while Varinn kissed Kitty goodbye. And as Varinn stalked stiffly away down the corridor, Thrain flashed Kitty a quick, conspiratorial grin, his eyes dancing with warmth.

"He'll do it," he said lightly. "Once Timo gives him that sweet pleading face, there'll be no turning back, ach? Truly, it's a brilliant idea, Kit, and I'm cursing myself for not thinking of it before. Thanks."

Kitty waved it away, but she again couldn't stop smiling as she accompanied Thrain first to their regular checkup in the sickroom, followed by one of his ongoing meetings with Rathgarr, too. And then it was back to the shop, where Ymir promptly informed Kitty that he'd added her very first salary to her credit-account, and she was free to spend it as she pleased.

It was a strange, surreal, wonderful feeling, and Kitty spent a few moments wandering through the shop, eyeing various items to purchase, either for herself, or for Varinn or Thrain. But in the end, she decided against all of it, in favour of just... leaving the funds there, on her account. And just knowing, for the first time in years—or maybe even her entire life—that she had a little cushion of safety. Something she'd earned from her chosen trade. Something she'd done for herself.

She felt even lighter as she launched herself into another busy morning's work at the shop, helping customers, sorting inventory, working away at repairs, carefully watching as Ymir showed her how to balance the week's ledger. And then attempting to talk down an irritable Killik, who had again come in search of chains, and was flatly refusing to purchase any of the remaining available options.

"All too flimsy," he snapped. "Too easy to break. Need stronger."

Thankfully, at this point Thrain strode in—and perhaps he'd scented Kitty's consternation, because he stalked over to loom beside her, slipping his hand around her waist. "Look, Killik, good chain's valuable, and damned useful, and it's not gonna oft end up lying around in a shop," he snapped back. "If you want it done properly, you'll order it new from a forge."

Killik frowned at Thrain for an instant, glancing up and down his soot-streaked apron. "Skai forge makes *weapons*," he said, curling his lip. "Best weapons in mountain. No time for *chain*."

"Ach, so we'll make you some in the *Grisk* forge," Thrain said, with a roll of his eyes. "Come on, then, and tell me what you want."

Killik visibly hesitated, but then followed Thrain out of the shop without a single look back. Leaving Kitty to exchange an amused glance with a nearby Ymir, who again had that rather calculating look in his eye. And when Thrain returned a short time later—ready for their daily trip down to the Ka-esh wing—Ymir shoved a piece of parchment toward him, covered on both sides with his crabbed handwriting.

"The Ash-Kai orders," Ymir said. "Still not sure you can handle them, but want to get them in before you load yourself down with fool Skai *chains*, of all things."

Thrain blinked down at the paper, and then back at Ymir.

His mouth opening, and closing, and finally pursing, as the breath slowly exhaled from his chest. "How much extra are you paying me, then?" he asked. "If you'll actually stoop to hiring an Aetha to smith for you?"

Ymir's mouth pursed, too, but he finally replied with an amount, which Thrain instantly countered with something else. Leading to an intense bout of haggling between them, both of them viciously glaring toward one another—but somehow, they eventually seemed to reach an agreement. And Thrain was wryly smiling and shaking his head as he and Kitty headed for the Ka-esh wing, his hand clasped in hers.

"Can't believe I agreed to that," he said dryly. "Gods, Varinn will never let me forget it, ach?"

But that night, Varinn only grinned with genuine-seeming delight at the news, and yanked Thrain close, squeezing him tight. "Ach, I am so proud of you, *krútt*," he said fervently. "You ken you have true promise, if even Ymir sees this."

Thrain huffed a disbelieving laugh at that, but he was still smiling into Varinn's shoulder, his ear-tips noticeably flushed. "And how was it with Timo today?" he asked. "Better than doing it alone, I ken?"

And wait, yes, surely he could smell it, and now Varinn was smiling, too. "Ach," he replied. "This was... good. He was delighted to come, just as you said. And he listened to me, and stayed out of my way, and even... helped. Not as much as you, *krútt*, and I yet missed you, but it was still—better. Easier."

It was perhaps the first time Varinn had actually admitted to missing Thrain, and Thrain had surely caught that too, his eyes shimmering as he squeezed Varinn tighter. "Och, well, you oughta thank Kit," he said, husky. "All her doing. She likes to put on that she's all fluffy sweetness, but she can be pretty sharp, too."

This was accompanied by his wicked, approving grin toward her—and without warning, he lunged over to gently tackle her onto the bed. Pulling her down onto the soft furs with him, and then rolling her onto her back on top of him. So Varinn could prowl down over them both, a devious, thrilling gleam in his eye.

"Ach, she is," Varinn purred, as he spread one big warm hand against her hip, and then gave it a light, gentle slap. "Such a pretty, naughty little kitten. Needs to be put in her place, now and then."

Kitty's gasp was harsh and betraying, her body writhing up against him, while Thrain chuckled with dark, satisfied glee. And soon they were both working her over with their mouths and gently slapping hands, and Kitty couldn't bite back her shout as Varinn finally knelt between her legs, and fastened his mouth against her.

He felt so different than Thrain, his tongue and lips more careful, deliberate, seeking out what made her moan loudest— and then relentlessly repeating it, over and over again. Until Kitty was utterly lost, incoherent, clinging to him with her tingling hands and trembling thighs. Gods, it was so good, he was so good, there was nothing but this, nothing—

But then Varinn rose back up over her, his face slick with her, his long black tongue sweeping his lips. And Kitty moaned again as he easily flipped her onto her hands and knees before him, tilting her arse up, opening her for him. But instead of sinking in where she'd expected, where she so desperately craved it, his prodding, dripping-wet heat slid... upwards. Catching against where she'd worn his *rassja* so many times now, but they'd never done this, oh gods, oh please...

"Oh," Kitty gasped, arching up more for him, opening as wide and brazen as she could. "Oh, please, Lord Grisk. Grant me your scent. Your favour. *Please.*"

And oh, Varinn was purring, his big hands stroking her in such indulgent approval, while Thrain shifted around to kneel before her on the bed, tilting her face up to look at him. "Och, you want your Lord Grisk up your rump, pretty kitten?" he breathed, his eyes flashing. "You want to open up all your tight little holes for him? Make yourself reek all through of his scent?"

Kitty fervently, frantically nodded, and oh, gods, Varinn was already pressing forward. Gently nudging that slick, dripping head into her tightest, most tenuous place, and it was so big, so blunt, so impossible. But she needed this, needed it so much, and she gulped down breaths, willed herself to relax, to open. To feel his oozing fluid easing the way, to welcome him in a little deeper, a little deeper...

"Ach, that's it," Thrain breathed, his blazing eyes flicking toward the sight, toward where Kitty was held wide open, stretched taut and trembling around Varinn's hot invading flesh. "You suck your lord up good and deep, Kit. Feel him split you wide open on his good Grisk prick. Let him fill you and feed you everywhere he wants."

Yes, yes, Kitty wanted that too, needed it, and she moaned again as she nodded, and arched back even more. Felt Varinn pushing in even deeper in return, sliding breath by breath, slow and careful and relentless. The feeling so overpowering, so overwhelming, and Kitty trembled all over as he filled her, her breaths sharpening to loud shameless cries. More, more, more, *please*—and oh, that was his deep grunt, the feel of his skin meeting hers, because he was buried all the way, jabbed as deep as he could go.

"Good, Kit," Thrain breathed, his hooded eyes still flashing on the sight. "Feel good, to have your lord rammed all the way up your rump, plugging you full? So full you'll never, *ever* stop scenting of him?"

Kitty choked and nodded, and oh, Varinn was gasping too, rocking gently against her, his hands still caressing up and down her flanks, flooding her with shivery wonderful warmth. As he seemed to swell even larger, opening her wider, pooling his sweetness so deep inside, oh hell...

"You too, *krútt*," Varinn ordered, hoarse, as he gently caught a handful of Kitty's hair, drew her head further up and back. "In her belly."

Oh, gods, oh please, because Thrain instantly groaned, and fumbled to comply. Yanking off his kilt, tossing it aside, baring his pierced bobbing length before Kitty's blinking eyes—and then he fed himself between her parted lips, deep into her mouth.

Kitty nearly shouted together with him, his hips reflexively bucking him into her throat, and she desperately fought to suck him, to draw him even deeper. To feel them both inside her, filling her at both ends, so hard and so hungry and so, so perfect. Varinn rocking a little faster, a little further, his growl steady and breathless, while Thrain cursed and moaned, and gouged in deeper. His taste and his scent so strong, so stunning, his hands tangling in Kitty's hair as his upper body pitched forward over her to meet Varinn's mouth. Their tongues catching as the pleasure swelled and soared, their bodies rocking into her again and again and again, making her theirs, theirs, *theirs*—

The release crashed over her in a wild, wheeling wave, plunging her beneath it, beneath the strength of the two orcs buried inside her. And oh, now they were shouting too, emptying out in sharp swelling surges, their mouths biting and nostrils flaring as pure, rapt ecstasy flashed up between them. And for an instant, Kitty was sure she'd never known anything so good, so right, so beautiful. Hers. Theirs.

She couldn't seem to speak afterwards, quivering all over as Varinn carefully set her down to the bed, and folded her into his arms. But those arms were still so warm, so safe, stroking up and down her back, her shoulders, even smoothing the hair out of her sweaty face, while Thrain's trembling body curled up behind her, his face buried in her neck, his hand spread wide against her belly.

"Ach, this was good, sweet *kisa*," Varinn murmured, as he inhaled against her hair, slow and deep. "You are so good. So soft, and so kind, and so eager. All we could have wished for, ach?"

It was an echo of what he'd said back in the crypt, and he was even holding her eyes as he said it, his mouth pulled into a tender, affectionate smile. As if he meant it, as if he really really meant it, and Kitty clung to that, to him, buried her face in his chest.

"You, too," she whispered, without at all meaning to. "You're *marvellous*, Varinn. Both of you."

She could feel Varinn's twitch of surprise, the catch of his fingers against her—and then the gentleness again as he drew her a little closer, and drew Thrain in tighter, too. Stroking them both, again and again and again, until Thrain's breath sank into a low snore, and the sleep curled up in Kitty's chest, too.

The next morning was even better, even brighter— especially when, after they'd taken their usual pleasures together, Varinn clasped Kitty's hand, and drew her over to his shelf. Snapping open his jewel-box, and then—Kitty froze— pulling out a beautiful, shimmering gold bracelet.

"For you, sweet *kisa*," he said, his face very slightly reddening, as he carefully fastened the bracelet around her wrist. "I ken it suits you, ach?"

Kitty's voice was trapped in her throat, her wide eyes staring at the gold gleaming and sparkling against her skin. It did look stunning, a distant part of her noted, and it was orc-forged, and surely another heirloom, and he was—he was really giving it to her? Without being prompted, without being obliged, without having a matching gift for Thrain. As if he really wanted to, as if he really meant it—

Before she'd even realized it, she'd thrown herself against Varinn, her arms flinging tightly around his waist. "I love it," she choked, into his chest. "I love it so much, Varinn."

She could feel his soft chuckle as his arms settled around her, drawing her close. "Ach, I am glad, *kisa*," he murmured, into her hair, as his hands stroked up and down her back. "It pleases me also, to see and scent my jewels upon you."

Kitty's words had failed her again, but she clung to him even tighter, her nose sniffling helplessly into his chest. And then there was the feeling of Thrain behind her, too, his arms circling around them both, wrapping her up in warm wonderful safety.

"Looks good on you, Kit," he said. "Nice choice, Varinn. As always."

Kitty was still sniffling and smiling when they pulled apart again, and for an instant, there was a sudden, selfish compulsion to beg Varinn to stay, even just a little longer—at least, until he glanced narrowly toward the door, and then strode over to pull the curtain open. Revealing the sight of a flushed, excited-looking Timo, bobbing on his heels, and hoisting a large pack on his shoulder.

"I hope I'm not too early, brother?" he asked, with a shy, beseeching smile toward Varinn. "I've already packed for the day. And briefed with Nattfarr, too!"

Varinn clearly couldn't find the will to argue, his shoulders sagging as he smiled back at Timo with palpable fondness in his eyes. And after their morning prayers—Timo joined Kitty and Varinn this time—they again went their various ways, Thrain to the forge, Kitty to the shop. Where she again spent a truly satisfying day, learning, chatting, helping wherever she could. Discussing a new shipment with Harthr and Grein and Knorr, working with Ymir and Rosa on their taxation proposal, enjoying her usual lunch with Thrain in the garden—and even dealing with a glaring Filak when he showed up again, this time with a glinting red stone in his hand.

"How very, *very* lovely!" Kitty said, with what she hoped was an appreciative smile, and an enthusiastic clasp of her hands to her chest. "Now, if you'll give me just one moment—"

She'd already been glancing hopefully toward the door beyond Filak, toward where—yes, thank the gods—Thrain was already striding in, wiping his sooty hands on his apron. "*Hvað nú*, Filak?" he asked, and then his eyes instantly lit up as they settled on the stone. "Och! *Falleg! Algjörlega dýrðlegur.*"

Filak again looked reluctantly pleased by this, and once Kitty had gone to fetch Ymir—who was packing the cart with Harthr and Grein at the back of the shop—they again launched into an intensive gem-purchasing discussion. However, this time Ymir plucked out the neat pricing-table Rosa and Kitty had drawn up, jabbing his claw imperiously at the appropriate row. And after glaring balefully down toward it, Filak jerked an irritable nod, and stalked from the room.

"That is a damn good stone, though," Thrain said once he'd left, studying it with a speculative gleam in his eye. "Ken I might ask Thrak if he'd buy part of it for Dammarr's *kíróna*, if you'll hold it for the day, Ymir?"

Ymir sniffed and frowned at this, but accordingly locked the stone away under the counter. And when Kitty asked Thrain if she could see his progress on the *kíróna* so far, he excitedly agreed, and all but dragged her down the corridor to the forge. Proudly showing her the beginnings of the gold circlet he'd begun to make, its delicate base almost weightless in Kitty's palm.

It was truly impressive work, and once Kitty had exclaimed extensively over it, Thrain also showed her the heavy chain he'd been working on for Killik, with some help from Fjorvi. "Ended up making it a bit of a jewel, too," he told her. "With more of a curb chain, and a good solid locking clasp here, ach? Polished it up nice and shiny, too."

Kitty blinked at that, but refrained from pointing out that the chain seemed a bizarre choice for a jewel, and Killik certainly didn't seem the type to appreciate such things... right? However, when Killik showed up the next day to collect his chain, Kitty was astonished to see him carefully fingering at the heavy, gleaming steel links, with something almost like eagerness in his eyes.

"Will that work, d'you think?" Thrain asked as he strode in again, clearly having scented Killik from down the corridor. "It should take a hell of a lot to break that lock once you fasten it, but"—he demonstrated, locking and unlocking it, pulling the chain taut—"but if it does fail, just bring it back, ach?"

Killik actually nodded, and he even gave Thrain a brief little bow before tossing some human coins on the counter, and stalking off again. And once Ymir had written up the sale, it turned out that Killik had left a very generous tip, which Ymir grudgingly added to Thrain's account, even as his eyes glinted with unmistakable glee.

"Never thought about those *Skai* wanting jewels," he said, more to himself than Kitty or Thrain. "An entirely untapped market! I wonder…"

This soon led to Ymir creating another detailed list of heavy chains for Thrain—an *experimental investment*, he called it— and then demanding why he wasn't off working on the Ash-Kai orders yet. To which Thrain rolled his eyes, and replied—with surprising magnanimity—that he was, and that Kesst's new *hálsmen* ought to be done by morning.

It was indeed done by morning, and it turned out to be a simple, elegant piece, showing off the lovely stone to its best advantage. And when Kesst and Rathgarr stopped by the shop that afternoon, Kesst eagerly snatched the *hálsmen* out of Thrain's hands, and beamed at it with genuine delight.

"Look at this, Rath!" he exclaimed. "It's lovely! Who would have dreamt that *Thrain*, of all people, would turn out to be an adequate smith?!"

Thrain looked—rightfully—rather affronted by this, but Rathgarr sharply elbowed Kesst in the side, and grasped his hand to Thrain's shoulder. "Before the war, the Grisk were always our best goldsmiths, son," he said firmly. "It is to all our gain that Thrain has found his way to this again."

He was giving Thrain a proud, toothy smile—surely hinting at all their meetings over these past few weeks—and beside them, Kesst was looking distinctly apologetic, and clasping his new *hálsmen* to his chest. "It really is impressive, Thrain," he said, his voice earnest. "Fatherhood is looking good on you. And"—he drew in a breath, his head cocking—"sobriety, apparently, too. Congratulations, on all fronts."

Thrain shifted a little uncomfortably, waved it away with a shamefaced half-smile. But once they'd all left again, it occurred to Kitty that it had been many days now, or perhaps even weeks, since Thrain had taken a drink. Maybe even—a month?

And that very night—perhaps even in acknowledgement of that fact—Varinn gave Thrain another gift from his box. Two long, delicate matching gold chains, not meant for his neck, but—Kitty stared, dry-mouthed, as Varinn put them on—for his current jewels, instead. One long chain attached to the gold handle of the *rassja*, and the other one clipped onto the round bead at the tip of his *typpavír*.

And then—Varinn stepped backwards, his eyes glinting—the chains just... hung there. Shimmering and glittering as they swayed down from Thrain, in both front and back, brushing the floor every time he moved. And even those slight touches made Thrain's breath catch, his lashes fluttering—and when Varinn gently caught both chains in his hand, Thrain staggered and moaned and shuddered all over, his entire body gone rigid, his grey skin gleaming with sweat.

It was quite possibly the most shocking scene Kitty had witnessed from them yet, but she soon found herself settling onto Varinn's lap in his chair, her back to his front, so they could both look at Thrain properly. Drinking up the sight of him standing before them, his lean, beautiful body bucking and groaning for them, blatantly bared, on display. The sight so damned arousing that Varinn soon shifted beneath Kitty, slipping his rock-hard heft up inside her, so they could gasp and grind together as they watched.

"So good, *krútt*," Varinn breathed, hoarse, as he ran the

chains through his fingers, his hardness swelling fuller inside Kitty's clutching heat. "So pretty, when you are so full of my good Grisk gold. I have never known such a stunning orc in all my days, ach?"

Thrain staggered and gasped, his eyes rolling back, his hips thrusting into empty air. And Kitty moaned at the sight of that familiar slick white, finally seeping out from around the tip of his *typpavír*, coating the delicate gold chain. Making it sparkle and glimmer even more than before, and when the fluid reached Varinn's fingers, he lifted the chain to his mouth, and then to Kitty's, too.

"He scents even sweeter, when he is stoppered and craving thus," he purred, as his tongue curled against it, against Kitty's. "How long do you ken he can hold out for us, *kisa*?"

Kitty laughed, breathless, twisting the chain around her tongue. "For as long as you please, Lord Grisk," she whispered back. "But you won't be too cruel, right?"

Varinn's answering laugh was dark and hot, and he tugged a moaning Thrain a little closer. "Never more than he can bear," he murmured. "I can always scent what my *krútt* wishes for, ach? What he most longs for."

And oh, Thrain's moans were guttural, now, desperate, as Varinn licked his way up the chain, running it between his sharp teeth. Pulling Thrain closer, closer, closer, until he fell a little forward over them, his hands flat to the wall above their heads, holding up his trembling body—and with one last, purposeful snap of Varinn's sharp teeth, Thrain's *typpavír* somehow came loose, lurching into Varinn's waiting hand. And instead, Varinn's mouth was there, clamping around the swollen, glossy head of Thrain's cock. While Thrain bucked and writhed and shouted, slamming the wall with his palms, every muscle in his straining body rigid and gleaming as he poured out into Varinn's throat.

This, too, was a sight Kitty had never seen from them before, and she stared, enthralled, as Varinn sucked Thrain dry with the same methodical intensity he'd used on her. His gulps smooth and steady as he drank, his eyes fluttering—and now he was surging out inside Kitty too, pulsing again and again as his groan rumbled through his chest, and surely through his mouth around Thrain, too.

Afterwards, Thrain couldn't seem to stay upright, and he collapsed down onto them in a sweaty shuddering heap, his face buried in Varinn's neck. "You *didn't* just do that, Varinn," he mumbled, his words badly slurred. "You've *never* done that. Everyone will know, they'll scent me in your mouth, on your breath, every time you *speak*..."

His body kept heaving into them, his previously softened length already swelling against Kitty's belly, and Varinn huffed a husky laugh, drawing him closer. "Ach, I ken," he murmured back, kissing at Thrain's wild hair. "I wished to, *krútt*. You taste just as good as I always dreamt you would, ach?"

Thrain made a helpless, choked little sound, almost like a sob, his face thrusting deeper into Varinn's neck. And as Kitty snuggled closer, too, it occurred to her that Varinn had done the same with her, a few days before. Put her scent on his mouth, so everyone would know, every time he spoke...

It made the next few days even lovelier, most of all because—after taking some time to source his preferred alloy—Thrain was now finally working on the so-called gifts for Ella, alternating the work with Ymir's ever-expanding list, and Dammarr's far more labour-intensive *kíróna*. Thrain even called Kitty in to give him more specifics about what Ella had wanted for the rings—what kind of clasp, and whether she'd specified a shape—which conveniently granted Kitty the opportunity to glean his own preferences, and then to firmly claim them as Ella's, as well. And finally, several days later, Thrain dropped two bright, perfectly matching rings into Kitty's hand, his chest puffing out with obvious pride.

"Didn't realize how tricky they'd be, with that clasp," he said. "Remade the damn things a half-dozen times. But I know

Nattfarr's a real stickler for jewels—as any Aetha should be, really—and wouldn't want him to be disappointed, ach?"

Kitty eagerly agreed, and fervently thanked him as she tucked them into her palm. And that night, it was an utter joy to watch the shock—and then the delight—flash across Thrain's eyes as Varinn held the rings out toward him, and coolly beckoned him close.

"You—you devious little *hellcat!*" Thrain exclaimed at Kitty, his grin splitting his face. "And you, Varinn! You—you—you—"

He appeared truly incapable of speech, his mouth uselessly opening and closing, and Kitty laughed with Varinn as she grasped Thrain's arm, and dragged him over. "It was all Varinn, really," she said lightly. "But of course we both wanted to make sure you would like them, right, Varinn?"

Thrain was still looking stunned, and then genuinely moved, his eyes blinking hard as he stared down at the rings, and then up at Varinn's face. And Varinn was blinking too, and then leaning in to press a long, purposeful kiss to Thrain's mouth, his breath inhaling deep.

"Ach, your scent, *krútt*," he murmured as he drew away, a fond little smile pulling at his mouth. "I would have had Katharine order us even more, had I known you would be so pleased."

Thrain was still blinking, and sniffing, and giving Varinn a wavering, watery smile. "Just—to know you think my work is"—he wiped at his eyes—"good enough, for *you* to give, as a Grisk gift. To me."

Varinn's smile was still so fond, and a little bemused, too. "Ach, you ken it is," he said softly. "It brings me great joy, to grant such a gift to one who has been such a gift to me."

Thrain sniffed again, shook his head back and forth. "But— I haven't been," he gulped, his eyes still shimmering on Varinn's. "Gods, Varinn, I abandoned you to work alone for this, you should still be furious with me. Not to mention everything else I've done, with the drink, and how I—"

His head kept shaking, his breaths heaving, but Varinn brought up both his hands, settling them against Thrain's shoulders. "But you have worked so hard against this, *krútt*," he said. "You have fought against the drink, again and again. You have shown yourself a good father, and a strong protector of Katharine and our son. You made us this promise, and you have kept it. You keep finding your way, even if it is not always the one I made for you, and I love you all the more for this, ach?"

The water was streaking down Thrain's cheeks now, his head still shaking, even as Varinn kept nodding. "And should you yet welcome this, *krútt*," he continued, husky now, "I should yet be honoured to ask you—"

His own shoulders were rising and falling now, his eyes shining with meaning, with affection, with hope. "Thrain Aetha, of Clan Grisk," he said. "Will you be my mate?"

46

For a hushed, hanging instant, nothing moved. Only Varinn's shoulders, heaving up and down, as he searched Thrain's eyes, and held that small, hopeful smile to his mouth.

But Thrain had gone—still. Utterly, uncharacteristically still, his body rigid all over, his face draining of colour. Until his mouth thinned, and then twisted, and... crumpled.

"Oh gods," he whispered, a ragged gulp in his throat. "Oh gods, Varinn. I—I *can't.*"

Wait. He couldn't. He... couldn't?

The air seemed to vanish from the room, the stillness wrenched into something hollow, something... wrong. Something that cracked cold and jagged up Kitty's back, as Varinn betrayed a faint, unmistakable flinch, his hands spasming on Thrain's shoulders.

"Why... why not, *krútt*?" he finally asked into the silence, his voice unnaturally even. "What is amiss?"

Thrain's mouth was still crumpling, his eyes squeezing shut, and his head wrenched back and forth, as if he were in genuine pain. "I—I *know*, Varinn," he croaked. "I know what you did. All of it."

The ice kept cracking up Kitty's spine, spreading wider, colder, as Varinn kept staring at Thrain, his body just as frozen as she felt. "What I did," he repeated, still so even, so empty. "What... have I done?"

Thrain's mouth twisted harder, into something much like a sob—and then he wrenched away, backwards, out of Varinn's reach. "You lied to me," he choked, flailing his arm toward Varinn, and... and toward Kitty. "About—this. You told me you spoke a vow. You told me you wanted Kit, wanted to make her your mate. But you were lying. Faking it. The whole fucking *time*, Varinn."

Oh. Oh, no, no, no, Thrain didn't know, he couldn't know, how had he possibly known—and Kitty's own horrified shock was there, etching into Varinn's face, into the painful-looking spasm in his throat. While Thrain was still shaking his head, dragging his hands through his hair, fighting to haul in breath.

"I knew something was off from the start," he continued, "'cause I can still *scent* you, Varinn, gods damn it. But then the memories started filtering back, and I—I remembered, what you said, when you punched me that day in the woods. *Everything.*"

The ice was fraying now, fracturing up Kitty's back, because those awful words of Varinn's were already here, rising so sharp and painfully familiar, as if he'd spoken them just a moment ago. *You ken I should wish to steal her? A weak, foolish, thoughtless, spoilt woman, with a hundred scents upon her? A woman who is for sale.*

Varinn's throat spasmed again, but he didn't speak, and Thrain barked a laugh, loud and harsh and bitter. "But it's been clear you both—wanted me believing this," he said, again flailing his hand between them. "So I've been trying to just ignore it, and just keep going, ach? Because it's still been so damn good, and it's everything I've ever wanted, *everything*. For me, and—and for our son. And I *know* how much I owe you both, I know how much I've fucked this up, I know I'm damned lucky to still have even this much from you. But—but—"

His voice was swallowed by his heaving breaths, by the awful aching misery beneath his words. "But I—I can't keep doing it anymore, Varinn," he gasped. "Can't speak a vow to you, when I don't know if it's real. Don't know"—his breath heaved again, his glimmering eyes finally shifting toward Kitty's—"what this even is between you two, ach? I ken you did speak a vow to care for her, Varinn, but—"

His voice broke again, his eyes shimmering on Kitty's face, as his hand rubbed at his mouth. "What did he promise you, Kit?" he whispered. "Did he offer to—to pay you?"

To pay her. The words seemed to thunder out between them, sinking like a fist into Kitty's undefended belly. Enough to make her stagger backwards, the breath surging from her lungs, but Thrain was drawing in more air, holding his miserable eyes to her face. "Was that it, then?" he choked. "He paid you off? Enough for you to forgive me, and still have my son? And even"—his mouth contorted again—"to keep welcoming me into your bed, when I behaved?"

Oh gods, no, no, no, Thrain couldn't be saying this, he couldn't truly have thought this, all this time?! But more comprehension kept slamming into Kitty's belly, harsh and vicious and horrifying. Because maybe—maybe that was what she'd done. Maybe that *was* exactly what she'd agreed to, at the start of all this. *I shall care for you and your son*, Varinn had said, *and you shall help me care for Thrain.*

That had been—the transaction. The deal. Varinn's care— including his coin—in exchange for Kitty's compliance. Her repayment of her debt.

He'd paid her, because she'd been—for sale. Just as he'd said. Just as they'd all always known.

And the ice was finally breaking, shattering Kitty apart, escaping in a rush of water, streaking down her cheeks. And she was biting her lip so hard it hurt, her hands clutching against her swollen waist, against—against Varinn's *thyrja*, oh gods. And her head was shaking, or maybe nodding, and what could she do, what could she say, how could she possibly, possibly fix this. She still owed Varinn, she still had her debt, and she—she loved him. Loved him, and loved Thrain, so much it was clawing at her, tearing her apart. There had to be something, anything, please gods, please, Lord Grisk, please...

"It wasn't—Varinn's fault," she finally choked at him, at them. "It was—it was *mine*."

47

I*t was mine.*

The words wrenched at Kitty's throat, her chest, her heart—but they were out. They were out, they were real, and they were—they were true.

"It was—my idea," she gulped at them, at Thrain's miserable face, at Varinn's blank, empty eyes. "I was the one who—suggested it. I was the one who first—propositioned Varinn. I told him I would stay here, and go along with everything he wanted, if he—took care of me. If he—helped me find a trade. If he—paid."

She could feel the truth in her words, could almost taste the bitter shame in it, and she couldn't even look at Varinn or Thrain anymore, couldn't bear it. "So of course—he agreed," she whispered. "For you, Thrain, and—and your son, because he would do anything, anything within his power, to help you, and keep you safe. And that's why I've been working at the shop all this time, it was part of the deal. Part of—my payment. That's all."

She had to bite out the last part, had to make herself keep standing there through the horrible, hanging emptiness.

Fighting against the waves of misery, of guilt and loss and regret, because she had been for sale, she always had been, why had she ever pretended otherwise.

But—she risked a brief, wet-eyed glance at Varinn's pale face—maybe, maybe this would do it. This would be enough to—pay her debt, once and for all. If she took all the guilt, all the blame, so there was none left for him. So he and Thrain could reconcile, they could swear those vows to one another, without her coming in between them. They could be the matched pair they'd always been meant to be. The lost orphan and his saviour, the worshipper and his lord, the wild magical Aetha and his wise Thjoth handler. Best friends, for always.

But Varinn didn't—look pleased. Or relieved. If anything, he looked almost—ill. His face so pale, his eyes so blank and empty, his bulky body so rigid and stiff. His hand skittering up, rubbing hard at his nose, as if—as if he couldn't bear the scent, couldn't bear to breathe.

While beside him, Thrain—scoffed. The sound loud and harsh and disbelieving, grating through the room. "What the hell, Varinn," he hissed, his voice cracking. "You're just going to let her spout this rubbish? Let her take all the blame for this?"

Kitty froze again, her eyes snapped wide on Thrain's face, because he—he was wrong, he was, he couldn't know, he couldn't. And she needed to keep trying, keep saying it, keep paying her debt, please—

"It is my fault," she forced out, into the agonizing emptiness. "It is, Thrain. Not Varinn's. He was only—"

"It is not your fault!" Thrain exploded at her, his hands in fists, his eyes suddenly blazing. "And ach, even if you won't blame Varinn, you need to at least blame me! This is still so much more my fault than yours. *So much more*, Kit!"

Kitty tried to shake her head, to speak, but Thrain made a strange, strangled sound, his hand flailing out between them. "I was the one who came onto you that night," he hissed. "I was the one who asked to walk a foxed, weeping girl home. I was the one who came inside your apartment, the one who touched you first. I was the one who was spiralling and losing his shit, I was the one who still had an attachment, and I damn well knew it! And"—he hauled in an unsteady breath, jabbed a finger toward her—"I was the one who looked at you, scented you, touched you, and had the fucking *audacity* to think—to think—"

He broke off there, his voice catching into a harsh, high-pitched laugh. And Kitty's heart was thundering, suddenly, too high and dangerous in her throat, and she only distantly noticed Varinn staring at Thrain too, his breaths audible through his nose. "To think what," he hissed, very quiet. "*What, Thrain.*"

Thrain laughed again, not a laugh at all, and dragged both hands against his hair. "I just thought—you would like her," he said, his voice heavy, wooden. "Just the kind of woman you always liked best, ach? Sweet, eager to please, likes to be told what to do, and to be looked after—but not a fearful fainting prude, either. You ken I haven't scented you around Alma? Or Rosa, with that pretty little *kraga* she wears?"

Oh. Oh, gods. The ice was creeping in again, closing around Kitty's chest, or maybe it was something rotten, something dark and jealous and wrong. Varinn had liked *Alma*... and *Rosa*, too? And he was just staring at Thrain now, unmoving, as Thrain laughed again, the sound grinding horribly through Kitty's ears.

"It wasn't—a plan," Thrain rasped out. "And I obviously still wanted Kit, and I was foxed, and spiralling into my rubbish. But the thought was still"—he heaved for more breath—"there, in my fucked-up drunken head. That maybe— maybe—it would work out. I'd put my scent on her, we'd have a roaring blow-out fight over it, and then—you'd meet her. You'd scent her. You'd—see."

Oh. No. No, no, no, Kitty couldn't move, couldn't think, could only stare with Varinn at Thrain's sweaty face, his shaky, twitchy body. "Because—you're getting older, Varinn," he choked. "Over thirty summers now. And you keep saying you want that woman, that son. You've said it for years, ach? You keep sneaking down to that damned foul crypt, longing for the scent of your own blood, but you've never actually—tried. Never sought out a mate. Never even looked twice at any of the women who've sniffed around you, even the ones without a single scent upon them. I could scent them, could scent *you*, but it's always been some fool excuse or another. The war, too risky, too busy. And when I brought up seeking out a woman together, you shot that down, too. Said we couldn't risk finding someone who didn't want both of us."

Varinn wasn't moving, Kitty wasn't moving, still just trapped in Thrain's words, in the helpless guilty misery glimmering in his eyes. "It was because—of *me*," he said, a hoarse scrape in his throat. "You were putting it off because you didn't want to lose *me*. And I love you for it, Varinn, I do, but you—you need that son, ach? You need that scent so much it hurts you. And I can't stand the thought of being the one who's kept it from you. Can't *bear* the thought of you—you going down into that crypt forever—leaving me here—without it. And you *could* die, ach? Every day you're out there, saving the world for the rest of us."

The silence echoed out after his words, clanging with truth, with loss, with grief. With Thrain gulping for air now, scrubbing both hands at his face. "So mayhap—mayhap I wanted to blow us up, too," he whispered. "Never meant to spark a son of my blood in it, *ever*, but mayhap I wanted to do something... unforgivable. And then you'd come in and pick up the pieces, just like you always do. Just like—your father did."

Oh. Oh, no. Oh, gods, that tale of their fathers, how Thrain's father had abandoned a woman, how Varinn's father had gone in to help her. How they'd fallen in love, and then—

"And because of my father's rubbish, *you're* here," Thrain's thick voice continued. "*You're* here, Varinn, and you've saved so many of us. You saved *me*."

There was even more silence, ringing, breaking between them—and then another one of Thrain's laughs, almost a sob. "But the whole idea was fucked, I know, and then I—fucked it up even more," he croaked. "When I woke up the next morning, and panicked, and ran. Left Kit alone and pregnant, just like my waste of a father did. And ach, you eventually went in and tried to fix it, but your problem was, you also tried to fix *me*. To keep me, and forgive me, when it should've been unforgivable. And I should have seen it, you've always sworn you'd never leave me, or forget me. And I don't think I really believed it, until—until—"

More silence, so painful it was crumpling in Kitty's chest, and Thrain waved toward her, another sob catching in his throat. "Until you did this," he whispered. "You pretended to care for Kit, to speak a vow to her, for me. And I've wanted to believe it so much, Varinn, more than I've ever wanted anything in my life—but I can't keep going on like this. It's not right, and it's not fair to her, or—or to you. Most of all after you've both been so, so good to me."

The tears were streaking down his face, now, the sobs shaking his shoulders, and somehow Kitty was weeping too, the hot liquid dripping from her chin. And without warning, Thrain lurched toward her, clasped her hand in both of his, squeezed it in his cold clammy fingers.

"You deserve better, Kit," he choked. "You've deserved better, all this time. And I ken you're just trying to take all the blame for Varinn, so the two of us will work it out, but all those things you said"—he barked another hoarse little laugh-sob— "that was all just him doing his damned *job*, ach? Sniffing out Grisk mothers who need help, offering what they need, helping them get back on their feet, mayhap with some training or some coin? He does that every second *week*. He's helped *dozens* of women like you. That's what he fucking *does*, it's what our clan pays him to do every day—and you know he fucking *lives* for it. You don't owe him a damned fucking *thing*."

Oh. And it was this, somehow, this unthinkably obvious realization, that suddenly kindled a spark of mortified heat, amidst all the ice frozen in Kitty's bones. Varinn had just been—doing his job. She hadn't been—special, in any way. And the debt, the deal, even that hadn't been a special pact between them, something that had mattered. It had been for—for—

I shall do all that is within my power. No matter the cost.

The heat kept licking higher, burning across Kitty's face, as her eyes dropped to—to her *thyrja*. Her rounded belly. Her ridiculous little kilt. To all the things she'd thought had meant something. To all the ways she'd again let herself rely on a man, let herself believe he cared, that he had her best interests at heart. When in truth—in truth—

You're a beautiful, helpful, charming girl. You know how to present yourself. You're a lot of fun, especially in bed...

"Katharine," broke in an urgent voice, Varinn's voice, and suddenly he was here, too close, clasping her other hand in his strangely hot fingers. "Ach, do not scent thus. Do not even *think* thus. I ken I have oft been—wrong, and even cruel, amidst all this. But"—he drew in a ragged-sounding breath—"I was not speaking false, when we spoke of this in the crypt, ach? Now that we have better learnt one another, you are just what I have most longed for in a woman. You have been a great gift to me."

But Kitty couldn't even look up now, couldn't bear to meet his eyes, because that—that was just what he would say, wasn't it? What he should say, if he was trying to fix this, to salvage this, to save face for Thrain. *I shall do all within my power...*

"Please, Katharine," Varinn's voice said, quiet again, unusually thick. "I ken I—I ought to have spoken truth to Thrain, upon this. For ach, he does not know—he could not know—all that has passed between us, since the start. And I ought to have known that he knew, I ought to have paid closer heed, it is clear I have not always been"—another ragged breath—"at my best, of late. I thought—I thought we understood one another, I thought we had settled this, and I am—very sorry to know I have failed you, once again. I wish to make amends for this, *kisa*, I wish to be a good and worthy mate to you. Please."

Kitty had never heard him sound like this, speak like this, with so much rushed desperation in his voice—but he would do anything, anything for Thrain, and she clung to that, to the dregs of her willpower, her awareness. Needed to stop believing everything a man said, just because he'd said it, because gods, even now, it was so bizarrely, blatantly untrue.

"But—you're not my mate," she somehow whispered, to the floor. "You never did—speak a vow. Not—that kind."

And gods, she could feel Varinn's flinch, could hear the sharp hiss from Thrain behind him. And then the sound of Varinn's breaths again, long and laboured, shuddering too close between them.

"I only wished," he finally said, "to wait until—you were ready, also. Until you had chosen—for certain—to stay. I did not wish to push you or bind you to me any further, after all I had already done to you. But"—another dragging breath—"should you wish, sweet *kisa*, I should be most honoured to offer you this. Today. Now."

And it was that, suddenly, that dragged Kitty's eyes up to his face. To where—he looked—ashen. Ill. His eyes bright and pained, blinking far too fast, as his lips pressed tight together, his breath again dragging through his nose. As if he again meant this, he couldn't mean this, he—

"My dearest Katharine," he began, his voice hushed, raspy, catching in his throat. "Before all my fathers and mothers, and all the Grisk, and all the gods, I wish to pledge you my—"

But Kitty was yanking away, tripping backwards, whipping her head back and forth. No. No, no, no, he didn't mean it, he couldn't, not like this, or—or—

Or did he? Because he was rubbing hard at his eyes, his shoulders shuddering, and behind him Thrain was looking suddenly alarmed, lurching up toward him. Gripping at Varinn's arm with all his claws, their black points sinking deep into his skin, but Varinn hadn't even seemed to notice, because he was—was he *weeping*? Weeping, over—over *her*?

But no, no, he would do anything, anything, except hurting Thrain—but Thrain was still looking hurt, and lost, and... frightened. His eyes on Kitty almost pleading, suddenly, as if she needed to fix this, and she needed to fix this, please gods, please, Lord Grisk, please...

"I just—need some time," she somehow gulped. "Just need—to think about this, for a while. Alone. Please."

And Varinn—didn't hesitate. Didn't even look at her. Just jerked a curt little nod, spun on his heel, and—strode from the room. Leaving the curtain wildly swaying in his wake, and Kitty stared blankly toward it, while the ice seemed to crack through her again, clamping around her throat.

No. No, he couldn't go, he'd gone, because she'd asked him to go. And there was the urge, sudden and almost overpowering, to chase after him, to catch him, to feel him wrap her into his warm safe arms. Because he would do that too, he would the instant she asked, but would he mean it, oh gods would he mean it...

"Fuck," whispered a voice, muffled and rough, and when Kitty whirled toward it, it was—Thrain. Still standing here, staring at her, with his hand clamped over his mouth, the whites of his eyes gleaming in the lamplight. "Fuck, fuck, fuck. Gods, Kit, I'm sorry. *Fuck*."

But the words seemed to wash through her without meaning, without consequence, even as her thoughts dragged up a similar memory from weeks—months?—before. Thrain in her apartment, his hand over his mouth, cursing under his breath. With that same raw panic shining, shouting, in his eyes.

"You should—go after him," she somehow said, through her constricted throat. "He shouldn't be—in the crypt—alone."

Thrain's head was rapidly nodding, his mouth grimacing, both his claws hands dragging at his face. But even as he lurched toward the door, he was already whirling back, catching her hand in his again. "I'm so sorry," he choked. "I shoulda better thought, before dragging all this up. Didn't realize you two were really—*och*. Leave it to me, to fuck it all up again."

He'd barked an awful, bitter laugh, and he rapidly shook his head, squeezed his eyes shut. "And gods, I know how all that must have sounded," he said, in a rush. "But I still— wanted you, Kit. Wanted you so damned much. Still do, ach?"

But the words still just felt so empty, washing over Kitty without meaning, because he'd kept all this secret, too. He'd promised to be honest, to earn her trust again, to be—a friend. And he had been, he had, and maybe that was why it hurt so much.

I wanted to do something—unforgivable. And maybe you'd come in and pick up the pieces.

Because again, it had been about—them. About Thrain and Varinn. Not about her. Maybe it had never been about her, for either of them, from the very start.

But she couldn't bear to say it aloud, not without breaking down sobbing, and she somehow felt herself nodding, and maybe even attempting a smile. "Of course," she said, through the waver in her voice. "We'll discuss it later, if that's all right? We certainly wouldn't want him to get locked in down there."

She'd spoken far too quickly, but she'd said it, and even managed that smile up toward Thrain's face—but he didn't smile back. If anything, he just looked sad, his throat swallowing hard, his eyes bright and bleak.

"Still too good for all this rubbish, Kit," he said gruffly, as he leaned in, and pressed a soft, brief kiss to her hair. "I'll be back as soon as I can, ach?"

Kitty nodded, fervent and rapid, because he just needed to go, now, now—and he nodded too, pressed another kiss to the top of her head. "Thank you, sweet kitten," he whispered. "I—I love you."

And as those impossible, assuredly untruthful words hung between them, Thrain spun toward the door, and fled.

48

K itty ended up in the shop. Pacing up and down the aisles, trailing her fingers against the familiar, neatly stacked shelves.

Gods, what was she doing. She should have stayed in their room, should have curled up and sobbed beneath the fur. But she hadn't been able to bear the smells, the shelves, the chair. All those memories of pleasure, of warmth, of... happiness.

So without thinking, without following why, she'd taken off her *thyrja* with shaky hands, and then her earrings and bracelet, too. And then she'd drawn over Varinn's box, and snapped it open.

And inside it, there were those painfully familiar jewels— the *rassjas*, the chains, the *typpavír*, Varinn's own large gold ring. But... nothing else. No other jewels she hadn't seen before, because Varinn had—he'd given them all of it, everything he'd had. Everything his dead parents had left behind. And Kitty had stared at it for far too long, as more hot wetness streaked down her cheeks, and gasping sobs choked from her throat.

She'd finally stuffed her own jewels back inside, snapping the box closed—and then she'd snatched up the lamp, and rushed from the room. Out into the thankfully empty sitting-room, the quiet dark corridors, just following the familiar path to—the shop. To a place that felt just—like hers. A place where she could think, could try to comb through the chaos still screeching in her skull.

Varinn had—tried to speak a vow to her. Thrain had said— he loved her. Varinn would do anything for Thrain, Thrain had known the entire time, Thrain had planned for this, had done this for Varinn, to gain Varinn a son. While Varinn had just been helping Thrain, just trying to save him. And also just doing his damned job, what he was paid to do, *he's helped dozens of women like you. You ken I haven't scented you around Alma? Or Rosa, with that pretty little* kraga *she wears?*

But no, no no no, that wasn't all of it, and it wasn't—fair, either. For all he'd done, Varinn had never shown the slightest interest in anyone but her and Thrain. He'd cared for her, he'd kept his word to her, he'd been unfailingly generous and kind. And even if he had helped other pregnant women, surely he hadn't... *fed* them. Hadn't shared their beds, hadn't let them kiss his feet, make him promises, put themselves in his debt. *You know how he gets off on the control, ach?*

But gods—Kitty sagged against the jewel-case, sank her head into her hands—they'd still both lied to her. They'd still done it for—each other. For—their son.

And maybe—Kitty's hands slid down her front, caught on her belly, as more water streamed down her cheeks—maybe that was the horrible, final crux of it. Varinn had done it to save Thrain from the drink. And Thrain had done it to give Varinn a son. And they—maybe they'd even succeeded, and now Kitty just needed to get—out of the way, just like she'd planned all along. Learn a trade. Run a shop. And then leave, and never, ever trust a man again.

"Kitty?" cut in a voice, deep and familiar—and Kitty flailed backwards, into the shelf. Her watery eyes blinking hard, squinting toward—oh. It was Harthr, standing a careful distance away, his head tilted, his brow creased. "Are you—well?"

Kitty sniffed and belatedly wiped at her wet face, her fingers clammy and trembly against her skin. "Oh, fine!" she heard her voice say, very far away. "Perfectly fine. I'm just—rather overtired, is all."

Harthr smiled, but it looked a little odd in the darkness, and Kitty could just catch his gaze flicking downwards, toward—oh. Toward where her *thyrja* should have been, gods curse it, and Kitty's hand fluttered to her bare collarbone, felt her heart thudding beneath her chilly skin.

"So I really ought to be getting to bed, then," she said, as brightly as she could. "Perhaps I'll see you in the morn—"

But the words broke in her throat, because Harthr had—lunged. Lunged toward her, swift and sudden, and—grabbed her. Clamping both her wrists in a tight, too-powerful grip, and yanking her close into his hot, sweaty skin.

"No, pretty pussycat," he said, his eyes alight with satisfaction, with... victory. "Tonight, you come with *me*."

49

She would come with him? With *Harthr?!*

Kitty stared at him, utterly frozen, as the shock and the nausea crashed and surged in her belly. As Harthr just kept looking at her, with that strange sickening victory lighting up his eyes.

"Thought those two would never leave you alone," he continued, with a grin that might have once been charming. "But I knew if I waited long enough, they'd slip up sooner or later, ach?"

Kitty's heartbeat was thundering, wailing against the still-rising nausea, the staggering incredulous disbelief. "But you," she gulped, "you don't—actually want—"

You don't want me, she'd been about to say, and her shaking hand had even waved down at her belly—and Harthr followed her hand with obvious distaste, his nose wrinkling. "Ach, no," he said flatly. "I don't want other orcs' used goods—let alone ones who already *reek* of men, as you do. Still shocked Varinn would go for that, either, but"—he shrugged and smiled, baring his sharp white teeth—"we all know he's desperate, ach? Runs in the family, I ken."

The nausea churned higher in Kitty's belly, and too late, she fought to yank her hands backwards, away—but Harthr's grip was far too strong, clamping painfully tight as he jerked her closer again. "Oh no you don't, pussycat," he growled. "I said, you're coming with me. Or rather"—he gave a cold, brittle smile—"you're running away, will be the tale I'll tell come morning. Begged me to take you home."

Kitty's head was shaking, whipping back and forth, but oh, gods, Harthr was already yanking her down the aisle, toward her mending station. And why was he doing this, what was this, please—

"But—why?" she gulped, through her screeching thoughts. "Why? Where? What—what have I ever done to you? I thought—I thought I was helpful, I thought we were friends?!"

Her voice had wrenched to a painfully high pitch in her ears, enough that Harthr grimaced as he glanced back toward her. "You're still a human," he said, with a dismissive shrug of his shoulder. "And ach, you *were* helpful. So helpful, in truth, with all those contacts, that our buyers kept running into that man Charles, ach? Charles Tatterham."

Charles. Damn him, Charles. And even the thought of him was flashing more bitter ice through Kitty's trembling body, as the nausea roiled and curdled in her belly. "And?" she made herself say, over her shaky, panting breaths. "I told you he's rubbish, you'll lose coin dealing with him, and—"

"Oh, give it up, pussycat," Harthr snapped back, with a roll of his eyes. "That man *reeks* of you, and you of him. And once he heard your name, heard you were here, he became *very* interested indeed."

What? Kitty gaped at Harthr, and wildly shook her head. "But—Charles and I broke up," she managed. "He left me. Wanted nothing—to do with me."

But Harthr only shrugged again, and yanked Kitty over toward—oh. To where the familiar cart was waiting, oh gods, already loaded up with goods...

"Ach, but you humans are so fickle," Harthr replied.

"Changed his mind, and decided he wants you back. Offered a price we couldn't refuse."

He was even smiling at her, *winking* at her, as if this was some relaxed trading discussion, and not—not her *life*. He was taking her back to Charles, because Charles had—had *paid?!*

"You must be mistaken," Kitty's voice babbled, very far away. "You have to be. Charles didn't want me. He took all his jewels back. He—he had me thrown out on the street to *starve*."

Her voice was badly hitching now, very close to sobs, or panic, or both—and that was a twist on Harthr's mouth, another shrug of his shoulder. "Said something about his business needing the help," he replied. "And his trading partners. How they've been asking after you, and falling off without you, or some such."

His lip curled with clear contempt, or even mockery—but the panic in Kitty's chest was wheeling higher, nearer to terror with every gasping breath. Because gods, that—that was just like Charles. Wasn't it? He'd taken her entirely for granted, ignored all her efforts toward him, toward his business, toward his associates and meetings and parties. And now that he'd begun to see an impact on his pocketbook, he'd decided he wanted her back. Of course.

"No," Kitty gasped, the word a thin, desperate croak. "No, Harthr. You can't. You can't take me back to Charles. Please. *Please*."

But Harthr wasn't even looking back at her now, dragging her with unrelenting force toward the loaded cart. Toward where—Kitty nearly tripped—Grein and Knorr were both striding out of the tunnel. Grein visibly hesitating as his eyes caught on her, while Knorr's mouth pulled into a chilly, satisfied smile.

"They're both trapped down there, then?" Harthr asked them, his voice damnably smug, as he kept dragging Kitty toward the cart. "You sealed the doors? Shut off the ventilation?"

Wait. Wait wait wait, Kitty was staggering again, the nausea surging dangerously close, because Knorr was nodding. Nodding, and eyeing Kitty, still with that cold, amused smile on his mouth. "All done," he said smoothly. "And confirmed that our other best scenters are out of the mountain now, too. So we should have plenty of time, and"—his smile sharpened—"those two arseholes won't be getting out of that crypt. Now, or ever."

And he was—they were talking about—*Varinn and Thrain.* In the—crypt. They'd—they'd trapped them. Sealed the doors. Shut off the ventilation, not getting out now, or ever...

"You—you didn't," Kitty gasped, as black spots flashed behind her eyes, the dread curling around her throat. "You didn't—lock Varinn—and *Thrain*—in the *crypt*? With—no ventilation? With—*gas*?"

But no, oh gods no, Thrain hated the crypt, hated being trapped, this couldn't be happening—but Knorr was laughing, *laughing*, as he strode over to the cart, and leapt up into it. "Just the way they both always wanted to go, ach?" he replied. "The way they should've gone years ago, after what their fool fathers did to our clan."

No, no no no, but beside Kitty, Harthr was barking a laugh too, and dragging her closer toward the cart. "Ach, it's about time the scourge of the Aetha was ended," he said flatly. "It's a shame about Varinn, but by this point he deserves it, ach? And if all goes well"—his cold eyes flicked down to Kitty, to her belly—"this should deal with the Aetha spawn, too."

Kitty staggered, stared, as the nausea speared higher, as the full comprehension began careening through her gasping, trembling body. They were trying to *murder* Varinn and Thrain, and they were—*selling* her. Selling her to Charles, who—who wouldn't stand for an orc son. Who would try to have her son—killed.

Kitty couldn't see, couldn't breathe, couldn't move through the panic, the terror, the rage. And Harthr had grasped her by the waist, lifting her up toward the cart, toward Knorr, his cruel clawed hands gripping her belly, pressing against her churning stomach, against her *son*—

And before she'd even followed it, Kitty heaved, and retched, and vomited into Harthr's face.

50

For an instant, there was chaos.

Harthr cursed and hurled Kitty away, sending her tumbling back against the cart, as he yanked off his tunic, and scrubbed at his face. And gods, even the sight of it, the scent of it, was enough to make Kitty's stomach heave again, but she had a moment, an opportunity...

She ran. Pitching off down the aisle as fast as she could, streaking straight for the door. Her feet pounding the stone floor, her hair flying out behind her, while her heartbeat screamed in her ears. She just needed to find anyone, anyone, so close, please, *please*—

But then something crashed into her. Something big and hot and horribly powerful, and though Kitty kicked and flailed against it, it was far too strong. It was Knorr, gods damn it, his face contorted with cold fury, and Kitty hissed at him, and spat at his eyes. "Get—off me!" she shouted, as loudly as she could. "Help! Anyone! *Help*!"

But there was nothing, only Knorr's painful grip, his furious growl thundering into Kitty's chest. "Silence, woman," he barked at her. "Lest you wish your son to meet my fists!"

The ice flashed up Kitty's spine, swarmed out more

horrified terror, swallowed the words in her throat. And Knorr laughed, hard and mocking, as he roughly gripped her arm, and yanked her back down the aisle. Down to the shelf with the chains, oh gods, and he snatched one up—one of Thrain's brand-new jewels for the Skai—and began binding Kitty's wrists behind her back. "Now, fool woman," he snapped, "we'll try this again. And you'll stay silent, else I'll gag you, also!"

Kitty desperately fought to think, to find some kind of mooring in the terror, and she shook her head, gulped for air. "You can't gag me, or hurt me," she gasped. "If Charles has really paid for me, he'll expect me delivered alive and well. If I've choked on my own vomit because of *your* foolishness in gagging me, he won't be very happy with you, will he?"

Knorr growled again, but that had surely been a displeased twitch in his eyes, so Kitty kept seeking, searching. Catching, suddenly, on the nausea, on how it had been so negligible, all this time, until now. Not because it had gone away, clearly, but because of... Varinn and Thrain. Because they'd made sure she was... filled, fed, with their seed, every single day. Just as Efterar had said...

"Also, my pregnancy has made me very, *very* ill," Kitty continued, rapid, breathless. "And it's only because of Varinn and Thrain's care that I've been faring as well as I have! So if you don't want me to wither away and *perish* on your watch, or keep sicking up all over you and your valuable goods, you need to take better care, starting now!"

Knorr's growl had deepened, but his grip on her arm was perhaps a little less painful, even as he yanked the chain tight around her wrists, and began pulling her back toward the cart. "I said, silence, woman," he snapped. "You're ours now, and we'll do with you as we wish!"

"You will not!" Kitty shot back, and with another burst of desperate courage, she kicked at Knorr, and writhed wildly against his grip. "And I am *not* yours, I'm Varinn and Thrain's!

And if you think they'll just wait down in that crypt and let you get away with this, you're out of your damned *minds*!"

Knorr barked in response this time, but Kitty didn't miss his uneasy glance toward Harthr, who was still scrubbing at his face—and now glowering viciously toward her as he hurled the soiled tunic aside. "Ignore her, Knorr," he spat. "That crypt is a sealed tomb, with only one way in and out, and not even their *scents* will escape it. Now get her into the cart, and let's go!"

Kitty kicked and squirmed, but it was useless against Knorr's punishing grip, and now against Grein's, too. Both of them hauling her up into the cart, although—Kitty distantly noted—they both were careful to avoid her midsection this time, and Grein's grip was as brief as possible as he lowered her down to sit on a large wooden crate.

"Is there aught else you need," Grein muttered, not quite meeting her eyes, and Kitty twitched as she searched his taut face, as her thoughts again skittered and swooped. He was offering to get her something. She had to think, damn it, think...

"Could I have—some warm clothes?" she managed. "A cloak, perhaps? And some water? To keep me from perishing from the cold—or dehydration—while you kidnap me?"

Behind Grein, Knorr barked another curt, irritated growl, but Grein had actually winced and nodded, and leapt out of the cart. And Kitty shot a bright, brittle smile toward Knorr, who was still looming menacingly over her. "Maybe I'll tell Varinn and Thrain to go easy on Grein, when they catch you," she said sweetly. "Of course, I wouldn't do the same for you."

Knorr bared his teeth at her, and spun around to yank at the metal contraption at the cart's front, perhaps its steering mechanism. "Keep dreaming, fool woman," he hissed over his shoulder. "They won't leave that crypt alive, and I'll be *glad* to finally scent their rotting corpses!"

The hatred in his voice was palpable, almost painful, and Kitty's false smile faded as she blinked at him, and the cart jerked into motion beneath them. "But—why?" she asked, her voice catching. "Gods, what have Varinn and Thrain ever done to you? They've both worked so hard to help their clan. To help orcs like *you*."

She only vaguely noticed Harthr and Grein jumping back into the moving cart, Grein indeed with a heavy cloak in one hand, and a waterskin in the other. "We don't *need* their *help*," Harthr snarled, frowning as Grein slung the cloak over Kitty's shoulders, and—after an uneasy glance toward Harthr—gingerly set the waterskin in her lap. Where Kitty couldn't possibly touch it, let alone drink from it, with her hands still bound like this, and she frowned balefully toward it, and then up toward Harthr's hard, narrow eyes.

"Our clan has had enough *help* from the Aetha to last us a dozen generations," he continued flatly. "They promised us a better life, a better future—and then they almost *destroyed* us, with their magic and their *lies*! When we were orclings"—Harthr's voice hardened, sharpened—"there were many hundreds of Grisk in this mountain. And now, thanks to the Aetha, most of them are *dead*!"

Kitty stared at him, her thoughts distantly screeching at the pain in his words, at how the cart was moving faster, faster, rolling down the tunnel on its own. "And," Harthr added, jabbing his claw toward Kitty, "Thjoth like Varinn have allowed this, again and again. You ken our clan would have ever left this mountain at all, had Varinn's father not gone with them? Ach, even now, you ken the Grisk would have welcomed Nattfarr and his reckless fool cousins as our leaders, without Varinn by their side?"

The nausea was distantly churning again, and Kitty gritted her teeth, searched for a reply. "Look, I understand you being angry over what happened with their fathers, and the attack," she managed, "but what, exactly, have Varinn and Thrain themselves actually done to you? Or Thrak, or Nattfarr?"

She didn't miss how Grein was looking away now, his gaze

intent on the rough stone wall sweeping past, but Harthr's eyes were still blazing, his lip curling. "Nattfarr spent *years* larking about the realm and leaving us without his magic, when we needed it most," he hissed. "Thrak is an arrogant overbearing *jester*, and Thrain"—he scoffed—"is a needy wasteful drunkard, who shall guzzle down all the strongest ale you can offer him, and then keep 'forgetting' how much he promised to pay!"

But—wait. Wait, was that—satisfaction, glinting in Harthr's eyes? Triumph? Because—wait, gods curse it, *Harthr* had been the one supplying Thrain with drink, all this time—and he'd even kept offering it that day in the shop. Even when Kitty had been there, even after Thrain had refused. And how had she forgotten that, forgotten how much Harthr had pushed that? And also—another suspicion surged up—would Thrain truly have kept forgetting how much he owed? Whatever his faults, he'd never seemed stingy or greedy over coin, had he? *Good Grisk gold is meant to be earned, given...*

"So, not only were you supplying Thrain with the strongest ale you could find," Kitty said, her voice very thin, "but you were lying to him about the price, too? So what, he wouldn't be able to pay it, and then"—the suspicion twisted, tangled with a memory from weeks before—"and then *Varinn* would pay it instead. And then they'd fight over it, and you'd keep driving a wedge between them, while pocketing the extra coin yourself!"

Her voice rang with certainty, with contempt, and Harthr's lip curled higher, his hands clenching at his sides. "We didn't force the ale down Thrain's throat," he shot back. "We were doing good business, to help the clan. And if anything, we were trying to do Varinn a favour! If he wasn't so fuck-drunk on the Aetha mayhem, he'd have tossed Thrain—and Nattfarr—out *years* ago, and helped the rest of our clan move on in peace! But no"—he barked a hard laugh—"it's too deep in his stubborn Thjoth blood. The need to pet and coddle the deranged Aetha, to keep them from destroying themselves, no matter the cost to the rest of us!"

Kitty's head had begun to ache, her nausea churning higher, as she stared at Harthr, and more comprehension coiled through her skull. Harthr had... wanted Varinn's help. Harthr was... jealous of the Aetha. Of... Thrain?

"So remind me again, what do you actually *want*?" Kitty snapped, her voice clipped, as her hands spasmed against the chain binding them. "What do you expect Varinn to do for you, that he isn't already doing? Other than"—her chin lifted, her eyes narrowing on his—"sharing your bed, perhaps?"

And yes, good gods, that guess had surely found its mark, flaring more raw, shuddering rage across Harthr's flashing eyes. "Oh, fuck off, you jealous little harpy," he spat. "Varinn and I used to be friends. Best friends. In full agreement on the useless Aetha, on the clan, on our future. On how the Grisk needed to focus on our strengths, on trade and wealth and *family*. Until that damned attack, when he got trapped underground with his precious *krútt* for weeks on end! Came back stinking of Aetha, and was never the same again! Bewitched, by their vile magic!"

Harthr was bellowing now, his voice carrying against the stone tunnel all around them. While the ache in Kitty's skull thudded even louder, her hands clenching tighter against Thrain's chain. "Rubbish," she snapped back. "Of course Varinn wasn't the same after that, his parents had just been *killed*! And has it never occurred to you that maybe he just fell in love with Thrain? Because it's been *years* since then"—she hauled down a breath—"and those two are still *brilliant* together. They support each other, they listen to each other, they make each other laugh, they balance out each other's worst tendencies, and they give each other joy and peace. And yes, Thrain absolutely blows Varinn's mind in bed, and Varinn does the same right back to him! And they both love every damned moment of it, as they should!"

The jealousy flared again in Harthr's eyes, but Kitty didn't care, her hands clutching, seeking, against Thrain's chain beneath the cloak. "And Varinn *does* still think all those things, about the Grisk," she hissed. "He supports trade. He supports the shop. He sent me to work there, for gods' sake! And how dare you say he doesn't support families, when he teaches *orclings* in his spare time, has essentially been a father to Timo, and spends every single day working out there in the realm, risking his life to help young orcs, and women like me! And"— her voice was still rising, almost shrill—"you still haven't even told me what more you expect from him, or from the Aetha! How the *hell* are they actually failing you, and the clan? Not years ago, but *now*?!"

Harthr was still glowering at her, but not actually replying—and to her distant surprise, it was Grein who cleared his throat. "With women, and sons," he said, his voice low. "With rebuilding our clan. Nattfarr is fixed upon his own goals, and his own mate and son. He knows many of our clan are not fighters, and we cannot yet risk running freely above ground, seeking out mates. But he does *naught* to bring mates to us. Will not even *think* of using his great gift of Speaking, to help us in this."

Wait. Wait, Kitty's thoughts were swirling once again, her eyes darting between Grein and Harthr, and even Knorr, still standing at the front of the cart, steering them down the tunnel. "Ach, for Nattfarr is already set," Knorr added coldly, over his shoulder. "He and his kin shall have their sons, ach? He and Thrain can use their Aetha magic for their own gain, but"—he laughed, thick and bitter—"gods forbid they should grant us the *one* service their fool fathers and forefathers did, and help bring more women to us!"

Kitty's thoughts were still spinning, skittering, slipping into something almost like—uncertainty. So they—they all knew about Thrain's magic, then. And *had* Thrain and Nattfarr's fathers truly used their magic to recruit women, before? Thrain had spoken of his father wielding his magic to manipulate women into his own bed, yes, but the more Kitty considered it, the more it didn't make sense, and...

"But—their magic doesn't even work that way," she said, tentative. "Does it? Thrain didn't use his magic to bring me here, or—coerce me. Not in the slightest."

"Ach, we know," Knorr snapped over his shoulder, his voice curt. "The Aetha magic does not *coerce*. It grants truth, and thus, it grants ease and safety. Has Thrain never looked at you, and spoken some truth you ought not to have believed, but you did? Have you never spoken truth back to him? Has he never made you feel safe thus? At peace? Able to trust him and his vows?"

Oh. And suddenly Kitty was indeed thinking of all those moments, all those times Thrain had spoken, and she'd... believed him. Trusted him. *I should never treat a woman thus. Are you sure you wanna. So sweet, woman. Will never, ever forget this. I shall earn your trust again.*

"This magic helps both the women, and us," Grein continued, his voice still quiet. "They can know that we ask in good faith, and we can know whether they truly wish to be here with us, of their own free will. We do not wish to force or harm them, ach? We long for women who will be good mates, and good mothers to our sons. Women who will help us rebuild our clan, amidst all we have lost."

Oh. And as she stared toward him, digesting that, Kitty almost felt a twinge of... sympathy, for perhaps the first time in this entire disaster. They wanted... women. Families. And...

"And Thrain's father—and Nattfarr's father—really used to do this?" she asked, uncertain now. "Seek out women, for their kin? Use their magic to make... promises, and reassurances? Broker vows and agreements, that kind of thing?"

All three orcs nodded, and Kitty's thoughts were again skipping back to those revelations in the crypt. To how Thrain's father had misused his gift. Broken that trust, perhaps, that pact with his clan. And yes, Knorr was grimacing, shaking his head as he turned away. "Until Thakfarr got drunk on the power, and started taking all the women for himself instead," he said flatly. "As they do."

Kitty swallowed, still considering it, frowning between them. "Well, you can't blame Nattfarr and Thrain for not wanting to involve themselves in that again, can you?" she demanded. "It sounds like a lot of risk and pressure to dump on two orcs—one of whom is a new father, and the other who doesn't even want to use his magic! Also, it sounds like a terrible long-term strategy to begin with, and there are surely dozens of other ways you can meet interested women. Granted"—her frown deepened as she glared at them—"their interest in kidnappers and *murderers* is likely to be very low indeed!"

Harthr sneered and rolled his eyes, while Grein was still looking sober, almost sad. "You say this, but it is not so easy," he replied. "The war is over, ach, but women still fear and spurn us. And even when there is no risk of attack, we are oft mocked and harassed when we walk above ground. We have all tried this many, many times, ach? Tell us, what should *you* do, if a strange orc came up to you on an empty road, and sought to speak to you?"

Right. Kitty's thoughts darted guiltily backwards, to her own initial reaction to Thrain in the pub—and to how Thrain, an experienced fighter, had still made obvious efforts to hide his identity. And what might have happened if she hadn't been so foxed, if instead of conversing with him, she'd just screamed for help instead...

"Well," Kitty said, on a deep breath, "you're traders, aren't you? You know how to work with human contacts, and how to make offers and broker deals. If I had been offered a fair and comprehensive proposal while I was, er, *working* in the city, I would have given it *serious* consideration—and I knew many other women who would have, too!"

And yes, yes, the more she thought about it, the more it

made sense. Many of the women she'd worked with in her mother's business had become weary of the work too, and would have welcomed an opportunity to safely move on to other prospects. And they had generally learned to be accepting toward all kinds of men, as well as toward a myriad of intimate preferences—and therefore weren't likely to be particularly shocked by the orcs' openness, or their copious seed. Or—Kitty's hands tightened against Thrain's chain, as a sudden miserable longing surged deep in her chest—their jewels.

"I could help you do it, too," she continued, speaking faster now. "Just like I have with the trading. I could write to the women on your behalf, and help to make your proposals. I have multiple contacts in the city, and I'm sure they could help me find more. Also, word travels quickly among women in such work, and personal recommendations carry a great deal of weight. I really think it could help."

Her voice had gone fervent, her gaze sweeping eagerly between them, and if she wasn't mistaken, that was surely a glint of interest in Grein's eyes. But Harthr only scoffed again, loud and harsh, his face again twisting with chilly contempt.

"We're Grisk, woman," he snapped. "We don't want harlots like you, who bear hundreds of scents upon them. We want women who scent only of *us!*"

Oh. Kitty's sympathy evaporated as quickly as it had appeared, and she felt her own lip curling, her hands fingering, searching, at the chain. "Of course you do," she hissed. "Because you're all such chaste and virtuous prizes yourselves, what with the kidnapping and murdering! Has it never occurred to you that no one has brought women to you because they *know* you? And because they've seen how you behave toward other women and Grisk sons?"

She shot a sharp, disdainful look down at her swollen waist, and at the waterskin still lying untouched in her lap. "Varinn and Thrain would never tolerate this rubbish, especially with a

Grisk child's life at stake," she snarled. "Varinn would give anything to care for the most vulnerable in this clan. He does, and he *has*. And it's no wonder he stopped being friends with you, and rebuffed your advances, because he's a thousand times the Grisk you are!"

Harthr was growling again, his fists twitching at his sides, but Kitty kept glaring back, kept grasping at Thrain's chain. "And when Varinn breaks out of that crypt," she continued, louder, "and finds out how you've threatened me and his son, *he's* going to be the one kidnapping and murdering around here!"

But curse him, Harthr just kept growling, as something much like mockery flashed across his eyes. "You really think he'll care?" he shot back. "I could smell you tonight, fool woman. I can see you. You *reek* of rejection, and you're not wearing Varinn's jewels, or his mating-gift, either. It's clear he's regained at least some of his senses, and realized he doesn't want a harlot for a mate! Let alone as his own Thjoth son's mother!"

The hurt and the rage surged in Kitty's chest, and she gulped for air, grasped for truth, for certainty. "Varinn would never reject a child," she choked. "Never. No matter who its mother is. He would do *everything* within his power to save it, and"—she hauled down another breath, courage—"and so will I!"

And with that, she leapt up, and swung out the long, heavy chain before her. The beautiful chain with that solid clasp, just like the one Thrain had proudly shown off to her and Killik, demonstrating how it opened and closed. The chain Knorr had so foolishly used to bind her, even using the clasp to lock it. And this entire time, Kitty had been working at it, attempting to pull it apart—and she'd indeed caught all three orcs by surprise, their eyes wide on the swinging shining steel.

Until Harthr growled again, and lurched toward her—but Kitty had already leapt backwards, sideways. Toward the edge of the cart, toward the large spinning wheel. And she silently breathed a prayer as she peered down into the wheel's whirling steel spokes, the axel's rod just visible behind them...

She swung the chain into the wheel with as much force as she could muster. Feeling its steel length catch and tangle, whipping painfully out of her hand as it swiftly wrapped around the axel. The loose end wildly flailing, flapping in the spokes, please, please, please—

And with a sharp, earsplitting screech, the cart skittered sideways, and jerked to a shuddering halt in the darkness.

51

For a moment, everything went still. The tunnel, the stunned staring orcs, Kitty's desperate gulping breaths.

But then—Harthr lunged again. Lunged straight toward Kitty, onto her, tackling her painfully against the cart's hard steel edge. "You scheming little *trollop*," he snarled at her. "You'll pay for that, you—"

Kitty was already screaming, the panic wailing behind her eyes as she kicked and flailed—but oh, oh thank the gods, Grein was here, tackling Harthr by the shoulders, dragging him backwards, away. "You cannot harm her!" he hissed, with surprising menace. "She bears a Grisk—"

His voice broke there, his eyes chagrined, but suddenly Knorr was beside him, yanking Harthr away, too. "We want that fool trader's payment for her, brother," he growled, in Harthr's ear. "We fix the cart, we dump her upon him, and make her *his* nuisance to handle. And you ken"—his eyes glinted coldly on Kitty's—"having a man douse her in his fresh scent will be even better vengeance upon Varinn and Thrain than harming her, ach?"

No, no, no no, and Kitty scrabbled away again, toward the edge of the cart—until Knorr lurched forward, far too quickly, and roughly grasped her by the arm. "I think not, pussycat," he snapped, as he swiped to yank a rope from around a nearby crate. "Henceforth, you'll be still, and behave!"

Kitty cursed and kept fighting, flailing against Knorr's powerful grip, but he was far too strong, and his binding was far harsher than before. Not only wrapping around her arms, but also her chest, and then—Kitty uselessly kicked and whimpered—even her feet. Leaving her utterly immobile on the cart's cold floor, and Knorr flashed her a vicious, mocking smile before leaping over the cart's side toward the broken wheel.

Harthr and Grein followed him—Harthr spat at her on the way by—and soon Kitty was left alone in the cart, while the sounds of irritated voices and crunching metal filled her ears. And despite her best attempts to frantically wrench and wriggle free, the ropes held fast, digging and scraping deeper into her skin with every movement. Until she finally sagged heavily against the nearest crate, and fought to blink back the water prickling behind her eyes.

Gods, what was she going to do. She was trapped in this horrid cart, trapped being dragged back to Charles. And Varinn and Thrain were trapped in that awful crypt, with no ventilation, with that horrifying threat of gas. Just like when they'd been trapped so many years ago, just like Thrain had hated and feared ever since. And what if it killed them this time? What if Harthr was right, and they would never escape? What if they were... already dead?

The water spilled from Kitty's blinking eyes, streaked hot and swift down her cheeks. Gods, what if Varinn and Thrain were already dead. What if they were already lying cold and empty in that dark, miserable crypt. Trapped in that awful vault of Varinn's, without even a son to carry on Varinn's scent.

Even the thought of it was so sickening, wracking with visceral strength in Kitty's belly, enough that she had to haul down more gasping breaths, fight against the nausea churning in her throat. No. No no no. They wouldn't. They couldn't. She had to believe it, had to believe they could find a way out of this. Varinn had saved Thrain last time, hadn't he? And if nothing else, he wouldn't give up on Thrain now, he would do anything within his power...

And surely—surely what Kitty had told Harthr was still true, too. Varinn wouldn't abandon a Grisk son. He wouldn't abandon Thrain's son. He'd already proven that back when he'd hated her, when she'd been nothing but a threat to him. So surely he would do so again... right? He wouldn't care if she'd left behind his jewels, if she'd perhaps thought... thought...

What? Gods, what had she thought? What had she hoped to decide, to accomplish, before any of this? Had she wanted to accept Varinn's vow? To work it out, to have more sons together? To believe him, and stay?

But Varinn had lied, and Thrain had lied, too. Thrain hadn't truly wanted her. He'd wanted to do something unforgivable, because of Varinn, because he'd wanted Varinn to have a son. While Varinn had just been doing his damned job with her, and he'd let her take on that debt, for—for Thrain. He would do anything within his power...

Kitty groaned and thudded her head against the crate, her eyes squeezing shut. She had to think, damn it, keep fighting, keep trying to escape this. Even if Varinn and Thrain didn't care. She needed to do this for her son, and for... for herself.

And that was a new thought, a strange thought, enough that her eyes blinked open, gazed blankly at the crate. She didn't want to go back to her old life with Charles, or the life she'd had with her mother, or—or any of it. She'd loved working in the shop, learning a trade, making her own coin, her own decisions. And even if she'd followed Varinn's guidance—and his orders—she'd still... wanted to do that. She'd chosen to do that. Just like she'd chosen to embrace orc fashion. To make so many new friends, to help others however she could. To help Thrain. To help Varinn.

And even without them—even if this nightmare reached the worst possible end—Kitty had still studied a trade, just as she'd intended. She'd still gained experience, and maybe even references. She'd made good decisions, smart decisions, for her future, for herself, for her son. And she could do so again. She could.

It was enough, somehow, to keep her breathing, thinking, as the cart finally creaked into motion again, trundling down the tunnel with far less speed than before. As Harthr and Knorr and Grein all finally leapt back into the cart again, Grein angling her a regretful look, Harthr still with a petulant scowl on his mouth.

"Not one *word*, wench," Harthr growled at her, as he stalked past. "Or we'll find something else to fill your mouth with."

But Kitty was done wasting her words on this vile greedy ingrate, and she only eyed Harthr darkly as he sank down onto a crate, and shot an uneasy glance back up the tunnel. Back in the direction of Orc Mountain.

And suddenly Kitty's heart was hammering, her thoughts whirling faster than before. Even if Varinn and Thrain were— well—her own absence would still be noted, at least when morning came, right? Ymir would notice, and so would Ella and Nattfarr and Dammarr and Thrak, and all her regular customers at the shop. And even if Harthr claimed she'd wanted to run away, surely they would wonder, right? Surely— her heartbeat skipped—they would at least send someone to check, at some point. Because that had been Varinn's whole job, hadn't it? The job he was paid to do? Helping Grisk families and sons?

So Kitty kept breathing, kept thinking, even as the cart slowly rattled on and on and on. Until finally Grein and Knorr leapt out to begin pulling it, moving even slower, while Harthr kept glancing uneasily back down the tunnel, and barking orders toward them in Aelakesh. Sounding more and more impatient with every passing moment, and Kitty just had to keep waiting, please, please, until—

They stopped. Stopped, in what appeared to be the middle of the tunnel, for no apparent reason—but Harthr exhaled a sigh of palpable relief as he lurched toward Kitty, and hauled her up again. His hands' grip rough and careless as he thrust her down over the cart's edge, and into Knorr's waiting arms.

"You take her," Harthr hissed. "Payment's supposed to be hidden at the top of the stairs. You'll scent it. Don't be seen."

Knorr curtly nodded, and Kitty's screeching brain distantly noted that he was now wearing thick gloves, and a heavy black cloak, with the hood pulled low. And even as she squirmed and fought in his arms, he growled and yanked her closer, his claws pricking through the gloves into her skin.

"Enough, fool woman," he snarled, as he dragged her toward the wall, toward a narrow, pitch-black opening, barely visible in the rough stone. But yes, oh gods, he was taking her into it, plunging them into utter darkness, and the fear surged again, rattling in Kitty's chest, in her gasping breaths. She had to keep thinking, keep hoping, keep believing. It was useless to try to overpower or convince Knorr, she was *not* wasting any more of her limited energy on him, but, but...

She twitched as they burst up and out of the darkness again, into what appeared to be a building. A rough, cramped-looking building, with a few sparse furnishings and a packed earthen floor. And through a small window, Kitty could see silvery moonlight, and perhaps—perhaps—just a hint of morning light in the sky.

She could almost feel Knorr's urgency, now, in how he swiftly pulled off her bindings, and tossed them aside. And how he roughly grasped her arm, yanking her toward the door, as his other hand clutched tightly at her back beneath her cloak, his claws pricking into her skin in a silent, menacing threat.

And then—they were out in the street. In Dusbury. In an area Kitty easily recognized, only a short distance away from her old apartment. And wait, wait, he couldn't be taking her back there, Mrs. Schultz had let the apartment to someone else... hadn't she?

But Kitty's searching glance at Knorr's face found only that same grim urgency, his gaze held straight ahead as he shoved her down the dark, empty street. Yes, yes, down her street, and toward her door—and then inside. Into the starkly familiar staircase, into even the familiar smell of it—and he shoved her up the stairs, up and up and up. All the way to the landing, where he kicked at a loose board in the floor, revealing a small cloth sack. And he even smiled at Kitty, cold and deadly, as he tucked the sack into his cloak, and reached for the door.

"Good riddance, wench," he said, under his breath. "I'm sure you'll enjoy this."

And with that, he yanked open the apartment's door, and shoved Kitty inside.

Kitty was—in her apartment. Her *apartment*.

And it was—the same. Almost the same. It had clearly been cleaned, aired out, but those were Kitty's hats, Kitty's boots, Kitty's furnishings. Kitty's frilly, frothy clothes, hanging in the wardrobe, and... was that her *jewel-box*? As if—as if she'd never left at all?!

And wait—Kitty froze, her breath catching—she wasn't alone. Because there, stirring awake on the bed, on *her* bed, still made up with her familiar bedclothes, was—Charles?

But yes, yes, that was Charles, good gods. Wearing a dressing-gown, and loudly yawning as he sat up, and blinked blearily toward her.

"Oh, there you are, Kitty," he said, around another gigantic yawn. "Finally. I've been waiting all night."

Kitty stared at him, and for a dangling, dizzying moment, there was the strangest urge to laugh—or, perhaps, to throw something sharp and heavy toward his handsome face. Charles was here, Charles had paid to have her kidnapped, and now— rather than asking how she'd fared during this horrible ordeal—he was complaining that she was *late*?!

But if Charles had registered his rudeness, he certainly

didn't show it, because he was already looking distinctly bemused, giving a puzzled little smile as he shoved up to his feet. "What is it, Kitty?" he asked. "Aren't you happy to see me? Weren't you kidnapped by orcs, and trapped at that vile Orc Mountain, for gods' sakes? Although"—his eyes ran up and down her cloaked body—"you're still looking surprisingly good, thank the gods."

Kitty kept staring at him, fighting the urge to shout at him, as the incredulous disbelief kept churning in her chest. Charles truly thought she'd been kidnapped and held captive at Orc Mountain for weeks, and his most pressing concern was her *appearance*?!

"I wasn't kidnapped," she finally managed, her voice clipped. "You kicked me out, remember? How do you still have the apartment? Why are all my things still here?"

Charles cast a brief, dismissive glance toward the apartment around them, and then twitched a careless shrug. "I had James pay the landlady," he replied. "It's a good location, nice and central, and easier than finding you a new place, right?"

The disbelief surged higher, escaping from Kitty's mouth in something almost like a laugh. Gods, how she'd fought and agonized over this damned apartment, how she'd pleaded with Mrs. Schultz to no avail—and meanwhile, Charles had just waltzed back in when the mood struck him, and paid to pretend as though nothing had even happened?

"You aren't going to thank me, then?" Charles continued, still with that puzzled smile on his mouth, even as his eyes glinted with impatience. "I rescued you from *Orc Mountain*, Kitty. For a shocking amount of coin, I might add."

His voice had gone sharp at the end, stern, a tone that would have once had Kitty instantly smiling and apologizing, and rushing over to tend to him. Reassuring him of her gratitude and her loyalty, her awe at his grand rescue, at him finding her, caring for her, even regaining such a lovely convenient apartment for her.

But as she stared at him, her disbelief seemed to harden, tightening into a cold, decisive contempt. Charles had never cared for her. He still didn't care for her. He cared about his own convenience, his own comfort, his own pleasure. And Kitty was finished giving him any of it, forever. She was making her own decisions. Choosing her own future. Doing this for herself.

"I didn't ask to be rescued, Charles," she said, her voice crisp. "I'm afraid you've made a poor investment, once again. I'm not interested in living here again, or working for you again. Ever."

There was an instant's stunned silence, during which Charles' eyes bulged, and his mouth fell open—but then he snapped it shut again, and gave her another smile, much tighter this time. "You're clearly confused and overwhelmed by your ordeal, Kitty," he said, speaking slower now, almost as if to a child. "You were at *Orc Mountain*. You needed to be rescued. And gods, you didn't *work* for me. You were my—"

But he broke off there, his mouth twisting, and Kitty heard herself laugh, bright and brittle. "I was your employee, Charles," she said flatly. "My job was to help run your life and your business, to make you look good at parties, and to keep you satisfied in bed. And I did an excellent job, well beyond what I was paid, for four *years*. And you still fired me with no notice, no provisions, and not a single consideration for my health and wellbeing! You had me thrown out of my apartment to starve on the *streets!*"

Her voice rang through the room, louder and sharper than she'd ever spoken to him before—and she could see the unease shifting, darkening, in his eyes. "Look, that was all just—a misunderstanding, Kitty," he said, still in that drawling, condescending tone. "The landlady vastly overstepped. Of course I wouldn't have had you thrown out. I even told you I would give you an extra month, remember?"

Kitty's laugh pealed out again, thick with fury and contempt. "Yes, and then you left town with your other woman, and didn't spare it a second thought!" she snapped back. "Let me guess, you only reconsidered when you found out she wasn't as business-minded as you'd expected? Or perhaps"—her lip curled—"you horribly underpaid her as well, and she was clever enough to realize her worth before shackling herself to you!"

Charles' mouth aimlessly opened and closed, suggesting Kitty had hit quite close to the truth, and she laughed again, not a laugh at all. "So here is my proposal for *you*, Charles," she said coldly. "You will pay me a severance. You will give me a reference, speaking particularly to my business and management skills. And you will allow me a few days to pack up my things, including"—her eyes flicked toward the jewel-box—"my jewels."

For an instant, Charles seemed incapable of speech, his mouth fallen open again—but then he shook his head, as unmistakable disapproval slowly crept across his eyes. "You can't be serious, Kitty," he replied, his voice hardening. "Why would I ever agree to such a preposterous proposal?"

Kitty scoffed, and gave Charles a chilly, withering smile. "So I will go away quietly," she replied. "And refrain from reporting you to the authorities for unlawful kidnapping! And failing that"—she raised her chin—"I know all your contacts, Charles. I can set up meetings of my own. I can show up at all your parties. And I can tell some *highly* compelling tales about your business acumen—or wait, rather, your complete lack thereof!"

Charles' eyes widened with shocked betrayal, his breath audibly catching—so Kitty kept going, jabbing a finger toward him. "All the bad deals," she hissed. "All the missing coin in your ledgers. All the lost imports and *rubbish* excuses you made around them. And"—her voice rose—"even today! Paying shocking amounts of coin to ransom someone against their will, without even *trying* to confirm whether they *wanted* it! Not to mention leaving said coin out in an open stairwell, without even supervising the trade-off? How many times have we talked about this kind of carelessness, Charles?!"

She was truly hollering now, waving her hands wildly between them, and she drew in breath, squared her shoulders. "If you want to stay in business, you'll accept my terms," she said. "And that's my final offer, Charles."

He still wasn't answering, just staring at her with his eyes goggling. And suddenly Kitty couldn't bear to look at him for another moment, and she spun around, and stalked to the wardrobe. To all her beautiful clothes, which she'd acquired and tailored with such care. And as she began carding through them, she distantly noted which pieces would fetch the highest prices, which could use some alterations, that wrap-around silk number would surely suit Dammarr, and...

"Kitty," cut in Charles' voice, strange now. "Are you... are you pregnant?"

Damn it. Kitty's eyes cut sharply sideways, toward where he was still gaping back toward her. But his wide eyes were now fixed on her waist, on where her hands' movements had shifted the fall of her cloak. On where her bare belly—and her revealing orc clothes—were now entirely visible to his shocked, staring eyes.

"My personal matters are none of your concern, Charles," Kitty belatedly replied, keeping her voice as steady as she could, as she yanked her cloak closed again. "And I'll thank you not to comment, or speculate. Now, are you accepting my offer, or not?"

But Charles wasn't replying, he was still staring at her, with that stunned disbelief in his eyes. With something that was slowly shifting to... disgust.

"The child's not mine, is it?" he said, an odd, menacing softness in his voice. "Because if it was, you'd have started with that, wouldn't you? You'd have come after me for everything I was worth?"

Kitty stared back at him, a cold clammy shiver creeping up her spine—and Charles stepped closer, his eyes unnervingly alight. "It's an *orc's* spawn," he breathed. "Of course. And this is all some kind of sneaky orc scheme, isn't it? I *knew* those orc traders were highly questionable, I knew I should never have gotten involved with them to begin with!"

His voice was rising, ringing with disdain and outrage, and Kitty had to draw down air, pull herself straighter. "Wrong, once again, Charles," she snapped. "Trading with orcs was a clever move on your part, for once! Getting in on a new market early, and making inroads and key contacts before your competitors catch up! And that has absolutely *nothing* to do with—"

But Charles cut her off with a harsh, high-pitched laugh, and a swipe of his hand toward her. Grasping her wrist, oh gods, and gripping it with sudden, surprising strength. "Oh, Kitty," he said, with a slow, pitying smile. "I see it all now. Those orcs have lured you into their devious clutches, and now they're using you to swindle me. Did they threaten you and frighten you, darling? Or make false promises to care for you?"

Kitty yanked against his hand's grip, but it didn't budge, and he came even closer, still with that strange light shifting in his eyes. "But the ruse is up now, my foolish, silly little Kitty," he said, his voice almost a croon. "Now, let's start this over again, why don't we? With the *truth*?"

Kitty opened her mouth to protest, but found that Charles' sticky hand had clapped over it, his tall body stepping even closer. "You needed my rescuing," he breathed, "even more than I could have *dreamt*. And you're going to apologize for threatening me, and speaking so inappropriately to me, aren't you? Because"—his mouth was smiling again—"no one will believe a single claim you make, Kitty, when you're pregnant with an orc's spawn. *No one!*"

The certainty shuddered through his voice, flashed smug and triumphant through his eyes. "You need me, Kitty," he said, his breath hot in her face. "You need me to help you out of this mess you've bumbled into. You need me to care for you, and pay for you, and cover for you throughout this pregnancy. You need me"—his smile twisted higher—"to publicly pretend this orc-spawn is *mine*."

Wait—what? He thought—what? He wanted to pretend her son was—was—

"And I might even consider it, my silly Kitty," he murmured, coming closer, "if you make it worth my while. If you retract everything you've said, and apologize. If you do your utmost to atone for your disrespect, and make this up to me!"

The rebellion and the rage were surging, flaring up in Kitty's chest, roiling in her belly. Charles was—blackmailing her? Blackmailing her into working for him again? Agreeing to pretend her son was his, so he could hold her ransom over it, for months on end? So she would attend his parties, manage his business, and—and share his bed? Still?!

Charles' hand was still over Kitty's mouth, as if he didn't need to hear her answer, because of course he thought she would fall all over him for his kindness, as she always had before. And gods, how had she ever tolerated this tedious little cretin for four entire years, let alone pretending he was the most wonderful man in existence? While he benefited from her labour, kept her in poverty, and—Kitty's fury surged higher—had never once even *attempted* to please her in bed. Gods, she'd had more pleasure with Varinn and Thrain in a few *weeks* than she'd had with Charles in four damned years.

And it was that image of Varinn and Thrain, choking through her thoughts, that had her dragging in more breath, more courage. Shifting slightly against Charles' hot, looming body, as if to move closer, closer...

She slammed her knee up into his groin, striking it with painful but satisfying force. Sending Charles loudly yelping and reeling backwards, clutching both hands at his trousers.

"You little wretch," he growled at her, his eyes wild with

rage. "How *dare* you. I've been extremely kind to you, Kitty, I've made you a very generous offer—and now you're conspiring with foul *orcs* to steal from me, and destroy me!"

Kitty was breathing hard, her nausea surging, but she rolled her eyes, and squared her shoulders. "You're the one who conspired with the orcs to kidnap me!" she shot back. "And now you're threatening me, and blackmailing me! I told you I don't want to work for you, and I meant it! Not now, not *ever!*"

But it wasn't working, Charles was spitting and wheezing and shaking his head, and staggering back toward her. "You've—you've lost your *mind*, Kitty," he sputtered. "Those orcs have clearly tainted you, and ruined you, and *broken* you! And maybe"—his eyes shifted, flared again—"maybe you don't care about your own livelihood, but what about theirs?"

Theirs? Kitty was backing away from him, angling toward the door, but he kept coming closer, still with that feverish light in his eyes. "What if I go tell everyone I know that I've been swindled by orcs," he hissed. "And they've also kidnapped and impregnated my mistress. The magistrates will enjoy hearing that one, won't they? All gross violations of the orcs' precious peace-treaty, don't you think?"

Oh, damn him. *Curse* him. And the uncertainty was already lurching, careening with sickening strength through Kitty's already-nauseated stomach. Gods, she hadn't once considered the treaty in all this, and Charles couldn't—he couldn't be right. Could he? Would the magistrates believe him? Would they—would they prosecute? Start another war? Over her?!

The vision of Varinn and Thrain was surging again, together with Ymir and Dammarr and Thrak, Ella and Nattfarr and Rakfi. And Alma and Baldr and Drafli, Timo and Cecily and Sune, Efterar and Kesst and Rathgarr, Eyarl and Valter and Trygve and Vragi. So many people, so many friends, and the very thought—the thought—she couldn't, she—

"Oh, so that's it, is it?" Charles' taunting voice continued, grating painfully into Kitty's skull. "They've infected you that deeply, have they? Don't worry, silly Kitty. We'll straighten you out, won't we?"

And gods, he was coming closer again, he was grabbing her wrist again, yanking her into his heaving chest. As the panic finally kicked and flailed, striking Kitty to helpless, horrified trembling, trapped here in his arms. No. No. No no no, please, please please—

When behind them, something cursed. Banged. And suddenly there was noise, movement, life, drawing her close, dragging her into his sweet-scented arms.

It was... Thrain.

53

Thrain—was here? Alive? Safe?

Kitty yelped and spun around, toward where—yes, yes, yes—Thrain was here. Here, oh gods, tall and familiar and so, so beautiful, his eyes searching hers with bright, desperate urgency.

"Och, Kit," he croaked, as he again clutched her into his arms, clasping her tightly against his bare, sweaty chest. "Och, we're here. Naught's going to touch you, or harm you, ach? Naught."

Oh. Oh, gods. Thrain was here, he was safe, and—and he'd said *we* were here, *we*. And Kitty yanked back again, desperately searching behind him—and then she twitched all over at the sight of Varinn, quietly closing the door, and striding up to stand beside Thrain. His big body sweaty too, his braid mussed, his face flushed, his jaw set. But he was here, thank all the gods, he was alive, he was safe, and they'd come for her, they'd *come*.

"Ach, *kisa*," Varinn said, very low, his eyes angling flinty and certain toward hers. "You are safe now."

It was like an embrace of its own, like the sweetest thing anyone had ever said to Kitty in her life—and somehow she was already weeping, the water spilling down her cheeks, the sobs escaping loud and breathless from her throat.

"I thought," she gasped, between her great, gulping sobs, "you were dead. I was so worried you were trapped in the crypt, dying down there, with the gas, and Thrain hates it so much—and—"

The sobs overtook her again, swallowing all her words in their strength, and oh, Thrain was yanking her closer, stroking his big hands up and down her back. "Shhhh, Kit," he murmured. "Naught to fret over. You ken no one's going to kill us by locking us in a crypt, ach?"

His voice had gone clipped, contemptuous, and Kitty fervently nodded, sniffling into his chest. "I—I know," she gulped. "But it was just—so awful—and so terrifying—and Harthr is so *vile*—and Knorr is just as bad—and now—now *Charles*! He's threatening me, and blackmailing me, and saying I'm going to start a *war*!"

Her voice was almost a wail, but Thrain's hands just kept stroking, his arms drawing her even closer into his sweaty, sweet-scented warmth. "Rubbish," he said flatly. "This fool's just jealous, and vexed that you got away. Naught to fear, ach? Now"—his voice lowered—"breathe for me, will you, Kit? Slow, deep breaths. Find my scent again. Find Varinn's in it, too."

Oh. Yes, yes, Kitty could do that, hauling in a hard, shaky breath, drinking up Thrain's warm, wonderful scent. And yes, yes, finding that faint familiar twinge of Varinn's richness in it too, and feeling—just for an instant—the brief touch of Varinn's hand, gripping gently against her shoulder.

But even as Kitty turned toward it, it was already gone. Because Varinn was moving, pacing slowly across the room, his flinty gaze fixed on Charles. And gods, Kitty had almost forgotten about Charles, but he was certainly still here, edging backwards toward the bed, his eyes wide and alarmed on Varinn's slowly approaching form.

And blinking between them, it distantly occurred to Kitty

just how *large* Varinn was. With his broad shoulders, his deep chest, his big clawed hands. Hands that were hanging with deceptive casualness at his sides, only hinting at menace, at danger.

"You wish to speak of laws and treaties, little man," he said to Charles, his voice so steady, so calm. "Then let us do so. What law have we broken? And where are your witnesses upon this?"

Charles' mouth opened and closed, and he sidled further backwards, stumbling over the edge of a floorboard. "You—you kidnapped Kitty," he stammered. "And you—you swindled me! You took my coin, to get her back!"

But Varinn didn't even blink, and his clawed hand reached for something on his belt. Something that was—a bag of coins? The bag Knorr had taken from the stairwell?

"We found this outside," Varinn said coldly. "You ought not to leave your riches lying about, where they can so easily be plundered. As for this kidnapping"—his lip curled—"why did you not report this, at the time? Why did you not seek out your woman, or send after her? Why did you leave her to crawl through the forest alone, with no food or drink or care?"

The contempt had crept into his voice, curt and brittle, and Charles eyed him with palpable unease, his throat visibly convulsing. "I didn't—know," he said finally. "I was—away. On a hunting-trip."

"Ach, for six weeks?" Varinn continued smoothly, the contempt sharpening on his voice. "If we inquire after this, and seek witnesses, none shall have seen you here in Dusbury? No parties? No meetings? No one-sided trysts with disappointed women?"

His nostrils flared with clear distaste, his eyes glinting hard and cold. While Charles kept staring, swallowing, as Varinn began walking a slow, deliberate circle around him. His hands still hanging at his sides, his big body still so deceptively, dangerously calm.

"Meanwhile," Varinn added, deeper now, "this woman claims you have threatened her. Coerced her. And ach, we witnessed you touching her, confining her, whilst she sought to escape you. We can yet scent her fear, and her fury toward you."

Charles was looking rather hunted, now, his shoulders hunching up around his ears. "We were quarrelling, that's all," he said, too quickly. "Kitty's *my* mistress, and she should never have—"

But without warning Varinn's waiting hand snapped out, slicing dangerously close to Charles' neck. While against Kitty, Thrain was growling, deep and angry in his chest—and after a brief little pat to her arse, he carefully guided her backwards, and then strode across the room. His tall body easily falling into step opposite Varinn, both of them now circling Charles in slow, prowling silence.

"No, human," Varinn said, with real menace in his deep voice. "Katharine is not yours, and you have no right to command her, or speak ill of her. Most of all after you *attacked* her, before two witnesses."

Charles sputtered, babbling some kind of excuse, but Kitty didn't hear it over Thrain's loud, furious bark. "Silence, you fool," he snarled. "Kit's not yours, and she's never been yours. She's *ours*."

She's ours. Those words ringing through the air, tilting oddly through Kitty's thoughts—and Varinn hadn't argued it, hadn't even faltered at it, his eyes still glinting with cold fury on Charles' pale face. "My wise partner speaks truth," he said evenly. "And you ken, he holds the power to make *you* speak truth, also. I wonder what he shall draw from you, when he asks?"

Charles visibly startled, but Thrain was smiling now, still walking in perfect step with Varinn opposite him. "Mayhap he'll speak of all the blood I scent upon him," he supplied, with deceptive lightness. "I wonder why such a prim-and-proper trader would smell like that? Messy affair, was it? Trade gone wrong, mayhap?"

Kitty blinked—Charles had never ever actually *killed* someone, had he?—but he'd gone even paler than before, his throat audibly bobbing. "I didn't," he began. "I mean—I wasn't—"

"Or mayhap the woman I scent, from several weeks past," Varinn cut in, with more low menace in his voice. "The one who reeks of pain and fear, and"—he inhaled deeply, his nostrils flaring—"ach, a husband. I wonder what became of her? Or whether her husband knows of you?"

Charles flinched this time, but didn't speak, and Thrain laughed again, soft and almost—almost—amused. "Och, I ken not," he said. "Or what about that other man, from just this week? Scents like he struck you in the face. I wonder what he was raging about? Surely not another bad deal? Wonder where that coin ended up?"

His eyes angled downwards, toward the bag of coins still clutched in Charles' fingers, and Kitty could hear Charles' sharp inhale as he clutched the bag close. "You—you're lying," he said, with creditable bravado. "You have no *conception* what you're talking about. And you're *orcs*. No one—*no one*—will believe you!"

But Thrain and Varinn's steps didn't slightly hesitate, and Thrain laughed again, while Varinn's clawed hands flexed at his sides. "Mayhap," Varinn said smoothly, as he glanced toward— toward Kitty. "But I ken they shall believe *her*. Most of all if she tells her own tales of her mistreatment, at your hands!"

Charles sputtered again, but his shoulders were squaring, his bottom lip jutting out. "I didn't mistreat Kitty," he countered. "I spoiled her *rotten*. I paid for her apartment, bought her food and coal, and gave her any number of expensive clothes and jewels and gifts!"

Varinn's answering scoff was harsh, derisive, and his claws seemed to jut out even longer, extending sharp and black from his fingertips. "No, you mean to say you did the *least* you could have done," he hissed, with a wave of his hand around the apartment. "After *four years* of her work and kindness on your behalf, this is all your faithful woman has to her name? An empty cupboard, a bare apartment, a few frocks and cheap trinkets? How much coin and trade has she gained for you, in all this time?"

Charles twitched, glancing uneasily toward Kitty, and opposite Varinn Thrain laughed, the sound scathing in his throat. "Och, I can scarce even *smell* the gold in that jewel-box," he said, with a jerk of his messy head toward it. "Kit already owns far more than this combined, with us. And you ought to *see* what else he's been planning for her. Sets your cheap, weak little gifts to *shame*."

Wait. Wait, Varinn wasn't planning other gifts for Kitty... was he? But his eyes had briefly flicked toward her, and then back to Charles again, as he jerked a hard, decisive nod. "For I see the true worth of such a woman," he said, his voice firm. "A woman who is kind, and eager, and faithful, and true. A woman who seeks to bring joy and peace and ease to those around her. A woman who is not ashamed of pleasure, and instead welcomes it, and seeks to grant it to those she cares for in return. A woman like this"—he exhaled, his eyes again flicking toward Kitty—"is a great gift, worth a great price."

Oh. Something was jangling in Kitty's chest, bright and vivid and wild, and now Thrain was looking at her too, a small smile curving at his mouth. "Ach, she is," he said, husky. "And unlike you, fool"—his eyes narrowed back toward Charles— "my partner sees all the real value Kit brings him, too. She earns coin for our clan. She helps with our trade and policies. She builds bonds within our home, and well beyond it. She does him credit in how she speaks, how she presents herself, how she cares for the people he cares about. She's an asset to his name and his clan, a boon to his reputation—and thank the gods, he's smart enough to appreciate that, and reward it! Not to shunt her into a cold little hovel, and throw her a few cheap baubles now and then!"

His voice was fierce, surprisingly vicious, and Charles glanced back at Kitty too, his eyes unreadable. "I made her another offer," he said, almost petulant. "I realized I was— underpaying her, after she left."

But now it was Kitty's turn to scoff, or maybe it was a laugh, carrying through the room. "You made me another offer?" she demanded. "You tried to blackmail me, you mean! You tried to use my son against me!"

Varinn and Thrain both growled in unison, the anger kindling higher in their eyes as their steps kept pacing, circling. "Is this truth, human?" Varinn asked, a low deadly snarl. "You threatened not only our woman, but our *son*, also?"

Charles' mouth opened and closed, his gaze uneasily darting to where Thrain was still growling, his clawed hands flexing hungrily at his sides. "Och, we can scent you, fool man," Thrain drawled. "I wonder if you're brave enough to speak these threats again, where we can hear you?"

There was a faint but undeniable tremble up Charles' back, together with a searching glance toward the door. Prompting a chilly laugh from Thrain, and a contemptuous snort from Varinn. "Ach, you ought to run," Varinn hissed. "But first, you shall vow to leave Katharine be. You shall swear to never speak her name on your foul lips again. And you shall forever forget this claim of orcs swindling you, lest you wish for all your secrets to be shouted in the streets!"

Another visible shudder wrenched up Charles' back, and Thrain huffed a low laugh, his eyes cutting toward Kitty. "Anything else you want from this fool, Kit?" he said. "Before he disappears from your life forever?"

Oh. Well. The wild sparkling warmth was still jangling, careening in Kitty's chest, and it took a moment to think, to dredge up words. "I wanted—a reference," she managed. "And severance pay. And"—she glanced around the apartment—"time to take all my things."

Neither Varinn nor Thrain showed any surprise at this, and both of them were frowning at Charles again, their steps around him still so slow, so deliberate. "And you shall swear to write Katharine a reference, and send it to Orc Mountain," Varinn repeated coolly. "You shall pay her a fair severance. And you shall grant her time here to take all her goods. And then"—his voice deepened—"you shall leave her be. Forever."

Charles grimaced, and for an instant he looked petulant, almost rebellious. "But," he stammered. "What if I don't *want*—"

But before he could finish, both Varinn and Thrain—lunged. Their big bodies moving in swift, furious tandem toward Charles, their teeth bared, the growls burning from their throats. And Charles yelped and wailed, cowering beneath his arms, bracing for impact, for—

Nothing? Nothing, because Varinn and Thrain had just—traded places, both of them hurtling past Charles without even a touch. And Thrain was laughing, cold and amused, while Varinn shot a distasteful, dismissive glance downwards. Toward where there was an unmistakable trail of wetness, running rapidly down the front of Charles' trousers.

"Get out, fool," Varinn snapped, with cutting contempt. "Before you piddle all over the floor, and leave us to bear even more of your foul reeking scent!"

Charles blanched, trembled, glanced downwards with abject mortification in his eyes—and without another word, he hurled his bag of coins toward Kitty's feet, and rushed past Varinn for the door. Yanking it open, dodging out, and then slamming the door shut with a deafening thud, before thundering down the stairs, his boot-falls fading away with him.

He was gone.

54

For a brief, hovering breath, there was only stillness. Only staring at that closed door, at where Charles had gone. Gone. For... for good?

But then a glance at Varinn seemed to confirm it, his eyes wry and soft and regretful on hers—and before Kitty had even caught it, she'd thrown herself toward him. Hurling her arms around his waist, burying her face into his solid, sweaty chest.

"Thank you," she gulped, muffled, into his skin. "Thank you so much. You were *wonderful*."

The fervency shuddered through her voice against him, and oh, that was the feeling of his big warm arms, wrapping tightly around her, folding her close and safe. "Ach, it was naught, *kisa*," he murmured, and she could feel his face pressing into her hair, his breath inhaling slow and deep. "I am so sorry it was not sooner. You ought never have needed to bear this, ach? We ought never to have left you alone and unguarded thus."

His voice wavered, his arms pulling her even tighter, and it distantly occurred to Kitty that until this, they... they hadn't left her unguarded, ever. Had they? There'd been that one day at the shop, but after that Thrain had stayed, every single day.

And what had Harthr said, back in the shop? *Thought those two would never leave you alone. But I knew if I waited long enough, they would slip up sooner or later...*

"You—couldn't have known," she managed, into his chest. "Harthr—he was—he was *waiting*. The whole *time*."

A choked sob had escaped her mouth, and in return Varinn growled, deep and menacing, even as his big hands ran firmly up and down her back. And wait, that was the feeling of Thrain's hand, too, joining Varinn's in the stroking, his tall body hot and twitchy against her.

"Fucking *Harthr*," he snapped, his voice scathing. "Always knew he was rubbish. And a fucking *fool*, if he thought he could get away with stealing *Varinn's* mate."

But at that, Kitty felt Varinn slightly stiffening against her, and perhaps she'd stiffened, too. Because she wasn't Varinn's mate, she'd never been Varinn's mate, and then she'd gone and confirmed it, by leaving behind all his jewels. And what must he think of her now, what if she'd still ruined this beyond repair, what if—

And then, without warning, Varinn—sank downwards. Down—onto his knees, on the hard floor. Kneeling before Kitty, good gods, and clasping her hand tightly in his, as his face tilted upwards, his eyes glimmering on hers.

"Katharine," he said, his voice rough and low. "I am—so sorry. I have been—so wrong. The way I have treated you has been—thoughtless, and selfish, and unspeakably cruel."

What? Kitty stared at him, frozen, her heart lurching in her chest—and he just kept staring back, his eyes so bright, so ashamed. "Not only did I speak such harsh and hurtful words toward you, when first we met," he continued thickly. "But against all my clan's ways, I also led you to believe—you owed me a debt. I pressed you to pretend to be my mate, and to—to serve me, and obey me. I pushed you to speak false to Thrain— to all our kin—on my behalf. For my own selfish ends."

Kitty couldn't move, couldn't think, and Varinn choked a

strange laugh, bitter and broken in his throat. "For again, I wished to hold—power over you," he continued, his voice cracking. "Over you, and over Thrain. And I told myself this was for Thrain's gain, and our son's. And ach, I ken there was truth in this, but this did not honour either of you, and—"

But. He was breathing hard now, his too-bright eyes flicking toward Thrain, and back to Kitty again. "And in truth, what I wished most was—to have you, Katharine," he whispered. "I wished—to keep you. I wished to have you longing for me, kneeling for me, sucking out my seed, calling me your lord. I wished to make you reek of me. I wished to make you *mine*."

His voice had gone deep, vicious, *hungry*—and he squeezed his eyes shut, shook his head. "But I—did not want to admit this," he continued. "To you, or to Thrain, or to—myself. I thought myself—above you. Above a woman who would"—he swallowed, exhaled, met her eyes with a pained grimace—"mate with an orc she had just met. Who would then—kneel and beg for another, in exchange for his care. And who—who bore so many scents, enough to suggest that she—oft did this. Oft traded her beauty for her gain."

Oh. Yes. Yes, Kitty had done that, because she'd been for sale, just as he'd said. And her heart was plummeting, her eyes dropping—at least, until Varinn gave her hand a desperate little shake, dragging her eyes back to his again.

"But I was wrong," he said, low and fervent. "I was wrong, to speak thus, to even *think* thus. I was proud, and I was self-righteous, and I was cruel. And in the face of my cruelty"—his mouth twisted—"you showed me only kindness. You helped me. You cared for me. You honoured me, before not only Thrain, but all our kin. You kept the vow I threw upon you, and you never failed or faltered in this. Not once."

Kitty swallowed, her hand spasming in his, and he abruptly brought it to his mouth, pressed a warm, reverent kiss against her skin. "You never once showed contempt or anger or bitterness," he continued, hoarse. "Even when you thought I might—abandon you, after this was done. Instead, you kept working, kept honouring me, kept granting me such pleasure and ease and peace. You embraced my clan, and my dress, and my gods, and all my deepest longings. You were so sweet, and eager, and true, and in this"—his glimmering eyes searched hers again—"you showed yourself a true Grisk, *kisa*. A far better Grisk than I have been. Far better than I deserved."

Kitty swallowed again, attempted a shake of her head—but Varinn was shaking his head too, making a sound that was half-growl, half-sob. "And when I saw how wrong I had been," he continued, faster now, "I did not speak truth to you, or to Thrain. Instead, I thought—I thought if I cared for you, kept you safe, brought you pleasure, gave you time and freedom to choose me in return, this would—cover my past sins. I thought I could pretend I had never done this, pretend I had never been so small or selfish as to hurt you, or speak so ill of you, or bring you such fear and pain. I wished to pretend I would never do this to one I loved so deeply."

Oh. Oh, gods, he hadn't just said that—had he? But he wasn't taking it back, wasn't looking away, despite that quiver on his mouth. "And I wished to pretend," he continued, very quiet now, "for Thrain. I wished to keep Thrain's fealty, and his hunger, and his—his worship. As I have always wished for, and longed for, but"—his eyes again glanced toward Thrain—"I have also not wished to admit this, ach? I wished to just—have all these gifts, for the taking, at my whim."

His eyes were so bright on Thrain's, his throat audibly convulsing. And when Kitty darted a look at Thrain, she found he was—weeping. Weeping, the water streaming down his face, as he barked a high-pitched little laugh, and—dropped to his knees on the floor beside Varinn. Yanking Varinn tightly against him, and burying his face deep into his neck.

"Och, always the martyr, Varinn," he said, with another shrill, muffled laugh, or perhaps a sob. "Naught about how I betrayed you, or lied to you, or blamed you for my own sins.

Naught about how I *knew* how much you wanted a mate and son, all those years. Naught"—another sob—"about how I kept throwing myself at you, doing my damnedest to give you everything you ever fucking *dreamt* of, so you wouldn't ever leave me."

Varinn's eyes closed, his inhale shuddering against Thrain's hair, and Thrain gulped, shook his head into Varinn's neck. "And naught about the drink," he choked. "Naught about how I sought to hide it from you, and left you to clean up my rubbish again and again. And worst of all"—his face tilted toward Kitty, his wet eyes blinking as they met hers—"naught about how I dragged a sweet, innocent woman into my mess. How deeply I hurt her, and hurt you. And made it so you didn't trust her, and wouldn't like her, from your very first scent of her upon me. It was *fucked*, Varinn, I was fucked, and"—he gulped another sob—"for me to have even *thought* about doing it on purpose, blowing things up between us for it, in hopes of maybe, maybe gaining you a mate and a son—"

His streaming eyes were darting between Kitty and Varinn now, and he roughly wiped at his face, shook his head. "You both should never speak to me again," he croaked. "Ever. Let alone welcoming me into your relationship, and your bed. And even pretending to be mated, all this time, for *me*."

Oh. Kitty was blinking hard, now, but the wetness had finally escaped her eyes too, trickling down her cheeks. While Thrain's eyes kept holding hers, searching hers, shimmering with molten, miserable truth.

"I'm so sorry, Kit," he gasped. "Gods, I'm so sorry. I've treated you so unfairly from the start, ach? From when we first spoke. You were foxed, you were alone, you told me how cruel this fool Charles had been to you, how he'd up and left you— and what did I do? I helped myself into your sympathies, into your apartment, into your bed. All while thinking about what *I* wanted, about what it might do for *me*. And the next day, after I sat there and watched you give away those damned jewels, I told you—you were fun, a good time, and then—I left you, too. Left you in an even worse state than that vile man did."

Kitty couldn't hide her wince, and perhaps Varinn had hissed, too—and Thrain's chest was heaving, his eyes still glimmering with such stark, shameful misery. "Even cursed the gods while I was at it," he continued, his voice hitching. "And then, after Varinn found you, and saved you, I still raged at him for my failings. For my shame. And I know you both, I know how good you both are, and I ken neither of you would've even *thought* about lying to me if I hadn't done that, ach? If I hadn't been such a fucking mess, between that, and the drink. Varinn was desperate, and of course *you* were desperate, Kit. You'd almost *died*, because of me."

Kitty's chest felt very tight, and it took too much effort to swallow, to keep blinking at Thrain's miserable eyes. To watch him struggling to draw in air, to let it out. "And just like with Varinn, you turned around and—helped me," he rasped. "You took me to Efterar. You did *everything* he told you to. You supported me, you stayed with me, you didn't push me away from you and Varinn, even when you should have. You made me laugh, you brought me such joy and pleasure, you got me a damned *typpavír*. You even helped me find forging again, after so long. And"—his eyes dropped to Kitty's waist—"amidst all this, you took care of our son, too. Such good care, Kit."

His voice hiccoughed, cracked, the water again streaking down his cheeks. "You deserved so much better than my rubbish," he whispered. "You deserved to be wooed, and courted, and cherished. Treated like the treasure you are."

Kitty's thoughts were spinning, her breaths dragging thin and ragged through her throat. Her wet eyes still held on Thrain's face, her thoughts catching on the strange, distant certainty that—thanks to that impossible magic he bore—this was his truth. Every damned word of it. He meant it, just like how he'd meant everything else he'd said to her, all this time.

All his failings, yes—but all his effort, his passion, his kindness. His heart.

"But," she somehow whispered, "you were also good to me, Thrain. You were."

He snorted, shaking his head, but Kitty had to say this now, needed to say it. "Both of you were," she managed, with a furtive, fleeting glance toward Varinn. "You both brought me— into your lives, and your home, and—your bedroom. You fed me, and clothed me, and kept me warm and safe. You introduced me to your kin. You supported me in finding a trade, and helped me work in the shop. You gave me beautiful gifts. You watched over me far more than I realized—enough to foil Harthr's plans all this time—and you came to me whenever I needed help. And throughout all that, you never once judged my—my past. My... work."

But Varinn was already grimacing, stubbornly shaking his head, and Kitty sighed, twitched a shaky shrug. "Well, except at first," she amended. "But let's be honest, you'd also just been very hurt, by the person you loved most, and you also thought I knew about you two, and that I had ulterior motives. *And*, you have one of the best noses in the mountain, you could smell Thrain all over me, and you were still stuck taking care of me. Of course you weren't having kind thoughts about me, right? Gods, who would?"

She attempted a wan smile toward Varinn, toward where he was still looking subdued, regretful. But he wasn't arguing or interrupting, either, perhaps waiting for her to continue, again giving her time, freedom, consideration. The way he so often had.

"And *you*," she said, her voice wavering, as she shifted her gaze back to Thrain again. "Yes, you did a lot of thoughtless and hurtful things. But you also worked to—to recognize that. To face that. You apologized, you sought treatment, you reorganized your entire life—and even quit your *job*, against your own kin's wishes—to make it work. And when you faced setbacks in your recovery, you were honest with us, every time. You did your very best to be a good father, and a good partner, and a good friend. You did everything you could to keep the promises you made to us, even when you thought—you *knew*—we were lying to you. The entire *time*, Thrain."

Her eyes were prickling again, streaking water down her cheeks, especially when Thrain clearly made to protest, to spout some rubbish again about how he deserved it—but Kitty was already shaking her head, flapping her hand toward him. "You didn't deserve it, Thrain," she countered. "You didn't. You were sick, and doing your best to heal, in the face of multiple challenges. Including"—her mouth tightened—"including that cretin Harthr. Who kept supplying you with the strongest ale he could find, and lying to you about the price, so he could keep driving a wedge between you two! Which he's apparently been trying to do this entire time, because he's still jealous that Varinn chose you over *him*!"

Thrain twitched, his gaze darting toward Varinn—and Kitty could see the swift, sudden comprehension passing between them, the silent communication of their eyes. Varinn's expression shifting into flinty hardness, Thrain's into disbelieving contempt.

"Fucking *Harthr*," Thrain spat. "He's *always* scented of spite around me, and I *knew* something was fishy about those bills of his! But ach, I ken he kept sending his lackeys to you to collect for me, didn't he, Varinn? Even—"

"Even Eyarl, and Valter," Varinn continued with a groan, rubbing at his eyes. "And twice he even sent Timo! Ach, I am not about to argue with Timo over a price! What should that teach him?"

"Och," Thrain replied, his voice scathing. "Harthr *knew* your greatest weakness, Varinn, knew you'd never want to show yourself wrong-footed or untrustworthy before your kin! Knew you'd far rather put the blame on—"

He broke off there, looking chagrined, but Varinn gave a

grim sigh, his head bowing. "Ach, on you, *krútt*," he said heavily. "He knew I should put my kin before you, and your safety. And I... I *did*."

Thrain winced, blinking at where Varinn had turned to look at him, his eyes bleak. "Just as I have also done with our work all this time," Varinn continued. "When I kept pushing you in it, well beyond what was best for you. And"—his miserable eyes raised toward Kitty—"just as I have done with you, Katharine, when I brushed aside Thrain's fears over Harthr. When I left you alone with one who I also did not fully trust. One who wished you great harm."

There was an instant's aching silence, dangling between them, until Kitty swallowed hard, attempted another smile down toward Varinn's drawn face. "But what Harthr did was *his* fault, not yours," she replied, quiet. "And maybe—maybe you taking the blame for his actions on yourself isn't an overly balanced way to see your clanmates either, is it?"

Varinn blinked, his forehead furrowing, and beside him Thrain huffed a little laugh, and elbowed him in the ribs. "Och, now you've been told, Varinn," he said. "Mayhap you'll actually listen to her upon this, ach? Gave up *years* ago on you ever listening to me."

Varinn's expression was now shifting between pained and discomfited and regretful, and he let out a shaky breath, rubbed at his mouth. "I shall—try," he finally said. "I shall seek to be wiser, stronger, for you both, to better keep you well and safe. To better see my own failings in this, and how I might—"

"Och, stop, Varinn," Thrain broke in, wry and a little sad, as he nudged his elbow back into his side. "Didn't mean you need to take even more on yourself. Gods, you *can't*, you ken? And you caring so much is one of the best things about you, one of the things that makes you so... *you*. But mayhap, just"—he shrugged, exhaled—"just keep listening to us, ach? Trusting us, respecting us, over the rest of our kin, and your obligations toward them?"

Varinn was listening, now, his full focus on Thrain's face, and surely Thrain had registered that, barking out another choked laugh. "And look, you *did* listen about Harthr, after that first day, remember?" he said. "And you listened to Kit about helping me get treatment—and you listened about my work, too. Gods"—he sniffed, ran a hand over his eyes—"you've just been so fucking *good* about the whole work thing, Varinn, even when I know how damned hard it's been for you. I don't deserve that either, ach? Don't deserve *you.*"

He was speaking very quickly, not looking at where Varinn was frowning, now, his nostrils flaring, his head shaking. Perhaps scenting something on Thrain, on the way Thrain was shifting on his knees, and looking up at Kitty. His eyes bright, pleading, painfully determined on hers, his hands gripping tightly at his knees.

"But *you* deserve Varinn, Kit," he whispered. "You deserve to be cared for, to be valued and cherished. And"—his eyes darted briefly to Varinn, and then back to her face—"I swear to you, if you accept his apology, you won't regret it, ach? He'll take such good care of you, he'll be the best mate and father you could have ever asked for. You two are so good together, and you deserve to finally be happy together, and at peace. Without me barging around and fucking up everything between you. Again."

But wait, wait, what the hell was he saying, and he was gulping for more air, his wet eyes rapidly blinking. "So once we're back home again, I can—move out," he continued, too wooden, too fast. "Move down to the Ka-esh wing, mayhap, where we wouldn't scent each other so strongly, and I could keep—keep apprenticing with Gary, and work in the Ka-esh forge instead. And mayhap you'll be kind enough to set up a schedule, after our son is born, so I can still see him, still try to be a good father to him. And no need to worry about me running back to the drink, because"—he dragged down another heavy breath—"I can't do that to our son. I *won't*. So it'll be fine, ach? I'll be fine, and you'll be happy. You'll see."

His voice was so fervent, his eyes so bright, so... so anguished. And he was even still trying to smile, to let on that this really was fine, this was what he really wanted. And as Kitty stared blankly back toward him, it distantly occurred to her that it was like hearing herself speak, like staring into her own pretending eyes. Into her own past, into repeatedly sacrificing her own desires, her own accomplishments, her own *future*, for someone else's benefit.

And without even feeling it, Kitty watched her hand slipping out toward him. Toward that silken mess of his black hair, sliding against it, her fingers sinking deep. Wanting him to look at her, perhaps, needing him to hear her, to know that she saw him. She understood.

"Now that's rubbish, Thrain," she said, her voice a shaky whisper. "You know we wouldn't be happy without you. We— we love you. And we're so glad you fought through your illness, and came back to us. So glad you brought us all together."

Thrain's wet eyes snapped wide on hers, disbelieving, and he bit his lip, shook his head. Glancing sideways toward Varinn, toward where Varinn was searching Kitty's face, a strange light in his eyes—but he was nodding, his mouth pulling into a small, wavering smile. Twitching with warmth, with gratefulness, with bare, startling affection. With hope.

"Our sweet, forgiving *kisa* speaks truth, *krútt*," he said, his voice husky, his shimmering eyes still on Kitty's face. "We are both so proud of you, and we love you too deeply to let you go, ach? You are part of this. Part of us. Always."

The certainty was so smooth, so stunning in his voice, in his slowly spreading smile. And somehow Kitty was smiling back, even through the tears again trickling down her cheeks. Needing Varinn to see how she understood him, too, and trusted in his judgement and his kindness. As perhaps she had since the very first moment they'd met.

And Varinn understood her too, still holding her gaze with such soft, approving affection, his breath inhaling slow and deep. As his tongue brushed his lips, and his shining eyes glinted with a familiar, dizzying heat.

"You are such a great, great gift to us, sweet *kisa*," he murmured. "And if you should allow it, we should be so honoured to—begin again. To show you our care, and our honour, and our pleasure. To woo and claim you as we ought to have done, from the start. Together."

Oh. Kitty's eyes widened, darting between them both. Drinking up that heated reverence in Varinn's gaze, and—and the sheer stilted shock, in Thrain's. Shock that was slowly fading behind his blinking lashes, giving way to a shy, uncertain awe, as his hand carefully found Kitty's fingers, and brought them to his lips. Kissing her with hushed, worshipful sweetness, his eyes intently searching hers—and when Kitty twitched her fingers closer, he breathed a hard exhale, and began slowly moving upwards. Kissing over her palm, her wrist, sparking out shivers of pleasure beneath her skin.

"Ach, *kisa*?" Varinn murmured, because oh, now he was kissing her other hand, his lips warm and gentle, his eyes also seeking, searching, on hers. "Should you welcome this, from us?"

And oh, could he truly want this, could he want to start over, to show her his care, and Thrain's care. Could he truly want to do it together, show her together—and suddenly there was only longing, crashing like thunder through Kitty's chest. Needing to see this, to know, so much it was breaking her apart...

"Yes," she whispered, pleading, praying to her lord. "Please. *Please*."

55

At first, Varinn and Thrain just kept... kissing. Kissing Kitty together, with such slow, sweet gentleness. Thrain's mouth trailing softly up her arm, while Varinn rose to his feet, and carefully slid her cloak off her shoulders. Letting it fall to the floor, so he could brush his kisses up the line of her bare shoulder, until he reached the sensitive curve of her neck.

"You taste so good, *kisa*," he murmured, husky into her skin. "So rich. So sweet."

Kitty gasped and shivered, leaning into that reverent press of Varinn's mouth—but he didn't deepen the kiss, or let her feel even a nudge of teeth. Keeping it light and feathery and soft, just like Thrain beside him. Who had slowly risen to his feet too, his lips now brushing up Kitty's arm to her shoulder, tasting her collarbone, his slick tongue lingering against her tingling skin.

Gods, it felt good, both their warm clever mouths caressing in tandem, scattering gooseflesh beneath their touch. And their big warm hands were touching Kitty now too, stroking up and down her back, spreading over her belly, cupping at her breasts. And oh, Varinn's hand had found her face, guiding her lips to his, seeking against her mouth with his soft delving tongue.

Kitty instantly opened for him, moaning into him, and she could feel—could taste—his growl, too, rumbling low and hungry through his chest, his tongue. And Thrain had gasped at the sound, too, his kiss stuttering up Kitty's shoulder, until it latched hot and hungry onto her neck—and it was enough to make her stagger, nearly collapsing into Varinn's solid form against her.

He huffed a heated little laugh, low with affection, and perhaps with satisfaction, too. And he and Thrain were already pulling off the rest of her clothes—her flimsy top, her kilt, her boots—and then their own clothes, too, before carefully guiding her down to her back on the bed. Their big powerful bodies sinking down on either side of her, cradling her close and safe between them.

Varinn's mouth instantly found hers again, his kisses firmer now, as his gentle hand stroked her cheek, her neck, her breasts. While Thrain began kissing steadily downwards, skating his hot hungry mouth over the swell of her belly, licking into her navel, the sensitive creases above her thighs. And then—Kitty yelped, gasped into Varinn's mouth—Thrain spread her thighs apart, and licked up slow and deep between them.

"Oh," Kitty gulped, and Varinn chuckled against her lips as his hand found Thrain's messy head, and pressed him deeper. Making both Kitty and Thrain groan at once, and Thrain's hands clutched at Kitty's thighs, pulled them even wider. So he could bury his face even harder against her, his fluttering tongue feasting deep within her, while Varinn's tongue did the same with her mouth. Both of them locked to her, drinking from her at once, almost too stunning, too overpowering, to be real.

But it was, it was, and it was still happening, still wrenching brighter with every choking breath. Even with how Varinn was gently drawing away, pressing a brief kiss to the tip of Kitty's nose—and now he was kissing downwards, while Thrain kissed up. Trading places, oh gods, and Kitty moaned at the feel of Thrain finding her mouth, his tongue slick and sloppy, tangy with the taste of her. As Varinn just kept kissing, so slow and sure and thorough, his hands caressing her rounded belly as he kissed over it, inhaled against it, even bowed his forehead to it, while his breaths shuddered through his chest. And then downwards, toward, toward—

Kitty's cry was more of a shout this time, her shaky body arching brazenly against Varinn's seeking succulent mouth, and oh, he liked that, he wanted that, rumbling that low satisfied purr into her. Enough to make her writhe and shout again, her cry muffled against Thrain's slick kisses, his soft satisfied laugh. "You like that, Kit?" he murmured, hot against her lips. "Like having Lord Grisk prostrating himself before you, feasting on you? Making you squirt and scream for him?"

Oh gods, oh Kitty was not doing those things, or was she, because her writhing, shuddering body felt like someone else, like something had possessed it, transformed it. Something that wanted her shouting and wailing, her entire awareness narrowing to sheer, staggering sensation. To how her swollen, spread-apart flesh was thrumming and throbbing beneath Varinn's intent hungry mouth, its control utterly lost, its convulsive spasms writhing, wracking, wringing out dazzling, dizzying surges of pleasure.

But amidst it all, Varinn only kept purring, and swallowing. Drinking her down in deep, audible gulps, even as his tongue kept curving, feasting, *appreciating*. While Kitty panted and shook and scrabbled at him, please, oh gods please...

"You want more, Kit?" came Thrain's heated voice, ragged against her mouth. "I bet you'd like to have your Lord Grisk's strong ploughing next, ach? You want to swallow up his fat, pretty prick? Suck out all his good Grisk seed inside you?"

Kitty's cry was helpless, desperate, her head nodding, her

tingling hands yanking wildly at Varinn's hair, his shoulders. And Thrain laughed, husky and approving, as he slipped his fingers down to where Varinn's mouth had been. Opening her, oh, so Varinn could shift up over her, his body huge and heavy, his eyes half-lidded on hers, as his long tongue swept across his shiny mouth. And one big arm was settling close beside her head on the bed, blocking her in, while the other hand again found her face, tilted it up…

And he kissed her again, so firm and sweet, as his slick, rounded head nudged between her legs. Jutting into where Thrain was opening her swollen heat wider, guiding them together, so Varinn could stay focused on kissing her like this, on his tongue sinking thorough and deep into her mouth, in perfect time with that bulging, driving cock.

Kitty shouted and writhed again, but it only pressed them deeper, tighter together, Varinn's heft swelling fuller inside her, stretching her wide and taut around him. As his mouth kept drinking up her cries, taking them into the strength of his huge, pressing body. Enclosing her utterly beneath it, upon it, in pure perfect safety, and Kitty nearly sobbed as he sank the rest of the way in. His groin grinding tight against hers, his strength flexing and flaring inside her, whipping her cries up higher, hotter. And then he was rocking, oh gods, meeting her again and again and again, and it was too much it was so much it was tearing her apart—

Kitty's release charged through her in more bright, brilliant bursts, thrashing her beneath him with spasms of staggering, glorious bliss. And now Varinn was the one groaning, his teeth very lightly clamping her lip as he stiffened all over—and oh, oh there it was, that surge of hot heady sweetness spraying inside her, filling her, marking her, claiming her as his own. His face almost pained, or even beatific, as he pumped it out for her, straining to pour out more, more, more, until she could feel the pressure of it growing inside her, swelling, distending, oh—

He drew out with a hiss, a regretful twist on his mouth—and Kitty gasped at the feel of that molten heat surging out between them, flooding all over her thighs, all over the bed-linens. But if Varinn had noticed, he didn't seem to care, and he was even caressing her face again, looking into her eyes with something like approval, or maybe even appreciation.

"Ach, you are so sweet, my beautiful *kisa*," he breathed, his lashes fluttering, before his lips found hers again, kissing her slow and deep. "You scent so good. Taste so good. Feel so good, upon me. It is a great honour to have you beneath me, so full of my fresh seed that it spills freely from within you."

Oh. Kitty could only seem to shiver and shake in reply, and she belatedly realized that she was clinging to him with her arms and legs, her hands somehow clutched against... Thrain's? Because wait, Thrain had been caressing Varinn's back throughout all this, his head bent into Varinn's neck. And now Varinn's head was turning to meet Thrain's, their mouths catching together with far less gentleness than they'd used on Kitty, their long tongues tangling, teeth scraping sharp against sweaty skin.

"Hungry, *krútt*?" Varinn murmured, into Thrain's mouth. "Wish for your turn?"

And wait, what had he just said—but yes, wait, he was already settling sideways onto the bed beside Kitty, while Thrain shifted up on top. His lean body hovering over her, his hazy eyes darting with unmistakable uncertainty between her and Varinn. Because he hadn't done this with Kitty, not like this, not since that very first night, in this very bed. And surely, that had been because of Varinn, because of Varinn's claim upon her, and—

And now Varinn's hand was the one slipping downwards, seeking between Kitty's legs, opening her up. Spreading her swollen, quivering, still-leaking heat even wider apart, for—for Thrain, just as Thrain had done for him. And did Varinn mean it, could he really mean it, his eyes catching on Kitty's, as his tongue swept across his lips.

"Shall you next welcome my wild, beautiful *krútt* inside you, *kisa*?" he murmured, both rough and soft. "Shall you welcome his hard, powerful Grisk prick, and his precious Aetha seed? Seed that has"—his hungry eyes angled toward her belly, and then to Thrain's face—"already shown you its great strength, and flowered deep within you?"

Kitty blinked, choked, searched that cool, crackling satisfaction in his glinting eyes—and then she rapidly, frantically nodded. While Thrain groaned above her, the sound hoarse, urgent, as his warm body shifted lower, his waiting, prodding flesh already seeking, sinking between her parted, trembling legs.

It already felt so different, so poised, especially with that cold curve of gold at the tip—and oh, it moved differently, too. With less of Varinn's steady, focused determination, and more hitching, barely restrained jerks. Jutting inside her breath by breath, straight into the thick slippery mass of Varinn's sloshing seed, already bubbling and squirting out around Thrain's invasion, coating him in its scent, its claim, perhaps even its command. Its control of this, between them, even now.

But Thrain certainly didn't seem bothered by this, and if anything, he felt almost... frenzied, somehow, against the clutch of Kitty's trembling hands. His lean body rigid all over, shaking with waves of tension, with badly fraying control. With his eyes rolling back, his teeth bared, as his hard strength inside her jerked deeper, deeper...

"Ach, I ken you are sweeter than my hungry *krútt* can bear, *kisa*," Varinn's low voice cut in, sounding almost amused, as his big hand stroked firm and reassuring up and down Thrain's rigid, sweaty back. "Should you mind, mayhap, if I allow him to rut wild upon you, for a spell? As long as I can scent no pain upon you?"

Oh. Kitty could scarcely follow what that all meant, but Thrain's straining stillness above her—inside her—was almost too much to be borne, and she was already furiously nodding, and dragging Thrain closer. But he still held himself there, shaky and stiff, staring heavy-lidded at Varinn, waiting for his brief, indulgent nod. And then Thrain moaned, half agony, half relief, as he shuddered all over, and plunged the rest of the way inside.

It was sharp, stunning, impossibly overwhelming, and Kitty's cry rose together with Thrain's, their bodies crashing together, locking hard and tight. With his long, rock-hard cock bobbing and lurching inside her, delving as deep as it could possibly go, as if it wanted to plunder into her womb itself— but then it snatched away, brief and disorienting, before slamming inside again. The sound thick and obscene, spurting out more of Varinn's fluid from deep inside her, but oh, that only seemed to surge the hunger harder, hotter. And Thrain was growling, groaning, as he did it again, again and again and again. Driving reckless and relentless into her, into Varinn's slick sticky leavings, until the seed was sloshing and sputtering around them, loudly squelching with every wild, desperate thrust.

And maybe it was a mess, maybe it was wrong or obscene or shameful. But Kitty's shaky, blinking glance sideways toward Varinn found him still looking indulgent, appreciative, even... enraptured. Almost like a god, perhaps, granting his greatest blessing upon his most favoured subjects. Wanting them to take their pleasure with his good fresh seed easing the way between them, marking them. Making them still his, even more than they'd been before.

And gods, it looked so good on him, his face so warm and open and dazzling, so alive. As if he'd always wanted this, always wanted to witness this—and wait, perhaps this was part of why he'd been so hurt by Thrain's betrayal, too. Because he'd wanted to be there, to see it, to approve of it. And he'd wanted to see Thrain like this, like...

Like he'd been sparked to life, too. Like he was blazing, on fire, his hair and eyes wild, his teeth bared and flashing white. As he kept plunging furiously into Kitty, into Varinn's slick spilling seed, again and again and again, his driving hips hammering with such fierce fervid desperation. Like he was about to explode, to shatter into a million streaming sparks, flying radiant into the sun—

He blew out with a raw, ragged roar, his cock buried to the base, his head thrown back. His entire body convulsing with every wracking spurt of molten heat, with every spasm of those rapidly emptying bollocks, jammed tight against her. And suddenly Kitty's release was flashing up, too, shrieking in a surge of sweeping, spinning euphoria. Her sparkling body writhing and gasping around him, welcoming him, milking him, drinking up everything he could give her—until she was utterly dazed, dizzy, drenched in it. Flooded utterly to the brim, and still spurting out more around him, spewing all over him, over her, the bed, everything.

But it still felt so good, so suddenly, stunningly blissful, so right. And perhaps Varinn and Thrain thought so too, because Thrain was still gently thrusting inside her, his eyes fluttering as more hot slick sloshed out around him, while Varinn was... inhaling. Breathing in slow and deep, his chest steadily filling, his eyes gone hazy and hooded. And he even leaned over into Thrain's neck, inhaling again as he buried his face in his flushed, sweaty skin.

"Ach, *krútt*," he purred, as he drew away again, his mouth pulling into a slow, affectionate smile. "So rash and messy and needy. My *kisa*'s sweet little womb was too much for you, ach?"

Thrain rapidly, fervently nodded, his eyes squeezing shut, his breaths hitching from his throat. But then his eyes snapped wide open again, seeking for Kitty's, looking almost—almost panicked.

"Ach, I—I'm—sorry, Kit," he said, too quickly, his voice hoarser than she'd ever heard it. "That was—I—gods. So much easier when—I was—foxed out of my mind. *Fuck*, I mean"—he shuddered, gulped for air—"I should've—shouldn't have—I—"

He squeezed his eyes shut again, frantically shaking his messy head back and forth, his panic almost palpable in the air—and Kitty was deeply, profoundly grateful when Varinn caught his mouth again, kissing him with hard, solid steadiness, as his hand firmly stroked up and down his trembling back. And Kitty could feel Thrain gradually settling, calming beneath it, his breaths slowing, his body sagging heavy against her.

When Varinn drew away again, Thrain's eyes were bright, blinking with gratitude, with unmistakable relief. "Thanks, Varinn," he whispered, before turning back toward Kitty, and pressing a tender, tentative kiss to her mouth. "And thank you, Kit. Forgot how fucking *good* this felt, how damn sweet you scent and taste. You're a true Grisk goddess, ach? Worthy of Lord Grisk himself."

He'd cast another weepy glance toward Varinn, but Varinn was smiling at Kitty too, that indulgent warmth again glimmering in his eyes. "Ach, she is more than worthy," he said, his voice such a soft, low caress. "She is a great, great gift to us. Just the kind of woman I have begged the gods to bring to us, all these years."

Something shimmered up Kitty's spine, hot and disbelieving, but Varinn was still smiling at her like that, like he really, truly meant that. "I asked for a woman who would be a boon to us, and to our clan," he murmured. "A woman who would not treat our kin or our ways with judgement or shame, but instead with warmth and kindness. A woman who would care for Thrain as deeply as I do, and would care thus for our sons, also."

Oh. The shimmery warmth was fizzing out wider, stronger, the shy smile pulling at Kitty's mouth—while above her, Thrain huffed a choked, disbelieving laugh. "Do you really mean to tell me, Varinn," he demanded, his voice far steadier than before, "that you've been putting this off for *years*, putting *me* off whenever I asked you, because—because you expected the *gods* to handle it for you? To show up and drop your dream mate naked into your lap?"

Varinn's glance toward Thrain was more than a little guilty, and he twitched a rolling little shrug. "Ach, mayhap," he said. "The gods have always been good to me. And"—his gaze flicked back toward Kitty, his mouth quirking up again—"she near *did* drop into my lap naked, ach?"

Kitty couldn't help a wry grin back, while above her Thrain loudly scoffed, and jabbed a claw toward him. "That had nothing to do with the gods, you overbearing tyrant!" he exclaimed. "That was me. All me!"

Varinn's grin was quick and affectionate, his hand slipping up to rustle in Thrain's hair. "Ach, mayhap," he said again, husky. "But I have also prayed every day for the gods to help you, ach? To teach me how to reach you. To bring the orc I love most back to me again."

Oh. Thrain's smile instantly faded, his eyes gone stricken on Varinn's, and thank the gods Varinn leaned in again, kissed firmly at his quivering mouth. "And here you are," he murmured. "My wise, rash, stunning Aetha, bringing me such joy, and such peace. And"—his eyes glinted—"reeking as if you have drowned your prick in a *vat* of my good seed."

Thrain's bark of a laugh was impossibly merry, and he grinned broadly between them, his eyes dancing. "You oughta scented him, Kit," he said. "I promise you, he's been thinking about that for weeks. Setting me loose on you when you're full of his fresh seed, so my scent will start shouting *that* about him, too."

But despite that roll of Thrain's eyes, he didn't actually seem bothered by this, and Varinn's smile had gone almost smug. "Ach, it shall," he coolly replied. "And any orc who scents you shall know you are mine, *krútt*. Your mouth, your rump, and ach, your pretty pierced prick, for it fucks only at my command, into my woman's womb. You are *my* Aetha, *my* rare beautiful truth-seeker, and you bow and beg only for *me*."

His voice had gone deep and almost scathing by the end, but Thrain still didn't seem slightly alarmed, not by Varinn's tone, or his words. And instead, he was even biting his lip, his face and ears flushing, his eyes lowering with something almost like shyness. "Ach, Lord Grisk," he murmured. "It is my honour."

And as Thrain had spoken, he'd even pulled up a little, so he could put his hand to his heart. Just the way they prayed to the gods in the shrine, and there was a strange, hushed stillness as Kitty and Varinn blinked at him—and as a flush stole across Varinn's cheeks, too. His expression almost dazed, almost reverent, looking for an instant as though Thrain was the god, and he the shy, awestruck worshipper.

But then Varinn seemed to shake all over, and pulled himself up too, onto his knees. Clasping Kitty's hand, drawing her up beside him—and then gripping his other hand into Thrain's. Blinking between them both, now, his jaw set, his eyes hot and flinty and bright.

"Thrain Aetha, and my dear Katharine, of Clan Grisk," he began, on a slow exhale. "You are both all I could wish for. All I could long for. All I have dreamt of, in all my days. And thus"— his throat convulsed—"it would be my greatest honour to serve you, to lead you, and to cherish you, as my bonded mates. To do all within my power to care for you, and our son. No matter the cost."

Oh. Kitty's heart was suddenly hammering, her wide eyes frozen on Varinn's earnest face, on the nervousness—the determination—in his eyes. On how he was looking at her, and then looking at Thrain, open, vulnerable, exposed. As if waiting for them to object, to challenge those impossible words—or even waiting, perhaps, for Thrain's magic to grasp him, to catch him in its thrall. But wait, it was, he was, Thrain's eyes holding Varinn's with glittering, vivid intensity, even as his breaths heaved from his chest, and water trickled down his cheek.

"And you're sure about Kit, too, Varinn?" he asked, his voice a whisper, as his other hand groped out, caught tightly onto her own clammy fingers. "You're sure you mean it?"

But Varinn didn't blink, didn't falter. Just looked at Thrain, and nodded, and breathed. Facing Thrain's magic, his... truth.

"Ach, I am sure, Thrain," he said slowly. "I ken I have oft been wrong, in how I have treated Katharine. But amidst this, I have always cared for her, and longed for her, even from the start. Have you not scented me, all this time? Do you ken"—he choked a thick little laugh—"I would have ever spoken false to you, had I thought my scent would betray the falsehood? And thus urge you to ask me of it, even once?"

Oh. Wait. He meant—he surely didn't mean—did he? And Kitty's whirling thoughts were spinning, suddenly, skipping and skittering backwards, thinking of all those times Varinn had looked at her, touched her, kissed her. All the times he'd so clearly wanted her pleasure and her affection—and how Thrain had never argued it, either. *Och, you oughta scented him, Kit. I ken he likes it. Don't stop.*

And Thrain was—nodding. Nodding, even as more wetness streaked down his cheeks, his breaths coming in short little sniffles. "It's why I kept on as long as I did, too," he whispered back. "Know all your scents, Varinn. Know what your love tastes like."

His love. His *love*, and Varinn nodded too, his eyes furiously blinking, as he raised Thrain's hand, brought it to his mouth. "Ach, I ken," he said, his voice rough. "Is there aught else you— or Katharine—might wish to ask?"

At that, Thrain's eyes broke away from Varinn's, and caught on Kitty's instead. Holding with that same strange snap of power, of *magic*, as his mouth gave an apologetic smile. "Aught else, Kit?" he asked, hoarse. "Aught you wish to know from Varinn, or me?"

But Kitty was sniffling too, and shaking her head, and then smiling back at him, slow and true. "I just—love you both so much," she gulped. "Want to stay with you both, for always."

Thrain's eyes squeezed shut, his shoulders sagging with palpable relief, and he choked a half-laugh, half-sob. "Ach," he whispered. "Me, too. So—ach, start over, Varinn, will you?"

Beside them, Varinn was rapidly nodding, and dragging in more air, as a small, hopeful smile quivered on his mouth. "Thrain Aetha, and my dear Katharine, of Clan Grisk," he began, a husky low rasp. "Before all my fathers and mothers, and all the Grisk, and all the gods, I wish to pledge you my troth. I shall grant you my favour, and my sword, and my fealty. I shall keep you safe. So long as I am able, and so long as you both shall wish. Shall you accept this vow, from me?"

And in that instant, there was only—awe. Awe, swinging out bright and joyful, so, so alive, beating with wild golden wings in Kitty's chest. And she was laughing, and crying, and—and somehow throwing herself at Varinn, her and Thrain tackling him down together. Pinning him to the messy bed beneath them, to that truth of their future, made real in flesh and touch and scent.

"Yes," Kitty sobbed, into Varinn's chest, into the warm wonderful embrace of his eager, powerful arms. "Yes."

56

Kitty couldn't have said how long she stayed there, wrapped so warm and safe in Varinn's arms. In... her mate's arms. Her *mate.*

It was still so surreal, so impossible, but somehow it just kept... being there. Being there, in the warmth of Varinn's solid body beneath her, in his big hands caressing both her and Thrain at once, drawing them closer. In how Thrain was already nuzzling hungrily at his neck, and how Varinn's hand slipped up to his messy head, guiding, approving, as Thrain's sharp teeth sank deep, and a low, contented moan vibrated through his chest.

And in how... something hard was already swelling, prodding, into Kitty's belly. And how easy it felt, how right, to push upwards a little, to flash her brightest, most stunning smile at her mate's flushed, contented face. And then to carefully guide him back inside her again, sinking him deep into the sticky surging mess, as she gasped and shuddered around him.

But again, Varinn didn't seem to take any notice of the mess, not even as it streaked across his thighs, his belly. And instead, he only settled his big hand to Kitty's bare hip, and watched with those hazy, approving eyes as she rode him, rocking to meet his own gentle thrusts again and again and again. Until the pleasure again crashed through her, clamping her against him, surging out more of the mess—but oh, he was pouring out again too, pumping her even fuller, his body grinding and arching beneath her as his nostrils twitched and flared.

The surging streams afterwards were even worse, especially when Kitty drew off again—but Thrain's hand had slipped down to smear in it, wiping it liberally against Varinn's abdomen, his chest. And then—Thrain pulled away from Varinn's neck, contentedly licking his reddened lips—he even brought his dripping hand to his own mouth, dragging his broad tongue up against his palm with smooth, sheer shamelessness.

"Our seed tastes so good, blended thus upon her," he murmured, his eyes gleaming on Varinn's. "Thought it would, ach?"

Varinn nodded, his eyes still so warm, so approving—especially when Thrain smeared his hand in the mess again, and then brought it to Varinn's mouth, instead. Slipping his fingers between Varinn's lips, watching as Varinn willingly sucked them off, one by one. His eyes fluttering, his purr rumbling low through his chest—and wait, wait, now he and Thrain were both glancing hungrily at Kitty, and then at each other. And then they both grasped her, their hands careful but firm as they bodily shifted her up and around, so she was—straddling Varinn's *mouth*?

And no, no, they couldn't want that, Varinn couldn't want that, especially with how the mess was already spilling out over his *face*, oh gods—and Kitty hovered uncertainly over him, her thighs already trembling, her eyes wide on Thrain. On where he was grinning back at her, devious and wicked, as his hands clasped her waist, and gave her a firm nudge downwards.

"Sit on him, Kit," he murmured. "Told you, he needs to be cared for too, ach?"

But wait, surely this wasn't caring—or was it, because Varinn's hands were spasming on Kitty's thighs as they tugged her downwards, too. And when she finally obliged, tentatively nudging herself downwards toward his mouth, he groaned, husky and hot, and instantly latched on with a deep, staggering kiss.

Kitty shouted and flailed, already shuddering all over, keening at the impossible feel of Varinn's seeking tongue, the sound of his throat eagerly swallowing—and curse him, but Thrain was laughing, easy and amused, as he swung himself over Varinn, too. Facing Kitty as he straddled Varinn's hips, his eyes glittering on Varinn's already-hard, dripping-wet cock— and then he casually took that cock in hand, and guided it back, behind his bollocks, between his arse-cheeks. And Kitty had a dazzling, unbroken view as he slowly sank down onto it, drinking it up inside him, while his own pierced, leaking length quivered and swelled, and Varinn's mouth groaned into Kitty's pouring, throbbing heat.

It was too much, so much, pure sweeping sensation and hunger, wheeling and crackling between Kitty's legs, before her eyes. With how this felt, how it looked, Thrain's lean body arching up, painted with a sheen of sweat, as he sank himself all the way down to Varinn's hips. Making Varinn moan into Kitty again, his hot slippery tongue thrusting up even deeper, drinking her from the inside out. His throat still audibly, repeatedly swallowing, and gods, he must have drunk so much, and—and—

"Good, Kit," Thrain breathed, as his eyes flashed, as he began slowly rocking, grinding Varinn's heft deep inside him. "You feed your lord like a good little mate. Let him revel in the scent and taste of what he's done to you, how he's claimed you. Smear the truth of it all over his face, so he'll scent it every time he breathes, ach?"

Oh. Oh, gods, was that what they were doing, and Kitty helplessly moaned again, nodded, held Thrain's gleaming eyes.

Watched as he began stroking his own slick, dripping length, easy and shameless, his hand moving together with his steadily grinding hips. "Ach, just thus," he breathed at her, between gasps. "Squeeze out all that fresh seed for him, ach? Gorge it deep into his hungry belly. Show him what a good lord he's been, how he's had you jammed full of so much good seed you can't even *try* to keep it all in."

Kitty's moans were almost shouts now, between the impossible sensation of it, the impossible words, the thrilling craving careening between her and Thrain, reeling them both up higher, catching in their linked crackling eyes. "Show him how he's been such a good Lord Grisk," Thrain gasped. "Just like his forebears. Taking in his clanmate's sweet woman as his own, and nourishing you, caring for you. Making you strong and fat and hale for birthing hearty Grisk sons. All of them grown by him, scenting of him, belonging to him—"

Kitty's pleasure was screeching, now, wheeling so close to the edge, and Thrain was surely close too, his breaths heaving, his body sinking down harder, faster onto Varinn, his hand wildly stroking, the slick sounds of slapping skin heavy in the air. "And mayhap they'll even—*be* like him," he continued, his eyes furiously fluttering. "He'll—change them, from the inside out. Rebuilding the clan in his image, pumping out more and more heirs from his fat Grisk bollocks, so his scent will never die, never fade. He'll carry on for generations, *forever,* just like the god he is—"

And oh, oh, his voice was cracking, breaking, because Varinn's body beneath them was curling up, his growl vibrating almost like a roar into Kitty's womb, into her very soul. And Thrain cried out as Varinn's hips locked up hard, his seed surely spraying deep, and his own cock bobbed, so close—

And perhaps it was Varinn, or her, or both, but suddenly Kitty's upper body was lurching forward, her mouth lunging wildly for Thrain's pierced, bobbing head. Catching it just in time, oh, as it spewed out, surging its hot sweetness deep into her mouth, into her throat. And as Kitty moaned and fervently swallowed, Varinn was still doing the same beneath her, even as he kept pouring out into Thrain. All of them filling, feeding each other at once, and oh, it was good, it was right, it was everything.

When it finally ended, and the world began slowly filtering back again, Kitty found herself trembling so uncontrollably she could scarcely hold herself up. And thank the gods, strong hands were again grasping her, turning her, tucking her down close and safe into Varinn's warm, sticky side. Into where his wet mouth was kissing her forehead, as his big hand gripped possessively at her arse.

"Thank you, sweet *kisa*," he murmured, into her hair. "You have brought me such joy, this day. Both of you."

Kitty smiled and snuggled closer against him, inhaling the familiar beloved scent of his chest, and hazily watched Thrain doing the same opposite her, his long arm slinging across her waist, his face again buried deep in Varinn's neck. "Smells so good thus, Varinn," he breathed, with a hushed reverence in his voice. "So damn good, ach? I ken our son will smell a bit thus too, when he's born."

Varinn nodded, gathering both Kitty and Thrain a little closer, as that low, contented purr thrummed through his chest. And gods, Kitty almost wanted to purr too, curling into the warmth of it, the sweet surrounding safety. "So you really think our son might smell like Varinn, too?" she asked, her voice soft, almost shy. "Enough that other orcs will... know? That he's his father, too?"

"Ach, yes," Thrain said, with a contented-sounding satisfaction. "There's something about the way the seed seeps in when we share a woman, ach? The sons will always scent of it. Oft bear signs of their second father, too. In looks, mayhap, or skills, or manner."

The words seemed to send even more warmth sparkling into Kitty's chest, and even more quiet, settled relief. So Varinn really had wanted this, then. Really did see their son as his. As *theirs*.

"But this has led to darkness also, ach?" Varinn said, his hand now absently carding through Kitty's hair. "Most of all when there are few women amongst us, and when many orcs long for a son. Or when"—he sighed—"orcs have feared their death, so they shared their women with their kin, in hopes of gaining better care and guarding for the son. Other orcs have even stolen women and sons from their kin, and claimed them as their own—or even forced other orcs to steal away women on their behalf."

Oh. Kitty winced, even as she abruptly pulled up, glanced between Varinn and Thrain's eyes. "So... about that," she said. "Did you know that Harthr and his cronies are also angry with you because—they've been expecting *you* to bring women to them? They seemed to think that was your responsibility. Especially Thrain's, and Nattfarr's, with their magic."

She shot another wince toward Thrain, but he was already scoffing, and rolling his eyes. "Och, that again?" he snapped. "After what my fool father did, you ken neither Nattfarr nor I have the slightest wish to wade into woman-hunting! And ach, each moon, Nattfarr hosts a Truth Revel in the main Grisk common-room, and welcomes all the clan to gain from his gift as they wish, and speak whatever vows they please. So they have *naught* to moan about, except for mayhap the truth that no women would want them! Gods, why would they?"

Kitty's relief escaped in a shrill chuckle, though she was still considering it, remembering Grein's quiet, pained words. "But I could see how it would still be... difficult," she said. "To meet women, with the mountain being so isolated, and the war still so fresh in people's minds. So I suggested"—she bit her lip, glanced uncertainly back to Varinn—"that I could try contacting my former colleagues, back in the city. I can think of at least some who would be very interested in a fair offer. Not to come and *work*, I mean, but just even... to visit for a while. To get to know the orcs here, and see if they'd like to settle down for good. Raise a family."

Varinn actually seemed to be considering this, tilting his head, so Kitty drew in breath, kept going. "That kind of work isn't always easy, especially as you get older," she continued, faster now. "And the lack of steady support and training in other fields is the biggest reason a lot of women stay. And they're likely to be more open-minded than most, and less likely to be shocked by another culture's preferences, or care about"—she half-laughed as she glanced downwards—"sticky messes. Although..."

Her voice had faded, and perhaps so had her enthusiasm, her eyes dropping back to Varinn's chest. At least, until his gentle hand found her face, guided her to look at him again. "Although what, *kisa*?"

Kitty grimaced, but then tried to smile, leaning her head into the comfort of his touch. "Well, all the men's scents," she said, wretched. "Harthr said no Grisk would want any woman who had—well. He said *you* shouldn't want a woman like me, either. A... a harlot."

Her smile had gone pained, miserable—but wait, Varinn was hissing a hard, low growl, and Thrain laughed, loud and scornful. "Fucking *Harthr*," he snarled. "As if he has the slightest fucking clue about what Varinn wants, or any other Grisk, for that matter! And I told you, Kit"—his eyes glinted on hers—"Varinn doesn't care. He doesn't, because you're his now. He's conquered them all, by *earning* your favour. Ach, Varinn?"

Varinn was firmly nodding at Kitty, the certainty flashing in his flinty eyes. "Thrain has always spoken truth upon this, *kisa*," he said. "You have chosen to grant your loyalty to us. To me. And this is what matters, ach? This is a great, great blessing. An unspeakable gift."

Oh. Kitty felt herself relaxing again, the smile pulling at her mouth, the relief unspooling in her chest. Though Thrain was still looking mutinous, and giving a firm clasp of his hand to her bare shoulder.

"So, ach, Kit, we'll write your friends," he said flatly. "It's a damned good idea, though"—his eyes darkly narrowed—"why you should be trying to help those cretins is beyond me! After what they did to you, Kit! Kidnapped you, and sold you! Risked your damned life, and for what? Och, even if they'd killed us, did they really think *no one* would wonder where Varinn's mate went? Fucking *really*?!"

His voice was sharp, satisfyingly enraged, and Kitty choked another laugh, smiled shyly at his flushed, furious face. "I did hope someone would come," she said. "So I did try to, er, hamper things, as well as I could. I stalled the cart with one of your chains, and even"—she made a face—"threw up on Harthr. He was... not pleased."

But Thrain was grinning approvingly back toward her, and Varinn was reluctantly smiling, too. "Och, we smelled it," Thrain said cheerfully. "Followed you out that way. It was the gods' luck that you still had some of Varinn's fresh seed in your belly, ach? Make the scent extra spicy for Harthr to enjoy, I ken. He won't get that outta his airways for a long, *long* time."

He winked at her, and though Kitty wrinkled her nose with distaste, she couldn't help laughing, too. Even as a surge of questions suddenly rose in her thoughts, because they hadn't even talked about this yet, had they? "So wait—how *did* you get out, then?" she demanded, her gaze darting between them. "How long were you down there? And how did you know it was Harthr? How did you know he'd taken me?"

Varinn and Thrain exchanged glances, and Thrain shrugged, gave her a twitchy smile. "You're mated to Varinn, Kit," he said. "And bearing his fresh scent. So the instant we got out, he knew where you'd gone, and who with. Don't think I've ever scented him so enraged in my life, ach? As for the crypt..."

His voice caught, his mouth twisting, and Kitty didn't miss Varinn's hand stroking him, firmly caressing his back, his shoulder. "The crypt was... not easy," he supplied, quiet. "For either of us. Most of all since we knew it meant *you* were in danger, *kisa.* And since the crypt is fully sealed from the rest of the mountain when the doors and vents are closed, we could not scent where you were, or where you had gone."

His eyes looked a little hunted now, too, his head tilting toward hers, dragging in a slow, deep breath of her hair. "We searched for a way out," he continued, "but those old Ka-esh builders knew their work, ach? I ken we could have found a weak spot and clawed our way out, but it should have taken days, or mayhap weeks, whilst you were at risk of grave harm. But then..."

"But then Vragi's damned kitten," Thrain said, with a wry shake of his head. "Escaped, again. And when Vragi couldn't find Varinn to help, of course he went for Timo, who sniffed out the whole mess pretty quick, ach? Followed our scents down there, and when he realized the doors had been tampered with, he ran for help. In the end, it was that damned Filak who sorted it out, since he's apparently a rock-sniffing wonder, and he found them another way in."

Oh, gods bless Timo, and Vragi, and Arni—and even Filak—and Kitty grinned delightedly between Thrain and Varinn, and then flailed down toward them, squeezed them both tight. "Oh, I'm *so* glad they found you," she said. "Timo is such a gift, isn't he? And Varinn, of course it would be your great kindness to your kin that helped you, in the end. Of course."

She was already sniffling a little, water pooling in her eyes, and when she pulled up again, Varinn looked a little bright-eyed, too. While Thrain grinned fondly between them, and then bent down, and gave a gentle nip to Varinn's neck. "Ach, of course," he said lightly. "Gods forbid they leave him alone for half an evening. He might *die,* you ken."

Kitty choked another weepy laugh, especially since Varinn's expression had gone predictably stern. "Our kin were a great,

great help to us," he said repressively. "I am glad to help Vragi with his kitten, whenever he needs this. And, Timo has returned my care toward him tenfold, ach? And granted this to *you* also, *krútt*."

Thrain looked slightly chastened, but the smile was still quirking on his mouth, his teeth again nipping at Varinn's neck. "Ach, ach," he said. "And if nothing else, you should be forever cured of going to brood in that damned crypt now, right? Never fucking *again*, Varinn. As long as you're still breathing."

His voice had gone low, almost pleading, and Varinn gave a heavy sigh, a curt little nod, as his hand again stroked up and down Thrain's back. "Ach, I will not," he said, quiet. "I vow this to you, *krútt*."

Kitty could see the relief in Thrain's eyes, could almost taste it in the air—but then, a strange little shift, as he twitched up to study Varinn, his head tilting. "Och, Varinn," he said, almost apologetic. "We haven't spoken vows back to you, or each other, have we? You'd like it, ach?"

Something spasmed on Varinn's mouth, and he swallowed, attempted a shrug. As if he would like it very much indeed, and Kitty found herself pulling up too, searching Thrain's eyes with genuine alarm. "Of course we'd want to, right?" she demanded, too shrill. "Were we supposed to? I didn't know we were supposed to!"

But Thrain was wryly smiling again, rubbing at his face. "Och, just forgot," he said, husky. "Distracted, by you both. And Varinn would never expect it of you, Kit, as it's an orc vow, ach? But if you yet want to..."

Kitty was already nodding toward him, rapid and eager, and he nodded back, too. That slow, true smile curving at his mouth, as he clasped her hand, and then Varinn's. And then Kitty gripped Varinn's hand, too, closing the circle, while Varinn blinked between them both, his eyes suddenly bright, blinking hard.

"Right, then," Thrain murmured. "Varinn Thjoth, of Clan

Grisk, and Kit, the sweetest woman in the realm. Before all our mothers and fathers, and all the Grisk, and all the gods"—his eyes briefly closed—"I wish to pledge you my troth. I shall grant you both my favour, and my sword, and my fealty. I shall keep you safe. So long as I am able, and so long as you shall wish."

It was the same vow Varinn had spoken, the exact same words, but Varinn was still looking shocked, almost awed. And Thrain smiled back toward him, the fondness glimmering in his eyes—and then he gave Kitty's hand a gentle squeeze. "Your turn, Kit," he said. "And you can say your own version, ach? Doesn't need to be the same, it's the meaning that makes it."

Oh. Well. So Kitty nodded, drew in breath, gave a warm, wavering smile between them. "Thrain Aetha, and Varinn Thjoth, of Clan Grisk," she managed. "Before you both, and all the gods, and Lord Grisk himself—I pledge you both my—my heart. I swear to be loyal and true, and to honour you both however I can. I want to be yours, and to make our home together. For as long as I'm able. And as—as long as you both wish."

It came out sounding jerky, stilted, not nearly as smooth and lovely as theirs had been—but in a rough, sudden movement, Varinn's arm clutched around her, and dragged her close. Pulling her back onto him, and he'd pulled Thrain in too, rocking them back and forth, as his breath came in strange, stilted-sounding gulps. As if he was weeping, oh gods, and perhaps Kitty was weeping too, and squeezing back at him as tightly as she could.

"I love you," she whispered, between her own shaky breaths. "Both of you, so much. I think—from the first moment we met."

She was thinking of Thrain's kindness in the pub, of Varinn's kindness in rescuing her—and she could feel Varinn squeezing her even tighter, his head nodding against hers.

"Ach, *kisa*," he whispered back, his voice tremulous. "From that first moment you knelt and kissed my feet."

Kitty gulped and nodded back, sniffling into his neck—while beside them, Thrain stiffened, and yanked up, away. Enough that Kitty and Varinn both turned to look at him, Kitty wiping a shaky hand at her wet face. And blinking at where he was looking shocked, and incredulous, and... delighted?

"Wait, you two," Thrain said, as a swift, stunning grin spread across his mouth. "Wait, wait, wait. Do you really mean to tell me that—you knelt and kissed his *feet*, Kit? The first time you *met?!*"

Kitty warily nodded, to which Thrain gave a loud crack of laughter, his head tilting back, his hand clutching at his shaking belly. "Och, I can't," he gasped, between guffaws, his eyes dancing on them both. "I can't. You win, Varinn, the gods are on our side after all, because"—he laughed again, wiped at his eyes—"of all the things to do, Kit! Kiss his fucking feet! Of course he was obsessed with you from the start. Gods, I didn't even need to *try*."

Varinn was looking far less amused, though his glance toward Kitty was rueful, maybe even regretful. "It was... not an easy matter," he said, quiet. "For either of us."

But Thrain was still laughing, still wiping at his eyes. "Not easy my arse, Varinn," he said. "Just like the day I got sick of your martyr rubbish, and propositioned you by blowing my load on your feet. Learned some things that day too, ach?"

He kept grinning at Varinn, wicked and triumphant, as a low growl burned through Varinn's throat—and with a sudden swift twist, he'd set Kitty carefully to the side, and lunged toward Thrain. Tackling him hard to the bed, his knees pinned to Thrain's sides, his hand snatching deep into his messy hair.

"You damned vexing menace," he growled, though Kitty didn't miss the suppressed smile on his mouth. "You are a terror, and a torment, and—"

And then Thrain kicked up beneath him, hard, fighting to

shove him off, his arms and legs flailing. While Varinn fought to keep pinning him down, and somehow they rolled onto the floor, swiping and kicking at each other, while their laughter rang through the room. And Kitty was helplessly giggling too, watching them grunt and squeal and roll on the floorboards, until Thrain finally pinned Varinn this time, holding his hands over his head, grinning broad and stunning down toward him.

"Och, you love it," he murmured, with such soft, caressing warmth in his voice. "Now what do you say to getting the hell out of here, and taking our mate home?"

And Varinn was already nodding, and smiling up at Thrain, and Kitty, too. "Ach, *krútt*," he replied. "Home."

 short time later, Kitty followed Varinn and Thrain down the stairs, and out into the bright morning sunlight.

Varinn and Thrain had packed up all her things with surprising efficiency, tying them all into some clean bed-linens, and then throwing them over their cloaked shoulders. And though Kitty had glanced worriedly at the messy—perhaps destroyed—bed, Thrain had only snorted, and shaken his head.

"As far as anyone else will know, it was only that vile man here," he'd said cheerfully, yanking up his hood. "Not likely that your landlady's going to go chew him out over his mess, is she?"

Kitty could admit to a rather resentful satisfaction at the thought of Mrs. Schultz needing to clean up a bed full of orc-seed, and she'd willingly waited at the bottom of the stairwell with Varinn and Thrain as they'd slowly inhaled through a tiny crack in the door, scenting for humans beyond. And at Varinn's signal, they all slipped out the door, and up the quiet street. Keeping their heads bowed low beneath their hoods until they'd reached the outskirts of town, and headed into the forest instead.

"You two are so good at all this," Kitty said, with genuine appreciation, once they'd stopped for a rest, and Varinn had started a small fire, cooking a grouse Thrain had caught. "I still can't believe how easily you dealt with Charles. It's almost a shame you aren't working together anymore."

But wait, what if they took that the wrong way, and Kitty shot a belated wince between them—but thankfully, neither of them seemed offended, and they both shrugged in unison. "It is better that Thrain is safe, and content, and happy with his work," Varinn replied. "He is too good a goldsmith to waste this, and rebuilding our Grisk smithing is also of great value to the clan, ach? And, after all this"—he grimaced, waved irritably around them—"it is clearer than ever that one of us ought to stay close to you, *kisa*. It is not wise for both of us to be at risk out in the realm thus, with a mate and son at home."

Oh. But even so, Kitty was still wincing, because that was still her fault, wasn't it? At least, until Thrain bumped her with his elbow, and dropped a kiss to the top of her head. "Stop worrying, Kit," he said firmly. "We've talked about it at length, and it's what we want, ach? And mayhap we'll still do some special projects together, now and then. And also"—he shot a hopeful grin toward Varinn—"now we'll get to be fathers together, ach? I ken that'll be even better."

Varinn grinned back, his eyes kindling with undeniable eagerness, or even excitement. And Kitty was smiling too, the relief sagging her shoulders, until—

"Wait," she gasped, pulling up straight again. "What about—what about *Harthr*? And Knorr and Grein? Where are they? What if they're still trying to—"

She clapped her hands over her mouth, glancing rapidly at the mass of trees around them, which could be hiding any number of would-be kidnappers—but Thrain was already drawing her close, rubbing a reassuring hand up and down her back. "Och, no need to worry about that either, Kit," he said.

"Our kin went after them, ach? We don't stand for kidnapping, most of all one of our own women and sons. Fucking *Harthr.*"

His voice had gone scathing again, and Varinn was looking contemptuous too, even as he carefully blew on the meat he'd been cooking, and began pulling off little pieces for Kitty to eat. "There was no way for them to escape this," he said flatly. "They cannot escape our noses, ach? And Harthr would have very well known this, so I truly cannot fathom why he even sought to try something so foolish."

But Thrain was already shaking his head, curling his lip. "It was a statement, is what it was," he snapped. "A rebellion, against you, against Nattfarr, against all of us, for daring to ignore his rubbish, and lead the clan in a way he doesn't like. I can't *wait* to see that snake tied up and bleating for mercy, ach?"

Varinn sighed and nodded, and then glanced toward the southwest. "I ken you shall soon be able to witness this," he replied, with grim satisfaction, "if I have not mistaken the scents."

Kitty blinked at that, but it soon turned out that Varinn's assessment had been entirely correct. Because once they'd travelled a fair distance through the forest, they strode into a small clearing, and found well over a half-dozen Grisk milling about within it.

"Brother!" Thrak joyfully shouted, streaking over to clasp Thrain in his arms, whirling him around. "Ach, it's good to see you safe. And our sister, and our son!"

He drew away to grin broadly at Kitty, giving her a brief little bow—and then he turned to face Varinn too, squaring his shoulders, his smile gone wry, maybe even apologetic. "And you too, Varinn," he said, quieter, holding out his hand. "I thank you, for all you have given, to keep my brother and sister safe."

Varinn easily waved it away, clasping Thrak's hand in his—and suddenly they were embracing too, their bodies rocking back and forth. "Although I still ken you should swear vows to my brother," Thrak said, a little muffled. "He's waited fucking long enough, ach?"

But Varinn was nodding, and clearing his throat as he drew backwards. "Ach, I ken," he said thickly. "And thus, we have spoken vows, just this morn. I am now honoured to call both Thrain and Katharine my mates."

He shot them both a small, hopeful smile, while Thrak crowed aloud and lunged back for Thrain, grasping him into a headlock this time. Leading into an impromptu sparring-match between them on the forest floor, while Kitty laughed aloud, and then allowed Varinn to guide her forward, toward the rest of the people coming to greet them. First was Dammarr, who congratulated Kitty and Varinn with a sincere smile, even as his clawed hand tugged awkwardly at the tight waistband of his sloppy trousers. And behind him were Nattfarr and Ella, both of them offering their felicitations too, Nattfarr with a knowing warmth in his eyes, Ella beaming with genuine delight. While behind them were Eyarl and Valter and Trygve and Timo, all of them taking turns dragging Varinn into their arms.

"Feared so much for you, brother," Timo said, giving a weepy, quavering smile into Varinn's chest. "Have never smelled your scent thus before, ach?"

Varinn was squeezing Timo back just as tightly, pressing a brief kiss to the top of his head. "You were such a great help, little brother," he said, husky. "I ken we might have been lost, without you."

Timo gave a choked, happy little hiccough, but then turned to frown behind him. Toward where—Kitty startled and stared—there were three more orcs, tied up beneath a tree. Harthr, Knorr, and Grein, all of them watching this with dark, uneasy eyes.

Varinn was already frowning back, and—Kitty startled again—even spitting on the ground as he strode over toward them, a sudden fury flaring all over his big, taut body. "You stupid, useless, *odious* fools," he snarled, as he swiped for Harthr's hair, and yanked his head up with vicious-looking force. "Did you ken you could harm *my* mates? And kill *my* son?!"

Harthr's mouth opened and closed, his face wincing with obvious pain. "It—it wasn't personal, Varinn," he babbled. "It was just—business, for the good of the clan! And I thought you'd dumped Kitty, and you really should have, she gave us *naught* but trouble, and—"

And without warning, Varinn drew back his big fist, and slammed it into Harthr's mouth. Sending blood spattering out in all directions, while Harthr's scream wailed through the air. And behind them, Thrain was loudly whooping, shouting Varinn's name, while Varinn set his jaw, and drew his fist back again. Flashing more terror through Harthr's watering eyes, his body trembling against its bonds, and—

"Ach, enough, son!" broke in Eyarl, rushing over to grab at Varinn's fist, yanking it downwards. "You ken the clan will choose his fate. Not you. Ach?"

Varinn instantly stilled, and Kitty could see his awareness returning to him, something like mortification flashing across his face. And already, Thrain had rushed over toward them, slipping a reassuring arm around Varinn's waist, even as he glared down at Harthr, too. "Och, are you sure, Eyarl?" he drawled. "We can't even kick him a little? Piss on him, mayhap?"

Eyarl gave a disapproving frown toward Thrain, who rolled his eyes, and then flashed Harthr a cold, vicious smile. "Och, I ken he reeks enough already," he said, with clipped contempt. "Not to mention the usual stink of envy, too. How sad for you, that you didn't ever get up Varinn's kilt. Lucky for us"—Thrain's smile went even colder, and his hand blatantly stroked up the hard lines of Varinn's bulky chest—"he's always had much better taste. He knows exactly what he wants. And he'd never, ever find it with the likes of *you*."

The triumph was cool, crackling in Thrain's voice, and he'd even bent his face into Varinn's neck, nibbling with slow, sensual familiarity. While his hand just kept brazenly stroking, caressing Varinn, showing off his access, his ownership. And oh, Varinn liked it, he wanted it, his body visibly relaxing, his chin lifting, as he glared down at Harthr with dark, dismissive contempt.

Harthr was looking mutinous, now, and also pathetically jealous, while beside Varinn Eyarl cleared his throat, and glanced toward where Timo was watching this with unmistakable interest. Prompting Varinn to wince, clasping Thrain's wandering hand, closing it against his heart. And then spitting at Harthr's feet before whirling around and stalking back toward Kitty, pulling Thrain close behind him.

"I ken we ought to leave," Varinn said, his mouth still very thin. "Else I may very well wait until Eyarl is elsewhere, and then go punch Harthr again."

Thrain barked a loud, approving laugh, and Kitty couldn't help laughing too, even as she tucked herself close into Varinn's side. "It was magnificent," she said shyly. "Thank you for defending me, Lord Grisk."

She could feel him softening against her, his face bending into her hair. "It was my honour, sweet *kisa*," he murmured. "If Harthr is wise, he will never again dare to *speak* your sweet name with his foul lying mouth."

Thrain harrumphed his agreement, and turned to glare over toward Harthr again, his lip curling. "He really has fucking lost it," he snapped. "For the *clan*, he said. Fucking really?!"

But Kitty was angling a regretful glance back toward them too, toward the three orcs she'd considered true colleagues, all that time. "They really did do good work, though," she said. "And it is valuable work, important work—and I'm sure the income is a great help to the rest of the clan, too. It'll be a shame if it's lost, after this."

Thrain gave a scoff of disbelief, tweaking Kitty's nose with exasperated affection, while Varinn kissed her hair, his chest hollowing against her. "It is very kind of you, *kisa*, to remember this," he said. "We will be sure to remember it, also. Now"—he sounded a little exasperated, too—"you shall no more think upon them, ach? You shall rest, and we shall go home."

Kitty meekly nodded, and allowed Varinn to sweep her up into his arms, before striding back into the forest. Curling her close against his chest as he walked, lulling her into ever-deepening ease with every smooth, steady step.

It was so lovely, and as Kitty began to slip in and out of sleep, it distantly occurred to her that it was so strangely surreal, too. It was as if this same moment had been lifted from weeks ago, with Varinn holding her like this, carrying her home—but instead of walking with Dammarr, with Thrain left drunk and angry behind, it was Thrain by his side instead, tall and easy and confident. And they were even speaking together in low, murmured Aelakesh, clearly in an effort not to disturb Kitty, though Varinn kept pressing the occasional soft kiss to her head, as though he couldn't quite resist. And Kitty felt herself smiling as she snuggled closer, into his warmth, his quiet, beloved safety.

She must have drifted off for good again, and then slept for some time, because when her awareness filtered back in again, she was... in bed. In their warm, familiar bed, cradled close between Varinn and Thrain's strong bodies. Their hands again entwined over her waist, and Kitty contentedly stretched out, and then curled closer. Into that heady rich scent of Varinn's chest, and she inhaled deep against him, touched her lips to his salty-sweet skin. And then began kissing downwards, while Thrain hummed approvingly behind her, his hand already spreading wide and hungry against her arse.

But then—Varinn's hand, gently catching her wrist, holding her still. And when Kitty darted a searching, uncertain glance upwards, she found him looking apologetic, and so affectionate, too. "I wish for it, *kisa*," he murmured, "but mayhap—could we go to the shrine first? I wish to—"

But he broke off there, angling a narrow, frowning glance toward the door. And Kitty could feel Thrain stiffening too, twitching up to look, as Varinn slid out of bed and made for the door, grasping for a kilt on the way by.

"What is it, brother?" Varinn asked, yanking the curtain open—and revealing Thrak behind it. He was shifting awkwardly on his feet, his messy hair standing all on end, and he grimaced as he glanced between them, rubbing at his face.

"Sorry," he mumbled. "Sorry, I know you're—och. But I just wanted to ask, brother"—his eyes flicked toward Thrain, almost pleading—"if you might've finished that gift for Dammarr? He's been caught in the most peevish melancholy all this past week, and now after *this*, he's—"

He flapped his hand toward the three of them, and then grimaced again, shook his head. "Sorry, but I ken it's—it's not been easy for him, ach? And I ken the gift might help. If it's ready. If you don't mind. Sorry. I would owe you, I know."

He was breathing hard, and looking truly regretful, but Varinn was already clapping him on the shoulder, and giving him a bracing little shake. "There is no debt, only brotherhood," he said firmly, with a brief glance over his shoulder. "Ach, my mates?"

Kitty was already rapidly nodding, eyeing Thrak with genuine concern, and after a brief glance toward her, Thrain nodded too, giving a relieved exhale. "Ach," he said. "And the *kíróna* is near finished, brother. I only need to spend some time polishing it, and giving it one last look-over. It'll take me a little while, though, and"—he winced, glanced at Varinn—"didn't you just say you wanted to—"

But Varinn was waving it away, and swiping for a kilt from Thrain's shelf, and tossing it toward him. "We are happy to help our kin," he said. "Whenever this is needed."

Thrain caught the kilt, smiling at Varinn with a sudden,

bright-eyed appreciation. And soon they were all striding through the sitting-room together—Kitty waved cheerfully at Ella and Rakfi on the way by—and heading down the corridor.

It turned out that Varinn had wanted to debrief with Ymir anyway, so he and Kitty headed for the shop, while Thrak and Thrain went to the forge. And Kitty was genuinely shocked by Ymir's gasp of relief—or maybe even delight—as he rushed around the counter toward them.

"You're back!" he exclaimed, almost scolding, but not quite. "Why did it take you so long? What in the gods' names did that Harthr do to you? Never quite trusted that sneaky Grisk, always argued a bit too hard over my prices, didn't he?!"

Kitty chuckled and nodded, and soon she and Varinn were regaling Ymir with the entire tale. And while Ymir was gratifyingly outraged by it all, his most vehement ire was upon learning that Harthr had falsely inflated the prices of his ale for Varinn, in an attempt to cause discord between him and Thrain.

"That's damned depraved, that is," Ymir snarled scornfully. "Cheating his own damned brother, who's worked his tail off in this shop for years, without once asking for pay! May the gods all shit upon him, I say. And"—his irate eyes flicked toward Kitty, as he jabbed his claw at the neat pricing-table on the counter—"good work helping bring in this price list too, woman. Wouldn't be able to pull off that rubbish now, would he?"

Kitty and Varinn both readily nodded, still grinning, and Kitty didn't miss Varinn's proud glance down toward her, the slight swelling of his chest. While Ymir raised an imperious finger at Varinn, and then spun and rushed off down the clothing aisle.

Kitty shot a questioning look at Varinn, but he twitched a mild shrug, a wry little smile. And when Ymir returned, he was holding a small, nondescript-looking box, which Varinn silently accepted, and tucked into the side pouch on his kilt without comment.

Kitty's head tilted, the question already rising on her mouth, but at that moment, more people spilled in behind them. Rosa, and Gary, and Kesst, and Rathgarr, and Geva and Jule, too. All of them smiling and exclaiming and welcoming Kitty safely home again, and demanding to hear the entire tale from the start.

So Kitty and Varinn told it all again, to many shocked gasps and questions and curses. And finally, at the end of it, Rosa put her hands on her hips, and frowned between Kitty and Varinn with surprising vehemence.

"But you're leaving something out, right?" she demanded. "Where's the part where Varinn betrayed you? Or kept some crucial revelation from you? Perhaps he *knew* that vile human man was trying to get you back, the entire time? Or perhaps"—her suspicious eyes flashed on Varinn—"it was all tied into some devious Grisk scheme, on your part? Maybe for some gold? Or a promotion? A tactical advantage against the humans?"

Varinn blinked at Rosa, nonplussed, his mouth turned into a distasteful little frown. "Ach, no," he said. "I ken we have had much to learn of one another, and"—he shot a regretful glance toward Kitty—"this has not always been smooth, or easy. But why should I have sought to trick my sweet woman with a secret scheme? I wished her to stay with us, and be happy."

For an instant, Rosa looked speechless, staring blankly between Kitty and Varinn, before dropping her eyes, and beginning to silently count on her fingers. "Impossible," she muttered to herself. "That can't be right. I can't need to rewrite the entire *Manual*. Right? No, no, of course not. You know, I think"—she twitched, and brightened—"an interview with Thrain is in order."

With that, she rushed distractedly from the room, while Jule and Geva grinned fondly after her, and Kesst made a show of elaborately rolling his eyes. "Well, I, for one, am not even slightly surprised," he drawled. "Deep down, you Grisk are all the same. All so sweet and devoted to each other, falling all over yourselves with gifts and cuddles and apologies. It's enough to rot all our teeth out of our heads, hmmm?"

He was indeed looking profoundly pained, drawing back his lips to rub his tongue at a sharp white fang, but Geva laughed and clasped his arm, shaking her head. "And lucky for you, brother, Efterar can attend to your teeth whenever you need," she said cheerfully. "And this is the part where you tell them congratulations, remember?"

Kesst rolled his eyes, but accordingly wished Kitty and Varinn all the best upon their matehood, and even—to Kitty's astonishment—included a lovely, surprisingly eloquent Ash-Kai blessing. Which was instantly followed by Thrain poking his head in, and eagerly announcing that Dammarr's gift was ready—a development that prompted Kesst to throw up his hands and stalk past Thrain out the door, muttering under his breath.

Kitty and Varinn soon followed, and found Thrak already waiting in the corridor, holding a conspicuously shaped, cloth-wrapped item. He looked visibly agitated, his tall body bobbing uncomfortably on his feet, and Thrain easily slung his arm over his shoulder as they walked, giving him a companionable shake. "I think he'll like it, brother," Thrain said. "It's better than aught you could've purchased, anyway, and has personal meaning to you. A good Grisk gift."

Thrak nodded, his throat convulsing, and Kitty found herself searching his profile, and smiling, too. "And it's the meaning that counts, right?" she said, her thoughts casting back to what Thrain had said about her vows, and then back to Dammarr's own words, too. "Especially if you're honest with him about why it's taken so long, and how you just want him to feel at ease in his own skin. However that feels for him."

Thrak nodded again, jerky and rapid, his nervousness

almost palpable in the air. And when they reached their sitting-room, Thrain took one look at Thrak's anxious eyes, and then squeezed his arm, and strode off toward Thrak and Dammarr's bedroom.

He soon returned with a tired, rumpled-looking Dammarr, whose narrow gaze swept across all of them, his trousers looking even more sloppy and ill-fitting than before. "What is it," he snapped. "Look, I am not in the mood for some kind of—"

But then his eyes widened, his voice catching, because Thrain had swept the cloth away from Thrak's hands, revealing... the *kíróna*. The coronet, Thrain had called it, but as Kitty stared at it, her breath stilled in her throat, she realized it was far more than just a simple coronet. It was almost—almost a tiara, crafted out of thin, featherlight filaments of bright, glittering gold. And studded into it, woven all through it, were tiny, richly coloured stones, sparkling in the light. Sapphires, and rubies, and—Kitty peered closer—emeralds. Filak's emeralds, surely. And gods, it was so stunning, and they were all Dammarr's favourite rich colours, and she belatedly glanced toward his face, toward where he was looking—pale. Shocked. Maybe—maybe even... afraid.

"W-what are you doing?" he choked toward Thrak, his voice a whisper. "And where—where did you get that? I thought it— it was lost? How did—how did you know?"

His wide, panicked eyes were darting between them, and then holding with painful disbelief on Thrak's face. On where Thrak's head was slowly tilting, as something shifted in his eyes. "It's—it's for you, possum," he said, his voice softer, more tender, than Kitty had ever heard it. "And it's—it's not Pa's old one. Didn't even know you remembered it, ach? Thrain made this copy of it for me. Thought—thought you'd like it. As a belated mating-gift."

He thrust it roughly out toward Dammarr, who was still staring at it as though it might explode at any moment. "You really—did not know?" he asked, his voice oddly high-pitched. "I mean, I always loved it, it was the best Grisk jewel in the mountain, but it is meant"—his voice cracked—"for a human. A *woman*."

His mouth twisted into something sad and bitter, his glimmering eyes angling almost accusingly down toward his rumpled trousers. And Thrak had surely noticed that, lurching a step closer toward him, giving him a brief, wavering little smile. "So?" he asked, thick in his throat. "I had it made—for you, Dammarr. For *you*. Fuck whatever my father thought about it, and who gives a damn about him, anyway? I thought you might like it, but if you don't, or you don't want to wear it, that's fine too. I mean that, ach? And I ought to have told you, I—"

He broke off there, rubbing at his face with his free hand, and then he abruptly thrust the *kíróna* sideways toward Thrain, and gripped both Dammarr's hands in his. "I didn't get you a mating-gift, all this time," he said, with visible effort, "because I was—scared. I was scared of fucking it up, and making you feel—wrong. And I shoulda told you, but I didn't want that to make you feel wrong either, so I just kept avoiding it, and fucking it all up even worse. And then even worse when you got the dresses, because you thought it was just a—a bedroom thing for me, something I wanted to get off to, when it's just—"

Dammarr was still staring at him, unmoving, unblinking, and Thrak swallowed, tried for another smile. "It's just you, possum," he whispered. "Just you. Just want to see you happy, and content in your own skin. And it's you being *you*, looking like you wanna be here, wanna be in whatever you're wearing, wanna make me work and beg you for it—that's what gets me hard for you, ach? Every fucking time."

Oh. Kitty's eyes were prickling, suddenly, and Dammarr was blinking now too, and rapidly shaking his head. "You cannot—mean that, Thrak," he whispered. "I scented you, when I was wearing them. And you said—lovely things. All those things you never say."

But Thrak's brows drew together, his mouth pulling down into almost a pout. "Ach, I ken I did," he said flatly, "but it's just—you usually dress *thus*, ach? In these"—he flailed his hand at Dammarr's trousers—"these black shapeless *things*, and I can scent how you don't even like being in them! And then you show up glowing in red silk and lace, scenting as though you command the room? Och, what do you ken I should do? Tell you I hate it, and then run off and blow my load in secret instead? Och"—his voice dropped, his eyes fluttering—"even the *scent* of you in them, possum. You were *happy*, and you liked it, and *I* liked it, and—"

Dammarr was still staring at him, waiting, perhaps not breathing, and Thrak tried for another smile, brought one of Dammarr's hands to his lips. "So just thought—you might like the *kíróna*, too," he murmured. "All the same colours, ach? Good Grisk colours. Would look nice with your hair."

And yes, yes, Dammarr's sideways glance toward the *kíróna* was wistful, almost longing, and Thrak had followed his gaze, and eagerly nodded. "So mayhap just—try it?" Thrak said, the hopefulness tilting in his voice, lighting his eyes. "Just—to see?"

Behind Kitty, Varinn had murmured something about fetching a looking-glass, and slipped toward the door, while Thrak turned and took the *kíróna* back from Thrain. And then, as Dammarr stood utterly, perfectly still, Thrak raised the *kíróna*, and carefully slid it onto his head.

And it was—stunning. Truly, breathtakingly stunning. The gold a light, elegant ring around Dammarr's head, the gems glittering and sparkling within his silken black hair, contrasting beautifully with the tips of his pierced pointed ears. The entire effect making him look undeniably regal, and a little ruggedly beautiful, too—as though he were some wild, long-lost royal elf, ready to command a council or a war. And Kitty was somehow flapping both hands at her face, and trying to fight back the water streaking down her cheeks.

"It's so stunning," she gulped, both a laugh, and a sob. "You all have wonderful taste. You were right, Thrak, it's *perfect* on him. Looks beautiful with his hair, and his other piercings, too."

Dammarr was still looking dazed, blinking at her with bleary, bemused eyes, and Kitty nodded and grinned at him, wiping at her wet cheeks. "It's really good," she said, glancing gratefully behind her to where Varinn had reappeared, holding a small looking-glass. "You'll see."

And yes, Varinn was handing over the looking-glass, so Thrak could hold it up before Dammarr's face. And Dammarr visibly startled, his eyes slowly growing wider by the instant, as he stared for a long, silent moment—and then he slowly tilted his head, watched the jewels gleam and sparkle in the lamplight.

"You like it?" Thrak asked, bobbing a little on his toes, and it occurred to Kitty that he was looking far less nervous than before, his nostrils flaring as he inhaled. "Looks good, right?"

Dammarr angled a brief, searching glance toward Thrak, his own nostrils flaring, too. Surely seeing, scenting, that rapidly rising hunger, far too visible on Thrak's form. And without warning, Thrak had even lurched forward, bending his messy head into Dammarr's neck, while Dammarr again watched in the looking-glass, his sharp tooth biting his lip.

"You gonna wear my crown, and tell me what to do?" Thrak murmured, husky, into Dammarr's skin. "Gonna take your rightful place as my king—or mayhap my queen? Whatever the hell you want, possum, as long as it means I get to have you. Get to have you wearing my jewels. Flaunting *my* claim upon you. Making me *yours*."

His voice had gone hotter, deeper, and Kitty didn't miss Dammarr's hushed choke of breath, the flutter of his eyes. The way his head had tilted into the touch of Thrak's hungry mouth, his own tongue brushing his lips. And his breath was suddenly audible, sniffling through his nose, as he finally squared his shoulders, and nodded.

"Ach, then," he said, his voice a whisper. "I—thank you, Thrak, for such a beautiful Grisk mating-gift. I shall be honoured to wear it."

Thrak jerked back upwards at once, his grin splitting his face—and then he punched both hands in the air, threw back his head, and howled his victory. To which Dammarr huffed an irritated-sounding groan, and met Varinn's gaze with a longsuffering roll of his eyes—but his face was looking decidedly flushed, too, a small, stunning smile pulling at his mouth.

"Now, less talking, more fucking," Thrak gleefully announced, as he slung his long arm around Dammarr's hips, and brazenly winked toward the rest of them. "Don't expect to see us anytime soon, ach?"

With that, he promptly dragged Dammarr away toward their bedroom, and while Dammarr groaned again, he certainly wasn't resisting, either. And it wasn't long before the sounds of loud moans and messy slurping began emanating from the room, enough that Thrain gagged, and even Varinn's smile had gone rather pained as he herded them away.

"This was good work, my sweet mates," he told them, with surprising earnestness, once they were all back in their own room again. "I am so proud of how you have found your own ways to serve our clan, amidst your own new callings. This is a great credit to me. A great honour."

Kitty smiled shyly back at him, tucking herself into his side, but he still held himself a little stiffly, his eyes darting between her and Thrain. "And it is thus my honour," he continued, quieter, "to offer you more signs of my thanks, and my care. To offer you..."

His hand fumbled down toward his kilt's side pouch, drawing out that little box he'd gotten from Ymir. Snapping it open with a sharp flick of his claw, and drawing out... gold. Gold that shone and glittered in the lamplight, and wait, it wasn't only gold, but it was also... green? Green, emeralds, *Filak's* emeralds, glittering large and bright on... two rings. Two stunning, matching emerald rings, one of them noticeably bigger than the other.

Thrain was gaping at them too, with just as much shock as Kitty felt, and his mouth opened, closed, opened again, as a distinctive flush crept up Varinn's cheeks. "I did not wish to ask you to make your own ring, also," he told Thrain, "so Ymir called in a debt, and moved me to the top of the Ka-esh list, ach? Gary made them both for us, in secret."

Thrain was rapidly nodding now, his throat bobbing, his palm rubbing at his blinking eyes. "Ach, I can tell," he croaked. "They're perfect, Varinn. Oh, gods, they're *perfect*, and the cost for stones that size alone, how did you afford it, you already spent all your—"

His voice broke into a choked sob, as Varinn's smile spread across his mouth, so slow, so affectionate. "I have good credit," he said, with a dismissive wave of his hand. "I wished to see my mates flaunting the finest gifts I can afford, ach?"

Thrain was truly weeping now, his head repeatedly shaking, but Varinn had firmly grasped his hand, and slowly slid the ring onto Thrain's finger. Where it looked even more stunning than before, flashing strong and gold and green, the colours setting beautifully against the lovely grey of his skin.

And Thrain kept staring at it, kept weeping, as Varinn gently clasped Kitty's hand, too. Sliding on her own marvel of green and gold, and though it was a similar design to Thrain's, it was far more delicate, the band thinner, the emerald smaller, but with even more brilliant facets on the stone. And the sobs suddenly lurched from Kitty's mouth, too, as she hurled herself into Varinn's waiting arms.

"Thank you," she whispered, sniffling into his chest. "You're so good, Varinn. So, so good to us."

A satisfied sound huffed from Varinn's chest, almost like a laugh, as he drew her tighter into him—and then Thrain was here, too, crushing himself against them, his long arms flinging around them both. "Ach, Varinn," Thrain croaked. "The best. Love you so damned much."

The sound from Varinn's chest had deepened, softened, back into his rumbling purr, and he drew them even tighter, swaying them back and forth. "I thought they should please you," he said, husky. "The way you scented when you spoke of that emerald, *krútt*. Much like with the *typpavír*, ach? And the piercings, also."

Thrain huffed another muffled laugh-sob, but at that, Kitty twitched backwards, searched Varinn's eyes. Because wait, what had happened to those piercings he'd had Thrain make—and surely he'd followed that too, reaching around behind them to grasp for something off the shelf.

"And if you should yet wish, *krútt*," Varinn murmured, holding out the glinting, matching rings in his palm, "I should yet be glad to see you wear these also."

Thrain's sobs hitched again, into an unmistakable moan, and he swiftly, desperately nodded. To which Varinn nodded too, that fond smile again pulling at his mouth, as he turned toward the lamp, heating the rings in the flame. And then he drew Thrain close again, and Kitty tightly clasped Thrain's hand, watching in hushed silence as Varinn carefully pinched Thrain's nipple, and stabbed the ring's sharp gold post through it.

Thrain's moan was harsh and hoarse, his hardness already visibly swelling beneath his kilt—and then again as Varinn closed the clasp, and bent down to draw that newly pierced nipple into his mouth. Gently caressing it with his lips and tongue, his eyes intent on Thrain's face, until it was only pure, raw hunger in Thrain's eyes, in his heaving dragging breaths.

Varinn finished the second side far more quickly, and when he drew back this time, he was moaning too, his eyes fluttering at the sight. Because gods, it did look good, both Thrain's deep grey nipples now glinting bright with rings of smooth, shining gold. With gold that matched his earring, and his nose ring, and his *thyrja*, and his stunning new emerald ring, and—Kitty fumbled for his kilt, yanking it off—that piercing, too. Which was already gleaming, dripping, as his cock bobbed out toward them, long and ruddy and full.

"Beautiful, *krútt*," Varinn murmured, grasping that bobbing length in an easy hand, as he leaned in, and pressed a brief, hard kiss to Thrain's mouth. "The most stunning orc I have ever seen or scented, in all my days."

Thrain was visibly flushing, his eyes dropping, but Kitty was fervently nodding, too. "You're gorgeous, Thrain," she repeated, in a strange, distant echo of the words she'd spoken that first night they'd met. "And you're brilliant, Lord Grisk. You have *such* good taste."

The appreciation was bare and earnest in her voice, and Varinn glanced warmly down at her, his hand slipping to gently grasp at her arse. "Ach, I ken I do, *kisa*," he said softly, his eyes gleaming on hers. "And now, I wish you both to dress for me. In all your jewels."

Oh. Kitty felt the hunger rippling higher, the eager curiosity rising in her eyes, as Varinn stepped backwards, the light shifting in his eyes. "And then meet me in the shrine," he murmured, low, hungry. "So I might present you to our gods, and gain their blessing."

58

Varinn wanted to present them. To the gods.

Kitty wasn't even slightly following what that meant, but she was already nodding, and Thrain was nodding, too. And with a grunt of satisfaction, Varinn swiped for something on his shelf, and spun around, and—left.

"Do you know what he means?" Kitty asked Thrain, with an inquisitive smile. "He wants to... say prayers together, maybe?"

But Thrain huffed a low, hoarse laugh, and twitched a jerky shrug. "Not by the scent of him, I ken," he breathed, as he carefully brushed a finger at his new nipple-rings, and then snaked his other hand downwards, wrapping it around his hard, swollen length. "Och, I can still scent it," he continued, huskier than before, as he began stroking up and down, smooth and hungry and brazen, already pumping out a string of thick white. "So *good*, Kit."

Kitty laughed and swatted at his hands, giving him her sternest pout. "He said to dress for him, not make a mess on the furs, you menace," she said cheerfully. "Now bend over like a good boy, and get ready for your *rassja*."

Thrain moaned again, mumbling helplessly about devious

pretty hellcats with their hidden deadly claws, but soon he was obediently bent over, shuddering and gasping, while Kitty eased the seed-slick *rassja* inside him, and then attached its dangling chain, also. And then turned him around, and reached for the *typpavír*, too—and this time, at Thrain's heated request, she put it on him herself, while he watched and groaned. First the ring for his bollocks, and then the cage part, and then—Kitty's hands only slightly shook—she carefully slid that gold rod deep inside, locked it all in place, and clasped that chain on, too.

By the end of it, they were both shivering and gasping, and Thrain nearly tore Kitty's clothes as he yanked them off, leaving her clad in only her *thyrja*, her earrings and bracelet, and her beautiful new ring. And then he snatched her own *rassja* out of Varinn's box, licking his lips as he made a shaky turn-around motion.

Kitty shuddered and moaned as he slipped it inside, easing its length deep with trembling fingers, and then giving her arse a firm little slap. And finally they were both ready, both dressed in only their lord's jewels, and Thrain abruptly clasped Kitty's hand, and dragged her from the room. Out into the dim, empty sitting-room, and then over to the familiar, sweet-scented shrine.

There was only one other figure inside it, kneeling silently before Lord Grisk, and it took Kitty a jolting, breathless moment to realize it was—Varinn. Because he was entirely unclothed, and he'd taken his hair out of its ever-present braid, letting it fall in loose, shining black waves over his broad shoulders. And there, around his own bared, swollen cock, he was again wearing that thick gold ring, its tight circle making him look even larger, more intimidating, than before.

His bowed head was slowly lifting, turning toward them with nostrils flaring—and then he smoothly rose to his feet and strode toward them, his bare feet silent on the soft furs. His body so big and bulky and powerful, his skin shining deep greenish-grey in the lamplight, his jutting, gold-encircled cock swaying with every smooth step. And his dark eyes glittered as they swept over Kitty's bare breasts and belly, so blatantly displayed with her *thyrja*—and then his gaze flicked toward Thrain. Holding on his *typpavír*, his chains, his new nipple-rings, and then his flushed, gasping face, the wild, desperate light in his eyes.

"Good," Varinn murmured, and it distantly occurred to Kitty that he'd wanted them to come to him like this, hungry, trembling, craving. "Now come, and stand before Lord Grisk."

Oh. Kitty swallowed and nodded, and then padded after Varinn across the furs, halting before Lord Grisk's kind, carved stone face. And Thrain had come to stand beside her, his steps jerky, his eyes bright and strange, almost pained, as they settled on Lord Grisk, too.

And blinking at him, and then at Lord Grisk again, it distantly occurred to Kitty that—she'd never seen Thrain in this shrine before. Not since she'd first arrived at the mountain. And that he'd clearly had a complicated relationship to the gods, perhaps due to his father, or the drink, or all the hardships he'd borne. *Fuck 'em all*, he'd told Kitty, that very first night. *Fuck 'em all.*

But now he was standing here, his throat bobbing, his eyes rapidly blinking. Doing this, perhaps, for Varinn. For Varinn, who gave a gentle, reassuring nip at Thrain's neck as he came to stand beside him, his head bowing toward his namesake.'

"My lord," Varinn said, his voice low and smooth. "I have brought my mates before you, to show you their many strengths, and ask your blessing upon them. To ask for a prosperous, plentiful union, that brings forth hale, hearty Grisk sons."

Kitty's hand reflexively slipped to her waist, her breath exhaling, and she could feel Varinn's eyes on her for an instant, before they settled back to Lord Grisk again. "Thus, I wish you to first again meet Thrain, of the Aetha," Varinn continued, as his big hand clasped to Thrain's shoulder. "He is one of only three living bearers of the old Aetha magic, and he is swift and lusty and wise. He sets at ease all who meet him, and has granted great help to his kin, oft at his own expense. Of late"—his eyes flicked toward Thrain, a small smile on his mouth—"he has brought the great Grisk art of goldsmithing back to us, and with your blessing, this shall then bear forth for many ages to come."

Thrain was biting his lip, his eyes blinking hard on Varinn, but Varinn had turned back to Lord Grisk, his hand slipping down to Thrain's chest, to his new nipple-rings. "You see the beauty of his work," Varinn continued, huskier, "and the beauty of his form, also. How handsome his face, how strong and straight his limbs. How long and ready his prick, and how fat and potent his bollocks. How they have already made me a son."

As if to demonstrate, Varinn had even reached his hand down to gently clasp Thrain's bollocks, rolling them, plumping them, for Lord Grisk's stone eyes. "And you can also see," Varinn said, even lower, "how my mate has eagerly granted himself to me. How he is filled and flaunted with my good Grisk gifts, and my gold, and my scent. For I have sought to be a worthy Thjoth, a worthy heir to your own greatness, and in this, I have tamed an Aetha, and made him my own."

Thrain visibly shivered, his caged heft spasming, straining against the *typpavír*, and Varinn betrayed a low little hiss as he tugged at the *typpavír*'s long chain, and then loosened its clasp with a flick of his claw. "You can see," he murmured, as he began slowly drawing the slick gold rod out, "how deep he has taken my gold inside him. And how"—the rod fully squeezed out with a wet sound, a thick spurt of white—"how wide he has stretched himself upon it. How he gapes soft and open for me."

And oh, gods, Varinn was showing that too, rolling Thrain's

crown with easy, familiar fingers. Displaying that lax, surprisingly large slit, yawning dark and open around his ring, and obligingly sputtering out a thick spurt of white. While Thrain moaned and shuddered, his head tipping back, and Varinn gasped too, even as he set the *typpavír* before Lord Grisk, and then gripped Thrain's shoulders, and spun him around.

"And here," Varinn breathed, as his hand slid over the hard curve of Thrain's arse, "he has taken my gold even deeper. He has learnt to make himself easy for me. Learnt to split wide open for my prick and my seed, whenever I should wish to grant this to him."

Thrain moaned again, especially when Varinn wrapped the *rassja*'s dangling chain around his palm, and then gently tugged that out, too. Drawing the hard gold into his hand with a loud, slick-sounding squelch, and setting it before Lord Grisk with the *typpavír*. And then Varinn caressed his proprietary hand up the length of Thrain's opened crease, his fingers nudging into the gaping darkness the *rassja* had left behind.

"You see how soft and open my Aetha is," he continued, through his heaving breaths. "You see how ready he is to welcome my good prick, and swallow me deep inside. To milk out my seed with his sweet Aetha rump, and make himself *reek* of me."

Thrain's moan was more like a cry this time, and for an instant, Kitty thought Varinn might make good on his word, and bend Thrain over here and now—but then, oh, Varinn glanced toward *her*. And now he was here, behind her, his big hands stroking down her shoulders, her arms, to her rounded belly.

"And next," he continued, still breathless, his eyes back on Lord Grisk, "I wish you to see my sweet *kisa*. I ken you already know much of her, for she has oft prayed to you here, and showed you her heart, and her strength. She is kind, generous, and true, and has brought great joy and peace not only to me, but to my Aetha, also."

Oh. A hot little shiver snaked up Kitty's back, especially as Varinn's hands kept stroking, showing, flaunting. "Katharine has bravely made her life here, and grown us a son, with my Aetha's good seed," he murmured. "And amidst this, she has worked tirelessly for me and my kin, and has freely shared her great skills and knowledge with us. She has gained the Grisk wealth, and reach, and fairness, and exposed the hidden thieves amongst us. She has again and again shown me great honour, before all our kin."

Kitty's breaths were hitching, now, her body leaning closer into Varinn's warmth at her back, into the touch of his hands cupping her breasts. "You see how ripe and sweet she is," he continued, gently rolling her nipples with his fingers. "How her pretty little form has flowered under my good care. How deeply she scents of me, after drinking so many loads of my good seed. And whilst I have not yet pierced her anew with my gold, or marked her with my teeth"—his voice lowered—"I am only waiting until our son is birthed, to be doubly sure of her safety. After this, her form shall bear just as much of me as my Aetha's."

Another quiver rippled up Kitty's back, because he'd never before mentioned any of that—had he? And the anticipation was already rising, fluttering in her chest, as Varinn's hand slid downwards again, toward the dark hair at her groin. "And she, also, has learnt to open all her holes wide for me," he murmured. "She has learnt to welcome my strong, fat Grisk prick deep inside her, and to milk out my good seed with all eagerness—and she does this for my Aetha, also, at my behest. She is so pretty, when she is working upon his prick, and pumping him dry for me. Putting her mouth—and now her sweet little womb—to good use for me."

Oh, gods, Varinn could not be saying these things, meaning these things, and Kitty was whimpering as his seeking fingers slipped deeper between her thighs, nudged gently up inside. "You see how ready she is for me," he purred, so husky now. "How dripping wet she is, slick with her juices. She could swallow me whole this moment, should I wish. Ach, pretty *kisa*?"

Kitty gulped and nodded, and oh, oh, wait, he was doing it. Gently bending her upper body forward with careful intent, placing her hands to the table before Lord Grisk. And then he coolly tilted up her arse, spread her legs, opened her wide, and—Kitty yelped—sank his swollen strength all the way inside her, in one smooth, dizzying stroke.

"See?" Varinn said, his voice damnably steady, as he drew all the way out with a squelch, leaving her wide open, waiting, clutching for more—and then he plunged back in. While Kitty trembled and cried out, sought to grasp tighter at the table, to keep herself upright, as her body wildly, desperately spasmed around his thick invading heft.

"She cannot help but seek to milk me," Varinn said, with dark satisfaction, as he drew out with another slick squelch, letting his smooth head nudge and tease against her convulsing, betraying heat. "She longs to bear me a strong Thjoth son, to carry on our line. But first, she shall bear me my Aetha son—and only after this, shall I fill her sweet womb to bursting with me."

His voice had gone hot, dangerous, commanding in a way Kitty had never heard from him before, and somehow it was writhing the hunger higher, sharper, her body straining for more of him, to open for him, oh. "Please, Lord Grisk," she gasped, without thought. "Please, fill me. Now."

But Varinn's laugh was cool, breathtakingly arousing, and his big hand even drew back, gave her arse a firm little slap. "Behave for your lord, *kisa*," he murmured, even as he sank himself inside again, gave a casual little circle of his hips, made her yelp and whimper. "You shall gain a son of my loins when I choose, and not before. And you ken I have yet greatly honoured you, by allowing my Aetha to fill your womb."

Kitty fervently nodded, casting a brief, regretful glance over her shoulder toward Thrain—but oh, gods, Thrain was looking just as wild and shaky as she felt, his heft bobbing at his groin, his tongue licking his lips. "So wise and generous, Lord Grisk, as always," he breathed. "Offering up your sweet woman's ripe womb to me first. Letting me fill it for you, ready it for you."

Kitty should not have moaned like that, shuddered like that, and oh, Varinn was drawing all the way out of her again, leaning over to briefly press his mouth to Thrain's. "Only the best for you, *krútt*," he replied, his voice rough. "Now come, and again fill her hungry womb with you, ach? Show Lord Grisk how well my *kisa* takes you, also. How sweet you both scent, when your good Aetha prick is buried deep inside her."

Oh, oh gods, because yes, now it was Thrain moving behind her, Thrain's pierced, jabbing length, prodding just slightly into her wet, wide-opened heat. "Ach, Lord Grisk," he whispered, in a strangled-sounding voice, as his hardness jerked in a little further, a little further. "I... thank you, for your great kindness, in sharing—your woman's—womb with me. She feels—so good—so—"

His voice broke into a groan as he slammed all the way in, as Kitty's own cry echoed through the room. Her invaded body frantically seizing against him, too, needing to keep him there, but oh, Thrain was already tightly grasping her hips, and drawing out, before plunging in again. And then again, again, his groans rising as he held her in place, and picked up speed. Furiously pumping in and out, hard enough to chatter Kitty's teeth, and—

And then the sound of a ringing slap, skin striking skin. And Thrain's hammering hips instantly stilled, his hardness held half-inside, flexing and straining against Kitty's own convulsing clutch. While Varinn shifted around behind Thrain, and Kitty could feel Thrain shifting too, his hands' grip slightly softening on her hips.

"But you see," Varinn's cool voice continued, "how my wild rutting Aetha yet lacks control, when he is inside my sweet *kisa*'s womb. How he needs to be taught, and tamed. How he needs"—his voice deepened, as Thrain grasped and flailed—"my command. My strength, inside him."

And gods, the way Thrain was shuddering, gasping, because surely Varinn was pushing in, now, sinking deep into Thrain's open crease, filling that gaping hole with himself. And when Thrain's hips convulsively lurched forward again, straining into Kitty, that was another sharp slap behind them, an answering bolt of stillness through Thrain's taut, rigid body.

"See how sweetly he submits," Varinn's heated voice continued. "See how easy he opens himself, and swallows me deep inside. See how he has learnt to behave for me."

Thrain's groans were rising again, his hardness again spasming wildly inside Kitty's clutch—but oh, oh, he was sliding out again, but far slower this time. Far more considered, more controlled, and surely that was because—Kitty helplessly trembled and moaned—it was Varinn in charge now. Varinn easing Thrain in and out, gently pumping him inside her, because he was buried deep in Thrain's arse, he was fucking her through Thrain, oh gods, oh hell.

"He is so sweet, when he behaves," Varinn's voice rasped, as Thrain's slow strokes moved a little faster, a little smoother. "When he fights his Aetha nature, and takes his pleasure how I wish. When he wields his good Aetha prick for my own gain. For my sweet *kisa*'s gain, also."

Kitty and Thrain were still moaning, gasping, shuddering against one another, and Thrain's hips kept smoothly rolling, their bodies meeting again and again. The pleasure sparking and simmering, wheeling higher with every breath, and Kitty could feel Thrain's heft shifting and straining inside her, his moans hitching toward cries—

"So good, *krútt*," Varinn murmured, as Thrain's hips rocked a little faster, a little harder. "So hot and soft and sweet upon me. And so hard and strong inside my *kisa*, filling her with my good Aetha prick. Granting her my pleasure, my favour, my good Grisk seed."

Thrain and Kitty writhed harder, their cries tearing through the room, but the thrusts kept coming, plunging bright and beautiful and almost unbearable, again and again and again. "Fill her for me, *krútt*," Varinn hissed, low and dangerous. "Feed her for me. Flood her again with your good Aetha seed, with your precious Aetha life. Make her mine, *krútt*, mine, again—"

His voice cracked, broke, Thrain's hips driving in fierce, one last time—and suddenly there was only pleasure, screaming through Kitty's body, her breath. Wracking her entire being in the strength of it, swallowing her whole beneath its wheeling shattering waves, as Thrain's molten heat sprayed out inside her, too. His own body spasming and straining, his shouts resounding in her ear, because oh, surely Varinn was doing the same to him. Pouring him full, completing the circle, locking them together with pleasure and seed and scent. Showing Lord Grisk their hunger, their bonds, their hearts.

And when the room finally stopped spinning again, Kitty's breaths dragging deep through her throat, she felt Varinn's warm hands stroking her flanks, and then slipping up to stroke Thrain's, too. Soothing them, approving of them, because they were—they were both still bowed before Lord Grisk. As if they'd prostrated themselves before him, worshipped him, as they'd worshipped his heir. Welcoming his command, his pleasure, his favour.

And somehow Kitty could feel Varinn's deep breaths, in and out, could feel his body shifting low over Thrain's, too. Bowing, also, his long hair falling over Thrain's back, his big hands coming up to clasp over Kitty's on the altar.

"You see how they honour you," Varinn whispered now,

with palpable rawness in his voice. "You see how they honour me. I beg you to grant them your blessings, and your mercy, and your strength. I beg you for a prosperous, plentiful union, and a strong, safe, happy home for our sons. Your sons."

The words seemed to ring out between them, dangling quiet but impossibly powerful—and when Kitty lifted her heavy head, blinked up toward Lord Grisk's kind, familiar face, it occurred to her that of course he would grant his blessing. Of course he would, and he already had, so many times over. She was so blessed, so truly deeply blessed, and so grateful. So lucky to have such love, and a home. So lucky to have a son.

And it was with that thought—with her hand slipping to spread against her belly—that she felt something... move. A tiny, almost imperceptible flutter, strange and low in her abdomen. And then again, even stronger this time. Enough that she gasped, twitched all over, felt her mouth quiver with something like a gasp, or a sob.

"I just—felt him," she gulped, and suddenly she was flailing up, away from them, away from Thrain's invading heat—but gods, she just needed to see their faces, needed to feel them beneath her hands. "I just—felt our son. Moving. *Alive.*"

Her voice was choked, her eyes blinking, pleading, between Varinn and Thrain, as her mouth pulled into a wide, weepy smile. And for an instant, they both stared back at her, Varinn's breath heaving, Thrain's eyes flashing sharp—and suddenly they both dragged her close, clasped her tightly in their arms. Varinn's breaths still powerfully shuddering through his chest, while Thrain whooped and laughed, his lean body almost bouncing with excitement. "Och, did you hear that, Varinn?" he demanded. "Our son is already quickening! He's going to be the best, brightest little orcling in all the realm, aren't you, little kitten? You're going to be so big and strong and clever!"

He'd fallen to his knees before Kitty on the fur, happily nuzzling at her belly, and Kitty choked a giddy little giggle at the sight of him, her hands sinking into his messy hair. Even as her body kept leaning into Varinn's solid strength, though he seemed a little unsteady too, his arm clasping tighter around her, his other hand spreading almost wonderingly on her belly. And his dazed, blinking gaze had angled back toward Lord Grisk, his head giving a brief, reverent little bow.

"Thank you, Lord Grisk," Kitty whispered, perhaps to him, or Varinn, or both, as she buried her own face into Varinn's warm, shuddering chest. "This was—so generous of you. All of it."

She could hear Varinn's throat swallowing, could feel his hand spreading wider over her belly. Warm and protective and safe, again claiming her son—their son—as his. Something he'd so selflessly done all this time, but after his prayer, his blessing, it somehow seemed even more real, more settled, than before. He truly considered Thrain his, all the way down to his prick and his seed—and therefore, when Thrain had touched Kitty, given her a son, that meant she and her son were now Varinn's, too. And perhaps—perhaps they always had been.

I should never resent my clan brother's own son, he'd told her, back when they'd first met. *He is my kin, also. My son.*

Kitty snuggled a little closer into Varinn's warmth, inhaled the deep familiar sweetness of his scent, and below her, Thrain was doing it now, too. Inhaling deep against the hollow of Varinn's hip, pressing his lips to his silken skin.

"So generous," Thrain murmured, repeating Kitty's words. "I see you, Lord Grisk, and I honour you. Long may your scent carry forth, and speak of the life you have made."

His voice was hushed, his eyes soft and awestruck as they met Varinn's gaze. As if this was his own prayer, his own worship, or maybe even his own blessing. The lord and his worshipper, come together as best friends, as fathers, as mates. To create that new life, here, beneath their clawed hands.

And Varinn was swallowing, smiling, dragging Thrain up, dragging him close. "The life we have made, together," he whispered. "The life that will speak of us together, and bear forth after us. Forever."

The words were hopeful, utterly certain, the voice of a god's son, here, in their arms. And Kitty nodded, clung to him, dragged in that truth, that hope, the sheer, impossible happiness. "Together," she whispered. "Forever."

EPILOGUE

Kitty was about to attend her first proper Grisk party in months, and already, she was tempted to cancel.

"You both *really* think he'll be all right?" she couldn't help asking Varinn and Thrain, yet again, as she cradled Thrandr's tiny, squirming green body against her chest. "For an entire evening?"

They were walking down the corridor to the Bautul wing together, and she didn't miss Varinn and Thrain's fond exchanged glance, or Thrain's low, indulgent laugh. "Ach, naught shall harm our son, *kisa*," Varinn replied firmly, with a gentle slap to her arse. "And if he were ever in danger, you ken we would scent this, and rescue him at once."

The tension in Kitty's shoulders slightly faded, though she clutched Thrandr a little closer, and tickled at his little green belly. Making him gurgle and coo in return, flailing his tiny green baby fists, and she grinned brightly back toward him, even as that familiar, ache again shimmered in her chest. Whispering of warmth, and affection, and pure, boundless devotion.

It was still an overwhelming feeling, sometimes, and one that she hadn't at all been prepared for—especially after the consistent discomfort of her later pregnancy, and the shocking, days-long pain of labour and childbirth. But once it had finally been done, and Gwyn had set Thrandr in Kitty's trembling arms, she'd taken one look at her son, and instantly broken into joyous, weepy laughter. He'd been such a tiny, exquisite, green-skinned marvel, squalling and squirming with unchecked enthusiasm, his long little arms flailing toward her, his little eyes long-lashed and bright.

"Oh, he's perfect," Kitty had sobbed, as Varinn and Thrain had both crowded close, their hands spreading against Thrandr's tiny back. And while Varinn had just leaned in and breathed, his nostrils flaring again and again as his eyes shimmered and shone, Thrain had burst into hoarse laughing sobs, as tracks of tears had streaked down his flushed cheeks.

"Ach, Kit, he's so perfect," he'd choked, as he'd stroked a reverent hand at their son's messy black hair, so reminiscent of his own. "Look at him. Oh gods, he's so perfect, and he's *ours.* We *made* him. He scents of *us.*"

His voice had cracked into more incredulous laughter, his head bending down to join Varinn's in breathing slow and deep. "Och, and he scents of you, too, Varinn," he'd rasped, with a teary smile toward Varinn's face. "Even more than I'd hoped. And ach, look at his nose! That's not an Aetha nose, Varinn, that's *yours.*"

Varinn had been shaking his head, wiping at his wet eyes, but upon Kitty's own closer inspection, Thrandr's little nose had looked remarkably like Varinn's. Broader and blunter than Thrain's, its tiny nostrils flaring with eerie familiarity as he'd drawn in a deep breath—and then he'd loudly sneezed, his little fists flailing, as if he hadn't been at all sure what to make of all these strange new scents.

"It *is* your nose," Kitty had gulped at Varinn, beaming through her still-leaking eyes. "Because he's yours. Ours. Together."

Varinn had twitched a nod at that, again wiping at his face, and giving Kitty a slow, quavering smile. And once they'd managed a spell of nursing—again with Gwyn's help—Varinn and Thrain had taken turns holding their son, too. Varinn again breathing so slow and deep, his face buried in Thrandr's messy black hair, his low purr rumbling through his chest. While Thrain had again laughed, and swayed with him around the room, and nibbled at his tiny fingers, as Kitty and Varinn had both beamed wet-eyed toward them.

It was a pattern that had steadily persisted, all throughout their six months of parenthood so far. Kitty fiercely, fervently devoted to their adorable little marvel, while Thrain had been the fun, laughing, playful parent, always ready with a toy or a game. And Varinn, of course, had been the one to ensure Kitty and Thrandr were always warm, comfortable, and well cared for, even going so far as to insist—despite Kitty's protests—that she take regular rests and breaks, and even do silly things like attending parties.

"It is good for you, *kisa*, to renew and refresh yourself with your kin," he said now, in his sternest voice, as he absently stroked at the neat, short new beard he'd grown of late. "And it is good for Thrandr to learn to spend time with others, also. And you ken the nursery"—his other hand gently nudged her toward the door—"shall take good care of him."

The nursery was indeed a cozy, comfortable, bustling room, full of soft furs and little orcs playing with brightly coloured toys, and Kitty relaxed even more as Gwyn came over, cradling Ella and Nattfarr's tiny new son Roarr against her chest. "Hi there, little fella!" she said toward Thrandr, with a cheerful grin. "You're going to have so much fun with us tonight, aren't you?"

Thrandr happily gurgled, his little limbs flailing, his bright eyes already fixed with interest on the nearest group of playing orclings. It included several other familiar young orcs, Rakfi and Barden among them, and Rakfi was currently racing in circles around them all, with what appeared to be a large carrot clutched between his sharp little teeth.

Thrain was already laughing, dropping down to playfully snap at Rakfi's carrot—to which Rakfi delightedly shrieked, and launched toward him. Resulting in an impromptu play-fight on the furs, and soon Thrandr began squirming to get down and join in, too. And Kitty leaned against Varinn's side as they both watched and smiled, and Varinn's hand stroked reassuringly up and down her back.

"You ken I shall scent for him all eve, *kisa*," he said, husky, with a brief kiss to her hair. "But mayhap I wish to have you and Thrain all to myself for a spell also, ach?"

Kitty couldn't deny her twitch of interest at that, or her eager smile up toward that telltale glint in his eyes. And it made it easier, somehow, to finally kiss Thrandr goodbye, and to turn her attention to the admittedly exciting prospect of the evening's entertainment. It was one of Nattfarr's monthly Truth Revels, during which anyone could draw upon his powerful magic to seek out truth, or speak vows. And Kitty knew from enjoyable experience that while the Truth Revels usually began innocuously enough, after bedtime they invariably became adult-only gatherings, during which pleasures could be freely shared, and orcs would openly flaunt their mates for all who might wish to see.

Of course, Varinn had always taken great satisfaction in flaunting Kitty and Thrain to the fullest possible extent, and Kitty's hungry anticipation only rose as he swiftly guided them back into their bedroom, and sank into his usual chair. "Now, my sweet mates," he purred, as he stretched his bulky body languidly in the chair, and gave them a slow, smug smile. "You shall ready each other for this party, ach? And for me."

Oh. The warmth was already coiling hotter in Kitty's belly, and she smiled shyly toward Varinn as she nodded, and hurried to obey. Fetching their new, much larger jewel-box from the shelf, while Thrain plucked out clothes, and the hairbrush, and the scented oil they'd begun using of late, too.

And then, their eyes shimmering and crackling whenever they met, she and Thrain took turns dressing and preparing each other, in the ways they knew Varinn liked best. Brushing each other's hair, oiling each other all over, and then adding on more jewels, too. Kitty in her *thyrja* and ring, of course, and her lovely gold bracelets and anklets and earrings, all of them gifts crafted by Thrain, and given by Varinn. And then, finally, Thrain carefully drew out the delicate gold *kraga* they'd given her after Thrandr's birth, and snapped it around her neck.

"You wish her to wear the chain also, Varinn?" Thrain murmured, with a heated glance toward Varinn. "And the *rassja*?"

Varinn coolly nodded, his eyes hooded as they flicked up and down Kitty's gold-studded form. "And the womb-ring," he replied, with damnable steadiness. "But soften her up a little first, ach? In both holes, I ken."

Oh, hell. Kitty's gasp choked out her throat, her hungry heat convulsing between her legs, and Thrain huffed a husky little laugh as he prowled toward her, the familiar long gold chain dangling from his fingers. "You heard your lord, Kit," he murmured, clipping one end of the chain to the loop on her *kraga*, before nudging her onto her back on the bed. "Open up, ach?"

Kitty gulped and obeyed, sagging onto her back, parting her trembling legs wide for him. Exposing her open, hungry heat, already slick with craving, but also showing that lovely gold piercing, embedded inside the top of her crease. It had been another post-birth gift, made to exactly match Thrain's, and Varinn had done the piercing under Efterar's careful supervision, once they'd been certain she was fully healed from childbirth. And though it still wasn't nipple-rings—Varinn had still firmly refused those, until Kitty was finished nursing—it had proven to be impossibly compelling, and she'd spent the first few weeks with it in a constant state of arousal, begging for relief from her orcs' laughing, licking tongues.

And worst—or best—of all, Varinn's next gift had been a long, delicate gold chain. One that was made to hook to her *kraga*, and then extended downwards to clip onto her new piercing. Creating a simple yet devastating piece of jewelry, one that only required the gentlest tug to set her gasping and quivering and obeying. And oh, Thrain was already grinning, wicked and insolent, as he clipped the chain onto her piercing, and gave it a light, experimental flick with his claw.

"Oh, gods," Kitty moaned, her body curling up, her head whipping back and forth on the bed—and both Varinn and Thrain laughed, husky and low, as Thrain leaned forward, let his own gold ring nudge and tease against hers. And then he slipped himself downwards, nestling his crown against her clutching hungry heat, before sliding slow and smooth inside. Making Kitty flail and cry out again, and Thrain was gasping now too, his eyes fluttering, his lean body straining to keep it slow, stay in control.

He still preferred it hard and fast, Kitty well knew, and some days, she did too—but again, Varinn was watching, allowing this, giving this. Expecting Thrain to behave, and honour this. And Thrain was, easing in and out with deliberate care, pumping his slick fluid inside her, until the sounds were slick and squelching, the wetness streaking down between them.

"Enough," came Varinn's mild voice, and Thrain instantly stilled, his eyes squeezing shut as he drew in a deep, bracing breath, and backed out, away. His glossy pierced length wildly bobbing and dripping, but he ignored it as he lurched toward the jewel-box again, and returned with a thick, gleaming gold ring. It was too large for a finger, but too small for a bracelet, because it was meant for—Kitty gasped as Thrain's familiar fingers spread her open—for there. To be hidden up inside an orc's woman, as a secret sign of one's affection, only revealed when she was opened wide for pleasure.

Thrain had made this one too, of course, and his eyes flashed as he watched his fingers slip it inside, deep into Kitty's slick, opened heat. The sensation shuddering her all over again, her body clutching hungrily at his touch, but he was already drawing away, and licking his lips as his gentle fingers spread backwards, down the length of her crease.

"Now here, Kit," he murmured, as his other arm guided her knees up, rolling her higher onto her back. "Open up nice and soft for me."

Kitty gasped and nodded, willing herself to relax as much as she could, to welcome the gentle prod of his pierced tip against her resisting tightness. It was easier to manage now, especially with Thrain, who wasn't quite as thick and blunt as Varinn—but she still writhed and moaned as she felt him slowly breach her, pressing in breath by breath. His slick, slippery length sliding in smooth, steady, oh, oh, until he was buried all the way, his swollen bollocks bulging snug against her skin.

"How is she behaving, *krútt*?" Varinn asked, his tone one of light, conversational inquiry. "Has she taken my good Aetha prick with ease, as she should?"

Kitty and Thrain both moaned at once, and Kitty could feel Thrain swelling fuller, his hips rocking tighter against her. "Ach, she has," he replied, choked. "So hot and tight. Would love to—"

"Not yet," Varinn cut in, and oh, he'd risen from his chair, striding smoothly toward the jewel-box, and plucking Kitty's *rassja* out of it. "You heard my wishes, *krútt*."

Thrain nodded and moaned again, drawing all the way out of Kitty with a pained-sounding hiss. And then he snatched the *rassja* from Varinn's hand, pulling Kitty's softened opening even wider with his fingers—and she shivered all over at the feel of the *rassja*'s solid gold, sliding swift and easy inside her, while both Varinn and Thrain watched.

"Good, *kisa*," Varinn murmured, with a gentle slap to her arse. "Now close up, ach?"

Kitty groaned, shuddered, fought to obey, to clamp her stretched-out skin as tightly around the *rassja* as she could. And that was another light, approving slap of Varinn's hand to her arse, along with a warm smile from his mouth, as he nudged her back to her feet. "Good," he murmured again. "Now your turn, *krútt*. The largest one."

Thrain shuddered and nodded, already lurching over to the jewel-box again, and returning with another gleaming gold *rassja*. It wasn't the first one Varinn had given him, but a new one he'd asked Thrain to create for them, soon after they'd spoken their vows. And rather than having it made entirely from new gold, Varinn had ordered Thrain to melt down all Kitty's old jewels from Charles, and to blend them in, too. Drowning them entirely in Varinn's own new gold, but for the various gems, which now adorned the *rassja*'s handle. And there was something strangely, satisfyingly compelling about watching Varinn's fingers easily stroke the jewels, casually showing his ownership of them, as his other hand bent Thrain double over the bed, exposing everything for their eyes.

"Good," Varinn purred, as he swiftly coated Charles' gold in his own dripping seed, and then coolly began sliding it into Thrain's upraised arse. Making Thrain choke and spasm around it, clearly fighting to open and welcome its considerable width and heft inside him. But he was doing it, arching and groaning as he swallowed it breath by breath, his body trembling all over with the effort. Until it, too, was buried deep inside, with only that jewelled handle exposed.

"Very good, *krútt*," Varinn murmured, bending to press a brief kiss to Thrain's back. "You are so sweet, when you so easily welcome my gold inside you."

Thrain fervently nodded, and shivered all over as he stood up again, his eyes hungry and pleading on Varinn's face. But Varinn only gave his hot cheek a cheerful little pat, and flashed him a smug, wicked smile. "Now dress, ach?" he said. "Both of you. We should not wish to be late."

Both Kitty and Thrain groaned in unison, while Varinn kept smiling, raising his brows toward them. And there was no use arguing, Kitty well knew, but it still proved remarkably difficult to focus on dressing, to the point where Varinn finally threw up his hands and did it for them. First choosing a lovely silk ensemble for Kitty, and then plucking out Thrain's heaviest leather kilt, clearly with a goal of concealing everything beneath.

"Now behave," Varinn murmured, as he palmed at Thrain's scarcely visible bulge beneath the thick leather. "And mayhap I shall reward you both later."

It was a brutally effective promise, as always, and Kitty fought to turn her focus to the evening's celebration as she accompanied Varinn and Thrain down the corridor. As usual, the Revel was being held in the large Grisk common-room, and Kitty could already hear the noise and music and laughter ringing through the air, growing louder and louder with every step. And bubbling her own eagerness higher too, almost— almost—enough to ignore the distant unease about Thrandr, still back there in the nursery.

"Our son is still well, *kisa*," Varinn murmured into Kitty's hair, as he guided her toward the common-room door. "Now settle yourself, and be at ease. Honour me, and do me credit."

That, too, was a powerfully effective order—as Varinn very well knew—and Kitty gratefully smiled at him, her body relaxing as she took in the excitement of the party all around them. There were drummers, and dancing, and games, and what appeared to be a mountain of food—and of course, all of their Grisk friends and kin, chatting and laughing together. And little Vragi was already running over to meet them, his kitten—now a dainty black cat—curled up close in his arms.

"Look, brother!" he said excitedly, his eyes bright on

Varinn's face. "We gave Arni a new collar today! Isn't she pretty in it?"

Vragi had of course bought the new collar at the Great Grisk Showroom-Shop—and he'd done so with Kitty's help, since she still worked there most mornings, with Thrandr tucked into a sling against her side. She'd continued to find it highly fulfilling and enjoyable work, especially with Thrain still just down the corridor at the forge, ready to step in at a moment's notice. Not only to help with Thrandr, but to help their kin as needed, too—and even today, he'd worked together with Kitty and the Skai tailor Gamall to make the adorable little collar for Arni, its gold clasp and shiny pale leather making a lovely contrast against her glossy black fur.

"Ach, Arni is stunning in this, little brother," Varinn told Vragi with a grin, kneeling to gently pat at Arni's silken head. "A good Grisk gift. I am glad my mates were able to help you gain this today."

He'd angled his approving grin up at Kitty and Thrain, surely having scented them on the collar, and Vragi's little chest puffed out as he gave a satisfied nod. At least, until Arni twitched up in his arms, gazing wide-eyed across the room toward Ella's dogs—and then she yowled and leapt to the floor, scampering toward the door.

Vragi instantly rushed off after her, the sounds of his giggles ringing through the air, while a fondly exasperated Varinn watched them go. And Kitty wasn't at all surprised when Timo suddenly materialized before them, a knowing smile pulling at his mouth. "I can handle this one, brother," he said, with a genial clap to Varinn's shoulder. "You enjoy your night with your mates, ach?"

Timo had grown nearly as tall as Varinn over this past year, and now sported multiple piercings in both his pointed ears— but Varinn still ruffled his hand in his hair, and flashed him a swift, grateful smile. "I thank you, son," he replied. "Most of all after that mess with the lost orcling today. You saw Efterar upon it, ach? And spoke with your friends, also?"

Timo easily nodded, and gave Varinn's shoulder a reassuring shake. "Naught to worry about, brother," he said. "I was glad to help, ach?"

With that, he turned and strode off out the door, leaving Varinn looking both pained and grateful, his shoulders sagging. But now it was Thrain clapping a hand to his shoulder, and squeezing tight. "He lives for it, Varinn," he said firmly. "Just like you. And you're taking damned good care of him in it too, ach?"

He wasn't wrong, because Kitty knew full well how much effort Varinn and Nattfarr and Rathgarr had gone to over the past year to safeguard not only Timo's physical health, but his mental wellbeing, too. Taking what they'd learned from Thrain's experiences, and not only keeping Timo away from particularly difficult situations, but also ensuring he had regular outside support, as well. They'd also set it up as a formal apprenticeship, with limited hours and a fair salary, which had seemed to work well for all involved—and soon afterwards, Trygve had begun a similar apprenticeship with Thrain in the Grisk forge. And to no one's surprise, Thrain had proven to be a fun, supportive, and easygoing teacher, and Trygve had already begun to produce some truly stunning work.

Of course, Kitty's own formal apprenticeship as a shopkeeper had continued as well. And in addition to her day-to-day work in the shop—stocking, mending, helping customers—she'd kept on with some intriguing larger projects, too. Not only the ongoing pricing and taxation frameworks with Rosa and Ymir, but also the mountain's larger trading efforts, which had continued to expand over the past year. In the ongoing absence of Harthr and Knorr—who had both been sent off to dig tunnels in the south—Eyarl and Valter had taken over the bulk of the trading management, with considerable support from Grein. Who, unlike Harthr and Knorr, had immediately confessed to his wrongdoing in kidnapping Kitty, and had accepted his punishment digging tunnels without complaint. And when he'd returned several months later—earlier than expected, due to good behaviour—he'd fervently begged Kitty's forgiveness, and brought her multiple gifts for Thrandr, as well.

And along with the gifts, to Kitty's astonishment, Grein had even written her a glowing letter of reference. Praising her poise, her professionalism, and her comprehensive business and trading skills. And while Thrain had scoffed and rolled his eyes afterwards, pointing out that a reference from Grein was worse than useless, Varinn had looked reluctantly pleased, and Kitty had carefully tucked the letter onto her shelf alongside the written reference Charles had sent, too. Not that she ever expected to need them, but they were her accomplishments, in her own chosen profession. Her own certainty that she had done this for herself, and if the need ever arose, she could support herself, and her son.

And over the past year, it had been truly gratifying to offer that same freedom to several other women, as well. Because as Varinn and Thrain had promised, they'd helped Kitty write to several of her former colleagues in the city with paid offers to spend time visiting Orc Mountain, and considering the possibility of staying long-term. And Kitty had been delighted to have received multiple expressions of interest in return, followed by a variety of visits. Not all the visits had been successful, of course, but none had been downright disastrous, either, and several had gone excessively well. And in a surprising development, Grein had been one of the first orcs to meet a new mate—a plump, bubbly brunette named Stasia. Who had turned out to have an excellent eye for fashion, and had enthusiastically joined Grein and Kitty in identifying new clothing and textile traders to collaborate with. And over the past few months, she'd even begun working together with Kitty and Gamall to develop some new designs to sell in the shop, all made in fabulous orcish style.

And it was Stasia rushing over toward them now, looking resplendent in an all-crimson ensemble, and pulling along an indulgent-looking Grein behind her. "Kitty!" she exclaimed. "Did you get a chance to go through that new shipment this afternoon? It was glorious, wasn't it?"

She'd clasped her hands to her chest in awestruck wonder, and Kitty eagerly nodded, glancing beyond Stasia toward where a nearby Kesst had visibly perked up, too. "It was incredible," she replied. "Brilliant work with that contact, Grein. And Kesst, I've already set aside some trousers from it for you, and a dress for Geva! And a beautiful robe for you too, Dammarr."

She'd grinned toward where Dammarr had come over with Thrak to join them, eyes lighting up with unmistakable interest. Dammarr was also looking truly resplendent, dressed in a deep blue robe that perfectly matched the sapphires in that beautiful *kíróna*, and in Thrak's latest gift, too—a dazzling new *thyrja*, forged by Thrain. And Thrak was already laughing as he strode over too, slinging an easy, familiar arm over Dammarr's shoulder. Showing off his own gleaming emerald signet ring—another gift from Thrain, and apparently a perfect replica of the one their father had once worn.

"Gonna spend me outta house and home, possum," Thrak said cheerfully, with a nip at Dammarr's pierced ear. "Keeping a gorgeous Grisk mate properly kitted out is a costly business, ach?"

Dammarr wryly smiled, but didn't argue, and Varinn and Grein exchanged amused glances, too. "Try having two of them," Varinn told Thrak, flashing a teasing grin toward Kitty and Thrain. "Most of all when they both spend their days surrounded by goods and gold, dreaming up new ways to spend my credit."

Thrain barked a bright, incredulous laugh, and lunged

toward Varinn, tackling him into a headlock. "You tyrant!" he exclaimed. "You love it, and for that, I'm gonna spend even more. You just *wait* until you see what I'm making us next!"

Kitty didn't miss the unmistakable flare of interest in Varinn's eyes, but he'd already launched himself back at Thrain, pinning him down to the fur. And soon they were both rolling around wrestling on the floor together, their laughter carrying through the room—and with a shout, Thrak leapt in too, followed by Grein and a nearby Baldr. And soon Kitty was backed up against the nearest wall with Dammarr and Stasia and Alma, and laughing and cheering as the match turned into a clan-wide free-for-all.

"You're sure you don't want to join in?" she cheerfully asked, once Dammarr had given a loud, piercing whistle at a brilliant tackle by Thrak. "I could hold your jewels, if you like."

But Dammarr gave her an easy grin, and wryly waved it away. "Ach, I am quite content to watch for now, away from my brothers' sweaty mess. But thank you, sister."

Kitty shot a swift, warm smile back, her eyes lingering with genuine appreciation on that beautiful ensemble, and the elegant ease all over Dammarr's form. It was still so good to see her now-dear friend so obviously relaxed, at home in such well-suited clothes and jewels, without any signs of the discomfort or tension she'd so often noticed before.

"I'm glad," she said now, and she meant it. "You're truly stunning tonight, sister. As always."

The *sister* was new, these past months, something that was just between their closest circle—though for some time now, they'd also been referring to Dammarr as *hán* in Aelakesh, rather than *hann*, or he. It had turned out that Rosa had been doing some research on the subject, and had made the intriguing discovery that some orcs from ages past had embraced a third way of being—one that walked a middle path between their orc fathers and their human mothers. And Kitty would perhaps never forget the look on Dammarr's face as Rosa had excitedly told them about it, and even brandished an old book with multiple illustrations of striking, beautifully dressed *hán*-orcs, who had often been highly regarded among their kin for their insights, wisdom, and creativity.

Afterwards, Kitty had borrowed the book from Rosa, claiming to want to review the fashions—and the next day she'd handed it to a grateful-looking Dammarr, together with a beautiful new dress. And afterwards, she'd frequently seen Dammarr and Thrak reading it together, and she'd also overheard them having multiple discussions about it late at night, often while she was dozing against Varinn and nursing Thrandr in the sitting-room. And amidst it all, Thrak had never once wavered from his consistent refrain that Dammarr was beautiful, and he wanted his mate to be happy, and content— and eagerly in his bed—no matter what that looked like.

It was after that that they'd begun to call Dammarr *hán*, which translated closest as *they*, in the common-tongue. And a few months later, following Thrak's example, they'd switched to using *they* for Dammarr in the common-tongue, as well. And while they still only used it among themselves for now, it seemed to suit Dammarr so well that Kitty struggled to think of them as anything else. Especially after the day a few months before, when Thrak had come to see Kitty at the shop with the book, shyly requesting a new kind of *typpavír* it discussed—one that didn't fill and flaunt an orc's prick, like Thrain's did, but instead cradled it tight and close, and safely out of the way.

As always, Thrain had accepted the job with his usual easy willingness, and when Thrak had given Dammarr the gleaming, gem-encrusted *typpavír*—a web of gold in a perfect half-moon shape—Dammarr had choked and gasped, and hurled both arms around Thrak's neck. And since then, the two of them had seemed to develop a new taste for flaunting their pleasures together, Thrak desperately gasping and rutting into Dammarr's languid, neatly svelte body, showing off the jewels glinting at his mate's groin and throat, and flashing against their beautiful hair.

And even now, a sweaty Thrak was prowling over, his messy hair all up on end, his eyes glinting hungry on Dammarr's face. And without a word, he snatched Dammarr's wrists to the wall above their heads, and then buried his face in their neck, both their hips grinding up together as Dammarr moaned and arched against him.

They certainly weren't the only ones enjoying pleasures together—the younger guests had all been sent off to bed by now, and Kitty could see several other heated clusters gathering against walls and corners. Baldr and Drafli had already come over to crowd against Alma, too, and even Jule and her captain mate were grinding together on a bench, his face bent deep into her throat.

"Och, not again," cut in Thrain's revolted voice, from where he'd come over too, pulling a sweaty Varinn behind him. "Do these two never stop? C'mon, Kit, before I need to burn out my eyes *and* my nose. Dancing, mayhap?"

Kitty laughed and willingly let herself be tugged over toward the drums, which were already surrounded by groups of dancing orcs and women. And soon she was tucked in close between Varinn and Thrain as they whirled and stomped and played together, until her face hurt from laughing, and she was just as hot and sweaty as they were.

After that, they cooled down with some refreshments, which thankfully didn't include wine or ale—Nattfarr had long ago asked the Grisk to forego strong drink at gatherings, out of consideration for orcs like Thrain. And once Kitty and Varinn and Thrain had all eaten and drunk their fill, they traipsed over toward the front of the room, where Nattfarr and Ella were seated on a raised bench together, with their three adorable little dogs—Teppo, Tommi, and Trot—pacing protectively around their feet.

As was often the case at these Truth Revels, there was also a short line of revellers standing before the bench, all waiting to partake of Nattfarr's gift—whether to speak vows to loved ones, or find truth, or seek inner insight. And Kitty smiled at the sight of Grein and Stasia at the front of the line, Grein holding Stasia's hand as she held Nattfarr's eyes, and told him how happy she was here with her new mate, and how deeply she wanted a son.

Grein and Stasia were both looking rather weepy as they left again, Stasia giving Kitty a quick, wavering smile. And next in the line before Nattfarr was the tall Skai Killik, his arms folding over his lean chest as he coolly eyed the massive, muscular orc beside him. Who, Kitty now knew, was a gruff, frowning fellow named Ulfarr, and around his thick-set waist—serving as a belt on his trousers—was Thrain's beautiful heavy chain, its steel links just as shiny as on the first day he'd made it.

"Speaker, I wish you to ask my clanmate," Killik was now saying to Nattfarr, his mouth pursing, "what he longs for most."

Nattfarr didn't even blink at Killik's request—Kitty now knew that he regularly fielded far more personal inquiries than this one—and easily held Ulfarr's eyes as he repeated the question. And in return, Ulfarr took a breath that heaved his giant shoulders, his swallow audible even amidst the noise all around.

"I long to be a good father to my heart-son Sune," Ulfarr said in his deep, growly voice, his gaze fixed unblinking on Nattfarr's face. "I long to regain my place amongst my Skai kin, as a true Skai son. And I long"—his voice lowered—"to beget a son of my own blood. I long to grant a son all the safety and peace that was stolen from me."

At this, Killik betrayed a brief, almost imperceptible grimace, as something like sadness flashed across his eyes— but it vanished just as quickly, in place of a cool, flinty determination. "We thank you, Speaker," he said crisply. "Now, Ulfarr, let us—"

But even as he'd turned to go, Ulfarr's huge hand caught his lean arm, and waved him back toward Nattfarr again. "You also, Killik," he said, in his heavy, gravelly voice. "What do you most long for, this night?"

Killik rolled his eyes, but gamely spun back to face Nattfarr, who caught his gaze, and then repeated the question toward him. And in return, Killik's pointed ears very slightly flushed, his breaths hitching in his throat. "I wish to chain Ulfarr to my bed," he said, husky, "and keep him there as long as I wish, whilst I wield my taunts and daggers against him. Until he screams my name, and soils himself with his seed."

Oh. Well. Now it was Ulfarr's face reddening, but he certainly didn't seem averse to this plan. And when Killik abruptly spun and strode off, his head held very high, Ulfarr rapidly lumbered after him, licking hungrily at his lips with his thick black tongue.

Beside Kitty, Thrain was chuckling as he watched them go, his hand gently slapping at Kitty's arse. "Glad my jewel's been holding up for them," he said cheerfully. "I swear, those Skai could rival the Ka-esh with their love for chaining each other up, ach?"

Kitty laughed together with him, and followed his eyes toward where none other than Filak was sitting sprawled on a nearby bench, with an excessively handsome Ka-esh named Julian kneeling naked between his thighs. And not only were Julian's hands bound behind his back, but he had a chain circled around his slim neck, its other end held casually in Filak's long, terrifying claws.

"Um, but didn't Filak tell you the other day that he'd begun sniffing out a woman to mate with?" Kitty doubtfully asked Thrain, her eyes on where Filak had yanked Julian's face up, his curved claws tracing coolly at his sweaty grey cheek. "And that he preferred to find one he could keep deep underground, where no other orcs could scent her? As if"—her lip curled—"his mate would be another one of his beloved precious rocks, that he can lock in a cabinet somewhere, while he goes off and enjoys his own pleasures elsewhere?"

She could hear the distaste in her voice—despite her best efforts, her opinion of Filak had not improved, these past months—and while the look of disapproval in Varinn's eyes rather matched her own, Thrain laughed, and shook his head. "Och, don't discount how much Filak loves those gems of his, Kit," he said cheerfully. "To him, that'd be the height of good treatment, ach? I ken he'll be in for a surprise, when he does sniff out a real-life mate to obsess over."

Kitty couldn't help already sympathizing with the poor woman, especially given the decidedly worshipful look on Julian's handsome upturned face. But before she could consider it further, Thrain nudged her forward, toward where a smiling Ella and Nattfarr were waiting, Ella now holding one of her dogs—Tommi—in her lap.

"Have you thought of a question for Nattfarr, Kit?" Thrain asked. "Or you, Varinn?"

Varinn nodded, as he always took these Truth Revels seriously, and felt a responsibility to publicly support Nattfarr, and ask him meaningful, thought-provoking questions. And Nattfarr was already reaching to clasp Varinn's forearm, flashing him a grateful smile as their eyes met.

"I have a question for you, brother," Varinn said, holding his gaze steady to Nattfarr's. "Now that we have gained so much, what do you believe is our next, greatest need? What ought we to seek, for our Grisk sons?"

Nattfarr hesitated, the warmth sparking in his eyes, because Kitty knew he appreciated Varinn's questions too, appreciated having his thoughts drawn, and made into truth. "I believe we need to keep building our home," he said finally. "We need to keep caring for our brothers and mates and sons, and thus return the Grisk to our former power. We are strong, we are steadfast, and we shall use our deep grounding to raise up all our kin around us. And good work like yours, my faithful brother"—he inclined his head toward Varinn—"is the bedrock of this truth. A great gift of life to us all."

His words seem to shimmer out between them, resonating with strength and promise. And Varinn was smiling back, slow and true, as his hand clasped tighter around Nattfarr's arm, and gave it a firm little shake.

"Now you, Kit," Thrain said, a little husky, as he nudged Kitty forward. "What do you want to ask? Anything at all."

Kitty blinked and twitched, because gods, how was she supposed to follow that, she needed to think of something deep and excessively profound—but Nattfarr's inquiring eyes had already caught hers, and held. And instead of something meaningful, Kitty blurted out the first thing that came to mind, something she'd perhaps wondered a little too often, this past year.

"I want to know what Varinn really thought," her traitorous voice announced, "the very first time he fed me, that day after we met. In the camp underground."

Oh good gods, what the hell had she just said, and she felt herself blanching, shaking her head, as Thrain merrily laughed, and gave an approving slap to her arse. And though Varinn was visibly grimacing, his eyes had again caught to Nattfarr's, his jaw flexing, his face and ears flushing a deep red.

"I thought mayhap I had died," he croaked, his voice not at all his own. "I had never felt aught so soft and tight in all my days. I wished for naught more than to pour Katharine's belly full of me, and make her reek of me—and then to fill all her other holes with me, also. I wished"—his voice hardened, deepened—"to make her kneel and beg and worship me, and to swear to open her womb for a son of my own blood, once she had granted my Aetha his."

Oh. Well. Kitty's face had perhaps flushed as red as Varinn's, especially when Thrain gleefully laughed again, and Ella flashed her a knowing, amused grin. And suddenly Kitty couldn't seem to look at any of them, and instead busied herself with crouching down to scratch behind Teppo's silky little ears.

"Och, that's the spirit, Varinn," Thrain was blithely saying, with another crack of laughter. "Though none of us are even slightly surprised by this, you ken. Now for mine... och. Mayhap... ask me about the best fuck of my life."

It was such a typical Thrain question—he always asked something light and silly and irreverent, and Kitty now knew it was because his and Nattfarr's magic sometimes worked strangely together. Calling up truths that were buried deep, or ought to have been forgotten—and once, when they hadn't been paying attention, Nattfarr had even told Thrain a memory that hadn't been his own. One that—as far as they'd been able to discover—had belonged to Nattfarr's great-great-great-grandfather, from over a hundred years before.

Nattfarr had already repeated the question back to Thrain, an easy smile on his mouth—and Kitty was suddenly, deeply alarmed to see Thrain twitch and choke, his eyes bulging, his face draining of all colour. As if he sought to look away from Nattfarr, but couldn't.

"The best fuck of my life," Thrain said, his voice wooden, "was a few months ago, on the day when I'd gone a whole year without a drink. And as a reward, Varinn and Kit both worked me over all night, until I was weeping and screaming, and blowing empty loads—and then, after Kit went to sleep, Varinn bent over for me, and let me plough him dry into our bed, until he was screaming, too."

Oh. That. Thrain had told Kitty about it the next morning, of course, his body still shuddering at the memory, the triumph flashing in his eyes. But beyond a very brief acknowledgement, Varinn had never spoken of it again, and Kitty hadn't brought it up again, either. Knowing, perhaps, that this was something Varinn had wanted to keep between him and Thrain, something that made him feel vulnerable, or even powerless. And oh, gods, the way he looked now, his face gone deathly pale, but for the splotches of deep red staining his cheeks.

And without at all meaning to, Kitty lunged over to clasp Varinn's hand, smiling up at him with genuine admiration, or maybe even awe. "It was just the kind of thing Lord Grisk would do," she said, low and fervent. "Giving up your own desires, your own control, to honour someone else. Giving them a great Grisk gift, something meaningful, something they'll never forget. Just like I'll never forget your kindness toward me when you fed me that day, too."

Varinn's glance down toward her was brief, but abjectly grateful, and Kitty kept beaming toward him, as her hungry hand stroked up his broad, bulky chest. And Thrain slid over behind Varinn, too, easing his arms around his waist, nibbling at his neck. "Sorry, Varinn," he murmured, a little choked. "It really was the best gift, though. Will never, ever forget it. Or"— he drew in a shaky breath—"how good you've been to me, throughout all this. How I'd never have made it a year without you, and your kindness. And yours, Kit."

His bright eyes glanced toward Kitty, glimmering with intensity, with truth. And Kitty smiled back toward him, nodding, because it certainly hadn't always been easy, and Thrain had almost fallen back into the drink several times—to the point where, during that last difficult month of her pregnancy, Varinn had found him sitting alone in a human pub, staring at an untouched tankard of ale before him. But like every other time, Thrain had fought it, and acknowledged it, and come home again—and then he'd immediately gone to Efterar and Rathgarr, both of whom he'd still continued meeting with, all these months. He'd kept his word, kept his promises, over and over again—and it had been just like Varinn to honour that, and give him a great gift in return.

And thankfully, Varinn was sagging against them both, his eyes closing, and Ella had quietly murmured something to Nattfarr, before drawing him up and away. Leading him toward the exit, while their dogs merrily trotted at their heels, surely eager to go collect their brothers from the nursery—and Ella even winked as she waved goodbye to Kitty, and glanced meaningfully at the empty bench.

Kitty didn't need telling twice, and she promptly smiled and nudged Varinn downwards, onto the bench. And though he'd cast her a wary look, he sank down without hesitation, his legs sprawled, his hand rubbing at his still-flushed face.

Kitty exchanged a brief glance with Thrain, the awareness passing swift between them—and then they both sank to their knees at once. Kitty stroking at Varinn's muscled calf, inhaling the rich scent of his skin, while Thrain bent down low, and pressed his mouth to the top of Varinn's bare foot.

"We adore you, Lord Grisk," Kitty murmured, to his shifting, watching eyes, as she trailed her lips down his leg, until she was kissing at his other foot, too. "You're so good to us. So kind."

Varinn didn't reply, but Kitty could hear his exhale, shaky and slow. And when she shot a glance upwards at his face, the redness on his cheeks was already fading, his expression easing toward relief, or maybe even appreciation. So Kitty kept kissing, kneeling, worshipping, slowly working her way up Varinn's calf, while Thrain kept kissing and licking his foot. One of his hands already moving beneath his own kilt, as his head tipped back, and his worshipful eyes met Varinn's face.

"So good, Lord Grisk," Thrain rasped, as his breath shuddered through his chest. "So kind, in caring for us as you have, and granting us so many gifts, and so much peace. Just as a god's son would."

Varinn's eyes had briefly closed, his nostrils flaring, his flush fading a little more. And when his eyes opened again, they were cool, crackling, flicking between Kitty kissing his thigh, and Thrain still bent over his foot, his hand still frantically working beneath his kilt.

"Undress, both of you," Varinn ordered, husky and soft.

"And anoint me, *krútt*. Whilst you, *kisa*"—his hand found her chin, tilted it up—"shall ready me for ploughing."

Oh, hell. Kitty and Thrain both moaned at once, both of them already fumbling at their clothes, and tossing them aside. Leaving them both fully bared and exposed at Varinn's feet, but for all their jewels. And Kitty desperately fought back the awareness of what it must look like, both of them naked and kneeling and stabbed full of Varinn's gold, with those glittering *rassjas* brazenly jutting out between their arse-cheeks.

But Thrain clearly didn't care—Kitty had long ago learned that he revelled in showing off his beautiful body, with all Varinn's gifts inside it—and he was already moaning again, his worshipful eyes fixed to Varinn's face. While his hungry hand kept blatantly stroking his swollen length, pumping out its early seed, and drizzling it down onto Varinn's bare foot. Anointing him, just as Varinn had ordered, while Kitty belatedly kissed up Varinn's thigh, and—after a brief, seeking glance toward his face—began unbuckling his kilt.

He was already rock-hard beneath it, bobbing up ruddy and full, and Kitty moaned again as she gratefully sucked him deep. Her tongue already seeking into his leaking cleft, her lips stroking and lavishing him, as her tingling hands stroked and caressed, just the way she knew he liked best. And she was rewarded with a low hiss from his mouth, even as—she slightly startled, but kept going—Valter strode up beside her, a piece of rumpled fabric clutched in his hand.

"Sorry, but I need a scent placed," he said to Varinn, thrusting the fabric toward him. "Should be quick."

And gods, of course Varinn was already nodding, his eyes easy and mild as he took Valter's proffered fabric, and held it to his nose. Inhaling slow and deep, his brow thoughtfully furrowing, as though this were his only consideration in this moment. As though he'd entirely forgotten the two naked worshippers on their knees before him, one of them desperately sucking his prick, the other still fervently pumping himself, and anointing his feet with thick drizzling white.

"It is Grisk," Varinn said slowly, his voice not even slightly wavering. "An elder orc, from the south, near the sea. I ken I have met him once or twice—Gunnar, I ken."

Valter nodded and curtly thanked him, before turning and striding off into the party again. And only then did Varinn's mild eyes drop back to Kitty and Thrain, to where neither of them had faltered their ministrations in the slightest. Just the way he'd wanted it, they both well knew, and Varinn rewarded them by settling his hands to both their heads, and sinking his claws into their hair. Watching them as they serviced him, worshipped him, readied him for whatever pleasure he might wish to grant them.

And yes, yes, Kitty could feel his sweetness pouring smoother now, seeping steady into her throat, and she carefully slipped backwards, pressing a soft, open kiss to his crown. "Would you prefer to keep using my mouth, Lord Grisk?" she shyly murmured, searching his eyes. "Or is there another hole we can offer you, instead?"

And gods, the way Varinn took a moment to consider that, coolly watching as Kitty kept kissing him, sipping on his steady oozing sweetness. "I ken you shall both need to show me your offerings, *kisa*," he murmured, as he made a lazy turn-around motion with his claw. "Tempt me, with what is mine."

Oh, hell. Kitty's eyes darted to meet Thrain's, to where he was looking just as dazed and hungry as she felt. And in a jolting flurry of movement, they'd both shifted around on their knees, now facing away from Varinn, toward the party. Both of them arching their backs toward him, showing him their bared behinds, so Varinn could view and evaluate their... offerings. And Kitty fought to ignore the sight of the various eyes watching them—some curious, some appreciative, some envious—as she felt Varinn's warm hand stroking up her flank. Tilting her up even more, so he could grasp the handle of her *rassja*, and gently draw it out, before all those watching eyes. And then he did the same to Thrain, removing his with a slick-sounding squelch, before neatly wrapping the jewels in a rag, and setting them aside.

Kitty's face was burning, now, her body trembling on her hands and knees, and she could feel the prickle of Varinn's eyes, looking, deciding, evaluating, before all these watching witnesses. And perhaps she was even arching more toward him, opening her slick, swollen-feeling body a little wider, because oh, she wanted him, needed him, needed him to choose her, to honour her—

"Good, my loves," he murmured, as his hand kept stroking, perhaps doing the same to Thrain, too. "I thank you, for honouring me thus. And thus, as your reward"—a gentle, dizzying slap to Kitty's arse—"I shall first offer your tight, pretty rump to my Aetha, *kisa*."

Oh, gods, yes, he was so good, so generous, and Kitty rapidly nodded, her moan choking in her throat. "Yes, Lord Grisk," she gasped. "Yes, please. You're so very, very kind. So good to us."

Varinn's low laugh was husky, approving, and Kitty could feel him tugging Thrain up, and onto the bench beside him. And then his warm hands drew her up and backwards, too, toward Thrain, toward... his lap. And though she was still facing forward, toward the eyes of the party, she could feel Thrain's hardness already jutting up, catching and pulsing against her. And then slowly delving its pierced, dripping head inside her, into where she was still stretched and soft from the *rassja*, from when he'd opened her before.

"Sit on him, *kisa*," Varinn murmured beside her, his hand giving another gentle slap at her arse. "Swallow my Aetha's good Grisk prick inside you."

Beneath Kitty, Thrain was gasping and groaning, his hands already on her hips, guiding her downwards. Sinking slow and careful inside her, and oh, it felt so strong, so good, filling her most secret places, anchoring her at her very core. And she and Thrain cried out together as she sank all the way, pinioned firm and safe on his lap, just as Varinn had commanded.

And yes, yes, Varinn was looking darkly, thoroughly pleased, licking his lips before leaning in to kiss both of them, tugging gently at the chain still clipped between Kitty's neck and her crease. Making her moan and flail into his mouth, and she could feel him chuckling as he drew away, and then... guided them downwards. Maneuvering Thrain onto his back on the bench, with Kitty still skewered on her back atop him, her shaky legs splayed wide.

Because oh, this was what Varinn had wanted, his legs now shifting to straddle the bench, his body settling between her thighs. While he kept watching her with warm, affectionate appreciation, his gaze lingering on her breasts, her chain, her piercing, on where she and Thrain were locked together. And on where—Kitty arched and moaned—Thrain's shaky hand had slipped down to her open, quivering heat, opening it even wider, and then slipping his fingers up inside. Catching on where she was still wearing that gold ring, hidden deep within—and then he carefully drew it out, and reached to slide it down over Varinn's poised, waiting length instead. Where it settled slick and gleaming against his base, adorning him, readying him for this, oh gods. And yes, Varinn was easing forward, lining himself up, and...

Kitty screamed as he drove inside, carving deep in one swift, staggering stroke. Filling her utterly full, jammed to the brim on both sides—and then he drew out, and did it again. And again and again and again, ploughing her smooth and steady and firm, while she and Thrain both writhed and gasped beneath him. And oh, Thrain's trembling fingers were playing with her piercing, too, wringing her cries higher, while Varinn's firm hand grasped her chain, and drew her up by the neck. Pulling her into a fierce, possessive kiss, his lips hot against hers, his tongue plunging deep into her mouth. Using all her holes at once, oh, filling her with him and his mate, while all these orcs watched, and bore witness. Marvelling, surely, at the strength and power of the god's son among them, bending two frantic worshippers to his whim, filling them with his flesh, his favour, his life.

Kitty's release flashed up in a furious flaring surge, clamping her helplessly against both Varinn and Thrain in pulse after dizzying pulse. And gods, she could feel Thrain tightening, arching, so close to the edge—and without warning, Varinn yanked free of her, and grasped Thrain's thighs, shoved them up. And then he sank deep again, burying himself inside Thrain this time, while Thrain cursed and writhed, and poured Kitty's innards full of his hot seed. And oh, Varinn was doing it too, his beautiful body arching up as he emptied himself, his eyes fluttering closed, his nostrils flaring, the ecstasy pure and bright on his flushed, worshipful face.

Kitty couldn't have said how long she hung there, shuddering and swaying with the aftershocks, with the slowly spreading relief. But at some point, she felt Varinn slipping her *rassja* back inside, and pressing a soft, approving kiss to her mouth. And then doing the same to Thrain, surely in part because he didn't want to leave a mess at a party—but also, Kitty now knew, because of the scents. Because every time the seed was stoppered like this, the scents sank deeper into Kitty and Thrain's flesh, their very selves. Marking them as Varinn's, and only his, from the inside out.

"Come, my loves," he murmured now, as he fastened Kitty's kilt back around her waist, and thrust Thrain's into his hand. "You ought to rest, ach, *kisa*? And Thrain, shall you fetch Thrandr for us?"

Yes, yes, that was exactly what Kitty needed, and she willingly accompanied Varinn and Thrain across the room, past multiple groups of revellers in similar states of enjoyment. And while Thrain headed for the nursery, Varinn guided her back into their cozy familiar bedroom. Drawing her down into bed, tucking her close against his chest, burying his face in her hair.

"Are you well, *kisa*?" he murmured, a little hoarse. "This was not... too much, ach?"

Kitty sleepily smiled and snuggled closer against him, inhaling his warm, rich scent. "Of course not," she replied, quiet. "I love honouring you, Lord Grisk. Granting you everything you deserve. Making myself yours, in every possible way."

She could feel his big body relaxing, gathering her even closer—but now it was Kitty slightly stiffening, drawing back to meet his eyes in the guttering lamplight. Seeing the instant concern in them, his head tilting, his nostrils flaring as he inhaled. "What, *kisa*?" he asked, sharper than before. "What is amiss?"

But Kitty was already smiling again, spreading her hand against the warmth of his chest. "I was just thinking about what you said to Nattfarr," she said, shyly now, "and wondering if you've thought any more about actually granting me... your son?"

Her words seemed to hover between them, perhaps too brazen, too precarious. Because after Thrandr's birth, Varinn had been very adamant about preventing another pregnancy, a demand that Efterar's magic had easily fulfilled. But it had been six months now, and the question, the possibility, had been hovering more and more at the back of Kitty's thoughts. And it distantly occurred to her that maybe Varinn had been right, and she'd needed the time to rest and relax tonight. To think, to evaluate her life and her goals, and... and maybe even to work up the courage to ask him this. To realize, perhaps, that she'd fallen into that old pattern of pretending, and that she wanted to be honest with him. To even be... selfish.

"I truly want it, Varinn," she told him, quiet but certain. "I've wanted it since—since maybe we first met. I love you, and I trust you, and I know you're a wonderful father and mate.

And I've loved being a mother, too, and it would mean so much to me"—she swallowed, held his eyes—"to create another life with you. To give us a son of your blood, who will bear your scent, and carry forth your line, and carry on your work and your goodness after you."

But oh, gods, Varinn wasn't speaking, was just looking at her like this, his eyes gone bright, strange, utterly unreadable— and at that moment, Thrain strode back into the room, holding a sleepily squirming Thrandr against his chest. "Och, what's this?" he demanded, as he slipped into bed behind Kitty, and settled Thrandr into her waiting, eager arms. "Out with it, you two. You ken I can't scent you?"

Varinn still wasn't speaking, the swallow audible in his throat, and Kitty took a shaky breath as she cradled Thrandr closer, felt him settling in to nurse against her. "I was just... asking Varinn," she finally ventured, into the silence, "if we could perhaps... start trying. For... another son."

The alertness flashed across Thrain's body all at once, and suddenly he'd jerked up in bed, beaming between her and Varinn. "Och, really?!" he demanded, his voice rising. "And did Varinn tell you he'll drag you to Efterar first thing in the morning, and lock you in here all day until it's done? We'll need more babysitting, I ken."

He was still grinning delightedly between them, and Kitty couldn't help a choked little laugh, even as she darted an uncertain glance toward Varinn's unreadable face. "Er, well," she began thickly, "I'm not exactly sure if he..."

But gods bless Thrain, because he only laughed again, and bent down to nip at Varinn's mouth. "Just struck him speechless, Kit," he murmured. "He's been dreaming about it for *weeks* now, ach, Varinn? Just waiting for you to ask, I ken."

Oh. Well. And Kitty could see Varinn's face flushing as he kissed Thrain back, as if drawing strength from him, the courage to be honest, too. And then he turned back toward Kitty, squaring his shoulders, giving her a small, wavering smile. "I should be—most honoured, *kisa*," he murmured, and oh, gods, that was a sob, choking from his throat. "Most honoured, that you yet wish for this, from—from me. Ach, I—I—"

His voice cracked, his eyes squeezing shut, as another sob choked from his throat. And then his body lurched toward her, dragging her in even closer, while Thrain clutched tightly against them, too. All of them rocking and weeping and laughing together, especially when Thrandr gurgled and popped up again, flailing his little fists with palpable excitement.

By the time they all settled again, Kitty's eyes were red and swollen, her cheeks wet, her face sore from laughing. And she was still smiling as she nuzzled into the warm safety of Varinn's chest, into the steady thud of his heartbeat within it. Into the safe, solid certainty of him, still here, still caring for her, still making her his. Her Lord Grisk, her rescuer, her mate. Her giver of home and love and life.

"New life," she sleepily murmured, with a happy little sigh against him. "Together. Tomorrow."

And his purr was softness, it was safety, it was everything Kitty had ever wanted, here beneath the warm, cozy fur. "Ach, my sweet goddess," he whispered, a caress, a prayer. "Tomorrow."

Varinn knew something was afoot the instant he stepped out of the tunnel, and into the bright, late summer sun.

His head snapped sideways, and his body straightened, his nostrils flaring, as he drew in a deep, searching breath. Drinking up the familiar, beloved scents of... his kin.

He breathed in again, combing through the scents—but yes, yes, they were all there. Thrain, Katharine, Thrandr, and Vikaell, all together at that little Skai cabin to the southeast. Together with—Varinn's brows furrowed—Timo's mates. Sune, and Cecily.

Varinn shot a searching look over his shoulder, toward where Timo was striding out of the tunnel behind him, and flashing him a bashful grin. "It is meant to be a surprise, brother," he said cheerfully, elbowing Varinn in the side. "You cannot ken how hard it is to keep secrets from you, ach? I ken I did well, to gain them half a day."

Varinn blinked, as their morning of tedious errands underground at once took on an entirely new light, and Timo grinned again, and jerked his head in the direction of the cottage. "Ought to go meet them, then," he said lightly. "See what they're up to, ach?"

Varinn half-laughed, half-growled, and slung his arm around Timo's neck, giving him an exasperated little shake. Which was much harder these days than it had once been, with Timo having finally grown into his full height, his tall, sturdy body now more than a match for Varinn's. But Timo humoured him anyway, laughing merrily as Varinn rustled his hair, and then companionably dragged him down the path.

"You have indeed bested me, son," Varinn said, with a rueful smile toward Timo's face. "And pulled your new mates into your scheme, too! Are you sure they do not mind this?"

Timo waved it away, though his cheeks instantly flushed, and the scent of his hunger filtered through the air. "Ach, you ken Cecy loves schemes," he replied offhandedly. "But I have sworn to reward them later, also."

Varinn was still smiling, though he couldn't help the wrinkle of his nose, the wry shake of his head. Timo had finally claimed Sune and Cecily as his mates a few moons before, and some days their scents on one another—loudly proclaiming all their joys together—were near enough to make Varinn gag. But he was yet delighted for his brother, deeply gladdened to scent him so sated and at peace. And he was already looking forward to the day when he would meet Timo's son, and scent the truth of his line carrying forth, just as it should.

"Ach, and no sons yet, brother," Timo said, with a too-knowing half-smile, surely having followed the thought in Varinn's scent. "I yet have no wish to be murdered by Cecy's kin, you ken. But"—his face went even redder—"last eve, Sune again told us how he wishes us to have my Grisk son first, ach? He wishes to see if he likes the son or not, before risking the need to put up with one of his own blood."

Varinn barked a disbelieving laugh—he knew Timo loved Sune, but Akva above, he would never understand Skai—and Timo flashed him another sheepish grin, and shrugged against

Varinn's arm still over his shoulder. "Ach, I ken he is just humouring me," he said, a little husky. "He knows how I feel about it, ach?"

Varinn's own smile softened, and he gave Timo's shoulder a reassuring squeeze, for ach, he well knew it, too. Knew how Timo longed for a son of his own blood to scent, just the way he himself had. And whilst Varinn adored both his perfect sons equally, and saw them both fully as his own, he'd almost felt something—healing, inside him, at his first scent of Vikaell in Katharine's womb. He'd felt peace, and hope, unlike anything he'd tasted before. He'd carried forth his father's scent, his line, for the ages to come. He'd created new life, new kin, from his own loins, from the love he'd made.

The thought quickened his steps on the path, and he stretched both arms over his head as he shot another curious, searching glance toward Timo beside him. "So shall you even give me a hint, then?" he asked lightly. "Please do not tell me my mates have tried to cook again?"

Timo laughed, clearly recalling the memorable incident in which Katharine and Thrain, in all their sweet eagerness, had decided to try cooking Varinn supper in the kitchen. The end result had stunk up the entire Grisk wing, and in his consternation, Varinn had roundly punished them both. Until both their gold-tipped rumps had been bright red with his handprints, and they'd both vowed—around large mouthfuls of his gouging prick—to never touch an oven again.

"No, you ken they know better now," Timo said, with a teasing wrinkle of his own nose toward Varinn. "And be a sport, brother, and try not to scent for too much, ach? Let them have their fun."

He was still grinning, but there was something a little deeper in his scent, something heartfelt and earnest. So Varinn nodded his agreement, and fought to ignore the urge to breathe in deeper, to seek through all the intricate, tantalizing threads of his sweet mates' scents. Scents that were easing closer with every breath, with every step toward that Skai cabin, tucked just there within the trees.

It was one of several above-ground hideouts that the Skai kept and maintained, mostly for meetings and trysts with humans, and—Varinn gave a few careful sniffs—it thankfully smelled like it had been cleaned, and aired out, too. And as they approached, he wasn't slightly surprised by the sight of Timo's slim, handsome Skai mate Sune, leaning casually against the cabin's doorframe, his arms folded over his chest. Not betraying even the slightest hint of having seen nor scented Timo, who was prowling eagerly toward him—though Varinn's inward disapproval was somewhat mollified by the way Sune instantly melted into Timo's biting kiss, the vivid scent of his hunger shuddering into the air.

"All ready?" Timo murmured at Sune, once he'd drawn back again, and Sune signed his assent before turning toward the cabin's closed door. Flinging it wide open with a sharp shove of his hand, so that—

"Happy birthday!" came the chorus of voices, and Varinn stilled, stared at the sight beyond the door. At his kin, his family, all waiting for him, dressed in bright beautiful colours, and wearing *strange hats*, and waving colourful fabric flags in the air. And they were all grinning toward him with flushed excited faces, and little Vikaell broke away from Katharine's arms, and rushed over to launch himself up into Varinn's arms instead.

"Happy bur-day, Papa!" he exclaimed, wildly waving his flag, and Varinn couldn't stop staring at him, at them—and especially at Katharine—as a hot tingling began behind his eyes, and a slow, stunned smile pulled at his mouth. And then Katharine and Thrain and Thrandr all rushed over too, flinging their arms around him at once, flooding him with the raw, wonderful truth of their scents.

"Are you surprised?" Katharine asked, beaming up at him

with her big, beautiful eyes. "You look surprised. Does he smell surprised, Thrain?"

Thrain was already nodding and chuckling into Varinn's neck, sending that hot, familiar shudder all the way through Varinn's form. "Ach, he's surprised," Thrain murmured, with deep satisfaction. "Though we might need to remind him what birthdays are, ach, Kit?"

He'd lifted his head to grin at Varinn, and Varinn was still smiling back, so broad his cheeks hurt. "Ach, I recall this," he said, for he did remember the mountain's women excitedly speaking of birthdays, and the Ka-esh had even drawn up a proposal to officially request the adoption of the decidedly human tradition at Orc Mountain. However, instead of keeping to the same detailed calendar the humans preferred—a prospect toward which many orcs, including Varinn, felt very little enthusiasm—the proposal had wisely suggested following the orcish traditions around births instead. And Varinn knew very well that he'd been birthed in the late golden days of summer, when the gods oft walked the earth, and—he glanced dazedly toward the still-open door, out at the bright, crisp sunny day—that would be around... now.

"We really just wanted an excuse to celebrate you, though," Katharine added, with another stunning smile toward Varinn's face. "And to have a little private party, just for us! Right, Thrandr?"

Thrandr had clambered up into Varinn's other arm, beaming brightly toward him, showing off his missing front tooth. "Ach, Papa," he said decisively. "Party just for us, with no one to de-tract you, or take you away from us!"

Varinn's smile toward him felt so fond, and deeply contrite, too—but Thrain had already scented it, nipping lightly at his neck. "No guilt or martyrdom allowed on your birthday, Varinn," he said firmly. "We all ken how important your work is, ach? But we just wanted you to ourselves for a day, is all."

Thrandr nodded his agreement, still beaming at Varinn's

face, and Varinn drew him closer, pressing a fervent kiss to the top of his messy, sweet-scented head, and then to Vikaell's, too. And then to Katharine's, and Thrain's, and ach, he was so blessed, he had so many great and priceless gifts, and—his nostrils flared, before he again shut the thought away—he was one moment, one deep breath, away from weeping.

"I thank you, my loves," he croaked at them, blinking hard. "This was—so thoughtful of you. So kind."

He angled his weepy smile over his shoulder toward Timo, too, who was grinning back, and looking decidedly pleased with himself. And then—Varinn blinked as another half-registered scent emerged—Timo waved his other mate Cecily in, too. And she was carrying a gigantic basket, one that wafted the strong, succulent scents of roasted poultry, and fresh-baked bread, and—Varinn eagerly sniffed—his favourite cakes from the kitchen.

"Happy birthday, brother!" Cecily gaily said, as she set the basket down on the cabin's small table with a flourish, and tossed her long blonde hair over her shoulder. "Enjoy your meal, ach? And we'll be waiting nearby, so when you're ready"—she waggled her brows at them—"we'll take the boys home for the rest of the afternoon, won't we? We'll hunt Timo all the way there, and we'll have so much fun, ach?"

Thrandr was excitedly bouncing in Varinn's arms, whilst Vikaell—who was always far more considered than Thrandr—shyly eyed his older brother, and then gave a careful little nod. And Varinn still couldn't stop smiling, at his sons, his mates, at Timo, at Cecily and Sune, at all the great, great gifts he'd been given. His *birthday*.

"I thank you all," he said again, though it sounded so weak, so ineffectual, his eyes still blinking back the wetness pooling behind them. "This was—so good of you. Ach."

They all smiled back at him, a flood of warmth and kindness swarming his senses at once, and with a cheery wave, Timo headed out the door, pulling Sune and Cecily after him.

Leaving Varinn alone with his mates and sons, and the basket of delicious-smelling food.

Katharine was already tugging him toward the table, and Varinn willingly complied, sinking into a sturdy wooden chair, and drawing both his sons closer into his lap. "So you both helped to keep this secret, also?" he asked them, with a teasing little smile. "Have my Grisk sons morphed into Skai, whilst I was off working this morn?"

Thrandr gleefully cackled, shaking his head, whilst Vikaell eyed Varinn with grave seriousness. "We never turn Skai, Papa," he replied, wrinkling his broad little nose. "Too stinky, you ken."

Varinn half-laughed, half-winced, but Thrain was cackling too, and bending down to nibble at Vikaell's pointed ear. "Don't let them hear you say it, though, son," he said, with a wink toward Varinn. "That's not good Speaker's Guard behaviour, ach?"

Vikaell gave a solemn little nod, and Varinn couldn't help drawing him even closer, again inhaling the familiar, beloved scent of his little head, with its neat little black braid. From his earliest days, Vikaell had been unnervingly like Varinn in almost every way, except—to Varinn's genuine delight—for his rare, stunningly Aetha smile. And Vikaell had long ago informed them all, with his usual steady decisiveness, that he was going to be a Speaker's Guard like Papa when he grew up, and he would keep Rakfi from doing foolish things like locking himself in the crypt. Which, in fact, Rakfi had already managed to do on three separate occasions, to the point where Varinn had personally paid the Ka-esh to disable the latches on the doors, for everyone's sake.

"So not only did our clever sons help keep it secret," Katharine was saying now, smiling fondly toward Vikaell, "but they also helped us choose what food to bring for you! So we have"—she began drawing out neatly folded packets from the basket—"roasted duck and bread, together with sweet-cakes, and baked apples, and berry cobbler, and three kinds of pudding!"

Varinn's mouth fell open at the sight of it all, his laugh again shaking through his chest. Leave it to his sweet sons to choose mostly desserts for his birthday dinner, and he grinned at them both, and drew them even closer. "Ach, these are indeed all my favourites, my loves," he told them, as firmly as he could. "This was such a good surprise, ach?"

His sons delightedly beamed back toward him, and soon they were all happily eating the delicious meal together. Whilst Thrandr and Vikaell regaled Varinn with all the devious ways they'd worked to keep the party secret from him, and—his brows rose—how they'd apparently brought him gifts, too.

"Ach, you brought gifts?" Varinn echoed, casting a searching glance toward Katharine and Thrain—but they were both warmly nodding, and Thrandr promptly hopped off Varinn's lap, and rushed over to pull out a large steel box from under the bed. And when he snapped it open, Varinn could instantly scent leather and new gold, the gold laced with Thrain's beloved scent, and Thrandr's, too.

Thrandr had carefully picked up the gold item from the box, his bright eyes dropping as he tripped back over toward Varinn. "For you, Papa," he said, with a shy, hopeful half-smile—a smile that, for an instant, reminded Varinn so powerfully of Thrain that it swallowed his breath. "Me and Thapa made it together in the forge, ach?"

He'd thrust out his little hands toward Varinn, opening his fingers wide, and Varinn blinked down at the item inside. At the... figure, carved entirely out of gold. It was small and slightly misshapen, but decidedly orcish in form, and it had been polished to a bright, beautiful shine. Suggesting many hours of hard work upon it, and Varinn's eyes were prickling again as he gently picked it up, and held it with true reverence in his fingers.

"This is stunning, Thrandr," he murmured, hushed, as his

eyes caught, held, on the familiar way the figure held out his arms. "It is our father Lord Grisk, is it not?"

"Yes!" Thrandr excitedly exclaimed, punching his little fist into the air, and flashing a triumphant smile toward Vikaell. "I told you it looks just like Lord Grisk, Vika! I *told* you!"

Vikaell was wearing a disapproving little pout, suggesting very clearly the exchange that had led to this, and Varinn gave a reassuring pat to Vikaell's little head, even as he kept smiling toward Thrandr. "But it is clear that this is Thrandr's own vision of our father, also," he said. "Which is just what a true artist should do, ach? And this makes it all the more yours, son. All the more precious to me."

Thrandr's little grin kept splitting his face, the pure scent of his utter delight careening through the air, and Varinn inhaled it slow and deep, treasured its truth on his tongue. At least, until a twinge of quiet uncertainty cut into it, and Varinn instantly glanced down toward Vikaell, who was biting his lip, and blinking helplessly over toward Katharine.

"And Vika chose a gift for you at the shop, Varinn," Katharine said now, with an encouraging smile toward Vikaell's uncertain face. "You put a lot of thought into it, didn't you, love? And used your own credits toward it?"

Vikaell gravely nodded, but then cast a brief, chagrined look up toward Varinn's face. "But I did not—make it, Papa," he confessed, his little mouth quivering. "So it is not—*precious*. Mayhap if you wait until later, I shall go seek to make a better gift, ach?"

Varinn could taste the sudden urgent alarm from both Katharine and Thrain, silently shouting on his tongue—but he was already drawing Vikaell's stiff little body closer into his arms, squeezing him as tightly as he dared. "Ach, no, son," he said, husky, into Vikaell's hair. "Any gift from you shall be precious to me, also. Most of all if you have put your own careful thought and coin into this. Do you ken, I have never once made a gift for Mama or Thapa myself? Ach, I have oft asked Thapa to make them for me! But I have meant all my gifts to them with all my heart, just the same."

He could feel Vikaell slightly relaxing, his wary eyes glancing toward Katharine and Thrain. Toward where they were both wearing so many of Varinn's jewels, Katharine with multiple piercings in her ears, and a lovely little ring in her nose, along with her bracelets and rings and *thyrja*. Whilst Thrain now sported gold all the way up both ears, and in his lip, as well as his nose. And even—in a deeply rewarding recent development—his tongue.

Vikaell's little body had relaxed a little more, and he gave a tentative little nod before sliding off Varinn's lap, and heading for the steel box. Where he drew out a shining, square leather item, and then brought it back to Varinn, setting it carefully in his lap.

"It is a pouch, to tie to your belt or your kilt, whilst you work," he said shyly. "I have oft seen that you do not have an easy way to carry small goods, such as coin or gems. So mayhap this shall help?"

The uncertainty again glimmered in his eyes as he glanced at Varinn's face, but Varinn's delight was already vivid and close in his own scent, in his broadly grinning mouth. "Ach, this is so thoughtful, son!" he said. "And look how well made it is! I shall have much use for this, and shall be most pleased to wear it every day. It shall grant me great joy to always scent your gift upon me whilst I am away from you, ach?"

Vikaell's relief studded through his scent, flashing his breathtaking little Aetha smile across his mouth, and Varinn again drew him close, and yanked Thrandr over, too. Swaying back and forth with them both, as the joy and affection choked tightly at his throat. "Thank you, my sons," he whispered. "You are both such a great gift to me."

He'd cast a wavering smile over toward Katharine and Thrain, and in return they both rushed over too, throwing their arms around them. Their shared relief almost overpowering in

Varinn's scent, and Thrain nipped softly at his ear, let his clever tongue linger and caress. "Too good, Varinn," he breathed, perhaps too low for anyone but him to hear. "As always."

Varinn inhaled deep, his head reflexively tilting into Thrain's mouth—until Thrain huffed a reluctant laugh, and drew away. "Later," he murmured, with a brief, purposeful sweep of that pierced tongue against his lips. "But next, we have games! Och, my sons?"

Thrandr and Vikaell both perked up at once, Thrandr loudly squealing with delight, and soon Varinn was caught in a whirlwind of orcling-led games and challenges, many of them slightly incomprehensible, but still thoroughly amusing, all the same. And as was so oft the case, the games inevitably devolved into an extended bout of wrestling on the fur rugs, both orclings shrieking and howling with sheer, unfettered delight, whilst Katharine watched and laughed.

But finally Vikaell betrayed a wide, squeaky little yawn, and after snatching him bodily up into his arms, Thrain strode for the door, signalling out beyond it. And soon Timo reappeared, looking rather dishevelled, and reeking of scents Varinn didn't want to examine too closely—but he was grinning at Thrandr and Vikaell, and waving them toward the door. "Now come home with us, little brothers," he said, "whilst your parents rest here for a spell. Do you ken you can hunt me all the way there?"

Thrandr was already excitedly whooping again, and after a round of tight hugs and farewells—and promises from Varinn and Thrain to scent their sons as they went, and see them again before nightfall—the little group traipsed off into the sunlight. Leaving Varinn smiling fondly at the closed door, already feeling the bittersweet loss of them, but also—he glanced at Katharine and Thrain—longing for this. With a craving that had grown almost overpowering, now, coiling in his belly, hardening his prick beneath his kilt.

And ach, the way Katharine and Thrain were both looking

back at him, Thrain already stalking closer, ducking his head into his neck. "Finally," he murmured, as he began unbuckling Varinn's kilt with swift, familiar fingers. "Time for your other gifts, ach?"

Varinn's inhale caught, shuddered with the fullness of Thrain's dark, determined hunger, and ach, Katharine was here too, her sweet, succulent eagerness teasing into Varinn's nostrils. "So come relax, Lord Grisk," she murmured, as she clasped his hand in hers, and tugged him toward the bed. "And allow us to honour you."

Varinn certainly wasn't about to argue, and he willingly allowed his mates to finish undressing him, and guide him down onto the large, fur-covered bed. So he was seated on the edge of it, and watching with rising appreciation as Thrain yanked off his own kilt, whilst Katharine knelt on the fur beside the bed, drawing out another steel box from beneath it.

"So first," she said shyly, "we have a new gift for you. For us."

She opened the box, again filling the air with the sweet scent of newly forged gold, and Thrain plucked out the cloth-wrapped item inside, and passed it into Varinn's hand. And when Varinn carefully unwrapped it, he found himself holding a heavy, shining, stunning new *rassja*. One that lacked the usual beaded shape, and was instead just a single slab of smooth curving gold—which was perhaps for the best, because it was quite possibly the largest one he had ever seen. Larger, even, than the last one he'd had Thrain make, and Thrain's scent was all over this one, too—but not in that way. Not yet.

Varinn's hunger hitched and heated, but his smile at Thrain was curious, and a little uncertain, too. "It is beautiful work, *krútt*, as always," he said, his voice hushed. "I thank you, for such a great gift. But—are you sure you wish to wear it? Are you sure you... can?"

He'd cast a doubtful, but decidedly greedy, glance toward Thrain's arse, because ach, how he would look, taking this inside him, wearing it, for Varinn—and Thrain flashed him a smug, satisfied grin in return, before bending down to nip at Varinn's mouth. "You'll have to find out, won't you?" he murmured back. "You wanna watch me try, Lord Grisk? Watch me work to take your big, fat, golden birthday cock inside me?"

Ach, Varinn did, and his groan vibrated through his chest, all the way down to his throbbing, rock-hard prick. Whilst Thrain and Katharine both merrily laughed, and Thrain promptly dropped to his hands and knees on the fur rug at Varinn's feet. Giving him a clear, mouthwatering view of his firm gorgeous arse, of how his hole was already soft and open. Suggesting that he'd already been working toward this, readying himself for this, and Varinn's hunger lurched higher, together with a stark, settled satisfaction. A satisfaction that only deepened as Katharine finished undressing too, baring her small, lovely body for Varinn's roving eyes.

And after bearing him two hale, healthy sons now, Katharine's body was softer and plumper than it had once been—but it had only served to ripen her rare beauty, and deepen the richness of her scent. And the same dark, ravenous part of Varinn that wanted to split Thrain wide open around him also craved this, this truth of his sweet mate's form forever altered for him, at his pleasure, and his command. She'd grown and birthed him two sons, granted him new life—and she'd thus given him the ultimate power, the ultimate gifts. Far beyond anything she'd ever granted any of those foul men before him, and it was only natural that such gifts would mark her, and make her even softer, even sweeter, even richer than before. She was such a jewel, such a prize, and she was *his*.

"You are so stunning, my sweet *kisa*," Varinn murmured, as his eyes next wandered to his gold rings embedded in her dusky nipples, and her navel, and her groin. "So lovely to see and scent, ach?"

Katharine's cheeks prettily flushed, the scent of her arousal swelling in the air, together with an even closer scent of—ach.

And Varinn swallowed over the lump in his throat, and again held his breath, smiled tenderly toward her, even as he raised his brows, and made a meaningful turn-around motion with his claw.

She instantly obeyed, as she always did, and Varinn's hunger flared even higher at the sight of his little gold *rassja* already embedded between her arse-cheeks, where it belonged. She oft wore it these days—she'd shyly told him that she just liked having the reminder of him there—and ach, what it still did to him, knowing that his sweet, perfect woman longed so deeply for his gold, and his filling. Just like—his gaze belatedly dropped back to Thrain, still on his hands and knees before him—his perfect orc mate did, too.

"And you are so stunning also, *krútt*," he murmured approvingly, as he shifted a little forward, ran his appreciative hand up the length of Thrain's open crease. "You are sure you are ready for this?"

He'd cast another doubtful, hungry glance down at the massive gold weight in his palm—Akva above, it was near as thick around as his forearm—but Thrain fervently nodded, and Katharine was striding over too, and kneeling sweetly beside Thrain on the fur. "Perhaps you can watch as I help further prepare him, my lord?" she asked Varinn, eyeing him beneath her long lashes. "And will you be so kind as to share your seed with us, as well?"

Ach. Varinn swallowed his reflexive groan, and gave a permissive wave of his hand toward his bared prick. Which was already fully swollen, and liberally leaking onto his belly, and he almost groaned again at the sight of Katharine's little tongue licking her lips, as her eager little hands came up to touch him. One of them already stroking his shaft with sweet, soft eagerness, whilst her other hand cupped under his slit, catching his oozing seed in her palm.

It still stole his breath to watch it, to feel it, to know the unmatched, unalloyed power in it. To just sit there, rock-hard and riveted, whilst his beautiful, sweet-scented, gold-studded woman pumped him, milked out his good seed, and then—he groaned aloud this time—carefully brought it to Thrain's open arse, and began slicking him with it. Sliding it liberally into his crease, and then even slipping those clever, shameless little fingers deep into it. First two fingers, and now three, and even four, easing in and out of his *krútt*'s soft, open arse without the slightest hesitation, the sounds slippery and squelching. Whilst beneath her ministrations, Thrain brazenly moaned and arched higher, opening wider, his proud, satisfied craving wheeling through the air. Knowing very well he was taking nearly his woman's whole hand, and knowing how much Varinn liked that, how deeply he approved.

And ach, ach, Katharine was already returning to Varinn, pumping him, collecting more of his good fresh seed, and again slicking it inside their mate. Who was steadily groaning, now, his arse reflexively bucking against Katharine's delving fingers, as the scent of his release surged closer—and Varinn chuckled as he reluctantly drew away Katharine's hand, and guided it back to the huge *rassja* he was still holding.

His *kisa* instantly complied, meeting his eyes with conspiratorial warmth as she turned her attention to slicking up the *rassja*, coating its massive gleaming bulk all over with Varinn's slick, heavy-scented seed. Until it was fully drenched, dripping of him, and ready to fill his mate's waiting, wide-open arse.

Varinn drew in a shaky breath, gave a brief flutter of his fingers toward Thrain—and again, Katharine easily followed the order, taking the *rassja* fully in hand, and finally settling its gleaming tip to Thrain's slack, open hole. To where Thrain gasped and arched higher, his body shuddering all over, but ach, he was already taking the *rassja*'s narrow tip, easily swallowing it inside. And then more, and more, the gleaming gold smoothly filling him, disappearing into his spasming heat—until it slowed, and finally stopped. Buried halfway inside, now, with Thrain's rim already stretched tight around it, and Varinn greedily watched as Katharine and Thrain began working it together, nudging it in and out, sinking it a little deeper every time. And Katharine had reached over to pump Varinn a little more, oozing more seed into her slick fingers, lavishing it onto Thrain's stretched hole, onto the gold opening it wide.

"Good, *krútt*," Varinn heard himself say, husky and low. "You are so pretty, when you bare yourself, and seek to take my gold inside you. When you open up wider for me than you ever have before."

Thrain choked and nodded, the gold slipping even deeper, and Varinn kept watching, enthralled, as they both kept working it, as the sweat began beading on Thrain's back, and on Katharine's brow, too. Betraying the true effort they were putting in for him, but ach, it was working, the gold sinking deeper, stretching out Thrain's taut rim even wider around it. Indeed perhaps larger than Varinn had ever seen it, and he hissed aloud as it opened wider, wider, wider...

"Good," he growled, as his hand dropped to Katharine's, closing over it, increasing the pressure, guiding the gold even deeper. "You shall take my good birthday gold all the way inside you, ach, *krútt*? You shall open for me, and swallow it whole for me?"

Thrain writhed and hissed and nodded, his frantic determination soaring through the air, his rim stretched so tight it was almost translucent, nearly enough to tear—but ach, ach, there it went. The bulkiest part of the *rassja* finally disappearing, slipping inside, whilst Thrain shuddered and shouted, his head thrown back. But it was done, it was jammed all the way within him, buried to the hilt. Locking all that gold deep inside him, surely more than he'd ever taken before. And Varinn could scarcely breathe around the pride and the hunger and the sudden, staggering gratefulness. For his mate to have granted him this, granted him such a gift—

And ach, for his mate to now carefully shift up, turning around, showing Varinn his flushed, sweaty face, his stunning, satisfied smile. And then to promptly bend down, with his full, beautifully adorned arse still jutting up, so he could kiss eager and ravenous at Varinn's bare foot.

"Ach," Varinn groaned, his head tipping back, as Thrain huffed a smug, husky laugh against his foot. And now Katharine was there too, kissing Varinn's other foot, before—he moaned again, his lashes fluttering—she pulled over a cloth, and a small basin. So she could begin washing him, Akva above, wash his feet and serve him, whilst Thrain kept licking and lavishing him, sending shudders of heated satisfaction all through Varinn's form.

It was truly like a dream, like a joy that never stopped unfolding, especially once they guided him back to lie on the bed, so that they both might kneel over him and worship him at once. Not only washing him and kissing him all over, but then coating him with his favourite scented oil, and rubbing it in with firm, eager fingers. Until he felt so languid and relaxed that he could scarcely move, even when Thrain rolled him onto his side, and finally, finally began kissing at his swollen, leaking prick. Whilst Katharine eased behind him, shifting low, so she could—Varinn's groan shuddered, deep in his chest—slip her little tongue deep between his arse-cheeks.

He groaned again and propped his leg up, greedily opening wider for her, because Nattfarr had been entirely accurate when he'd first spoken to Varinn of this, so many years before. Of the utterly unspeakable joy in it, in having a clever little human tongue blatantly seeking into one's arse, spiking wild streaks of bliss out from one's deepest core. Not to mention the brazen, blazing power it bore, the visceral, unspeakable command. Not only in having Katharine's sweet little human lips latched to his arse, drinking up his most vivid, most fundamental flavours—but also, afterwards, the way she would walk about scenting of it, of him. And Varinn had found himself taking a deep, distinct pride in it, in the undeniable truth that his woman was one of very few in the mountain who scented thus—a number that included Ella, and Grein's mate Stasia. Showing their great Grisk grounding, their pure shamelessness in their pleasure, and their incomparable devotion to their mates.

Varinn couldn't have said how long he revelled in it, gloried in it, holding off his release as long as he could. But his mates' hot wonderful mouths were just too sweet, and he could feel the ever-increasing pressure of his gradually growing load in his bollocks, almost about to burst into Thrain's glorious sucking throat—and finally he reluctantly nudged Thrain backwards, and clasped his hand on Katharine's head behind him, too. "I thank you, my loves," he croaked. "But mayhap you shall now trade places, ach? Make us ready for—"

He couldn't finish, his breath catching in his throat—but his mates both groaned in unison, and their thrumming hunger surged even higher in the air, in Varinn's deeply inhaling breath. And now it was Katharine's small, soft body easing around to face him, pressing eagerly against his front, whilst Thrain shifted around to lie behind him. His arm gripping tightly around Varinn's waist, as his hard, dripping prick ground against Varinn's bare arse.

But Varinn had already pressed closer into it, and even reached around to grasp at it, settling it into place against him as Thrain helplessly bucked and moaned, the stunned disbelief spattering across his scent. For ach, this had taken some getting used to, and in his misplaced selfish pride, Varinn had admittedly spurned it, for far too long. But he'd finally overcome his foolishness, and faced the truth that it brought great pleasure, for him and Thrain both. And that there was also a deep, transcendent power in it, in wielding his mate's perfect Aetha prick as he pleased, consuming it whole into his own body, making his seed his own. Claiming Thrain as his, in every possible way.

And also—Varinn hissed as Thrain plunged in, sinking deep in one jerky, greedy stroke—it was in this, and mayhap only this, that he could truly let his ravenous Aetha rut feral and free, thrusting and thrashing and slamming to his wild heart's content. His Aetha couldn't hurt him the way he could hurt Katharine, not even close, and Varinn truly didn't care if he ended up bloody or bruised afterwards. Not with the way it tasted on Thrain, the way his hunger soared and flew like it did with nothing else, the way the relieved, easy contentment would shimmer around him afterwards for days, or even weeks.

"So good, Varinn," Thrain was already gasping, choked and helpless behind him, as his hips plunged in faster, sending Varinn jerking with every thrust, scattering even more blazing heat through his body. "So—fucking—*good*. Och. *Och.*"

A hoarse, gasping chuckle escaped Varinn's mouth, and his hungry eyes found Katharine's, as his greedy hands drew her closer. Wanting her, needing her against him, around him, the yearning so desperate he was almost weeping—and ach, bless his sweet goddess, she was here, just as eager and frantic as he felt, as his magnificent Aetha felt, still driving away behind him. And Varinn shouted, and mayhap even sobbed, as his huge, dripping, distended prick finally sank into her slick, hot, eagerly pulsing clutch, gripping around him with perfect, aching intensity.

"Ach, *kisa*," he moaned, scrabbling to draw her closer, as his hips began bucking, all on their own. Needing to be deeper, needing to part her around him, to gouge himself as far as he could possibly go. Needing to feel the perfect, dizzying sensation of his weeping, spurting slit kissing up against her, rutting against that soft, waiting head of her womb. Urging it to relax, to open, to seep its own rich seed back toward him. The seed that reeked so powerfully of readiness, now, of ripeness, and Varinn groaned and sobbed and shook as he rutted harder, kissed it deeper.

"Open for me, *kisa*," he gasped, without even hearing it. "Open up wide for me, for my good Grisk seed. Drink me up into you, milk me dry for you, make us a—"

He couldn't finish, couldn't, but his prick was there, there, so close, so deep—and Thrain's grinding hips were helping now too, pushing him even closer, helping him open Katharine wider, perfect, perfect. "Make us a son, Varinn," Thrain gasped, lost, helpless, into Varinn's ear. "Give our mate your good fat load, give her all that good Grisk seed, spray it up from your full bollocks deep into her womb. Until she blooms for you, ripens for you, until she bursts with your scent. Your son. Your *life*."

And ach, ach, ach, Varinn was bucking, breaking, obeying—and his seed surged, sprayed, spurted out so hard it was pain. It was pain, and pleasure, and pure, devastating ecstasy, reeking of power and triumph—triumph that only wailed higher at the truth of his *kisa* breaking, too, her bliss shuddering her all over, milking him dry in hard gripping flares of pleasure. Milking his seed deeper inside her, flooding it into her, and ach, now Thrain was flooding out, too. Flailing and thrashing and shouting behind him, pouring Varinn's innards full of him, as his teeth sank hard into Varinn's neck.

And ach, there was no truth like this, no power like this, and somehow Varinn's desperate gasping mouth had found Katharine's neck, too. His bite clamping messy and uneven, entirely unlike his usual careful precision, but bless his goddess, she only moaned and shuddered even closer as her sweet, rich lifeblood filled his mouth. Her pure, dizzying euphoria whirling into Varinn's breath alongside it, whipping up his own greed, his own furious, unbearable rapture. And for a bright, careening instant, he was certain this was what the gods felt like, this was heaven, it was glory and wonder and unspeakable joy brought to earth, dwelling within his breast, his breath, his heart. Bringing forth warmth, and hope, and... life.

Life.

Varinn's ravenous swallowing mouth on Katharine's neck had faltered, his teeth trembling against her skin—and suddenly, somehow, his breath escaped in a surge of raw, ragged sobs. Sobs that tore through his chest, his throat, as he floundered backwards, and found Katharine's familiar, beautiful face. Catching it in his hands, cradling it in his tingling fingers, as he frantically searched her own bright, weeping eyes.

"You are—sure, *kisa*," he choked. "B-both of you."

He'd darted a wild-eyed look at Thrain, too, who had shoved up a little behind him, wiping at his own wet eyes, even as his pierced tongue swept at his red lips. "Ach, we're sure, Varinn," he murmured, though his voice hitched. "We've all spoken of it, haven't we? You can't be *that* surprised."

His expression was so adoring, but perhaps fondly amused, too, and it took a concerted effort for Varinn to find words, to find the means to speak. To even think, beyond the shuddering wondrous truths, filling his scent stronger with every jolting breath. A son. A son. *Life*.

"Ach, I ken," he somehow replied, around another shaky, reverent inhale. "But we had not—settled this. Not for certain. Not with—Efterar. And we had not spoken of our son being—"

Mine, he wanted to say, but even the thought had set him weeping again, the tears streaking down his cheeks. His. Their son would be his. A second Thjoth son, to carry on his line, and bind forward his fathers' scents. And the scent would be twice as strong, the line twice as strong, and it couldn't be truth, it couldn't be—but Katharine was nodding and smiling tearfully toward him, whilst Thrain gave a familiar, fundamentally reassuring nibble to his neck.

"Och, your scent, Varinn," Thrain murmured, the affection hitching into his scent. "But of course he was going to come from your seed, ach? We ken how much it means to you. We ken how happy you've been, since Vika was born."

Varinn twitched and winced, for he'd been truly overjoyed with Thrandr's birth, also—but that was another nip at his neck, harder this time. "Och, we ken you love them both," Thrain continued, harder, "and if it ever scented that you didn't"—another nip—"mayhap I'd feel differently about it, ach? It wasn't your *love* that changed with Vika. Just your own—peace around it all, mayhap. How calm and settled you've been. Can't even remember the last time I scented you vexed or annoyed, ach? And"—his nip came with a husky laugh this time—"it was after Vika that you settled down about *this*, too."

His hips had bucked brazenly against Varinn's arse, shifting his prick inside him, and Varinn choked a weepy laugh, glancing back to where Katharine was smiling tearfully at him, too. "We both wanted it, Varinn," she said softly. "I've loved being a mother, and you've been such a wonderful and generous father—you and Thrain both. And Efterar and Gwyn both confirmed that I'm healthy, and that this is a good time, especially now that Vika's been fully weaned. And in truth, I've been finding"—her face prettily flushed—"I miss having a baby. I've been wanting you to give me another one."

Her expression had gone a little defiant, now, her bottom lip adorably pouting, and Varinn felt his fond chuckle vibrating his chest, his arm drawing his sweet mate even closer. Whilst behind him, Thrain was still nuzzling his neck, his breath inhaling, his contentment twining deeper into the air around them. "And also," he murmured, "I don't know about you two, but I don't think I can handle another Aetha yet. Poor Vika would drive himself ragged trying to keep them all in line, ach?"

The rueful affection was bright and clear in his scent, echoing the truth behind his words, and Varinn choked another shaky, relieved chuckle as he found Thrain's hand, and tugged him a little closer. To which Thrain instantly complied, wrapping both his long arms around Katharine and Varinn both. "Also," he continued, with satisfaction, "it was a good birthday present, ach? A good surprise?"

Varinn nodded, though he winced again, too—for despite his best attempts to ignore it, he'd still smelled it. Still scented that new, succulent richness—that hope—on his sweet ripe woman, the instant they'd opened the cabin door. And all throughout the party, his hunger and his longing had kept rising, until it had felt like he'd been vibrating with it, thrumming with the inviolable promise of it. A son. Of his own blood, his own seed, his own scent.

And as he was breathing it in again, filtering it in slow and reverent, Katharine's scent—shifted. Changed. Only a touch, a twinge, but enough to snap Varinn's body to utter stillness, his nostrils flaring, his breath juddering in his throat. And then he flailed downwards over her, dragging Thrain with him, even keeping Thrain's prick clamped inside him, so they could kneel together over their mate's belly, and scent it together. Scent the staggering, miraculous truth of Varinn's seed finding Katharine's, and... fusing. Twining together, somehow, strand by strand, in some great magic from the gods, to create something... else. Something that scented like Varinn, like Katharine, like Vikaell—but also entirely new. His son. His *son*.

Varinn's sobs again tore from his throat as the scent of it filled his breath, his soul. Spreading out wide and warm all through him, settling him heavier on the furs, his lips reverently kissing Katharine's silky-soft skin. As his eyes again found hers, holding with true, overpowering gratefulness, with genuine, heartfelt awe. His woman, his mate, his sweet, generous, perfect Grisk goddess, was granting him another son. Making life with him, together. And with their wild, wise, perfect Aetha, who had brought them all together in the first place.

And if his Aetha was growing hard in his arse again, and giving an eager, experimental little thrust against it, Varinn could only seem to smile and gasp, and arch back to meet it.

Welcoming his mate's good strong Aetha prick, his deep furious ploughing, meant only for him. A true gift, too, especially when Thrain's strong, capable hands guided Varinn upwards again, settling his own already-seeping prick back against Katharine's dripping open heat. And Varinn moaned as he sank home again, as his seed sloshed out around his plunging prick, shouted of the truth he'd made. The life.

It was again pleasure unlike any other, ringing and resounding between them, deepening in Varinn's breath, in the fundamental peace enfolding his heart. And as he buried himself deep in his sweet goddess, meeting her again and again, it was almost a prayer of thankfulness, of worship, for all the great, great gifts he'd been granted. His kin. His calling. His sons. His birthday. His life.

It was all he'd ever wanted, all he'd ever longed for, his prayers multiplied into blessings, into the crown of his own bright glory. And he came like a god himself, caught between his two worthy worshippers, whilst the whole world screamed his name.

~

THE END

~

THANKS FOR READING!

Thank you so much for joining me for this epic adventure among the Grisk! I truly loved writing this one, and finally giving our Grisk Disaster Trio their happy ending. I really hope you enjoyed the ride too!

I also wanted to share a little about what I've learned writing this book, especially around Thrain's substance use. I had the privilege of hearing from multiple readers who had personal experience with substance use disorder (including several professionals in the field), and their stories were so humbling, inspiring, and enlightening. Through them, I learned that despite what popular media tells us, recovery IS possible, and it happens far more often than we think. Not only that, but reframing the ways we think and talk about substance use can make a real, tangible difference in actually encouraging people to seek treatment.

So! Throughout this book, I really wanted to portray a positive and hopeful recovery experience, one that highlights the factors proven to help people most. This includes access to support from loved ones (and employers), reliable and affordable medical help, accountability partners, food and housing, and financial support. Throughout the book, Thrain also has help avoiding triggers, seeking out new hobbies and habits and passions, working through the inevitable (normal!) relapses, and beginning to face the trauma and PTSD that his substance use was helping him cope with. In an ideal world, this kind of comprehensive support would be available to everyone who needs it, and I truly hope that we as a culture can keep moving away from all the judgement and shame around substance use, and shift our focus to uplifting the people who need our help.

Now, what's next for Orc Sworn? I am still LOVING writing these books, and I'm definitely keen to return to the Ka-esh clan... and the Skai and Bautul too! I think Filak will definitely give us some top-tier Ka-esh drama, and Killik and Ulfarr still have a LOT of unfinished business to tie up too, ha. If you have thoughts, I'd love to hear them at my Facebook group, on my Discord server, or on my Patreon! (You can find them all linked on my website at finleyfenn.com!)

Also, if you'd like to spend even more time with these characters, you can also find a bonus prologue for this book on my mailing list at finleyfenn.com! It tells the tale of a certain spicy, long-ago adventure between Varinn and Thrain in the crypt... it was so much fun to finally write this scene! And for even more bonus chapters from Varinn's point of view throughout this book, please check out my Patreon!

Thank you again for joining me on this adventure! Your support truly means so much to me, and I'm just so grateful to you. Until next time, ach? :)

ACKNOWLEDGMENTS

Once again, I'm eternally grateful to my unbelievably awesome community of readers, supporters, and friends. Your generosity and enthusiasm is just such a gift, and truly makes it possible for me to keep writing these books. Thank you!

I especially want to thank the advance readers, proofreaders, sensitivity readers, and subject matter specialists who supported this book: Amy F., Amy G., Aquila Editing, Ari, Carlotta Hughes, Cookie, Erin, Jane Mwaniki, Jen M., Jen R., Judi S., Kahaula, Lauren Mauchley, Lexi K. Jordan, Miranda Sapphire, MK, Otto, Serena, Stacy, West Dente-Ferguson, and Þórey H. And of course, I remain forever thankful to Goddess Ruby Dixon, whose guidance and wisdom has just been such a true blessing to me.

I'm also extremely grateful to all the readers and friends who took the time to share their substance use insights with me, including Angie C., Carla, Erin, Lauren, Molly, Otto, S.C., and Vio. And special thanks to the substance use professionals who gave me their detailed and immensely helpful guidance: Kass O'Shire and Keely Adams, LMSW, CAADC.

I also want to mention just a few of the friends who continue to go above and beyond to support me and the Orc Sworn community. My deepest gratitude to my own wise Bautul Enforcer Marykate, for managing my day-to-day life and keeping everything running; to the fabulous Amy and Elizabeth, for their invaluable support on my Discord server; to Erin, fearless leader of the Skai Mafia PR team, for all the delightful art and encouragement; to Morning Dove for all her generous insights and beautiful tales; to Coco for the mountain of gorgeous artwork; to EJ and the Skai sisters for the Tales from the Orc Den podcast (it's SO much fun!); to Katie at Romantically Inclined Reviews for the ongoing and hilarious support; to narrator extraordinaire Shane East and my publishers at Podium Audio for the awesome Orc Sworn audiobooks (this one is on the way soon!); and to the many incredible artists and author friends who have so kindly shared their brilliance with me.

I also want to say a special thank you to all the readers who have supported me on my new Patreon over this past year. I cannot overstate the genuine difference your generosity has made in my life, and on my ability to focus on writing these books. Without you, this book would have been multiple months later coming to you, and I am just so, so grateful for your kindness and support. Thank you.

And finally, as always, my most heartfelt gratitude to my own generous Lord Orc, who always takes such good care of his needy Grisk wife. You honour me, my lord.

ALSO BY FINLEY FENN

THE HEIRESS AND THE ORC

Once, he was her dearest friend... but now he's a brutal, terrifying monster.

In a world of recently warring orcs and men, Ella Riddell is determined to ignore it all. She's the wealthiest heiress in the realm—and soon, she's to wed a lord, and become a real lady.

Until the night her engagement-party ends in utter *disaster*, and Ella runs for the forest—**and straight into the powerful arms of a hulking, deadly orc.**

And it's not just any orc. It's *Natt*. The orc Ella made a secret, foolish pledge to, many years past...

He's huge and shameless and vicious, not at all the gangly, laughing daredevil Ella remembers. **And he's here with one shocking, scandalous aim: to wreak vengeance on Ella's betrothed. With *her*.**

With her hunger.

Her surrender.

Her undoing.

Ella knows she should run, even if this deadly enemy was once a friend. Even if his scent drags up a dark, forbidden longing. Even if his kisses are the sweetest, filthiest thing she's ever tasted in her life...

But will Ella truly risk her perfect future, for an orc? Will she face the bitter truths of the past, and brave the terrifying Orc Mountain, before more war rises to destroy them all?

ALSO BY FINLEY FENN

THE MAID AND THE ORCS

She's fallen for an angel... but he's mated to a monster.

In a realm of orcs and powerful men, housemaid Alma Andersson is drowning—in grief, debt, and drudgery. And when her awful employer makes his darkest demand yet, she flees for the forest, and tumbles toward her doom...

Until she's snatched to safety by a **huge, vicious green beast.**

An *orc.*

He's utterly terrifying, with his towering bulk, sharp teeth, and deadly black claws—but his touch is gentle, and his eyes are kind. And his scent is a deep, decadent sweetness, sparking a furious flame between them...

But it's only more disaster, because **Alma's shy, soft-hearted rescuer is already mated... to another** *orc.* A tall, silent, snarling monster named Drafli, who loathes Alma on sight, and clearly longs for her death.

Yet Drafli will do anything for his sweet mate, even if it means tolerating a weak, worthless human. So he makes Alma a cold, calculated offer: **he'll share his mate with her... but only on his terms.**

He wants her silence.

Her surrender.

Her servitude.

And with Alma's fate firmly in Drafli's ruthless hands, how can she face her own dark desires—or all the secrets hidden behind Orc Mountain's walls? **Can a lost, lonely housemaid come between two orcs... without being crushed?**

ALSO BY FINLEY FENN

THE GOVERNESS AND THE ORC

He'll make all her dreams come true... but only if she can pretend to love him.

In a realm of orcs and powerful men, Geva Okoro is a proud, impoverished governess, trapped in a dismal, dead-end post—until the day the orc breaks in.

He's a huge, insolent, arrogant brute, swaggering with smooth, shameless wickedness. But unlike the orcs from the terrifying tales, he only wants one thing from Geva...

Her employers' gold.

There's no escaping his devious clutches, and soon a furious Geva is reduced to raiding her employers' house with an orc. Compromising her career, and destroying all her dreams... until the orc proposes another shocking scheme.

He'll split the day's plunder with her—*if* she'll pretend to be his mate. For one month. At Orc Mountain.

Sharing his rooms.

Smiling sweetly at his side.

Smelling all over of his deep, decadent scent...

He's offering more wealth than Geva's ever dreamt of, but there's no way she can trust this treacherous thief... can she? Let alone convince all of Orc Mountain that she *loves* him?!

And surely, even her best play-acting would never start to feel real... or win over an orc's cold, broken heart?

ABOUT THE AUTHOR

Finley Fenn is "the queen of dark orc romance" (Virgo Reader), and her ongoing Orc Sworn series has been praised as "sexy, romantic, angsty, and captivating ... utter brilliance" (Romantically Inclined Reviews).

When she's not obsessing over her stories, Finley loves reading, drooling over delicious orc artwork, and spending time with her incredible readers on Patreon, Discord, and Facebook. She lives in Canada with her beloved family, including her very own grumpy, gorgeous orc husband.

For free bonus stories and epilogues, special offers, and exclusive Orc Sworn artwork, sign up at www.finleyfenn.com.